Praise for *In the Wake*

"Rick Barton's *In the Wake of the Flagship* brilliantly turns the historical novel on its head. At once hilarious, thought-provoking, and ultimately tragic, this novel is an opus, the work of a writer at the peak of his powers."

—Joseph Boyden , author of *The Orenda*

"In this time-warping, genre-blurring novel, satirist Fredrick Barton skewers four centuries of American idiots, from the "vicious lying rat bastard" Puritans of the 17th century to the self-righteous politicians, small-minded university administrators and bumbling FEMA officials of our own time. Unlike his narrator—a foul-mouthed Native American warrior, who would rather fire off one-liners than destroy his enemies— Barton takes no prisoners."

—Miles Harvey, author of *Painter in a Savage Land* and *The Island of Lost Maps*

"*In the Wake of the Flagship* is absorbing, head-turning, absolutely brilliant."

—Gary B. Nash, author of *The Unknown American Revolution*

"*In the Wake of the Flagship* is a delightfully imagined, often hilarious tale about greed, territory, bigotry, and the lies hidden within American history, as told by Metacom, a fierce truth-teller brought back from the dead. Barton brilliantly links the legacy of the past to this contemporary moment, in a way that asks essential questions about justice and power. As in all of Frederick Barton's novels, the prose is lucid, the story engaging, but this might be his best novel yet—outrageous, ambitious, smart, funny, and poignant."

—Rene Steinke, author of *Holy Skirts*

IN THE WAKE
OF THE
FLAGSHIP

Book and cover design: Alex Dimeff
Cover image: "M. Palacio's Design for a Colossal Monument
in Memory of Christopher Columbus" from *Scientific
American*, October 1890.

UNO PRESS
unopress.org

For
Joyce Markrid Dombourian, of course
Proofreader, Companion, Fellow Traveler, Friend
and
In Loving Memory of
Peter Mampreh Dombourian, 1920-1992
Joyce Boyle Dombourian, 1919-2004
V. Wayne Barton, 1925-1997

"Woe unto them that call evil good and good evil."

—Isaiah 5:20

"Blessed are the peacemakers, for they will be called the children of God."

—Matthew 5:9

"The weak are meat, and the strong do eat."

—Tom Hanks, *Cloud Atlas*

ACKNOWLEDGMENTS

I am indebted to my administrative colleagues at UNO, especially Rebeca Antoine, Libby Arceneaux, Delores Julian, Judy Scott, Dennis McSeveney and Scott Whittenburg, for their daily support over many years, so often bridges over troubled waters; to my esteemed UNO creative writing colleagues, Randy Bates, Amanda Boyden, Joseph Boyden, Carol Gelderman, John Gery, Richard Goodman, Henry Griffin, Erik Hansen, Carolyn Hembree, Barb Johnson, Joanna Leake, Justin Maxwell, Kay Murphy, Neal Walsh; and to my treasured Valparaiso friends for their years of encouragement, Mark Schwehn, Dorothy Bass, Peter Lutze, David Nord, Martha Nord, Ed Uehling, Marilynn Uehling, John Feaster, Sue Feaster, Buzz Berg, Arlin Meyer, Sharon Meyer, Renu Juneja, Mel Piehl, Eileen Piehl, John Ruff, Gloria Ruff, Al Trost, Ann Trost, Lenore Hoffman, Joe Otis, Lorraine Brugh, Gary Brugh, Allison Schuette, and Margaret Franson; to the rocks of my life, my sister Dana and my mother Joeddie; to Will D. Campbell; and to Joyce Markrid Dombourian, my partner of 38 years, most of all, of course, to Joyce.

I also want to acknowledge the central role in my life of my beloved students, a partial list, of which, includes: Glenn Adams, Lindsay Allen, Jason Altman, Jamie Amos, Amanda

Anderson, Rebeca Antoine, Mark Babin, Matthew Bains, Matt Baldwin, Robin Baudier, Robert Bell, Ken Berke, Arin Black, April Blevins, Joseph Boyden, Robert Brown, Amanda Buege, Corina Calsing, Carin Chapman, Hannah Choi, Melanie Christensen, Maxine Conant, Cara Cotter, Chrys Darkwater, Denise Dirks, Lucas Diaz, Lea Downing, Leo Dubray, Jessica Emerson, Neil Fears, James Fenton, Robert Ficociello, Brendan Frost, Eli Gay, Danielle Gilyot, Erin Grauel, Paula Hilton, Abram Himelstein, Anna Hunter, Barb Johnson, Glenn Joshua, Kevin Kisch, Tom Kizcula, Carr Kizzier, Peter Keith-Slack, Sheryl Kohlert, Jennifer Kuchta, Katheryn Laborde, A.C. Lambeth, Jonathan Leavitt, Casey Lefante, Stephen Leonard, Joe Longo, Sue Louvier, Michael Mahoney, Nick Mainieri, J.G. Martinez, Paula Martin, Allison McNeill, Craig McWhorter, Carolyn Mikulencak, Daniel Morales, Andrew Moore, Kyle Mox, Brian Olzewski, David Parker, Jocelyn Paxton, Amanda Pedersen, Joyana Peter, Matthew Peters, John Pusateri, Allison Reu, Kathleen Rief, Elizabeth Rosen, Nancy Rowe, Marisa Rubinow, Maurice Ruffin, Richard Schmitt, Brent Scott, Darren Smith, Jennifer Spence, Ariel Spengler, John Tait, Shana-Tara Regon, Neil Thornton, Woodlief Thomas, Johnny Townsend, Linda Treash, Joyce Tsai, Kristin Van de Biesonbos Gresham, Jessica Viada, Stephen Walden, Missy Wilkinson, Kelly Wilson, Cooley Windsor, Mark Whitaker, Summer Wood, Larry Wormington.

My especial thanks to the friends who read this book in manuscript and gave me key advice on how to proceed: Ed Uehling, Arlin Meyer, John Feaster and Gary Nash, who taught me anything I may know about Colonial American history. The book is so much better for their suggestions. Its limitations, of course, remain mine alone.

FREDRICK BARTON is the author of the novels *The El Cholo Feeling Passes*, *Courting Pandemonium*, *Black and White on the Rocks*, and *A House Divided*, which won the William Faulkner Prize in fiction. He lives in New Orleans, Louisiana.

UNO PRESS

IN THE WAKE
OF THE
FLAGSHIP

FREDRICK BARTON

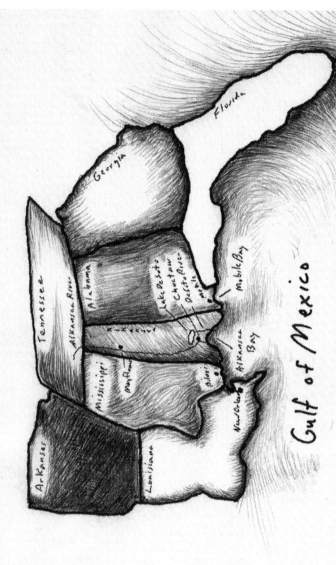

Georgia

Florida

Tennessee

Arkansas River

Alabama

Lake Pesoto

Chactaw

DeSoto River

mobile

Mississippi

Arkansas

Mississippi

Mayflower

pilow

Arkansas Bay

Mobile Bay

Louisiana

Nueva Leon

Gulf of Mexico

Massasoit Metacom, 2014

200 miles

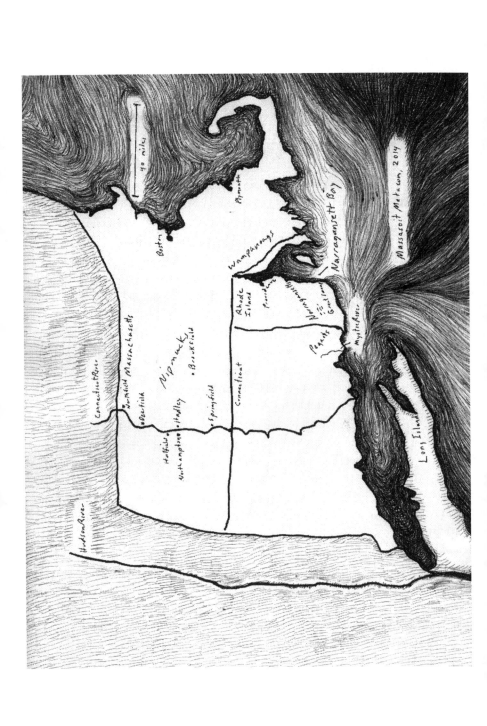

Massasoit Metacom, 2014

40 miles

Boston

Plymouth

Wampanoags

Narragansett Bay

Rhode Island

Providence

Narragansetts

Canonicus

Pequots

Mystic River

Connecticut

Connecticut River

western Massachusetts

Nipmuck

Deerfield

Northampton

Hadley

Springfield

Brookfield

Hudson River

Long Island

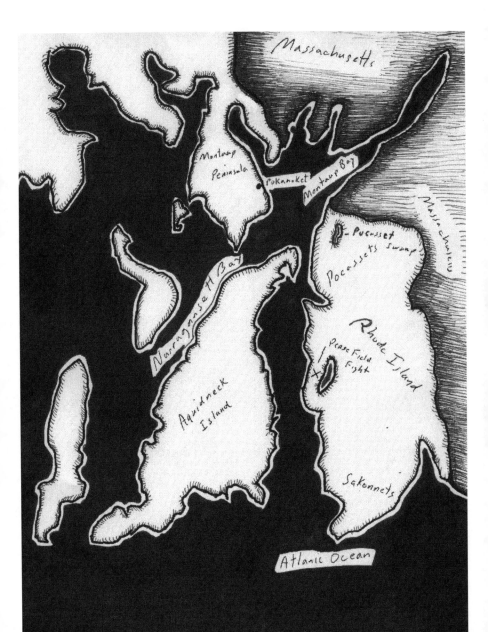

Massachusetts

Montaup Peninsula

Pokanoket

Montaup Bay

Massachusetts

Pocasset

Pocassets Swamp

Narragansett Bay

Rhode Island

Peace Field Fight

Aquidneck Island

Sakonnets

Atlantic Ocean

PROLOGUE

PART ONE

Call me Metacom.

Yes, yes, that is only one third an original opening line. But thirds is twice the fraction I ended up, about which more anon.

Call me a pessimist. Even though a black man twice got elected President of the United States in something like a miracle, I am still a pessimist. An African-American in the White House hardly eradicates four centuries of history. American's forefathers and postfathers have distinguished themselves mightily through the centuries for invading other people's property and taking things that didn't belong to them. I ought to know; one of the things they took from me in the early going was my name.

The Puritans called me Philip. *King* Philip, if you please. And in their usual self-justifying way, the war they started by invading my land and taking the property and lives of my Wampanoag people, they called *King Philip's War*, as if the whole genocidal horror was my doing, instead of theirs. King Philip's War, which Indians such as myself prefer to name for the Governor of Plymouth Colony and hence call That Vicious Lying Rat Bastard Josiah Winslow's War, raged across the plains and swamps and hillocks and waterways of Massachusetts, Rhode Island, and Connecticut from June of 1675 until August of 1676, during which period my allies and my steadfast Wampanoag warriors kicked some serious, sanctimonious Puritan butt.

Rather than a list of our astounding victories you're going to need more information to comprehend fully, let me adduce at this point just a single, telling fact: In March of 1676 we attacked and laid waste to Clark's Garrison, the fortress just outside Plymouth itself where all the rat bastarding got started in 1620. Had my Narragansett brothers joined our efforts in the late summer of 1675, we would have sent the English scrambling for their boats and off to invade somebody less testy than the likes of me and my warriors. Since the Narragansetts' efforts to remain neutral only brought them their own personal English invasion, they got nothing for their efforts at diplomacy other than a ball of flintlock lead in their tribal forehead, the slashing steel of racist blade in their fleeing backs, and the genocidal flames that laid waste to their homeland in what is now western Rhode Island.

The English and their American allies like to decry the diplomatic blunder in Munich in 1938 when Neville Chamberlain and his compatriots sold out Czechoslovakia to the Nazis, but for my money the great negative example of appeasement was that attempted by the Narragansetts. It bought them nothing but months, and it brought them almost total annihilation. Early on, the English perfected the art of playing us off against each other, and they've kept up both the dividing and conquering ever since.

The Pequots, a Connecticut tribe, tried resistance, and that didn't work. Then the Narragansetts tried appeasement, and that didn't work either. Aren't many of either left. Aren't many of my Wampanoags left either. I tried accommodation and then a fight to the death. The latter worked: I'm dead. But as you will see, though I am down, I am not out. And I am demanding that my twentieth- and twenty-first-century buddy, Richard Janus, return to his calling and put me back on my historical feet. "Get back to where you once belonged," Paul McCartney said. The Beatles are still my favorite. Get back Rich-Rich.

IN SUM, AFTER FOURTEEN months of scaring the landgrabbers into a whole bunch of praying and logic-flaying self-justification, we lost. We lost our land. We lost our identity. Most of us lost our lives. And thanks to those who took things from us, we lost our place in history. Yes, we're not alone in that. Few people today recall that the might and splendor of Carthage once rivaled that of Rome, and fewer still reflect on what a different world it might be had the Carthaginians prevailed in the Punic Wars. Americans and Europeans might all eat less pasta and more tabbouleh, and might all be Muslims for all I know. On the other hand, a triumphant Carthage might have crushed the Muslim movement in its infancy. The Earth turns on a small axis. The winners write the history of the pivotal moment, and the losers are quickly forgotten.

The occasional American colonial historian comes forward to look at our Indian contributions to the early days of English habitation in New England. Some of them get it right: the great Jill Lepore, for instance, or Francis Jennings. But I'm very little satisfied with much that has been written about me and my role in seventeenth-century history. For the longest time I was just a blood-thirsty savage, a liar and a vicious, heartless monster, this despite the fact that I was a family man and a popular leader of my people. More recently, by an infuriating writer I shall allow to remain unnamed (why call attention to his libelous work?), I've been depicted a grafter, a conniver, a coward and a quitter, who, upon defeat and capture, deserved scorn to accompany savage torment. Not surprisingly, I resent the second picture more. For somebody who was purportedly an incompetent, it's interesting, isn't it, how many warriors answered my call to war and under my command managed to inflict the damage we did, how many stood bravely with me to the very end. Did it ever occur to these modern white writers to question the authorial motives of the sources from which they built their images of me?

No matter my depiction, though, my story hasn't stuck one wrong way or the other. And any truly sympathetic portrait? Gone with the wind. My allies and I were pretty big news for a time around the three-quarter mark of the 1600s, but we've been losing recognition ever since. Ask a friend who King Philip of King Philip's War was, and the answer will sooner be the Spanish King who wasted his armada attacking Queen Elizabeth than it will be yours truly.

My people aren't around much, and save for a bunch of history profs with allergies from ancient manuscript dust, nobody much talks about me anymore, despite the fact, if I do say so myself, that I remain one of the most fascinating and emblematic figures in the four-century history of America.

Some version of all this would still be true if I had told the stupid English they could shove the "Philip" bullshit up their unwashed butts. But folks haven't been talking a lot about Tecumseh, either, and frankly, he was up to at least as much mischief as I was and against a lot longer odds.

So call me by my true name: Metacom.

I know how we New England Algonquians sometimes took new names at pivotal moments in our lives. But not me. Metacom's the name I was born with, and you can bet it was the name my wife and Wampanoag pals called me when we sat around what the English called our *wigwam* and we called, depending on the season, our *weetoo* (summer) or *nashweetoo* (winter). Yes, I confess I cooperated in the Philip bullshit because that seemed to make the English comfortable somehow. I had a name like theirs. I was polite (most of the time). I learned to make a P to stand for myself and signed a bunch of shit they wanted me to sign.

White historians like to say that I embraced the name Philip. I don't know why they feel so compelled to make this point or why it never occurs to them that absolutely everything they know about me they conclude from looking at documents written by the English, who didn't like me much from the outset and really hated me by the end of my days. But just to set the record straight, I concede that I used the name Philip when I was dealing with white people. But go look at those documents, and they almost always say down at the bottom "alias Metacom." Who do you think that was for? The English wanted me to be "Philip." But I always had that lying Judas interpreter John Sassamon put "alias Metacom" on the deed or contract or whatever BECAUSE THAT'S MY NAME.

I am Metacom, son of Massasoit Ousamequin, and younger brother of Wamsutta, whom the English called Alexander. Yes, Wamsutta and I did "sign" some papers acknowledging the name change. So what? We were trying to get along with these self-righteous thieves. We hoped that if we took English names they'd treat us with greater respect. But these were names for their use, not ours, names for diplomatic purposes only. And a lot of good it did us. They poisoned Wamsutta in 1662. Fourteen years later they had more fun sending me into the next life.

One of my enduring joys in the names Alexander and Philip, though, is my knowledge that the fucking English didn't seem to understand that the classical Philip was the older man, not the younger, and that Philip and Alexander were father and son, not brothers. These guys could read, but they didn't bother to read much other than the Bible, and boy, they sure paid a lot of attention to that.

Jesus.

Anyway, Massasoit, whose given name was Ousamequin but was known to the English by his title, which means Great Sachem, and Ousamequin's sons, Wamsutta and I, were all sachems or chiefs from the settlement named Pokanoket. Given their own political organization, the English thought of

Ousamequin, Wamsutta and me as kings. But we weren't. As with other Algonquians, a Wampanoag sachem didn't rule but led. And his or her (there were female sachems) leadership was largely exercised by persuasion, by building a consensus among the village sachems and the people who constituted the broader community.

The Pokanokets belonged to a large group of indigenous American people called Algonquians, who spoke similar, mutually understandable languages and lived in a huge swath of American coastal lands that stretched from the Carolinas all the way to Labrador. Though all these people had a great deal in common, just as human beings always have, they saw themselves in terms of their differences. They divided into nations that might be as small as an individual town and were always limited to a particular region, a fertile valley, a stretch of river, a coastal peninsula. Our division into so many different regional identities was a critical weakness that the English were able to exploit when they moved in with us beginning in the 1620s and 1630s.

Through my father Massasoit Ousamequin's leadership, a number of people from separate New England towns who had gone by different names, Manomets, Nausets, Cummaquids, Pocassets, Sakonnets, Pokanokets, came together in the confederate nation called Wampanoag, a term that means "people of the first light." Originally we employed this name because of our residence along the Atlantic coast where we saw the sunrise first. Later, we were people of the first light because we were the first to realize that the seventeenth-century English were ruthless, conscienceless, genocidal monsters.

The New England Algonquians dressed in a variety of ways. The women wore deerskin skirts that hung to the knee, cinched at the waist with woven rope belt. Many women painted their faces with ochre, sienna or umber and so did some of the men. My sister-in-law Weetamoo liked to paint her face with charcoal and then use red ochre for special occasions. My wife Wootonekanuske used purple ochre under her eyelids and striped across her cheekbones. The men wore belted deerskin breechclouts with flaps that hung to mid-thigh and leggings tied with leather strips. All of us wore moccasins, and all of us wore bracelets and necklaces made of seashells. Some of us tattooed our arms. Though the women usually wore their hair long and pulled back with a beaded leather headband, as did many men, like me, others of the men had their wives or other family members shave their heads with sharpened clam shells into a single scalplock that hung from the middle of the head down the back. We were proud of our bodies, and neither the women nor the men wore shirts during warm weather, though, noting the habits of the English, some of the women would slip on vests when the English were around.

We looked strange to the English who moved in with us. But then they looked strange to us too, with their long, curled hair in the French style, their ruffled collars and shirt cuffs and their sometimes powdered hair. We were all human beings, but we were better at realizing that about the English than they were about us. Because we dressed differently and decorated our bodies in different ways than they did, they termed us savages. But as we shall see, savage is as savage does.

Some white scholars have questioned the Wampanoag identity, speculating about it as an artificial entity, subtly undermining the extent of my father's authority and ultimately mine. From my perspective it's like questioning whether George Washington was really a leader of the American people because, before he came along to serve as President, the American people were divided up into thirteen separate and only faintly confederated independent states.

From this perspective it's fascinating how people endeavor to challenge my legacy. The Wampanoags weren't a real nation. So Dad and I weren't as important as we thought we were. The English and their American successors get to have it both ways. They get to blame me for waging war on them, and then they get to disrespect me too. I don't like this comparison one whit, but as a villain, I get lumped in there with Saddam Hussein. They say it's my fault they had to come in and take my land; then they razz me for being a weak leader. Well, it's not a contest I like to compete in, but I will point out that I killed a lot more white people on "American soil" than Saddam did.

Look, people disagree about stuff. It's human nature. Neither Dad nor I would maintain that every idea we ever had achieved unanimous popularity among our people. Such a notion is ridiculous. What leader has ever had universal support? But the breast-thumping Puritans never questioned that Dad was *the Man* as long as he lived. And though I certainly acknowledge that things got way more complicated by the time my own sachemy came around, I find it damn annoying that they name after me a war that I didn't start and then subsequently undermine the notion that I possessed the authority to make the landgrabbers sorry, if only for a while, that they fucked with me one time too many.

So get back Richard Janus, and tell them they can call me Metacom. That's my name, and this is my story. I am Metacom. And until Janus finally finishes his work, I am your metacommentator.

PART TWO

Ages and ages ago, Richard A. Janus set out to tell my story, an intention I appreciated. And he would have told it correctly; that is, he would have depicted me as the complicated but ultimately courageous leader of my people that I see myself to be. If Rich told my story, I would at least be forgotten by history as an admirable person and not a scoundrel and coward as some are forgetting about me now. But Rich never got around to telling my story, his life complicated by sadness and various shenanigans by the same kind of conscienceless but powerful white men who made me so miserable.

Rich, you can take over whenever you're ready.

Not yet?

Then I am going to tell Rich's story along with mine. Or at least I am going to relate some background and then tell a particular part of Rich's story which is kind of an analogue to my own, though some readers will no doubt scratch their heads at that assertion. Racism was there at the beginning. The English tried living with us as long as we were useful, and when we weren't any longer, they tried marginalizing us. Ultimately they enslaved us or killed us. Richard Janus spent the bulk of his life as an educator in urban public schools where minority and working-class young people were housed in an undeclared isolation, raised to be useful as laborers. And when the economy changed, and society needed more educated skills, they were moved to impoverished urban universities and trained for low-level, white-collar jobs. And when those jobs could be performed more cheaply by poor people abroad, those urban universities were systematically strangled, their students, not yet enslaved or murdered like their Wampanoag brothers and sisters, were ignored, stranded and abandoned to the meager circumstances and second-class citizenship they were born to. Powerful men make calculated decisions to serve their own kind; the rest of us suffer the consequences.

Rich and I got to know each other pretty well in the years that he prepared to tell my story. Yes, the dead can communicate with the living. And if Rich would only listen to me, then I wouldn't have had to learn to write.

Because I have cared about Rich and followed his pretty much bizarre life rather closely, I think I'm a pretty good authority on what has happened to him. Rich is both typical and exemplary, a brave guy and a fuck up: a guy after my own heart. (And I need someone after my heart since the Puritan Fathers cut mine out and fed it to their dogs.)

I will provide more details in a little while, but in overview, Richard Janus is a Southern white boy who grew up interested in the activities that fascinated most boys of his post-World War II generation. He came from good parents. His mother was a grade school teacher with a heart full of love, and his father was a liberal intellectual of the kind you could find on university faculties in the 1950s and, in some instances, in the Southern Christian pulpits up until about 1963 when the racists suddenly realized that the eggheads might actually make legalized integration viable and that black people might start getting elected to public office, first as sheriffs, then as mayors and governors, and ultimately as President of the United States.

Six foot three and wiry, Rich played basketball and baseball and football. He made good grades because he was supposed to. He passed the ball, laid down a good sacrifice bunt and mastered the cross-body block because he knew that there was no "I" in the word "team." He was as selfish as most people and as horny as any other guy his age, and he was ashamed of himself on both counts because he knew he should be better than he was.

Fair-skinned, sandy-haired and blued-eyed, Rich grew up in New Orleans where he enjoyed an all-American, blissful, white-bread, middle-class boyhood that left him entirely unprepared for the rough and tumble that life really is. His family lived in an 800-square-foot, prefabricated bungalow that was made out of ticky tack and looked exactly the same as the other houses in his neighborhood where everybody's dad had a job. Some of the dads drove Greyhound buses and some were gas station mechanics; some were traveling salesmen and some worked for oil companies. Many had gotten college degrees on the G.I. bill, but some hadn't finished high school. And yet all the dads were more or less the same. They mowed their grass or trained their sons to do so. Remarkably, from the standpoint of the early twenty-first century, everybody, whether blue collar or white collar, made about the same amount of money. But, of course, everybody was white. Though his family's income was modest enough, Rich grew up a privileged nincompoop without a clue about how other people lived.

Rich somehow managed to live in New Orleans, raised at his father's knee with a generally benign attitude about race, without actually knowing any black people who were half the city's population during his childhood. Rich went to a neighborhood school four blocks from his house and played sports year-round on the spacious playground adjacent to the school. Everybody he went to school with and everybody he played sports with were just the same. All the kids got allowances, which they spent on candy, gum and baseball cards. All got nice presents for Christmas and their birthdays. Everybody had a bike and a pair of roller skates and a sack of marbles. Everybody was nice and said "sir" and "ma'am" to all the adults.

Everybody in Rich's neighborhood had it swell, a fact they all, at least dimly, recognized. They weren't rich, however. Few families could afford to eat at restaurants, and when they did, the kids were taught to order the least expensive item on the menu. But they wanted for little, and compared to the great majority of people who have endured life on this earth, they had grand lives.

There's no telling how close Richard Janus came to being the sort of soft-brained liberal who spent more time in self-congratulation and obeisant political correctness than in trying to find some niche in which to do a bit of right. But then, he was blessed with some hardship in his life that got his head twisted around in a way that was ultimately good for him. Right out of college he had to spend two years fighting the Vietnam-era draft, during which time he made a colossally bad marriage. He studied history in graduate school at UCLA, but when his marriage broke up, Rich moved back to New Orleans and taught social studies at an inner-city school for two years.

After that he went into the Peace Corps where he was assigned to teach English in a village twenty-five miles northwest of Kisumu in Kenya. There he became involved with a Luo girl whose age he was never able to ascertain. Rich always hoped she was at least twenty but always feared that she might have been as young as sixteen. Njoki Ngilu was an orphan who had been raised by her aunt after both her parents were killed in a raid by their Kalenjin rivals.

Njoki was tall with long arms and graceful, surprisingly strong hands. Her skin was as dark and shiny as anthracite, and she had huge ebony eyes that shined with a merriment Rich found entrancing. She had a quick smile that she seemed to think forward and usually hid behind her hand and swallowed down with a giggle. Njoki was provided to Rich as a housekeeper and cook by the people of the village. The first day she arrived at the small wooden house that had been built for the teachers the Peace Corps sent every two years, she cooked Rich a morning and evening meal, and without asking him, found a pile of dirty clothes and hauled them off to the stream to wash. That night she slept on a thin pallet in the kitchen, one of the house's two rooms. Rich had been provided a reasonably comfortable bed for the other room, which also had two tattered chairs and a small wooden desk where he could prepare his lessons and set up his typewriter to compose letters and maintain the journal he kept.

Shortly, Njoki made plain that sex was part of the service she was supposed to render. As Rich lay reading inside his mosquito netting one night not long after Njoki arrived, she came back from the stream with her face and arms still damp from bathing. Her long white smock was unbuttoned from neck to hem. At first she just walked back and forth alongside his bed, inquiring about what he would like for breakfast. But finally she said, pointing to the empty expanse of sheet next to him, "I sleep there you want."

Rich knew what she was offering, but he pretended not to. "Your pallet is uncomfortable?" he said. "It's only fair that I should sleep there sometime. I should split it with you. We could switch every other night." He got up and went to lie down on the pallet in the kitchen. As he left the room, he said, "Best button your dress before you catch a chill, Njoki."

But the next night, as Rich was getting into bed, Njoki entered the room with a solemn face. "I sleep there," she said.

Again, Rich understood the overture. This time he tried to deflect it by saying, "I thought we agreed: one night on the pallet, one in the bed. I slept on the pallet last night."

"Bed big for two," she said.

"You want to sleep beside me," Rich said.

"Yes. My job. Keep house. Sleep there." Then she smiled, covered her mouth with her hand and giggled.

Rich knew better, but he let her into the bed, telling himself that sleeping was all that would go on.

Three nights passed without their touching. On the fourth night, once Rich had laid his book aside and quenched the oil lamp, Njoki curled against him and said, "You no ring. Not marry, yes?"

Rich ignored her body pressed against his side and the long leg she had hooked at the knee over his thigh. "No, I'm not married," he said. "Not any longer."

"I know," she said. She rubbed her knee on his leg. "My job. Keep house for you."

Rich didn't say anything. She nuzzled her face into the curve of his shoulder and neck. He lay as still as he could. Then she placed her hand on the crotch of the khaki shorts he'd worn to bed each night. He was hard. And when he turned to her, he was lost.

Rich cared for Njoki greatly. During the time he spent with her, her English improved rapidly, and he fantasized about making sure that she got enough education to find decent work in Nairobi or Mombasa. Sometimes he pledged that he would find a way to send her to college in London. But Rich's plans for Njoki never included taking her back with him after his service years were completed. No words of her following him to America ever passed between them. Njoki was precious to him. He thought she was beautiful and that she exuded an almost unearthly goodness. But she was simple, not in terms of intelligence, but in terms of knowledge and experience. She was thoughtful, kind, and sweetly accommodating, but she was not the woman with whom he wanted to live out his years.

Nor did Njoki ever seem to think beyond the specific time they had together, a time she knew would end. But though she assumed nothing for the future, though she requested nothing whatsoever of him, Rich felt ashamed of himself for sleeping with her. He loved her, but he wasn't *in* love with her, and he was raised not to become sexually involved with someone he wouldn't want to marry. In his isolation, in his flight from his own life, her sweetness and her availability functioned as a narcotic. He knew he shouldn't involve himself with her, but he lacked the strength to halt that which he had allowed to begin.

At least, after the first time, Rich insisted that he use a condom. But the condoms available to him were of poor quality and broke on two occasions that he knew about. How many other times they failed he couldn't be certain. But their relations continued, and Rich panicked when she became pregnant. He was convinced he had ruined his life. And when, a dozen weeks later, she began to miscarry, he felt a relief akin to a pardon from prison.

But horror followed: Njoki bled to death.

No one in the village blamed Rich. No one even commented that Rich was the father, or that his involvement with her led directly to her death. Njoki's aunt stood by him and held his hand at her funeral.

But for the rest of his life Rich felt that he had taken the life of an innocent young woman he should have protected and taught rather than embraced as a sexual partner. He had not curbed his desires, and she died because of it. He returned to the U.S. in an attitude of penance from which he was never entirely able to free himself. Over the course of the rest of his life, he confided these events to but a single person. But to a good friend once, when asked about his time in Africa, Rich said, "I did something unspeakable there, and now I have my soul to save."

1

So that you can understand my story properly, I need to go back to the beginning.

First there was the Big Bang, and then there were galaxies . . . OK, I'm kidding. I am Massasoit Metacom, not James Michener. So let's confine things to a millennium or so.

My Algonquian ancestors had been in New England for more than a thousand years. We were a settled people. Our men hunted, trapped, fished and gathered clams and lobsters to supply our diets with protein. They built our housing and boats and mastered weaponry for self-defense. Meanwhile, our women tilled the soil with hoes of hickory and birch fastened to strong clamshell heads. The land on which we thrived was thickly verdant, with scores of species of trees rising everywhere to the sky. White pines, those magnificent trees from which we built our canoes, our *mishoons*, soared almost 200 feet. The soil was relatively thin, but we knew how to fertilize it with fish parts, and it yielded crops of such bounty that we never knew hunger. Our gardens, carved from the forest by controlled burns, produced such an abundance of corn, beans and tubers that we were able to stock our storage baskets with plentiful supplies from the autumn harvest to keep our bellies full from one year to the next. The English decried our region as rocky and barren, and in the early days after their arrival, they spent a lot of their time starving to death. This was because they were ignorant and unwilling to learn from our prosperous example.

We lived in villages with each family in its own thatched cattail-reed *weetoo*, which was relatively cool in the summer, and in winter in its own bark-sided *nashweetoo*, which was considerably warmer than the drafty clapboards the English would build in our midst, way warmer than the pitiful lean-tos the first Pilgrims erected in the late fall of 1620. We New England Algonquians grew a lot of corn, beans, peas, squash and other vegetables. We cultivated grapes and strawberries and mulberries. We grew and smoked tobacco but never abused it like the idiot Europeans. We were taller than the Europeans and leaner, and we enjoyed a longer lifespan. Unfortunately, we weren't as ruthless. We noticed that their skin was lighter than ours, their hair and eyes in various hues where both our hair and eyes were black, but we didn't think of them as fundamentally other.

We should have.

Europeans of various nationalities began to sail up and down our coast in the 1520s, occasionally putting in for supplies and doing a little trading with my forebears. The cod banks brought back fishing vessels year after year. We were, relatively speaking, a populous people living in a series of villages along the waterways of the coast. Captain John Smith sailed by in 1614 to declare our shores well populated and prosperous. A year later another Englishman reported that the New England shores were too populous to represent a promising prospect for European colonization.

Well, that didn't last. For the more the Europeans came around, and the more we interacted with them, the more we exposed ourselves to their sorry, unhygienic ways. We put up with the fact that these guys stank to high heaven, had never

taken a sweat bath in their entire lives and wore the same filthy
clothes until their rags rotted off their backs. But we had no clue
that they were walking toxic waste dumps and that just inviting
them into our *weetoos* was putting us in mortal danger. Then we
found out. Starting in 1616 and lasting for nearly three years,
our people suffered through a plague that wiped out more than
half of us and left entire villages depopulated. Our neighbors
across the bay, the Narragansetts, were miraculously spared this
pestilence, but my father Massasoit Ousamequin saw 80% of his
people die. So we grew cautious when the stinkers came around,
usually taking refuge off the coast where they had little success
finding us. And that's exactly what we did when the Bible-
Thumpers showed up in 1620 with plans not to infect us but
rather to move in with us.

1620. Boy, that was a year, the beginning of the end, though
I concede we didn't see it coming. 1620 was when the belted hats
showed up on a pitifully banged-up vessel called the *Mayflower*.
Many of them had been hanging out in Holland for twelve years
where they had been practicing "freedom of religion" since they
had departed their native England where religion was available
but seldom involved much freedom. Still, I put the term
"freedom of religion" in quotes because the Pilgrims believed
that they should be free to practice the religion they believed in
and that you should be free to practice the religion they believed
in, too.

These separatist Puritans did pretty well in Holland.
They had a magnetic leader in a guy named John Robinson,
who led a prospering congregation of English Jesus freaks
in Leiden, Holland, and tripled the size of his faithful flock
in little more than a decade. But then, the damnedest thing
began to happen. All the offspring of the praying Brits began
to speak Dutch, wear wooden clogs and bug their parents
about planting tulips. That absolutely just wouldn't do, so the
fundamentalists of their day decided to come to New England
and bother us.

Well, these guys that history ultimately took to calling the Pilgrims (makes them sound so saintly, doesn't it?) suffered various setbacks in trying to get out of Europe and didn't manage to set sail until September. That meant they didn't get here until November, by which time it is way too late to plant anything, and, in case you studied your geography in an American public school, beginning to get way cold, even colder then, in what has been called the "Little Ice Age" of the seventeenth century. With the slightest bit of luck, half of the rat bastards would have frozen to death just before the other half starved to death. But luck is something American Indians have enjoyed very little of in the last 400 years.

The *Mayflower* captain dropped anchor in what they called Provincetown Harbor in our month of *Pepewarrkesos*, on November 11, 1620. But before our invaders ventured off the ship, they all got together and signed something they called the Mayflower Compact which has made its way into America's collective sense of itself as evidence of what a remarkable bunch of democrats we have always been, as long as we understand the democratic impulse as one reserved for people who think just like we do. This compact grants to the stinkers of the *Mayflower* the "right to enact, constitute and frame such just and equal laws, ordinances, acts, constitutions and offices, from time to time, as shall be thought most meet and convenient for the general good." How about them apples? Just before I drop in for an uninvited visit to your house, I invest myself and my kind with the right to make up the rules we're going to use while I take up residence in your bedroom.

And people have maintained that the Jews invented chutzpah?

Well, after declaring themselves, as a group, the men in charge of the hereabouts, the Pilgrims dicked around for a while. They spent a whole day praying, and even if it was a Sunday and they were religious fanatics, that seems to me like an injudicious way to behave since the weather grew colder by the day. Then they futzed with a boat to carry them ashore for so long that I would have thought they would have all expired from the inertia of their own incompetence. Finally, they got their fetid butts on the Cape Cod sand where they marched around under the leadership of Miles Standish, belovedly known by his shipmates as "Captain Shrimp" to honor the fact that he was shorter than a fire hydrant. (Yes, an anachronistic metaphor, but then I am an anachronistic narrator, right?) It would be perfectly fair to make fun of Standish for being a self-righteous prick who couldn't find his own ass with two hands except for the fact that his viciousness has got him lodged in the same chamber of hell with Pol Pot.

We had been sick as dogs for four years, and we knew the plague came from Europeans, so they looked like the rot of death to us. When we saw them coming we ran and hid. We didn't want to interact with these pink stinkers, and we didn't even yet know that Standish was a world class thug. The first chance he got, he stole a basket of our corn and sat down to thank his God for endowing him with the will and fortune to be a fucking thief.

Eventually the Pilgrims made their way from Provincetown Harbor over to Plymouth Bay, prayed about matters as usual and set up shop. Only three years earlier we would have had the manpower to tell them, "Don't let that skank of a ship sail up your ass as it carries you on to somewhere else." In 1616 my dad had 3,000 warriors under his command. But by 1620, he had only a few hundred. We still had large enough a force to have wasted the interlopers, and we definitely should have, but we hadn't the foresight or the excuse. So we let them come on across Cape Cod Bay and plant themselves on the site of our abandoned town of Patuxet, which was located on a hill with a nice view of the sea, beside a stream that supplied fresh water. In 1616 Patuxet had been a thriving settlement of 2,000, but the few people there who survived the plague had moved west and south to reside with relatives in other villages. Liking the environs of the place they renamed Plymouth, the high hats thanked their God for sending the sickness and death that made a place for them. Had they ever read the Beatitudes?

Since we weren't using the land they parked on, and they were such a pitifully bedraggled lot, Massasoit Ousamequin let them set up camp and calculated maybe he could utilize a connection with the English to bolster his diminished position vis-à-vis the Narragansetts and their Sachem Canonicus who had started big-shotting around over to our west. Judged within the confines of his own life, Dad was right. But judged within the confines of all of us who came after him, he couldn't have been more wrong if he had jumped into the twenty-first century and voted for George W. Bush.

In short, we let the holy rollers get a foothold from which they climbed right up our butts. We even helped them. They were so completely incompetent that they barely made it into a second year. One hundred two of these Pilgrims disembarked the *Mayflower* in November of 1620, but by the spring of 1621, forty-five of them had died, including thirteen of the sixteen unfortunate women. If we'd just ignored them, they would never have made it to 1622.

Boy do we wish we could have a do-over on that one.

2

Richard Janus went to Lancaster College on a basketball scholarship where he distinguished himself as a guy who liked to find the open man but always left his own man open – good hands, slow feet, good O, weak D. An injured knee playing football in high school and repeated ankle sprains throughout his basketball days left him gimpy by the time he turned thirty and with a regular limp a decade later. But he earned a double major in history and English from Lancaster and was good enough in the classroom that he was nominated for a Rhodes Scholarship, which he did not win. He did win a fine graduate fellowship from the Fortran Foundation, however.

Right after college, Rich married a red-headed cheerleader named Faith Cleaver who had identity issues he hadn't recognized when he was a star athlete and she dedicated herself to reminding him whenever she could that he was a star athlete. After they were married, this tempestuous firetop became a tongue-speaking evangelical Christian which she kept blabbering about until she became a radical feminist and after that a devoted Communist. She also became a lesbian. Ultimately, she became a professor of English with a specialty in Marxist-feminist-lesbian literature. Make your own jokes about how her tongue-speaking days played into her professional credentials and her sexual practices. Suffice it to say, Rich suffered during the days of his marriage to Faith, sometimes deservedly, often not.

Rich went to UCLA on his Fortran Graduate Fellowship, and that's where he began to read about and form his opinions about me. He even undertook a doctoral dissertation about me that was finally going to set the record straight about how I was a stand-up guy who just got Josiah Winslowed by a vicious lying rat bastard and all his pink-toned rat bastard comrades. As you might imagine, I was really looking forward to the book Rich was planning to write. And I want to say to him right now: "It's not too late, my friend. You have a UCLA education, and I'm just a dead Indian. Who are they more likely to believe?"

Unfortunately, Rich went through a divorce. And he lost a certain measure of faith in himself. So he did what dissertationists often do when their personal lives start getting in the way of their scholarship: He quit, leaving my story to be told by others, frequently not to my liking. Needing to eat and enjoy the pleasures of shelter, depressed or not, Rich landed a position teaching high school social studies and coaching a sport each season at Fortier High School in New Orleans, where he had grown up. For a savored while, he dated a woman he knew from Fortran Conferences, Cally Martin, a classics professor at the University of New Orleans, a brown-haired beauty with sparkling emerald eyes and a spirit as profoundly warm as anyone he had ever known. Cally Pappas Martin was a young divorced person too. Rich and Cally should have made their connection work. But they didn't. Rich's fault entirely, so bruised by his first marriage that he was terrified of another committed relationship. Cally understood. She wanted more, but she gave Rich no ultimatums, and they remained friends.

But when Cally married a UNO colleague, Rich couldn't face the idea of having to run into them around town. So he made an abrupt decision to enter the Peace Corps, a worthy enough choice, far superior to moving over to Skid Row, but the Peace Corps produced the tragedy of Njoki Ngilu.

After the Peace Corps, Rich drifted around the country for several years, working construction, trying to hold himself together with hard physical labor. The only constant during this period was his regular volunteer work as a football, basketball and baseball coach in whatever municipal league needed his assistance. Finally, in 1983, when he was 35 years old, Rich came to the conclusion that he should settle down and begin pursuing the career he was obviously fated to follow. He began applying for high school basketball coaching positions again, and he found one in Choctaw, Alkansea, that historic metropolis of about a million souls on the Alkansea River about twenty-five miles north of Alkansea Bay.

I find it fascinating that Rich ended up in a city named for an Indian nation. The Creator likes his inside jokes. A settlement at Choctaw was first founded by Spanish deserters in 1540 and has eerie connections to events in my own history. The deserters were wounded and dispirited soldiers in the hapless expedition of Spanish conquistador Hernando De Soto and survivors of the fierce resistance by the famous Black Warrior, Tuscaloosa.

Hoping to board ships in the Gulf of Mexico that could return them to Spain, they set up camp on the lower Alkansea River on the last high ground above Alkansea Bay. But the ships didn't come, and gradually they took Choctaw wives and disappeared into the Indian community.

Over the next two centuries, Choctaw passed through the official ownership of Spain, France, and finally, the United States. Not surprisingly, it developed a rich and diverse culture with a European sophistication pulsating with the rhythms of the Caribbean. By the time Rich Janus arrived in 1983, Choctaw was a black majority city suffering serious financial problems resulting from white flight to the suburbs and the hostile neglect of the policy makers in the Alkansea state capital of Mayflower, 150 miles up the Alkansea River.

At Choctaw High, Rich settled down for what he then assumed would be his life's work: English teacher and head basketball coach. In this, he was fabulously successful, winning seven state championships in the next sixteen years. As a basketball coach, he was a canny evaluator of talent, an inspirational motivator of his players and a keen pregame strategist. He was also an excellent game manager with an instinct for the right substitutions in critical situations, the right moment to call a time out and the right time to resist the expected time out.

In order to earn step pay increases, he began to take graduate classes at Urban University, the large state institution in the northern part of the city. Urban had been founded in 1955 under the name Alkansea State University—Urban, but just as those who teach, work and study at Indiana University-Purdue University Indianapolis hate that their school is widely called "Oo Eee Poo Eee," those affiliated with the Choctaw institution despised that in its early days their campus was called "Ahh Shoo," a name the speaker often followed by guffawing, "gesundheit." As a result, in a campaign waged by its students, the name was changed in the 1960s to Urban University. But the people in state capital Mayflower, if they spoke of the school at all, routinely called it U.U., pronounced "Ewe Ewe," a formulation that infuriated both Urban employees and Choctaw community supporters.

At Urban, Rich concentrated on American literature, first earning a Master's and then moving into the Ph.D. program. Working around his coaching schedule, taking classes at night, on weekend mornings and in the summer, he moved through the program slowly. It took him eight years. But unlike his abandoned work at UCLA on me, this time he completed a dissertation on sports themes in twentieth-century American literature and film. He wrote his thesis in a single frenzied summer. Rich called his book, *Reading Between the Lines*, and though he worked on it carefully and thoughtfully, he was pleased most of all just to finish it.

So Rich became Dr. Richard A. Janus after all, but without telling my story, an act of negligence which I am still coaxing him to rectify. Rich was proud to earn his Ph.D., even though he wasn't really all that proud of his dissertation which seemed too easy after abandoning the more difficult task of telling my story. But damned if he didn't publish the thing, and damned if it didn't actually sell a bit, a feat dissertations, as almost every academic knows, are almost forbidden to do.

And double damned if the publication of *Reading Between the Lines* didn't land Rich a contract to write a second book, *Pick and Roll*, a memoir about his first season as head coach at Choctaw in 1983-84 that produced the least likely of his state championships when an unranked team of role players without commanding height and without dominating stars came together, defied incredible sporting odds and accomplished something all involved would treasure the rest of their lives. *Pick and Roll* is an ode to the pleasure of team sports and an account of the affection a coach can develop for his players.

Central to the narrative of *Pick and Roll* was Rich's affectionate and admiring relationship with the best of his players on that first championship team, Alphonse Jackson, a 6'3" swing man who had the greatest burning drive for success Rich had ever encountered. Alphonse had grown up in Choctaw's Mitchell Hardwicke Housing Development. His mother cleaned houses to put food on the table; he never knew his father, who died in Vietnam before Alphonse was born. Alphonse might well have gone the way of the gang-infested world in which he lived. But he possessed uncommon vision and inspiring grit. Even during the success he enjoyed in that one season Rich got to coach him as a senior, Alphonse understood that his playing days would not extend beyond college. He had no false dreams of a professional basketball career. He wanted to be a journalist, and he dedicated himself to that pursuit as fiercely as he chased after a loose rebound. Rich loved him. And as proud as Rich was of that first, unlikely state championship team Alphonse led, Rich was even prouder that Alphonse realized his dream. He graduated first in his class at Choctaw High, won a scholarship to Urban where he started at shooting guard for three years and graduated in four, and went on from there to the Journalism School at Columbia. Eventually, he became a staff writer at Newsday.

Pick and Roll did not sell as many copies as *Reading Between the Lines* had, edged out in the publishing scramble by books ghostwritten for such high-profile college coaches as Rick Patino, Dean Smith, Jimmy Prince and Jerry Tarkanian. But *Pick and Roll* was a better book than Rich's first, and he was prouder to have written it.

Something even better than winning championships, getting his Ph.D. and seeing his books published happened to Rich after he began his career at Choctaw High. Something good out of something bad. The bad was that Cally Martin's husband turned out to be an unrepentant perambulating gland, and she decided she wasn't going to put up with it. They were married six years, happily for less than six months. The good was that to get away from the memory of her failed marriage, Cally left the University of New Orleans to take a job as chair of the Classics Department at Urban University in Choctaw. She had an aunt who lived there and who rented her a small apartment on the ground floor of her large Edwardian house in Riverside, a quaint middle-class neighborhood in the northwest area of the city snug to the Alkansea River levee. The apartment had low ceilings, and it got little light. But the space served her in the short term. And Cally lost focus on buying a home of her own when she and Rich became involved again.

Though Rich and Cally hadn't seen each other in the six years after Rich left New Orleans, they had kept in touch with a volley of postcards. Mostly, they just sent each other brisk, silly messages of no import other than the unstated implication that they continued to think about each other. They found picture postcards of mundane things such as the front of a hotel or a scene in a park, cards they could pick up for free. On the back, each would write a nonsense greeting. Cally sent Rich a card showing the colorful parrot cage at Audubon Park in New Orleans. In the small space on the reverse side she scribbled:

> The girl parrot is saying to the boy parrot, "If you weren't so fresh, we wouldn't be in this jam." And the guy parrot replies, "Are you a twit or what?"
> I think birds are deep. What about you?
> Love, Cally

She liked to grab postcards off hotel reception desks. She sent Rich one from the Drake in Chicago. On the back she wrote:

> When I checked in, the clerk asked me, "When is Mr. Janus arriving?" And when I said, 'I don't think he's coming,' she said, "Oh well,

then, I fear we shall have to declare bankruptcy
and consider suicide."
    Do you think she was overreacting?
    Write me.

Love, Cally

Rich made his own card from a photograph that had come
out almost completely blank and wrote on the back:

    I would remark that your recent card was
    for the birds, but I'm not nearly so twitty as all
    that. Really, I think you should strive for greater
    artistry in your card selection, such as I have
    done in making this astonishingly excellent
    card with my own hands.

Love, Rich

After reading about street flooding in New Orleans during
a torrential thunder storm, he found a postcard of Niagara Falls
and wrote on it:

    As I recall, this is your driveway.

Love, Rich

The notes seldom strayed beyond the silly, although they
occasionally included at least a spot of genuine information.
After Rich decided to accept the coaching job at Choctaw
High, he sent Cally a card showing a grandfather clock in a
hotel lobby. On it he wrote:

Someone has told me it's time to grow up. Ignoring that advice, I've decided to become the head basketball coach at Choctaw High in Choctaw, Alkansea. Go Warriors.

Love, Rich

Later that year, Cally sent him a card of a couple in cocktail attire in the Carousel Lounge at New Orleans' Monteleone Hotel. They're being served drinks by a woman in a miniskirt and black mesh stockings. The greeting read:

This is a picture of me and hubby. I'm saying, "I wouldn't go home with you if you were actually a human being." He replies, "Excellent sentiment. You wouldn't have the waitress' home number, would you?"

Love me, Cally

Rich tried to call her after receiving the Carousel Lounge card, but her number had been disconnected. After arriving at her aunt's house in Choctaw, however, Cally called Rich and invited him out to dinner. They talked at the Bayside Inn over turtle soup, baked oysters and a bottle of Merlot; then they adjourned to Rich's Victorian shotgun camelback cottage for after-dinner drinks. They talked until after one a.m., hungry to be together again. They had been friends for a decade, and they possessed no need for coy flirtation. They had been lovers before, and they became so again that night.

Cally continued to use her aunt's apartment as her home office, but she relocated her clothes and personal items and her better pieces of furniture to Rich's house. Cally took up her duties as department chair, and Rich taught his English classes, pursued his graduate degrees and coached his teams. Cally became a regular at Rich's basketball games. They loved the theater and became season ticket holders and sponsors of the productions of the Urban Theater Department and fond acquaintances of its chair, Joseph Alter, whose work as a director they greatly admired. In the summer they traveled, most often to Europe.

They felt no urgency to wed, however, and they decided to marry only on the spur of the moment while on vacation in Mexico. They found a priest in the dusty village of San Jose del Cabo and exchanged silver rings they had purchased earlier in San Lucas. Cally wore a paper umbrella she'd saved from a pina colada in her hair. They weren't even certain that the wedding had legal standing in the United States. But they didn't care either. They never merged their finances, not even after their Mexican wedding, but they gradually began to own things in common, a new stereo, a nice Oriental rug, first one car and then another, finally a house, a split-level Mediterranean on comfortable Venice Boulevard. And though they were just teachers, with two salaries, they felt affluent.

And most important, they were happy. How unmodern of them.

3

We never could teach that first group of Pilgrims how to fish. Maybe they got so traumatized by their time on the Mayflower that they just never wanted to go near water again. Whatever the reason, the early pinkies were like twentieth-century white boys trying to learn to dance. They could do the squeeze-eye squint and bite their lips and nod their heads, but they couldn't dance worth a damn. Any one of us could probably have fed the lot of them just with seafood, but these guys couldn't catch a crab if it was clinging to a toe. If we hadn't taught the high hats how to farm New England soil, they would have starved to death. But we helped them, and like a spinning top that bangs its sides a few times in the early going, they finally got themselves upright and more or less stable. Silly us, we thought that was to our advantage. We traded them pelts, which we had in abundance, for metal pots and pans and knives and ultimately muskets. These European goods were better than the clay utensils and shell-bladed weapons that we had. The English were more than a little standoffish from the beginning, but since we were looking for allies not buddies, that didn't much matter to us.

The Pilgrims divided themselves into two groups. The main contingent stayed in Plymouth and built a little town of single-room, dirt-floored, clapboard houses heated by chimneyless fireplaces. These dark and smoky abodes were strung along a single street and surrounded by a picket fence that is listed in the Guinness Book of World Records under the category Hilariously Flimsy and Useless Fortifications. If we had chosen to attack, their fence wouldn't have slowed us down an entire minute. And though they had bothered to build the fence, they understood this well enough that they soon erected a meeting house (read: church) that could double as a fort. (Kind of makes you think, doesn't it, of that crucifix that can be unsheathed to become a dagger.) Because Massasoit Ousamequin strategically chose alliance over belligerence, this group of bumblers in Plymouth survived and eventually thrived.

But a more piteous band, single men mostly, were deposited twenty miles north in a little town they called Wessagussett right next to a village of the Massachusetts. The English built a second fort at Wessagussett, but the men there could barely figure out how to feed themselves. So their fort was just a place they could hide while starving. By 1623 a number of them had abandoned the skinny life behind their pickets and moved in with the Massachusetts. Our traditions demanded that we accept visitors into our homes and feed and care for them, and this the Massachusetts did without hesitation. The English who took up residence among them made a smart move since the *nashweetoos* were warm and the food was plentiful. Those white men who stupidly remained in their freezing fort were so hungry they were offering the Massachusetts the very shirts off their backs for a sack of corn. The Wessagussett Pilgrims couldn't seem to grow anything and couldn't stir themselves to gather the clams and oysters that were there for the picking up. Their lethargy was mysterious to us because they seemed to lack the will to perform the tasks necessary to stay alive.

Then, the hardier guys down in Plymouth got this idea that Massachusetts Sachem Obtakiest, who had only about forty warriors under his command, had hatched a plan to attack the Wessagussett fort and wipe out all the baggy britches inside. The Pilgrims were forever claiming that Indians were about to attack them, even though we hadn't.

The truth is that the sociopath Miles Standish was looking for an excuse to settle a stupid score with Wituwamat, an obnoxious Massachusetts with a big mouth and a fancy knife he liked to wave around. Standish was down in Manomet finalizing a trade with Sachem Canacum when Wituwamat showed up and began flapping his lips about what a tough guy he was and how he wasn't afraid of anybody. Or at least that's what Standish *assumed* he was saying. But since Standish couldn't speak a word of our language, Wituwamat could have been saying that he'd just nailed the hottest babe in the Northeast. Whatever, being a stupid hot head, who suffered mightily from his short-guy complex, Standish decided he was being dissed and blew off every effort Canacum made to get him to settle down.

When Standish returned home, he began to ask anyone with an ear just what a Massachusetts Indian was doing in Manomet anyway. Why, he must have been there to conspire! Or so Standish began to declare. The Massachusetts to the north and Manomets to the south must have been cooking up a bloody scheme to attack the English. Of course, there could have been a thousand reasons why Wituwamat came calling on Canacum. Standish had come to Manomet to trade. Might not Wituwamat have been there for the same reason?

"Not so," a wild-eyed Standish declared on a cold and gray *Namassackesos* morning while standing before the licking flames in the fireplace of the Plymouth Meeting House on March 24, 1623. He had convinced Governor William Bradford to convene an emergency meeting where the men of the colony could devise a strategy for confronting the threat of Indian attack. "He wasn't trading, I tell you," Standish almost shouted. "I didn't see him ask to trade anything. All I saw and heard was him bragging about what a big man he is, and how he killed a meadow's worth of enemies, gutted them with his fancy knife, he said, slit their throats. He as much as threatened me directly."

"But he didn't go to Manomet to threaten you," William Brewster argued. "He couldn't have known you were there."

"Just my point," Standish said, striding back and forth before the fire. "The only reason he could have been there was to convince Canacum to attack from the south while Wituwamat and the Massachusetts have at us from the north. We must strike first, lest we have to meet our enemies standing back to back."

"Canacum has never been our enemy," Brewster said. "And the Massachusetts have been trying to teach our brethren in Wessagussett how to feed themselves for nearly a year."

"I have to stand with our Captain," Edward Winslow said, pious papa of that Vicious Lying Rat Bastard Josiah Winslow. "I have received word from Massasoit that the Massachusetts are planning to attack Wessagussett. Even if Captain Standish is not right about Canacum and the Manomets, we must meet the threat where we know it lies. Were the fort at Wessagussett to fall, we would be the next to hear the natives' war whoop."

Winslow loved to tell a story about how he once saved Massasoit Ousamequin's life when Dad was sick. What happened was that Winslow came around once when Dad was constipated and fed him a laxative broth. Wasn't even an English potion but an herb mixture prepared by our medicine woman. Winslow just handled the spoon. But when it worked Winslow took the credit, and Ousamequin saw it useful to portray himself as in Winslow's debt. That way Dad could feed him information or misinformation as it suited his purpose. Dad was no big friend of Massachusetts Sachem Obtakiest, and the Massachusetts were never members of our confederacy, but you can rest certain that whatever message Massasoit Ousamequin sent to Winslow, he didn't mean to endorse what followed.

But Winslow's alleged message from Massasoit swung the undecided, and Governor Bradford, a man with no military experience or affinity, elected to authorize a military expedition to relieve the residents of Wessagussett from their "peril." What peril those at Wessagusset were facing from the Massachusetts remains unclear. Obtakiest didn't need to waste his arrows on the slackers who were doing a fine job of dying all by their own lazy, depressed selves.

But Standish and Papa Winslow had figured out what the Indians were up to. First they would wipe out Wessagussett, and then they'd move on Plymouth. In fact, as Standish assembled his assault team, the rumors swept with a rocket's red glare from one Plymouth house to the next. The Indians weren't just going to attack; they were going to kill every English man, woman and child then in New England. Never mind that these were the same Indians who had some of the smarter Wessagussett folks sharing their *nashweetoos*. Never mind that these were the same Massachusetts people who had been trying to teach the Wessagussett layabouts how to survive. Never mind that the Wessagussett residents were desperate skeletons who constituted no threat. In short, never mind that Obtakiest had no incentive for launching a war. For Standish had figured out what the Massachusetts sachem was planning, and that was that.

And we know (Gulf of Tonkin Resolution), we know (Bush Doctrine), just what you do when you've figured out, or think you've figured out, or made up so you can justify some preemptive attack, that the other guy has weapons and is planning a mass destruction. Why, you strike first, of course. That's right folks, it started way back then.

So two days later, on March 26, 1623, still cold and gray, Standish and his squad of praying slayers headed up to Wessagussett, where they found a bunch of skinny guys who immediately informed him that they had no reason to fear the Indians who had been nothing but nice to them. Standish announced that he would give the Wessagussett people something to eat if they'd help him fight the Massachusetts. I'd love to tell you that they declined. But, alas, they didn't. Gratitude so infrequently comes in a European shade of pink.

Standish invited Wituwamat and some other Massachusetts Indians to come have a meal with him in the Wessagussett fort, where they could discuss new trading initiatives. Obtakiest passed. Lucky him. As the Pilgrims entered the drafty room in which the banquet was to be served, they made a dramatic point of stacking their muskets in a corner and motioning for their Massachusetts guests to do the same with their own muskets, bows and quivers.

They all sat down in straight-back chairs around a rough plank table covered with white linen for a meal of venison, corn, peas, tubers and squash. There were some serving spoons on the table and some wooden bowls but no dining utensils. Englishmen would not begin to use the fork, which they considered an Italian pretension, until the next century. Each diner would brush the vegetables from the bowl into his mouth with his fingers and would use his own knife to slice and spear the meat. Since the meal had not started, the Indians' knives were still sheathed.

Standish asked all present to bow their heads in prayer to give thanks for the food they were not about to eat. The Indians weren't Christian, but they had dined with white people and knew their habit of praying before meals. "Oh Heavenly Father," Standish said, "we thank thee for the bounty before us in this land that thou hast given us for our dominion." Standish lifted an opened eye for a glimpse of the Indians at the table who had learned some English but hadn't a clue what *dominion* meant. They stared at the table, at the walls and at each other, all silently wishing he'd finish this mysterious ritual so they could eat. "Guide and protect us Lord God," Standish said, "as we seek to follow the course thou has set for us." And while he prayed, the runt slipped his dagger from his belt and held it ready under the table. "Amen," he finished, an ending the Indians had come to understand.

But as soon as the last of the prayer was spoken, Standish spun on the Indian sitting next to him, a tall handsome man named Pecksuot, and began stabbing him in the chest, over and over again. Till now, there had been no hostilities between our people and the English. We had cultivated them as allies against our rivals to the west. Our culture did indeed employ the ambush as a strategy of war. But we did not attack people with whom we sat down to eat. Pecksuot's first reaction was one of utter surprise. But he was mortally wounded before he grasped Standish's incredible treachery. The other Pilgrims in the room launched identical attacks on the other Indians gathered there. Edward Winslow fell upon Wituwamat with the same shocking violence, as did William Latham on the man next to him. All but one of the Massachusetts were stabbed to death before they could even draw their weapons to fight back. The lone survivor was Wituwamat's teenaged brother who was stabbed but instead of struggling surrendered. He was taken outside and hanged.

Then Standish, Winslow, Latham and the other Englishmen ran throughout the area and killed any Indian they came across. They attacked the Massachusetts village and killed still more people until Obtakiest managed to lead the survivors into a swamp where the English could not follow. Standish returned to the dining room in the fort, cut off Wituwamat's head and wrapped it in the tablecloth so that it could be carried back to Plymouth and displayed on a stake, a trophy for all to see.

War was hardly unknown to my Algonquian brothers in New England. But we had never witnessed unprovoked viciousness on this scale, and it terrified us. This was Standish's exact intention. So how should we remember this man memorialized in Longfellow's poem? Miles Standish, heroic founding father? Or Miles Standish, terrorist?

Standish's attack on the Massachusetts sent the message that the English would kill suddenly, relentlessly and without mercy. At the time the separate villages of the region functioned independently and without a tradition of cooperative military action. Could these English in so few numbers have conquered the local inhabitants outright? Not in 1623. Certainly not if the Indians banded together. But would that be a lesson we New England Algonquians would learn in time?

4

In 1999, Richard Janus' professional career took an unexpected bounce (so to speak). Urban University CEO Francis Saurian invited all the high-school coaches in the area to apply for the Urban Ungulates head basketball coaching position that had become vacant when, after two years at the school, he fired the incumbent, immediately after firing the athletic director for refusing to fire the incumbent coach. Saurian was an executive who thought it his job to shake things up. By the end of his second year as rector at Urban he had changed out all his deans and half his vice rectors. Embarrassed by the men's basketball team's pitiful attendance and inability to win even ten games a season, he was determined to shake things up in athletics too.

A short and pudgy man of Armenian ancestry with a fringe of white hair around a shiny, olive-hued bald pate, but a man who possessed a silver tongue, a stubborn determination to achieve his objectives and truly impressive reserves of energy, Saurian was also an executive who thought that he didn't really need subordinates because he was better suited to do most of the jobs in his organization himself. He subscribed to the saying, "If you want things done right, do them yourself." So when Saurian fired the A.D., he decided not to appoint another one, taking that job, among others, for himself. Fortunately, for Ungulate fans, of whom there were literally tens, Saurian (in a rare instance of self-knowledge) understood that he knew nothing about basketball, so he didn't try to coach the basketball team himself.

The invitation to the local high school coaches had some merit. Being taken seriously as possible college coaches flattered them and made them more likely to encourage their star players to consider becoming Ungulates. But Saurian's motives had nothing to do with recruiting and everything to do with race. Saurian was obsessed with the fact that he had taken the rectorship of a university in a black majority city, so foremost, he wanted an African-American coach. Furthermore, he wanted to brag of having hired an African-American coach drawn from the largest number of black applicants for any Division I basketball head coaching vacancy in history. Saurian relished circumstances that would allow him to claim first or biggest or best. And so, Rich made it onto the list of finalists from the written application pool because Saurian assumed Rich was black.

The enduring joke was that Saurian charged himself with hiring a new coach without so much as a committee to consult with. Saurian understood so little about basketball that he was befuddled about why sometimes a basket counted three points but other times only two. And he thought the situation completely unfair when the referees stopped the game and made one guy shoot from darn far away with everybody in the arena yelling at him and his team got only one point. Saurian wasn't incapable of understanding the rules of the game, but he cared too little to ask for an explanation, and he was not a man to whom subordinates volunteered instruction. But ignorant as he was about the fundamentals of the sport, Saurian was an excellent peruser of resumes and thought Rich's seven state championships were pretty impressive.

If Saurian had asked anybody who knew anything about college basketball, such an expert would have told him that the leap from high-school basketball to a head-coaching position at the Division I level was gigantic, that such a move was seldom risked and less often successful. Even Rich would have told him that. But Saurian, who trusted his own instincts and sneered at expert advice, didn't ask Rich or anybody else. He looked at Rich's accomplishments, called him in, interviewed him and offered him the job. He did so in part because, when they met, he liked Rich, insofar as Francis Saurian could like anyone other than himself. Rich got on the list because he was supposed to be black and got hired because he had a Ph.D., especially one in something other than higher education administration or educational leadership, a real, genuine, regular traditional academic Ph.D. of the kind that even shithead engineering faculty would have to respect. Not that Saurian suspected many shithead engineering faculty cared about basketball, since they all came from countries where people wet themselves over soccer.

Saurian had been thinking about all the fun he was going to have bragging about having hired Urban's first African-American coach. Now he was thinking of the even more fun he was going to have boasting about having an Ungulate head coach with a Ph.D. in English and two books. Yes, Saurian thought, he would introduce Rich as *Dr.* Janus and never afterwards allow anyone at the university to refer to him in any other way. And whenever Saurian himself went to academic CEO meetings around the country, he would be the envy of all his peers for having hired a Ph.D. and author as his head basketball coach. Saurian was sure that his brilliant idea to hire Rich would quicken his move from Urban to the presidency of a Southeastern Conference or, better, a Big Ten university, the underlying goal of everything he did.

Cally was not completely convinced that Rich should make the move to Urban. "You've got a real touch with these high school kids," she said. "They're hungry, and they listen to you. You're able to teach them as much about life as about basketball or about life using basketball as your hands-on metaphor."

"Why can't I do the same thing at the collegiate level?" he asked her.

"Oh, you probably can with some of them. But how many times have I heard you say that the college game is about recruiting first, recruiting second and coaching *only* third?"

"You have heard me say that," Rich admitted. "And, OK, no doubt to a large extent it's true. But you know there is still important off-court work to do with college players too. Maybe even more so."

"How can that possibly be true?" Cally asked.

"High school kids are more provincial, but because of that less subject to delusion. They haven't been out of their own neighborhoods, most of them, and know almost nothing about the outside world. The farthest they've ever been away from home is to an away game. So their dreams aren't too big for them. But those kids who get a college scholarship, every one of them thinks he's going to the NBA, thinks he'll settle for a pro team in Europe. Every one of them wasn't just the best player on his team; he was the best player in his league. You can tell him that his statistical possibility of landing a pro contract is close to nil, and all he'll conclude is that you're talking to the guy standing next to him. I want to show them a different model. I want to show them Alphonse Jackson."

"I can see them learning something from Alphonse," she said.

"Fucking A," Rich said. "Alphonse might win a Pulitzer someday maybe. Some kid gets a pep talk from a guy like Alphonse . . ." Rich shrugged. "You see what I'm saying."

"What you're saying is that you think you want to make this move?" Cally said.

"Finally be a university person like the gorgeous woman in my life."

Cally wrinkled her brow. "I hope you're not serious."

Rich laughed. "Of course not." Or so he said now and would always say, but the truth was Rich didn't like the vibes he got off some of Cally's colleagues. Nothing overt. Just a faint hint of condescension that he was only a high school teacher. And a coach at that.

"So you think you might help get some college players focused on life after basketball," Cally said. "OK. I can see that. But other than that, what's the appeal?"

"The challenge." Rich folded his lower lip between finger and thumb. "Turn the page in life and find one more chapter. Climb the mountain one more time." The truth was that Rich burned to make a difference, to live a life that mattered, not to win championships but to touch souls, to touch souls in order to save his own. "Climb a different mountain."

"Then I guess you ought to do it," Cally said.

"But you don't think so."

"Well, I don't trust Francis Saurian," Cally said. "You know that. He'll say anything at the moment to get what he wants and renege on it later without the first hint of embarrassment. You need to protect yourself. Saurian is septic. I've seen these careerist university administrators. Everything is about themselves and their next job. They make changes so they can list those changes on their resumes. They promise people whatever is required to get their cooperation. But keeping those promises isn't even on the dial of their moral compass."

"He's going to pay me five times what I'm making now. That's protection."

"And if he fires you, you don't have the salary or a job either. You don't care about money, but you've never impressed me as someone who's going to be content without a job."

"That's the risk, I guess," Rich said. "I don't like it, but there it is. Part of the challenge."

"Make him give you tenure," Cally said. "Point out that you've got tenure at Choctaw High and you won't move without it."

"He'll never go for it," Rich said. "It's a great idea, but coaches don't get tenure. Not even in high school. My tenure at Choctaw is in English, not as head basketball coach."

"Can't hurt to ask him. Man is a walking, talking wild card. He might do it just because it isn't done. Another first he can list on his resume. And I am not kidding about that."

So Rich asked for tenure, and Saurian acceded for two reasons. Most important, he could list that arrangement as another first on his resume. And what did Saurian care if a basketball coach had tenure, particularly at Urban University where Saurian had no intention of remaining one second longer than it took him to land a more prestigious job at a bigger school?

But Saurian had been through enough academic infighting in his career to know that a CEO dare not commit to tenure on his own, lest he stir up a roiling snake pit of unrest among his faculty. Thinking of faculty as snakes, Saurian believed, was quite appropriate, since snakes are cold blooded, come out of their holes only to eat and, if kept properly fed, are content to do almost entirely nothing for their entire lifespans. The only problem with the notion of tenure for Richard Janus was that Saurian couldn't use his coaching record to park him in the Department of Physical Education because Rich had taken not so much as one P.E. course in his entire college career, not even at the undergraduate level, much less any graduate courses. Consequently, Saurian would just have to secure tenure for Rich in the English department, the only real problem being that Rich had never taught a college-level English course.

As a contractual condition of hiring, common academic practice grants to appointees from off campus for positions such as president or chancellor or rector, provost, dean, and even department chair, the lifetime security of tenure in departments where the recipient hopes never to be forced to teach anything. (Well, chairs may have to teach a course once in a while, but no more often than they can help.) But even in such positions of academic administration, tenured appointments are still moved forward through the regular review process. The faculty in the "home" department is consulted by the department chair, and in some cases a vote is taken. The chair is not constrained by that vote, however, and makes his or her own recommendation to the dean who does the same to the provost and then the provost to the CEO and the CEO to the Board, and in the cases of religious institutions, the Board to God, who always reserves the right to send down brimstone and fire against recommendations not to *His* liking.

On rare occasions, departments may rise up and try to tweak the upper administration by denying the prospective appointee his or her desired tenure. But even in the face of anemic resumes, departmental faculty usually choose to approve tenure in hopes of securing political clout with the new appointee as well as his boss. From the outside, of course, this will appear odd since political clout on a university campus is of almost no value whatsoever.

In the half-century history of Urban no department had ever faced down a CEO and blocked an external appointment by denying tenure. Rich's application for tenure, though, was extraordinary since he had never held a university teaching position, and he wasn't being considered for an appointment in academic administration. What sense did it make to tenure Richard Janus in English when he was going to coach the basketball team? Well, it made sense to Francis Saurian because Rich had won seven state championships in the last sixteen years, and the Ungulates hadn't won seven *games* in any one season in the last eleven years. And he wasn't going to let any nit pickers in the English Department interfere with his plans.

5

After Miles Standish's murderous expedition against the Massachusetts, in the season we called *Namassackesos,* or late March of 1623, Edward Winslow wrote of the terror that gripped the people in our settlements near Plymouth. Winslow claims that many more died in the months ahead because we were too frightened to plant our crops. In short, my brothers and sisters were scared to death. But how likely does it seem to you that people so skilled at providing for themselves became too unsettled to feed themselves? And how gamy a coincidence do you find it that within months Canacum was dead at Manomet, along with Sachems Aspinet at Nauset and Iyanough at Cummaquid? These Pilgrims, the founding fathers of the nation that would become America, considered themselves chosen by God. Killing was a privilege bestowed upon them. What they made, I cannot say, of a Jesus who decreed the responsibility to "turn the other cheek," and chastised a disciple for raising a sword in His defense against arrest in Gethsemane.

But to me self-righteous violence sounds like the guys who flew airplanes into the World Trade Center in 2001. Doesn't it? Mohammed Atta was pretty sure he was flying on the wings of divine direction as well.

In the short haul, Standish's villainy had unintended consequences. Before the physical, moral and spiritual pipsqueak launched his attack on the Massachusetts, my brothers in the region had been supplying the Pilgrims with a goodly number of skins and pelts, which were shipped back to England in exchange for European goods they couldn't provide for themselves. After the slaughter at Wessagussett—surprise, surprise—we weren't much interested in having any more to do with the Pilgrims. So just that quickly their cash trade dried up, a fact they boohooed about plentifully in their diaries and in letters to their supporters on the other side of the Atlantic. Of course, in their telling, we were the bad guys in this.

Additionally, when all the sachems in the area were suddenly extinguished, their kinsmen decided to relocate to the west, into the area where my father Massasoit Ousamequin was the head guy. Before the massacre at Wessagussett, the Nausets had more warriors than did the Pokanokets. With their Sachem Aspinet dead, the Nauset fighters shifted their allegiance to Ousamequin. Ousamequin was a judicious leader. Sandwiched between the English to his east and the Narragansetts to his west, he saw his best course of action as diplomacy, rather than warfare, and he successfully pursued a policy of strength and cooperation for all of his long life. In this he was ultimately aided by Edward Winslow, one who was wrong about Wessagussett, but one who learned as he grew older. He was an imperfect man, but one who saw the inherent weakness of his people's plantation in their first decades and therefore the advantages of negotiation and compromise over a default resort to arms. Edward Winslow was the George H.W. Bush of his generation, a limited and flawed person who showed more wisdom than might have been expected. Edward's son Josiah, That Vicious Lying Rat Bastard, was the W of the family, a prejudiced, shallow and violent man whose arrogance led his people to the brink.

Had Massasoit Ousamequin lived much longer, his policy would have frayed in his own hands as it did first in my brother Wamsutta's and then in mine. The problem for us with the English was that more and more of them kept showing up. First they were in Plymouth. Then in 1630, arriving in an entire fleet of seventeen ships, fully one thousand belted hats arrived in Massachusetts Bay and took up residence in the area of Boston. Overnight, almost, the number of Englishmen in the vicinity quadrupled. Not long later another bunch of Bible thumpers planted themselves at the mouth of the Thames River and declared their presence the colony of Connecticut. By the mid-1630s we had plantations of English to our east, north and west. We were being surrounded. And they still kept coming, their hunger for land causing problems for those who had lived on it for over a millennium.

Our abiding problem was disunity. The Pilgrim attack on Wessagussett scared the people of southeast New England into the Wampanoag confederacy. But that new nation led by my father never really came to a meeting of minds with the Narragansett nation across the bay to our west. And the Narragansetts felt themselves to be squeezed on *their* west by the Pequots who lived along the southern Connecticut coast and on the banks of the Thames and Mystic rivers.

The Pequots were a prosperous people living on fertile land and involved in coastal trade with the Europeans and other Indian nations as well. In the mid-1630s they played a more prominent role in the fur trade than did the Puritans of Boston, Plymouth or Connecticut. And in the eyes of the English settlers, that was an unacceptable act of impudence for which the Pequots needed to be punished. The punishment arrived in 1636 and 1637, and it made what we had seen earlier at Wessagussett look like a hootenanny of racial harmony. In what the Puritans called The Pequot War but we Indians preferred to call The War of the Ubiquitous Johns, the goal was not just to scare the bejesus out of native peoples in order to get them to behave in a properly deferential way. No, the objective this time was genocide. Why merely scare the Indians into a resentful obedience when you can just wipe them out and appropriate land?

Now, you're going to really love the way the Puritans worked out a justification for this particularly sanguinary instance of evil. They said that the Pequots had to be punished for killing the Englishmen John Stone and John Oldham. Let us take up the case of Stone first.

It is scant exaggeration to say that the Puritan excuse for war on the Pequots was like Stalin saying that the Germans had to be punished for burning the body of Hitler. John Stone was not a citizen of Plymouth or Massachusetts Bay, and he was reviled in both places. He was a West Indian trader who engaged in acts of piracy just about any time he thought he could get away with it. In Plymouth, William Bradford had condemned him to death for trying to steal a trading ship. In Boston, he was exiled after being denounced for Biblical knowledge of another man's wife, a sin for which he managed little in the way of contrition.

With no more sanctuary to be found in New England, Stone decided to sail to Virginia where Englishmen were notoriously less uptight. On the way there, though, he sailed up the Connecticut River in search of people he could kidnap and then either ransom to their families or haul away to be sold into slavery farther south. Jewel of a man, John Stone. And he got just what he deserved. While he was ashore one night and behaving in his usual arrogant, irresponsible and violent way, the Pequots snuck up on his camp and sent him to meet Old Scratch by planting a hatchet solidly in his cranium and scattering his brains in the dirt. Good riddance. You'd think the English would be pleased that the Pequots effected what the English had edicted.

But no, of course not, no.

The case of John Oldham is equally outrageous. Oldham undertook a trading mission among the Narragansetts in 1633 and sold them goods infected with smallpox. Some 700 Narragansetts died as result of this villainy. But the Narragansetts deduced his perfidy, and when he next came among them in July of 1636, he was publicly charged before a council of Narragansett elders, tried in accordance with their traditions, found guilty, formally sentenced and publicly executed for mass murder, as, indisputably, he ought to have been.

Take note now: the Narragansetts killed Oldham, not the Pequots. The Narragansetts were the Pequots' traditional rivals and enemies. And the Puritans knew exactly what had happened and why. But the truth was of no interest to them. What they wanted was to make war on the Pequots. Why? Because the Pequots had the best trading position in the whole of southern New England, the Dutch from New Amsterdam central among their clients. They had good land to boot. Now, capitalizing on the deaths of the first two Johns, the God-fearing Puritans had the excuses they craved. The Pequots had killed "good Christians" and must be punished. In August of 1636, the Puritans, under the executive leadership of a third John, John Winthrop, Governor of Massachusetts Bay, dispatched a fourth John, John Endecott, to wreak their vengeance.

You have to love the actions of these guys who came to the New World more purely to pray to a Jesus they obviously hadn't a single wisp of a distant scent of understanding. Among Endecott's explicit, written, unconcealed charges was to sail to Block Island, where Oldham had died, kill all the men living there, capture all the women and children and sell them into slavery. No matter that the Puritans' declared war was with the Pequots and that the Block Islanders were Narragansetts, the human bounty from the sale of the slaves would fund the rest of the military expedition. Hallelujah and hand me a bayonet, we've the Lord's work to do.

However, if you were John Endecott, you wouldn't do your job very well, or at least not the killing part. Endecott and his scripture-quoting sidekicks attacked Block Island, but the residents refused to fight or even to show themselves, so Endecott resorted to burning their uninhabited *weetoos* and stealing what corn he could locate. He then journeyed on into Pequot territory where he met with the same reception. Endecott challenged the Pequots to come out and fight him in the open, European style, and the Pequots said, no, but if you'd like to come into the woods where we can sneak up on you, we'll be glad to meet you there. Endecott's primary accomplishment was not to agree to their suggestion. With nobody willing to advance in order to be killed, Endecott sailed away with little to show for his efforts, save the enmity of the Pequots who had sense enough to understand that they probably hadn't seen the last military incursion they were going to face at the hands of the light skins.

This is where the story gets sad, as, alas, it always did when we Indians tried to resist the white man's murderous ways. The Pequots knew within reason that the English had not finished screwing with them. So the Pequots approached their old rivals the Narragansetts and said, to coin a phrase, let's the bury the hatchet; in fact, if it comes to it, let's bury a lot of hatchets in the brains of the English. If the Narragansetts had agreed to an alliance at this point, the whole history of New England, and thereby maybe of America, might have turned out differently. The Pequots and the Narragansetts were easily the two most powerful Indian nations in the region, much more so than Dad's Wampanoags. Together they could have put far more fighting men into the field than the English. And with the Narragansetts standing strong on the Pequots' eastern flank, the English could not have attacked over land into Connecticut or maintained overland communications between battlefields in the Connecticut valley and home bases in Boston and Plymouth.

The Narragansetts were tempted. Buggers were always tempted. But before deciding what course to take, they sought the counsel of the white man they regarded as their friend, Roger Williams, the founder of Rhode Island, protector of Quakers and theological antagonist of the Puritans. "The Pequots are your historic enemies," Williams argued to Narragansett Sachem Miantonomi as they sat around the fire in Miantonomi's *nashweetoo* in *Wapicumniilkesos*, in early March of 1637. "Fifteen years ago they fought you and took land that had always belonged to your people."

"But the English are a savage people," Miantonomi responded. "They kill without mercy and without provocation. We are not friends of the Pequots, no, but how long will it be before the English pick a quarrel with my people?"

Williams was an outcast from the Massachusetts Bay colony from where he was banished under threat of death, and he could count no friends among the zealots at Plymouth. He had come into the area only a year earlier and had made a point of negotiating a land sale from Miantonomi for his plantation at Providence. "My brethren English are hardly perfect beings," Williams admitted, "but they are not now your enemies. If you stand with them, you will continue to have peaceful relations with them. The Pequots have always been your enemies. If you help defend them, even if you succeed, you will face enemies on both your front and back."

Miantonomi puffed at his pipe for long seconds before replying. "Even though we can see the past more clearly than the future, your arguments are strong. You can send this message back to the English. My people will not join with the Pequot. I will even send 500 of my warriors to accompany the Boston men into Pequot country. Once the fight is finished, I ask only that our lost land be returned to us."

Williams was pleased and extended his hand toward Miantonomi to shake. The sachem was startled by this gesture, and though he had encountered it previously, he first drew back before he gathered himself and clasped with Williams. "What you ask is perfectly reasonable," Williams said. "And it shall be done."

"And one other thing," Miantonomi said. "The fighting must be in the way of our people, not yours. Such killing as shall be necessary must be restricted to those wearing the colors of war on their faces. The women and children and old people must not fall under fire from your musketeers, must not feel the cold metal of your blades."

"That goes without saying," Williams said.

Williams is hailed by history as a man who preached universal religious tolerance and was a friend of the Indians. By comparison with the men who hounded him into exile, perhaps he was. But it's difficult to believe that he would have lobbied Miantonomi the way he did purely out of a sense of where the Narragansetts' best interests lay. For even Williams must have feared the might of a Pequot-Narragansett confederacy and its impact on his own activities at Providence. Unfortunately, this won't be the last we'll hear of Williams whom history often treats as a saint but who, in fact, always ended up on the wrong side when the invading whites made war on their bronze-skinned neighbors.

In the aftermath of its alliance with the Narragansetts, as the English began to gear up for a more concerted attack than John Endecott had managed, they sent a couple more Johns down to Fort Saybrook at the mouth of the Connecticut River. John Mason came down with reinforcements from Hartford, and John Underhill came in with another contingent from Boston. In May these two men were instructed by their superiors to attack the Pequots at Sachem Sassacus' strongly defended main village on the Thames River. That would have proved a fight history would have recorded differently, for even had the English prevailed, and they might well not have, they would have shed much of their own blood in the pursuit of victory. Johns Mason and Underhill understood that and so opted for another tactic. Instead of attacking the village on the Thames, they attacked another settlement on the Mystic River. Wily them since Sassacus had his warriors on the Thames while only women, children and old men were then resident on the Mystic. So much for what goes without saying by Roger Williams.

The Pequot settlement on the Mystic was a palisaded fort with only one entrance/exit to be defended. Along with their Narragansett and Mohegan allies, the English could no doubt have taken the fort by just marching in. But *some* warriors *might* have been inside.

So Mason proposed another idea. "How about burning them out?" he suggested to Underhill, one John to another, as they huddled under pine, birch, elm and oak. They had yet to engage with the enemy, though they were now in musket range.

"Torch the fort?" Underhill asked, surprised. "We haven't made a single sally. We aren't even sure of the fighting force lurking inside. Surely we must test them first." In fact, Mason had strong reason to believe that only the smallest number of warriors were inside the Mystic fort. He had earlier seen hundreds of Pequot warriors along the banks of the Thames, presumably headquartered at the larger fort there, and had no reason to think that they had relocated here. Underhill's reservations stemmed from a momentary surrender to conscience. "There may be few true combatants inside," he said, "and fire is an indiscriminate weapon."

But Mason persisted with his argument to proceed with the torch, and finally Underhill agreed to put the matter to Chaplain Samuel Stone who had marched with Mason from his church in Hartford. The Reverend Stone said he would like a night to pray about the question, and so the English and their Indian allies lay down in the forest for the night, only the shortest paces from the replication of hell they would shortly make. In the morning this man of the cloth said that God had granted approval to proceed with fire, although, of some Pontius Pilate note, the Reverend set off toward Narragansett Bay before the first spark was struck.

The "battle" at Fort Mystic was a cold-blooded massacre of civilians. You can defeat your enemy by breaking his will to fight sometimes more easily than defeating him in combat. Isn't that what the firebombing of Japan during World II aimed to accomplish? Isn't that what dropping the atomic bombs on Hiroshima and Nagasaki was for?

The English surrounded the Pequot fort, then set it on fire and burned up anyone who tried to remain inside. Those who tried to flee in terror they sworded and musketed down like lambs in a slaughter house. Witnesses at the scene reported that perhaps five Pequots managed to escape. By fire, blade and bullet, the English sent 700 souls into the next life while losing only two of their own men, both of whom died of "friendly fire." Mason was so aware of the inhumanity of what his troops were up to that he ordered the Narragansetts to the rear for fear the Indians would try to stop the carnage. And indeed Underhill later recorded the Narragansetts' protest that what the English did was "too furious and killed too many," though he dishonestly tried to represent this attitude as one of cowardice.

Sassacus and two hundred of his warriors finally arrived at the Mystic fort, but they were so overcome by the horror they found there that they were surrounded and captured by the Narragansetts. Under the traditions of New England warfare among the Indians, those who surrendered would have been spared and even provided for. But the English took the captives away from the Narragansetts and sold them into slavery in the West Indies in exchange for enslaved Africans. Hereby, the first direct connection was made between my people and those from another continent with even darker skin. The English had the good if evil sense to understand that none of us would have worked very well as a slave anywhere in New England because an Indian captive would have slipped away into the woods and back into his or her own community at the first chance. African slaves had been imported into Virginia a couple of decades earlier, but now the practice had expanded northward.

And though the holding of slaves would die out sooner in New England than elsewhere in the American colonies, the shipping tycoons of Boston and Newport were made rich by the slave trade and continued to traffic in human cargo until the last of its infamous days.

Pequot Sachem Sassacus himself escaped capture at Mystic and tried to take refuge with the Mohawks. But the Mohawks, seeing their interest in promoting trading relations with the English, killed Sassacus and sent his scalp to Boston as an indication of their good will and reliability. (The Mohawks scalped their victims; we New England Algonquians did not practice this barbarism.) Throughout the rest of 1637, the dispirited Pequot survivors were hunted down and killed or captured and sold into slavery, their former lands taken over by Mohegans, Narragansetts and the unending stream of English immigrants.

One might have thought that the English pretense of Christian charity would have been offended and guilt stricken by this genocide. But in that presumption one would be sorely mistaken. Mason and Underhill were welcomed back to their English settlements as heroes where they made little effort to conceal what they had done. Mason bragged about his exploits and credited his God Almighty as the inspiration for the "fiery oven where did the Lord judge among the heathen, filling Mystic with dead bodies." Back in Plymouth, Governor William Bradford wrote, "It was a fearful sight to see them thus frying in the fire and the streams of blood quenching same, and horrible was the stink and scent thereof; but the victory seemed a sweet sacrifice, and we give the praise thereof to God."

Man, oh man, though more evidence is coming your way, I am sure you already see why John Lennon would dare imagine a world with no religion.

6

On the ridiculous theory that naming rights to university buildings might be sold to wealthy alumni willing to fork over $2 million a pop to put their family's name on a three-story rectangular configuration without a whisper of architectural grace, none of Urban's buildings had names. Just numbers. Each building was given its number in the order of its completion. By the time Rich was hired as head basketball coach, the university owned 83 buildings on its rectangle of desirable real estate along the Lake De Soto shoreline. But since the founding CEO in the mid-1950s was cannily determined to protect his property from being taken away by a state profoundly disinclined to support his university, the buildings were always erected as far from each other as possible. Each of the first four buildings was constructed on a different corner of the campus. The library was placed in the middle; at least that made sense. But each new construction was placed as far from the others as possible. These policies of numbering and strategic distance were as confusing as an address in Tokyo and meant that undergraduates spent years unable to find their classes. And once faculty members located their own offices when they were first employed, they seldom left the vicinity thereafter.

Francis Saurian knew that this was idiotic and confusing, and sometimes he thought of doing something about it even though he had no plans whatsoever for hanging around any longer than necessary. He had the naming of his buildings on his mind as he stepped from his office into that of Kimberly Kane, the raven-haired executive assistant he'd inherited from his predecessor, to direct her to set up an appointment for him with the chair of the English Department. Kimberly's eyes were fixed on the screen of her computer, and Saurian flicked his tongue over his lips as he looked at her. He would think she was scrumptious if he concerned himself with such things. But he was a man of considerable discipline, and he knew that sexual scandal was the quickest way out of administration and back to a teaching career. If it was extra-marital sex he needed, he'd just pay for it like any other intelligent guy who made a lot of money.

So he steeled himself to temptation and quickly looked away from Kimberly through her open door into the outer office of his suite. Walking past at that very moment was Sheila Pyrite, one of his employees, and one of his most vexing. Sheila Pyrite reported directly to Francis Saurian and had a small office in his own suite where she could sometimes be found, but he didn't know what she did. The Urban workday was from 8:30 till 5:00, but Sheila seemed to come in later in the morning, always after 10:00, when she bothered to come in at all. As Saurian understood matters, Sheila was the only child of Joshua Pyrite, the now deceased founder of Pyrite Fruit, a company he sold for $100 million to the United Fruit Company in the late 1950s. After divesting himself of his company, Joshua dedicated the rest of his career to public service or attempts thereunto. He served three terms on the Choctaw School Board and ran unsuccessfully for mayor on two occasions. Not long before his death, Joshua talked Saurian's predecessor into hiring Sheila because he thought it would be good for her to have a job, and he thought a job in education would be the best way for her to enjoy a meaningful life. Sheila was now approaching forty, and she'd just divorced for the third time. She had a degree in psychology from Alkansea State and had done graduate work at Urban, ultimately earning a Ph.D. in Academic Counseling in the College of Education. Some of this Saurian had learned from Kimberly Kane, some from poking through Sheila's personnel file one night where he learned that her title was Special Assistant to the Rector for Assigned Project Management. Sheila's salary was $75,000 a year, which seemed to Saurian a goodly amount for someone who evidently wasn't expected to work a forty-hour week. Somewhat spooked by both Sheila's job description and her personal history, especially her immense fortune, Saurian was reluctant to interfere with her activities too much. But he would like to know what she did or was supposed to do. When he asked that question of Kimberly shortly after he'd taken the rectorship, Kimberly had responded, "She handles special projects."

"Right, I see," Saurian said. "What's she working on right now?"

"Oh, I wouldn't know that," Kimberly responded. "She doesn't really interact with us a lot. Not that she's not nice and all."

"Oh, I'm sure she's more than nice," Saurian said. "I was just curious about her portfolio. You know, what all she's up to, how I might work her into some of my objectives."

"Well," Kimberly said, slinging her mane of black hair back over her shoulder. "Rector Beauregard gave her what he said were some 'broad guidelines,' and she's been going with that pretty much since then. She has a lot of meetings off campus."

As Saurian was jostled now by seeing Sheila come into the office at 10:23, he said to Kimberly, "I want you to set up a meeting for me with the English chair. Can I presume he knows where 6 is?"

"He's never been here before, as far as I know. But he probably knows."

"Well, get him over here and give him directions if you have to. And while I'm on this business of numbering our buildings, what do you think of the idea of giving them names?"

"What kind of names?"

"I don't know, names for historical figures, I guess, something like that. Maybe for important people from the State of Alkansea or for explorers who founded the area."

"Maybe for the Indians who lived here before us?" Kimberly said. "That would be neat." She said that, I'm sure, just to please me because I'm the one telling this story.

Saurian shrugged. "Yeah, I guess we could do that. Anything's better than just a list of numbers. Nobody can find anything. How about if I put Sheila Pyrite on it?"

Kimberly wrinkled her brow. "I don't know. I guess you could ask her."

Ask her? Saurian thought. He was her fucking boss.

Kimberly said, "I don't think Rector Beauregard ever asked her to manage one of his own projects, but maybe she'd be up for that."

Saurian thought he'd damn well put Sheila on the building-naming project. But when he asked her to do it, she said that she'd prefer not to, that her plate was pretty full. And when he asked what all she had on her plate, she raised the back of her hand to him and ticked off a series of names with her thumb against her fingers. He had no idea what she was talking about but dismissed her without asking her to explain. Since he would be leaving his current position for a better one before long, he didn't really care whether the buildings got named or not.

Meanwhile Urban University administrators, even unappreciated lowlings like department chairs, did usually know that the CEO's office was in 6 and that 6 stood on the quad between 12 to the south and 16 to the north. So at the appointed time Dr. Chockley Stinchcomb showed up for his meeting with the big boss bearing with him no small measure of anxiety. He hadn't a clue what Saurian wanted with him, but he couldn't imagine anything good.

Dr. Chockley Stinchcomb was an aging linguistician who, at 5'6", was even shorter than Francis Saurian whose bald pate poked the height bar at 5'7". Dr. Stinchcomb had grown up in Choctaw where he attended Rich's own Choctaw High School back in the long-ago day when white people went there, even the children of white people with the means of the Stinchcombs.

Chockley's father had inherited considerable wealth from his father who had done the same. The family had amassed a fortune owning land on which slaves raised sugarcane, though nobody in the family mentioned that anymore. The Stinchcombs no longer needed to work and so did not work. Chockley's father did not work. His grandfather did not work. And his great-grandfather had slaves who worked for him. Chockley was unusual in the line of Stinchcomb heirs in that he had stirred himself enough to have a job. This, however, did not mean that he worked.

Chockley Stinchcomb held a B.A. in English from Tulane and a Ph.D. from Harvard. He had attended Harvard during the 1960s, graduating in 1969, without evidently noticing the cultural revolution that changed the way most everybody else thought about everything. At Harvard he had studied vowel inflection variation in the formation of regional accents. His dissertation studied the host of accents in the city of New Orleans, some sounding as if the speaker hailed from Brooklyn, others sounding more like something you'd hear in Virginia, and still others that rang with the twangs of Mississippi and Alabama.

Dr. Stinchcomb was quite the authority on the subject of New Orleans accents, and his satisfaction about his expertise was so great that he never felt the need to pursue additional scholarly work. He was occasionally asked to drive over to New Orleans to speak on the subject of local accents, mostly to Uptown and Garden District audiences of retired people, but he never published his dissertation or anything else other than a series of letters to the editor of *The Choctaw Straight Arrow* about random events of no enduring interest. Given that Stinchcomb's letters were all intensely boring, all who read them presumed that they were printed because of the influence of his family, although no one could state exactly what influence the Stinchcomb family exercised or, with the exception of the editorial staff at *The Straight Arrow*, over whom. Chockley signed all his letters with his name, followed by the words "Ph.D., Harvard University, 1969." His graduate degree was seldom relevant to the topic of the letter, but the paper printed his educational credential anyway.

Dr. Chockley Stinchcomb arrived at Urban after finishing his work at Harvard, and the members of the English Department were so impressed with themselves for having a colleague with a Ph.D. from America's most prestigious university that they granted him tenure three years later despite a mediocre teaching record and no published scholarship. I hasten to point out that That Vicious Lying Rat Bastard Josiah Winslow also had a Harvard degree, and *I* didn't find that fact much of a recommendation. Stinchcomb shared Winslow's disdain for anybody not like himself, though his viciousness was limited by his astonishing self-satisfied laziness. His appalling lack of productivity meant that had he not come up for tenure in Urban's first years, he wouldn't have gotten it. But, he was a Harvard man, and now in 1999 he was a full professor and department chair, the latter a story in itself.

While at Harvard, Stinchcomb had developed an affinity for tweed suits and pipe smoking. The suits were inappropriate for the climate in Choctaw, leaving him with a permanent shine, as if he'd just wiped his face with the wrapping paper from a pound of ham. Meanwhile, the pipe smoking left him smelling like an ashtray with B.O. He had a full head of unruly gray hair, which he wore longer than might be anticipated for a man of his patrician hauteur. He mysteriously fancied himself a wit and was always chuckling smugly at his own remarks. But, actually, he was a stifling bore and one oblivious to the fact that at department social gatherings people were always walking backwards away from him for fear that they would get trapped into one of his endless monologues, which might ultimately cause them to collapse into a stupor and topple into his stink. Yes, this description is largely unkind, but I got to thinking about Chockley Stinchcomb in connection with That Vicious Lying Rat Bastard, and I fell into a foul mood.

After Stinchcomb was escorted into and seated on the burnt umber sofa in the CEO's office in 6, he was asked by Francis Saurian to look over Richard Janus' resume. The office was furnished as if it were a living room. A baby blue sofa faced the one on which Dr. Stinchcomb sat. Beige wing chairs at either end made for a comfortable meeting space. The CEO paced about on the Oriental rug that covered the center of the room, talking as he strode back and forth.

"*Dr.* Richard Janus," the CEO began. As Stinchcomb fumbled for reading glasses in the breast pocket of his tweed suit coat, the CEO began to argue about how Rich and Jesus were just about the same because their names both started with a J and ended with US.

OK, Saurian was not really so direct as all that, but he was giving Rich a big-time boost and talking with such forcefulness that Dr. Stinchcomb wasn't able to study the resume he'd been handed. Frankly, Saurian's whole approach to this situation reminded me of the procedures followed in the execution of a number of treaties and land-sale agreements the English made me sign and subsequently waved in my face when they damn well knew I couldn't read them. Not that I otherwise identify with Chockley Stinchcomb, I hasten to add.

"As you can plainly see," the CEO said, pacing back and forth in front of the English chair, "*Dr.* Janus is a very well qualified individual." He stopped and spun around to face Stinchcomb directly. "*Very* well qualified, indeed. *Exceedingly* well qualified, one might say."

"Yes," Stinchcomb agreed, though he hadn't figured out what to. "Yes." He brushed his fingers over the top page of Rich's resume, his eyes sweeping back and forth like search lights, trying to take in something to say that might please the CEO. "Mr. Janus does seem well . . ."

"*Dr.* Janus," the CEO said. "*Dr.* Janus. The man has a Ph.D. From your very own department, in fact."

"My Ph.D. is from Harvard," Stinchcomb said.

"Well, good for you," the CEO replied. "I hope you aren't insinuating that your degree is superior to Dr. Janus'. Given that you've spent your entire professional career here."

"Oh, no," Dr. Stinchcomb said, mopping at his forehead with the back of his hand, smearing a streak of grease across his reading glasses in the process. He stared down at the resume growing damp in his fist and tried again to take something in.

"There's no reason for you to disparage Dr. Janus just because his Ph.D. is from Urban and yours is from hoity toity Harvard."

"Oh, no," Stinchcomb said. "I thought you meant that Dr. Janus' Ph.D. was from Harvard."

"Well, it isn't. It's from right here, and that's good enough for me. I assume it's good enough for you too."

"Of course," Dr. Stinchcomb said, his eyes down on the paper that had dissolved into a spidery blur in front of him. He coughed, looked up at the CEO, and managed, "Dr. Janus seems very well qualified indeed."

"Ah, excellent," the CEO asserted. "Then we agree that tenure for Dr. Janus in your department should prove no problem."

"Tenure?" Stinchcomb wondered, finally ascertaining why the CEO had summoned him.

How, I can just feel you wondering, did someone as inept as Chockley Stinchcomb end up the chair of the largest department at the second largest institution of higher learning in the state of Alkansea? One word, *the* word (no?): *politics.*

Chockley Stinchcomb became Urban's English Department chair because he had no friends and thus belonged to none of the department's bitter pedagogical, ideological and territorial factions. It isn't quite true that because he belonged to no side that he was neutral, but it *is* true that no one wanted him as an ally.

The English Department had three warring groups all wanting either to dominate the department or at least be immune from attack. The Brit Lit faction thought the department ought to concentrate on literary texts produced by writers from the British Isles (unlike the Brits themselves, they were willing to include Irish writers) who had completed their major works by the time of World War I. In their view not enough time had passed to judge the merit of more recent British writers while American writers were not worth discussing. Some in the Brit Lit group thought that literary studies should start with Beowulf and end with Shakespeare. Others thought that Shakespeare alone was sufficient. But to keep the peace, the Brit Litters offered inclusion to Swiftians and Miltonists, Romanticists and Victorians.

The Modern Lit contingent wanted to include all writing by American authors and all twentieth- and twenty-first-century literature produced by writers anywhere in the world. The members of this group prided themselves on their embrace of diversity and considered themselves the most politically correct.

The rhetoric/composition and popular writing faculty, which included the creative writers, wanted to dignify the contributions of their colleagues who taught basic writing, traditionally the field hands of university employment. This group was important for protecting the least powerful members of the department, the non-tenure-track Instructors who did far and away the most work and, as is always the way of the world, were the most poorly paid and least appreciated. The problem was that the rhetoric/composition folks, who all had Ph.D.s, resented the fact that they weren't highly regarded and were forever hoping to be accepted by the lit crew. Meanwhile, the creative writers just wanted to be left alone and resented the fact that they constantly had to be pulled away from their latest poems or stories to fight political battles.

In the waxing and waning of departmental political struggles over matters that no one could recall as short a time as a year later, the Modern Litters usually wielded the balance of power.

The ancient traditionalists were contemptuous of the training and the scholarship of any save their own. The Modern Lit people despised the disdain of the traditionalists. On the other hand, the modernists themselves looked down on the training and scholarly or creative product of the rhet/comp and creative writers. Chairs often came from their group as they played the other two off against each other. And if this sounds like the strategy of the Pilgrims with regard to the Wampanoags and the Narragansetts, then you're paying pretty good attention after all.

Chockley Stinchcomb ascended to the position of chair because he had no support from anyone and thus could be safely supported by everyone. We might think that as a linguistician (professionals in the field prefer *linguist*, but Chockley was hardly professional), he belonged to the rhet/comp group, but they were appalled to be associated with him because he never published. Meanwhile, he thought the creative writers shouldn't have university jobs because writing could not be taught. Once when Chockley made such a statement in a faculty meeting, a fiction writer whispered to his poet colleague, "Well, it evidently couldn't be taught to him."

As the politicking commenced, the traditionalists were convinced to support him for chair because what, after all, was more traditional than a Harvard man. But they had no other use for him. So the modernists promoted his candidacy and pretty soon he was the department's top administrator even though he had evidenced no skills in management or human relations. In the semester that Stinchcomb had been chair, he had endeavored to do nothing, if he could, and if he *had* to do something, he tried to get someone else to do it instead. This had yet to make anyone seethingly mad, and so even though he accomplished nothing and lacked an ounce of personal support, he maintained the endorsement of two-thirds of his colleagues.

However, this sudden issue of tenure in the English Department for Dr. Richard Janus was another matter altogether. About this, Dr. Chockley Stinchcomb was not going to be able to avoid doing something. He was going to have to consult with his tenured colleagues, and after that he was going to have to make a recommendation.

"Is Mr. Janus applying for a position in our department?" Stinchcomb inquired of the CEO, a bead of sweat running between his glasses, down his nose and plummeting with a wet splash onto Rich's resume.

"*Dr.* Janus, Dr. Stinchcomb."

"Yes, Dr. Janus," Stinchcomb replied. "Didn't I say that?"

Still pacing, the CEO ignored his question. "We *are* going to be OK with *Dr.* Janus' tenure, are we not?"

Stinchcomb swallowed audibly. "I'm sorry, Mr. Rector, I mean Dr. Rector. Is Dr. Janus applying for a position in our department?"

"No, he's not."

"I see," Stinchcomb said, though, of course, he didn't.

"He's not applying for a *position* in your department; he's applying for *tenure* in your department. Or let me put it this way, *I* am applying for him to have tenure in your department. And as you acknowledged just a moment ago, Dr. Janus is very well qualified." The CEO stopped in front of Dr. Stinchcomb again and tapped on the top page of Rich's resume. "Guy really is a beaut, isn't he? Hell of a record."

"Excuse me, Mr. Rector, Dr. Rector. I'm sure this is my own fault. Please pardon my confusion. But, but, if Mr. Janus, Dr. Janus, isn't applying for a position in our department, why, why, is he applying for tenure in our department, why are you applying for him to have tenure in our department? Please forgive me, but I don't understand."

The CEO nodded vigorously and made a punching motion with his fist. "Because he wants it, don't you see. And because I want him. Hell of a record. My god, hell of a record. And I am not going to get him without tenure, which I think illustrates what a catch he really is. And that's why I am sure you and your fellows over in the English Department are going to help me."

"I'm sorry, Dr. Rector. If I may ask. You are going to get him for what?"

"Our basketball coach, of course. Didn't you look at the resume? The man has won seven state basketball championships, and he has a Ph.D. in English. Published two books too. Like I said, hell of a record. I don't quite understand why we're still talking about this."

Stinchcomb cleared his throat. "If I may. I see all the points that you are making. And I concur heartily, of course. If the decision were up to me alone. Well. But, as I know you understand, my colleagues will want to study this situation. And some may express concern that. Well. Well. Mr. Janus, Dr. Janus doesn't seem ever to have taught."

"What are you talking about? The man has been teaching for nearly two decades. Quite successfully as I understand it. I'm sure we can get letters attesting to that if you want them."

"Well. Of course." Stinchcomb swallowed and almost choked on saliva. "Of course, I meant at the university level," he croaked.

"Oh, here we go," the CEO said. "The usual elitist crap I can always count on from you boys over in the Humanities. English especially." Saurian's own Ph.D. was in sociology, a field he always felt looked down upon by the likes of people from English, history and philosophy. Saurian hadn't ever practiced that much sociology, of course, because he had determined while still in graduate school that the only money in academics lay in administration. Yes, the power and glory were intoxicating, but if you weren't in it for the money, why were you in it? "I don't take kindly to discriminators. My record in that regard is exceeded by none I'm proud to say."

"Well, that's not my own view, of course," Stinchcomb said. "I have the utmost respect for secondary teachers."

This was not remotely true. Chockley Stinchcomb had almost no respect for secondary teachers whatsoever.

"They work very hard under very trying conditions, I'm sure," Stinchcomb continued, "but I feel certain that some of my colleagues will raise the issue of university-level teaching experience and the greater scholarly demands and whatnot."

"Whatnot?"

"Yes. The scholarly demands and whatnot."

"Look," the CEO said in a flat tone. "Let's cut to the chase."

"The chase. Yes," Stinchcomb said.

The CEO rolled his eyes. "I'm sure you acknowledge that I'm the CEO around here."

"Yes, of course."

"Well, as the CEO I'm hiring Dr. Richard Janus to coach our basketball team. *Dr.* Richard Janus with his Ph.D., his seven state championships, and his two books. I'm the CEO, and that's what I'm doing. And as chair of the English Department, you're going to see that Dr. Richard Janus gets tenure. You guys over in Humanities think that CEOs don't pay enough attention to you, but *I* have paid plenty of attention since I've been here, and I know that your average faculty member gets promoted to full professor on the basis of one book. My new basketball coach has two, which, the way I count, makes him twice as good as the rest of you. I don't know by what factor that makes him better than you, since, as best I can tell, you got your degree from Harvard, ate it and have been sitting on the crapper ever since. So let's be just as clear as possible. This meeting is coming to a close. You are going to leave here, and you are going to get me that tenure recommendation I want, and you can damn well know that if you don't, I will find me someone in your department who will prove delighted with your chair stipend and will be glad to get me what I want just to make me happy."

Chockley Stinchcomb was surprised at how easily matters played out. Several faculty members whispered in his office that the department was being railroaded, but with the CEO's determination in the matter known to all, no one was willing to oppose Rich's tenure openly. In a department as divided and suspicious as Urban's English Department, anyone inclined to speak against the arrangement was convinced that his or her opposition would be conveyed directly to the CEO by an enemy. Stinchcomb sent the paperwork forward where it was approved by Dean Turner and by Provost Alton Centry, who was a palpable suck-up that Saurian was biding his time to get rid of anyway. The CEO affixed his signature and sent it to the Board of Trustees via the Under Viceroy of Higher Education for Academic Affairs, the inveterate babbler Margaret Lockhart, and then the Viceroy of Higher Education, the unprincipled Elia Lipscom, both of whom signed it without looking at it, knowing what it entailed or, given that it had to do with Urban University, caring about it one micron of a whit.

So that's how Rich left Choctaw High and arrived at Urban as head Ungulate basketball coach and tenured full professor of English.

7

We Indians learned from the Pequot War two very sobering lessons. First, an Englishman's word was good only until he had a selfish motive not to stand by it. Second, the English fought with an astonishing immorality that honored no humane boundaries and granted no mercy. As friends, the English were not trustworthy; as enemies they were fiends.

Those lessons influenced my father as he tried to lead the Wampanoags over the next quarter century. We lived in closest proximity to the English at Plymouth, but we could really do little more than try to maintain a show of force married to a conciliatory demeanor. After the mid-1630s, without cooperation from at least the Narragansetts, the Wampanoags could be dispatched as ruthlessly and as thoroughly as the Pequots and the Massachusetts before them. So Ousamequin ever endeavored to get along. The problem was that the English ever endeavored to procure more of what was ours. As more and more of them showed up, they wanted more and more of our land. Some snake-brain-sized remnant of a conscience made them willing to enter into contracts for our property. *When expedient.* Lacking an iron-clad charter with the British crown for their operations in the New World, the Plymouth leadership felt like its best long-range protection, should the Motherland ever decide to meddle very seriously in their affairs, was a series of deeds of transfer. "See," the colonists could say, "they sold it to us. It's ours because they sold it to us." But cognizant of both Wessagussett and Fort Mystic, Ousamequin knew full well that the English would take by force what they could not extract by "legal" transactions.

So Dad's strategy was to sell land that Wampanoags were not using a little at a time for as much as he could get. In 1642 he relinquished the property where the Pilgrims built the town of Rehoboth. In 1650 he gave up territory for Bridgewater and in 1652 still more land for Dartmouth. By mid-century, southern New England was trapped out, our supply of skins gone. Now our land was disappearing too. And as Ousamequin's long life drew toward a close, his options became more and more restricted.

The changing of the guard began after the sale of Dartmouth. Given that Dad was now in his late seventies, my older brother Wamsutta was beginning to exercise more influence with our people. Ousamequin affirmed Wamsutta's leadership, and to make sure that the English understood, he removed himself from our Pokanoket settlement at Montaup and took up residence many miles away in the land of our Nipmuck cousins, in territory still largely untouched by English settlement.

Ousamequin stayed in touch with us for the rest of his life and was always free with his counsel, but he remained with the Nipmucks until his death in 1660. His connection with the Nipmucks served us well, and in the years to come, they would prove our staunchest allies.

In 1654, without Ousamequin as a signatory, Wamsutta frustrated Plymouth in their determined monopoly of our land sales by selling a Wampanoag island in Narragansett Bay to a Rhode Islander. Then in 1657, Wamsutta refused to allow a sale of land to the Pilgrim town of Taunton, even though Plymouth alleged that Ousamequin had agreed to it. They had no documentary evidence, however, and were unable to produce Ousamequin to confirm this allegation. So Wamsutta refused to relent and in the process again pissed off the short-tempered Plymouthites.

Changing the pattern of our interaction with the leaders of Plymouth, Wamsutta proved unwilling to let our nation's land go at fire-sale prices, but he wasn't looking for a fight with the English. That's why in 1660, not long after our father's death, with me in tow, he showed up in Plymouth to initiate the whole name-changing ritual. "Hey, I'm a regular guy, a good guy to have as a neighbor. I'm not spoiling for trouble. Au contraire, I want to be one of you. Why . . . why don't you start calling me one of your own names so we'll know we're buddies. Alexander? Sure, Alexander's excellent. Alexander it is. I am Alexander now. Philip for my brother Metacom? No problem. Philip he is. We all have names just alike, and we are just alike. I'm going to treat you with respect, and I am sure you will do the same for me. We'll all just get along famously. We'll always be the best of pals."

Not.

In 1662, Wamsutta sold still more land to a Rhode Island colonist. And then the crap started again. Whenever we did something the English didn't like, somebody started a rumor about how a bunch of us were getting together to go to war.

This time, the story began to circulate in those drafty English clapboards that Wamsutta had asked the Narragansetts to help him make war on the Bible thumpers.

Can anybody say "Pequot"? How about "Wessagussett"?

The rumors got so rampant that then Plymouth Governor Thomas Prence dispatched That Vicious Lying Rat Bastard Josiah Winslow to bring Wamsutta into town for some scolding and humiliating. Winslow and ten thugs set off to arrest Wamsutta in Pokanoket. But he wasn't there. Instead, he and his wife Weetamoo (my own beautiful wife Wootonekanuske's lovely older sister) were with a group of friends fishing on Monponsett Pond, a small lake to the northwest of Plymouth. On this beautiful *Towwakesos* or July day, the sun up and warm, the lake a shimmering blue, Wamsutta was in such an unwarlike mode after an early morning swim with his wife, that he and his companions had stacked their muskets outside their lake weetoo and were inside eating breakfast when Winslow and his goons stormed up and seized all the Wampanoag weapons before Wamsutta and his friends realized what was up.

That Lying Rat Bastard started right in with his accusations, which was pretty easy for him to do given that he was armed and my brother wasn't. Wamsutta was some pissed. Here he was on vacation, enjoying a fresh-smoked brown trout and tasty corn porridge with goose and lentils, and in comes this seething white jackass to stomp about waving a single-shot pistol, pointing fingers and making unwarranted threats.

Wamsutta told him straight out: "If I were in a conspiracy to kill you and your sorry lot, would I be miles from home, closer to your garrisons than the villages of my warriors? Would I have failed to post a guard, as I obviously did, so that you could sneak up on me?"

Winslow pressed his handgun against my brother's breast. "I have my orders, *King* Alexander, and as Jesus is my savior you stinking savage, I will do as I am commanded." Now most of you even vaguely familiar with the New Testament won't recall Jesus handling a lot of weapons, but according to Josiah Winslow, the Good Lord was riding shotgun with him.

Wamsutta controlled his instinct to spit in the man's face. "Stink, Mr. Winslow?" he said. "You would know of stinking." Wamsutta was almost five inches taller than That Vicious Lying Rat Bastard and looked down on him with a sneer.

"You stink of greasy fish and Indian mush."

"And you stink of white man's filth."

Wamsutta had brass balls. If a fight broke out, he was an instant goner, even if his friends might have been able to get some payback before all the blood was shed.

Winslow jerked his pistol up under Wamsutta's chin. "I have a mind to send you into internal darkness, you creature of Satan."

"Have at it, Christian, but make sure you kill me, because if you don't, I am going to tear your arms off and feed them to my hogs."

Winslow stepped back, his gun still pointed at Wamsutta's chest. He probably figured that his bullet would kill my brother but then leave himself weaponless and vulnerable to any knife the Indians had concealed beneath their clothes. He stepped back again. "Get him out of this festering hole," Winslow said to his men, waving with his pistol toward the skin-draped *weetoo* door. But when two of Winslow's men tried to seize him, Wamsutta shook them off.

"I have no fear of going with you," he said, striding on his own outside, followed by Weetamoo, her long black hair hanging wet on her neck from their swim. Outside he said to Winslow, "Take me to your Governor Prence. We have met often before. I will answer any charges he has and disprove them. For I have truth on my side, and whoever says I have been planning for war has only lies." Wamsutta then thought of taking Winslow's gun away while the white man's accomplices rifle-shivered the rest of the Wampanoag party outside. Would that he had. Winslow might have killed him then, but Wamsutta might have sidestepped the bullet and then wrenched the Rat Bastard's head off instead. He was definitely strong enough.

Winslow kept backing away until his men were outside with him; then, still holding his pistol on my brother, he mounted his horse and told Wamsutta to walk ahead, and they would follow him through the woods. Winslow's men had gathered the Wampanoags' muskets, and one man covered Wamsutta's six friends while Winslow ordered Weetamoo and the rest of the party to stay put. "If you follow us down the trail, you will never see home again."

"No," Weetamoo said, her black eyes flashing and her fists gripped at her side. "No, we will not remain behind. My husband will not walk while you ride, and you will not take him off alone. He is a sachem, whereas what are you? Are you even what your people call a soldier?"

"We could shoot you where you stand," Winslow said. "Every one of you. Then your insolent husband too. We could shoot you and throw your fiendish bodies into the lake where you would never be found."

Weetamoo laughed, all in her mouth, her eyes wide and without mirth. "Surely even a white man knows that bodies don't stay buried in a lake."

"Of what matter to us?" Winslow said. "We aren't here. We weren't ever here."

"Whatever you may do to us," Wamsutta said, "will ultimately be known. If you want to avoid war, you won't shed any blood today. I have no plan of war, and because of that I will go with you, but Weetamoo is right; I will go as a sachem, and my party will come with me."

"And you will ride," Weetamoo said.

WAMSUTTA, WEETAMOO AND THEIR friends were escorted to the coastal town of Duxbury, east of Monponsett, and Plymouth dispatched officials to give Wamsutta the third degree. Wamsutta

defended himself against accusations that he had attempted to
foment an Indian conspiracy, pointing out once again that an
Indian about to go to war seldom instead went on holiday. That
Lying Rat Bastard remained sullen throughout most of the
encounter, frustrated that his fellow beige skins didn't decide
to arrest Wamsutta for the unspeakable crime of being a Native
American and a disrespectfully uppity one at that.

But the other interrogators announced that they believed
Wamsutta innocent, and all of a sudden That Lying Rat Bastard
Josiah Winslow was all strawberries and grapes. Why, now that
the matter of the conspiracy had been laid to rest, why didn't
Wamsutta and his men come on up to Winslow's house in
Marshfield and the whole bunch of them sit down together for a
meal, just as Massasoit Ousamequin had all those years ago when
English and Indian dined together at the first Thanksgiving.
Winslow had slain a deer only the day before. And Mrs. Rat
Bastard just loved roasting some flesh and whipping up a stew
for unexpected guests.

I think it's the clearest proof of Wamsutta's basic determination to continue our father's policy of cooperation that he
agreed to follow Winslow five miles up the coast.

When they got to Winslow's two-story house, with its
large barn and its rising fields on all sides, the Rat Bastard
invited everybody in. Mrs. Penelope Rat Bastard even seemed
to have been expecting guests. She had a large cauldron
of venison stew bubbling from a hook in the hearth. And
she had onions, radishes and green beans each simmering
in skillets on the coals. As Wamsutta, Weetamoo and their
six Wampanoag friends stepped into the one-room lower
floor with its double bed in the corner, Mrs. Rat Bastard
addressed them with words of welcome. Winslow and
Franklin Ferguson, one of the soldiers who had helped arrest
Wamsutta earlier in the day, moved a table from against the
wall where it doubled as a desk and set it in the center of
the room. Straight-back, narrow seated chairs were shifted

to the table from various places around the room. Though there were eleven people, and only seven chairs, nothing was said about the inadequate number.

Mrs. Rat Bastard opened a standing cupboard and brought out eleven metal bowls while her husband fetched spoons and laid them on the table. Ferguson went outside to the stream that whispered behind the house and returned with a pitcher of water. The Rat Bastard set out ten glasses and opened two bottles of wine. Taking one of the bowls from the table, he went to the stew pot, filled it, waited for his wife to place the cooked vegetables on top and returned to hand the food to Wamsutta. "Here, Alexander," he said. "Let us dine together and make peace."

Wamsutta accepted the bowl and nodded his thanks.

Winslow then turned to his other guests, waved his hand palm up across the table and said, "Please, let my wife serve you. Let us enjoy together the bounty of God's earth."

Weetamoo and the other Wampanoags stepped forward to the table, where each took a bowl and spoon, then moved to the hearth to let Mrs. Winslow ladle out the stew and vegetables. The table could seat six but not comfortably. When they had been served, Winslow and Ferguson sat on the gathered chairs and poured themselves glasses of wine. All of the Indians poured themselves water from the pitcher. They were not unfamiliar with the white man's alcohol, but they had long since realized its danger. Wamsutta and Weetamoo seated themselves at the table, but their friends sat on the floor, their backs against the rough wooden walls. Each of the men made sure that his breechclout was modestly tucked between his legs. Penelope Rat Bastard had fixed herself a bowl, but she remained standing at the hearth. Three chairs remained untaken, enough to have seated all the Wampanoag women, but none moved from the floor to take one.

"Let us bow our heads," Winslow said, even though some of the Wampanoags had already eaten a spoonful or two. "Our

Heavenly Father, please bless this gathering. Please bless this food and drink that it might be the agent of your will, to feed our bodies and send us on our way filled with the nourishment of your objectives. Amen."

"Amen," Ferguson echoed.

Then they ate without a great deal of conversation but with relish. They had all put in many miles that day, and they were hungry. When the first bowls were finished, Winslow took Wamsutta's back to the huge black pot to be refilled. Weetamoo waited to be served likewise, but the Rat Bastard served himself and then sat back down. The others returned to the hearth themselves and ate heartily. The brown stew was thick with chunks of venison and delicious.

As darkness drew on, blankets were brought down from the second story, and Wamsutta and Weetamoo were offered the bed in the corner. The other Wampanoags were invited to curl up on the floor around the fireplace. The Indians were all surprised they weren't shown to the barn. Mr. and Mrs. Rat Bastard went upstairs where they had other beds for their own rest.

Wamsutta had lain in the Rat Bastards' downstairs bed for less than an hour before he became violently ill and had to rush outside. He did not make it to the privy before throwing up. And he couldn't return inside because he continued to throw up. Weetamoo held his head when he lay down on the trampled earth of the yard, holding his belly and gasping shallowly for breath. The sound of Wamsutta's retching awakened the others in the house, and his friends came out to help attend to him.

"You have been poisoned, my husband," Weetamoo said, rubbing a worried hand across Wamsutta's brow. "We must get you away from here." She turned to the others and told them to prepare the horses. "We must leave at once," she said. "We must get him to Medicine Woman before it is too late."

When they had Wamsutta on his horse and were preparing to lead him back home, Josiah Winslow came into the yard and said, "What has happened? Has Alexander taken ill? Were the trials of the day too much for him?" Mrs. Rat Bastard stood in the doorway in her dressing gown. She said nothing.

"We know what you have done," Weetamoo said. "You believe in a fiery hell. If you had not prepared your place there already, the flames await you now."

Weetamoo was right about him. Winslow was a monster. What Miles Standish would have executed with a dagger thrust, Winslow performed with poison. But exactly like Standish, That Vicious Lying Rat Bastard knew no remorse. In the days to come, he even charged the colonial till for supplies required to "rid the populace of a pest." The homicide was executed with such precision that no one else was even sickened. Winslow had obviously sprinkled the fatal powder into Wamsutta's bowl each time he served my brother. And in his final words in Wamsutta's hearing, "Were the trials of the day too much for him?" Winslow had already begun to spin his account of what had happened.

The ride back to Pokanoket was over forty miles, and Wamsutta did not make it half that far. Though his friends tried to steady him on his horse, he could barely keep himself astride his mount. Eventually they had to take him down and try to warm him beside a campfire. His head was on fire, but he was shivering. They tried to soothe him, tried to coax him into taking sips of water, but he fell into a coma and died before daybreak. He was forty-four years old, a fit, splendid specimen of a man, tall, straight and strong. And then: gone.

YOU HAVE TO MARVEL at how the English endeavored to cover up this murder. Wamsutta had died of indignation, they wrote, a hot-headed savage unable to control his rage. Yeah? If he was still in such a rage, why was he dining with the enemy? Others speculated that he had become exhausted in traveling from his holiday *weetoo* to the meeting six miles away. About the latter, give me a break. Our people thought nothing about *walking* three times as far as Wamsutta *rode* the day he was poisoned, farther even than that. Hunting trips might take us forty miles on a single day. Those of our young men who acted as couriers could travel farther than that. And in his youth, Wamsutta had served Ousamequin as a messenger.

And about the idea of death from rage, well, few in the twenty-first century will fail to spot the nasty racism festering there. In hopes that, somehow, a founding father the likes of Josiah Winslow wasn't a lying, vicious murderer, modern doctors have offered speculation that Wamsutta came down with appendicitis. But how about this: Wamsutta was a leader of considerably more will than our father Ousamequin had needed to exert. He was falsely accused and lured into an English town. Afterwards, he was fed at the home of a man who had threatened to kill him earlier in the day. After dining, he became ill. Shortly later, he died. It hardly takes Sherlock Holmes or Lieutenant Colombo or Joe Leaphorn or Jim Chee to sleuth out that he was poisoned. Charge: Murder. Verdict: Guilty. Conspiracy was afoot after all. Josiah Winslow no doubt shook the death potion into Wamsutta's bowl, but his accomplices held the highest positions in Plymouth Colony.

Come, Richard Janus, come my friend, you know this story demands to be told.

Wamsutta was dead, and I was next in line for the duties of leadership. Don't think for a fleeting second that the proposition of becoming sachem of the Wampanoag nation and spending my forthcoming days dealing with the likes of That Vicious Lying Rat Bastard Josiah Winslow didn't depress me. It depressed me every living second that it didn't scare me shitless.

8

Francis Saurian's success in getting Rich the head coach job and tenure seemed like wonderful news to Rich at the time. Rich's Ungulates won eleven games his first year, and he coached his team to a 17-14 record in 2000-01, Urban's first winning season in over a decade. Saurian was so pleased with a winning season that he extended Rich's original five-year contract to a new five-year term through 2006. In fact, Saurian promised Rich that as long as the program progressed, he was ready to extend his contract a year for every year of success so that Rich would always have a five-year safety net under him.

And despite a disappointing loss in the semifinals of the conference tournament, Rich was expecting a second extension when his third team finished 19-12. He felt that his program was on the upswing, and that in another couple of years he would have the Ungulates competing for a Deep South Athletic Conference championship and a seat in the NCAA tournament.

But that vision of the future didn't come to be. Shortly after the end of his third season, while Rich was on the road trying to recruit a new shooting guard and a new power forward, he was fired by Francis Saurian who had fallen in love with another idea for attracting publicity to himself after Rich's Ph.D. hadn't attracted much national attention. Saurian didn't understand that national sportswriters cover teams who win twenty games and only *then* look for the color angle. Rich and his Ph.D. might have brought Urban, and therefore Saurian, the kind of attention he wanted had the CEO given Rich the time to build a program. But he didn't.

Rich learned that he was no longer Ungulate head coach while watching ESPN in Minden, Louisiana, where he had an appointment to visit with power forward recruit Keeshawn Lutze the next morning. In and of itself, Rich's firing probably would not even have been covered by the national media. He was a former high-school coach with a three-year Division I record of 47-46. But Rich's otherwise unnoteworthy demise was tied to one of the biggest college basketball stories of the year. For though Francis Saurian had yet to notify Rich that he no longer had a job, he had announced at a huge press conference back in Choctaw that he had just hired legendary former Illinois coach Jimmy Prince. Two days earlier, after a career of controversies arising from his explosive temper and foul mouth, Prince had been fired at Illinois for allegedly calling the president's executive assistant an ugly name for the female genital orifice. Prince denied the accusation, claiming that he had said, "Why are you always such a nut?" But no one in Champagne, or for that matter, anywhere on the planet, believed that the assistant was lying. Prince was out. And just like that, Prince was *in* at Urban. And Rich Janus was out. Wonderful the way the world works, no? Believe me, I should know.

Well, while the President at Illinois had had enough of Prince's embarrassments, and was delighted with the excuse to send him packing, Francis Saurian was even more delighted at the opportunity to stand in the national spotlight next to a coach who had won four national championships and stood second on the list for all-time Division I victories. Saurian didn't care that Jimmy Prince was a jerk. He didn't care that Prince hadn't won a national championship in fifteen years or a Big Ten championship in a decade. He just knew that Jimmy Prince was a guy constantly in the news, and for Francis Saurian, even bad publicity was better than being ignored.

Hiring Jimmy Prince seemed to Francis Saurian such a cracking great idea that he was sure someone else would soon hit upon it. There was no time to tarry. There was no time to inform

Rich Janus what he was up to. So Rich was fired for over forty-eight hours without being notified. Confused, but loyal to the job that wasn't even his anymore, he kept the recruiting appointment with Keeshawn Lutze and signed the young man to a letter of intent. Lutze might have made a significant contribution to Coach Prince's team, but Prince withdrew the scholarship offer as soon as he learned of it. Lutze subsequently signed with Mississippi State and led them in rebounding for four consecutive years.

Rich made repeated calls to Saurian but was unable to speak with him on the phone. And Rich wasn't able to get an appointment to see the CEO until two days later. When they finally did meet, the rector wasn't even sheepish. "I'm sure you understand, kid," Saurian said.

"I can't say that I do," Rich replied.

"The man has four national championships," Saurian pointed out. "Urban basketball got big time just by landing his name on a contract. One fell stroke: Nowheresville is Somewheresville. Two days ago we were invisible; today we're on the map with a star by our name. You really do understand; I just know it. Given that I like you, I didn't want to do this. But I really couldn't pass it up."

"We've had back-to-back winning seasons," Rich said. "We've got four starters coming back. Recruiting is going very well. We were going to get there."

"I don't doubt you were, kid," the CEO said. Rich was five years older than his boss, but Saurian always called him "Kid." "You worked hard. I believe that. And you showed progress. No doubt about it. But how long was it going to take? Three more years? Five? Longer? School like this is a tough sell. People want the big leagues. Cyclopes and Crows sell out, just like teams do in all the NFL and NBA cities. But we're still not averaging 2,000 fans at our games."

"That's four times the attendance when I arrived," Rich argued. "And attendance will grow. We win, people will come. We're winning now, and we're gonna win more."

"But we aren't on the map, kid. Fucking Mayflower Monsters up at America's Sports University are the only collegiate sports teams anybody in this state cares about or that *The Straight Arrow* covers. Mayflower plantation masters treat us like field hands and all the sports guys here in Choctaw mutter 'yassa.' You won seventeen games last year, nineteen this time, we still got no ink. People on our own faculty and staff wear Monster brown on football game days. We can either keep on taking it, or we can do something to shake things up. I think you might get us to the NCAA tournament in a year or two. But that's still not going to cut it. We got to go to the Sweet Sixteen and the Elite Eight. We got to go to the Final Four. When that happens, people will take notice. You're a good coach, kid, but Final Four, I don't know. With Jimmy Prince, I know. He's been there. And he's won. Chance to get a Jimmy Prince doesn't come along every day. When it does, you don't think twice, you gotta sign him."

"I've got a contract," Rich said.

"Come on, kid, this is the real world. Contracts are made to be broken. Go read the fine print in yours."

"I've read the fine print, Francis," Rich said. "My contract is guaranteed. All of it. Base salary, plus TV and radio, plus camp. $250,000 a year for four more years. One cool million."

"And you're the kind that would fight me on this, I gather."

"For every last penny."

"What I figured," the CEO said. "Yeah, you tenacious S.O.B. Why I hired you, I guess."

"I took you at your word. I gave up a job I liked. I have performed, and only last year you extended my contract and promised to do it again this year if we improved, which we did. You can take away my job as head coach, but you still have to pay me. You don't, and all the publicity you've gotten for hiring Jimmy Prince is going to turn around on you. Press loves sensation. But it loves controversy even more."

"Want to be first assistant coach under Jimmy?"

"Not even if he offered it to me himself."

"What I figured," the CEO said again.

"Anyway, Prince doesn't want his predecessor on his staff. I recruited those guys, and they're loyal to me. Prince has got to turn them to himself, and he couldn't do that if I was in the huddle with him."

"I'm sure I could count on you not to sow dissension."

"Won't work, Francis."

"I could insist."

"Talk about reading the fine print. Go look at the contract you just signed. I'll bet my ass you don't have the power to tell Prince who to put on his staff."

"Probably right." The CEO shrugged.

"Count on it. The contract I signed, you didn't have the power to tell me who to put on my staff."

"Well, it was an idea."

"Yeah, but not a good one. Prince and I have very different coaching philosophies. I wouldn't have wanted to work with him."

"We'll figure something else out, I'm sure," the CEO said.

"You promised me a chance, Francis. I believed you."

"Well, that was a big mistake on your part, wasn't it? You should have learned by now not to trust a man like me." The CEO laughed as if he had said something funny.

"So you just lied. You admit it."

"Nothing of the sort, kid, so I don't admit it. I told you the truth when I hired you. I said you were the best man for the job, and you were. Then. But this is now. Now Jimmy Prince is the best man for the job. I didn't lie because the truth changed. I gotta do what I gotta do."

"What you gotta do is pay me one million dollars over the next four years. You want to write me a check up front, I'll be happy to cash it."

"So you're going to make me pay you for a job you're not doing anymore?"

"Wouldn't you, if you were in my place?"

"I'm sure I would," the CEO said. "But I'm not in your place. I'm in my place. And in my place I've got to do what I think is best for me."

"You mean for the institution. For Urban University."

"There's a difference?"

A WEEK LATER, RICH was summoned back to the CEO's Building 6 office. When Rich entered, Saurian seemed almost electric with excitement. He asked Rich to sit on the blue sofa and perched for a second on the umber one before leaping back up and beginning to pace.

"So here's the deal, my young man," the CEO began. "And it's a sweetie. It's so goddamn good I believe I have absolutely outdone myself in thinking of it." He looked at Rich who made no response. "Aren't you curious?" He laughed.

"I haven't a clue what's going on," Rich said.

"OK, here's how it goes. Only people at this university who make $250K a year are me, the head basketball coach and the provost. You ain't me, and you ain't any longer the head basketball coach. Follow my thinking?" Rich shrugged. He thought Francis Saurian was nuts. "You ain't me and you ain't the head basketball coach. But I'm gonna have to pay you $250,000 a year because my lawyers say I can't get out of it. So I guess that means you're gonna have to be the provost."

Rich thought he was joking.

"Is that brilliant or what?" the CEO said, chortling.

"I am presuming that you aren't serious, though I haven't a clue where you're heading with this."

"I am serious as diabetes. I put old Fussy Britches Alton Centry on notice when I came here that he should think about retiring, and he's dithered around long enough now. Far as I'm concerned, as of the end of this conversation, he's out and you're in."

"And you're not concerned that I know absolutely nothing about being a provost?"

"Nobody does, don't you see; that's the beauty of this deal. Fact is, as you will shortly learn, nobody even knows what a provost *does*. You're going to spend the next several years of your life answering the question from countless people, 'What *is* a provost, anyway?'" Saurian laughed warmly at the wily solution he had concocted. "Let me assure you that Dr. Fussy B across the hall, whom I inherited from my do-nothing predecessor, sure as hell doesn't know anything about being a provost. You can take my word for that. I was a provost once and a damned good one as the fact that I am now a rector indisputably demonstrates. Why be a provost if you're not determined to be a CEO? But F. Britches just wants to kiss my ass. Or he makes like he wants to kiss my ass. He has no idea I know all about the conspiracies he's waged against me with the usual bunch of campus do-nothings who run for the faculty senate instead of doing research and keeping their office hours. I'll be glad to be shut of Old Fussy."

"And you're not concerned that I have never, unless you count the supervisory aspects of my coach duties, held an administrative position?"

"Oh, I suppose I am concerned about it. But I'm not bothered by it."

"And you think the Viceroy for Higher Education isn't going to be bothered by it?"

"You asking if I'm worried that Viceroy Elia Lipscom might block my appointing you?"

"Precisely."

"You got a Ph.D., man. You've written two books. You're a tenured member of the English Department, and I think there's some unwritten law in the Bible of Academia that at least half the provosts in the nation at any one point have to come from an English Department. I can and will make the case for you. But your question insinuates that Elia Lipscom gives one shit about who the provost at Urban University is. Like every other official, elected and appointed, in this entire godforsaken state, our viceroy doesn't care about anything at all that happens at Urban or anywhere in Choctaw for that matter. If it's not something happening on the Mayflower campus, then it's off the radar screen of official concern. I could appoint a cretin as provost and Lord Viceroy wouldn't care. Hell, I could appoint a dachshund."

Rich knew at least in part that what the CEO said was true. He had learned as much in trying to promote the Ungulate basketball program. So few cared. In college sports the only thing that mattered was what happened on the Alkansea State University flagship campus upriver at Mayflower. The Ungulates could pull an upset as they did last year against a pretty good Georgia team, and a routine loss by a mediocre Monster squad was still the lead story on the local TV stations and in *The Straight Arrow*. The State Board of Trustees for Higher Education had repeatedly thwarted Urban's hopes for fielding a Division I football team, but that proceeded less directly from an antagonistic attitude toward Urban than from perplexity about why, when America's Sports University already had the Monsters, anybody else would want, much less need, another football team.

"All right," Rich said, "let's say you're correct that the viceroy isn't concerned enough with what we do down here to bother scrutinizing your appointing me as Urban's chief academic officer. Why would you want to do it? Why would you think I'm qualified?"

"Aside from the fact that I evidently have to pay you $250,000 whether you do this job or twiddle your thumbs?"

Rich stared at him without responding.

"Come on, kid," the CEO said. "You gotta have a sense of humor about this. You and I are about to have a lot of fun together."

"What makes you think that our deans and vice rectors and the other top administrators who report to the provost will accept me as their boss?"

"See there, kid. I knew this idea was a keeper. Maybe not even half the people on campus know what a provost does, and nobody off campus knows. But you know. You're so far ahead of the game it makes my heart go giddy up."

"You're making jokes about cretins and dachshunds, but if you're serious about this idea, you have to help me understand how I could capture the respect of the people I would work with. I have no credentials in this area of leadership, no qualifying experience whatsoever."

"Jesus, man? Credentials for a provost are an earned terminal degree and a scholarly record sufficient to merit a full professorship. If that ain't an exact quote off the credentials page, it's close enough for government work. Universities out there even have provosts with an MFA for the terminal degree nowadays, and you have a Ph.D. So much for the credentials discussion."

Rich's discussion with the CEO was interrupted at this point by Kimberly Kane, who popped in to say that she had the phone call he had been expecting. Saurian responded to Kimberly with narrowed eyes and a knit brow. "Beatrice Florin," Kimberly said.

"Can you put her off?" the CEO asked. "We're not quite done."

Kimberly pursed her lips and posted a hand on her right hip. "You've been trying to reach her for three days. You really want me to tell her you're in a meeting?"

"No, you're right," Saurian said. "Give me thirty seconds; then put her through."

Along with everybody else in Choctaw, Rich knew who Beatrice Florin was: the widow of Fordyce Florin, who had recently died of arrogance and accumulated vitriol. Fordyce was the founder and president of Florin Oil, the largest off-shore drilling operation in the Gulf of Mexico. Before his recent death, he had easily been the richest person in the state, a status his wife had now inherited.

"Can't not take a call from Beatrice Florin," the CEO said to Rich.

"I understand," Rich said.

"Let's wrap up this discussion tomorrow," Saurian said.

"Have Kimberly put you down for tomorrow at the same time. Tell her I said to move anybody she has to to get you in."

"Including Beatrice Florin?" Rich said.

"Not including Beatrice Florin, smart ass. But assuming we meet tomorrow, I hope you arrive with a positive answer. You don't accept the job by tomorrow, I may figure out a way to take the offer off the table."

AFTER DISCUSSING THE MATTER at length over dinner that night with Cally, Rich decided to seek additional advice and arranged to meet with Humanities and Social Sciences Dean Ben Turner at a smoky dive called Park Central on South Main Avenue near Municipal Park. Over a pitcher of beer on the front patio of the tavern, Rich confided to Turner that Francis Saurian had offered him the provostship to satisfy the buyout provisions in Rich's coaching contract.

Ben Turner was a highly visible man on the Urban campus and a scholar of some accomplishment. Turner's book on the political strategies of Andrew Jackson had made the front cover of *The New York Times Book Review* and had earned him significant royalties, money he hadn't needed since, after abandoning his "starter marriage" to his college sweetheart, he'd exercised the wisdom to marry the only daughter of a Mayflower shipping baron. A man about Rich's age, Turner was a devoted supporter of Urban athletics and a big basketball fan. He and Rich had met through the Ungulate Athletic Association, to which Turner was a generous donor. Turner was also dean of the college where Rich held his negotiated tenure and where Rich would now begin to teach full time if he turned down the CEO's offer.

Ben Turner was an avid tennis player, so fit he looked ten years younger than he was. Turner was less than six feet tall, but his erect bearing made him seem taller. Rich had seen him operate in meetings where he exhibited charm, wit and charisma. He had the sheen of a man with money. He drove a black Jaguar and owned a Greek Revival house in the Exchange District. He always wore an expensive suit and starched dress shirt and had his nails manicured. He never looked like he needed a haircut but never looked like he'd just gotten one, either. Rich didn't know him well enough to know whether his personal financial resources were limited to his university position and his book royalties or whether he'd been affluent even before he married his second wife. Rumors about Ben were rife on campus in significant part because he dressed and carried himself in a way that most academics didn't, wouldn't or couldn't. People whispered that Ben's first marriage collapsed because his wife caught him with a graduate student whose thesis he was directing. Rich didn't know whether this rumor was true or just the product of jealousy over Turner's posh lifestyle.

Rich had heard that Ben had made a killing in the stock market in the eighties, bailed right before the 1987 crash and then made another killing in the 1990s, again bailing before the Dot Com bubble burst. Rich had no idea if any of these rumors were true and, in fact, they were matters of little interest to him. Rich liked money well enough. He liked to be comfortable. But money was never a goal for Rich. Perhaps it wasn't for Ben Turner either. Rich was impressed with Turner's generosity to the Athletic Foundation and what Rich had heard were other charitable organizations as well. Moreover, on the few times they had been together, Rich and Ben had gotten along very well. Ben was a good storyteller, and he was quick to laugh at the funny tales of others.

Still, Rich and Ben Turner weren't friends exactly. They had never socialized apart from university functions where they'd been seated at the same table. But they were on friendly terms. Turner had always been encouraging about Rich's efforts as Urban's basketball coach, and he had called to offer his condolences when he learned that Rich was being replaced by Jimmy Prince. Rich appreciated that support, so he contacted Turner to hear the dean's reaction to Saurian's offer. Rich figured there was no reason even to consider becoming provost if Turner thought such a move would be greeted with derision by the university's academics.

"If you're talking about the faculty in the classrooms and in the labs," Turner told him, "few will even notice. A provost appointment is like the appointment of the Ambassador to the United Nations. People understand that it's important but not that it has a direct impact on their lives. What goes on in 6 is a mystery to all but a few faculty and a concern to few as well. The working faculty are almost frighteningly disassociated from issues of university leadership. But it's among their strengths that most of them are focused on their students and their own research. They don't have a clear understanding of what a dean or a vice rector does, except make more money than they do, which they resent when they bother to think about it. But whereas a dean or a V.R. will make $50,000 more than they do, what they really resent, what they'll get livid and litigious about, is learning that the guy in the office next door makes $5,000 more than they do."

Turner took a long pull from his beer mug and then continued. "Most faculty know that the provost is the number two executive officer on campus, but only a minority have a clear concept about what a provost does. If a university were a democracy, they might demand that a provost or a rector or dean present a platform of some kind. But universities are democracies in pretense only, and though most faculty would not state that proposition directly, at some critical level they understand it. And that's why they pay so little attention."

Rich said, "So you're telling me that if I become provost, most faculty won't care one way or another."

"Some faculty will no doubt complain," Turner said. "Some faculty would complain if Jesus were named provost. But if Saurian presents your appointment in an aggressive way, which I'm sure he will, the grumbling will be short lived, and people will go back to doing what they would be doing if you *or* Jesus were named to the position. The faculty care passionately about who their chairs are because their chairs control their teaching schedules, their office assignments and their merit pay increases. But they care less about the identity of their dean and less still about the provost."

"OK," Rich said. "What about others in administration? The vice rectors and deans?"

"The vice rectors are totally beholden to the CEO for their jobs. Some of them will report to you. But they all know who's king of the hill. They're going to hip hip hurray for whomever Saurian anoints. You. Jesus. Or Hitler for that matter. 'Gee, Hitler's the new provost. What a grand idea. I hear he really got those trains running on time back in Germany.'"

"I think that was Mussolini," Rich pointed out.

"Not in Germany," Turner said, laughing. "And if Hitler were named provost, the V.R.s would happily give him credit for getting the trains running on time in Italy. They would jump to grant him whatever credit they could imagine, just so they could keep their jobs and their six-figure salaries."

"What about the deans?" Rich asked.

"Deans are a little different," Turner said. "And a lot the same. The deans will get together and complain. That's why they call a group of deans a *gripe*. Herd of buffalo. Pride of lions. Gripe of deans. Each of my colleague deans no doubt thinks he or she should be the next provost. We work with the provost every day, and so we know pretty certainly, even if we're dead wrong, what we would do differently than whatever provost we've served under. That makes each of us think this position should go to us."

"Including you?" Rich asked.

"Sure, of course, including me," Turner said.

"So why should I take the job if you should have it?" Rich said. "You're way better qualified. You have the experience to prepare you to serve as chief academic officer, and I don't."

"First of all," Turner replied, "Saurian isn't going to appoint me. So you don't have to worry about accepting a job that should have gone to me."

"Well, what about the other deans? Why will they accept me in the position if they think they should have gotten it?"

Turner laughed. "They'll accept you because they'll be glad the position didn't go to me or any of their peers. They'd each feel insulted and resentful if they didn't get the job but another of the deans did. If you get the job, they'll just get together to gripe that Saurian is a nut."

"You think Saurian is a nut?" Rich asked.

"Absolutely he's a nut. But he's a nut who is also a wily fox. He probably won't, but if he stayed around here long enough, he might even do the place some good. As a mere byproduct of doing himself some good, of course. But good is good."

"I wasn't here when he was hired, obviously, but I hear you were the inside candidate."

"Your wife *is* one of my department chairs, after all," Turner laughed. He took a swallow of beer. "I was *an* inside candidate. There were others."

"But you had the most support as I understand it."

"Perhaps," Turner said. "But it doesn't really matter. I didn't get it, and life goes on."

"Life goes on," Rich said, "with a nut as the boss. But I should go to work for him?"

"Well, just because he's a nut doesn't mean he doesn't need a capable and scrupulous provost. And I think you can be the provost he probably doesn't even think he needs. But don't worry. He won't appreciate you if you become the greatest provost in the history of higher education."

"And the deans will accept me?"

"Some will. Some won't. Those who do will help you. Those who won't will look for the opportunity to stab you in the back. But they won't cause a public ruckus at the announcement of your appointment because they won't want to piss Saurian off, given that he still rules the roost. Nor will they want to piss you off either, because whatever they think of your appointment, you'll be their new boss. You'll be the guy who either approves or blocks their next pet project. You'll be the guy who either will or won't back them up if one of them shows the balls to make a tough and unpopular decision. Most important, you'll be the guy who decides how much raise they get the next time the state deigns to fund one."

"But they'll look at me as unqualified."

"They'd look at Jesus as unqualified. But, in fact, save for your ever having headed an academic unit, in the way that matters most, you *are* qualified."

"How so?" Rich asked.

"Qualities you need in a provost," Turner said, "are primarily those of leadership." He began to tick off a list on his fingers. "First, you have to have the ability to make tough, often unpopular decisions. Second, you have to be thick-skinned about being constantly second-guessed by people who don't know what you know and would run crying to their mommies if they ever had to make a choice between two unpleasant and unclear choices. You didn't win all those state championships without being able to do exactly those two things while standing up to every daddy and every momma who thought their baby wasn't getting to play enough."

Rich looked out at the silver-lighted avenue as a sedan braked hard and made an abrupt left turn across the median, barely avoiding a collision with a passing streetcar.

Turner seemed not to notice as he continued, "A provost has to be well organized. He has to be able to do more than one thing at a time, like a coach has to prepare for Saturday night's opponent while practicing earlier in the week for Thursday's game, all the while he's trying to recruit those two important kids that will make his team better a year from now and trying to get that famous coach from Big Deal University he met at a coaching conference on the phone to ask the favor of a game two years from now that might land on national television and help raise the profile of his program. A provost has got to be able to handle budgets, has got to understand what he can afford to fund and what he can't. Just like a coach has got to manage that big guarantee for supposedly taking a licking at Big Deal U in order to take his team to a game in Hawaii, which he's been using as recruiting bait."

Turner reached his mug across the table and clinked it against Rich's, then raised it in toast. "You've been that coach, Janus. Here's to you. I'm sure I will enjoy working with you. Provost is just another managerial assignment, and you should take it. We aren't going to do any better on campus, and we could do a whole lot worse if we go outside."

CALLY DIDN'T AGREE WITH Turner's position at all. "That's why you negotiated tenure," she said. "You obviously can't trust that son-of-a-bitch Saurian to tell you the truth about the time of day. He's screwed more people than Warren Beatty and Bill Clinton combined. Just go teach English. And if you don't like that idea, go back to coaching high-school basketball. I can guarantee you that the next vacancy in this region is yours for the applying."

"What about the money?" Rich argued. "Nobody is going to pay me $250,000 for coaching high-school basketball."

"Screw the money," Cally said. "We have what money we need."

As usual, Rich should have just listened to Cally's advice. Cally was right about the money, though Rich was motivated by the principle of obligation that the money represented. And he did worry that he was going to miss the coaching. But he figured he could always get his gym fix by doing volunteer coaching the way he had in the past. And he was heartened by Ben Turner's support. Moreover, he was intrigued by a very different kind of challenge. Speaking from experience, I can say that some people keep stepping on the same hoe. I kept thinking that I could find a diplomatic solution to my problems even though I knew That Vicious Lying Rat Bastard Josiah Winslow was determined to steal my land. Rich believed that Francis Saurian could be reasoned with even though Rich had determinative evidence that Saurian's notion of truth was whatever served his interests at the moment.

Still, as he entered the CEO's office the next afternoon, Rich remained uncertain as to how he should respond to Saurian's offer. He felt himself to be smart and capable enough to handle the duties of provost, but he didn't feel himself experienced enough.

Once they were seated opposite each other on the office's two couches, Rich said, "Disappointed as I am in your decision with regard to my position as head basketball coach, I will admit that I find the idea of becoming chief academic officer intriguing."

"Excellent," the CEO said.

"At the same time," Rich continued, "I'm having trouble overcoming the idea that your proposition is perhaps crazy."

Saurian leaped to his feet and began to pace. "Crazy is the flip side of genius," he said. "One works; the other doesn't. It's a crazy idea if you prove a screw-up. It's genius if you pan out. You're going to make an excellent provost. I know it."

"Why do you know it?

"It's in your nature."

"It's in my nature," Rich said, "if I agree to it. But why would I agree to it? As they say in the film business, what's my motivation?"

"It's in your interest," the CEO said.

"Why isn't it in my interest to make you pay me one million dollars over the next four years to teach three classes of English each semester?"

"'Cause English professors don't make $250,000 a year."

"But I've got a contract that says you have to pay *me* that much."

"Not what it says. Not exactly."

"It's what I think it says. And I've got a good lawyer."

The CEO laughed and clapped his hands. "The meaning of a contract is inevitably subject to debate. That's why we have lawsuits. You've got a good lawyer. I'll get one just as good. You'll pay your lawyer with your own money. I'll use the state's money. You'll end up paying your lawyer most of your million even if you win. It's easier to do it my way and agree to become provost. You get to keep your mil."

"I'll get to keep my million no matter what. You think I won't fight you on that, but I will."

The CEO stopped to look Rich squarely in the face. "Christ, kid, you think I don't know you'll fight me. Of course, I know it. But you got to listen to me: it's not in your interest. You think you've got a good hand. But I've got a better one."

"How so?"

"My lawyer says if I relieve you as basketball coach, and you want to collect the salary provided for in the contract, you have to accept those duties I assign you."

"Duties commensurate with my professional accomplishments," Rich said.

"Yeah, yeah," the CEO chortled. "And when we signed, we didn't think it would ever be invoked, and if it were, that you'd do something like work as an associate athletic director or a director of scouting or some such shit."

"Or teach English. That's why I asked for and received tenure as a professor."

"Well," the CEO said, "here's where it gets complicated, see. And here's where it seems I'm holding aces, and you're holding jack squat. You ready for it?"

"Ready for what?" Rich asked.

"Ready for the truth that will make you provost."

Rich shook his head. Saurian was a piece of work.

"See, I'm not going to assign you to teach English," the CEO said and then laughed high in his throat. "Your tenure says you can go teach in the English Department if you want to. But if you do, I am free to fix your salary at the average of the other full professors in your department. That would put you at just over $62,000. Shameful, I know. Downright pitiful. But that's what the poor suckers make, and so that's what you'd make. You have the right to turn down my administrative assignment, but the consequence is you make sixty-two rather than two fifty."

"I'll have my lawyer study that," Rich said.

"I'm sure you will. And he'll tell you I'm right. You only get the $250,000 if you accept duties I assign you. I'm assigning you to be provost. And look, kid, it's not that bad a deal in the long run. You might like the job. And even if you don't, if you stick it out for three years, you can go back to the English Department then at the administrative to nine-month conversion rate of 9/11ths or nearly 200K a year. Helluva lot better than sixty."

"Why are you doing this, Francis? There have to be other people you can get to serve as provost for you."

"Of course, there are," the CEO said. "Wouldn't do any better than you'll do. Sure, I could find somebody. But the way I figure it, the only way I will really draw much scrutiny from the viceroy and the other shitheads up in Mayflower is to have too many people down here making the kind of money you do. You force me to pay you two fifty for doing something worthless, I'm gonna have four of us making a quarter of a million or more. Jimmy Prince held me up for 375, twenty-five more than I make, for Christ sake, and bitched that I couldn't pay him the million he pulled down at Illinois. Him, me, a provost and you. That's a million and a quarter flowing into only four bank accounts. Looks bad. This is the way to go, kid. Trust me."

"I trusted you when I became head basketball coach. And now here we are."

"The only way you lose is if you don't serve three years as provost and thus don't put yourself in position to become the highest paid English teacher in the history of the university."

"I'm where I am now because you fired me."

"Yeah, but people care who the basketball coach is. People only care who the provost is if he starts closing down programs or firing people. You won't have cause to do that, and I won't have any incentive but to let you remain provost for as long as you like."

Rich stood up and walked to the large window in the CEO's office that looked out over the campus. He thought back to his years as a graduate student and how much better the grounds looked now than then. Landscaping had finally been introduced in the late eighties, and trees planted then were now maturing and providing shady places where once there was only scalding sun. This was a place with such potential, he thought. He had been proud to come here to coach. The kids who went to school here were hungry for education the way those who went to private universities and the big state schools weren't always. Rich wanted to make a difference. Maybe he could make a difference in this way here. He turned to the CEO.

"You know I wouldn't take this position, Francis, if I didn't think I could handle it."

"Nothing different ever occurred to me, kid."

"You won't mind if we don't shake on it," Rich said.

"Nah," the CEO said. "But do let me be the first to call you Provost Janus."

"Beware, Rich Janus," I called out.

But he hasn't heard my plea for him to write my story, and he didn't listen to me now.

I was twenty-three years old when my brother Wamsutta was murdered. I'd like to contend that I was an instant hit as leader of my Wampanoag people, but that was neither true nor likely. In the aftermath of my brother's death, I made some hot comments about That Vicious Lying Rat Bastard Josiah Winslow, which were reported back to him. I said I'd like to take a dozen of my best men, sneak into his stinky little village of Marshfield, grab the fucker by his horns and skin him like a skunk. The way Winslow heard it, or at least the way Winslow claims to have heard it, I had conspired with every Indian in New England to wipe Plymouth Plantation off the face of the earth. Every time we turned around they were accusing us of plotting to foment a race war. I can't help but conclude that they thought they had it coming. Reluctantly, and as a last resort, I did, eventually, wage war on these pig-skinned monsters. I think maybe I got the idea from them.

Two months after Wamsutta's death, in *Matterllawawkesos*, in August of 1662, they sent a message to my village at Montaup, where Bristol, Rhode Island, is now located, that they wanted me to come to Plymouth. So I went. These Pilgrims were still our biggest trading partners. I grant I hated them because they were lying racist religious fundamentalist murderous hypocrites, but just like Wamsutta, I felt trapped in a vise of my enemies. I wanted to avenge my brother. But my responsibility was to see that my people got the best chance to prosper, so I tucked my yearning for personal vengeance into the tightest compartment of my heart and forced myself to seek an interracial accommodation. When I got to Plymouth, they demanded that I appear before their General Court where they began the crapola about how I was conspiring against them. I waxed goddamn indignant at that accusation and hotly denied it. It pissed me off to be falsely accused. I was twenty-three, I hadn't figured on becoming Wampanoag sachem for years, if ever, and I was still trying to figure out what all I might be able to accomplish. Then the white stinkers, to whom we had been nothing but good neighbors, treated me like a criminal.

That Vicious Lying Rat Bastard rose from his seat on a bench against the meeting house wall to address the court. "We register, *King* Philip, *new* King Philip, that you deny plotting with Narragansetts and Mohegans against us."

"Indeed I deny it," I replied. "Have I not denied it repeatedly?"

"But that is not what others of your people report to us," Winslow said. The day was warm, the air outside humid, and little breeze stirred through the windows of the meeting house. Winslow took off his hat and slicked back his damp, thinning gray hair with his palm. "Why would your people bear testimony against you?"

"Where are these people?" I demanded. "I have heard no testimony against my word today. If you have such witnesses to conspiracy, bring them here and let them testify."

Winslow continued as if I had not challenged him to produce witnesses. "And shouldn't we consider it in your own interest to deny conspiracy, if you were planning to foment war?"

"Only you say I am planning war," I responded.

"And those of your people from whom we learned it."

"Produce them, then. PRODUCE THEM," I thundered.

"And isn't it convincing evidence that you become so agitated when we try to discuss this with you? Isn't your anger and lack of self control evidence that you are lying?"

"No, what I think you should take as evidence that I am not lying is the fact that I haven't attacked you already since you POISONED MY BROTHER."

Some people in the room gasped, and others spat out indignation. But Winslow laughed, spun around to face his fellow filthy britches on the court and made a sweeping bow with the hand holding his hat. "Gentlemen of the court," he said. "You see how this savage thinks. You see how he boils with lust for an excuse to wreak violence on God's holy community?" Chortling again, the Rat Bastard turned to me: "*King* Philip. If I had meant to see your brother *King* Alexander in his grave, I would not have chosen poison as my weapon. Ask the men who were with me at Monponsett if I did not have him in the sight of my pistol."

"I know what you did," I said. "I know what you did."

"There," Winslow said, pointing at me but looking at the court. "A threat. Here right in our open court, the man threatens me."

"What threat?" I said. "I have come here to put rumors of threats to rest, not to make them."

The acrimonious debate volleyed on, and That Vicious Lying Rat Bastard continued to accuse me of conspiracy and to deny having anything to do with Wamsutta's "hysterical" death. I continued to deny any plans for war and to search for a peaceful way forward.

They had an idea. How about I sign a treaty with them saying that I wouldn't sell any of my land for the next seven years to anyone without their permission? Well, the last thing I ought to do as sachem was sell *anybody* any more Wampanoag land. But who were they that I had to have their permission to do what I wanted with my own property?

Still, I was a realistic person, even as a twenty-three year old. And the document didn't require me to sell land, just to sell it to them if I was going to sell, and I had already adopted my no-sell strategy. With the Pilgrim Belted Hats already squatting in Rehoboth not far off the northern neck of my peninsula, I figured I'd better hold on to what I still had, lest we lose the ability to grow enough corn, beans and greens to feed ourselves. The Plymouth English said that by signing their document, I could prove my friendship to them. I took this to mean that I wouldn't have to come back and defend myself on trumped-up charges again. So I signed, and we did all the smiling and bowing formalities that go along with these kinds of things. And they didn't bother to tell me that the document on which I inked my P didn't say anything about the agreement expiring in seven years, the terms to which I had acceded.

And these people promoted themselves back in England as having arrived in the New World to bring salvation to the likes of me and mine. For the next decade, a guy named John Eliot, who founded the famous "praying towns" where Indians were converted and taught to read the Bible, kept trying to bring me to his Lord. Why would I want to go to his Lord? Why would I want to believe in a God who taught his followers that to screw people with a different skin pigment was righteous behavior?

So the Plymouthites didn't really believe their own rumors that I was about to start a race war in 1662. They just wanted to get my P on a piece of paper that would allow them to contend that I was their subject. This was because Rhode Island was just about to land a royal charter, which it did just a few months later, drawing a map of New England showing that my Wampanoags belonged to the Rhode Island pinkies. Rhode Island was headed by that notorious loner Roger Williams who tolerated Quakers and other heretics and liked to think of himself as a friend of the Indians. And if you had to choose between Roger Williams and That Vicious Lying Rat Bastard Josiah Winslow, and you were an Indian, you definitely chose Roger Williams.

But that's only to say if you had to choose between Poppy and W, you'd choose Poppy because he might kiss you before he fucked you.

The problem for my sachemy in the 1660s was primarily economic. I needed to hold on to land for purposes of subsistence. But I no longer had a beaver population to use for trade. And my people had come to regard as necessities the metal pots, tools and other goods, including muskets and gun powder, that we could only get from Europeans. What were we going to buy them with? I came up with what I thought was a cracking good idea: whale oil. And to that end I tried to exert control over the native whaling activities centered on Nantucket Island. Seemed a winner when I thought it up, but I mainly just pissed off the Nantucketites, who remained so mad at me that they fought on the side of the English during That Vicious Lying Rat Bastard's War.

I am sure that I should put this more delicately, but a considerable problem was occurring in our little corner of the world because, well, the English were fucking like bunnies. We

Indians normally had only two children, and that helped keep us in balance with the resources of the land we lived on. After the European-induced plague of 1616, we had more land than we had people to utilize it, so we had adequate room for the English when they dropped in on us in 1620. But by the mid-1660s, land was growing scarce. The wives of the English were squeezing out little cotton tops and carrot tops at nearly eight kids per. Go do the math over forty-five years. Two make eight or the equivalent of four couples who make thirty-two or sixteen couples who make one hundred twenty-eight. And they all want a square of land to park a cow or two on and a sty for some hogs and enough dirt to raise corn and vegetables. Things would have been bad enough had every square inch of my homeland been suitable for farming, but maybe eighty percent of it wasn't. I'm certainly not saying one couldn't live well in southern New England. Until the sneering white collars moved in, we Indians lived very well. We knew how to supplement those things we grew with things we could collect, and we got all the protein we needed from forest game or the sea, which was just a giant pot of food for us. The English ate seafood and game as well, but from the beginning they were more dependent on what they could raise from the soil, and unoccupied ground was in increasingly short supply.

Meanwhile, I had nothing with which to buy pots, knives and guns except my patrimony soil. I had sworn I was done with selling it to them, but after a time, the best I could manage was to jack up the price. Already by 1665, I was forced to trade off bits of land for cash. My revised strategy was to sell the English only parcels of my property that lay adjacent to towns they'd already established. My people didn't want to live near them anyway.

Then in 1667 the Plymouthites established a new town at Swansea on some property that Ousamequin had sold them years earlier. The land wasn't particularly good, and we didn't think they would ever try to use it. But then there they were, right on top of us, squeezing us down onto the Montaup peninsula and blocking our freedom of movement to the north and east.

That's when the white monsters hit upon a new swindle. They'd identify an Indian they knew to be in some financial difficulty and offer to lend the man some money, accepting a mortgage on his farm. The Indian could almost never repay the mortgage, so pretty soon the white man owned the land and kicked the Indian off. Guess who was a prime practitioner of this little game of legalized thievery. Yep, none other than That Vicious Lying Rat Bastard Josiah Winslow. I could ruminate for ages on the connection between the mortgage crisis of the 1660s and the one orchestrated by George W. Bush's free marketeers in the first decade of the twenty-first century. But let me just summarize with two words: *naked greed*.

1667 was supposed to have been a joyous year for me and my wife Wootonekanuske. Our son Neksonauket was born that year. But even the miracle of his birth led to ashes in my mouth over how deceitful the English were. They had infected our land, not just with the plague of 1616 and the viciousness of Wessagussett and Mystic River, but with a sickness of the soul, a collapse of honor. John Eliot, the great misguided missionary, had sent unto me the aforementioned John Sassamon, a Christianized Massachusetts Indian and Harvard man of some considerable skills as a linguist, scribe and translator, which just goes to show you that educational institutions don't hand out consciences with their diplomas.

Sassamon had done some document work earlier for my brother, and I liked him well enough, particularly since he only made perfunctory efforts to convert me. Eliot wanted him hanging around with me, so that he could get me praying to their Jesus. But I told Sassamon straight away not to bother wasting his time, and though he'd occasionally make some little feints in the direction of religious discussion, he mostly kept his mouth shut about the matter, so I let him hang around. From what we could tell, he enjoyed being with us, even though he dressed like the English and had lived among them, rather than his own kind, for most of his life.

Why wouldn't he like being with us, instead of with the English? It's not as if the white people of New England in the seventeenth century lived like the white people of New England today. It's not as if they had insulated suburban houses. The English had a monopoly on gun manufacturing and a ruthless willingness to do anything to advance their own material interests. But the life they lived was uncomfortable and unclean. And though Sassamon was a despicable English bootlick, he was smart enough to recognize a superior lifestyle. We ate better. We smelled better. And not being religious fanatics, we had a lot more fun. The Pilgrims spent their free time going to church and worrying each other about "scripture." Smiling was almost a felony. But while they were worrying about lives in the next world, we were enjoying ourselves in this one, singing and dancing, running races, staging contests, playing tug-of-war or lacrosse or field hockey, in short, having a good time in the fleeting years the Creator grants us.

GIVEN THAT THINGS HAD changed so very much since the English had arrived and begun overpopulating the place, Wootonekanuske figured we probably ought to get documents in place to make sure that those possessions that were indisputably mine and hers would be preserved after our deaths for the well-being of Neksonauket. Wootonekanuske was not only beautiful and sexy, she was also really smart. But I didn't always listen to her, usually to my regret. This time I did. I dictated a will to John Sassamon. He wrote it up in English, and I signed it with my large English P and directed, as always, that Sassamon append the words "alias Metacom," so that Indians and English alike would know that this will was mine and was designed to provide for my beloved first born.

It's an embarrassing thing that I couldn't read. John Sassamon had been instructed to teach me to read, so that I could read the Bible and be converted. But I was cold to that reason, and I couldn't figure out needing to read when I had Sassamon around to do it for me. Put that one down on me. Sassamon's lesson for me about my illiteracy was bitter and infuriating. Everywhere I stated that this parcel of land, and this horse, and these cattle and hogs were to become the property of Neksonauket, Sassamon wrote that they were to become the property of, get this: John Sassamon. The only thing worse he could have done was to have assigned my possessions to That Vicious Lying Rat Bastard Josiah Winslow himself.

Upon discovering what he had done, I banished Sassamon from Montaup, and he's lucky I didn't have him executed. I didn't because I knew he was fondly regarded by John Eliot, for whom, I concluded too late, he was merely a spy. Up in Boston, That Notorious Praying Prevaricator Increase Mather always sneered at Sassamon for spending the years he did working for me, but then Mather had little use for Eliot, either. And That Vicious Lying Rat Bastard treated Sassamon with the contempt he reserved for all Indians. Still, the way the Puritans played the game, the Praying Indians were a rung higher on the godly level than guys like me, and though I denounced Sassamon and actively wished him ill, I saw no good coming from killing him, no matter how much he deserved it. Sassamon went back to work for Eliot, but he didn't leave the vicinity, and we shall see more of him in due time.

1667 also saw the rampaging of another set of rumors that I was planning to entice the French and Dutch into joining me in an attack on the English. Once again I had to go into Plymouth and stand before their court to defend myself. Both the Dutch, who had recently been kicked out of New York, and the French, who had ambitions to control the Hudson River, had plenty of reason to want to disable the Puritans in New England. But they didn't contact me about it. I always figured that my Niantic rival Ninigret was behind this most recent rumor, and that's what I proposed to the Plymouth court. Later on, it occurred to me that the rumor came from John Sassamon. You'll see why shortly.

DURING THE NEXT FOUR years, things began to grow increasingly tense between my Wampanoag brethren and the Englishmen in the township at Swansea. Their ground wasn't much good for corn or vegetables, so the settlers there tried to sustain themselves by raising livestock: cows, goats, sheep and pigs. We were naturally irritated just having the pinks so goddamned nearby, but how they endeavored to support themselves was their own affair as far as I was concerned. Or I would have been content for it to be their own affair had they kept their animals penned. But they didn't, and their ungulates were forever intruding onto our property and eating and trampling our corn and other crops. You can imagine how irritating this was.

Finally, in *Namassackesos*, April of 1671, a bunch of my men became so pissed off that they put on their war paint, shouldered their muskets, slipped war clubs into their waistbands and marched up to Swansea to put on a demonstration of you-better-quit-this-shit-or-the-next-time-we-show-up-it-won't-be-to-display. (Kind of pun there if your ear is supple enough.) What my fellows did was go to the edge of town, let out some battle whoops and brandish their weapons. They didn't hurt anybody; they didn't even fire off any shots into the air. They were just saying, we're here in battle gear, so change your ways or live in fear. (Rhymes, puns: is this a literary tour de force, or what? I'm sure you could do even better, Richard Janus, but you can see I am trying as hard as I can.)

All in all, my guys behaved pretty darned well. Still, my brothers hadn't alerted me to their intentions before they took off for Swansea. If they had, I would have tried to talk them out of it, as they probably knew I would. I hardly blamed them for being pissed – I was pissed too. But a sachem's job is to rise above anger, however righteous, and seek out solutions to difficult problems without resorting to war (something George W. Bush never worked out about his job – but then working wasn't W's long suit). In my case, recognizing that they outnumbered us now, I was continually looking, forlornly, for some way to get along with the trout skins.

Word reached me that a party of English from Swansea had gone up to Taunton to complain to their fellows that they had been threatened and were now afraid for their lives. The usual drinking and boasting followed, and talk arose about putting together a squad of men to teach those of us at Pokanoket a lesson. Two days later a man from Swansea named Hugh Cole, who had come among us to trade on many occasions, arrived in my village to tell me that an important meeting was being arranged in Taunton and that I should attend.

So I gathered a small party of men, and we rode up to Taunton to parlay. We carried our muskets, but not our clubs, and we traveled without paint. The business itself was serious and worrisome, but the trip was lovely, and I was reminded of my many days traveling these paths with my father and brother. Daffodils, crocuses, hyacinths and mayflowers were everywhere in bloom. The air was perfumed by a rejuvenating earth, and I harbored an unwarranted hopefulness that calm talk could defuse the bomb of war one more time.

I sent ahead unarmed my chief captain, Annawon, to alert the residents of Taunton and Swansea that we were coming as they had requested, and they were gathered at their meeting house waiting for us. To demonstrate that we were arriving to talk, not fight, we left our muskets with my young cousin Mauconset, who remained on the edge of the woods with our horses. White men on the porch held their own guns at port arms as we passed, but every man inside the meeting house was carrying a weapon. One was Plymouth Governor Thomas Prence. Another was That Vicious Lying Rat Bastard Josiah Winslow.

"I come in peace," I said as I entered.

That opening was greeted with shouts, curses and threats, and I thought we might be slaughtered without discussing a thing. My men thought so too and drew in close around me, thickly muscled Annawon on my right and tall, strong Adonoshonk on my left. His scalplock falling against my neck, Annawon leaned in to me and whispered, "I have my knife sheathed in a legging, and whatever happens I will take Josiah Winslow with me to the grave."

I clapped his back and whispered in response, "May that be years from now, my brother."

Finally, the din of angry white voices quieted, and I said, "I come to sustain the peace that has endured between us since my father was sachem and you were few and vulnerable."

"We'll show you who's vulnerable now," one angry fellow in a pointed brown hat said.

"You sent painted warriors to threaten our people at Swansea," Thomas Prence said. He wore a white shirt and a cutaway coat buttoned at the waist despite the growing heat in the room.

"No, I didn't," I said.

"Liar," Brown Hat said. "Stinking redskinned liar."

I tried to speak as matter-of-factly as possible and stepped forward from my men, with whom I had been standing shoulder to shoulder. The white men flinched back as if I were attacking them and many pointed their muskets at my chest. I forced myself to smile and raised my hands to the level of my shoulders. I addressed myself to Prence. "I do not dispute that a party of men went to Swansea last week. And I do not dispute that they were unfriendly. But I did not send them. They went to Swansea without my permission."

"You ordered them not to go?" Winslow asked.

"I didn't know they were going," I replied.

Winslow sneered and said to the English in the room, "Some king this King Philip is."

"Despite your years in our midst," I said, "you have no idea about the ways of our people."

"We know your people threatened us last week, and that must never happen again," Prence said.

"I cannot promise it will never happen again," I said.

"You will if you want to leave here alive," Brown Hat said.

"We have complained repeatedly that you don't pen your animals and that they trample our gardens, destroy our food."

"Fence your gardens then," Brown Hat said.

"Provide me the fencing and I will," I replied. "But you will find it a lesser drain on your treasury just to pen your animals. Then we can live as neighbors."

"Neighbors?" Winslow said. "What kind of neighbors threaten mayhem to the residents of the next town?"

"In fact, they did not really threaten anybody," I said.

"You're not just a liar, but a damn liar," Brown Hat said.

"My warriors put on a show for you," I argued. "They displayed their anger and their frustration. I agree that they did not act wisely, but I do not agree that their behavior implied any immediate threat of violence."

"A ridiculous argument," Winslow said. "You might as well cease. Not an Englishman in this room believes that our people were not threatened."

"I have explained how to ease the bad feelings between us," I said. "What else can I do?"

"I will tell you what else you can do," Winslow said. He turned to a table behind him and unfurled a document already drafted. "You will sign this agreement that you do not plan hostilities against King Charles' subjects in New England and that as evidence of your good faith you will surrender your firearms and those of your warriors."

I looked at Rat Bastard's smug face. Another document. Another concession. Each more foul than the one before it. My men scuffed at the floor with their moccasins and chewed at their lips in dismay. Muskets could only be procured from European traders, and though we could find French and Dutch who would sell them to us, they were expensive.

"Sign it," Brown Hat said. "Sign it in ink or we'll sign it for you in blood."

This was absolutely humiliating. But what choice did I have? Save for the knife in Annawon's legging, we were unarmed. Winslow read the agreement to us. But who knows if he read to us what it really said? I didn't even have John Sassamon along to read it to me. Along with surrendering our weapons, the document proclaimed that we agreed we were subject to the governance of Plymouth, this to bolster their claim with the British crown that Wampanoag territory belonged to them and not to Rhode Island.

Surrounded and outgunned, I inked my P at the document's bottom. We were then marched back to our horses where I directed Mauconset to surrender our muskets. I would love to say that we rode back to Pokanoket with our heads held high. But the meeting at Taunton was an unqualified defeat and an indignity. So on this lovely spring evening, we rode through our beautiful wooded world in an atmosphere of despair.

I signed this infamous document because I was not ready to die or, at best, be put in irons if I didn't. But I also signed because I was nearing the end of my rope. It seemed hardly to matter what compromises I was willing to make in the interest of peace. There just seemed no getting along with the English. They were thoughtless neighbors, they were completely paranoid, and like many mentally and morally unstable people, they were first suspicious and then vindictive.

Later, That Vicious Lying Rat Bastard Josiah Winslow claimed that I had agreed to surrender not just the guns of those in my immediate party but the muskets of all the warriors in our confederacy. But I had promised nothing of the kind, and I couldn't have achieved such a disarmament had I ever agreed to it. That Winslow lied, of course, did not stop him from using the fact that Indians throughout southern New England still carried muskets as evidence that I could not be trusted.

10

The first year of Richard Janus' service as Urban University's provost was marked by his responsibility to reduce his general operating fund by four percent or roughly five million dollars, due to a state-mandated budget cut. His first week on the job, in July of 2002, he had to terminate the employment of ten individuals who reported either directly or indirectly to his office and to charge each of the deans and vice rectors who reported to him to reduce their budgets through either layoffs or the red-lining of vacant positions. This task did not make him popular on campus even though he had no alternative. Rector Saurian had Rich announce the cuts to a meeting of the faculty when Saurian was out of town.

Rich tried to discuss the situation with the CEO before Rich made his presentation and wondered aloud to his boss about the wisdom of such an announcement's being delivered by a provost so new to the job, especially one who only months earlier had been the basketball coach. But Saurian waved him out of his office with the direction to "go be the provost. That's why I hired you. I've been a provost, and I don't do provonomo. If I'd wanted to be provost as well as rector, I wouldn't have needed you."

Rich's second year as provost brought him even more misery. The state didn't cut Urban's budget that year, but Rector Saurian abruptly promised the faculty a three percent pay raise with money he didn't have. Rich protested and tried to get Saurian to rescind his promise, but the rector refused.

"Faculties get restless when they don't get raises," Saurian explained as the two met about the issue in the rector's office. Saurian was emailing when Rich came in and didn't stop as the two discussed the unfunded promised raise. Saurian typed even while he talked. "When the faculty don't get raises two years in a row, they get pissed. Our faculty hasn't had a raise in three years. And when faculties don't get raises for that long, they get irrational and vindictive. And when they get irrational and vindictive, they blame the administration."

"But the lack of raises isn't our fault," Rich said.

"What's that got to do with the faculty getting irrational and vindictive?" Saurian replied. "And as I said, when they get that way, they blame the administration."

"They won't blame us," Rich argued, "if we explain that they aren't getting raises because the state hasn't provided us any money to do so."

Saurian laughed out loud. "Boy, after a year over there a-provosting, you still have some things to learn about university administration. Of course, they'll blame us. If we try to say it's the state's fault, they'll say it's our fault for not convincing the state to increase our funding."

"But the legislature didn't fund raises for any of the state schools," Rich said.

"And what's that got to do with the price of roasted chestnuts on Fifth Avenue?"

"Our faculty is in the same situation as every other professor in state higher education."

"So?" Saurian asked.

"So, if we explain this to them in a calm, clear fashion, they won't get, as you put it, irrational and vindictive. They'll just get depressed."

"They're already depressed," Saurian said. "They're faculty. And every time they open their pay envelopes, they ask themselves why they're professors instead of doctors and lawyers. And since they don't have a reasonable answer to that question, they get and remain depressed. They never quite recall that they only have to work nine months a year, and not all that hard then, and that, in fact, they have the best jobs on earth, with the lifetime security of tenure for most of them to boot. No, they look at their paychecks and they boohoo about how little they're paid. So they can't get any more depressed. They can only get irrational and vindictive, and that's exactly what they'll get if we don't give them a raise."

"I'd love to give them a raise," Rich said. "But we don't have the money to do so. I assure you, I can't find a three-percent raise in the budget. It simply isn't there."

"Of course, it is," Saurian said. "It's only three percent. Three percent is always there."

"Not if we meet our obligations."

"Then don't meet our obligations. Who cares about our obligations? The faculty doesn't care about our obligations. All they care about is that three-percent raise, and that's all I care about, too. I'll bet you can find most of the three percent in the money you've set aside for replacing last year's retirements and resignations."

"I can maybe find two percent there," Rich acknowledged. "But you explicitly promised the faculty that last year's state budget cut would not affect educational programs. If we don't replace retirements and resignations, then we won't have faculty in all the programmatic areas we claim to offer in our catalogue. And that's only two percent anyway, not three."

"So we don't start the raise until the November paychecks. That means we won't need but two percent this year."

"Yes, but we'll be on the hook for the whole three percent next year without any guarantee that we can identify revenues to cover it."

"Kid," Saurian said, still typing away. "You gotta learn to take one year at a time. Go process that raise. Make us both popular. And don't talk to me about money any more. I am sick to death of people trying to let money stand in my way."

"So are you going to inform the faculty that in order to fund their raises we will not be filling vacant positions this year?"

"Of course not," the rector said. "Why would I do that?"

"Because they all have searches under way."

"Let them search."

"Let them search?" Rich said. "And what will we do when they've identified the candidates they want to hire?"

"First, we'll tell them that they'll have to wait a month."

"And at the end of that month?"

"That they'll have to wait still another month. By the end of the second month, the candidates they originally wanted to hire won't be available anymore, so they won't be nearly as disappointed as they would have been earlier."

"So then we call the searches off?"

"Of course not," Saurian said. "We counsel with them about the dangers of second choices and all that. But we let them identify secondary candidates if they choose."

"Then what?" Rich asked.

"By then, the spring semester will be almost over, and everybody will be looking forward to summer." The rector yawned and typed away.

"So by delay and subterfuge, we buy a year."

"So by delay, subterfuge and a three percent raise that we don't start till November, we buy a year, yes."

"But our problems will be compounded next year."

"And that's when we will worry about it," Saurian said. "Something always comes along. Kind of amazing that way. We enroll more students. Or the state increases our allocation. Or the legislature lets us raise tuition. Any of those things happens, we'll be fine."

"And what if none of those things happens?" Rich asked.

"Then we'll think of something else."

Rich was anxiety-ridden about this strategy, but when he executed it, he found that it worked just as Saurian predicted it would. The faculty weren't joyous about their raise. The faculty always feel that they deserve whatever raise they get, in fact, that they deserve more. But they are mollified when they get a raise the way a Holstein is mollified when it backs away from the feed trough with a full belly. As the year went along, they were frustrated when they weren't allowed to do the hiring they had been promised, but not nearly so frustrated as Rich thought they ought to be. But with a little more money in their pockets, they were oddly hopeful, especially in light of Saurian's promises that things would be different in the year to come.

Rich particularly worried that he was setting up a disaster in the 2004-2005 academic year when he'd have already exhausted his pool of vacant positions and would still have to find the last third of the prior year's raise. But then Urban enjoyed a record enrollment in the fall of 2004, and the problems Rich had lain sleepless over for a year were solved with the new tuition and fee revenues. Rich still thought that Saurian's approach to budgetary management was irresponsible and that Urban was lucky to have escaped, but he was glad for the relief.

Francis Saurian would no doubt have been glad for the relief as well, cocky, self-satisfied and oh, so, I-told-you-so, but nonetheless glad. Only Francis Saurian was no longer Urban rector when the 2004-2005 year rolled around. For his plot to land a CEO position at another, better financed institution had borne fruit. And the hiring of Jimmy Prince was the decision that propelled Saurian into a new job. Prince did just as Saurian predicted he might. In his first season, Prince took Urban to a league championship and a first-round victory in the NCAA tournament. Of course, he did it with the players that Rich had recruited and trained, but no one made mention of that fact. Without a sports tradition of any kind, Urban was suddenly a Cinderella. Jimmy Prince was deemed still to have the touch.

The second year, Prince took Rich's players to the Sweet Sixteen, a feat so exquisite for Urban's suddenly numerous fans that not even a subsequent thirty-point shellacking by North Carolina lessened its sweetness. For a month, Prince was Choctaw's biggest hero. And Francis Saurian was hailed as a genius higher education executive for spotting a chance to land a coaching legend and jumping on it. That's the picture of himself Saurian promoted every time a news camera appeared on campus, and he made sure he got himself in front of it, even if that sometimes required stepping in front of Prince.

And that's why the chairman of the Board of Trustees at the University of Memphis nominated Saurian to fill their presidential vacancy when the incumbent dropped dead of a heart attack while watching Internet porn and masturbating. Memphis had a storied basketball tradition, but its program had fallen on hard times. The school needed a man at the top who understood his priorities and would take such steps as needed to restore the primacy of the basketball program. Saurian had hoped to move to the presidency of a major conference school with a huge foundation and perks that would enable him to live like a potentate without having to report most of his luxurious lifestyle on his tax return. Memphis wasn't exactly that place. It wasn't Florida or Georgia, much less Michigan or Ohio State or UCLA. But it was far better than Urban, another rung up the ladder. And from Memphis, Francis Saurian could clearly see the top as his next step.

So that's how Provost Richard Janus became Interim Rector Richard Janus.

11

The one thing we Wampanoags had going for us was the division among the English and their desire to protect the interests of their individual colonies against those of their neighboring colonies. The pinkies up in Massachusetts Bay didn't much like the document the Plymouth bastards made me sign in *Namassackesos* of 1671 and invited me up to Boston to tell my side of the story. They were concerned that Plymouth had extracted the right to extort some of the Wampanoag land that they wanted to reserve the right to extort for themselves. I seemed to make some divide-and-conquer headway with the Bostonians, and they agreed to have a joint meeting with me and the Plymouth peckerheads to see if we could work something out more to my (and their) satisfaction. But by the time that conclave commenced in September, my old buddy John Sassamon had told the pinks of whatever plantation that he'd heard I was trying to hook up with the Narragansetts to commence the old race war conspiracy.

I don't want to claim that the humiliation I endured in 1671 led me to plot war. That would state the case far too conclusively. I was just despairing of the prospect that the Wampanoags were going to be able to live in peace with the English. Think of a chess game in which the white pieces outnumber the red. As the King (Philip) of the red pieces, I was still searching for moves. I entertained little prospect for victory. I was hoping for a draw. But there is no doubt that after 1671, I began to contemplate for the first time that maybe our only recourse for survival was the very Indian confederacy the English had been predicting since Miles Standish carved up his dinner guests at Wessagussett nearly fifty years earlier. Now, when I say contemplate, that's precisely what I mean. I was not settled on a bellicose strategy, for I was hardly certain that even if I could put together allies enough to make war that we would necessarily win. But the English showed no signs of ever treating us with fundamental human decency. So our options for long-term survival were shrinking.

What I will admit to is beginning to have conversations with other sachems about what they saw as our alternatives in the face of unrelenting English pressure. For a year we talked. Some wanted to go to war immediately. Others, particularly the Narragansetts, who were under far less immediate stress, were cold to any idea of trying to deal with the English via flintlock and tomahawk. Meanwhile, I recognized that if war were to come, we had to have weapons and that procuring weapons was going to require money. I had nothing to exchange for cash save my shrinking supply of land. And so in August of 1672, I broke the key principle of my sachemy and began to sell any and all land that my people weren't then living on and farming. It is testimony to the Englishmen's almost utter disregard for me that they bought the land with a frenzied hunger, paying me prices I had never before commanded in the process. They obviously didn't give much thought to what I might be up to. They paid me top pound while I used the cash to assemble the arsenal I required, assembled it here and there as quietly as possible but from the very same people who had taken my weapons away only a short while before. As the stratagem gradually proceeded, I sometimes laughed with bitter irony that, at least, if war finally came and I could prevail, then the land I was letting go would return to me. The cost in volume of blood, though, was not something I liked to contemplate.

THOUGH THE HISTORY BOOKS don't date it exactly as such, That Vicious Lying Rat Bastard Josiah Winslow's War got started in *Squocheekesos*, late in the month of January, of 1675, and if war was to come, and it did, it came earlier than I would have chosen it. I still didn't have the Narragansetts convinced that if war came they needed to fight with us, and I didn't have my stockpile of weapons built large enough. Nonetheless, I maintain the war started when our relentless turncoat old pal John Sassamon journeyed from his home in Nemasket, where he was serving as pastor to a bunch of Praying Indians, to visit with Josiah Winslow at That Vicious Lying Rat Bastard's house in Marshfield, the very same drafty clapboard hellhole where Winslow had murdered my brother thirteen years earlier. Thomas Prence's having died two years earlier, That Vicious Lying Rat Bastard was now the Plymouth Colony governor.

On January 28th, the ground white with fresh snow, the streams frozen, the sky gray, the trees bare and Winslow's chimney belching smoke, Sassamon dismounted his horse and knocked on the door of Winslow's one and one, two rooms stacked on top of each other. Winslow's wife Penelope answered, and after a brief exchange admitted the traveler who removed the ridiculous belted-hat he wore as a sign of his identification with the English. Winslow was working at a desk in the far corner of the twenty-foot-square downstairs room. The draped marital bed was in the front corner opposite. This was the very room where Wamsutta was poisoned. Winslow rose as Sassamon entered, and he and Penelope pulled out the dining table which had been moved back against the wall after the family's midday meal. Here the governor and his visitor sat as Penelope then turned to the fireplace hearth and busied herself over the blackened pots that stood on stands at the fire and with utensils that hung from hooks in the chimney bricks.

That Vicious Lying Rat Bastard was a long-faced, sallow-skinned man with thinning curly hair gone pewter in his forty-seventh year. Dressed in a billowy black suit with a high square white collar buttoned up against the cold under his chin, he was dour, slow to smile, quick to snarl. He knew who Sassamon was, and he knew the two of them shared an enmity for me. But Winslow was not a hospitable man even to his fellow Englishmen, and he had never concealed his contempt for all men of my race, a condition Sassamon could not escape however much he might pray to Winslow's god and dress in English clothes. So Winslow showed his visitor no more warmth than a lurking snake to a field mouse.

"What brings you this way in the cold?" Winslow said to Sassamon.

"I come with alarming news," Sassamon said, nodding his head ever so slightly, always deferential, always hungry for the approval of whatever white man he encountered.

Mrs. Rat Bastard, who really was just one of life's unfortun-
ates, condemned by the religious views of her father to the
sorry life of hardship in a colonial outpost far from her London
rearing, was not herself a Rat Bastard. She stepped to the table
with a pot of tea and a small plate of hard biscuits and bid the
men to sup at this foul table where Wamsutta ate his last supper.
Sassamon had never been served tea before since its import
to the New World was brand new, and the governor disliked
that his wife had offered it to an Indian. Ignorant of what tea
was, Sassamon did not truly appreciate her gesture, but he was
delighted by the extension of even so meager a repast and was
voluble in his expression of gratitude.

Winslow cut him off in mid-grovel by demanding, "Your
news, Sassamon. If it's alarming, then we had no doubt best get
down to it."

"Yes, of course, sire." Sassamon took such a large swallow of
tea that he scalded his mouth. Choking a little, he continued, "I
have come to warn you that Philip has been seen in the council
nashweetoos of the Pocassets, the Nemaskets, the Sakonnets and
the Nipmucks. He argues that the Indians are in their last days
and must make war while there is still a chance of victory. When
they ask with whom the Indian will trade for European goods
if the English are defeated, Philip says the French and others
who will come in the sailing boats but will stay only to trade and
will not be allowed to make settlements as the English have. He
has even been among the Narragansetts. If he draws them in, we
English will be in grave peril."

Winslow snorted. The presumptuous man seemed not to
understand that learning English and even learning to read
and write did not turn a savage into a civilized being. Winslow
had heard this story of revolt from Sassamon countless times
before. Sassamon was always saying that I was plotting war,
but Winslow dismissed the notion this time with a sneer of
contempt. That Vicious Lying Rat Bastard hated me well
enough, but his disdain for my person was such that, despite

his repeated accusations of conspiracy, he never believed that I was plotting anything other than another scheme to put pots on the fires in the Wampanoag *nashweetoos*. Winslow detested me and judged me a dissembler with an egotist's love of my own voice and the impertinence to think myself and my people as equal to the English. But Winslow was tired of hearing the incessant rumors of my alleged conspiracies. When the time came, Winslow calculated, my relentless, self-aggrandizing talk would die with the sound of my voice. All Winslow had to do was call me out, and he would bet a season of corn that I would sooner sue for mercy than raise a musket against an Englishman.

"And how do you know that Philip is planning to attack?" Winslow asked.

"I live among the Christian people of Nemasket," Sassamon said. "They have relatives among those who still practice the old ways."

"Give me a name of someone who has heard Philip plotting war," Winslow demanded.

"My people would not reveal such a name from among their family members. But they have confided in me. That is why I am here."

"Give me the names of those among your own who are your sources," Winslow said.

"They would not come forward, sire, and anyway, I cannot betray them. But you can count on what I am revealing to be true."

Winslow thought that he could count on Sassamon sticking his hand out for a reward as he always had in the past. Inwardly, Winslow scoffed at the idea of Sassamon's being too loyal to his people to betray them.

"Bring me someone who can testify to what you are saying," Winslow said, "and we will talk further."

"I will do what I can," Sassamon promised. "It might help if I could provide a witness some measure of appreciation for the risk he might take in coming to speak with you."

"And something of the kind for yourself?" Winslow asked, delighted that his prediction of the man's behavior was proven accurate.

"If you might be so kind," Sassamon said.

"I might be so kind—when you return with a witness." Winslow rose from the table and walked to the door, Sassamon following after slipping a biscuit into his coat. "It grows dark so early in winter. I wouldn't want to keep you from wherever your travels lead you next."

When Sassamon was gone, Penelope asked her husband the reason for the man's visit. "It is no matter," Winslow said. "The words of an Indian are not worth the air they travel on, and that proposition abides even when they tell the truth."

John Sassamon had hoped that Winslow might show him the hospitality of a place to sleep that night. He dared not hope for a bed, but a spot on the floor by the fire would have been welcome. Even permission to overnight in the cold barn would have been appreciated. But he had encountered this kind of response from the white men before. They had taught him to read, even sent him to their Harvard for a term, given him first rank stature among those they called the Praying Indians. But he was still a man in between. I regarded him as a white man with skin the copper color of my own, but to the English he would always remain just an Indian.

Sassamon made camp on the banks of a stream about halfway between Marshfield and Nemasket. He built a fire, melted ice in a pot for both himself and his horse, and prepared himself a stew of ground corn and dried venison. After he had eaten, he wrapped himself in a blanket to wait for the long night to give way to an icy dawn. As he huddled against the cold, he wondered if he could find a partner among his fellow praying men in Nemasket who would endorse his latest story about me. He had not entirely made it up.

The Nemasket Prayers spoke together often about the prospect of war. Like all Indians, they were as quick to gossip as white people. The Praying Indians harbored complicated concerns. Some were fearful that the English might push me into war and use that as an excuse to cast them out. A more resentful group, having embraced the English god, having put on the tight English britches and confining shirts, having separated themselves from those of their blood who still lived the freer traditional life, this second group of Prayers was frustrated to still be treated by the English as other, and as less. For this group, a fire of bitterness already smoldering in their bellies, That Vicious Lying Rat Bastard's War would put the torch to their storehouse of indignation and fury.

John Sassamon knew all these complex and even contradictory emotions because he felt them himself. He had concluded that he could best pursue his own interest by enticing the English to arrest, incarcerate and execute me. But was there anyone else among the Nemasket Prayers who could be convinced to reach the same conclusion? If Winslow had been more definite about a reward, Sassamon thought the answer might be yes. Dare he promise a reward that Winslow might not deliver? Such speculations stimulated Sassamon throughout the night and left him weary and unsteady as day broke and he prepared to complete his journey home.

The last part of Sassamon's return from Marshfield took him along the frozen shores of Assawompsett Pond. This was a lush area three seasons a year, and even though the lake froze over in winter, it remained an area of good hunting where rabbits and waterfowl nested in the marshy reeds and deer came to drink from the puddles sunlight melted in rock hollows along the shoreline. Having arrived at the lake by mid-morning, he might as well take advantage, he figured. He tethered his horse and began to stomp through the stiff brown vegetation to flush such quarry as might be hiding there. Within the hour his game pouch held a grouse and two mallards. Then he drew bead on a plump grey fox that he shot through but did not bring down. The furry mammal would be tasty in a potage with squash and chickpeas, and his skin could be converted into cash. The animal was obviously mortally wounded as it careened from the brush out onto the ice and skittered away from shore, falling on its side once but managing another ten yards before collapsing and panting its last.

Eager for the bounty of food and money, John Sassamon laid his musket and his hat on the lake's frozen edge before walking out onto the ice after his prey. But the morning sun had turned yesterday's snow into a slick film. Two feet from the dying fox, his feet in hard leather English shoes shot out from under him, and he fell down heavily on the seat of his European britches, his head whiplashing back and smacking against the lake's frozen surface. He was not knocked unconscious, but he was dazed. And he lay back, arms and legs outstretched until he heard the crack like that of a musket shot. Then, as he started to sit up, the ice opened underneath him. First, only his buttocks fell through, but as he tried to pry himself upright, the ice gave way under his hands. And as the whole of him fell through, a jagged edge of ice knifed him open from the middle of the neck to the crown of his scalp, a bloody and painful but minor wound. Then he was under, flailing and panicked. With legs like lead weights, he kicked for the surface. Someone or something had moved the hole through which he had fallen. Trapped and desperate, he tried to ram his head upwards, bruising himself without gain. He opened his mouth to scream out for salvation to the English god he had served, and his mouth and lungs filled with water so cold it burned like fire.

Three of his Nemasket townsmen, themselves hunting for winter fowl and whatever other meat they might spot, spotted his body trapped under the ice several days later, his head twisted back, his final agony frozen in his features. The Indians recognized what had happened. He was hardly the first person to have fallen through thin ice. They took for their own families the game that Sassamon had shot, and they carried his body back to town for a service where his fellow Prayers paid their respects before laying him in the ground, a Bible tucked under one arm, the lesson book with which he had tried to teach me to read under the other.

That should have been the end of John Sassamon. He should have disappeared from history without a trace. Only what followed has preserved for him his infamous role in the holocaust about to descend on all who tried to make human society in New England.

Because I had never tried to keep my enmity for Sassamon a secret, and because he died alone, whispers began that I had ordered him murdered. Gossip was so rife among the New Englanders of the day, you'd think the whole bunch of them, English and Indian alike, were faculty members in a university department, famished with dissatisfaction, nourishing themselves with rank, slanderous speculation. On other occasions the repetition of nasty rumors would produce witches to torture in Salem; now it made homicide out of an accidental drowning.

Unpleasant and personally repugnant as these rumors were, nothing came of them for weeks – until That Vicious Lying Rat Bastard Josiah Winslow decided that the time had come to acquire the Montaup Peninsula and all other remaining Wampanoag land for Plymouth, both as a reserve for Plymouth colonists, and as a bulwark against the claims of Rhode Island. In Winslow's view, the time had come to launch a genocidal blow against us in the tradition of Mystic River. All he had to do to push events in that bloody direction was trot out the story Sassamon told him the day before he died. People knew I detested Sassamon. Winslow's account of Sassamon's tattling established my newest motive for having him assassinated. An "official" investigation was launched by the governor, and various belted hats moved about the region gathering "evidence," none of which amounted to a pellet of hummingbird dung.

I was aware of the trouble Winslow was trying to cause, and finally I had had enough of it. In March, in the moon of

Namassackesos, I set aside my bear cloak and deerskin leggings, donned the English outfit I always wore when dealing with the pinks, and rode to Plymouth to address a town meeting on the issue. In the square, fortified meeting house that sat at the top of the hill on Leyden Street, That Vicious Lying Rat Bastard and some of his henchmen tried to entrap me with nasty insinuations and leading questions. "Did you kill John Sassamon yourself, or did you have someone do your dirty work for you?"

The men with me squatted on the floor near the door or leaned back against the rough gray wall. I turned from them to address the white men who were either sitting on the meeting house benches or standing on the opposite side of the room. "Look, my English neighbors," I told them, "you have let your fears and our differences cloud your reason. We need not relate to each other this way. Most of us in this room have known no time when we were not together on this land. Our whole lives we have been partners rather than adversaries, however often we have looked upon each other at moments with suspicion. You accuse me of a hand in John Sassamon's drowning. But I am innocent, and you have no evidence otherwise. It is well known that I had no use for Sassamon who tried to cheat me in the vilest manner. Were I to have killed Sassamon, I would have done it in 1667 when he tried to steal my son's inheritance. But however much a scoundrel Sassamon was, I knew your great missionary John Eliot loved him, and so I let him return to the reverend's embrace. Why would I kill him now, if I did not then?"

I turned my eyes directly to those of That Vicious Lying Rat Bastard. "I know you say that Sassamon had warned that I was plotting war. How many times in the past has that accusation been raised against me? I have led my people now for thirteen years and have endured many a slight during that time. But where is the first Englishman that I have slain?"

I turned now to address the others in the room, men who might be open to reason. "But let me make still another point. For the sake of argument, let us suppose that I did order

Sassamon killed. Were it true, and it is not, what business would it be of the people of Plymouth? As an Indian, he was subject to my authority, not that of Governor Winslow. Sassamon may have dressed as English, but he was not English. He may have led a congregation but a congregation of Indians, not of English. He did most dearly wish to be English, but all his prayers did not alter the color of his skin. He was an Indian, he was on Indian land, and I am sachem of the Wampanoag nation. If I had ordered him killed, and it would have been within the prerogative of my authority to have done so, such an act would not have been murder, but a legal execution. But again, I did not do it. My motive for killing him lies in the mist of winters long past. So, what now was my reason? The answer, your esteemed governor speculates, is that I killed him because he warned that I was engaged in conspiracy."

Once more I stared directly at That Vicious Lying Rat Bastard. "But how did I know he confided such a warning to your governor? I can assure you that Governor Winslow did not tell me, a point, despite our history of disagreements, with which I think the governor will agree. So how else might I know? Did the governor sound an alarm? Did he order your garrisons reinforced? Did he raise your militia to march after me at Montaup? No, he did none of those things. From all evidence before us, the governor granted no credence to what Sassamon told him, and in dismissing his tale, he provided no mechanism for me to have known it was told. And just as the governor dismissed the villainy of John Sassamon's slander, so now all of you must dismiss the slander that I ordered him slain or had any reason to do so."

Count that contest as a triumph for *moi*. A lot of blah-blahing ensued about how this one or that one wasn't convinced because that one or the other one was a bleeping racist asshole. But in the end they admitted finding no evidence to substantiate the rumors that most of them had been guilty of passing along. I was dismissed just as I demanded to be—though not without prejudice, a term I employ with both its meanings attendant.

If it was evidence they lacked, then by golly it was evidence they would have. As the leaves began to bud in *Sequanankesos*, they found someone willing to testify that he was an eyewitness to the murder. Interesting isn't it that with all the falderal of the winter, the "witness" didn't think to report to a single living soul that he WITNESSED A FUCKING MURDER. But now when they had flat run out of ways to prosecute me, here comes a Prayer named Patuckson who just happened to be behind a tried-and-true tree over yonder, just right over there where the hiding was perfect and the seeing superb, yes, almost right on the spot when the deed went down.

Patuckson's pathetic prevarication went thus: Sassamon was out hunting when three of my men, Mattashunamo, Tobias, and Tobias' teenaged son, Wampapaquan, came up on him, over-powered him, twisted his neck until he was dead, chopped a hole in the ice on Assawompsett Pond and shoved his body into the water so it would look like he died by accident. Man, you almost have to stifle laughter at a proposition so preposterous. But the Plymouthites seized on it as if it had been chiseled by their Almighty on one of Moses' tablets. They arrested all three men and put them on trial for murder. No attention was paid to the fact that Patuckson had recently lost a significant amount of money gambling with these three men.

The trial was held in late *Nimockkesos*, the time the English designated the first week of June. Only the monsters of the Inquisition were better at pretzeling logic to achieve their predetermined ends. Winslow presided. My men protested their innocence and produced witnesses that they were nowhere near Assawompsett Pond on the day they were accused of killing Sassamon. English law required two witnesses to gain a conviction, but even Winslow and his co-conspirators couldn't find another liar. Patuckson told his palpably ludicrous story. And then for their second witness, they dug up and hauled Sassamon's body into the meeting hall. If you wanted conclusive evidence that the English were sick fuckers, this ghoulish nonsense, I think, will do. They made each of the accused walk up to Sassamon's rotting corpse, which had been in the ground for four months, and then they jumped around the room and claimed that the body began bleeding afresh as his "killer" came near. Yeah, and O.J. Simpson spent all his years after being found not guilty of murdering his wife looking for the real killer.

Well, surprise, surprise, all at the bar were found guilty as charged. A gambling debtor and a slab of decomposing meat never lie. In pronouncing that all three of the accused would hang, Winslow made much of how six of the "most indifferentist, gravest and sage Indians" who sat with the jury, but weren't actually *on* the jury, concurred with the guilty verdict. He failed to mention that they were all Prayers, beholden to the English, fearful of personal repercussions if they crossed their masters, and therefore eager to do whatever the pinkies wanted.

With no excuse for wasting time, the executions were set for June 8. That Vicious Lying Rat Bastard had one last trick up his sleeve, a particularly cruel, though hardly unprecedented, one. When the traps were sprung on the gallows, Tobias and Mattashunamo were hanged dead. But the rope around young Wampapaquan's neck "broke," and he was informed that if he now told the truth he would be spared. Scared shitless and amazed to be alive, taking notice that his father and friend were gone, he made a quick calculation and confessed that Tobias and Mattashunamo had indeed killed Sassamon, but that he had only watched. Asked if they had done so at my direction, he said, no, that they had their own grudges against Sassamon. So having gotten only half of what they wanted, still lacking an indictment of me, they shot him on the spot, fiends to the end.

What was all this about? That Vicious Lying Rat Bastard had determined that if his colony was to have a future, he had to have my people's land, and he had to have it before Rhode Island had legal title to it. To get it, he determined to kill most of us and drive off any who survived long enough to run. But in order to protect himself from the meddlesome authorities back in merry old England, he needed to have an excuse to kill us. He needed to provoke me into an attack. And don't think I wasn't pissed when he wantonly murdered men of my community for a crime they obviously didn't commit. But pissed as I was, I was neither ready nor eager for war. I could have used another year of weapons procurement for one thing. But even then, and That Vicious Lying Rat Bastard would not be deterred until then, I would only have gone to war as a last resort. I knew when war came it would be a fight to the death, not just for the Wampanoags but for all in New England, English and Indian alike. And unless you are a man of the judgment of Josiah Winslow or Donald Rumsfeld, you do not instigate such a war casually.

Winslow declared that the conviction of Tobias, Mattashunamo and Wampapaquan of murdering another Indian was evidence that hostilities by the Wampanoags had commenced. He ordered that preparations for war begin and directed the English living closest to Montaup be relocated to a fortified site named Miles Garrison. Knowing my special enmity for him and fearing I would endeavor to settle with him personally if I could conceivably manage it, he sent his wife and children to Boston. Then, he moved troops into the vicinity of Swansea, right on top of us, poised for invasion.

Rightly fearful that a Plymouth attack on Montaup could escalate into a race war all across New England, the Quaker John Easton, Deputy Governor of Rhode Island, tried to mediate. As *Nimockkesos* ebbed toward *Towwakesos*, as June marched toward July, Easton sat with me in my *weetoo*. Over the course of three days we shared my pipe and ate together plates of baked flatfish, bluefish or eel, clam chowder thickened with artichoke hearts and fresh berries for dessert. Easton accepted my account of the difficulties we were facing, and I agreed to have our differences with Plymouth arbitrated by the governor of New York and a sachem from outside the Wampanoag nation designated by me. Trying desperately to cool things down, when some of my men arrested a contingent of pinks riding through our territory

ostensibly searching for stray horses, I ordered them escorted off
our peninsula and released. But Winslow refused to negotiate.
He sneered at a diplomatic solution and never acknowledged
any of my ameliorating gestures, informing Rhode Island that
he intended to subdue me by force of arms.

Blood was finally shed when a group of my men led by my
capable captains Adonoshonk and Annawon marched north of
the Montaup neck to scout enemy activities. There they found
in the southern portion of the township of Swansea, the area
closest to our settlement lower on the peninsula, that the village
of Kickamuit was almost abandoned, its inhabitants drawn away
to Plymouth and Miles Garrison on the other side of the Palmer
River. The few people who were left around were very skittish,
obviously quite frightened, Winslow's orders to evacuate
their property having spooked them badly. Adonoshonk and
Annawon, like many Wampanoags, had visited this village on
sundry occasions to trade and even interact socially. On two
different occasions my men stopped to talk with Englishmen
they knew. Both times the conversations were terse and edgy.
Though we all understood that the dogs of war were loose in the
flowering vales of New England summer, we were not prepared
for the English simply to turn tail and run away. Indians would
have fought before running. My men were perplexed and were
inspecting the vacated residences when an English teenager ran
out of a house they were approaching and shot one of my men,
my beloved cousin Mauconset.

Adonoshonk flung Mauconset over his own shoulder
and led a retreat to the safety of the woods. Then after a brief
council, they decided to try to reach Pokanoket Village while
Mauconset still drew breath. After they departed, the terrified
English burned down two of their own houses. Within days the
English had snuck back into Kickamuit and burned the entire
community to the ground, acts of arson that were later blamed
on Wampanoags and therefore me. Why would the English
burn their own homesteads? Ask the Israelis who were ordered

to abandon their seaside villas in Gaza but torched them instead. Ask the Israeli government who placated these homeowners by bulldozing property that was perfectly usable. Ask the Russians who destroyed what they could not carry away as they fled before Napoleon and Hitler. The English burned their own houses so that we could not have them after they were gone.

Obviously, events had moved beyond my control. As is so often true when men go to war thinking they are righteous and will prevail with little consequence, as with the American Civil War, World War I, and the Iraq War of W, Cheney, and Rummy, few in New England either English or Indian would prove unaffected by what was now upon us. That Vicious Lying Rat Bastard Josiah Winslow's War had come.

12

Always on the lookout for all the credit he could commandeer, Francis Saurian assured Richard Janus, when Saurian took the presidency at Memphis, that he had nominated Rich to succeed him at Urban. Rich allowed as how that was not necessarily a favor, and Saurian showed humor enough to laugh.

"Nah, we've gotten this place into good shape," Saurian said. "Enrollment's up. We've managed the butt-holing budget cuts Mayflower has jammed up us. We've got a basketball team coming off the Sweet Sixteen." He looked at Rich and shrugged. "OK. Sore subject, I guess."

"What? You think I'm not proud of our NCAA run?" Rich said. "I cheered louder than anybody."

"Course you did, kid. That's who you are. Team guy from the get go. Why we got along so well."

Rich was unaware that Saurian thought of them as having gotten along well.

"You'll do good, kid," Saurian said, Rich mentally correcting the *good* to *well*. "You got the chops."

"I'm only in for a year, Francis," Rich said. "Just interim while they search for a permanent rector."

"Oh that's what his royal highness Viceroy Elia Lipscom says now. Just gives him more leeway to fuck with you. But he'll come around."

"But I'm not really interested in becoming rector. I'm a placeholder, and I'm happy with that."

"You say that now, kid, but *you'll* come around too. You weren't interested in becoming provost either, and look how you've taken to it."

"We'll see," Rich said. "But I'm not chomping at the bit."

Saurian shrugged and knitted his brow. "Well, if Elia Lipscom is stupid enough to pass you over as permanent rector, I just might bring you up to Memphis. Like to have my own people, you know. Got to have your own guy as your number two. Probably get you a raise; bet you'd like that."

Rich didn't even bother to say that he had no intention of serving under Saurian at Memphis, that he'd sooner return to a high school position.

Saurian laughed. "Hell's bells, kid, you know I'm going to try to steal Jimmy Prince from you. But you know what, if I can't get him, I might just put you back on the basketball sideline. I bet you'd take that."

Rich was shocked at such a statement, all the more because it just might be true.

IN FIVE YEAR'S TIME, Richard Janus had gone from being a high school English teacher and coach to the CEO of the second-largest institution of higher education in the State of

Alkansea. As interim rector, he was in charge of a university without ever teaching at one.

Was this a job that might grow on him? Were there things he would like to accomplish at Urban, initiatives he'd like to pursue?

Aside from landing Jimmy Prince to replace Rich, Francis Saurian hadn't succeeded at much of anything. That would have required the State Board of Trustees for Higher Education to allow new program development at Urban and to allocate an appropriate level of funding, neither of which it was about to do.

But despite his lack of concrete accomplishments, Saurian was such a busy bee, he was a buzzing annoyance. He showed up at everything and was always dropping names and claiming friendship with rich and influential people, people like Fordyce and Beatrice Florin. So the people in Mayflower were glad to see him go. Saurian wasn't allowed to lead Urban anywhere, but he made so much noise some people in Choctaw and even some in Mayflower thought he might. And the only thing that mattered in state higher education circles was the success of the Alkansea State University flagship in Mayflower. And for that matter, mostly its sports programs. People didn't jokingly call it America's Sports University for nothing, and the joke on most lips carried no pejorative judgment. All ASU sports must succeed, and ASU football must succeed most of all.

Sports were so dominant at Alkansea State that when its current rector was hired, the headline in the *Mayflower Monitor* read: "ASU to Be Led by Former Wide Receiver." Stephen Hopkins played split end for the Monsters in the early 1960s, and that, far more than his scholarly or administrative achievements, secured him the job as his alma mater's CEO. The first question at Hopkins' first press conference was not about improved graduation rates, increased admission standards, or faculty recruiting objectives, but rather, "What plans does your new administration have to get the Monsters back in the BCS title game?"

Alkansea pride was so focused on ASU that the Viceroy for Higher Education, Elia Lipscom, wanted nothing more than to become the ASU rector. At 53, his thick girth hidden under monogrammed shirts and two-thousand-dollar suits, Lipscom was almost handsome, and people flattered him by saying he resembled Harrison Ford, but unlike Ford, he was a Monster through and through. His bachelor's degree in educational counseling was from ASU. His master's in education leadership was from ASU. His doctorate in higher education administration was from ASU. He had season tickets for Monster football, basketball and baseball games, and he habitually wore an ASU brown and green striped tie. Unfortunately, however, while at ASU, Elia Lipscom earned his varsity letter in nothing other than fraternity carousing and incessant bullshit. And if he wanted to succeed the football player currently in the job, Lipscom had his work cut out for him.

Ostensibly, the ASU rector was subordinate to the viceroy, but the flagship rector made more than twice as much money as the viceroy and enjoyed far more prestige and public attention. Thus Lipscom's entire agenda was to be seen as unstintingly supportive of ASU while doing everything he could to undermine Hopkins without, of course, getting noticed doing just that.

So when Saurian resigned to go to Memphis, Viceroy Lipscom saw an opportunity to appropriate a slice of Urban's budget. During the same phone call in which Lipscom notified Rich he was being appointed interim rector, the viceroy also told him that the Board of Trustees maintained a policy to draw upon the salary and benefits lines of a rectoral vacancy to support the Board's search for a new CEO. Translation: the viceroy was going to use as a slush fund the $350,000 plus the $87,500 in fringe that used to pay and support Saurian. This was money Elia Lipscom could use on such more important matters as getting himself appointed rector at ASU.

The viceroy and his people loved that in Rich they had themselves a greenhorn they could boss around easily, or even better yet, ignore. But they did hope that, out of jealousy, Rich would can Jimmy Prince. Given Prince's success, a new, permanent rector would probably prove reluctant to replace him before he choked a player, slapped an assistant or boffed a cheerleader, all of which he would probably do eventually. But Mayflower didn't want to wait for that when Rich could take care of Prince for them.

And Francis Saurian was right that his Prince hire had given Urban national visibility. If and when Viceroy Lipscom became rector at ASU, he didn't want his basketball team having to contend with a competitive squad at Urban. The two schools didn't even play each other because ASU didn't want to dignify Urban's program by actually competing against it. But people in Mayflower were still pissed that the Monsters had finished near the bottom of the SEC and hadn't even gotten an NIT bid whereas the Ungulates had gone to the NCAA two years in a row and most recently had become a national media darling by advancing to the Sweet Sixteen. That aggravating noise needed to stop.

Viceroy Lipscom came down to the Urban campus about a month after Saurian resigned. His stated purpose was "to solicit input from Urban stakeholders on leadership priorities for the next stage of the institution's development." But Lipscom wasn't remotely interested in input and was glad the turnout was small; it assured him of the apathy he counted on to let him do exactly what he wanted without any interference from Urban faculty.

Still, even a small group of faculty members, or just one loud mouth for that matter, could ask difficult questions and push the meeting in an unpleasant direction. To head that off Lipscom talked the entire hour of the meeting, frequently repeating the premise that his job was "to make sure the Urban team was headed toward the goal line and make sure a good quarterback was under center," a somewhat inappropriate sports metaphor given that the Board of Trustees had always blocked Urban's desires to field a football team. Nonetheless, Lipscom waxed eloquent about finding just the right person to "become the face of your institution" and emphasized the care he was going to take in the process.

In love with the sound of his own voice, Lipscom wasn't aware that no one was listening to him, but since he was interested only in being able to say that he had consulted with the faculty, he wouldn't have fretted much if someone had drifted off to sleep and fallen out of his chair. The fact that Lipscom appeared on the Urban campus was all that mattered. He wasn't going to just field and vet applications and nominations but would "comb the country like the scouts that discovered Jerry Rice catching passes at Mississippi Valley State."

He was going to use a national search firm, he asserted. He didn't say that for this they would be paid $100,000 from the Urban budget, even though no one at Urban was invited to discuss the value of using an executive search firm. Most important, the managing partner of the search firm would make a $20,000 donation to the Board of Trustees Foundation, a fund managed by Elia Lipscom. One hand does need to wash the other, now doesn't it? Lipscom was always fervent about adding funds to his foundation account since he used it to reimburse the expenses of his attendance at every meeting of higher education administrators he could conceivably get to. Lipscom was the highest ranking higher education executive in the state, but that didn't require that he do much. And though he loved being in Mayflower on game days of whatever sport was in season—see and be seen, you know—the rest of the time Mayflower sucked. So why be there when you could be in any of all the other places that were better?

Meanwhile, with Rich as an interim rector, Urban was left in the limbo Lipscom and all the Mayflower people thought it should reside in permanently. The search procedure for campus CEOs is always a lengthy process. New appointments are seldom made in less than a full academic year. Lipscom had had very little interaction with Rich to this point, Saurian's never wanting to share the limelight of bullshitting bigshots with his provost or anyone else. But Lipscom knew that Rich had managed Urban's finances since becoming provost and could be relied on to balance his budget, and that was critical. As far as Urban went, all Lipscom cared about was that it didn't produce some gaping deficit while he was still viceroy, a disaster that could affect his plans to become rector at ASU.

Meanwhile, as Rich headed off embarrassment for all involved and lived inside his budget, Lipscom and his team could easily defer any set of proposals for programmatic development or funded research initiatives by telling Rich at every turn that such issues should really await the input of the new CEO. Who could argue with a logic so mild and sensible? And such a strategy put Urban's various impertinent ambitions on hold for at least a year.

"On hold . . . on hold is where Urban ought . . . ought to remain permanently," Under Viceroy for Academic Affairs Margaret Lockhart said in a meeting with her board staff colleagues after Elia Lipscom returned from his encounter with the Choctaw faculty. "I mean, really, do we even need the place? Obviously, not . . . obviously not when we have ASU to . . . ASU to educate our young people. No one would ever choose Urban . . . Urban over ASU." Five-feet ten and erect as a totem pole, dressed in a brown suit accentuated with a green scarf, Lockhart nodded her head with earnest indignation, her sprayed pageboy of dyed-black hair moving with her face like the helmet of a bobblehead toy.

"Certainly no one other than the colored kids and the blue collar rift rats they've got now," Under Viceroy for Fiscal Affairs Ronald "Ronnie" Shade offered. Like the other two administrators in the room, he was a lifelong Monster man. His B.A. and M.S. in accounting and his Ph.D. in higher education administration were all from ASU. "And we need their kind to do the sort of work they were born to. Somebody's got to run the cash registers and stock the shelves and mechanic the cars and keep the air-conditioners running, and you don't need four years of college to learn how to do that. Exactly why we have our junior colleges and trade schools. And we got both for them right there in slum-hole Choctaw, where they sure as hell got more old Caddylacks need fixing than anywhere else in the state." His red hair now turning sandy, his pants held high above his waist with brown and green suspenders, freckle-faced Shade grinned at Margaret to assure her they were on the same page.

"Those people had any sense," Lockhart said, "they'd get out of Choctaw on the first Greyhound north."

"It's just an old honky tonk of a place full of bars, drugs, prostitutes, drag queens and gang bangers," Shade agreed. "Most of 'em colored. Except for the whatdayacallem fags? Homo sapiens?"

"Homosexuals," Viceroy Lipscom said.

"Yeah, homos," Shade said. "You know who I mean."

"Well, our fellow citizens in Choctaw," Lipscom said, "do like to brag about how their city has been around even longer than New Orleans."

"So what? The place is a dump," Shade said.

"Why does the wonderful . . . the wonderful State of Alkansea have to have a place like Choctaw . . . like Choctaw as its largest and most famous metropolis?" Lockhart asked. "We ought to have a big city like Dallas or . . . like Dallas or you know. A refined place."

"Absolutely," Shade agreed, "a place without so many people of the ebony persuasion?"

"Their . . . their pride in their obnoxious old . . . obnoxious old Mardi Gras is half what's wrong them," Lockhart said. "It's disgusting, people running around . . . running around drunk out of their minds, dressed in those . . . dressed in those ridiculous costumes."

"And women flashing their titties at anyone who wants to see them," Shade said, "which, of course, is everyone."

"Ronnie, really. Language," Lockhart clucked. "We aren't in ... aren't in a barnyard."

"Well, sometimes they flash a lot more than just their tit ... their," Shade made a cupping gesture with both hands against his chest, "their doorbells. And that's against the law."

"Not that they really have anything like law down in Chocolate Town," Lipscom said.

That was the real problem for the Viceroy and his associates. In public they were more politic and thus less candid, but they all found it persistently annoying that Choctaw and Urban University were so cram packed with black people. Over a quarter of the students who went to Urban were black, most of them first-generation college students. All the while the state funded several colleges just for black folks.

"What I can't calculate," Shade said, "is what enrolling all these coloreds has to do with our state priorities. Everybody knows these Afro-Americans are just going to smoke crap, make babies and elect corrupt, uppity colored politicians who are going to take bribes and shake people down and embarrass the state before the whole nation so that good businesses like car companies and steel mills and chemical plants won't locate anywhere in the state, not even in a decent, God-fearing, church-going place like Mayflower where the women never show their titties, not even to their husbands." Shade looked up with a snaggle-toothed smile of embarrassment. "Sorry, Margaret. I didn't mean to say titties. Is it OK to say doorbells? My granny used to always call 'em her dinners. But that sounds kind of crude now."

"Why don't you not speak of them at all, Ronnie," Margaret replied.

Their faint dispute about the proper word for breasts notwithstanding, the three higher education officers did agree that what Alkansea needed was to get together all those Choctaw Negroes and faggot artists and smack-addicted musicians and pointy-headed hippie intellectual counter-culturists, and have them transferred somewhere else. If justice were to reign in the world, that's what would happen. Then Mayflower could become the state's Dallas. Just reduce Choctaw to its Old Town. And move the white people who weren't gay or wouldn't vote for a Democrat up to Mayflower. Close down that stupid Urban University and turn Choctaw into a nice little tourist place, like Seaside, Florida, nice, clean, safe, and unthreatening. Then the new Choctaw could become a place the Mayflowerians and everybody else in the state could be proud of rather than embarrassed by. The new Choctaw could brag about its history all it wanted, and it wouldn't even be obnoxious anymore. That's what the state needed, its own version of Williamsburg, Virginia. Only maybe with one street still showing some titties, Ronnie Shade thought. But he didn't say so.

Then in August of 2004, the Mayflowerian dream seemed poised to come true. People in Mayflower had long shared the notion that the state would benefit if only Choctaw would disappear. Some who watched Fox News and Pat Robertson and believed that Jesus was a gay-hating, race-baiting Old Testament character full of fire, brimstone and a spaceship full of kick ass even prayed for such an event, sometimes out loud. Pat Robertson swore that his god wielded hurricanes as an engine of divine retribution. And then along came Hurricane Hosea raging through the Gulf of Mexico to hit Choctaw with the devastating power of an atomic bomb.

And when the storm howled and the waters rose, Richard Janus had to embrace his fated responsibilities to lead Urban University as its interim rector.

13

The first man to die in That Vicious Lying Rat Bastard Josiah Winslow's war was my young cousin Mauconset. He was just twenty. We were well aware that something ominous was going on because the Puritans were abandoning their homes and showing great fear when they encountered any of us on trails in the area. Mauconset was wounded in the upper chest early in *Towwakesos*, on the morning of June 23, 1675, from a musket shot by a red-headed English teen named Jeremiah Smith. Mauconset was carried into the woods by his companions, including my field captain Adonoshonk. As the group of Wampanoag scouts tried to minister to my dying cousin, they watched as Jeremiah Smith and his father Edward left their homestead in haste. My men made no attempt to interfere with their departure, but Adonoshonk sent one of our men, Pawtonomi, to follow them to the fortified house the English called Miles Garrison about three miles farther to the north. There Pawtonomi saw an armed company of fifty men camped around the garrison house, their horses tethered and guarded. Pawtonomi's intelligence made clear that the English were rapidly positioning for a war they were determined to pursue.

The Indians of New England had shed not one drop of English blood. Three of my Wampanoag brothers had been executed on the ludicrous charge of having murdered John Sassamon, who, being an idiot, died in a one-man hunting accident. So the only homicide victims before my cousin Mauconset were my countrymen Tobias, Wampapaquan, and Mattashunamo. Yet, on June 21, That Vicious Lying Rat Bastard Josiah Winslow ordered seventy men to march from Taunton and Bridgewater to Swansea and for twice that number to reinforce them on the next day. Moreover, on June 21, Winslow wrote to Governor John Leverett of Massachusetts, asking him for assistance in the war that hadn't even started.

Winslow's letter makes his intentions clear. The colonies of Massachusetts, Rhode Island and Connecticut all cast lustful eyes on the territory across Narragansett Bay from Montaup. The land there was unusually fertile for southern New England, and that is precisely why the Narragansetts who lived there were so prosperous. Winslow's June 21 letter said that he didn't think he would need military assistance from Massachusetts for subduing the likes of me and my Wampanoags, but he would like to be able to call on his larger and more powerful neighbor if needed. Then, given that he didn't get his full name that begins That Vicious Lying Rat Bastard for nothing, he warned them that he had intelligence that the Narragansetts were preparing to "Join *Philip*" in a war, I hasten to add, the English were starting.

"If we can have fair play with our own, which with the help of God we hope to accomplish in a few days," Winslow wrote, meaning, if he could count on a free hand to attack my villages without interference, then Winslow would be willing to recognize Massachusetts' jurisdiction over the Narragansetts. Did Hitler and Stalin study this exchange before they signed their pact about divvying up Poland and the Baltic States? History provides few clearer examples of wanton, naked aggression.

But I didn't know any of this at the time. I was still trying to figure out some strategy for avoiding war. Then on the afternoon of June 23, with south Swansea practically empty and the northern part of the township teeming with English militia, Adonoshonk and our men hurried into our seaside summer village with the body of Mauconset who had died of his chest wound. My chief captain Annawon and I were seated under an *apawonk*, a thatch-roofed shade arbor, beside the work area where we had been discussing the current crisis while laboring on a new *mishoon* or dugout canoe that we were burning and scraping into shape from the trunk of a white pine. My wife, Wootonekanuske, was tending the cooking fire, preparing *hasamp*, a corn porridge flavored with raspberries for a light midday meal. Wootonekanuske became horribly distraught over Mauconset's death, since he was one of her favorites and she had always appreciated the mentorship he had shown to our son Neksonauket.

While Wootonekanuske went to fetch Mauconset's mother and his father Wantonocon, my mother's brother, Adonoshonk reported to me what had happened and what Pawtonomi had observed in the northern part of Swansea. The women of the village were already crying together over the horror of this murder by the time Adonoshonk finished his report. When he was done, I directed him to set up a defensive perimeter around our town. I then saddled my horse and rode with Annawon, Pawtonomi and several fleet scouts on foot to Miles Garrison where Jeremiah Smith and his father had taken refuge. A bright sun shone that day, and the *Towwakesos* air was pleasing and fresh, the summer's sting of heat still some weeks away.

We rode out of a thick canopy of foliage and showed ourselves from a distance out of musket range, making clear that we had come to talk, not fight. Then with Annawon on my right and our men spread out on either side, we moved slowly forward. On foot, several of the English came out to meet us, our longtime acquaintance Hugh Cole in the forefront.

"Hugh Cole, I know," I said. To the others I said, "I am Metacom, sachem of the Wampanoag. The English know me as Philip."

"*King* Philip," one of the men said in a sneering tone.

I replied, "I have long since answered to that name in the interests of peace."

"We know who you are well enough, Philip," Hugh Cole said. "What do you want?"

"I am told that a boy in this house has killed my cousin," I said.

"What of it?" Cole replied.

"I have come to ask why a boy among you would shed the blood of my relative when matters between our two nations have become so raw."

"I doubt he knew the heathen he shot was kin to a *king*," the sneering man said.

At that point, Jeremiah Smith and his father Edward walked forward to join us.

Pawtonomi said to me in our tongue, "The carrot-headed young one is the murderer."

"Is this the boy who shot my cousin?" I asked Cole.

"Yeah, I'm the one who shot him," Jeremiah Smith said. "What of it?"

"Why did you do this killing?" I asked.

"He was an Indian," Smith said. "He had no business in my town."

"He had been to your town many times," I said. "Your town and many other English towns. All of us have."

Jeremiah Smith spat on the ground. "He was an Indian," he said.

"He was my cousin," I said. "He was of my own blood."

Jeremiah Smith sniffed loudly and said, "I'd known that, I'da shot him twice."

I turned to Hugh Cole. "This boy has admitted to murder. You must surrender him to me so that I may take him to my village and hang him."

"You may be the *king* of your people," Cole said, "but you ain't the king of Swansea or any other English town. Anything gets done to this boy, will be done by the people of Plymouth Colony, not by the likes of you."

"He was just an Indian," Jeremiah Smith said to no one in particular. "Lots of Indians gonna be shot before long now."

"I will bring this matter to the attention of the authorities in Plymouth," I said, though such a statement was made for Cole's immediate benefit only and without the slightest hope that I could procure justice for Mauconset from the likes of That Vicious Lying Rat Bastard.

"You go do that," Cole said. "You might get off toward Plymouth right now, in fact." The others remained facing us, but Cole turned his back and walked back toward his encampment.

THAT NIGHT IN MY reed-roofed *weetoo*, my captains were angry over Mauconset's death, over the racist comments of Jeremiah Smith and over the lack of respect Hugh Cole had shown me. Some proposed that we surround Miles Garrison and attack at first light, and a mumble of agreement spread around the gathering, particularly among the younger men who were Mauconset's friends and companions. Even Adonoshonk nodded.

Wootonekanuske said, "I think a plan to attack is the right course. We have feared this day for years, Metacom, but we have planned for it too, five years on now. They are massing to strike us. We must raise our war clubs against them first and hit them hard before there are too many of them gathered for us to attack."

But I didn't agree. "I acknowledge that the war the English have tried to thrust on us for decades has presumably now come. But this will not be a fight we will easily win. We can't count on the Narragansetts. Our Nipmuck brothers, yes, but not the Narragansetts. And we must win, for if we don't, the Wampanoag as a people will pass into the next world as a morning mist lifts away into nothingness before noon. I think, if there yet remains a chance for peace, I must remain, if only for a day or two more, determined in its pursuit."

Still, I agreed with Wootonekanuske and the others that an assault by the English appeared imminent. If we could dodge it, perhaps peace was still possible. I didn't know that Josiah Winslow had gotten Rhode Island Governor William Coddington's promise to deploy his colony's boats to intercept any effort we might make to escape from our peninsula by sea.

But my scouts kept me informed that That Vicious Lying Rat Bastard was clearly moving an army of men into the neck of Montaup. We were being pinned down.

As Wootonekanuske and I lay on our sleeping bench that night, our arms around each other, my hand stroking her back and flank, we continued to discuss what strategy to pursue. "Dreams of peace have become dangerous, my husband," Wootonekanuske whispered, so as not to wake Neksonauket. "I know you know this. A surprise attack might be our only chance."

"The fact that I demur, my love, doesn't mean that I don't respect and appreciate your advice. But this war, if it comes upon us, will risk everything for both sides. These English don't fight awhile and then go home. Those who resist them disappear completely. We must not go to war unless we have no other choice. And if war is thrust upon us, we must try to end it before all chance of ending it disappears."

Early the next morning, I called my captains together and ordered them to assemble ten-men squads, each with a young runner to act as a courier. "I want a squad on every trail from Swansea down into the heart of Montaup," I said to Annawon, Adonoshonk, Pawtonomi and Nimrod. If a battalion of English move onto our peninsula, you are to avoid engagement if at all possible and dispatch your runner here to Pokanoket where I will lead our warriors out to meet them. You and your men conceal yourselves in the woods and let the English pass, then close in behind them, keeping hidden until you hear musket volleys. If you encounter a smaller group, just a handful of men, take them hostage and escort them here to me."

On that day of June 24, one day after my encounter with the militiamen at Miles Garrison, Annawon's squad did arrest an Englishman on our land and positioned me after interrogating him to make a diplomatic move, which, by releasing him unharmed, I hoped might yet pull the fuse from the powder keg of war. Unfortunately, on another trail to the east, the

English dispatched a larger advance party to reconnoiter our positions under the pretense of being out to gather corn and other food stock to feed the large number of men gathered at Miles Garrison. This squad of six mounted English included Jeremiah and Edward Smith. The Wampanoag contingent that intercepted them was headed by Adonoshonk.

As was necessitated by the dense covering of tree and brush, the English rode single file, making it a simple matter to flank their column fore and aft. Surrounded, the English were outnumbered almost two to one.

"Throw down your arms," Adonoshonk ordered.

For a fleeting second the fate of our part of the world hung in the balance. The horses snorted and turned. The English gave no answer as they tried to assess their circumstances.

Then young Jeremiah Smith spat out, "I'll take no order from the likes of a greasy red savage like you," and immediately raised his musket. His shot wounded only the calm. My men bolted forward before the others could bring their muskets up. Adonoshonk's tomahawk took off the back of the English teenager's head, and the other five in his company were killed as well with knives and war clubs.

Adonoshonk directed that their bodies be left in the open as a warning to other English that we would not be attacked without responding. The English have made much of this decision ever since, voicing their outrage at what they termed "murders," claiming that the corpses were "mutilated." As if the bodies of soldiers who have died at the hands of sharp implements commonly look like someone who has died in his sleep at home in bed.

14

Richard Janus was a proud interim rector when he left his Building 6 office on the late afternoon of Friday, August 13, 2004. Registration for the fall semester had just ended, and Urban University had achieved its all-time high enrollment. Urban had been growing steadily since its founding as a commuter college in 1955 with 750 freshman, on its way to a presumed stable enrollment of around 3,000 undergraduates. But propelled by the nation's emphasis on college education and fueled in part by the African-American community's determination to see its children edge their way into the expanding middle class, and mirroring comparable enrollment patterns at metropolitan campuses across the country, Urban never stopped growing. Master's degrees were added in the early 1960s, and Ph.D. programs came shortly later. But even as its enrollment and curricular diversity attested to its critical contribution to the needs of Alkansea higher education, Urban was always funded at a lesser rate per enrollee than its, may I say, monstrous, big brother in Mayflower.

As classes got underway in the fall 2004 semester, Urban had a student population of 20,362, its first time topping the 20,000 mark. The Choctaw school was still only about two-thirds the size of ASU, but by achieving an enrollment number that started with a 2, Urban had crossed a significant threshold, one that did not go unnoticed by those in thrall to the interests of the flagship Alkansea State University campus.

Rich knew that Urban's new enrollment profile was hardly the product of his fledgling leadership. Francis Saurian and the Urban rectors before him had all pursued enrollment growth as a strategy for commanding greater attention from state educational authorities and therefore the capture of greater state resources. Moreover, more students meant more tuition dollars in the budgetary pot. And more money translated to more flexibility inside a budget that was always tight as a Kardashian bikini. But the Urban rectors' relentless recruitment and retention efforts were not the key to the institution's steady enrollment increase. Universities like Urban were burgeoning everywhere due to demographic and economic transformation. More people were locating in the sprawl of America's metropolitan areas, and more young Americans were pursuing college degrees.

Furthermore, Urban had the specific appeal of Choctaw going for it. Choctaw's Sun-Belt climate facilitated year-round golf and outdoor tennis. The cost of living was low compared to most American metropolitan areas. And the city's rich, diverse culture had made it a choice destination for capable young faculty members for Urban's entire five-decade history. As a result, Urban had built academic programs stronger than their funding. Young faculty came to Urban routinely thinking that they would stay only a handful of years, but fell in love with Choctaw, decided to stay, and put up with the chronic financial challenges to build a school that students across the region trusted to deliver quality education. ASU offered the panache of a nationally competitive football program that captured a national championship every decade or so. And ASU had a far better on-campus party atmosphere. But even many ASU students would confess their belief that Urban was a more demanding and academically challenging school.

Now that Urban was a school with more than 20,000 students, it was beginning to look less like an afterthought little brother and more like a rival.

THE LAST THING RICH'S data management director did on August 13 was send Urban's enrollment statistics to the Board of Trustees and the office of Viceroy Elia Lipscom. The first thing Lipscom did on Monday, August 16, was call Rich about the numbers.

"You Urban folks been taking lessons from Mayor Daley's political machine?" Lipscom asked. "Maybe Edwin Edwards over in Louisiana? Though I guess old Edwin was more interested in stealing money than votes. And people in Louisiana dumb enough to vote for Edwards on their own volition." The viceroy treated himself to a long laugh at his cleverness.

"Not sure I'm following you, Viceroy," Rich said, recognizing that something unpleasant was up but not yet sure what.

"Just interested if you Choctaws been registering dead people down there in Chock Town?" Popular throughout the central and northern parts of the state, "Chock Town" was short for Chocolate Town. Rich was shocked to hear such an epithet come from the Viceroy's lips.

"I'm still not grasping what you're driving at, Elia," Rich said. He restrained himself from calling Lipscom "Vice" as did most of the higher-ranking people on his staff.

"Come on, Coach. Y'all sent me figures up here saying you've registered over 20,300 students this fall, up nearly 1,200 from a year ago. Y'all counting people by their first names and their middle names too?"

"That's our enrollment, Elia," Rich said. "The extra tuition will give us some needed budgetary relief this year after the recent cuts we've had to endure. I assume you're pleased."

"Jesus in sack cloth, Coach, of course, I'm pleased. I'm just giving you the needle. Old baller like yourself, I know you can take it. I'm Hubert Humphrey pleased as punch. I'm gonna remember the fine work you've been doing for us when raise time comes around."

Rich dismissed the implied promise of a raise as pure bullshit. He was still making his provost salary, and that hadn't been increased since Francis Saurian hired him. "Not a good time to put money on your top people," Lipscom had told Rich when he'd named him interim rector, "not when we're cutting budgets. Makes us look bad." This in a season when he'd raised the salary of the rector at ASU by 15%, from "only" $390,000 to $455,000. All part of the viceroy's long-view scheme to land the ASU rectorship for himself. Lipscom's own salary was $295,000, but money was only one slice in the pie chart of his ambitions to become ASU rector. And his strategy toward Hopkins was a lot more cagey than That Vicious Lying Rat Bastard Josiah Winslow's toward me. By giving Hopkins a raise at the time, Lipscom could turn his pockets inside out if Hopkins was offered a job elsewhere, a prospect the viceroy dreamed of nightly. And, tastily, when Lipscom finally succeeded in becoming his own subordinate, his successor could hardly pay him a nickel less than Lipscom was paying Hopkins. Lipscom relished how brilliant all this was.

"I'll take any raise you want to direct my way, Elia," Rich said, "but credit for our enrollment growth belongs to Hart Thompkins and his team of recruiters." Hart Thompkins was Urban's Vice Rector for Student Affairs and Enrollment Management.

"Well, I'm glad you've brought up Enrollment Management," the viceroy said. "People up here in Mayflower are really pretty shocked by the numbers you've sent us. Pleased, as I said. But shocked. Some of my staff have suggested we need to get the new student profile numbers up here for us to take a look at."

"Meaning what?" Rich steeled himself so as not to let his irritation creep into his voice.

"Oh, meaning nothing. You know how Ronnie Shade is. Loves to crunch his numbers." Like Lipscom, Shade saw his job as promoting the interests of ASU in whatever way he could and making sure that none of the other schools he supervised did anything that might interfere with or diminish the interests of his alma mater. "Ronnie says that if y'all got something going on the rest of us ought to know about, then we ought to know about it first, up here at the Board."

"Once again, I'm not following, I'm afraid."

"Ronnie ain't saying y'all are doing something wrong."

"What could we be doing wrong?"

"Oh, you know, keeping too many men in the huddle. And that's a penalty. Or lining up off-sides when the ref ain't looking."

Rich chose to ignore this analogy.

"You follow what I'm saying?" Lipscom asked.

"Can't say that I do," Rich responded.

"Oh come on, Coach—don't play dense. I'm talking about y'all admitting some students who don't meet your enrollment regulations. The Board mandates the standards and y'all are obliged to follow them. But I know how it is. These enrollment management guys, they feel a lot of pressure to get their numbers up. Enrollment falls, everybody starts pointing fingers at them. They start worrying about the mortgage and their own kids' tuitions. Hardly blame a fellow for sneaking in a few extra students who oughtta gone to a community college."

"Hart wouldn't have any reason to cheat," Rich said. "If you want to know what we've got going that y'all ought to know about, it's called Choctaw, one of the nation's most interesting and diverse cities. Students want to come here to live and study. And that's why our numbers have risen steadily for years. We don't have enrollment problems; we've got space problems. I need another dorm and a modern science building."

"Let's not get ahead of ourselves," Lipscom chortled. "Here I am talking enrollment issues, and you're talking about new buildings in a state that's broke."

"If my memory serves, three new buildings opened on the Mayflower campus just last year. Not to mention the gazillion-dollar addition of 15,000 more seats at Monster Stadium. You add any more seats, you're going to have to hand out oxygen masks for those in the upper deck."

"All that's completely beside the point, Rector Janus. What goes on at the flagship is not connected to what goes on down at Urban."

"Same state, same state budget, same taxpayers. And the parents of Urban kids pay taxes at the same rate as those who go to Mayflower."

"Yes, well," the viceroy said, "I'll give you credit for representing your institution with passion. And we should, of course, take up these issues in due course. But I really called to let you know that we think the solution to your problems . . ."

"What problems? I haven't brought up any problems."

"You were just talking about needing new buildings."

"A dorm will pay for itself; so will the second one we need. Our science building was built in 1958 and hasn't ever been updated. Our kids have to study in labs that look like they were designed for Dr. Frankenstein."

"Yes, well, again," the viceroy said, "Ronnie is of the opinion, and he's hardly alone up here, that we probably ought to adjust your admissions threshold. Every year when you make your annual presentation to the Board, y'all emphasize your academic achievements."

Yeah, Rich thought, we emphasize the awards our students have won and the books our faculty have published, and right afterwards ASU brags about the football team's won-lost record, and everybody gives Stephen Hopkins a standing ovation, and the viceroy closes that and every other meeting by saying, "Go Monsters," as if they had the only sports program in the state, more important, as if ASU's football ranking was the only thing that mattered about state higher education.

"And it's right, absolutely," the viceroy continued, "to be focused on your academics. That's why we're all in this business, right?"

"Right," Rich said, trying to strip his voice of sarcasm.

"So we've been thinking, Ronnie and the other staff, that if we raised your ACT floor a couple of points, you'd do even better yet. Whaddya think? I'm sure Margaret would be happy to work with you to identify the right number." Margaret Lockhart was former dean of the College of Education at ASU and prided herself on her way around educational statistics. Rich was sure that Margaret Lockhart and Ronnie Shade belonged to the same coven.

"Probably cost us 500 or so students a year," Rich said. "Over four years it would push us back down to around 18,000 students."

A female voice chimed in, "With fewer students entering Ewe Ewe with a higher ACT average, your graduation rate . . . graduation rate . . . would probably go up. And maybe then a higher percentage of your graduates would turn out for . . . turn out for commencement ceremonies. Everybody always looks so . . . so presentable in their academic robes, especially your colored students. On campus they so often look as if they can't afford nice clothes to go to school." Margaret Lockhart. Rich hadn't realized she was listening. Francis Saurian had warned Rich that Lipscom frequently had members of his staff on extension lines. But this was the first time Lipscom had pulled this trick on Rich. That Rich knew of.

"Hello, Margaret," Rich said. Rich had been told that the under viceroy liked to be addressed as Dr. Lockhart, but he could never remember to do so.

"Hello, Rector Janus," she replied.

"I hadn't realized you were on the line."

"Well, you know how . . . know how concerned I always am about Ewe Ewe, especially matters like its graduation rate and its . . . its commencement ceremonies. I just want to see more of your students with their nice . . . nice robes on. You know I never miss a graduation."

"I know you don't," Rich said. Margaret Lockhart loved nothing more than dressing up in her academic regalia. Rumors circulated that she even went to all the high school graduation ceremonies in Mayflower, always in cap and gown. And she once wondered aloud at a Board of Trustees meeting why the Board didn't require professors to teach in their robes the way they had to in England and at the University of the South.

"Even at a commuter school like . . . like Ewe Ewe, graduations are important," Lockhart said. "That's why we call them commencements—because they're not an ending . . . not an ending but a beginning."

Rich abruptly understood why university presidents suffered from a high suicide rate.

"Well, we're working on our graduation rate," Rich said. "But I don't much like the idea of denying enrollment to the young people of this region who have come to rely on Urban for an educational opportunity others in their families may not have enjoyed. And we're kind of jazzed down here about surpassing 20,000. I don't know anybody in the community that would want to take a step back at this point."

"Solve your space concerns," Lipscom said. "That'd be nice."

"Eventually take 2,000 tuitions away from us. How do we run the place?"

"We'd completely protect you from harm," the viceroy promised. "You can take my word about that."

15

Shortly after the skirmish that cost the lives of Jeremiah and Edward Smith, Adonoshonk reported back to me that English blood was now on the ground, and I knew that there remained little chance of avoiding war. In fact, I suspected, and I was obviously correct in my suspicion, that Adonoshonk's killing of the Smiths and those with them was just the excuse That Vicious Lying Rat Bastard was craving to unleash the hounds of hell upon us. What Josiah Winslow didn't count on, however, was that things would not go so easy for the English as they had gone earlier at Wessagussett and Mystic River.

If you want evidence that the English were determined to initiate hostilities with us, look at the fact that the Governor of Massachusetts sent orders for his militia to march toward Montaup on June 25. Yes, that was one day after the skirmish in which the Smiths and their contingent were dispatched into the next life. But lest you forget, the only communications available back in the seventeenth century were either mouth to ear or letter exchanged from one hand to another. According to the Puritans' own records, word of Adonoshonk's response to young Smith's foolish violence didn't reach Boston until June 26.

Meanwhile, down in Swansea, Plymouth's officer in charge, Captain James Cudworth, had dispatched a self-righteous braggart named Benjamin Church to parlay with my sister-in-law Weetamoo, who lived on the eastern side of Montaup Bay. Weetamoo had succeeded her father Corbitant as sachem of the Pocassets. Weetamoo was older sister to my beautiful Wootonekanuske, and she had been married to my brother Wamsutta. She was always an independent-minded person, and she had responsibility to the people of her own township, but she was blood of my blood.

The Pocassets were great fishers and were renowned for their canoeing skills. Church's mission provides further evidence of how much the plan afoot was to trap me in Pokanoket Village and murder everyone there with me. I had always had good relations with Weetamoo, but she, like me, feared the coming of war between the English and those whose people had been there when the pinkskins arrived. Cudworth sent Church to Pocasset to make sure that Weetamoo didn't employ her *mishoons* to ferry my people away. The English wanted to make sure that Wamsutta's widow didn't act to save our lives.

To provide you an idea of how stupid I was during this now very late date, with the blood of English and Indian alike already staining our land, I continued to hope that, at the very least,

I could keep our hostilities limited to soldiers from Plymouth Colony alone. I had hardly enjoyed unqualified success in my diplomatic contacts with Massachusetts, but I'd had better luck with the Boston men than with the Plymouthites, now, I realize, largely because the Massachusetts villages were more distant and the Bay settlers looked west for additional land rather than south into Wampanoag territory. I did not know that an army of over 100 men had marched out of Boston toward Swansea on June 25 or that Massachusetts leaders had already decided to throw in their lot with their Plymouth brothers. So when my men brought me a white man they caught crossing into our territory, I let him go after I questioned him and found that he was a Bay colonist. In the last week of June, 1675, with the boots of marching soldiers pounding through the woodlands, the prospects of peace seemed dim. So how could we confine our enemy to the men of Plymouth? War with Plymouth alone was far more winnable than war with all the white men in New England. But in this, as in all else, my wishes, my strategies, and my will were frustrated.

THE FIGHTING BEGAN IN earnest on June 28. My men took up a defensive position in the woods on the east side of the Palmer River, within musket range of the bridge which led to Miles Garrison. Benjamin Church led a squad of Englishmen on a charge across the bridge, and my guys opened up on them, quickly sending them scurrying back across the river to the safety of their fort, killing several in the process, unfortunately not including the insufferable Church.

In a driving rainstorm the next morning, the English marched across the river in a larger force and bid us to come out into the open field and meet them in the kind of battle they fought in Europe: two lines blasting away at each other, the occasional cavalry charge being defended by pikemen who wielded long spears to pierce the mounts and turn them away. They called us cowards, and we told them they could go pike themselves. If they wanted a piece of us, they were welcome to come into the woods and fight us the way men fight: behind trees.

We lost no men that day because the English were not willing to engage us on our ground, and we were unwilling to lay down our lives in the mindless slaughter of the way they fought. They frightened us, though, and from the woods, Annawon and I realized the extent of our vulnerability. They outnumbered us, and they were obviously intent on war. If they marched directly on Pokanoket Village, we did not have adequate forces to defend the *weetoos* and fields of our families. Leaving an adequate force to harass and delay, Annawon and I rode forthwith to Pokanoket to prepare our people for our only viable response.

The English had put together an army of more than 500 men from Plymouth and Massachusetts, and though they whispered to each other in their fear that they would face 500 frenzied warriors, in fact, I had fewer than 200 fighting men with me at Pokanoket. Yes, as I have admitted, I had undertaken conversations with Narragansetts, Nipmucks and others about whether they would stand with the Wampanoags if the English forced war on us. These conversations are still cited as justification for their attack. I was the aggressor for having tried to forge a defensive pact. Stalin and his successors didn't much appreciate NATO, but they didn't turn the Cold War nuclear, and NATO really existed. To this point I had a firm defensive agreement with no one. And I was trapped on the peninsula of my homeland, facing a force nearly three times my own, and without allies I had only two choices. I could lead my men into a battle we would surely lose. Or I could retreat.

I sent Nimrod and Pawtonomi with an urgent message across the water to Weetamoo in Pocasset. If she sent her *mishoons*, we could live to fight another day. If she did not, the Wampanoags would that day become as the Pequots before them. While Nimrod and Pawtonomi were seeking our sister's critical alliance, I gave the order to my people to pack our own *mishoons* for flight. Everyone was to prepare transport for as many of their possessions as possible, recognizing that if Weetamoo did not send her canoes, much of what we owned would have to be left behind. I ordered all my people to give priority to foodstuff and weapons. As we had reached summer, Weetamoo's fields were adequate to feed us, but bringing food with us was still essential. We would diminish resentment by providing as much for ourselves as we could. Our weapons, of course, were our first priority.

Along with the others in Pokanoket that day, I devoted much of the day to filling boats with our possessions. The fierce rain let up, but the skies continued to drip, making our preparations more onerous. We were, fortunately, good packers. We moved from our summer village on the sea to our warm inland winter *nashweetoos* and back every year. We were well supplied with strong sacks and baskets for carrying and storing our belongings.

For our immediate family, Wootonekanuske made the hard decisions about what to take and what to leave behind. She was, as always, a rock, working without complaint and without rest. Tears wet her cheeks throughout the long day, but she never cried out, never mopped her face, never called attention to herself, just kept choosing, binding what was to be taken, setting aside that which wasn't, issuing orders to me and eight-year-old Neksonauket about what she wanted us to do next.

Like the other children in the village, Neksonauket attended to the chores his mother assigned him without a full understanding of what was at stake. He was too young to know fear, even though the English would no doubt kill him along with all the rest of us if the retreat were not successful. But a child of his age doesn't understand the finality of death. Neksonauket knew that the adults of the village were somber and on edge; he knew that his mother was upset, and he would occasionally wrap his arms around her waist and lay his head against her belly, telling her that he would allow no harm to come to her. But when he was out of his mother's sight, like the other children with whom he interacted as the *mishoons* were being packed, like Gulf Coast children in another century as a hurricane approached, he showed the excitement in his eyes. For our lovely, precious children, children who had never known the brutality of war, our preparations were, O Creator help us, yet an adventure.

Near sunset on that gray, drizzly, 29th day of June, Annawon and I walked down to the shoreline of Montaup Bay to prepare for departure. The Pokanoket *mishoons* were packed with as much as they could hold, some dangerously full for a five-mile paddle across open water. Foodstuffs which we had no room to take with us, particularly our extra supply of corn, had been taken into the forest, buried in our storage pits and covered over so that the English could not find and raid them. We could only hope to return some day to draw on the fruits of our labor.

As the rain diminished, the bay fell calm. Had it not, I would have ordered that additional items in the *mishoons* be removed and buried rather than risk canoes sinking from overtopping waves. Still, much of what we owned was stacked out on the dry sand beyond the wave crest, no place for storage in our slender boats, perishable foodstuffs we would prefer to take, bear rugs from our *weetoos*, fur robes we would need for warmth come winter, metal pots we had bought with skins and corn from the English.

The few of us who had horses had no recourse but to abandon them, me among them. And this would place us at considerable disadvantage in the days to come since we would have to flee and fight on foot. Historians have made much of the fact that I left without my horse, citing this fact as evidence that our departure was panicked and poorly planned. I grant that I might have proceeded differently, might have brought the bullet and blade of war to the English at an earlier time. But I thought then that peace was our best hope, and I doubt that any attack on the English up through the Montaup neck would have succeeded. So my horse was lost. A sadness for me, to be sure, but the losses to come would prove infinitely more painful.

Historians have also noted that I left behind at Montaup my English belted hat and mark it down as another indication of my haste. What nonsense! I didn't forget my hat. I discarded it. I never wore it save on those occasions when I went into an English town and endeavored to present myself as the white man wanted to see me. That time was clearly past. The hat was left behind because the days when I would have need for it were gone.

The rain had lifted, and we would enjoy a good moon to navigate by that night, but we could not wait much longer to learn of Weetamoo's decision. Just as I was about to announce that our departure would commence, just after last light, Annawon clapped me on the back and pointed out into the bay. Low on the water, a flotilla of Pocasset *mishoons* paddled toward us. On other occasions, when we visited or gathered to feast together, the canoers would have sung songs of greeting and celebration as they stroked their paddles through the water. But they understood clearly what was at stake and came toward us without a sound, feathering their paddles so as to silence even a splash.

Weetamoo wished that she could avoid getting involved in this ugliness. But at the critical juncture, she was unwilling to let the white hearts do to the Pokanokets what they had done to others before us. Her Indian heart was too huge for that. With Pocasset canoes at our disposal, we loaded as many of our possessions from the cache on the shore as we could, including those few small livestock we maintained whose feet we could bind in order to carry them with us. And in the joint navy of Pokanoket and Pocasset *mishoons*, we fled over the waters of Montaup Bay to safety.

The English have their Dunkirk, an operation that was largely the product of mismanagement but is remembered with triumphant pride. Like the Wampanoags as a nation, this Pokanoket Dunkirk is not remembered at all.

Like the Dunkirk evacuation, our desperate retreat was not tidy, and for that I take the blame. I had stubbornly held out hope that war could be sidestepped or at least limited in scale. And I had been wrong. As my people paddled across Montaup Bay, they were forced to leave their corn still mere buds on slender shoots, and other foodstuffs still in the ground. Our mature livestock, the cows and hogs we had learned how to raise from the English, were similarly abandoned. In a day's time we had given up our dry summer *weetoos*, the teeming shores where our fathers had fished, and the lush fields our mothers had tilled before us. In the morning we were rich. By evening we were poor.

SOME STORY RICHARD JANUS. The pain it causes to tell it myself.

FINALLY, ON JUNE 30, the English came across the Palmer River with their whole army and marched down Montaup to Pokanoket Village. We were no longer there. They joked about what cowards we were and how they had scared us with their obvious superiority. But the English were greatly relieved not to have to fight us, for though they were confident they would have vanquished us, they knew they would have taken many casualties in the process. This they were spared, at least for now, at least on this occasion.

But relieved as they were to have sidestepped battle this day, they were most certainly not relieved of their determination to take for themselves that which had only hours earlier belonged to us. They took our pigs, cows, goats, sheep and horses. They claimed our land for themselves and immediately began to speculate about its value in pounds and shillings, calculating even as they set torch to our weetoos how to handle the riches they had just awarded themselves. Would it be of greater value to occupy it directly, sell it to others who needed land they couldn't find in "safe" areas of New England, or merely hang on to it as a real estate investment?

As they plotted their future benefit from our soil, they undertook immediately to erect a fort which they could use to defend themselves should we reappear with the intention of taking our land back. And most viciously, they uprooted our corn, not to eat, but to destroy. Even if we somehow prevailed in a fight for our land, we would starve in the aftermath of that unlikely victory.

General William Tecumseh Sherman had nothing on these guys.

16

Two weeks after Rich's unpleasant conversation with Elia Lipscom and Margaret Lockhart about Urban's huge fall semester student registration in August of 2004, circumstances produced an enrollment reduction at Urban that not even the viceroy and his deputies would have dared. When Rich got home from work on Wednesday the 25th of August, he got the first inkling of what was about to happen when Cally told him that a Category 1 storm named Hosea had cut across the Florida peninsula into the Gulf instead of heading up the Atlantic seaboard as originally predicted. This marginal hurricane probably wasn't anything to worry about, she said. The storm was supposed to go back into Florida around Apalachicola, hundreds of miles to the east of Choctaw. Still, they ought to watch it.

Rich had grown up on the Gulf Coast where hurricanes were a seasonal annoyance. He understood that they were dangerous, but like most Gulf Coast residents of his generation and all those before, he regarded them as a nuisance to be endured. One hunkered down during a hurricane. Families supplied themselves with containers of drinking water, filled the bathtub with water for flushing the toilet if needed, kept several kerosene lanterns in the garage or work shed, stocked up on candles, packed in cans of soup, potted meat and Vienna sausages and made sure to have an adequate supply of batteries for flashlights and radios.

The New Orleans of Rich's youth endured some street flooding during Hurricane Flossy in 1956, but the water didn't rise into homes. Hurricane Audrey inflicted extensive damage on Cameron Parish in the western part of Louisiana in 1957, taking over 600 lives in the process. After that, people began to flee the swampy coastal area and barrier islands of Louisiana, but flight was still not a hurricane ritual for the residents of Rich's New Orleans hometown. So Rich's family remained in their little pre-fab home when Hurricane Ethel came in 1960 and Hilda in 1964. The Januses stayed home when Betsy caused traumatic flooding in the eastern part of the city in 1965, and though Rich was away at college, his family remained home when Hurricane Camille sideswiped New Orleans and obliterated the Mississippi shoreline in 1969.

The decision to remain in one's own house in inland metropolises like New Orleans and Choctaw was considered neither courageous nor foolhardy. Hurricanes were an aggravation, but inside a levee-protected city, not a matter of life and death. Residents rode them out and always had. And they continued to do so for another generation after Rich's childhood, even as fearsome Hurricane Andrew blew by in 1992 and Hurricane Georges gave Choctaw a pasting in 1998. But prodded by consistent reporting on the issue, the public had a much greater awareness of the dangers these storms represented, particularly for places like New Orleans and Choctaw that were built on drained swamps and depended on levees to keep a storm surge at bay. Global warming was rendering the storms more frequent and more fierce.

And the various canals the industrial titans had convinced their states to cut from sea to city had eaten away at fragile ecosystems and plunged once vibrant wetlands into the Gulf's rising brine, removing a defense of vegetation that had for centuries protected the cities behind them by soaking up the rushing water and sucking the force from the wind before it reached human habitation. No one worried about such an eventuality before the 1990s, but now people stood warned that the right storm on the right angle could push water over the levees of New Orleans and Choctaw, either or both, and fill their engineered topographies with the speed and force of a wide-open faucet into a salad bowl.

So when Carolyn took aim at the Alkansea coast in 2003, Rich and Cally and most of the residents of Choctaw took flight. The experience was pure misery. Fleeing west took Choctaw citizens right into traffic from New Orleans which had also ordered an evacuation. Fleeing east risked being overtaken by the turning storm from behind. So Rich and Cally headed north toward Nashville where they could turn east on I-40 and ultimately find refuge with old friends Jerry and Anne Schwartz. That drive normally took only six hours. Fleeing from Carolyn, it took them 23, and though they lost none of their newly acquired fear of killer storms, they were so uncomfortable inching along for 400-plus miles that they swore, the next time an evacuation was ordered, they would do everything they could to book an airline flight out of harm's way.

Hurricane Hosea had tracked slightly west when Rich got home from work on Thursday, August 26. But the storm was still predicted to go into Panama City when he left for his office the next morning. Unfortunately, Hosea strengthened to a Category 2 and kept tracking west all day Friday, bringing it ever closer to Choctaw. At 4:30 that Friday afternoon, Rich called Urban's deans and vice rectors to his office for an emergency preparedness meeting. Computer models now showed a Category 3 Hosea striking Pensacola, only ninety miles to Choctaw's southeast. If the storm did the predicted hard right turn, Choctaw should suffer little sustained damage. But Rich and his administrators agreed that the situation should be monitored overnight. He asked everyone to plan to meet with him at 9 a.m. the next morning unless he emailed them a cancellation before 8:00. They then adjourned across the street to Building 5, which housed the university's largest dining facility and several meeting halls. Rich was hosting a reception for new faculty and staff, to which all faculty and staff were invited.

"This really sucks," Dean of Humanities and Social Sciences Ben Turner said to Rich as they were walking over to the reception.

"The party or the hurricane?" Rich asked.

Ben laughed. "You're giving the party, Rich, so I'm sure it will be remembered for hours. I hope you weren't expecting to be appreciated for this gesture."

"On the contrary, I expect to be cursed because we're only serving beer and wine."

"That's the spirit," Ben said.

"Or the absence thereof," Rich countered.

Ben wrinkled his brow before smiling. "Oh, I get it. Very clever. But what sucks is this fucking hurricane shit."

"It's getting to be an irritation. I'll gladly own up to that."

"Everybody just acts like such pussies," Ben said. "I've never left for a hurricane, and I'm never going to."

"You didn't go last year for Carolyn?"

"Of course not. This city's been here for 300 years. Seen plenty of hurricanes in its time. But it's still here. Don't tell me you left last year."

"First time," Rich said. "Pretty annoying. Sat in a parking lot that stretched from here to Nashville."

"That's exactly why you'll find me in my den with my feet up while all the yellow bellies turn tail. The runners will sweat. And my new generator will keep me as cool as George Clooney."

"Generator won't do you much good if the levees overtop."

"Ain't happened before; won't happen now."

"Well, we both sure hope that's the case," Rich said. "Better yet, hope that this mother just goes and makes somebody else miserable. Florida's OK with me. Got a Bush there, and who better deserves a bashing than a Bush."

"I voted for Bush," Turner said.

Rich wasn't sure Turner was serious. "You're joking, right?" he said.

"Voted for W once and plan to do so again," Turner said. "You Democrats can't do any better than men like Al Gore and John Kerry, you're going to remain in the minority till my kids are voting for Jenna Bush's kids." Rich liked Gore and Kerry both and couldn't understand why Republicans spoke about them with such naked contempt.

Rich also never understood why political scientists were often the most conservative faculty members in the social sciences. But Rich had no clue that Turner was a Republican and found the idea in one part disturbing and in a larger part appalling. He didn't know quite what to say, and they walked the rest of the way to the reception in an awkward silence. Inside Building 5's ballroom, they quickly fell into conversations with others.

Ben Turner wasn't quite right that Choctaw had never been affected by a hurricane. It had flooded on numerous occasions in the eighteenth and nineteenth centuries. Of course, the levees were much higher in 2004 than they had been a hundred years earlier. And technological advances in pumping had transformed swamps into subdivisions. Still, Ben was wrong to dismiss the possibility of catastrophic flooding so cavalierly. Gulf of Mexico water had come within eighteen inches of topping levees in Hurricane Georges just six years earlier. This Hosea storm was now bigger and therefore more menacing than Georges. Thirty years ago, thousands of square miles of wetlands stood between Choctaw and open water. They were gone by 2004. Rich knew all this, and he was surprised that Ben Turner scoffed at people's concern so easily.

The storm was the topic of most every conversation at Rich's reception that evening. It dominated the exchange Rich had with one of his favorite faculty members, Joe Alter, who was chair of the Drama and Film Department and the director of numerous university productions that Rich and Cally had attended for years, even before Rich had begun working at Urban. Rich thought Joe's plays were underappreciated jewels. A short, stout, but sunny man just turned fifty, his curly bush of red hair starting to gray, Joe managed to be positive and fretful at the same time. Joe was concerned now that the looming hurricane threat was going to cost him rehearsal time for the year's first production, Tennessee Williams' *The Glass Menagerie.* "Things are going great," Joe said, "but we have so much to do. We open in only three weeks."

Hurricane Hosea also dominated Rich's conversation with Cecilia Lagasse, who was Urban's longtime Dean of Nursing, now serving as Rich's interim provost. Cecilia was another colleague for whom Rich felt a particularly fondness. A seventy-five-year-old widow, Cecilia was a devoted sports fan and an enthusiastic member of the Ungulate Athletic Foundation. She was present at every Urban sporting event she could get to. She had center court seats for men's basketball and could bawl out the refs with as much vigor as any fan in Ungulate arena. In Rich's first season as coach, after a hard foul on the Urban point guard, who was then her favorite player, she screamed out at a mustachioed referee, "Hey, Nosebeard, keep that thug off my baby," so loudly that she cracked up half the people in attendance. Rich loved her, and he and Cecilia became real friends during the two years he served as provost.

But in the typical party swirl, Rich was spun away from first Joe and then Cecilia sooner than he wanted and found himself trying to allay the fears of a new faculty member named Wayne Black, a philosopher who had just arrived, worrisomely sans Ph.D., from his graduate training at Minnesota. Black had two young children, a three-year-old boy and a baby girl. What should he do, he wanted to know. His dean (Ben Turner) had laughed and told him not to panic. But he did feel sort of panicky. He was from the Midwest, and he didn't know anything about hurricanes.

Rich told Professor Black that Dean Turner was probably correct. Still, Rich told Black, just to put his mind at rest, he should maybe plan on heading out of town the next morning. If he made preparations tonight and got on the road early the next day, he might manage to beat the crush of traffic. This caused the young professor to inquire whether he could expect the university to compensate him for having to leave.

Unable to control himself, Rich laughed out loud. "I don't know that there's a university in America that would compensate you," Rich said, astonished by the man's combination of naiveté and chutzpah. "But there sure isn't one in this state."

"Compensation is the wrong word," Black said. "I mean, you know, cover my expenses."

"I don't think our comptroller is going to view fleeing from a hurricane as reimbursable," Rich said, quickly tired of the young man's amazing pushiness. He'd only taught two weeks' worth of classes, and here he was hounding the CEO about money. By the standards of Rich's Southern rearing, this was not cool, and in that regard, not smart.

"I guess I didn't really think so," Black admitted. "But it never hurts to ask, right?"

Rich shrugged, his eyes sweeping the room for someone less annoying to talk to. Then the man stuck a knife in Rich's heart.

"Problem is," he said, "I spent most everything I had getting us moved down here from Minneapolis. We don't get our first paycheck until next Wednesday. I'd like to take your advice and go on, maybe even later tonight, but I'll have to calculate whether we can afford it."

"You have credit cards?"

"Maxed out," the man replied. "That's how we got down here. Had to put up most of my cash, you know, first month, last month and security deposit, just to get into our apartment."

Urban's credit union could issue Professor Black a salary advance, but the credit union was closed and wouldn't reopen till Monday. Rich made a mental note to put this kind of issue on his fix list for the future. Then he reached into his wallet and took out the eight twenties he found there. "Here," he said. "I would do more, but that's all I've got on me. That should buy you some gas and a cheap hotel for a couple of nights. Let's hope that's all you'll need."

"Oh, no thanks," Professor Black said. "I couldn't accept your charity."

"Consider it a salary advance," Rich said. "After all, I know where you work, and I have a lot of influence with your boss."

WHEN MOST OF THE faculty and administrators had headed home, Rich grabbed one last beer and wandered out to the courtyard bounded by the university fitness center and the west gate to Ungulate Arena. The courtyard here was one of the nicest areas at Urban, shaded by two giant water oaks and equipped with benches and concrete tables where students could eat outdoors or gather to talk. Student Affairs was hosting a social, and the area was teeming with undergraduates looking for free food and a chance to hang out with friends or make new ones.

Vice Rector Hart Thompkins and his staff staged this party as a "hoedown." They had hired a Country and Western band that was playing "Stand by Your Man" when Rich ambled into the area. All the staffers had on Western shirts, string ties, jeans and straw cowboy hats pushed back on their heads. Some were wearing cowboy boots. The students were encouraged to dress the same way and some had. But being students, some hadn't, too, and that was fine.

The sun was just setting, and out over the lake the sky was crimson and yellow, the color of fire, fading to pink overhead. It was hot, as it always was in Choctaw this time of year, but the humidity was unseasonably low, and so the evening was almost comfortable. Rich took up a spot in shadow just outside

Building 5 and leaned against the brick wall to sip his beer and observe, he hoped, without being noticed. When Rich first took over from Francis Saurian, Vice Rector Thompkins had made an appointment to discuss with him theme proposals for the year's student social events. Saurian, it seemed, wanted to approve Hart's plans before they were implemented. Rich stopped that practice shortly after the first meeting got started.

When Rich first came to Urban, he thought Hart's themes were silly and undignified. As he'd become a part of the campus community, however, Rich's attitude changed. The themes were silly and undignified. But so what, they were also a hoot. Hawaiian night with everybody in floral shirts, baggy shorts and flip flops. Gangster night with staff and students in pin-striped suits and long slinky dresses. Seventies night a fashion nightmare of plaid leisure suits. These theme parties were fun, and Rich could see that even the kids who didn't dress interacted comfortably with those who did. But his changed judgment about Hart's themes didn't mean Rich wanted a role in picking them. Hart appreciated this smidgen of new authority and had thanked Rich for it at length. At the time, Rich still didn't understand the power of his office and the trepidation it caused in those who had to interact with it.

Hart Thompkins wasn't the most popular man on campus, his personality a little stiff. Many of the vice rectors and deans thought Hart was a lightweight and dismissed his ideas out of hand. But in his time as basketball coach and then provost, Rich had worked with Thompkins a lot, and unlike other administrators on campus, Rich thought Hart was good at his job. He worked hard, never griped about the evening hours his job required and genuinely liked students, something not true of all university employees. Faculty often joked that university life would be great if it weren't for those pesky students. Administrators said pesky students and pushy faculty.

Rich looked out at the throng of those pesky students in the courtyard, some dressed in costumes, many not. Some were dancing in front of the band. Most were just gathered in shifting groups, talking and laughing, munching off paper plates of ribs and barbequed beans. Urban students were an amazing rainbow of colors and ethnicities, white, black and every shade of brown and tan in between, and Rich was delighted to see the extent of the racial and ethnic intermingling. The Asian kids were the ones most likely to be outfitted with a hat or a Western shirt, the Indians as well as the Japanese, Chinese, Koreans and Vietnamese. There were plenty of white and black kids in Western gear as well, though not as uniformly. Many youngsters of whatever skin color wore Ungulate black and orange T-shirts with jeans or baggy shorts.

However they were dressed, everybody seemed to be having a good time, and this gave Rich a jolt of pleasure he wouldn't have predicted. Rich had come to Urban to coach basketball. But he always thought of himself as a teacher. He liked teaching his literature classes in high school, and he considered his career as a basketball coach a teaching endeavor. Now, he was a university administrator, a professional undertaking more thrust upon than chosen. His job as interim rector was not one Rich had sought; he hadn't even sought the provost's position, of course. But watching this scene of young humanity interacting so comfortably and enjoying each other's company provoked a sense of pride he wouldn't have understood not so long earlier.

Rich finished his beer and made a round through the crowd, stopping to speak with each of the staffers on duty to congratulate them for a job well done. Hart thanked Rich profusely for his brief words of appreciation. Before heading home, Rich stopped just outside the bustle of the party to overlook the activities again. He was a man without children. And many of the students in front of him hadn't any idea who Urban's rector was. But on this warm summer night, he discovered himself with a brimming heart thinking, this is my chance. This is where it can happen. Here, here, right here, as, yes, as rector. These are my kids; these are mine.

17

For about a year before That Vicious Lying Rat Bastard Josiah Winslow started the war he named for and blamed on me, the puritanical New Englanders had been feeling pressure from Governor Edmund Andros and his humorless Anglicans in the former New Netherlands, now named New York for its most recent owner, the English Duke of York. Safely back in the old country, the Duke had collected all sorts of pieces of paper granting him majesty over just about every place in New England except Plymouth, Boston and Rhode Island. The Duke's documents said he was proprietor of everything west of the Connecticut River, which chopped off more than half of Connecticut Colony where Massachusetts' John Winthrop, Sr. had years earlier implanted his son John Winthrop, Jr. as Governor. For good measure, the Duke also laid claim to Delaware, Pennsylvania, New Jersey, the whole of the Hudson Valley, Vermont, New Hampshire, Maine, Nantucket, and Martha's Vineyard. The Duke's directive to Governor Andros was simple: "Go take possession of all that's mine." And Governor Andros set out to do just that.

This did not sit well with John Winthrop, Jr. or, in fact, with any of his brethren New England Puritans. So he did what the pinkies so often did. Junior said to Andros, "Hey, instead of yours and mine getting crosswise, why don't we just work together to kill some redskins."

When he began assembling the invasionary force that marched on Montaup and my Pokanoket village in the month of *Towwakesos*, late June of 1675, That Vicious Lying Rat Bastard offered to let Massachusetts and Connecticut divide the

Narragansett territory if they would provide him some needed reinforcements to attack me. The excuse the English devised for attacking the Narragansetts was an allegation that they were in league with me. Oh that they had been, but they weren't. John Jr.'s son, Wait Winthrop, along with Edward Hutchinson from Massachusetts and Roger Williams from Rhode Island, met with the Narragansetts even before That Vicious Lying Rat Bastard attacked Montaup, and all reported that the Narragansetts had no plans to support me. But that didn't stop Junior from dispatching son Wait and a Connecticut army to march on Narragansett territory on July 1 or from writing Andros on July 4 that the Narragansetts had joined me and that the New Yorkers ought to hold off messing with Connecticut until Connecticut could finish messing with the Narragansetts.

Yes, it's so complex, amazing, and nasty, you'd think Dick Cheney had devised it.

But if you need evidence that the whole of King Philip's War was about the white man's taking Indian land, contemplate the simple fact that the first move John Winthrop, Jr. made in a war that was ostensibly started by me and my Wampanoags was to send son Wait to invade the land of the Narragansetts, who hadn't joined my side. Their Massachusetts brethren had the same idea, and so instead of marching east to cut off my retreat, they sent Edward Hutchinson and most of the Massachusetts army west into Narragansett country, arriving there sooner and with a larger force than the army from Connecticut that Wait Winthrop commanded.

Now we really get to the sweet stuff of land greed. Hutchinson arrived in Narragansett territory on July 7 and sat down with the Narragansetts for negotiations on July 8. What Hutchinson basically wanted was for the Narragansetts to declare they lived in Massachusetts territory (this despite the fact that Ye Merry Olde King of England had already designated it as belonging to Rhode Island). One won't have to work terribly hard to imagine that the Narragansetts, who didn't recognize

Rhode Island's authority, were not now eager to bow to Boston. When they said, thanks, but no thanks, Hutchinson's crew undertook discussions about commencing to kill them.

But then, on July 9, the magically named Wait Winthrop (How could his mother have known?) finally showed up to counsel, yes, delay. Some historians have made much of Wait's arguments, suggesting that he was less bloodthirsty than his white fellows. Not. Others have noted that eastern Connecticut's nearby settlements were vulnerable should a war with the Narragansetts get out of hand, a more likely motivation.

But the biggest part of Wait Winthrop's policy of delay had to do with numbers. Massachusetts had them, and Connecticut didn't. Wait's papa, John Junior, had sent sonny boy into Narragansett territory with a smaller army than he might have otherwise because he was holding troops back along the Connecticut River in case New York Governor Andros should attack. (And, in fact, Andros did show up with a naval force on July 8.) Being outmanned by a significant number, Wait determined that if war came immediately, Massachusetts was going to come away with the lion's share of the land booty. So, "Let's wait," Wait said.

MEANWHILE, BACK AT MONTAUP, that self-important martinet Benjamin Church was stalking around, whining about how his commander, James Cudworth, was making a fatal error by not chasing me into the land of Weetamoo and her Pocassets. Church was a thirty-three-year-old carpenter (and, yes, he most certainly *did* suffer from a messianic complex) whom I have always suspected must have hit himself in the head too many times with his hammer. Cudworth was a greedy but cautious man, happy to set down roots on Montaup and build his fort to assure that my Pokanokets would never be able to return. But he kept getting reports of Church's second guessing. He considered having Church arrested and confined in stocks until he could be tried, fined, dismissed from the military and perhaps even jailed. But then he got a better idea, and on July 7 he summoned Church to my *weetoo*, where Cudworth had set up his field headquarters.

Short, and fidgety, Church reported as ordered, at last worried that he might have overstepped his bounds. Cudworth, seated on a straight-backed wooden chair he'd had nailed together once he saw that Pokanoket was his to occupy until further notice, did not rise as Church came in, and the little man kept batting his knee with his hat until Cudworth ordered him to stop. Even then, Church just couldn't stand still.

"I understand you're of the opinion we ought to give chase to King Philip," the commander said.

Church equivocated about how some of the men thought that and, well, yes, he thought there might be some wisdom in that view, although, of course, building the fort was an important undertaking as well.

Cudworth said, "You'd be willing to lead a contingent of men in pursuit of Philip, if I saw fit to dispatch you to that duty?"

Church exclaimed that yes, indeed, he would, by cracky. Then he launched into so long a tale about how he was on very good terms with Weetamoo and also with Awashonks, the female sachem of the Sakonnets, and how his own farm was right in the area and so he knew all the trails and swamps, that Cudworth finally had to cut him off.

"I am not completely convinced of the wisdom of such a venture," Cudworth said. "We don't know what Philip is up to, although I take notice that he hasn't showed much will to fight just yet. Still, your urgency impresses me. So I am going to let you select four squads of ten men and wish you godspeed as you give Philip chase."

Cudworth had multiple motivations for allowing Church to depart. Most important, he was sick of the little blowhard and glad to be rid of him. Also, Cudworth found pleasing the idea that Church might really encounter me and be greeted with a few tomahawk whacks in his presumptuous head. And on the off chance that Church might manage to give me a licking, Cudworth, as invasionary force field commander, having ordered the pursuit, would be delighted to assume credit for the venture.

Church started to list the provisions he'd need, but Cudworth cut him off again, saying, "Muskets, powder and shot only. Given your vast knowledge of the area, as you have promoted, I am sure you will find no trouble in providing for yourself while on the march." Church started to say something else, but Cudworth flipped off a limp salute and said, "You will make the crossing at first light."

A less, shall I say, self-confident man would have spotted the acid of sarcasm in Cudworth's instructions, but, feeling invigorated, Church set off with enthusiasm to identify forty men with an itch to fight Indians. Idiots are always plentiful, so he soon had himself a regiment and set off for the eastern shore of Montaup Bay the next morning, a feat accomplished as if the wandering perambulations of Moses through the Sinai were condensed into a single day. Church and his men went south to catch a ferry to Aquidneck Island where they stopped to trade with some Rhode Islanders for provisions and to hunt for an hour to provide themselves with several fat geese. That accomplished, they turned north again and hired some Rhode Island fisherman to take them over to the mainland, finally arriving just as the sun was setting over Montaup Peninsula behind them. Alas, as they made their spare camp, they were not able to dine on the provisions they had procured because the man Church had placed in charge of them had forgotten them back on Aquidneck.

You can see why the English were going to have a very tough time in the fourteen months that lay ahead.

18

In the three and a half hours that Interim Rector Richard Janus spent hosting his new faculty and staff, then subsequently observing his students' first campus social, things got much more alarming on the Hurricane Hosea projection maps. The computer models moved the storm dramatically to the west. The computer consensus at eight o'clock on Friday night, August 27, was that Hosea was going to slam into the east coast of Mobile Bay as a Category 4 storm some time on Sunday night, taking its fury through Gulf Shores, Alabama, and the quaint town of Fairhope. Mobile was only about fifty miles from Choctaw and that shortened distance ramped up the danger in Choctaw significantly. A hurricane's counterclockwise air flow would put Choctaw on the "good side" of the storm, if this current projection held true, but Hosea was so large that Choctaw was now unlikely to escape some kind of impact.

Rich emailed his senior administrators and moved their meeting for the next morning up to 8 a.m. He was not yet ready to announce a cancellation of classes, but he was increasingly convinced that he was going to have to undertake and manage some sort of response. Before putting two rib eyes on the grill, he called Hart Thompkins and told him to make preparations for implementing the evacuation plan, if necessary, immediately after the meeting in the morning.

After dinner, Rich and Cally watched Bogie and Bacall in *Key Largo*, and when the movie was over, they checked the National Weather Service website again for current landfall projections. Nothing had changed. Perhaps they would experience only a glancing blow. Probably still have to cancel classes on Monday, but might be able to resume a normal class schedule on Tuesday. Rich went to bed with a feeling of unwarranted relief and fell asleep with the pleasant memory of watching his students at their party earlier in the evening.

A Boston girl still uncomfortable with the annual ritual of hurricane watches and preparations, Cally stayed up later and checked the computer models at midnight. The National Weather Service was now projecting that the eye of Hosea would come right through Choctaw as a Category 5 sometime around midnight on Sunday. Knowing that Rich was going to have a hectic day, she did not wake him to give him this information. She rose at five a.m. on Saturday, August 28, and went directly to her computer. The storm projections had shifted farther west.

Cally washed her face, brushed her teeth and made a pot of coffee. When it had brewed, she took two cups upstairs to their bedroom, placed one on the night table next to Rich and sat down on the bed next to him at five thirty. He stirred as she sat on the bed and came awake from the smell of the coffee, checking his wristwatch for the time. Without her saying a word, he knew things were worse than when he fell asleep.

As he sat up and reached for his cup, Cally said, "We are really fucked."

He looked over at her. "I should brush my teeth if we're going to fuck."

"Not funny," she said. " They're saying it's one of the most powerful storms in history."

"I can make it funny," he said. "I can tickle you."

"You're not funny. I'm really upset. This is scary. It's going to hit Biloxi, and we're going to get beat to pieces by the northeast quadrant."

"So it's still tracking west," Rich said. "Maybe it will keep going, miss New Orleans and hit Baton Rouge. I hate those fuckers at LSU only slightly less than the cannibals in Mayflower."

"It's going to come right into Biloxi, then make the right hand arc that was supposed to take it to Florida and instead bring its western side into Alkansea Bay pushing a twenty-foot tidal surge in front of it. Twenty feet will top the levees south of the city. Things couldn't be worse."

"Or maybe it'll keep going west and hit Texas. Pat Robertson says God uses hurricanes to punish bad people. Who needs cyclones up their butts worse than W and Rick Perry?"

"Stop it. This is serious."

Rich took a deep breath. "If it's as serious as you say, then we should definitely return to the idea of fucking because no one deals well with a crisis while horny."

Cally started crying, and Rich felt like a jackass. This was not the first time he'd persisted with nonsense beyond the point of her tolerance. He set his coffee cup back on the night table, threw off the covers, got up and walked around the foot of the bed to sit next to her. He pried her cupped hands away from her face, put his arms around her and pulled her head against his shoulder. As her tears dripped down his chest, he stroked the back of her head.

"I'm really scared," she said. "We ran in front of Carolyn, and this is a lot worse."

"You're sure the storm has stopped moving west?"

"The computer models have all converged. Biloxi's going to get it. We're probably going to get it worse. The storm is enormous. It fills the entire Gulf."

"All righty then. What are we looking at timewise?"

"The eye hits the Mississippi Coast midnight tomorrow. We get it around three a.m."

"Then Biloxi will take the bite out of the storm before it gets here."

"No," Cally said. "Biloxi will take wind from the north. We're going to get the storm surge. Guys on TV are talking about it pushing the whole Bay in on us from the south then pushing Lake De Soto over us as the eye passes and the winds shift around to north-south."

"This is the doomsday track."

"That's exactly what they're saying on TV. The mayor has ordered a mandatory evacuation. He said that everybody should be out of the city by noon tomorrow."

"What should we do?" Rich always let Cally take the lead in situations like this because his foremost concern was her comfort and sense of security.

"We shouldn't wait until the evacuation deadline. The weather will start to go to hell by tomorrow afternoon. And we're talking the same traffic jam as last year."

"Maybe we can get on the road tonight," Rich said.

"I would feel better if we did."

Rich squeezed Cally hard. She was a pretty tough cookie, but the idea of drowning in a hurricane terrified her, and Rich hated little in life as much as Cally's being upset.

Once on campus, Rich brewed two pots of coffee and poured them into the pump thermos which usually sat in the waiting area to his outer office. He took the coffee and some pastries to his conference room and set out napkins and cocktail plates. Then he turned on the conference room television and waited for his administrators to arrive.

Urban's administrative team arrived at eight, everybody dressed in T-shirts, jeans and running shoes. They quickly reached consensus on a course of action. So that students and faculty already on campus would not have wasted a trip, they would allow Saturday classes to continue until noon, and then they would shut the campus down. Director of Public Information Sally Reasoner would contact the local media to announce that classes were being cancelled until the following Wednesday morning. Vice Rector for Physical Plant Services Charlie Lobovich and his staff would begin the process of securing buildings immediately.

The administrators were nearing completion of the meeting when Sheila Pyrite entered the rector's conference room wearing a powder blue suit with a turquoise blouse, dark stockings and patent leather high heels. "Sorry I'm late," she said to the gathering. She pulled a chair from against the wall and began to push it toward the conference table, forcing those already seated to adjust their chairs to make room for her. "I didn't get notified of the time," she announced as she opened a large stenographer's notebook, placed it in front of her and found a yellow No. 2 pencil she had arrowed into her black coif above her right ear.

"I'm sorry, Sheila," Rich said, "but what are you doing here? You said you weren't notified about the time of this meeting. You shouldn't have been notified at all."

"I wasn't," she said. "But I didn't want to embarrass anybody. I'm not a grudge holder, as anybody who knows me will attest."

"But what are you doing here?" Rich asked again.

Rich had debated confronting Sheila when he first was named interim rector to inquire about her responsibilities. Francis Saurian had never made clear what Sheila did, and Rich didn't know. Instead of confronting her, he had had a conversation about her with Kimberly Kane that simply added to the mystery of her presence in the rector's suite. Later, Rich asked Elia Lipscom if he was acquainted with Sheila. "Of course," Lipscom said. "Everybody in Alkansea knows Sheila Pyrite. She's a legend." Rich wasn't ever able to discern what made her legendary, but he got the distinct impression the viceroy was telling him not to mess with her, so he didn't. This capitulation to what smelled of a no-show job bothered Rich, but he consoled himself that he was just the interim rector and that it would be the responsibility of whoever accepted the job on a permanent basis to deal with her peculiar employment arrangement.

"This is *the* Hurricane Committee, is it not?" Sheila asserted now.

"I guess, yes," Rich said.

"Well, I'm a member of the Hurricane Committee," Sheila said. "I have served on this committee under three rectors. Three counting you."

Rich started to tell Sheila that she wasn't needed but, instead, shrugged and turned the discussion back to dealing with the student population.

Most Urban students lived off campus and would handle whatever evacuation process they undertook on their own. Hart Thompkins would direct the shuttering of the dorms that housed about 5,000 students. Those who had automobiles or could secure a ride with a friend (a buddy system had been in place since orientation) were to evacuate on their own. Several hundred students, however, most of them international students, were caught without automobile access. For this very purpose, after renting transport a year earlier, Rich had bought a small fleet of used buses. Hart's student activities staff were required to acquire and maintain chauffeurs' licenses and would serve as drivers. By prior arrangement, Urban students would be driven from Choctaw to the ASU campus in Mayflower where they would be afforded shelter in the basketball arena. Students being evacuated on university buses were alerted to bring blankets and other bedding since they would have to sleep on the arena floor. At least there would be plenty of bathrooms and, if necessary, access to showers. The buses would roll at three p.m. and perhaps then get a head start on the mass exodus that would probably begin about dawn the next morning.

Going down their emergency checklists, each vice rector and each dean read aloud his or her evacuation contact information. This list of phone numbers, cell phone numbers and email addresses, including alternative email addresses with non-campus carriers like Yahoo and Google, had all been gathered earlier and printed by Kimberly Kane on laminated cards that could easily be carried in one's wallet. Once this double checking of contact information was completed, Rich wished his team safe travels and told them they should plan to report to work at 8 a.m. on Wednesday, September 1, unless developments made that impossible. It was 9:30.

Rich asked several members of the group to remain with him as the others gathered whatever materials they had brought and began to leave. Sheila Pyrite did not depart, and when she didn't, Rich asked her more brusquely than he should have why she was still present. "I am waiting for my assignment," she said.

"What assignment?" Rich inquired.

"Whatever assignment you might want to give me. You just gave assignments to the others who were here."

"The others have dozens or even hundreds of people who report to them," Rich pointed out, anxious to move on and in no mood to deal with an employee who didn't seem to have a job.

"Yes, and I don't even have a secretary," Sheila said.

"No, you don't," Rich said.

"I don't think that's fair, but I haven't complained about it. I spoke to Rector Saurian some time ago, and he explained that the financial situation of the university at the time wouldn't allow it. I assumed that hasn't changed."

Rich sighed audibly. "No, Ms. Pyrite . . ."

"*Dr.* Pyrite, Rector. I have a Ph.D. just as you do."

"Dr. Pyrite, forgive me. But no, the financial situation of the university has not changed."

"Then I shall carry on as always," Sheila said. "If you'll give me my assignment, I will let you get on to your next item of business with those you've requested to remain."

Rich thought of asking her to remove her shoes, get a good long run down the hall where she was then to jump up her own ass and disappear forever. Instead, he said, "There are people you work with on regular basis, are there not? Some people on campus, many off?"

"Most certainly," she said. "I am not anyone's supervisor at this time, but I do work with many people, as you say, on a regular basis."

"Excellent," Rich said. "I want you to leave campus now because we are closing the university. But when you get home,

I want you to contact those individuals and tell them what we decided here today."

"Is there any information I should hold in confidence?" Sheila asked.

"No, none at all," Rich said.

Sheila Pyrite then stood up and said to all as she moved to leave the room. "You can count on me. I won't let you down."

When she was gone, Rich's interim provost, Cecilia Lagasse, said, "We'll give you a second to get back from *The Twilight Zone*, boss."

Everybody laughed, and then Rich asked Hart to make his calls to the dorm directors from the rector's Conference Room so that Rich could listen in and contribute to the conversation where and if appropriate. He asked Cecilia to remain as well as new University General Counsel Regan Hooks, a tall, forty-year-old brunette, a single mom with a daughter in high school. At seventy-five, Cecilia Lagasse was a slender, small-boned, white-haired woman of medium height and astonishingly plucky disposition. She had been the Dean of Nursing since the school was founded in 1970. Rich had appointed her interim provost in part because she would not stir the jealousy of any of the other administrators on campus, none of whom saw a woman of her age as a serious rival. If and when the viceroy ever got around to finding a permanent rector, Rich would return to his duties as provost and Cecilia would return to hers as Dean of Nursing, nobody put out, nobody threatened. Pretty smart. Only that's not the main reason Rich asked her to serve as interim with him. He appointed her because he liked her immensely and completely trusted her judgment. His only apprehension had to do with her health. She was so slight of build, she appeared frail. Rich wanted to make sure not to overtax her, and the circumstances they were now entering were not those he could control.

The process of initiating the dorm evacuations went smoothly. The whole campus had gone through this almost exactly one year earlier. The directors and staff knew the drill. So did most of the students. The first real problem arose when Rich was about to send everyone on his or her way and Regan wanted to know if the school nurse had been contacted. Since it was Saturday, school Health Services nurse William Tinsel was not on campus. Regan had the university's policies and procedures manual open on the conference table and was skimming through it to make sure Rich was doing everything the manual said he was supposed to do.

"I don't know if he's been contacted," Rich said. "Whom does he report to? The Dean of Nursing? He report to you, Cecilia?"

"Bill reports to me," Hart said. "Student Health reports to Student Affairs."

"Have you contacted him?" Regan asked Hart.

"No," Hart answered. "Not yet. What about?"

"Says here," Regan said, brushing her fingers across an open page in the policies and procedures manual, "the school nurse shall accompany those students being evacuated in university vehicles."

"Did we do that last year?" Hart asked Rich. "I don't remember telling Bill to do that." To Regan, Hart said, "Your predecessor didn't alert me to this regulation, I don't think."

Regan looked at Rich, who shrugged. "Hell if I know. Do you know, Cecilia?"

"I don't think so," Cecilia said. "I think I would have known. I really doubt Bill Tinsel accompanied an evacuation bus. That much I can say with confidence."

"Why?" Rich asked.

"Well," Cecilia replied. "His wife left him about three years ago. And his fifteen-year-old son Greg is severely disabled. And he's a big kid, as tall as a normal kid his age, and a lot heavier. But he can't feed himself or anything. Hell, he's still in diapers."

"Jesus," Hart said.

"Bill has assistance during the day, but he's the sole caregiver the rest of the time. I don't see how he could have managed the boy while also supervising students during an evacuation."

"Says here it's part of his job description," Regan said.

"Does he know that?" Rich asked Hart.

Hart shook his head. "I don't know. I'd guess not. I didn't know it. Ashamed to admit that."

"The deal is, guys," Regan said, "Bill Whatshisname . . ."

"Tinsel," Cecilia said.

"Bill Tinsel is going to have to get on that lead bus this afternoon."

All the others looked at her.

"My job is to protect the university from legal fuckups," Regan said. "Maybe we didn't even have to promise it, but we've put in writing that evacuation buses will be accompanied by the school nurse. One of our students gets hurt somehow and we've not provided promised medical personnel, some parent is gonna walk away with a lot of money we don't have. Hell, some kid gets VD and a parent will sue because the school nurse wasn't there to pass out condoms. Excuse me, Cecilia."

"Why should I excuse you?" Cecilia asked. "You think I don't know what a condom is."

"Well, I shouldn't be crude. I apologize."

"Apology not accepted," Cecilia said. "I know what a condom is. I've distributed condoms. And I've employed condoms. You're new here, Regan, so you are perhaps unaware that I haven't been seventy-five my whole life."

"Well, I . . ."

"I was seventy-four only one year ago. I have known about condoms for a long time. Rubbers we called them. And ever since my fifties, or my sixties, anyway, I have known what a fuck up is."

Everybody laughed.

"Knowing what it is now for over a decade," Cecilia said, "I would agree that this is a fuck up. You say the school nurse has to accompany the evacuation buses, and I'm pretty certain Bill Tinsel can't do it."

"Well, he has to," Regan said.

"Tell him he has to, and my money says he quits," Cecilia said.

"That would be a real shame," Hart said. "This situation aside, Bill does a great job. Students really like him. I do end-of-the-year surveys on all the areas that report to me, and Student Health always gets high marks from the students. Whole operation and Bill personally."

"This really is a fuck up," Rich said. "What are we going to do?"

"Seems obvious to me," Cecilia said. "I'm going to take a seat in the lead bus this afternoon. I may not be the school nurse. But I am a nurse, and I work at the school."

"I think that would cover our tail," Regan said.

"Absolutely out of the question," Rich said.

"And why not?" Cecilia asked. "Regan says it covers our butts, and I don't have to get stuck in the 300-mile traffic jam I got stuck in last year. Or at least I don't have to be doing the driving myself. Moreover, our buses have restrooms. If I may be perfectly frank, I was afraid I was going to wet myself last year. And that's a very embarrassing development for a lady of my age and rearing."

"I am not going to approve your assuming the duties of the school nurse," Rich said.

"Why not?"

"I am not going to let you ride up to fucking Mayflower with a bunch of fucking undergraduates to sleep on the fucking gym floor in fucking Monster Arena."

"My, my," Cecilia said. "Mention a toilet and the rector goes all, shall I say, fucking potty mouth."

"Jesus," Rich laughed. "I won't approve it. I'm serious."

"Why not?" Cecilia insisted.

"Because you are, by your own admission, seventy-five years old. That's why not."

Cecilia turned to Regan who had not been privy to Rich and Cecilia carrying on like this before. "Madame Counselor," Cecilia said. "Will you inform your boss that if he doesn't let me ride that evacuation bus, I will sue him for age discrimination, and I will call all of you as witnesses. And even the rector will have to testify against himself because in my experience, though he's a potty mouth, he's not a fucking liar."

Rich sighed, conceding that Cecilia's willingness to provide the required medical presence solved a critical problem in an ever tightening time line. "But when you wake up tomorrow morning unable to move," Rich said, "just remember I told you not to do this."

RICH TOLD HIS ADMINISTRATORS that he would remain in his office until all called to confirm they had been in contact with their immediate subordinates. At 11 a.m. the television in Rich's office, tuned to WALK, the local NBC station, announced that Urban was closing at noon and would reopen on the following Wednesday. Sally Reasoner called to inform Rich that all local media had the story and would be repeating it throughout the rest of the day and weekend. While Rich was still on the phone with Sally, WALK announced that Ettons University, the large private school across town, had also called off classes until the next Wednesday.

At about 11:30, Rich got a call from Elia Lipscom. Without introduction Lipscom began, "I'm glad to see you know how to answer the phone, Coach. Now we need to get you remedial lessons in how to make an outgoing call."

Rich was startled and annoyed enough by the viceroy's nasty tone that he didn't respond.

"You still on the line, *Rector* Janus? Or do you think you can hang up on me now, too."

"I'm here, Viceroy Lipscom. Awaiting clarification."

"Interesting that you address *me* as Viceroy, Dr. Janus. Way things are shaping up today, I thought maybe you had become the viceroy without anybody notifying me."

"I'm afraid I'm not following," Rich said. "Sir," he added after a beat.

"You're not following because you haven't been on the phone with that asshole Don Sharpe, your fucking counterpart over at the Medical School."

Donald Sharpe was the rector of the state's independent Joseph Gall Medical School, which was located in downtown Choctaw. Elsewhere around the country, the state Medical School was headed by a dean and affiliated with the local comprehensive state university. But Gall Med relocated from Mayflower to Choctaw in the early 1920s, gained its independence in the '30s and sneered at the idea of becoming a part of Urban when the latter opened in the 1950s. Several efforts had been made to combine the two operations, but Gall Medical School and its phalanx of physician supporters had fought off every such initiative.

The doctors had money, and when you're talking about any action that requires a vote in the legislature, money talks. Also, those who had gone to ASU as undergrads, and they were in the majority, didn't want to see Urban enhance its power and prestige by taking over state medical education. The whole Gall enterprise was an immense political football. (Nice metaphor, no, given that everything in higher education in the State of Alkansea always required reference to football.) All educational leadership positions in the state were subject to massive political influence, but despite his political connections Elia Lipscom (and the viceroys who preceded him) had the least amount of control over what happened at the medical campus.

Don Sharpe, who had grown up in Choctaw but had gone to Princeton undergrad and then Harvard Med, had basically been forced on Lipscom by the state's medical big shots who thought Sharpe brought Gall considerable prestige. Before going into medical administration, he had been a researcher of some renown. He had been on the team that hailed acetaminophen as a miracle drug for treating routine pain. Of course, acetaminophen was subsequently shown to cause liver damage, but that was long after Sharpe was pushing paper rather than pills. So whether he added prestige to Gall Medical School was a matter of some debate. Lipscom and Sharpe hated each other, and Lipscom despised any development that gave Sharpe a platform for showing him up. Unintentionally, Rich had supplied Don Sharpe just such a bully pulpit.

Faculty and students at the Medical School began to contact Sharpe as soon as they saw on television or heard on the radio that Urban was closing at noon. The Gall campus had Saturday afternoon classes, and Sharpe wanted them to meet. Rather than just telling his people that campus would close, for instance, at six p.m., he instead called Viceroy Lipscom to complain that Urban's noon closing was making things difficult for him.

"I am so pissed," Lipscom said to Rich, "that you put me in the position where he could get all self-righteous on my ass."

"Again, not following," Rich said. "Sir."

"You closed your goddamn campus, Coach. Don't you know you don't have the authority to do that? The plays come in from the sidelines; they fucking get called by me. You may be Ewe Ewe's quarterback at the moment, but you don't have the authority to audible. Now Don Sharpe is all up my butt about my not consulting with him and the pressure *my* decision to close Urban has put on him. Blah, blah blah blahdety fucking blah."

"Did you tell him I exceeded my authority and closed Urban without contacting you?"

"Are you crazy? Of course, I didn't tell him that. Why would I want him to think that someone would have the audacity to close his campus without getting permission from me to do so? Sharpe undermines my authority all the time already. You think I want him to think everybody does?"

"You realize," Rich said, "that we're going to get whacked by a Category 5 hurricane in less than 48 hours?"

"Come on, man, you don't know that. Hurricane predictors say a storm is going to hit Miami and it hits Corpus Christi."

"We've been monitoring this pretty closely down here, Elia."

"So you've been watching the hysterics on TV. You think we don't have television up here in Mayflower too?"

"Look," Rich said. "I apologize for exceeding my authority. If you like, I will call Don Sharpe and apologize to him too."

"You'll do nothing of the goddamned sort. You've already made me look bad. I'll not have you confirming that you've made me look bad."

Rich waited a bit before saying, "Well, again, I apologize for my ignorance about protocol, but you need to understand that the computer models have all converged now. This Hurricane Hosea is going to push a twenty-foot tidal surge right at us and hit us with its northeast quadrant. We're sitting down here in a bowl, and we're going to get smacked. There's no time to waste. We've got to give our students and employees maximal time to get out of here."

"All that may be true, although I am hardly convinced of it, but only *I* can close a goddamn campus."

Rich thought about pointing out that Urban was already closed, abuse of authority or not, but decided there were few advantages to provoking the man further. "Then, belatedly," he said, "let me request your permission to close my campus."

"You think I'm an idiot, don't you?"

Yes he did; he was convinced of it. "No, of course not," Rich said.

"If I am going to give you permission to close Urban, how do I account for the fact that the medical campus is still open? RIGHT IN THE SAME FUCKING TOWN?"

Rich held the phone away from his ear during this outburst. Then, bringing the phone back to his lips, he said, "Order Sharpe to close the Medical School at 6 p.m. If somebody asks you about this apparent discrepancy, tell them that Urban is a larger and more complicated campus. That it has 5,000 residential students whereas the Medical School has none, and that many of the resident students at Urban lack individual evacuation transportation. Prudent leadership requires studied distinctions."

"If I do that, I would have to close the community colleges right now too," Lipscom said.

"You ought to close them, Elia," Rich said. "This is serious business. We may err, but we have to err on the side of caution."

"Well, those of us up here in Mayflower aren't as convinced as you are how serious the threat is at this point."

The people in Mayflower were not convinced, Rich thought, because the people in Mayflower hated Choctaw and would be delighted if this hurricane or the next one wiped the city off the planet. "Ettons is closing at noon, too," Rich said.

"They are?" Lipscom hiccupped. Like everything in Choctaw, Elia Lipscom hated Ettons University, but Ettons attracted a lot of rich students from all over the country, and they usually turned into rich alumni who thought that the transcendence of their richness gave them the right to hold forth on all sorts of matters including higher education. As a result, Elia Lipscom did everything he could to kiss as much Ettons ass as he could find willing to bend over for him.

"You don't want to have the state schools seem less sensitive to the safety of their stakeholders than the private schools," Rich said.

"Well, you should have brought this matter about Ettons to my attention immediately," the viceroy huffed. "I didn't realize that you were just following their lead."

Rich saw no value in pointing out that he hadn't followed Ettons' lead.

Lipscom said, "I'll just contact all state media to inform them of my decision to close Urban, Carver C.C. and Choctaw C.C. at noon. I ought to close Gall at noon, too, just to piss off that son-of-a-bitch Don Sharpe. But then he'd just get some of his proctologist lackeys up my butt, so I'll follow your suggestion about closing the Medical School at six."

"That seems a judicious plan to me, Elia."

"Yes, well, I know you're just an interim, Coach, but in the future, you need to brush up on your procedures. Still, I think I've seen the right way out of this pickle. I assume you agree."

IN THE AFTERMATH OF the storm, all the students, faculty and staff at Gall blamed the medical campus' delayed closing on Donald Sharpe. Most folks at Gall, students and staff, even many faculty, had never heard of Elia Lipscom and had no clue what role the State Viceroy for Higher Education played in the governance of the Medical School. They didn't understand that Lipscom was Sharpe's boss. They didn't know Sharpe *had* a boss. They thought Sharpe *was* the boss.

Suddenly Sharpe's Ivy League pedigree turned from shiny shield to knotted noose. Who was this arrogant, know-nothing outsider anyway? Who was he to be so cavalier about something as deadly serious as a killer hurricane? Medical School employees and students bitterly resented that they had been made to follow the established class and work schedule while everybody else in Choctaw was packing up to get the hell out of town. The professional scalp of the suddenly friendless Donald Sharpe was required for payback. Seizing the moment, Elia Lipscom put his opportunistic surfboard on the wave of indignation and relieved Sharpe of his rectorship. But when Lipscom got a little unexpected push back from some of Sharpe's historic supporters, Lipscom named Sharpe a Distinguished Research Professor and let him keep his full rectoral salary while requiring that he teach only one course per term.

And they say that people go into education in answer to the whispers of a higher calling.

19

On July 8, Benjamin Church's Plymouth regiment arrived on the eastern shore of Montaup Bay with the stealth of a marching band playing John Philip Sousa. Even Church became aggravated enough to try shushing them—to no avail. Had it been our strategy to do so, we could have waltzed into their open camp that night and dispatched them without our working up a sweat. And just in case we might have lost them in the darkness, they would have lit our way since the whole bunch of them spent the dark night smoking tobacco, the cherry embers of their pipes visible for a mile.

The next morning, July 9, in a feat of soldiering that will not win Church a posthumous Crazy Horse Military Strategy Award, Church divided his forces and sent half his men north toward the Pocassets under the leadership of his nitwit friend Matthew Fuller. The other half he led south toward his own farm.

I knew within reason that I would not be able to spit the bitter bit of war. Still, I thought it worth the trouble of making one last effort to get the pinkskins to negotiate. Perhaps not so much blood had yet been spilled that no way back could be found. If that be the case, however, we absolutely had to avoid additional killing. I called Annawon and Adonoshonk to my side and told them how we were going to proceed. "Make sure we avoid killing that jackass Benjamin Church or any of the other Bible beaters under his command."

Adonoshonk nodded and otherwise made no comment. Not surprisingly, Annawon objected. "But they are practically defenseless," he pointed out. "We can take out this platoon almost without risk to our men. And that'll be twenty Englishmen we won't have to face later."

I always hated being at odds with Annawon, who was the strongest and most loyal man I had ever known. "I know what I want to do is a gamble. And I understand why you would resist the idea. But if we show mercy today, maybe we can bring the English from Massachusetts and Connecticut to a peace council. And maybe they can bring That Vicious Lying Rat Bastard Josiah Winslow along with them."

"They will just think that we are weak and afraid," Annawon argued.

"Probably," I said. "So we must show strength and mercy in the same moment. We must demonstrate that we could kill them to the last man but instead choose to allow them all to live."

Annawon remained unconvinced, but he followed my directions and made sure our entire war party knew that we were to fire our muskets high, wide and short. My distasteful plan to spare Church was popular, however, with my ally, Sachem Awashonks of the Sakonnets, who knew Church well and liked him. I had good relations with Awashonks, but I regretted her fondness for Church because I knew that it stemmed from the Englishman's insidious habit of getting her drunk on his whiskey. What she took as generous conviviality, I knew was evil manipulation. Church had tried not long earlier to divide the Wampanoags against themselves by getting Weetamoo's Pocassets to sit the war out and Awashonks' Sakonnets to throw in with the English. Awashonks didn't do that and stood by her own countrymen until the last days of the war. But like Weetamoo, she hoped the war could be stopped at this early stage.

What followed was the event that Church and the English subsequently recorded as the Pease Field Fight. Like the moron he was, Church led his men clanking down the shore of the Sakonnet River until he had squeezed himself out onto an isthmus of land known as Punkatees Neck. The shore route was the fastest way from his overnight camp to Church's own farm farther south in Awashonks' territory. His primary motive in marching south in the first place was to protect his own holdings. The self-seeking little prick deserved a lot worse than he was about to get. Any military strategist will quickly conclude that he couldn't have chosen a more ill-advised course. It is often remarked in the Indian community that George Armstrong Custer prepared for Little Big Horn by studying the tactics of Benjamin Church. We watched this whole progression with amazement because it possessed the military insight of the Charge of the Light Brigade or any number of "over the top" orders by the morally clotted trench-warfare generals of World War I. Church placed his men in a vice from which they had no mobility and no refuge. They were sandwiched between the river on their right and the heavily wooded shores of Nonquit Pond on their left, and we could have attacked from the north and the south simultaneously and cut his entire little brigade to ribbons without even exposing ourselves to much risk.

But we did not do this. Instead, my captains Annawon and Adonoshonk sent our men Pawtonomi and Nimrod ahead to show themselves just outside English musket range. With only two men in sight, Church and his militia reacted as we planned. They gave chase complete with racist oaths and blood-curdling taunts, all the while firing their muskets uselessly. Nimrod and Pawtonomi lured them within range of the woods where they stupidly found themselves panting and without loaded weapons. Then Adonoshonk gave the order, and two hundred Wampanoags, one hundred of my Pokanokets and a like number of Awashonks' Sakonnets, showed themselves at the edge of the woods.

One of Church's men shit his filthy britches when he saw that they were outnumbered ten to one and completely exposed. Church screamed for his men to retreat, and he was first among them running toward the rocky sand of the Sakonnet River bank. As ordered, our warriors fired into the air, off to the side and into the dirt of the field of peas where the English gathered to make their stand. Then through hours of "fighting," from late morning until sunset, not one of our bullets struck human flesh. (And, of course, from that point forward, through every John Wayne movie ever made, Indians were depicted as the lousiest shots in human history, though in fact, we were crack marksmen, much superior to the English who stood before us.)

Throughout the day, we held ourselves at a distance and out of harm's way. And when the English had exhausted their powder and lead without so much as scratching one of our men, Annawon and Adonoshonk led our fighters forward, muskets shouldered, bows drawn, war clubs raised. At this point we wouldn't even have had to shoot them. We could have just strolled over at our leisure and bashed their pea brains out with our war clubs. But close enough to smell their stink, Annawon ordered a volley fired over their heads. The English fell on their knees and cried. And Annawon smacked his chest with his fist, and spit in the dirt in front of them. Then he turned and led our men back to the woods and away.

We had made our point. You are outflanked and outnumbered. DO NOT FUCK WITH US. You are not just defeated but humiliated. You are ours. And we CHOOSE to spare you.

But, of course, because Church had the brain of a pigeon inside a head the size of Nantucket, he didn't get the point. In Church terms, we didn't miss on purpose, as one last bid for truce; no, in the view of Benjamin Church the devout, we missed because whitey god almighty steered every bullet and every arrow away from English flesh. So rather than recognizing himself as the object of a lesson about tactics and the beneficiary of a demonstration of mercy in the hopes of finding peace, Benjamin Church rose up from the sand where he thought he would breathe his last, threw his arms toward the sky and thanked his god. Thanked his god and not Annawon. Thanked his god and not me. Thanked *his* vengeful and racist god and not our beneficent Creator for letting him live on.

ON THE VERY SAME days that we were trying to teach Benjamin Church a lesson he was too blind to learn, troops from both Connecticut and Massachusetts marched into Narragansett country to pressure the residents there to join their side in the war on me. As recently as June 24, the senior Narragansett sachems, Pessacus, Quinnapin and the "old queen" Quaiapen pledged their neutrality to English emissaries. And I knew from years of trying to persuade them otherwise that the Narragansetts sincerely believed that their best interests lay in trying to sustain peace with the English. They were wrong about that, but that was their insistent position.

Now, with my Pokanokets in Pocasset country, the English wanted more than neutrality from the Narragansetts; they wanted alliance. Alliance now as an emblem of submission, land in the days to come. And they were determined to have it by whatever means necessary. As Puritan historian William Hubbard summarized the English position, the Massachusetts men went forward to forge a partnership "with a sword in their hands." Hutchinson arrived with an army of pugnacious Massachusetts soldiers on July 8. His plan was to secure a pledge of allegiance from the Narragansetts or to murder their leaders if they resisted. Had he tried violence, he may well have been sorry because Pessacus, Quinnapin and Quaiapen arrived for negotiations with an angry band of warriors of their own. Wait Winthrop showed up with a Connecticut regiment on July 9, and talks, aggressive on one side and sullen on the other, carried on for a week.

"We will not take the field against the Wampanoags," Quinnapin told Hutchinson and Winthrop. "We have no stake in your war with them."

"But you want to remain our friends," Hutchinson said.

"We have no quarrel with you," Quaiapen said. "We will not lift a musket against you either."

"But you understand that we find your position unfriendly," Winthrop said.

"We do not have to be friends to share the same world," Quinnapin said. "We have lived beside the Wampanoags and the Nipmucks for generations without resorting to war over whatever disputes we may have had."

"That is insufficient!" Hutchinson asserted. "I would like to believe that you are truly neutral, but many of my English brothers do not. They believe you will stab us the moment our back is turned. I must have your assurance this is not so."

"What more assurance can we give you?" Quaiapen asked. "You have lived near us for many years, and we have never raised a war club against you."

"You must attack Philip," Hutchinson demanded.

"We will not," Quinnapin said.

"Then there may be severe consequences," Hutchinson said.

"How about this compromise?" Winthrop said. "We draw up a treaty for your signatures in which you pledge your allegiance to us. But we will not require your warriors to take up arms against Philip."

"We could perhaps agree to that," Pessacus said.

"But since you will be our ally," Winthrop continued, "you will have to agree not to provide refuge for any of the Wampanoags who are displaced by fighting."

"And for this support," Hutchinson said, "we will provide a bounty for every Wampanoag you capture and turn over to us."

The three Narragansett sachems looked at each other.

"Hell," Hutchinson said, "you don't even have to feed them before you turn them over to us. Just bring in the heads. We'll pay you for each one."

Sweet, these Christians, no?

"On any Wampanoag?" Quaiapen asked.

"You bet," Hutchinson said. "Man, woman or child. Not a dung beetle's worth of difference to us."

"We will have to counsel with our people about this arrangement," Pessacus said.

After Hutchinson and Winthrop departed, Quaiapen said, "These white men are monsters. We do not kill women and children, nor do we turn away the destitute."

"But are we ready for war?" Pessacus asked. "They have barely concealed their intention to attack us if we resist what they have proposed."

"I will never agree to their terms," Quinnapin said.

"Nor I," Quaiapen said.

"Our great fort nears completion," Pessacus said. "Our best strategy now is delay."

On July 15, when the English brought forth their hideous treaty, not one of the Narragansett sachems showed up to ink his or her mark. Four Narragansetts without any authority signed the document while Quinnapin, Quaiapen and Pessacus melted away with their people into the Rhode Island woods. The Narragansett sachems withdrew in expectation of attack, but the English scrambled in different directions. Wait Winthrop hurried back to Connecticut to help protect against Andros' New Yorkers. And Hutchinson's services as a soldier, rather than a strong-arm diplomat, were needed to the north. For the dogs of war were unleashed.

The day before the coerced treaty with the Narragansetts, on July 14, the Nipmucks, many of them numbered among John Eliot's "converts" and living in "praying" villages, allegedly, but not actually, at my direction, fell on the southern Massachusetts town of Mendon and burned much of it to the ground. This attack was led by Matoonas, the sachem of the mission town of Pakachoog. Matoonas was himself a Prayer and in earlier days, together with the infamous John Sassamon, had made an attempt to convert me to Christian belief. Nonetheless I never had much confidence in the sincerity of Matoonas' own conversion. New England Indians undertook various strategies for getting along with the English. Like my father and brother, I pursued a policy of accommodation. Matoonas took the path of practicing their religion. But as the English began to beat their war drums, he heard a rumor that all the Prayers were going to be disarmed and relocated to islands off the Massachusetts coast. Infuriated by the idea of such treachery toward the very Indians who had reached out to the English most extensively, Matoonas struck a blow before he lost the weapons needed to do so. And in one fiery afternoon, Mendon was no more.

IN THE DAYS LEADING up to the attack on Mendon, the war panic gripped Indian and English colonist alike. On July 9, while our men were aiming at everything but the bodies of Benjamin Church and his men, my sister Amie's husband, Tuspaquin, one of Weetamoo's Pocassets and sachem of the village at Wamasket, got into a dispute over a hog in the tiny town of Middleborough, just north of Assawompsett Pond.

Before the English arrived with their sheep, cows, horses and hogs, we Indians had domesticated only dogs. Over the half-century since the English moved in with us, however, we took to raising animals ourselves, although we were never as committed to it as were our pink neighbors. We liked the horses, but they were expensive both to purchase and to feed. And we didn't like the taste of mutton and pork nearly as much as that of bear and venison and wild fowl.

Still, in the right circumstances we would raise sheep for their meat and warm fleece and pigs for their flesh and tough hides. Tuspaquin had found a piglet munching acorns in the woods near his weetoo the summer earlier. He put it in a pen of birch poles, expecting some white man to come claim it, but none did. So he fed the swine with whatever lay handy, mildewed corn, scraps, deer and turkey innards, fish heads. And it had grown enormous, nearly 400 pounds, he estimated. He thought of skewering it and treating the people of Wamasket to a pig roast. But all his neighbors preferred tastier meat. So he took the sow into Middleborough to sell it.

While entertaining bids for the animal in the small square in front of the meeting house, Tuspaquin was confronted by a drunken townsman who demanded to know where Tuspaquin had gotten the animal.

"I raised it myself," the Wamasket sachem said.

"How likely is that," the Englishman asked knowingly of his fellow residents of Middleborough. "Stole it is more probable, wouldn't you say?"

"I said I raised this pig myself. I shall not say it a third time. And I suggest you either bid on this animal or be off." Tuspaquin stared arrows at the man who was dressed in baggy gray pants, a faded blue shirt and a cone-like woven cap pulled low on his forehead.

"Where'd you get the pig in the first place?" Cone Hat asked. "They don't grow on trees like apples."

"It's no business of yours where this pig came from," Tuspaquin said. "I raised it. I found it in the woods near my village, I built it a pen, I fed it for a year, and now I am offering it for sale. It will feed many. So make a bid or move off."

"No Indian can tell me to move off in my own town," Cone Hat said. "And I will tell you that's my pig you've got. Mine. I lost it a year ago, just like you said."

Tuspaquin turned to the four other men he'd been bargaining with. "Any of you remember this man losing a pig a year ago?" None volunteered that he did.

"I say off with you sir before we come to blows," Tuspaquin said to Cone Hat. "You'll regret tangling with the likes of me."

"I'll show you a tangle, I will," Cone Hat said, moving toward Tuspaquin with raised fists.

Tuspaquin took one step to his right and knocked the man to the seat of his pants with a right-hand punch to the cheek. The other white men barked at them to stop, but they did not step in. Sputtering, Cone Hat got back to his feet and came at Tuspaquin again. But when he threw a punch, Tuspaquin grabbed his arm, and spun him around with his arm twisted behind his back.

"I could hurt you bad, now," Tuspaquin snarled in the man's ear. "Break your arm. Make it hard for you to keep your field weeded." Then he released his hold and kicked the man in his rump with the bottom of his moccasin. "I said, off. So it's off you go."

"I'll not have no savage tell me to be off," Cone Hat said, but he stumbled on in the same direction Tuspaquin had kicked him, muttering oaths as he went.

Tuspaquin returned to negotiating with the other four men, not yet able to settle on an agreeable price. And before he got it, Cone Hat returned with a musket, pointing it at Tuspaquin who backed away with his hands raised. The other Englishmen yelled at Cone Hat to put his gun away, but he cursed them, and when he swung the musket in their direction, they turned and ran away. Cone Hat then swung back wildly and shot Tuspaquin's pig. The shot fired, Tuspaquin stepped forward, wrenched the musket out of Cone Hat's hands and with its butt hit Cone Hat right between the eyes, knocking him unconscious. Tuspaquin threw the gun behind him, snatched the knife from his breechclout belt and knelt over the fallen man, meaning to slit his throat. But he stopped himself and called out for the original bargainers to return.

"Come out, English," he yelled. "Somebody must pay for my pig this man has killed." But no one came. Tuspaquin waited, contemplated again killing the vile wretch underneath his knee, and again put that idea aside. Finally, he stood and stomped away from the meeting house. When he reached the far end of the street, he turned back and yelled out. "I will come back, English. And I will not come alone. And when I come you will pay for my pig either with your pounds or with your blood. Mark my words. Your pounds or your blood." He raised his knife like a scepter, before slipping it back in his belt.

Then he turned and marched out of town.

Shortly later, a grease fire set Cone Hat's house aflame and burned it down. The people of Middleborough were terrified and assumed that Tuspaquin had done it. The real story was that Cone Hat had knocked a pan of lard into the fireplace when he'd stumbled home to get his musket. But the people of Middleborough did not know that and concluded that Tuspaquin would soon return with his warriors to kill them all. The following morning, in rising panic, the Middleborough villagers packed what of their belongings they could carry and, swearing never to venture out into the wilderness again, burned down their clapboards so they would not fall into the hands of Indians who didn't want them in the first place. Then they fled to Plymouth.

SAVE FOR THEIR OCCURRING in the atmosphere of fear and hostility that That Vicious Lying Rat Bastard Josiah Winslow had loosed upon the region, the incidents at Mendon and Middleborough were fundamentally unrelated to the war that bears my English given name, and some histories do not include them, though those that do habitually cite them as early skirmishes in King Philip's War. They weren't.

In the months to come, I still sought ways to find a path to peace, but from July 14 forward those efforts were no longer to prevent a war but to stop a war I hadn't sought.

20

At 2:30 on Saturday, August 28, 2004, Rich got a call from Hart Thompkins that the evacuation buses were ready to depart from the parking lot behind Ungulate Arena. This was the last call on Rich's checklist. He had already unplugged the office coffee pots, televisions and staff computers. The rest of the campus was already secured. If the students were on the buses, then Physical Plant Services would already have begun closing down the dorms. Rich told Hart that he'd be at the arena in two minutes. He then shut down and unplugged his computer, slid his laptop into its backpack, and turned out the lights in his office, forgetting to grab his well worn blue blazer as he departed. His office would not look the same when he next saw it.

In the arena parking lot, Rich stepped up into each bus and wished his students safety and as much comfort as possible. He asked them to listen to the Student Affairs personnel who were with them on each bus. And he told them he hoped to see them back on campus to sleep in their dorm rooms on Tuesday night. The seriousness with which everyone was taking this evacuation was manifested in the fact that not one student asked a question when Rich invited them to.

On the lead bus, Rich found Cecilia Lagasse sitting in the first seat, opposite the driver. When Rich greeted her, she patted the fat roll of bedding in the seat next to her. "Got me a foam ground pad, sheets, army blanket and two pillows," she said. "Didn't know I used to take my daughter Girl Scout camping, did you? You were worried about my sleeping on the floor. I've got the Hilton in the seat next to me."

"I wish you weren't doing this," Rich said.

"It's my job," she replied.

"No, it's not. It's not your job as provost, and it's not your job as dean."

"It's my job as a nurse," she said.

"Jesus," Rich said, shaking his head. "Can I have you represent me when I come before St. Peter at the Pearly Gates?"

"Well, the odds are I'll get there ahead of you."

Rich didn't know what to say.

"Only problem is that I'm not much of a believer," Cecilia continued. "I'm pretty sure the world is the worse off for someone's having invented religion."

She could look to my short life for evidence of this proposition.

"I can't counter the analysis," Rich said. "But I remain a stubborn if uncertain believer."

"Well, if I'm wrong," Cecilia said smiling, "I will count on you to put in a good word with St. Peter for *me*. But not anytime soon, I hope."

"Mind if I give you a hug?" Rich asked.

"I think at times like these we are allowed to set aside professional decorum," she replied. Rich stepped up into the bus to embrace her. "When you get to be my age, every day is a time I'm allowed to set aside professional decorum. Remember that the next time we see each other."

RICH WATCHED THE BUSES pull out, got in his new Ford Escape, and headed home. When he arrived, Cally had gathered various pieces of luggage in the front hallway, including the valise in which, after the evacuation a year earlier for Hurricane Carolyn, they had taken to storing their financial records and insurance policies. She hadn't packed for Rich; she never did. But she had gotten out his roller duffel and had laid out jeans, shorts, underwear and socks. When Rich had left in the morning, Cally had agreed to start working the Internet and the phone in search of a motel somewhere out of harm's way for them to hole up in for a few days. Rich asked her what she'd accomplished as he began to shift clothing and toilet articles into the bag. She told him that she hadn't been able to a find a room anywhere within a three-hundred-mile radius of Choctaw but, almost miraculously, had been able to get them airline tickets for Richmond, Virginia, where her parents now lived in retirement.

Cally said, "I told the Delta agent that I wanted two tickets to anywhere in the world. She thought I was crazy. Said she couldn't help me unless I named a destination. I said how about Las Vegas. Might as well go have ourselves a vacation, right? No seats. Tried New York, Chicago, L.A. Tried Seattle. Everything was booked. Finally I asked if she had a flight to Richmond we could get on. Bingo."

"That's great," Rich said. "I guess. What time?"

"Nine p.m. Get in at midnight. Called Mom. She and Dad'll pick us up. We're welcome to stay as long as we want."

"Three days. More than that, then something that's not going to happen will have happened."

"I have return tickets on Tuesday afternoon. Mom and I will visit. I'm sure she's got some chore saved up I can help her with. You and Dad can play golf and talk about sports. We were going to visit sometime this fall anyway."

"So we'll get it out of the way."

"Hey," Cally said, "that's not nice."

"I don't mean it not nice. You know I love your parents."

"Yeah, I do. And it's one reason I love you."

"I hope you also love me because I am a fucking stud."

"I know I'm supposed to laugh now, but I am too freaked out."

"Would you laugh if I said that you also loved me because I am your stud fucker?"

"No."

"What *would* make you laugh?"

"I would laugh if you said, I promise never to refer to myself as either a fucking stud or a stud fucker for the rest of my life."

"Too high a price."

Cally shook her head. "This shit scares me, Richie. It scares me, and it pisses me off too."

"It's going to be OK. It's just a big pain in the ass. But thanks to your diligent efforts, at least we're not going to have to drive out of here at ten miles per hour. Speaking of which, I think as soon as I pack this bag, we'd better go to the airport. It's nearly four o'clock. It took us two and a half hours last year to reach the airport. We'll have a little time to kill, but that's OK."

"What do you think parking will be like at the airport?" Cally asked.

"You didn't call?"

"I didn't think of it till right now."

"Well, we better call." Rich said, "If we get to the airport and the parking lots are full, we're completely fucked."

Rich made the call, but got no answer. "Everything about this is just so asshole," Rich said when he gave up. "How do we decide what to do?"

"I think we better take a cab," Cally said.

So they called Choctaw Cab Company and were told they'd be picked up at 4:15, twenty minutes away. Rich hurried to finish packing and placed his bag next to those Cally already had put in the front hall. He then parked his black Escape in the garage next to Cally's silver Mustang convertible, a surprise gift from him on her last birthday. The cab had still not arrived at 4:30. At 4:45, Rich called the taxi company back. The dispatcher told him that he no longer had contact with the driver who was supposed to pick them up. No one else was available. In a panic Rich called Yellow Cab, and a driver honked for them at 5:10.

The drive to the airport from their house usually took twenty minutes, though it could take twice that long in evening rush hour. But with people already evacuating, traffic crawled, and Rich and Cally began to fret they were going to miss their plane.

Rich struck up a conversation with the driver, a neatly dressed African-American man in a pressed, white, short-sleeved shirt worn tail out over black slacks. He had a short nap of almost white hair poking out from under his snap-brim cap. Rich judged him to be about seventy.

"I guess this is gonna take a while," Rich said.

"Yessir," the driver said. "Made two earlier runs today. Slower each time. This morning not too bad. Over an hour but not too bad. Right at two hours last time. Gonna be a sight longer than that this time around. Last one for me. I'm gonna drop you folks off and call it a day."

"Jesus," Rich said. Then he saw that the man had a Christ figure magneted to the dashboard. "Sorry. I'm just worried we're not gonna make our plane."

"I understand," the driver said. "No offense taken."

After a moment, Rich asked, "How long you been cabbing?"

"Oh, long time. Yessir. Long time. Lessee, I guess forty-eight years now. Used to just work downtown. Hotel to Old Town. Restaurant to hotel. Short hops. All the time to the train station back when the trains still ran. Now I just do the airport run as much as I can. Easier than cruising for a fare."

"What did you do before you started driving?" Rich asked.

"Went to work for Yellow when I got out the army. Korea. Bad business, but did me good, I got to admit. Worked in the motor pool and got trained up as a mechanic. Worked at Yellow as a mechanic when I got back. Didn't have black drivers in those days save with the black cabs. Even when I started driving, some white people would get right back out of the cab when they saw me at the wheel."

Rich shook his head.

"What work you do?" the driver asked.

"I work at Urban," Rich answered, deliberately not adding that he was the interim rector.

"What you do? You a professor?"

"I am."

"I thought maybe you was a professor. What you teach?"

"English," Rich said, not adding that he didn't actually teach anything.

"Wonder if you taught my grandson? He's an Urban student. Majoring in business, but I know he took some Englishes. Two or three of them. Said they was hard. His name's same as mine. Lionel Broussard. You have him in class?"

"Can't say that I did. We run hundreds of English classes every semester. Department has over eighty professors. Urban's a big school."

"Yes indeed. Mighty big. Guess almost as big as ASU these days. But Urban still ain't got a football team. Ain't that a shame. Y'all ought to get a football team. I always said that."

Rich laughed. "I will agree with you on that. Don't think they'll ever let us, but you're right that we oughtta." Rich was convinced that a major factor in Urban's second-class status lay in the fact that it lacked a football team. Urban's academics might be better than ASU's, but Mayflower had the Monsters, and so ASU was big time, and Urban was basically no time.

"I follow your basketball and baseball. Y'all beat them Monsters once in a while. Be nice if y'all had a football team that could whup em."

"You ever go to any Urban basketball or baseball games?" Rich asked.

"I just follow y'all in the paper. Always pretty tired when I get home."

Rich had been toying with the idea of mentioning that he used to coach Urban's basketball team, but decided not to, and the conversation fell away for a bit, and after the earlier friendly exchanges, the silence felt awkward and uncomfortable to Rich. "You said we were your last fare for the day," Rich said.

"Yessir. Once I drop you folks off, I'm done."

"Going home to pack up so you can get out of here?"

"Aw, I don't know about that. Where y'all heading?"

"Up to stay with family in Virginia. Hope to fly back home on Tuesday. Once it's over."

Lionel didn't comment on this plan, and Rich felt acutely the vast economic difference between them. Rich hadn't even asked Cally how much she'd had to pay for the tickets. It didn't matter. Whatever the fare, they'd never miss it. For Lionel Broussard, Rich presumed, such an expense was an utter impossibility.

"You don't want to take this storm lightly," Rich said. "The weather guys say it could be a killer."

"What they said last year about that Carolyn," Lionel said. "I took 'em serious last year. Me and my family. My daughter and her husband stay with me, them and my grandbaby, Keisha, and that grandson I mentioned, Lionel the Third—we call him Trey. Last year all of us and my brother, Arthur, and his wife and my mother, who stays with them and who was eighty-nine at the time, we got in our two cars, and we drove out together up toward Tennessee. Man that was a hassle. Traffic just like this."

"I know," Rich interjected. "I was on the same highway with you. That's why we're flying out this time. If we ever get to the airport, that is."

"I might fly, iffn I had a ticket. But I don't know if we'll try driving again. Last year was a bad mess. All those people on the road. We musta stopped at two dozen different motels that didn't have no rooms. Ended up sleeping in the car, all of us packed in on top of each other like Vienna weenies in a can. Tried stopping at one of those rest stops where they have restrooms and all, but the state police said we couldn't stay there after dark. Finally just got off the Interstate and parked on the side of the road. Then that storm went over to Florida, so the whole trip wasn't for nothing. Waste of time and a working man's money. Don't know that we'll do it again. My Oldsmobile was leaking a little oil before that trip. Now it's got a rod that's about to go."

"This taxi seems in pretty good shape," Rich said.

"Yeah, but this car ain't mine. Belongs to Yellow Cab Company. Don't expect they'll be inviting me to take it out of town with my family stuffed in it like I said, like bread crumbs and garlic in a artichoke."

"Well, you need to keep a close eye on the news," Rich advised.

"Oh, I will," Lionel said. "I do take a hurricane serious. Had four feet of water in my house when Camille came through. So I know what they can do. But we survived Camille up in our attic, and that might be what we have to do this time again."

Lionel finally pulled his cab up to the Delta concourse at 8:35. A trip of twenty minutes had taken three and half hours. Their plane was scheduled to board beginning ten minutes ago. Rich and Cally unloaded their luggage as quickly as possible. Rich gave Lionel two twenties and refused to accept the twelve dollars he had coming in change. Lionel thanked him profusely. Yanking their rolling bags behind them, Rich and Cally ran into the airport terminal desperately hoping any line at security was minimal. They were able to relax at baggage check, for the moment, anyway. Their flight was delayed to 11:00.

Rich had expected to find a madhouse at the airport. Instead, the terminal seemed like a vaulted venue for a funeral service. Far fewer people were around than usual. The shops and kiosks outside security were closed. The Richmond flight was scheduled out of Gate 1, the closest in. The far end of the concourse was dark. The only food service open wasn't even serving hamburgers or French fries. Rich and Cally bought cold, prepackaged ham and cheese sandwiches and Diet Cokes. The lights at the restaurant were switched off behind them as they walked away. Management was clearly letting their employees go home to make their own evacuation plans. By 10:10 the whole concourse was dark except for Gate 1. They were on the last Delta flight out. Or, at least, they hoped they were on the last flight out. No gate agents had yet appeared.

After Rich and Cally took seats along the concourse in the Gate 1 waiting area to eat their sandwiches, no one else came in. There was no hum of conversation. All the passengers in the gate house, Rich and Cally included, spoke to their companions in whispers.

"Where are the gate agents?" Cally asked, when the flight desk remained empty at 10:15. "We should be boarding in fifteen minutes."

Rich looked at his watch. "I don't know," he said.

"This fucking plane better fly," Cally said.

"It'll fly," Rich responded. "Why wouldn't it fly?"

"Why wouldn't there be any lights on? There's nobody here. That's why it wouldn't fly."

"There are still lights on here. The plane is going to fly. I know it."

"How do you know it?"

"The pilot is from Richmond," Rich said.

"How do you know that?"

"It just makes sense. Somebody's got to be from Richmond. Why not the pilot? The stewardesses too. The plane is going to fly so the pilot and the stewardesses can get home."

"You're supposed to call them flight attendants," Cally said.

"OK, so the flight attendants and the stewardesses can get home. To Richmond. Where they're from."

"You are insane. Why did I marry you?"

"I would say because I am a fucking stud and your own personal, erotically exceptional stud fucker."

"You *would* say it?"

"Yes, I *would* say it."

"But you're not saying it now."

"No, I'm not."

"And why not? Because I would have to kill you?"

"I find that a perfectly defensible reason," Rich said. "I have always said that life is sacred, and my life is not just sacreder, but sacredest. Save for your life, which is the most sacredest."

Banter aside, Rich was as concerned as Cally now that their flight might be cancelled. His job was to remain positive. This was an unspoken but expected dynamic in their relationship. She always worried about the worst possible developments. And he always assured her that things were going to work out. But as he contemplated their circumstances, he calculated all the things that could result in a cancelled flight. The airport personnel seemed to have disappeared. And yet someone was going to have to put bags on their aircraft. And someone was going to have to put jet fuel in the plane. And if anyone save maybe the ticket taker went home early, they were thoroughly screwed. If the plane didn't fly, Rich and Cally were miles from their house without a car. If the other cabbies were like Lionel Broussard, they were at home with their families, not waiting to provide transportation for abandoned airline passengers.

A bedraggled dark-haired woman in a pink business suit with a ruffled blouse, panty hose, and black high heels walked up and said, "Do you mind if I ask you a question?" She seemed to be out of breath.

"Of course not," Rich said.

As if exhausted, she parked her rolling carry-on bag and sat down in a chair across from them, brushing a wisp of hair off her forehead. "Do you think I might be able to get on this flight?" she asked.

Cally and Rich looked at each other. "Gosh, I'd be surprised," Cally said. "I tried all day to find two seats out of here tonight, and this was all I could get. We would have gone anywhere."

"I'm willing to go anywhere," the woman said. "This flight is going to Richmond, right?"

"Yes," Cally said.

"I'm from Chicago," the woman said. "I came into town for a conference at the Sheraton. I have a return flight to O'Hare on Monday, but I need to get out of here tonight. They've cancelled all flights for tomorrow."

"Oh, we hadn't heard that," Rich said.

"I wonder why?" Cally said. "The weather's not supposed to get bad until tomorrow evening."

Rich hadn't thought about any of this before, but he presumed that the next day's flights were cancelled out of concern for the ground personnel. Either a positive concern to let them take their own evacuation measures. Or a negative concern that they'd just call in sick or not show. Couldn't better planning by somebody—who? the airlines? the F.A.A? the fucking Bush administration?—address the issues of ground personnel? Keep evacuation planes flying until the last safe hour and then take the bag checkers and the gate agents and refuelers out on the last plane. Have to take their families too, of course. And who was going to define the limits of family? Spouse and children? Aged parents? Obviously complicated. Too complicated for anyone working purely within a profit-oriented mindset to undertake. Much cheaper to just cancel the flights. Keep the planes themselves out of harm's way in Atlanta and Cincinnati or wherever. Tell your employees to run for high ground. Wait to see what happened.

"Did you fly in on Delta?" Rich asked the woman in the pink suit.

"American," she said.

"I bet you'd stand a better chance to land a stand-by seat on an airline that's cancelled your flight," Cally said.

"They haven't cancelled *my* flight," the woman said. "My flight is on Monday. They've cancelled all the flights tomorrow."

"But the storm is supposed to hit on *Monday*, not tomorrow," Cally said.

The woman shrugged. "I asked them about that," she said. "I was told that decisions about Monday flights would be made at a later time."

"This is like an LSD trip," Cally said.

The woman cocked her head.

"Well, everything about this situation is bizarre," Rich said. "But Cally is right that your best bet would have to be with American. We sort of think this Delta flight is a small plane."

"Last American flight departed twenty minutes ago," the woman replied. "Last flight out of here period. Except for this one."

"Well, I sure hope they have room for you," Cally said.

"I will ride in a jump seat," the woman said. "Happily."

"I don't blame you," Rich said.

"Oh," the woman said, her voice reinvigorated, "here come some Delta people. I'm going up to the desk." She stood up, smoothed the skirt of her suit, and grabbed her roller bag.

"Good luck," Cally said, as the woman turned to walk away.

Three uniformed female Delta employees walked slowly to the front of the gate house. They were talking in low voices, but Rich and Cally both overheard a snatch of conversation. Here's what they heard. "All this and now we're over . . ."

Over what?

"Did she say this plane is overbooked?" Cally said way under her breath.

"I don't know," Rich said. "Surely not. Surely they wouldn't have let people sit here all this time waiting for a plane with too few seats." But he was just performing his required role of positive thinker. Jesus, he thought, after all this, had they sold Cally tickets on a full airplane? It was nearly eleven o'clock at night in a city quickly falling into disarray. And they could conceivably get bumped off the last flight out of hurricane hell because of airline overbooking policies. If they couldn't get a cab, they wouldn't be able to walk back home in time to drive out. Given his damaged left ankle and ever aching knee, Rich wasn't sure he could walk that far, period. They were going to have to call someone. Who was still here to come and get them? Rich's heart began pounding, and he took two deep breaths to calm himself.

Cally was thinking more strategically. "If this fucking plane is overbooked, then you and I are going to be the first ones to board. Grab your stuff. We're moving up there." She pointed to two seats right across from the jetway door. As they changed positions, the lady in the pink suit walked slowly back toward them, her head down, her shoulders slumped. As they were about to pass, she lifted her wet eyes to them and moved her head slightly back and forth.

"I am so sorry," Cally said to her, but the woman did not respond.

Rich never forgot the woman in the pink suit, and for the rest of his life he wondered what happened to her. He hoped maybe she had been able to rent a car to drive out of town. That's what he thought his own next move would be if, indeed, his plane was overbooked, and he and Cally got bumped. He worried that, in his preoccupation with following Cally to seats next to the jetway, he'd been amiss in not stopping to suggest such a course of action to the woman in the pink suit. But, of course, he had no idea if the car rental companies were still open downstairs at arrivals or if, like the airlines, the rental companies had released all their employees to make their own evacuations. Without ever solving the riddle, Rich wondered if he should have felt some moral imperative to offer her his own ticket, or if he had a greater obligation to stay with Cally. Situations like the one in which he found himself now posed questions to which there were no easy answers. Whatever he *should* have done, he let her walk away into a difficult and uncertain night, and he wouldn't ever feel right about it.

At about ten of eleven, one of the three women at the desk announced that they were ready to begin boarding the flight to Richmond. The volume of conversation instantly vaulted higher, and people moved quickly to form a line, none more quickly than Cally who lined up first while wind-milling her arms for Rich to join her. Without incident, they made their way down the jetway to the plane and into their assigned seats about halfway back on the right. The aircraft was a seventy-seater with one column of seats down the left side and two down the right. Cally and Rich stored their unchecked luggage overhead and squeezed quickly into their seats. They could sense a spirit of relief as their fellow passengers got into their assigned places. Rich was not ready to relax, however. He kept a wary eye on everyone who approached him, fearful that the next person to reach his row was one with a duplicate seat assignment. But the boarding process concluded without a squabble breaking out between two people assigned to the same seat. When everyone was seated, and Rich determined that no one else was coming aboard, he dared to relax. This was a mistake.

For shortly after Rich relaxed, a male pilot and one of the three uniformed Delta women, evidently the flight attendant, entered the front of the plane. The pilot let the flight attendant deliver the bad news. "This plane is overweight," she announced.

Groans of incredulity, frustration and alarm reverberated throughout the tiny aircraft.

"We are going to need four passengers to deplane," the flight attendant continued in a voice brighter than the situation warranted. This announcement hushed the groans and all other conversation as if someone had pushed a mute button.

"Would anyone like to volunteer?"

No one raised a hand, although some, like Rich, did begin to rustle slightly in their seats. Cally placed a hand on his thigh to make him stop moving.

"For anyone willing to volunteer, we are offering a two-hundred-dollar Delta travel voucher good for one year on any domestic Delta flight and two nights' accommodations at the Choctaw Hilton right downtown."

There were no takers.

And when after an awkward interval of searching fruitlessly for raised hands that weren't forthcoming, the two Delta employees concluded that no one would volunteer, and the pilot took the mike and said, "Folks, we've got a safety situation here aboard the aircraft. We'd prefer to have volunteers, but we have no choice but to have four people deplane."

Still, no one stirred into the aisle. And when no one did, the pilot and the flight attendant looked at each other with raised

eyebrows, slipped the mike back into its slot on the wall and
stepped back out of sight into the jetway. A general hubbub
erupted upon their disappearance. The conversations weren't
loud, but everyone consulted with a fellow passenger about how
the airline might try to decide whom to kick off the plane. Rich
and Cally distinctly heard the man in front of them say to his
wife, "They aren't going to get anybody off this plane unless they
come back with armed security. And they'd have to shoot me."

Cally wondered if they would factor frequent flyer accounts
into the equation. Both she and Rich were Medallion Members
and had hundreds of thousands of miles in their accounts.
Rich worried that they might use a last-served, first-screwed
procedure, and he figured his and Cally's tickets could well be
among the last purchased. He also worried about his own size.

"If they ask me to get off because I'm one of the biggest
people on the plane," he said to Cally, "I think you should stay
on. Go on to your mother's."

"Shut up," she responded. "Shut up, slump down, fluff that
sport coat up around you, suck in your cheeks and start looking
skinny."

A few minutes later, the captain entered with his co-pilot.
They went into the cockpit and closed the door. Right behind
them, the flight attendant signaled for the jetway to be rolled
back and closed the cabin door. No one had been made to get
off. The flight attendant took the mike and announced that
Delta Flight 1818 was ready for immediate departure. Rich and
Cally looked at each other. What about the problem of being
overweight?

As the plane taxied away from the terminal, Rich and Cally
stared out the window. The airport was almost completely dark.
With no other planes on the runway, they were first for departure.
As the pilot revved his engines, Rich and Cally clasped hands.
They always did this when they flew together, but this night their
hands were sweaty and tense. What was with the overweight
business and the safety issue the captain had warned them about?

The pilot set the small plane into motion southward on the north-south runway. It reached speed quickly and lifted off, a little sluggishly, Rich thought, seeming to make a dip downward again before making a sharp-angled climb. When the plane was safely up a thousand feet, applause burst throughout the cabin. Others, it seemed, had also been gritting their teeth over the weight issue.

The plane flew south over the lights of the city and on out to the water of the Gulf where Hosea was churning. Then it banked right and made a sweeping right turn into a long semi-circle that brought it back over the western suburbs. For some miles before eventually making another right turn to the east, the plane flew north right over Interstate 61. Below them, with their headlights pointing north, traffic seemed to be parked for as far as the eye could see.

21

When we arrived among the Pocassets early in the month of *Towwakesos*, on June 29, 1675, Weetamoo and her people had just finished erecting their summer village on the eastern shore of Montaup Bay. The reeds were still green on their seaside *weetoos*. She and I did not know when the English would come after us, though we presumed it would be sooner than it turned out. Immediately, we began to erect a refuge in the heart of the Pocasset Swamp that lay to the east between Pocasset Pond and South Wattupa Pond. So that they might not be seized during the presumed English attack, we dragged our canoes into the woods behind us and covered them with leaves and branches. This marsh of cedar and dense fern was to provide us the perfect ground on which to meet the English, even if they came in superior numbers.

James "Fortman" Cudworth left behind a contingent of men to continue working on his Montaup fort to ensure that my Pokanokets and I could never return to our homeland. But with the entire Massachusetts regiment under Sam Moseley now returned to Montaup from Narragansett country and its pointless excursion to Mendon where the Nipmucks had simply faded into the forest, Cudworth dispatched an expeditionary force on July 19, across the water and over land, to show me the strong arm of the Puritan law. Though still a stuttering commencement, King Philip's War began in earnest that day. Our gesture of mercy toward Benjamin Church and his band of nincompoops was not even noticed.

With that last bid for peace wasted, we took up the war in earnest, and we made the English pay immediately as we brought them under fire while they tried to beach their canoes near Weetamoo's summer village. But even with the Pokanokets, Sakonnets and Pocassets joined together, we were still outnumbered and did not rush to engage them with our war clubs, instead using our muskets and bows on them from the safety of our cover in the woods. They hated this and derided us as cowards even as they fell to our arrows and lead. We laughed and sneered at them in reply, and as soon as we judged we were too few to deny their landing, we fell back, as we had planned from the beginning, into our swamp refuge. The English gave us chase there, but they mightily wished they hadn't.

Sam Moseley and his Massachusetts militia led the way with Big Mouth Ben Church holding at the rear with the Plymouthites. The Bay men were out of their element, and we had the better of them the entire time they tried to dislodge us from our stronghold. We smeared our faces and chests with mud and green clay, made crowns for ourselves of plaited fern, and tied cedar sprigs to our arms. In this way, we were able to move about in the dense shadow as if invisible. We were at one with the boggy forest, and we could strike at will.

The English stamped about the marsh in great and increasing frustration. Their best strategy was to try to stay together. This made them easier for us to hit with our muskets and bows but made it more difficult for us to take them with a charge for we could not afford the casualties that would have come from massive hand-to-hand combat. We liked it when one or two came after us, and we repeatedly showed ourselves to tempt them to do so. Adonoshonk and Pawtonomi were particularly adept at this tactic. Strong as bears and swift as deer, they could move about unseen and unheard. They liked to circle around a group of English and surprise them from behind. The whoosh of arrow and following war whoop with which they announced and showed themselves was almost enough to scare to death those English not felled by their bows. And the English never chased in force. The one or two who followed a darting Adonoshonk or Pawtonomi into the deep woods were quickly separated from each other and lost, crept up on from behind and propelled into the next world with a war club, then covered over with leaves and never seen again.

Somehow the English must have thought that Moseley was going to rout us from the swamp and drive us into the hands of Church who never entered the thicket. This we would never have done under the minimal pressure they managed that day, but once again we benefitted because the English brought less than their full force against us. In exasperation, Moseley divided his men into three regiments, and sent them after us in different directions. Nothing could have served us better. With their numbers reduced, we could more easily flank them and hit them at the edges of their lines. Within minutes, we had all three units twisted in knots, and to our immeasurable delight we had them discharging their muskets at each other. We did more damage to them that day than they did to each other, but the casualties of their "friendly fire" (yes, accidentally shooting your own wasn't invented in Vietnam) added to the magnitude of our victory.

Finally, Moseley reassembled his troops and ordered a retreat. Though they were too pig-headed ever to have admitted it—the braggart Church barely mentions this battle in his post-war blowhard memoir—we didn't just administer them a licking; we humiliated them. But somehow, being so convinced of their racial superiority, they still didn't understand what they were up against.

The next moves the English undertook were almost staggering in their stupidity. I think Donald Rumsfeld must have internalized the strategy the colonists alit upon next so that he could fuck up as hugely as possible when he invaded Iraq in 2003. First, James "Fortman" Cudworth gathered all the English together just outside Pocasset Swamp where we were safe in our sanctuary. Then, he announced that he thought the situation was well under control. They knew where I was. So they'd, yes, just build a fort and wait for me to come out, whereupon they'd capture me and punish me severely. I had to come out eventually, Fortman reasoned, because I had a lot of Pokanokets and Pocassets in the swamp with me and sooner or later we would exhaust our supplies, get hungry and either die in the swamp or come out where they could kill us.

Having just taken a severe whipping and hardly eager for any more wandering around in the muck, the stink britches rallied enthusiastically to Cudworth's logic. Then he read everybody a letter from That Vicious Lying Rat Bastard Josiah Winslow himself. Seems Governor Winslow in his infinite wisdom was worried about how much money the war was costing poor pitiful Plymouth Colony and wondered if Cudworth really needed all the soldiers under his command. Well, no, Cudworth asserted, he didn't. Even after the pasting we gave them, he still commanded an army of more than 500 men. And the fort-building and waiting activities he'd settled on didn't require nearly the force amassed before him. In his view, the end of the war was at hand. George W. Bush studied this reasoning before declaring "Mission Accomplished" in Iraq years and years before anything approaching a mission was accomplished.

With that, Cudworth dismissed four of the five companies that Massachusetts had contributed to the seizure of my property, and Sam Moseley promptly led most of the Bay Colonists back to Boston with a small regiment dispatched back toward Mendon to look for the Nipmucks they hadn't been able to spot when they had five times as many soldiers nosing around. Then Cudworth assigned Daniel Henchman (really, even Dickens couldn't make these names up any better) to command the fifty remaining Massachusetts troopers and an equal number of Plymouthites to build that Pocasset fort and remember to kill me when I came out looking for some food. Having tidied things up to his myopic satisfaction, Cudworth departed with the rest of the Plymouth militia back across the bay to Montaup where he could supervise his more important fort on my now empty land and set about the important business of devising strategies by which he could claim as much as possible of my peninsula for himself.

For the next week, we sat at stalemate. The English would not venture into Pocasset Swamp to engage us on our terrain, and we would not come out to face them in the open. Due to "Fortman" Cudworth's brilliant soldiering, he had left a force under Henchman that we outnumbered and could have overwhelmed. But had we instigated such a fight, our victory would have proved Pyrrhic, for the casualties we would have suffered would have left us weakened beyond recovery. So we bided our time in the thicket, while the English built another fort.

I will concede James Cudworth one insight, however. He was correct that all of the Pocassets and all of the Pokanokets could not remain in Pocasset Swamp forever. Eventually, we would exhaust our supplies and have to locate food. We needed to move. And neither Weetamoo nor I liked the position in which we generally found ourselves in Pocasset country. The whole of Plymouth Colony lay to our east. The Atlantic opened up to our south. James Cudworth and the bulk of the Plymouth army were busy carving up Montaup but still hemming us in to our immediate west. And Massachusetts squeezed down on us from the north. Our best bet, I determined, was to make a run to the northwest, into the sparsely settled area of Massachusetts east of the Connecticut River but far to the west of Boston. This was Nipmuck territory, and the Nipmucks had already shown that they were ready to fight.

But moving nearly a thousand people this distance of seventy-five miles across tilled farmland and the open meadows of the Seekonk Plain was no small undertaking. We would almost certainly be spotted. And if even the remnants of Cudworth's force he had assigned fort-building duty in Pocasset were hot on our trail, our chances of successful escape were diminished. So we did what every magician does when he wants to make things, us in this case, disappear. We endeavored to get the English to look in the wrong direction.

My strategy was as old as the concept of war. If it's to your advantage, and if you can, get your enemy to fight on two fronts at once.

At twilight, my captain Totoson led an advance party of four right into the center of Dartmouth, which was isolated on the Atlantic coast in the most southern part of Plymouth Colony. With cooking smoke rising from the brick chimneys of the town's clapboards, Totoson and his compadres stumbled down the main street of the village, yelling slurred curses at the English and jostling into each other as if inebriated.

"Bugger you all, you stinking swinish English," Totoson yelled, spinning in a circle and pointing at the opening doorways and the beige faces that peered around them. Totoson and his men had knives concealed in their leggings and war clubs stuck in their waist belts, covered over with breechclout flaps. But they did not reach for their weapons, not even as musket-wielding Englishmen ventured cautiously from their homes and surrounded them.

"I've a mind to put a ball in your bloody savage eye for talk like that around women and children," one of the Dartmouth men said to Totoson.

"And I've a mind to make you pay me good English money for the damage your hogs did to my wife's corn and beans," Totoson replied, swirling around as if off balance and pointing to a series of men encircling his squad. "You and you and you and you and you," he said, flicking his index finger at the faces of each, rattling the shell bracelet he wore on his right wrist.

"Me too," one of Totoson's men said, pointing at his bare red chest which he had decorated with a slash of ochre. "You owe me good English money for my wife's corn and beans, which your animals have trampled and destroyed."

"And my wife's squash and lentils," another of Totoson's men added.

"Get out of this town, you sons of whores," an Englishman barked, echoed by the taunts of a dozen others. "You're so drunk you probably stomped your gardens yourself."

Jeers, accusations, denials, demands and threats bounced back and forth between the two groups. The English were so routinely negligent about keeping their livestock penned, that Totoson's complaint had the ring of truth, even though the Dartmouthians vehemently refused to admit it. And all the while they argued, Awashonks and two dozen of her Sakonnets stealthily set fire to a half dozen houses. When the alarm finally sounded and the English ran for their clapboards, Totoson sounded his hawk's call, and all the Wampanoag confederates fell ferociously on those who were no longer massed together. The raid was a total rout for our side, our second unqualified victory in little over a week.

Then as noisily as they had arrived in town, the Wampanoag war party slipped into the woods in silence. The survivors in

Dartmouth were terrified and sent word to That Vicious Lying
Rat Bastard Josiah Winslow in Plymouth that they had come
under attack and feared that the Indians would return shortly
to finish them off. Winslow responded with reliable idiocy. He
sent Cudworth word that he wanted a regiment dispatched to
support the Dartmouth townsmen, and "Fortman," always the
kiss ass, anxious for the approval of his Governor, decided that
this was a mission he should lead himself. So he had himself
canoed back over to Pocasset and relieved Henchman of almost
the entire force of men he'd assigned to guarding us and building
the Pocasset fort. At the beginning of *Lawawkesos*, on July 29,
when normally our women would be busy harvesting squashes
and beans, Cudworth, with Blowhard Benjamin Church in
tow, marched 112 men south toward Dartmouth, looking
for Sakonnets who weren't going to provide him so much as a
glimpse. When the English got to Dartmouth, the people were
already packing and denouncing themselves for ever having
ventured so far out into the wilderness. With Cudworth and
crew providing them pointless cover, the Dartmouthians
completed their scorched-earth preparations, burnt those
dwellings that Awashonks' men hadn't torched previously,
abandoned the settlement entirely, and fled, en masse, back to
Plymouth.

   While they were doing so, the Pokanokets, the Pocassets
and the Sakonnets got the hell out of Dodge. Granted, Daniel
Henchman was left with so few troops to "guard" us that he
couldn't have done anything anyway, but he had his head so
far up his "fortified" butt that he didn't even realize we were
gone until several days later when a man from Rehoboth told
him that he'd seen a large party of Indians, men, women and
children, crossing the Taunton River on July 30. By the time
the men That Vicious Lying Rat Bastard assigned to trap and
capture us figured out what was up, we were gone, baby, gone.

22

Rich and Cally arrived in Richmond, Virginia, at 2:45 a.m. on Sunday, August 29, 2004. They were greeted by Cally's parents, Matteo and Maria Pappas. Cally's mom looked exhausted and frail, her white hair gathered in a ponytail and covered by a Baltimore Orioles baseball cap. Matt had circles under his eyes that were almost black against his tawny skin. But he had lost none of his erect naval-officer military bearing and his bulldog, thrust-chest physique.

As Rich and Cally waited for their luggage in the sleepy airport, the Pappases recounted their day and now nightlong vigil before The Weather Channel. Hosea was going to give Biloxi a bad wallop in just about twenty-four hours. Choctaw was predicted to get the full-measure of the northeast quadrant shortly later. People along the coast who were unable to get out of their cities were taking refuge in the New Orleans Superdome, in the Biloxi Coliseum and in the Choctaw Arrowdome. Wealthier people who weren't leaving town were booking rooms in the high-rise hotels downtown. CNN had done an interview with the manager of the Waldorf in Choctaw who explained that they were accepting guests on a three-day pre-paid basis only. He wouldn't say how much rooms were going for, but he did say that all meals were included and that all guest rooms were above the fifth floor in the unlikely event that doomsday flooding occurred.

"They also interviewed a guy from y'all's school," Maria said. "You probably know him. They said he was the Dean of Humanities and Social Sciences, I think. Was that it, Matt?"

"Dean of something," Matt said.

"Ben Turner," Rich said. "Was it Ben or Benjamin Turner?"

"I don't know if his name was Turner," Maria said, her tired brow wrinkling. "Ben Turner? Oh, it might have been, I don't know."

"Guy maintained he hadn't ever evacuated for a storm and wasn't going to start now," Matt said.

Rich laughed. "Anybody from CNN point out that when you move out of your house into a high-rise hotel, they call that 'vertical evacuation'?"

"Somebody did use that term," Maria said. "Your friend . . . is he your friend?"

"If it's Ben Turner we're talking about, he's a friend," Rich said.

"Well, your friend said he was just going to enjoy Downtown and Old Town while everybody else made a run for the hills. He said maybe he'd watch the hurricane blow by from the terrace on top of the hotel. Afterwards, he was going to have a nice late brunch, then get a taxi home to sleep in his own bed Monday night."

"Sounds like Ben," Cally said. "Arrogant and full of himself."

"You don't like Rich's friend, honey?" Maria asked.

"Oh, I like him OK," Cally said. "He's my boss, and we get along fine, just as long as I meet with him in a room large enough to accommodate his ego. He's the kind of guy who knows everybody else's field better than the person in it. And if he doesn't know anything, like he doesn't know anything about classical history, literature, art and architecture, then it's a so-called elitist field populated by snobs and not worth knowing anything about in the first place."

"Oh, I don't think Ben is serious about any of that," Rich said. "It's just his way of teasing you. I think he means it to be affectionate."

Cally snorted. "He may make such pronouncements with a big old smirking smile and devilment in his eyes, but I think he means it."

"This is an issue Cally and I have agreed to disagree about," Rich said to Cally's parents.

"Meanwhile, where are our fucking bags?" Cally said.

Maria's mouth wrinkled in distaste, and Rich threw his arm around Cally, giving her a thump of quiet reprimand with his forefinger. He knew she was just stressed and tired. She had a filthy mouth, but she routinely kept it in check around her parents.

"Really," Cally said, ignoring Rich's physical remonstrance, "the only things on that carousel are three suitcases that must have gone around a hundred times each. They were probably here before we were. Where in the hell are our bags?"

The answer was that Rich's and Cally's suitcases, along with the bags of twelve other passengers on their flight, had been pulled off their plane to solve the overweight issue and left behind in Choctaw. A couple of the other passengers got upset, but Rich and Cally couldn't very well wax indignant at that decision since it's one they would have made themselves. Delta issued receipts for their two bags. But they never saw that luggage again.

AFTER WAKING AT NEARLY noon later that Sunday, Rich and Cally parked themselves in front of the television in the Pappases' den and remained there the rest of the day watching CNN and mulling over what was about to happen. It seemed that New Orleans, Coastal Mississippi, Choctaw and Mobile were populated only by reporters who interviewed city officials, all of whom said exactly the same thing: they were hoping for the best.

Rich tried to get Cecilia on her cell phone to see how she and the Urban students were faring in Mayflower at the Monster Arena, but all he got was busy signals on dial after dial. The storm hadn't even come ashore yet, and critical communications were already breaking down.

Tired from staying up so late to meet Rich and Cally's plane, Matt and Maria went to bed shortly after nine that Sunday night.

Fatigued themselves, Rich and Cally nonetheless continued watching the news until midnight. Nothing changed. Hosea was going to make a direct hit on Biloxi. Choctaw was going to take a pounding from the storm's northeast quadrant.

Rich and Cally lay awake in her parents' darkened guest room for a long while after they went to bed. They were exhausted, but they were too apprehensive to sleep. No storm of this magnitude had threatened the northern Gulf Coast in their lifetimes. Global warming, rising seas, eroded barrier islands and depleted wetlands made communities from Texas to the Florida Panhandle vulnerable in a way they never had been before.

Nonetheless, neither Rich nor Cally really believed anything life changing was about to happen. Lying in the dark, the winds already howling, the waters already rising, and the storm just scant hours from landfall, they were frightened, but in an almost calculated way, the way you are frightened when you feel an unexplained stomach pain and wonder if you've just felt the first stab of an abdominal tumor. You acknowledge the possibility to ensure that it will not be true. You know that natural disasters kill people, and you know that your own death is inevitable, but until the lightning bolt strikes you, until you close your eyes for the last time, you think that catastrophe is what befalls communities elsewhere, that death is what happens to other people.

On Monday, August 30, when Cally and Rich awoke, they turned on the television in their bedroom as they put on the same clothes for the third day. One reporter and her camera operator had ventured out into the street in Choctaw but retreated in a panic as a freeway sign came slicing down the street like a giant, tumbling razor. In Biloxi, another reporter tried to capture the fury of the raging storm while clinging to a flag pole on the rooftop terrace of a Back Bay, high-rise hotel. The transmission went dead within seconds.

In the few hours that they slept, the storm had made a slight jog to the right, the beginning of the long predicted right arc, shallower and later than the prognosticators had originally expected. This move brought the eastern portion of the eye wall directly over Choctaw.

"Shit," Cally said, as soon as this news was delivered. "Shit, shit, shit." She began to cry.

Rich put his arms around her and pulled her to him, and he felt her tears soak through his shirt and dampen the skin of his chest as she began to shake with sobbing.

"Come on, baby," he whispered, kissing the top of her head. "We don't know that a thing is any different. We took a little more of the storm, but we were always going to get plenty. We have to be calm. Take things one step at a time. Wait and see what the news reports are once the storm has cleared." She answered this counsel with another temblor of sobs. Rich felt he had made perhaps unforgivable mistakes in his life. He had suffered defeats and disappointments in a variety of situations. But he had been conditioned with an athlete's resolve to get up and keep on going. Now he felt a hopelessness he had not known previously. What happened eleven hundred miles away was completely beyond his control. He could not affect the outcome, and he could not affect the impact of the storm's wrath on the person he cared about most.

Rich and Cally watched televised news reports for the rest of a long day. The bulk of the storm had cleared Biloxi by noon and Choctaw about four hours later. By mid afternoon, once streets were no longer wind tunnels for flying debris, reporters ventured out to assess the damage. The reports from Biloxi were ominous. The storm had wiped away the strip of hotels and gambling casinos along Highway 90. But the situation in Choctaw appeared dramatically better. The initial thrust along the Mississippi coastline had taken a larger bite out of Hosea's wind speed than had been predicted, and the hurricane was blowing at only about 105 miles per hour as it ripped through Choctaw, a menace still, but less a monster than feared. Windows were blown out. Power lines were down. Trees were uprooted.

But for the most part, damage in Choctaw appeared limited to that which would yield to concerted clean-up efforts in a matter of weeks. The worst of the damage appeared to have taken place in Mississippi and on the shores of Alkansea Bay twenty-five miles south of Choctaw where Hosea's record-setting storm surge had sent a mountain of water crashing through water-side residences and businesses, shattering them into splinters and then washing them out to sea. Choctaw and Mobile, meanwhile, were repeatedly said by all major news organizations to have avoided major damage.

Rich and Cally retired to the guest suite about midnight that Monday. They showered and went to bed in a state of edgy optimism. They wondered if they would be able to fly home the next night on the six p.m. flight they had booked. More important, they wondered what lay in store for them at home when they got there. Their beloved Mediterranean house was surrounded on three sides by seventy-five-foot water oaks. One or more of them could easily have been blown into the house or the garage behind it, which held their two cars. The largest of the limbs on the trees were massive, tree-sized themselves. Had one been snapped by Hosea's fury and punctured the roof or slung through a window? The news reports indicated that power was out throughout the region. Even if they *could* get home tomorrow night, ought they yet to go? Rich imagined a complicated day upcoming as he would try to contact his administrators and check in with Elia Lipscomb for the view from Mayflower.

Still, Rich and Cally embraced each other with a relief that felt like that of narrowly avoiding a deadly auto accident. They were worn out. They were not certain they were out of the woods. But the worst had passed. They meant only to kiss goodnight, but their gentle caresses soon became more urgent, and they found themselves making love.

Rich and Cally rose late the next morning, almost eight, still groggy from days of anxiety. Dressed only in the terrycloth robes Maria had supplied them, they made their way to the kitchen, poured mugs of coffee, and went out to find Cally's parents watching a network talk show. As they sat down, hoping to nudge a change of channels, Cally asked if her parents had watched any news yet, if they'd heard anything to report.

Yawning, Maria said, "Yes. There's some levee problems. Isn't that what they said, Matt?"

"Yeah," Matt said. "No big deal, I don't think."

"Levee problems? Where?" Cally asked, her voice suddenly tight.

"What I gathered," Matt said. "Something on a river north of Biloxi. One in Choctaw, but not on the Alkansea River, just on a canal of some kind. Like I said, no big deal. How much threat can there be from a leaking canal levee?"

"Fuck, fuck, fuck," Cally said. Maria grimaced at the expletive. "I can't believe you didn't wake us."

"There's no reason to get upset, honey," Matt said. "Really. I'm sure things are going to be fine."

"What canal levee in Choctaw?" Rich asked.

Matt said, "I don't recall that they said a name. Just said a canal levee."

"The Vienna Canal," Maria said. "That's it, wasn't it, Matt? The Vienna Canal?"

"The Venice Canal?" Cally asked

"I think that's right. Yes," Matt said. "They probably have the situation under control already. We haven't heard anything about it in an hour."

"You're watching a fucking talk show, Dad," Cally said. "You don't really expect them to interrupt their insipidity to report breaking news."

"We'll gladly switch to CNN, honey," Maria said. "Won't we, Matt? We don't have to watch this. It is kind of silly; you're right."

"Hand me the remote," Matt said to Maria.

"No," Cally said. "Please continue watching this shit. Rich and I will watch in the bedroom."

Cally left the room in a huff. Rich, both understanding Cally's concern and frustration, and wishing she hadn't tried to make her parents feel bad, looked briefly at Matt and Maria with pursed lips, shrugged with raised eyebrows and left the room to follow Cally.

They had just gotten the television on in the guest bedroom when Soledad O'Brien stated the accepted wisdom, "Biloxi is devastated, but remarkably, it looks like Choctaw has dodged a very serious bullet. We have reports of leakage along some of the outlet canals, but the Corps of Engineers states they expect to have the matter under control shortly."

Cally breathed a sigh of relief and turned to Rich. "How unlikely that Mother got the details wrong. But who can blame her? She doesn't know the city, and news reports have that way of garbling things. How many times has she worried our house was under water because she saw a report of some asshole in a pickup sending waves into people's houses in street floods after heavy rains? Let's just hope the Corps of Engineers is as good as its reputation."

Cally got the little pocket-sized calendar she kept all her appointments in out of her purse and began to thumb through it.

"Whatever's in there for today, you're not going to make," Rich said, stating the obvious.

"Step class at 6:30," she said, referring to her workout session. "Missed that."

"I could put some books on the floor if you want and call out up, down, right, left."

"Right," she said, continuing to study her calendar. "What's in it for you?"

"You'd have to do it naked, of course."

"If you were any more predictable, you'd be a geyser."

"Exactly what I had in mind."

"Ho, ho, ho."

"You ain't my ho, you my woman."

"Shit," she said. "My mammogram is today." Though Cally's mother had so far been spared, breast cancer ran in her family. Both her mother's sisters had been stricken. As a result, Cally got mammograms every six months.

"You can go later this week," Rich said. "In fact, call your doctor right now and have him schedule you for Thursday or Friday."

Cally picked up the phone next to the bed and dialed her gynecologist's office. After nearly a minute, she put the phone down. "No answer. Why did we even think someone would be at work?"

"We'll call again tomorrow," Rich said. "Meantime, if your tits need some squeezing, I will be delighted to step forward."

"If you were any more predictable, you'd be a geyser," Cally said. "Have I ever mentioned that?"

"Have I ever mentioned that's exactly what I have in mind?"

"You might perhaps have, but you're going to have to handle the matter yourself."

"Handle my own geyser? I'd so much rather visit the Grand Canyon."

"How about you take matters into your own hands, and I'll watch and cheer."

"That is perverted."

"Yeah? So."

23

M aybe the humiliations the English suffered at Pocasset and Dartmouth, followed by the escape of the main force of my Wampanoag people from Pocasset Swamp, triggered the incredible meanness that followed. The Indians of New England were hardly of one mind, and we greatly needed the Narragansetts to raise their bows and muskets at our side. But still they didn't. Moreover, lots of Indian folks who were interspersed among the Plymouth towns to our east never contemplated joining us. Many had become Christians, some even genuinely so. But their primary motivation was geography rather than religion. They were surrounded by English and couldn't imagine surviving if they took up arms against them. And right after Totoson, assisted by the hysterical English themselves, sacked and destroyed the town of Dartmouth, the Indians of eastern Plymouth felt rightly fearful that enraged Plymouthites would turn on them out of raging racial paranoia.

So on August 1, several hundred Indians from various eastern villages flocked into Plymouth to declare their fealty to the English. They were not greeted with the embrace of Christian charity. Rather, they were penned up like cattle and fed only enough slop to keep the majority of them alive. On August 4, That Vicious Lying Rat Bastard went before the Plymouth Council and recommended what he argued was a deserving fate for all of them, men, women, and children, who had come before the English as a display of their loyalty. Now that I had escaped, That Vicious Lying Rat Bastard pointed out to his fellow hypocrites, Plymouth was going to have to endure a greater financial burden than he had anticipated when he thought he had me pinned down in Pocasset Swamp. Land and money, money and land.

The perfidy of my escape and the fact that my Pokanokets and I were accompanied to the west by Pocassets and Sakonnets proved beyond a doubt that the Indian race just couldn't be trusted.

"They are spies or worse," Winslow told his council members about those who had sought protection among the whites, "but they are under our control, and they have immense value. Value as *slaves*. They'll bring treasure for powder and lead when we sell them to the next slaver who sails into port. We know they can't be allowed to remain in our midst less they slip their bonds and cut our throats in our beds. We must sell them before it's too late."

The council couldn't have been more enthusiastic in its endorsement of the Rat Bastard's proposal. And weeks later the whole contingent of those who had sought refuge in Plymouth's bosom were sold to a Spanish slaver and carted away to misery and almost certain doom.

As the local Indians were being herded aboard the Spanish galleon, That Vicious Lying Rat Bastard remarked to a council member with a splash of racist sarcasm, "We are only enabling them to accomplish that which brought them here in the first place. They wanted to help us defeat Philip, and the gold they are yielding will be of far more service than anything they might have contributed to our efforts in the field."

And yet, Josiah Winslow professed astonishment on his Judgment Day when he awoke from the slumber of his earthly demise and found himself in Hell.

UNFORTUNATELY, AS WE FLED out of the northern end of Pocasset Swamp, we had no recourse but to leave our camouflaged *mishoons* behind. So when we reached the point of our crossing over the Taunton River, we had to take the time to build rafts to get our people across. This requisite delay cost us precious time as we knew that Henchman would eventually discover that we had escaped and would pursue us.

Once we had gained the west bank of the Taunton, we continued on toward the sanctuary of our Nipmuck brothers, traveling as fast as we could with as many children, women and old people as were in our number. I pushed everyone hard, believing that we could not begin to feel any reason for safety until we had crossed to the western side of the Pawtucket River, at a point about seven miles north of Providence, Rhode Island, and ten miles northwest of Rehoboth. We did not know yet that we had been spotted and that Englishmen from Rehoboth and Taunton were marshalling to chase us. As we forded the Pawtucket, we felt safer than we were, but we couldn't have traveled any farther anyway. Our people were exhausted and growing ill with fatigue. With so many of our people simply unable to walk another mile, Awashonks, Weetamoo and I ordered a halt on the late afternoon of July 31, and we began to set up camp on the banks of the Pawtucket, just south of Nipsachuck Swamp. We were still a full day's march away from resting our ravaged bodies around the hearths of our Nipmuck relatives.

Daniel Henchman had learned of our departure from Pocasset earlier in the day, and he immediately assembled a force to come after us. But it was not Henchman who approached our camp in the predawn of August 1, rather the joint militia of men from Rehoboth and Taunton. We had hoped not to have to do battle again before reaching Nipmuck country where we could avail ourselves of their reinforcements. But that was not to be our fate. When our sentries brought me word of the arriving English, I ordered that our people be aroused and escorted into the swamp to our north. My warriors and I would stand between them to meet the enemy and defend their retreat until they had reached safety. The fight that followed was fierce, costly and infuriating because our most ferocious foes that day were a contingent of fifty Mohegans under the command of

Uncas' son Oneco. Uncas the Perpetual Rat Fucker. Uncas had sent Mohegans to fight with the English against the Pequots at Mystic River an entire lifetime ago, and he lived long enough to send his son out against me. So just in case you think this book is a one-sided denunciation of white men, let me make clear that Uncas the Perpetual Rat Fucker inhabits an uncomfortable chamber in Hades right next to his buddy Josiah Winslow.

I lost nearly twenty-five men in the fighting, including my brave captain Nimrod who was felled by the bullet of a Mohegan. But at about 9 a.m. we were finally able to fall back into the Nipsachuck Swamp with our people, and not even the despicable Mohegans were willing to come in after us. Unfortunately, our retreat from camp had taken place under such distress, we lost much in the way of needed clothing and equipment. We were now down to the clothes on our backs and what weapons we had in our hands. Moreover, we were growing perilously low on powder. If the enemy came in after us, we would have to defend ourselves and our loved ones in hand-to-hand combat.

About an hour later, as we regrouped, tended to our wounds, and prepared battlements should our enemies brave the gloom of our hiding to attack us again, Daniel Henchman and his Plymouthite regiment arrived. Henchman's appearance with a hundred new troops was a two-edged development. There now remained no prospect of victory, and our discussions turned solely to strategies for escape. Fortunately, Henchman came from a long line of keen English military men, following in the tradition of his great mentors That Vicious Lying Rat Bastard Josiah Winslow, James "Fortman" Cudworth and that aptly named dawdler Wait Winthrop. For reasons known only to himself and God, Henchman ordered that the Rehobothians, Tauntonians and Mohegans stand down. They had such numerical and fire-power superiority that had they come in after us immediately upon the arrival of Henchman's regiment, we could have done little other than resist unto death. But as he had done at Pocasset Swamp, Henchmen halted outside. He made camp, and he and his men feasted over three deer they had slain. Henchman finally ordered an attack on the morning of August 2. The English and Mohegans stomped into Nipsachuck Swamp and shot up a goodly number of cedars and vines. But they didn't manage to kill any more Wampanoags because we had slipped away to the north and west during the night.

ALAS, OUR ESCAPE FROM Nipsachuck Swamp brought with it a painful parting. My sister-in-law Weetamoo squatted around the early morning campfire with me and accepted from Wootonekanuske a light wooden bowl of corn mush seasoned with salt black crappie and sweetened with cranberries. We did not speak as we ate. But when we were finished, Weetamoo said to me, "We must take different paths from here, brother."

Weetamoo hated the English as much as I did. They had killed the love of her youth, my brother Wamsutta. I wanted her to continue with me into Nipmuck territory, for I felt that we could make a successful stand there.

"Yes, you must travel on to find refuge in the *weetoos* of our Nipmuck cousins," she agreed. "I think you have no other recourse. But I am going to take my people south to the Narragansetts. We will be provided shelter there, but you and the Pokanokets might not be."

"I see," I said.

"I would rather you remain at our side," Wootonekanuske said.

"In my heart I am always with you," Weetamoo responded. "You know that. But if the Wampanoags are to endure, indeed if all our historic people of this land are to survive, we have to bring the Narragansetts into the fight. Once we've arrived, I will send my warriors to you. But I must convince my husband that we must have his men too."

Many years after Wamsutta's murder, Weetamoo had made a political marriage to Narragansett Sachem Quinnapin. The two had never lived together, but they liked each other and got along, visiting with each other on numerous occasions back and forth across the bay that divided their homelands. Weetamoo knew that Quinnapin would provide refuge to her and her Pocassets. She didn't know if she could convince him to come into the war on our side, but she was committed to make the effort.

When we reached the trail fork that Weetamoo would take south, we halted for a rest. Wootonekanuske and Weetamoo held hands and walked off into the woods away from us. Wootonekanuske never told me what they talked about, nor did I ever ask. They knew, as did we all, that they might never see each other again, and when they returned, the cheeks of both these commandingly strong women were wet. Weetamoo spoke softly to Annawon, whom she greatly admired, and clasped the shoulder of Adonoshonk. She then squatted to put her arms around Neksonauket and cradled his head against her shoulder. Last she came to me.

"The great Creator has blessed me by my connection to your family," she said. "Your father made one people of the Wampanoags. And my Wamsutta tried to protect us. You have done the same. Fate has not been kind . . ."

"The fate of having the English come among us," I said through tight lips.

"Fate has not been kind to you. But I know you have led us well. And I know we find ourselves in this wood under these conditions not from any circumstance that you chose. I am proud to have fought at your side. And if my husband Quinnapin makes it so, I will fight again in the days to come."

Then she embraced me, and as she did so, I wet her hair with my tears.

24

The relief that Rich and Cally experienced from Soledad O'Brien's "dodged a bullet" comment on Tuesday morning was yanked away from them when she announced less than an hour later that the Corps of Engineers was reporting, not a leak, but a breach, on the Venice Canal, the city's largest drainage canal that took water from Old Town, the Exchange District and Riverside and dumped it into Lake De Soto. O'Brien now stated that the breach was a quarter of a mile long and that some neighborhoods near the lake were sustaining serious flooding. The rest of that long Tuesday involved relentless channel-switching as Rich and Cally tried to determine the prognosis associated with this breach. How long would it take to fix? How much water was pouring into the city, and what neighborhoods beyond those on the Lakefront were being affected?

Choctaw was founded on relatively high Alkansea River bank land but had expanded in the twentieth century into surrounding, low-lying swamp areas that had been drained with new pumping technology developed in the 1910s. As a result, much of Choctaw was below sea level and therefore protected from surrounding water by a circle of levees. The levees to the west channeled the Alkansea River to the Gulf. Those to the north held back the waters of Lake De Soto. The eastern levees ran along the bank of the small but nonetheless flood-prone De Soto River that drained the lake into the Gulf. And the southern levees came in two sets, one just north of Alkansea Bay, twenty-five miles away, another right at the city's southern border along the Saybrook Canal, a still navigable but industrially obsolete waterway connecting the Alkansea and De Soto rivers.

On that long, stressful Tuesday, the news reporters only slowly caught up with the story of the levee breaches. Coverage of downed limbs in Pensacola and Mobile were gradually abandoned for footage of civilization flattened on the Mississippi Gulf Coast and Alkansea Bay and stories about the levee breaches in Choctaw. The Corps of Engineers talked for several hours about dropping railroad boxcars into the quarter-mile-long breach on the Venice Canal. Rich and Cally were practically prone with concern because they understood, as did the other evacuated residents of their city, but, for the longest time, the national news media *did not*, that the streets and then the yards, and ultimately the houses and other buildings would fill up with water if the Corps couldn't figure out a way to staunch the flow of water quickly. Not until Wednesday, however, did the extent of the devastation become clear. Not until Wednesday did the media begin to track Coast Guard helicopters plucking desperate people off rooftops. Not until Wednesday did the national news organizations understand and communicate that a disaster of Biblical proportions was under way. And even on Wednesday, and even on Thursday, national newsmen did not report that the levee breaches weren't single, isolated instances, but were ubiquitous throughout the region. Venice Canal had the longest breach. But every outflow canal in the city had also breached, as had the Saybrook. By Thursday the city was filling up like a bathtub. But only days later did the media understand that Hosea had simply collapsed the levee *system* throughout the region. The levees were so poorly constructed and even more poorly maintained that when they were finally tested, they failed, not here and there but everywhere.

RICH AND CALLY HAD to stop talking to Cally's parents, who, deriving their information from the behind-the-curve news media, kept chirping that things weren't so bad. Long after Rich and Cally had concluded just how very bad things were, Matt and Maria kept uttering declarations of pointless hope that served only to reduce Cally to tears of frustration. The question wasn't whether Choctaw had flooded; the only question was how high the flood waters would rise in individual neighborhoods. Although the basement of Rich and Cally's house had almost certainly flooded, wrecking their heating and air-conditioning systems that were situated there, and though a ground-level floor that housed Cally's home office, a garage with their two cars and an appliance room with washer, dryer and freezer, had presumably taken on water, the primary living areas sat nearly five feet above the street. Their living room, kitchen, den, dining room and bedrooms would only be affected if the water rose higher than five feet. News footage from certain sections of the city showed water far deeper than five feet. But no footage was shot in their neighborhood. From their vantage point in front of a television set in Richmond, Virginia, they couldn't tell what had happened to them and their immediate neighbors.

Meanwhile, Rich was finding himself infuriatingly isolated from his responsibilities. All the preparations that he had made to facilitate communications among his administrative team had failed. What Rich had on the little laminated card in his wallet was a series of cell phone numbers. And in the chaotic aftermath of the storm, cell phones simply did not work.

With the extent of the disaster still not clear by Wednesday morning, Rich did manage to get a landline call through to Elia Lipscom in Mayflower. Rich was hoping that Lipscom would have the benefit of a better-informed Alkansea media and therefore might be able to provide Rich more definitive information, might possess some idea of a timeline about the prospects of returning to the Urban campus. But Lipscom had less intelligence on these matters than Rich hoped. Rich's call did enable him to acquire a landline number for Cecilia Lagasse, however. Lipscom did have that, but he was none too happy about it.

"We got ourselves a historic crisis down here, Coach," Lipscom informed him early into the conversation, delivering this news as if Rich were somehow ignorant of it. "We got ourselves an elephant-sized fucking mess, and I got your so-called provost up my ass, which I very much do not need. Am I making myself clear? Just a little bit clear?"

"We're pretty much in the dark up here," Rich responded. "We're not even clear about the extent . . ."

"Where the fuck are you?"

"Richmond."

"Richmond? Where the fuck is Richmond?"

"Virginia. We're in Richmond, Virginia."

"What the fuck are you doing in Richmond, Virginia?"

Rich explained about Cally's parents and how they had flown out ahead of the storm.

"Well, that's all fine and dandy, Mr. Interim Rector," the viceroy said. "But I need your ass in Mayflower, not in Richmond fucking Virginia. I need your ass here, and I need you to pull your shrew of a provost out of my butt where at any moment she will no doubt try to open an umbrella. Now. This afternoon. Yesterday. Am I making myself clear?"

"Perfectly, Elia," Rich said. "I will make arrangements to come to Mayflower immediately. Meanwhile, may I ask why you are so upset with Cecilia? I have never found her anything other than a perfectly reasonable person."

"She's as reasonable as a goddamn Mack truck."

"Yes?" Rich said.

"Yesterday afternoon she shows up at the Board office saying she needs to see me. Ethyl told her I was in a meeting. She says, well get me out of the meeting. Can you believe that shit? Who does she think she is? She's not even a real provost. She's a fucking *interim* provost appointed by an *interim* rector. No disrespect intended. But still. Tells Ethyl to get me out of my meeting. I'm the general goddamned fucking manager of team higher education in this state and somebody who isn't even really an assistant coach of one of our minor league teams is telling my assistant to get me out of my fucking meeting. Then when Ethyl says she'll see what she can do, Provost Ball Buster says she'll just wait in my office. And when Ethyl opens my door your provost bolts past Ethyl as if she's Walter Payton bursting off tackle into the end zone, right into my office where I'm sitting watching the hurricane nonsense on the goddamn TV. I thought maybe she was going to shoot me or something. People have gone totally fucking nuts down here, you know."

"I doubt that Cecilia Lagasse would shoot anyone, Elia," Rich interjected. Not even you, Rich thought.

"Well, she had no business storming in on me like that. I was doing the state's business. Monitoring things. Staying abreast. Keeping myself informed."

"I'm sure she must have had an important reason," Rich said.

"I am telling you, man. We have an unfucking believable crisis going on here. We've got more of your Choctaw Negroes in this town than we know what to do with. The Convention Center is full of them. And they're starting to act up about food and shit. And now in comes your provost to inform me that she's got three busloads of your students been sleeping at the Monster Arena, and she wants me to find them dorm rooms because their poor little backsides are all tired out from sleeping on that hardwood floor. Wonders while I'm at it if I can find some sort of housing for her, too, since she's been sleeping on the floor too. Says a dorm room will do for her too, if that's all that's available."

"Well, that seems reasonable, Elia."

"Reasonable? What am I, a goddamn dorm director? I'm the fucking viceroy for fucking Higher Education."

"Well, you are the boss."

"Goddamn right about that."

"So I'm sure she thought you'd want to help. Perhaps she should have gone directly to Stephen."

"Aah, she did try to go to that asshole Hopkins," Lipscom said. "Bastard managed to give her the slip. Said that's why she just barged into my office. Didn't want the same thing to happen again."

"Well, then, there's a context, isn't there? I'm sure you can see that. Cecilia was just trying to do her job the best way she could. She's real old school, Elia. She was an army nurse in Korea. M.A.S.H. and all that. She's a take charge person. You'd like her if you had the chance to get to know her. Anyway, were you able to help her?"

"Who the fuck knows," Lipscom said. "Probably. I got fucking Stephen Hopkins on the phone and told him he was to take care of her problem. I presume he did. She hasn't been back here, and you fucking better make sure she doesn't."

"So ASU had empty dorm space?"

"How the hell should I know? But yes, I presume so." This fact, if indeed true, relieved Rich. He still wasn't clear about what he and his students (and all his fellow citizens of Choctaw) were facing, but if there were beds to sleep in, he wanted his students off the floor. At the same time, the fact that ASU had empty space pissed Rich off. He'd been campaigning for additional dormitories at Urban since he was first hired as the basketball coach. ASU had empty rooms. Urban didn't have nearly enough rooms.

As it happened, ASU did have dorm space for the three busloads of Urban students and more empty rooms than that. In the days to come, when circumstances made clear that most of Choctaw was not going to be habitable for months, additional students from Urban arrived to occupy even more dorm rooms. These rooms were not, however, offered to the Urban students without charge. Nor were they offered without attendant conditions. First of all, to remain in the dorms, the Urban students would have to enroll at ASU and pay its usual tuition and fees. With much fanfare, Alkansea State University Rector Stephen Hopkins, a Monster through and through, announced that ASU was opening its doors to *all* Urban students "regardless of their qualifications," an insidious little announcement that made Hopkins seem paternalistically magnanimous and rendered Rich's students suspect and second class from the moment of their arrival on the manicured lawns of their sister school.

Rector Hopkins crowed that he wouldn't even require the displaced Urban students to apply or otherwise go through the ASU transfer admissions process. If the student had been enrolled at Urban, he or she could study at ASU for the entire 2004-2005 academic year, and all who maintained their academic standing during that year could continue at ASU right through to graduation. The only paperwork the old Ungulates/ new Monsters would have to fill out was that attached to their tuition payments. If they were on Federal Aid, which *most* Urban students were, then they had to complete paperwork transferring their federal tuition support from Urban to ASU, a nasty little requirement because Urban still had employees that Rich needed to pay with the tuitions and federal grant monies that Stephen Hopkins was appropriating for ASU as quickly as he could snatch it. The shit storm in Choctaw was being alchemized into a gold mine for Mayflower. The powerful just never stop enriching themselves at the expense of the powerless, do they? Stephen Hopkins was no Josiah Winslow. But they were definitely related.

Hopkins may have dodged Cecilia at the outset, but that was before he spotted the opportunity nesting in the detritus of disaster. And once he spotted it, he embraced it with the enthusiasm of a second-rate actor marching down the red carpet on Oscar night. Or a Winslow starting a war to grab my land over the death of a man who fell through thin ice. Hopkins arranged for members of the Monster football team to help Urban students move into their new dorm rooms, a manufactured photo op that the Mayflower television and newspaper reporters ate up like five year olds devouring ice cream at a birthday party.

The Urban students didn't have any possessions that they couldn't carry in their own two arms. So they hardly needed the muscle power of Monster footballers to lug their back packs and bedrolls into a building. And, in fact, the football players didn't do much lugging other than for a few of the attractive Urban women who practically had their packs wrenched away from them so that the players could earn their Good Samaritan merit badges. Most of the players just stood around grinning, spitting between their shoes and punching each other on the arm. The quarterback, of course, offered himself to a phalanx of microphones to mouth barely coherent platitudes about how Monsters always aimed to be leaders off the field as well as on. Rich and Cally watched a bunch of this footage on television, wondering how in the world they were going to control their gag reflexes, a skill they needed to master because they would have to employ it repeatedly in the days to come.

Somehow, with Stephen Hopkins as their most visible spokesman, the people of Mayflower came to believe that Hurricane Hosea, which caused their campus and their city no damage whatsoever, was nonetheless about them. Pursuing this theme, Hopkins bragged to anyone who would listen that Alkansea State University had triumphed over the greatest crisis ever faced by a university in the entire history of higher education and made that claim the centerpiece of a self-congratulatory book he wrote about ASU's response to Hosea that he called *Front and Center*, a slim, self-important volume of preening self-regard that Rich and Cally always referred to as *Irrelevant and Off to the Side or Smugly Out of Harm's Way*.

ON THE WEDNESDAY AFTERNOON after the storm, Elia Lipscom hosted a conference call that included his two under viceroys Margaret Lockhart and Ronnie Shade, Rich, Stephen Hopkins and the rectors of the two state community colleges in Choctaw. The purpose of the phone conference was to structure a response to the developing presumption that neither Urban nor the other public institutions in Choctaw were going to be able to resume operations soon, not that fall for sure, perhaps not that year. The conversations raged on for over an hour with

Hopkins contributing repeated breast beatings about how, as the flagship, ASU was fully prepared to provide the leadership needed to navigate this crisis. Rich didn't even bother responding that unless Hopkins could find housing in Mayflower for over 20,000 students, ASU couldn't even provide navigation for displaced Urban students, much less those at the community colleges.

But nobody really knew *what* to do. Choctaw was closed until further notice, sitting pitifully in a toxic soup of sea water, lake water and leaking sewage. Neither state nor federal officials were able to supply any timetable for when citizens would be able to return to Choctaw. No one had any idea when the city would be drained or when fundamental services would be restored. At this point, no one even knew what the damages were neighborhood to neighborhood. For Choctaw, the Urban campus stood on high ground, but that didn't mean it hadn't gotten wet. And even if Urban's buildings had managed to escape the flooding, that didn't mean it could reopen for business any time soon since faculty, staff and students had no place to live in order to work or study there. How soon electricity and sewage and water service would be restored anywhere in the city was not known.

Still, Rich had to presume, that at some indefinite point in the future, Choctaw would be restored and would require a public university to educate its populace. If that were to be the case, Rich felt it imperative to hold onto his faculty and staff. And that meant paying them at this pivotally important time. Just like Rich and Cally themselves, Choctaws had been splattered into the homes of friends and family all over America. No place was available for them to work. But they still had food to buy and mortgages to pay on homes they couldn't live in.

Stephen Hopkins wanted to know what Rich was going to use for money. Rich responded that Urban had plenty of money in the bank, having just collected fall tuitions and federal tuition grants. Hopkins pointed out that a whole host of Urban students were now being admitted to ASU classes, and that those classes would have to be paid for by somebody, presumably by the monies in Urban's bank accounts.

"Unless, of course, you just plan to steal that money from your students," Hopkins said.

Rich didn't answer that charge directly, instead arguing that the job of the state's educational leadership was to address matters in the long term. The dimensions of the current crisis were unclear, but if the state failed to hold onto Urban's faculty and staff, then the university would have to be restarted from scratch when Choctaw was finally reoccupied.

"Who's to say it's going to be reoccupied?" Ronnie Shade asked. "When it comes to the nuts and boats of the situation, way I look at it, nobody down there now. Maybe nobody down there for a long time to come."

"Though I am sympathetic . . . sympathetic to your legitimate concerns . . . legitimate concerns," Margaret Lockhart chimed in, the words, as always, fluttering in her mouth like the wings of a caged bird, "Mayflower *is* the biggest . . . is the biggest city in the state now. And we . . . and we . . . and we *are* going to have to consider . . . to have to consider the needs of the flagship first."

"My point, exactly," Hopkins said. "I don't think we can afford to ignore the elephant on the table. We have no idea what a rebuilt Choctaw will look like. It may well just be a quaint little tourist destination. I understand that Rector Janus' old basketball instincts make him want to keep competing no matter how far behind he is. But I don't think we should presume that Urban is ever going to reopen or that, in the near future, there will be any need that it should."

In fact, Viceroy Lipscom and his entire administrative team agreed with Hopkins on this point, distasteful though Lipscom found it to agree with Hopkins about the direction of east. Still, the conversation had taken a dangerous turn. Lipscom didn't want any report of this conference to emerge, establishing the idea that he wasn't fully supportive of one of his universities.

Fredrick Barton

His job all along was to be entirely *pro* ASU without ever being *anti* anything else. No matter that these two positions were incompatible.

Lipscom always had his eye on the state capitol and on the governor's mansion, and he got the shakes when he thought of either now. Choctaw might be empty now, but until a radical redistricting took place, it still had a whole host of state representatives and senators who represented the flooded areas, and not one of them would be pleased at talk about Choctaw becoming a quaint tourist destination. For whatever reason, Choctaw's elected officials had never been fervently supportive of Urban, but they were sure to get pissed at the idea of closing it forever. Urban was a huge operation, and everybody in the city had some relative on the payroll and some child or niece or cousin enrolled there. Lipscom had to be very careful lest Hopkins and his own Monster staff manage to rock the boat enough to drown Lipscom's career in the Choctaw flood.

Moreover, the state's racial politics were not on Hopkins' side in this matter. Democrat Harlan Lebear had captured the governor's mansion by marrying huge majorities in the African-American community with his Catholic base in the counties along the Alkansea where original settlement had taken place. Lebear could not have been elected without the overwhelming support of black voters in Choctaw, and he couldn't be reelected without them. Urban is where middle-class African Americans sent their kids, and they wouldn't tolerate the idea of boarding the school up. Lipscom could hear the howls of racism that were sure to erupt at the very idea. And he could imagine just how far Harlan Lebear would crawl up Lipscom's butt at his not squelching the idea when first raised.

So Viceroy Lipscom brought the phone conference to an inconclusive end when he announced, "Thanks to everybody for your input. We have some tough days ahead of us. But I am sure we will stand united. And for the record, I want to let Rector Janus know that you have my full support. I pledge to everybody involved right now that whatever steps we have to take, Urban University will be utterly protected from a tragedy beyond its control."

This was not the only lie that Elia Lipscom would tell Richard Janus. But it would do for the moment.

25

After we escaped from the attack on our sanctuary in Nipsachuck Swamp, Edward Hutchinson and his Massachusetts battalion trailed behind us into Nipmuck country. He wanted most of all to apprehend me and those traveling with me. But his second objective in moving into central Massachusetts was to try to force the Nipmucks into a treaty like the one he had extracted under duress from the Narragansetts. Quinnapin, Pessacus and Quaiapen had at least consented to sit down with Hutchinson, but my Nipmuck brothers refused to talk with him at all.

A smarter leader than Hutchinson would have gotten the point that the Nipmucks weren't going to negotiate with him. What did he think they were up to as he marched through Nipmuck country in *Lawawkesos* on July 28 and found town after empty town? Well, since he came from the same distinguished crew of military geniuses as Josiah Winslow, James Cudworth, Benjamin Church, Wait Winthrop, and Daniel Henchman, he evidently didn't think anything at all, or at least not anything to worry about. Eventually, Hutchinson arrived in the hilltop English village of Brookfield, located right in the heart of Nipmuck country. Brookfield was a small town, but it had mightily pissed off the Nipmucks since its establishment a decade and a half earlier, increasingly so as more English kept arriving every year. The Nipmucks, who were already being boxed in by English settlers on the upper Connecticut River to their west, had only to look at what was happening to the Pokanokets to imagine what lay in store for them as Brookfield grew and a first Brookfield begat another and two more after that.

Finally, Hutchinson's scouts discovered that the Nipmucks had gathered as an entire nation at Menameset on the Ware River about ten miles north of Brookfield. Nothing if not persistent, incredibly stupidly so, Hutchinson kept sending out emissaries begging the Nipmucks to talk with him. Finally, Nipmuck Sachem Muttaump agreed to meet him at a site deep in the forest about halfway between Menameset and Brookfield. Hutchinson was delighted, sure that he could get Muttaump to ink a non-aggression pact.

What a blasé guy Edward Hutchinson was, leading a band of Englishmen numbering about twenty-five north on the winding, ever narrower trail that led from Brookfield to Menameset. What an arrogant idiot. Did he not notice, as the woods grew in upon him from either side, as his company was forced into single file, that he had maneuvered his troops into a position from which they could not defend themselves? Did that prospect occur to him for even one bleeding second before the first Nipmuck volley ripped his party to shreds?

Hutchinson's militia was without a strategy to defend itself. Eight lay dead almost immediately, a like number wounded, including Hutchinson and his second in command. Trapped in the tunnel of a forest canopy, they could not even see who had laid them waste. All the English who still drew breath could do was turn their mounts and ride through a blizzard of bullets back in the direction from which they had come.

Brookfield provided the badly wounded Hutchinson a temporary refuge as the entire township turned its meeting house into a garrison. Arriving not long later, Muttaump's warriors held the Brookfield garrison under siege for the next twenty-four hours, while they systematically appropriated tools and other usable goods from the vacated houses. On August 4, an English relief unit arrived from Marlborough, and Muttaump chose not to sacrifice his own men by attacking this large force. Nor did the Nipmucks strike as the English withdrew with all of Brookfield's inhabitants, still another English town lost, sacrificed to the racist land greed of men like Josiah Winslow. Edward Hutchinson survived the trip back to Marlborough but died there of his wounds, the last casualty of his own inept soldiering.

MY FATHER MASSASOIT OUSAMEQUIN was a legendary figure among the Nipmucks, viewed as a man of wisdom and insight. As his son, I arrived to flattering support. After the siege of Brookfield, I sat down with Matoonas and Muttaump in the latter's wigwam (the Nipmucks *did* use this term for their homes) at Menameset. My Pokanoket force was significantly reduced, and I lacked sufficient numbers of warriors to make an extensive contribution to the fighting that would follow. But I still had good, strong, experienced men in my company, Annawon, Adonoshonk, Pawtonomi, Totoson and Tuspaquin among them. And I took Annawon, Awashonks, and Totoson with me to Muttaump's wigwam. Wootonekanuske accompanied me as well, for I valued her counsel as all my people knew. The issue before us was how to proceed.

"I think we should select another target to the east," Muttaump proposed. "We have wiped out Brookfield like a ripe grape plucked and devoured. The English vine is heavy with fruit. We take one at a time until only the Boston grape is left. And then we put *it* to our teeth."

"How about Marlborough?" Totoson asked. "It lies closest to here."

"They'll expect us next at Marlborough," Matoonas said. "So I think we should attack at Groton. The English will have to stretch themselves to defend Groton, and if we strike with enough stealth we can destroy the town before reinforcements can even be dispatched."

"I concur with Matoonas' thinking," I said, "but we should extend it. Boston and Plymouth are our ultimate goals. I pray to the Creator to live to see the day both burn. But we mustn't leave ourselves open to attack from the rear. So I propose that first we secure the Connecticut River. The towns there are less well defended. We can pick them off one at time."

For some time we discussed the advantages of attacking Groton versus the settlements on the Connecticut. Some worried that the Connecticut River towns were small, and therefore of less value in sacking. Matoonas and Muttaump pointed at the successes we had enjoyed in the east at Mendon and Brookfield.

"We did have good victories in the east," I said. "Add Dartmouth to that list. But I think the small size of the Connecticut River towns is an advantage, not a detriment to our choosing them. We need to destroy as many English towns as possible and as quickly as possible. For if we can demonstrate that Pokanokets, Sakonnets and Nipmucks are a viable force, if we can prove that the English are vulnerable, then our sister Weetamoo may be able to convince the Narragansetts to come in on our side."

I asked Wootonekanuske what she thought, and she responded, "I can certainly see the arguments for attacking either east or west. I think Metacom makes a good case that we can more easily succeed along the Connecticut. And that has obvious advantages. We will lose fewer warriors. At the same time, we would throw a greater fear into Boston and Plymouth by attacking in their direction as Matoonas and Muttaump have argued. If our goal is to scare the English on the Atlantic, that is what we should choose. But I think, right now, our audience is in Narragansett country. Quinnapin and the sachems in his council. My sister promotes our case every day. What will enable her to succeed? I think the Narragansetts most of all need to believe that we are going to succeed. If they do, they will join us."

We did not vote, but after a time, as was our way, we reached a consensus to stage a diversion and then pursue my strategy of striking to our west. If our victories there had indeed brought the Narragansetts into the war in the summer of 1675, who knows what this part of the world would be called today? As likely New France as New England.

Better, what about Algonquia?

26

Given the loose talk about closing Urban for the rest of the year and maybe forever, Rich Janus realized he had to get to Mayflower as quickly as possible. But planes weren't flying, so how was he going to get there, and every hotel in Alkansea was full of displaced Choctaws, so where were he and Cally going to live? Despite Elia Lipscom's assurances that Urban would be "utterly protected," Rich didn't trust anyone who lived in Mayflower to look out for anyone from Choctaw. Rich was convinced that his institution was in jeopardy, that ruthless state politics were at work, and that his own advocacy was imperative. But to fight for his university, he had to identify a place to live in or near Mayflower.

Finally, Rich thought of calling Althea Feaster, head women's basketball coach at Mayflower Central High School.

"How well do you know her?" Cally asked, when Rich brought up Althea's name. "I sort of remember your mentioning her, but not for a while."

"I haven't seen her since I took my coaching job at Urban," Rich admitted. "We were coaching-conference buddies. But then I started attending college coach conferences and our paths didn't cross anymore. You think maybe she won't even remember me?"

Cally laughed. "Who could ever forget *Dr.* Richard Janus, state champ coachest with the mostest?"

Rich kissed Cally on her forehead. "I hate Francis Fucking Saurian," he said.

"If you call Althea," Cally said, "what are you going to say? Hi, remember me? Can my wife and I come move in with you for an indefinite period? We're quiet and clean, and we'll leave at the first opportunity. And we're so depressed, we won't want to make love, so we wouldn't make any distracting noises while you were trying to sleep."

"You make things sound so hopeful," Rich said.

"Aren't they?"

"I don't want to call her," Rich said. "But I don't know that we have any other choice."

"I know," Cally said.

"At least I can promise her that, unlike the Pilgrims who moved in with my old Wampanoag friends, we harbor no plans to take over their house."

See, I knew he was still thinking about me.

"Or that we haven't any plans to fill up their house with our children."

"So we've got two things going for us."

"Absolutely," Cally said. "Pacifism and menopause."

IF EVERYBODY IN MAYFLOWER had been like Althea Feaster, Rich would have developed a higher opinion of the place. When Rich called her, Althea said that she and her husband had two spare rooms, a guest room and that of their daughter, Keisha, who was away at the University of Tennessee playing for the great Pat Summitt. The guest room was currently occupied by a physician working for Doctors Without Borders who was providing emergency medical care for evacuees living in public shelters. The guest room had a double bed in it, whereas Althea's daughter's had only a single bed. But that was no problem, Althea urged. Who could be picky in times like these? The physician could move to Keisha's room, and Cally and Rich could have the guest room.

"Y'all have to come," Althea said.

Rich apologized profusely for making the blind call and promised that he and Cally would do everything they could to find housing somewhere else as soon as they got into town.

"Honey," Althea said, "y'all just come on, and what happens after that is what happens. I'll be curious to hear what caused you to lose your mind and give up basketball for the snake pit of administration. I know you got pushed aside for that asshole Jimmy Prince, but I also know you could have found someone else to put a whistle back in your mouth. Since you haven't so far, I figure that's going to take you a long time to explain, so y'all just plan to stay for six months if you have to."

"I'm sure it can't possibly come to that," Rich said.

"Well, we'll see," Althea said. "Just know we'll be glad to see you."

"Treasures in heaven," Rich said.

"What's that?"

"Your generosity is storing up treasures in heaven."

Althea laughed. "If I knew God was impressed by my letting an old friend use a room that was empty anyway, I'd have invited you to move in with us years earlier. Given the number of vile things I've said about referees, I need some plus marks to offset all the minuses."

WITH A PLACE TO stay lined up, Rich and Cally turned their attentions to transportation. Choctaw Airport was closed indefinitely, and Mayflower Airport had been commandeered by the federal government for the deployment of emergency personnel. Mayflower might reopen by Monday, but Rich did not want to wait that long. They found that they could get flights into Mobile, Birmingham, or Jackson, Mississippi, but there were no cars to rent at any of those locations. They were going to have to buy a car.

They found a low-mileage Ford Escape coming off a lease. It had a cigarette burn down into the foam on the driver's seat, but Rich and Cally both found comfort in the car's familiarity. They started back to Alkansea the next morning, the Friday after the storm. They drove south to Durham, North Carolina, then turned west on I-40 over the Appalachians. They spent the night with Jerry and Anne Schwartz, old friends of Rich's family, now retired on forty acres of woodlands and fields near the town of Rockwood, Tennessee, about fifty miles west of Knoxville. Jerry and Anne were in their mid-eighties now, but still full of vinegar. They insisted on cooking a meal, and they opened the bottles of Jack Daniel's (for Jerry) and Tanqueray (for Anne), which Rich had stopped to purchase as gifts.

Rich had known Jerry and Anne since he was a child. Jerry had worked in the Civil Rights Movement across the South as a colleague of Ed "Preacher" Martin, Jeff Caldwell and George Washington Brown, though always as a volunteer and never as an organization staffer. In the mid-1960s, Jerry had lost the Baptist church he pastored in Baton Rouge, Louisiana, when he tried to convince his congregation that Jesus demanded they accept the applications of Negroes to join their fellowship. After that, he worked as campus chaplain at LSU, where he was fired for inviting Preacher Martin to speak, and subsequently as head of "employee relations" at the big Avondale Shipyard in New Orleans.

Barrel chested, blessed with a full head of silver hair, Jerry Schwartz looked like a retired Cary Grant, including the black-rimmed glasses Grant wore late in life. Jerry was a man quick to laugh and eager to express a withering opinion, particularly about the insensitivity of Republicans in general and George W.

Bush in particular. "No-good bastard's flat-out evil," he liked to say of Bush. "The Axis of Evil he goes on about is him, Cheney and Rumsfeld."

Anne's recent hip surgery medication made her sleepy, and she went to bed soon after they ate. Jerry insisted that Rich and Cally join him on the porch for "toddies." As they sipped their Jack Daniel's, into which Jerry had splashed some Peychaud bitters, Jerry lit up a sequence of Camel Lights which he smoked after breaking off the filter tips.

Jerry was concerned about Rich's mission to save his university. "I know you gotta do this," he said to Rich. "But there's a place about a mile from here for sale, and I wish y'all would just go buy it and settle down here with me and Anne. Bush has done fucked up the whole Gulf South too bad to get it fixed again anytime soon. He's let global warming rage out of control. We got hurricanes in the Gulf now like we used to have redfish. Mark my words, with that man in control, Choctaw is screwed rude. The man's either a vicious motherfucker or a fool. And at this point it doesn't much matter which. I know you gotta go tomorrow, but when you get up, let me show you that place I'm talking about. You find you can't save things down in Alkansea, you come on back up here. You and me can fish for bream, and Anne'll teach your lady how to grow tomatoes the size of volleyballs. You can get a job coaching basketball around here somewhere and do something good in the world instead of wasting your time bossing around a bunch of airbags who've got their heads crammed so full of information it's crowded out whatever good sense they might have had."

Rich smiled into the rural night at his old friend's persistent but only half-believed assertions that, along with his degrees, an educated man acquired a great deal more in the way of arrogance than of wisdom. Jerry wasn't really hostile to universities, though his experience at LSU had been a significant disappointment, but he liked to tweak his friends, his way of displaying affection.

"You need to listen to me, nephew," Jerry said, exhaling a puff of gray smoke and then pulling a shred of tobacco off his tongue. "I used to believe that a better day for this old world was just around the corner. But I don't believe that anymore. I wonder if we're going to make it another hundred years. You doing some good down there at Urban, so be it. Go save 'em. But don't let them eat you up. Make sure you *can* do good. You were a helluva basketball coach. You need to get back to that before they get your soul."

"Come on, Jerry," Rich said. "I can't even account for how I find myself where I am. You're old as dirt, but I'm no spring chicken either. Whatever choices I've made, good or bad, I have to live with them now. I often wish otherwise, but my coaching days are in the past. Even if this job at Urban doesn't kill me, I don't see myself living long enough to get back to coaching."

"You miss it, son?"

Rich laughed. "I still dream about it."

"Coaching the Ungulates?"

"Never," Rich said. "Coaching the Choctaw High Warriors."

Jerry made a sniffing sound and then took a drag on his cigarette. "And you think you're too old to coach a high school team now?"

"Yeah," Rich said. "I guess."

"Just plain stupid," Jerry said. "You're not even sixty years old. And if you'd learn to live like me, smoke and have a couple of toddies every night, you might live to be a hundred like I'm going to. Nearly half your time left."

"Yeah, well," Rich said. "Right now I've got other business to take care of."

"I know, son. And I don't even know what you're heading into. From what the TV says, it's hell down there. And I'm sure they aren't on top of even half of it." Jerry rattled the ice in his glass, and stubbed out his cigarette. "So join me for one more. Might be a long time before you have the space for a proper drink every night."

That, unfortunately, would not be among the problems Rich was facing.

RICH AND CALLY HAD breakfast with the Schwartzes the next morning, now five days after the storm, and then set out west for Nashville where they turned south on I-65 and ultimately southwest on I-61. Traffic heading south was not heavy, but it was steady. Rich and Cally were not the only ones heading back into the storm zone. While driving, they were able to travel comfortably at seventy miles per hour. But they still couldn't make decent time. Problems finding gasoline began as soon as they crossed into Alabama. Lines at gas stations grew so long they backed up onto the Interstate and sometimes took nearly an hour to move through. In fairness to those in line, the station owners employed ad hoc rationing, no place that they stopped willing to sell more than ten gallons, some stations refusing to sell more than five. Rich and Cally became so paranoid about running out of fuel that they would not drive one hundred miles without getting into another gas line.

As a result of the gas station delays, a trip that should have taken little over seven hours took nearly eleven. They had hoped to arrive in Mayflower by mid-afternoon, but they didn't get there until nearly eight.

Rich had never met Althea's husband. In fact, he didn't even know the man's name. But here they were without a choice. Here they were about to take up residence with the family of someone that Rich knew fondly but not well and that Cally didn't know at all.

27

Just in case my Nipmuck allies and I weren't enough of a headache for the English, they kept helping us. They had gotten away with such cold-blooded slaughters as those at Wessagusset and Mystic River for so long that they thought they could strike at an entire people with impunity. Though the attacks at Dartmouth, Mendon and Brookfield were warnings of what was to come, the English leadership was yet too arrogant to be afraid. In their view, they'd only had to say boo and the Pokanokets, Sakonnets and Pocassets had cleared out and left behind, now unpeopled, huge swaths of coveted land.

Such an attitude of indomitability no doubt led to Captain Samuel Moseley's attack on the northern nation of Pennacooks who had always lived in peace with the English along the Merrimack River. This unprovoked act of viciousness brought more of our neighbors into the war on our side. Moseley burned an entire Pennacook village and killed all the residents. He subsequently bragged about unleashing his dogs on a captive woman and relishing the horrible spectacle as they tore her innocent body to pieces. Moseley was a monster, but he was a hero to the English. This was what we were up against.

But unintentionally, Moseley had, in effect, stepped into a pool of piranhas he would have been better advised to avoid. No doubt alarmed and infuriated by what the English did to the Pennacooks, the Abenakis exploded into action with such ferocity that, by October, they had sacked all the English settlements in Maine. Pressure from the north was so great, in fact, that the Massachusetts Council undertook serious discussions about building a palisade barrier below the Merrimack in hopes of keeping the Abenaki Confederacy at bay.

In our part of the world out on the western frontier, in *Matterllawawkesos*, on August 22, we initiated an unrelenting two-month offensive. On that date we launched a diversionary attack on the town of Lancaster, thirty-seven miles west of Boston, burning some houses and killing seven English. The purpose of this action north and east of Brookfield, and not far from the town of Marlborough, was to lead the English to think that we were focused on those settlements to the immediate east of Nipmuck country. We wanted them to dig in there and to lull them into complacency in their more isolated villages along the Connecticut River.

The English along the Connecticut did not become quite as careless about their vulnerability as we hoped, but they continued to behave as stupidly as their countrymen had since That Vicious Lying Rat Bastard Josiah Winslow fomented this madness on us all. The attack on Lancaster panicked the people of Hatfield, a Connecticut River town approximately in the middle of the line of Massachusetts settlements that stretched from Springfield in the south to Northfield up near what would become the New Hampshire border. On August 24, the Hatfieldians marched out to a settlement of Quabaugs, Nipmuck cousins, who lived nearby and demanded that the Quabaugs surrender their weapons. Right, the Quabaugs thought. You English have been killing whole towns of defenseless people for a half century now. So we'll just hand over our muskets, bows and tomahawks.

Or then again, maybe we won't. They didn't. And not remarkably, fighting broke out. The Quabaugs retreated from their village into advantageous terrain, in this case Hopewell Swamp. The English, led by Captains Richard Beers and Thomas Lathrop, followed the Quabaugs into the soft darkness and sacrificed the lives of nine men before they withdrew in defeat. Heretofore the Quabaugs had not joined our confederated army, but now they did.

The next two months went well for us as we put our
Connecticut River strategy into action. In *Micheeneekesos*, when
our women should have been in our homeland harvesting corn,
on September 1, we attacked Deerfield, killing an Englishman
outright and burning several homes. The next day we attacked
the most remote English outpost at Northfield, killing eight
and, again, burning several buildings. Slyly, we let two English
riders pass through our lines to carry the word of fighting at
Northfield to their brothers farther south. They sounded the
alarm in the town of Hadley, and the English residents there
responded to this news just as we knew they would. They paid
dearly for their predictability.

On September 3, Captain Beers headed north from
Hadley with three dozen men and a force of horse-drawn
carts. His mission was to evacuate the residents of Northfield
to towns farther south where they would be safer. I think
Pete Seeger perhaps had Beers in mind when he penned the
words, "When will they ever learn?" Just as the Nipmucks
had lured Edward Hutchinson into a trap in the hours before
the siege of Brookfield, we now did the same to Beers. About
two hours after he and his company broke camp on September
4 and had marched within two miles of Northfield, at a
spot where the trail narrowed and his maneuverability was
limited, we opened up on Beers and his men from every
direction. Altogether, we killed twenty-one English that
day, including Captain Beers himself, and by September 6,
Northfield was empty of human habitation. The top grape
was picked. Adding Beers' death to that of Hutchinson, the
English should have grasped that there were mortal liabilities
in leading men against us. But arrogant men being arrogant
men, they were slow to learn this lesson.

On September 12, we attacked Deerfield for the second
time, again letting English riders carry the word south. These
guys just couldn't seem to stop stepping on the same old hoe, and
as long as they were so ridiculously willing to bash themselves in

the head, we were ready to lay down the tool for their stomping. Just as they had determined about Northfield, the English now decided that Deerfield was indefensible. Duh!

To evacuate Deerfield, the English sent Thomas Lathrop with three times the force we had cut to ribbons outside Northfield. He arrived on September 16 and supervised loading what the English planned to haul away with them before setting out for Northampton on the 18th. This time we let the pinkskins load up their carts and complete the abandonment of still another town before we set about to deal with them. Otherwise, it was déjà vu all over again. Only more so.

We laid our ambush six miles south. We watched them come down the river at a steady pace until, as we knew, they had to pause to cross Muddy Brook, a small sluggish stream that emptied into the Connecticut a short way to the east. While they were trying to keep themselves dry, we let them have it. If I hadn't had such cause to hate them so very much, I would have felt sorry for their pathetic ineptitude. Once again, the careful design of our attack allowed us to surround them. Eventually, they were reinforced, first by Samuel Moseley and subsequently by a company of troopers led by Major Robert Treat and a squad of Uncas' despicable Mohegans. If not for the arrival of additional forces, we would have killed them to the last man. As it was, while losing just a handful of our own men, we took sixty-four English lives that day, including that of Thomas Lathrop, the third of their commanders to fall before our onslaught. The dying was so great that day that the English forever after referred to Muddy Brook as Bloody Brook.

Our triumph at Bloody Brook finally got the attention of the English leadership. Four days later on September 22, the United Colonies, a confederation that included Massachusetts, Plymouth, and Connecticut, but not heretical Rhode Island, called for an army of 1,000 men, 500 of whom were immediately to take the fight to us in what was left of their territory on the Connecticut River. Major John Pynchon, a wealthy Springfield merchant and civic leader, was placed in charge of the western force. Here's what we thought of that: On September 26 we burned Pynchon's mill.

But despite that insult, Pynchon still couldn't grasp what he was up against. It seemed not to dawn on him that if we could use a scalpel's precision to slice him personally, we were able to measure our blows and deliver them at the places of our choosing and to our maximum advantage. Because along the Connecticut River we had attacked and ultimately razed first Northfield and then Deerfield, Pynchon was convinced that we would next strike at the nested towns of Hatfield, Hadley and Northampton. To protect against that he located his 500-man army in the middle town of Hadley, which was the home base of second-in-command Robert Treat.

Pynchon's fellow Springfielders beseeched him to leave a minimal force to provide for the defense of their town, Massachusetts' largest and most prosperous of its western settlements. But Pynchon counseled his fellow citizens that they had no reason to fear because my forces always retreated into the woodlands of Nipmuck country and his army would stand between them. Moreover, he promised, I would be unwilling to attack Springfield because of Pynchon's personal relations with the local sachem, Wequogan, with whom he had traded for many years and whom he trusted beyond any doubt. But, of course, Pynchon was blind to the fact that for all the years they had traded, Wequogan had resented Pynchon's high-handed ways. And Pynchon did not know that Wequogan had led the raid that burned Pynchon's mill. In the end, Pynchon made a token gesture to popular will and left to defend his hometown a vestigial force of about a dozen men under the command of a young and untested lieutenant named Thomas Cooper with the assistance of town constable Thomas Miller. I shake my head. For even this last decision was the wrong one.

On October 4, Pynchon led all the troops in Springfield, save for the dozen to remain with Cooper, north toward Hadley. His stated objective was to use Hadley as an operational base from which to mount as many excursions into Nipmuck territory as necessary to bring me and my allies into submission.

What Pynchon didn't know was that Muttaump and I had dispatched several hundred of our warriors to join with Wequogan's men to ready an attack the moment Pynchon made his predictable move to Hadley. The arrival of some of our warriors was noticed and reported to Lt. Cooper, who in an act almost outrageous in its foolhardiness, led his tiny regiment out to investigate. Wequogan's sentries intercepted them and killed most of them, including Constable Miller. Lt. Cooper was gravely wounded but managed to ride back to Springfield to sound the alarm before expiring from his injuries. Of course, Springfield possessed no military force to respond to Cooper's warnings. All the remaining townspeople could do was to hurry to a garrison house. The homes, barns and other outbuildings in this settlement of five hundred English were completely undefended when our men arrived, and thus they encountered no resistance as they burned everything but the garrison house to the ground. Pynchon would have been better advised to take Cooper and the dozen soldiers he left behind with him to Hadley. The material losses at Springfield would have been no greater, and he would at least have saved the lives of a dozen fighters.

Our victory at Springfield meant that only three English settlements remained on the Connecticut River, those defended by Pynchon's troops at Hadley, Hatfield and Northampton. On October 19, we started a fire in the forest within sight of the village at Hatfield. Our old friend Samuel Moseley was in charge there, and though he was even more heartless and bloodthirsty than some of his fellows (none of whom would be termed a bleeding heart), he was comparably stupid. See a fire: send out a squad of ten men to investigate what's happening. We almost couldn't believe these guys.

We killed eight of the ten.

On October 20, we attacked Hatfield directly, on October 25 Northampton, and on October 26 the small settlement of Westfield on the path from Springfield to Albany, New York. Our successes in these battles were not as overwhelming as those up and down the Connecticut River had been earlier. But we did damage. We killed English and burned houses in every settlement. We were inside the heads of the English now, and we knew it. They were not so arrogant anymore, not those in the field, anyway, who knew that we might be lying in ambush around the next bend along any path they had to traverse, and not those who were now living elsewhere as refugees because we had destroyed their homesteads and emptied their entire towns.

In Massachusetts Colony, most everywhere outside of Boston, the settlers were in panic mode. Even far from the western front where all the fighting was taking place, English townsmen were fortifying their garrison houses, terrified that our whoop of war might fall on their ears next. The rural farmers were devoting so much of their energies to erecting defenses that they neglected their fields and their dairy cattle, and soon the English were frightened by a sudden food shortage to go along with the other problems their warmongering had spawned.

The sage English leadership in Boston and Plymouth responded to the disasters along the Connecticut and the attendant fear raging throughout their colonies with decisive action of a particularly English brand. First, as *Arrkesos* dawned, on October 30, they sent their army into the towns of Praying Indians that stretched along the eastern rim of Nipmuck country wherein lay our major force. The citizens of these Praying towns of Hassanamesitt, Makunkokoag, Natick and Nashobah were forced from their homes at musket point and herded into an internment camp on Deer Island in Boston Harbor.

The majority of the Prayers who were going to join us had already done so, primarily the young, strong and courageous. So what the English accomplished when they emptied the Praying towns was not a military advantage but merely an act of cruelty.

They forced more than five hundred women, children, elderly people and the infirm to occupy a hostile environment at the edge of winter. More than half of them died of exposure and hunger over the next five months. Several dozen others were captured and spirited away into bondage by slave ships that preyed on them without resistance. The people jailed on Deer Island represented no military threat whatsoever. And they prayed for mercy to an English god who did not spare them. They suffered and died for no purpose other than the racial meanness of the English—Creator damn their evil souls.

The second English response to the defeats they suffered along the Connecticut River was further evidence that the war they named after me was all about their greedy lust for land. Lose some towns to the Nipmucks and the Wampanoags on the Connecticut River. Bummer. What shall we do, what shall we do? How about this: Let's pick on a nearby people who have remained stubbornly neutral. Let's declare war on the Narragansetts.

28

The Feasters' house was a modest, brick, one-level ranch-style residence in a neighborhood of similar houses. Rich and Cally exited the Escape, and as they headed toward the house, they joined hands, each giving the other a silent squeeze. At the front door, Rich took a deep breath and blew it out between pursed lips. He did not look at Cally, fearful, he told himself, that if he did so, she would begin to cry. Actually, Rich didn't look at Cally because, if he did so, he feared that *he* might cry.

He rang the bell. Althea opened the door wide. She was about five eight and solidly built. She wore her black hair straight and flipped forward about halfway down her neck. Her skin was the color of pecans, and her face was sprayed with freckles. She was drying her hands on a kitchen towel.

"Rich," she said, smiling broadly. "Welcome." She handed her husband the towel and opened her arms. Rich stepped into her embrace, and they each gave the other warm pats on the back. When they stepped back, Althea said, "And you must be Cally." Cally nodded. "I know it's such an old cliché, but Rich has told me so much about you." Then she embraced Cally as well.

Althea then turned and introduced her husband, Robert. Robert, not Bob or Rob. Robert was about six feet tall and very lean, not skinny, but slim-waisted and sinewy. His skin was cordovan-colored, and his close-trimmed hair was reddish brown with flecks of gray. Robert had retired five years earlier after a thirty-year career with the U.S. Postal Service. He'd had various assignments through the years: at the front desk, on the receiving dock, in sorting. But his favorite job was always as a carrier. He liked being outdoors, even in bad weather, he said. He liked the courtesy most people showed him. Yes, he'd had the occasional run-in with people's dogs, but he was good with animals. And he carried a can of pepper spray on his hip if it ever came to that, which it had, but not often.

Since retiring, Robert hired himself out for small fix-it projects. He could put up a fence or install a new toilet. He could hang new porch lights, hook up a new dishwasher. Just things he'd learned how to do through the years, mostly at his own house. He didn't want big jobs, didn't do lawns or gardens. He would paint to finish off something he'd fixed or built, but he wouldn't take a straight painting job. He liked a challenge, liked solving a problem for somebody who might not be able to handle the job himself or might not have the time. He did a lot of projects for Althea's fellow teachers at the high school.

Althea and Robert showed Rich and Cally to the guest room. They had already relocated the volunteer doctor into Keisha's room, which stood directly across the narrow hallway that ran back to the front door and beyond it to the kitchen and small, over-furnished living room. At the end of the hall was the bathroom that Rich and Cally would share with the doctor.

The guest room was so small that once Rich and Cally had brought their suitcases into the room and placed them on the floor at the end of the bed, the room was full. Rich was very grateful to have a place to lay his head, but he was inwardly dismayed at how very cramped everything was. He and Cally had a king-sized bed in their master bedroom in Choctaw. Moreover, in their Choctaw home, Rich and Cally didn't even share a bathroom. Rich used the master bath. Cally used the bathroom in the guest room. Now the two of them were going to be sharing a toilet and shower with someone they didn't know.

Rich was ashamed even to think of such matters when so many people throughout the world were grateful for a public hose to bathe with and had no alternative to squat latrines over open trenches.

Once Rich and Cally had deposited their few belongings in the guest room, they were shown to the tiny dining table jammed into a corner between the kitchen and the living room where Althea brought out steaming plates of stewed chicken and turnip greens. Rich protested that Althea shouldn't have prepared food for them, but she said such a notion was too silly to answer. As they ate, the four of them engaged in a combination of small talk and speculation about what the future might hold. Rich wanted to know what they were going to do when Keisha came home, and Althea said that both of the living room sofas were hide-a-beds. Cally said it seemed perfectly horrible for Keisha to come home for vacation and have to sleep in the living room, but Althea laughed and said that Keisha had so many friends in town that she didn't spend much time sleeping anyway.

Though Rich was humiliated by the realization, some part of his dismay over the cramped accommodations the Feasters had to offer must have crowded out onto his face, because as the meal was ending, Althea said, "Robert and I talked about this while y'all were getting your stuff out of the car. I can't believe that we didn't think of it earlier, and I'm sorry we couldn't get it ready for tonight. But in the next couple of days, we're going to move the two of you into our bedroom. We've got a king-sized bed in there that I know would better fit Rich's long legs. And you could have your own bathroom in there, which would give you more privacy, which, Lord knows, I'm sure you have to be craving."

"Absolutely not," Cally said.

"We wouldn't think of putting you out of your own bedroom," Rich said.

Althea said, "All we need to do is get our toiletries moved down to the other bedroom and go through our closets for those things we need on a daily basis. I am really embarrassed that we didn't have this done by the time y'all got here."

"I won't hear of it," Cally said. "*You're* embarrassed? You're like an angel. I'm the one who's embarrassed. Rich and me. Calling you on the phone like this out of the blue and . . ." Abruptly, from the strain and dislocation, Cally began to cry, biting her lip, trying to control herself, finally covering her face with her hands. Rich sat frozen over his dinner plate, but Althea jumped up and came around the table to put her arms around Cally, pulling Cally's sobbing face against her bosom.

Cally had never felt more humiliated. Here she was a Harvard Ph.D., a full professor of classics and a department chair reduced to blubbering in front of people she didn't know. What was wrong with her? Why couldn't she control herself? As she began to recover just a bit, she patted Althea on the back. "Thank you," she said. "Thank you for your incredible kindness." Cally got to her feet and mopped at her cheeks with the back of her wrists. "Let me just go put some water on my face," she said, and walked away toward the bathroom.

"I'm so sorry," Rich said when she had gone. "The stress, I guess, is just greater than . . ."

"Don't be sorry," Robert said. "We've got a town full of people from Choctaw in the same condition. I can't imagine. All of y'all, cut off from your homes and everything. It's the job of us lucky ones to help you where we can. It's our privilege."

Rich swallowed hard and felt angry at himself. He too felt on the verge of tears, though he managed to steel them back. This was his fault somehow. If he hadn't let himself get enticed by the coaching job at Urban, if he hadn't let himself be seduced by Francis Saurian a second time and then Elia Lipscom too, he wouldn't be in this situation. He would be a coach and English teacher at Choctaw High. He'd still be evacuated from his home and job. But he wouldn't have all this responsibility on his shoulders. His and Cally's house would still be sitting in flood waters, but they could have stayed in Richmond. They could have found housing near Matt and Maria and set up a temporary base in Virginia until matters in Choctaw became more clarified.

But that wasn't the situation. Rich couldn't just look out for himself. He might only be the interim rector, he might have agreed not even to apply for the job permanently, but for the time being the fact that he was just interim meant nothing. He was the guy in charge, and he had the weight of all his employees and all of his students on his shoulders. Their livelihoods and their futures were hanging in the balance. He had to be in Mayflower. And that meant he had to impose on people who were obviously better, more decent, more deeply generous than he was. What had he been thinking? How did a guy who regarded himself as intelligent and savvy allow himself to get into such a mess?

While Cally was still in the bathroom, Dr. Peter Flanagan returned from his duties at the emergency clinic. Flanagan seemed about twelve to Rich, though he must have been in his early thirties. Dressed in green scrubs, he was rail thin and wore his sandy brown hair in a buzz cut. He was so fair, his skin seemed almost alabaster, and his eyes were a shade of pale blue that was almost white. As Robert was making introductions, Cally came back to the tiny dining room. She shook Dr. Flanagan's hand, and then started moving plates and utensils from the table to the kitchen sink. Althea told her that she didn't have to do that, but Cally kept cleaning up. Althea didn't try to dissuade her again.

Rich asked Dr. Flanagan questions about his practice but received little elaboration. He had an internal medicine practice at a large clinic in Philadelphia. Save to inquire if they had any health problems, prescription refills they needed, for instance, that he could help with, Dr. Flanagan didn't ask questions about Rich and Cally. Althea fixed the doctor a plate of food, and as she brought it out, he thanked her, saying that he was "famished."

As the food was being set before the doctor, Rich said, "I guess Cally and I have run you out of your room. I'm sorry about that."

The doctor didn't look at Rich as he responded, "We're all in this together. All of us just doing what we can." Then with his elbows on the table, he interlaced his fingers, bowed his head and said grace over his food.

Dr. Flanagan ate so quickly, Cally and Althea were still loading the dishwasher when he brought his plate into the kitchen.

"Would you like to join us for a nightcap, doctor?" Althea asked. "I'm sure Rich and Cally will need something to wash away the road."

"No, thank you," the doctor said. "I need to log some patient histories, and I want to be back at the Civic Center before six a.m." He turned to address Rich. "I like to shower before bed, but I can wait until the morning if you and your wife need the bathroom tonight."

"Oh, no," Rich said. "Please go ahead tonight. I haven't even figured out a schedule for tomorrow. Cally and I can wait for the bathroom until after you've finished."

"Please," Cally said.

Althea said to Rich and Cally, "Well, I'm counting on the two of you for that nightcap." She gestured at Rich with her thumb and said to Cally, "I've had one or two with this guy, if he hasn't mentioned it."

Everybody laughed, though why wasn't entirely clear.

"So what'll it be for y'all?" Althea asked. "I know y'all are tired, so I'm not proposing a party or anything."

"Scotch," Rich said.

"Vodka soda?" Cally said.

"Geez," Althea said. "Here I am proposing a nightcap and already I'm realizing what an unsophisticated hostess I am." She bent over and opened a low cabinet between the dishwasher and the refrigerator. "I think I may have some gin in here that one of the guys in my department brought over one time. Robert and I don't drink liquor very often ourselves. Would gin do? What do you mix gin with anyway? I really don't know a blame thing about cocktails."

Cally looked at Rich with heavy eyes. She detested gin. She liked margaritas, which obviously weren't an option, and occasionally had a light vodka soda. She had drunk whiskey with Jerry, but that was unusual. Rich wanted to shoot himself. Why did he ask for a Scotch? Why did he think Althea and Robert Feaster would keep a bottle of Scotch in their house? In berating himself with that question, Rich realized that he hadn't a clue what kind of alcohol most people kept in their houses. Althea and Robert were prosperous enough, certainly solidly middle class, but they didn't have near the income that Rich and Cally brought in together. Scotch was probably a luxury that people in the Feasters' income group seldom indulged in.

"Althea, stop that," Rich said as she pawed through the cabinet. She stood up and put a two-thirds empty bottle of Crème de Menthe on the counter followed by a bottle of Bacardi containing perhaps two fingers of rum.

"I don't see any gin," she said. "What about these? I bought the Crème de Menthe to put over ice cream as a fancy desert at one point." She flicked quotations around the word *fancy* and laughed as she did so. "I guess people just drink it over ice sometimes. Do they?" She picked up the other bottle and looked at it quizzically. "Where this rum came from I can't rightly say."

"No, no," Rich said. "We don't need any liquor. What are you and Robert having?"

"We were just going to have a beer."

"Beer is fine," Cally said, although she almost never drank beer.

"Beer it is," Althea said. "What's your pleasure? I got everything from Miller Lite to Budweiser regular."

"Miller Lite would be excellent," Cally said.

"Me too," Rich said.

Althea opened four bottles of Lite, placed them on a plastic tray with four short, clear glasses, carried the tray into the living room and set it on a black lacquered coffee table vaguely shaped like the top of grand piano. When everyone was seated, Althea handed out the glasses and bottles. She filled hers halfway, the foamy head cresting to the rim, and raised it toward Rich and Cally. "To our guests," she said smiling. "Glad y'all could come be with us."

Neither Rich nor Cally cried. Then. But both were afraid they were about to.

AFTER THEIR BEERS, RICH and Cally excused themselves for the night. It was only about 10:30, but they were exhausted from the drive and the runaway emotions they were battling to control. The bathroom was still humid from Dr. Flanagan's shower when Rich went in to brush his teeth. When he came back to the small guest room, Cally had turned out the light and, facing the wall, had curled herself into a knot in one quarter of the bed. Rich undressed and slipped into bed next to her. He lay on his back, staring at the dark ceiling, waiting for his eyes to adjust. When they did, he rolled onto his left side and let his arm stretch down Cally's body from her shoulder to her thigh. They both normally slept naked, but she was dressed in a T-shirt and running shorts, in case, he concluded instantly, she had to get up in the night. Before he went to sleep, he thought, he'd need to put his own running shorts on the floor next to the bed.

A few seconds after Rich touched her, Cally began to sob, her whole body shaking. Rich curled himself against her, nestling his head in the hair at her neck, which smelled of her shampoo and the dab of fragrance she put behind her ears each morning. She smelled of herself, of his Cally, and his heart swelled with sadness that she was so distraught and with frustration that he didn't know how to help her. Shamefully, as he always did when he lay close to her as he did now, he felt a hint of arousal, a primal, unthinking instinct that he mentally barked out of existence. He knew there was nothing he could do at the moment to console Cally, so he just nuzzled her, lightly kissing her hair and shoulder. He thought of Yossarian in *Catch-22* trying to comfort the dying Snowden, saying over and over, "There, there." His own words, "It'll be OK; it'll be OK," were little more efficacious.

In the long run, Rich was certain that things would be OK. Rich and Cally had insurance on their house and furnishings. All their losses might not be covered, but they were protected against unqualified disaster. They had savings to draw upon. Most important, as long-time members of the state retirement program, they would have comfortable pensions in their old age. The financial safety net under them was wide and strong. He and Cally had talked extensively of this protection on their two long days of driving from Richmond, volleying the details back and forth between them as a constant reminder of their bedrock security. He thought of listing these details again for Cally now but decided against it. She didn't need to be argued out of her distress; she couldn't *be* argued out of her distress. So he understood Yossarian's simple, impotent "There, there," for perhaps the first time. "It's going to be OK, baby," he said. "I promise. It's going to be OK." And accompanied by rubbing his hand in slow circles on her arm, side, hip and leg, he kept saying these words until Cally finally lay still.

For her own part, Cally was deeply ashamed of feeling so helpless. She prided herself on being a self-reliant person. Moreover, she knew the absolute truth of Rich's promise that things were going to be OK. Of course, they were going to be OK. Individually and together, the two of them had suffered disappointments in life, their failed marriages most prominent among them. But other things too. The loss of a game that Rich knew he should have won, a championship he should have won that somehow slipped away. The rejection of an article that Cally still felt should have been published. Heavy things at that moment. But passing, ultimately insignificant things. On the whole, Cally knew that she and Rich were among the luckiest people on the planet. They had professional accomplishment, financial security, their health, and most important, each other. And yet here she was bawling like a baby.

Yes, they didn't know the status of their home and possessions. Yes, their house could be severely, even permanently, damaged. But meanwhile, so many of their fellow citizens of Choctaw were cooking inside the Arrowdome, wallowing in filth at the Choctaw Center, crammed into gyms and public meeting buildings all over the region. There were lives lost in the flood waters. How many? Hundreds? Very possibly many more than that. How could anything happening to her possibly compare to the suffering of so many who had never known her advantages. And yet, her disgust with herself for feeling distress that she regarded as undeserved seemed to be part of what fueled the distress. If she could manage it, the blankness of sleep might provide her the only available if fleeting relief.

When Cally finally lay still, Rich kissed Cally's hair one last time and rolled on his back, one arm flung across his eyes. He did not regard himself an old man, yet his body felt profoundly old. A knee injured playing football in high school ached every night, and both his ankles, but his left one especially, incessantly screamed from the repeated sprains he had suffered throughout his basketball days, which stretched beyond college to adult recreation leagues and scrimmages with his high school players and didn't end until after he turned fifty and only when he finally couldn't move well enough anymore to guard anyone. He was uncomfortable in his upper body as well. Elbows and hands ached, he guessed, from gripping and swinging a tennis racquet. He'd prefer to sleep on his back as he had for all of his youth, but that somehow left him waking with a back so sore he had trouble getting out of bed. But sleeping on his side made his shoulders and neck sore, problems he countered at home by using three pillows under his head and another snugged to his chest to keep his upper shoulder straight. Four pillows. What a puss he was, he thought. And yet he knew he slept better and awoke in less discomfort if he had four pillows. There weren't but two pillows on the bed in the Feasters' guestroom, one for him and one for Cally. He would solve that problem the next day with a trip to Wal-Mart. But for tonight, he would have trouble sleeping, and in the morning he would awaken in more pain than usual.

Rich doubled the one available pillow and propped it under his head, wondering as he twisted his already aching neck if he would be able to rest at all, relieved that Cally had evidently managed finally to sleep. He wished Cally weren't so upset. They had talked exhaustively about how their circumstances ought to be classified as "aggravating" or "inconvenient." "Disastrous" was what was happening to the people who were still trapped in attics or who had already lost loved ones to the flood waters. "Tragedy" was the experience of those too poor to have evacuated for lack of a car or money for gas or a credit card for a hotel room and a meal, people like, God forbid, Lionel Broussard, the cabbie who had driven them to the airport. Yes, of course, what was happening to Rich and Cally was dispiriting, even righteously infuriating. But especially measured against others, they were lucky, really, very lucky. They were safe, and once the crisis passed, assuming their city recovered, they would be much as they had been before. Rich knew that, and he knew that Cally knew it too.

Still, Rich felt much of the distress that Cally was struggling to control. The prospect seemed inconceivable that Choctaw wouldn't recover, but on the other hand, the whole town stood under water. The only people remaining there were finally being forcibly evacuated by the National Guard. No businesses were operating. News reports wondered if the city would be uninhabitable for six months, possibly even longer. The mayor speculated that 10,000 people had drowned. Rich and Cally were employed by a university that was out of business with no reopening date on anybody's schedule. Rich's employees were godonlyknowswhere. His students were rapidly enrolling at other institutions, including the Satanic Alkansea State University. So Cally was right to feel that their lives had taken a brutally bleak turn. Everything they had worked for, their home and their careers, was in a state of suspension. Whether or not they would ever return to the lives they had led before the storm was unknown.

And in the meantime, they were homeless and living in the tiny bedroom of strangers. Wonderful, kind, generous strangers to be sure, but strangers. So Rich understood that Cally felt off balance, as if the floor of reality had just dropped out from under her.

Lying there in a sleepless daze, cramped in a bed smaller than he was used to, unable to cushion his head, his legs aching as always, a little warm in a house where he had no authority to touch the thermostat, reluctant to move for fear of disturbing what for Cally was no doubt fragile sleep, Rich felt himself rush to the precipice of his control. He had never before felt so vulnerable, so helpless, so lost.

His chest heaved, once, then again. His cheeks were wet. In a second he would be sobbing as pitifully as Cally had earlier.

And if he did, he would wake her, and his own collapse would terrify her. He cursed himself as a weakling and a coward and an ungrateful fool. His chest heaved again. Rich flared his nostrils and gripped both lips between his teeth. Not now, he ordered himself. Not now.

29

If Matoonas had not attacked Mendon, and if New York's Governor Edmund Andros had not menaced Connecticut at precisely the same time, Edward Hutchinson might have attacked the Narragansetts in mid-July of 1675. Though Narragansett country lay almost entirely within the royal charter of Rhode Island, Massachusetts and Connecticut unquestionably regarded this valuable expanse of real estate as their payment for letting That Vicious Lying Rat Bastard Josiah Winslow destroy the Wampanoag nation.

The problem for me and my Nipmuck allies was that the Narragansetts were stubbornly clinging to their strategy of neutrality. They were defying their "obligations" under the treaty they sent nonentities to sign. They had welcomed Weetamoo and more than four hundred of her Pocassets to their protection, along with elderly Pokanokets and Sakonnets who also sought refuge with them. They had killed none of our people and exchanged no one for an English bounty. But they had sent not a single warrior to join our fighters in the field.

That Narragansett country was located farthest from the major Puritan plantations, along the Atlantic coast north of Cape Cod on the one hand and dotting the Connecticut River on the other, meant that the Narragansetts had experienced fewer interactions with the English than any other Indian nation in New England. Thus, despite their knowledge of the murders at Wessagusset and Mystic River, both now two generations back, and despite their understanding that the English had recently driven both the Pokanokets and the Pocassets from their homes, the Narragansetts persisted in believing that they could do what the others of us could not: get along with the English.

Our daily runners kept the Narragansetts fully apprised of our victories along the Connecticut River, but despite repeated entreaties, they did not march to our sides. They rooted for us. Of that I have no doubt. They even assisted, just a little, around the edges, mainly with arms and ammunition. But they never deduced that their interests and ours were identical. They weren't complete fools, of course. They understood that the English were untrustworthy and capable of viciousness, but they thought they had a defensive ace in the hole. All the while we were fighting and dying northwest of them, they were erecting a monumental fortress they fiercely believed would protect them until That Vicious Lying Rat Bastard Josiah Winslow's War had played itself out to whatever end. Confident of their diplomatic skills and the protection of their mighty fort they sat the fighting out while the time for their participation was optimal, while the winds of war blew at our back. France made a similar error, did it not, when it took cocky refuge behind its worthless Maginot Line?

Even as we continued to do battle on the upper Connecticut, the English were already starting the disinformation phase of their campaign against the Narragansetts. This was all about collecting paperwork to present to royal authorities back in Merry Olde England so that the atrocities they were about to commit would possess the appearance of contractual validity. Ass covering, it would be called in a more modern vernacular. The kind of thing George W. Bush and his boys Cheney and

Rumsfeld would cram into the mouth of Colin Powell and jam through Congressional legislation to protect themselves from being prosecuted as war criminals.

To this end, in the harvesting time of *Micheeneekesos*, on September 22, Boston sent the Narragansetts a demand, in accordance with the strong-arm treaty of July 15, that the Narragansetts turn over any Pocassets and Pokanokets that might be living among them. Save as potential slaves, the Wampanoags with Weetamoo were of no value to the English. I had all the fighting men with me. She had taken charge of the young, the old and the ill. The Narragansetts tried to deal with this demand, not by complying with it, but by sending sachems Ninigret and Canonchet to parley with the Bostonians.

On October 18, under direct threat against their individual persons, Ninigret and Canonchet signed a new agreement that the Narragansetts would hand over any Wampanoags in their villages by October 28. Had Ninigret really been in charge of anything, he probably would have done it. But Ninigret's southern band of Niantics hardly exercised pivotal power among the Narragansetts. Canonchet, meanwhile, brave and strong though he was, remained the youngest and, at the time, the least influential of all the Narragansetts sachems. His very presence at the October 18 meetings in Boston was a sly insult the English didn't ever get. In short, the October 28 deadline came and went without the Narragansetts handing over any of our people.

When the Narragansetts neglected to deliver any of my people into the hands of the English for the certain enslavement, torment, and death that would have been their fate, the English began to whisper that the Narragansetts were sending warriors to assist me along the Connecticut River (oh, that such had only been true!) and that Canonchet was going to lead the Narragansetts into war. Who was doing this whispering? Why, those preparing the documents on which all the histories of me and mine are based. The United Colonies were planning another major land grab and needed an excuse for doing so. The English had been whispering about Indian attacks since five minutes after they got off the Mayflower. You could always tell when they were about to do something unspeakable to us because they complained we were about to attack them first. An attack was coming all right. But it wasn't going to be an attack *by* the Narragansetts, it was going to be an attack *on* the Narragansetts, and it was going to be led by our old Mephistophelean buddy himself, That Vicious Lying Rat Bastard Josiah Winslow.

In *Arrkesos*, on November 12, the United Colonies voted to raise another army of 1,000 men, 527 from Massachusetts, 325 from Connecticut and 158 from Plymouth. The purpose of this army, those ever so reliable documents prepared for the prying eyes of the King state unequivocally, was to enforce the terms of the treaty of July 15. Yes, just like George W. invaded Iraq to punish Saddam Hussein for those weapons of mass destruction he didn't have. Powerful men do what they want and sell you whatever reason you're foolish enough to buy.

Because the land the United Colonies were planning to "liberate" from the Narragansetts was to be divided between Massachusetts and Connecticut, even though most of it lay in Rhode Island, Plymouth's head Lying Rat Bastard was placed in charge so neither Boston nor Hartford would get the advantage in the planned on-site divvying. Not that anyone needed to assign him a referee's role to get That Vicious Lying Rat Bastard Josiah Winslow to lead a force to dispossess Indians of their property.

And what might be the incentive of the individual Englishman in arms, you ask. With their brothers dying out along the Connecticut River, why might a farmer from Connecticut, a blacksmith from Plymouth and a sailor from Boston shoulder muskets to shoot at peaceful Indians in Rhode Island? Filthy lucre, baby. The lure of riches. The English leadership understood the name of the game. Greed. And they were direct about it. Everyone who served in this campaign would get a piece of Narragansett land that could be lived on or sold. An interesting offer for a military action undertaken to assure compliance with a treaty obligation, no? Moreover, the soldiers themselves would be allowed to keep the proceeds from selling into slavery any of the Narragansetts (or Wampanoags) they managed to capture.

Are these guys Pilgrim Fathers or what?

That Vicious Lying Rat Bastard didn't even wait for his Connecticut allies to show up before he started trying to kill people. The Massachusetts and Plymouth regiments marched out of Rehoboth in *Keekesos* on December 9, and already on December 10 Winslow dispatched Captain Isaac Johnson to attack a Narragansett outpost near Providence. Winslow didn't send Johnson out to *talk* to anyone, to *ask* if someone near Providence knew when the sachems farther south would be sending those promised Wampanoags over. Nope, he sent Johnson to attack a people at peace. But the Narragansetts heard him coming and beat it. So Johnson had to content himself with the less sanguinary pleasure of burning up their warm winter *nashweetoos*.

Two days later, as his army approached the upper Pawtuxet River, That Vicious Lying Rat Bastard sent Johnson out to attack the village of Sachem Pomham. Again, the English made no effort to negotiate. They didn't ask anyone about when the Narragansetts would begin complying with the July 15 treaty that required them to surrender Wampanoag hostages. The only question asked that day was which of the *nashweetoos* in Pomham's village should be torched first. Understanding what was going on, Pomham and his townsmen hadn't stayed around for a chit-chat they knew would never take place.

On December 13, That Vicious Lying Rat Bastard marched his men into Wickford, the tiny trading town about halfway down the western coast of Narragansett Bay. Massachusetts and Plymouth had agreed to wait at this location for the Connecticut regiments who were to come around from New

London by boat. Not content to just sit around when there were nearby Indians to torment, That Vicious Lying Rat Bastard sent Johnson and Sam Moseley out on December 14 to attack the village of "Old Queen" Sachem Quaiapen. Once again they found no one home; once again they burned the village to the ground.

The Narragansetts responded to these repeated acts of arson on December 15 by burning Bull's Garrison, a trading post nine miles south of Wickford. This bit of preemptive offense was part of their larger strategy of defense. Since Bull's Garrison was the point of closest English habitation to the place where the Narragansetts had hidden themselves, their strategy was to deny the English a nearby place from which to attack them. That accomplished, the Narragansetts retreated to their swamp fortress, what they thought was their impregnable sanctuary.

Major Robert Treat and his Connecticut force of over three hundred, supplemented by one hundred fifty rat fucking Mohegans, arrived on December 17. And on December 18 the whole force of over 1,000 set off from Wickford. A bitter little Narragansett Praying shithead Judas named Peter had showed up to betray his people and show the English where his brothers and sisters were hiding. On the whole, human beings are a pretty despicable species.

The day was perilously cold, and That Vicious Lying Rat Bastard proved what an evil idiot he was just by ordering the attack to commence, for he marched his troops off without their having been resupplied. The only food the English soldiers possessed was whatever they had in their knapsacks. That night, they slept on the bare ground amid the ashes at Bull's Garrison. The next morning they rose before dawn to march toward their date with enduring infamy. Though that's not the way the story would be told for the next three hundred years.

The Narragansetts hoped the English would not come at all. And the Narragansetts greatly hoped that if the English did come, they would turn away once they saw what the

Narragansetts had waiting for them. On a five-acre island in the middle of the Great Swamp that lies north of Worden Pond and west of the Chippuxet River, the Narragansetts erected an immense wooden fortress inside of which huddled five hundred warm *nashweetoos* housing more than 3,000 people. The English had never before encountered anything like this structure. Its outer palisades were anchored in the ground and rose to sixteen feet. Its base was reinforced with felled tree trunks and piled brush twelve feet thick, making it practically impossible to gain a position from which the walls could be scaled. Moreover, jutting blockhouses atop the walls allowed the fort's defenders to fire down on any enemy that approached. Had the weather not been so cold that the swamp had frozen, the English would have been cut to ribbons had they dared try to slog through the muck toward the fort.

This massive structure had two entrances. One required climbing atop a gigantic tree trunk that functioned like a drawbridge across a moat. Anyone trying to enter the fort across the tree trunk was frightfully exposed, and the prospect of making such an attempt constituted a suicide dance. Getting into the fort this way seemed so impossible that the English didn't even try. On the opposite side of the fort stood a slightly less imposing entrance, although one that was itself difficult enough. Here, in front of an unpalisaded aperture, the Narragansetts had laid a horizontal series of tree trunks four feet high. The opening was wide enough for several people to enter at one time, but only after scrambling atop the wooden barrier the English labeled "the death trees." The opening was further protected by one blockhouse just inside the fort with point blank firing range at anyone entering and two flanking blockhouses outside the fort from which the Narragansetts could lay down a withering crossfire. This is where That Vicious Lying Rat Bastard decided the fort should be attacked, a decision his men appreciated all the way to their graves. And as if things were not bad enough once the battle started, the jittery English at the rear kept shooting the guys in front of them as they tried to blaze their way inside.

We indigenous Americans wouldn't have any luck if it weren't for bad luck. The Narragansetts had planned for every contingency in this battle with the English save for one, but that one was determinative. They hadn't planned for the English to show up in such large numbers. They had packed in tons of food stuff. Every nashweetoo was stocked with corn, vegetables, berries, meat and dried fish. They could have stayed in their refuge for months. But when the English showed up with more than twice the force the Narragansetts had expected, they found that they didn't have enough gun powder to kill them all. And they did kill plenty; perhaps a hundred were slain on the spot or subsequently died of their wounds. Another two hundred survived wounds, some serious enough that the sufferer was maimed for life. But in the end, Winslow sent enough English into the fort that he was regarded by Robert E. Lee as a model for how to slaughter his own men, and he subsequently became the hero of those pigheaded British generals who kept whistling their entrenched men over the top in World War I. Of course, being the kind of man he was, That Vicious Lying Rat Bastard abused the men he cared about least. Only by sending wave after wave of English into the breach, could Winslow's forces, through the superiority of numbers, finally prevail. So who did he order to lead the charge? The men of Plymouth? The men of his nearest neighbors in Massachusetts? Of course not. The men who soaked up Narragansett lead with their bodies came extensively from Connecticut.

But in the end, the Narragansetts did the majority of the dying. When the English forces had shed enough blood trying to take a fort that would require far more blood to be taken, That Vicious Lying Rat Bastard Josiah Winslow, just as his predecessors had done at Mystic River, ordered the fortress torched and positioned his men to musket down those who tried to escape the inferno. Canonchet and Weetamoo and her husband Quinnapin led some of their people on a successful break into the woods, a miracle of daring and fortitude for those who survived it. But hundreds of women, children and aged people, too little or old or enfeebled to run, expired in the furnace that Josiah Winslow made of their homes.

30

On Sunday, September 5, 2004, while the Feasters went to church, Rich and Cally went to a Wal-Mart that was so crowded they had to park on the street a couple of blocks away. They were joining scores of Choctaws, most of them black, shopping for reasons identical to their own. Just like Rich and Cally, untold numbers of Choctaws had fled the hurricane with clothing for only a few days. They were now living in motel rooms or, also like Rich and Cally, in the guest rooms of family, friends or strangers. They needed more, and more variety of, things to wear. And they needed other supplies as well. Rich and Cally were there to buy underwear, socks, knit shirts, pullover tops, sandals, shorts and jeans, four pillows, and a computer printer. Purchasing dressier clothing would have to wait until another time and another location.

The check-out lines stretched back into and clogged the merchandise aisles. After Rich and Cally finished selecting their purchases, they stood in a queue that inched forward so slowly they resigned themselves to at least an hour of waiting to check out. Their wait was aggravated by two Mayflower women immediately behind them in line who were loudly vocalizing their annoyance at the store's crowded condition.

"This has been going on all week," the taller of the two women said to her companion. "I tried to come in here on Wednesday, and it was just as bad." The speaker was fiftish and dressed in a gray suit, panty hose and patent leather high heels. Her steel gray hair was shoulder length but sprayed stiff. Her friend was wearing a knee-length dress with puffy sleeves and white lace at the collar. The second woman's hair was dyed ink black and also sprayed rigid. Rich presumed they were trying to shop either before or after church.

"I don't like this," the gray-haired one said.

"I don't like it either," the brunette responded. "It's never like this."

"And on a Sunday morning," the first woman said.

"I don't understand why something can't be done," Dark Hair said.

"We didn't ask for this. This isn't our problem."

"Who are these people?"

"They aren't from here; that's for sure."

"Look at them. Look at all the trash they're buying."

"Mayflower does not have anyone like these people."

"Excuse me," Rich said. "I couldn't help but overhear your conversation."

The two women glanced at each other. Gray Hair looked at Rich and raised an eyebrow.

"We only overheard because you were talking so loud," Cally said in a helpful tone. "We're just shoppers. We're not eavesdroppers or anything."

Gray Hair snorted and said, "Well!"

"I thought we should alert you," Rich said. "I gather I'm supposed to be ashamed of it, but I more or less can't help it. I, my wife and I, we're some of *these* people."

"Yes, we're homeless," Cally said. "We're practically vagrants. We've moved in with people we don't know. We don't know either of you; maybe you have more room than the people we're staying with. And look," she said, pointing at their shopping cart, "we have our own pillows and pillow cases. So if we were sleeping in your guest room, our nasty heads wouldn't get your linens all fouled with *these*-people grease."

"I think we should leave," Dark Hair said to her friend.

"Great idea," Rich said, making a sweeping gesture with his arm. "That'll leave more products for the two of us and *these* people."

"I'm going to report this to the manager," Gray Hair said.

"Check him out first, though," Rich said. "You know how Wal-Mart is. They hire a lot of *these* people."

"Never in my life," Gray Hair said as the two women stalked away, leaving their cart where it stood in line behind Rich and Cally.

"Wait," Cally called after them. "We didn't get your address."

RICH AND CALLY LEFT the Feasters' early the next morning. They entered a nearby Starbucks shortly after 6 a.m. where they commandeered a table near an electrical wall outlet and Cally set up her laptop. For an hour, they drank coffee, shared a bagel and read the newspaper. Just after 7:30, Rich left Cally to work in her makeshift coffee-shop office and drove over to the Board of Trustees office, located in a square three-story building across the street from the ASU campus. He arrived at 8:00 as a uniformed security guard was unlocking the front door. Rich was dressed in a black, short-sleeved knit shirt, a pair of blue jeans, running shoes and his blue blazer.

Elia Lipscom arrived at 8:30 wearing a crisp shirt of gleaming white with a scripted EL monogrammed over the breast and on each cuff, a striped Monster tie of brown and green, and a dark gray suit. Lipscom was short, 5'7", and stocky, but the tailored cut of his suit made him look slender. His over-sized head of swept-back graying hair and black-rimmed glasses made him look, Rich suddenly thought, not like Harrison Ford as some people liked to say, but like George Reeves, the television actor who played Clark Kent and committed suicide after his series was cancelled. Lipscom carried himself with the bluff swagger of a comic book hero, but Rich suffered no delusions that he was Superman.

Lipscom greeted Rich with a smile. "Good to see you, Coach. 'Bout time you got here."

"Soon as I could, Elia," Rich said. "Had to buy a car, you'll recall. Two pretty hard days' drive."

Lipscom pumped Rich's hand. "Next time you won't go away so far. Am I right?"

"If there's a next time," Rich said, "it won't matter where I go."

"Well, that's certainly oracular. Like that about you old coaches. Always with the non-prediction prediction. Anyway, come have a seat, and I'll bring you up to speed. Glad to see you came casual today. That'll be appropriate for what we've got lined up."

"I didn't really come casual, Elia," Rich said as he took a chair across from the viceroy's desk. "These are all the clothes I've got."

"Flood didn't wash out your credit card, did it?" Lipscom laughed.

Rich didn't share the mirth. "Had more important things to do than shopping for a new wardrobe," Rich said. "Put a high priority on getting here."

Lipscom clapped Rich on the shoulder as he made his way around his desk. "There'll be time to shop in the days to come. I'll be happy to give you an introduction to my tailor who can fix you up in no time." He took off his suit jacket, hung it on a hanger, slipped it into a little blended-in closet that Rich had never noticed before and sat down in his high-back, black leather chair, clasping his hands behind his head. "But as I said, if anything you're overdressed for today, about which, more in a bit. First, what you got for me?"

"I'm going to need your help on a whole host of fronts."

"What am I here for?" Lipscom said. "Hit me with your list."

"First, I'm going to need a place to work. Me, Cecilia, and whoever else on my team I can locate and get in here for however long we're going to have to stay."

The viceroy opened a desk drawer and brought out a white lined tablet. From a holder, he selected a pen and wrote on the pad. "Gotcha," he said. "Coach needs an office. Perfectly reasonable. Consider me on it."

"I'm going to need more than one office, Elia. I can't run a university in isolation."

Lipscom looked up at him. "Well, you're pretty isolated from it, if you know what I mean. 'Bout one hundred fifty miles."

Rich did not smile.

"OK, I gotcha," Lipscom said. "Office space. Whatever. Office suite, let's say. What's next?"

"I am going to need a bank of computers, as many as you can get us. I want to get the word out to whichever of our employees are evacuated here to Mayflower or in areas nearby that they need to get here on a daily basis. I need a place for them to work and computers for them to work on. I need to put them onto those computers to communicate with our students and with those of our employees who aren't anywhere around here. We need to locate everybody, and we need to get the word out that we may be down, but we're a long way from finished. We need to make sure they hang in there."

Lipscom made three short whistling sounds through his teeth. "Computers," he said, writing on his pad. "Ten?"

"Ten?" Rich echoed. "A hundred."

Lipscom looked up at him, drew his chin into his neck and raised his eyebrows.

"A hundred, ultimately," Rich said. "Even more. But by tomorrow or the next day I need a room with at least twenty. Thirty would be better, forty better yet. And I need a laptop for everybody on my administrative team."

"Still sounds more like fifty than a hundred."

Fredrick Barton

Rich shook his head, but Lipscom wasn't looking at him. "Get me fifty, and I'll come back to you when I've got people here and no computer to work on."

"How you gonna pay for this?" Lipscom asked. "I don't exactly have a budget with a line that reads, 'fifty computers for Urban University.'"

"Surely this state is insured," Rich said. "If I can find Hue, she'll know our coverage exactly." Hue Nguyen was Urban's Chief Financial Officer. "I presume Ronnie Shade does too."

Lipscom shrugged. "Not clear what all the state has covered. But you wait around for the state Office of Risk Management to approve your computers, and you'll start using them just about the time you're ready to retire."

"There's always FEMA," Rich said.

Lipscom barked a laugh out loud. "FEMA?" he laughed again. "FEMA couldn't get starving people bussed out of your bathtub. I wouldn't be relying on FEMA for anything."

"I suppose you're right," Rich admitted. "Look, fix me up somehow to get the computers brought in, and I'll figure out a way to cover it. I've got a huge utility budget. And right now we're not using much in the way of utilities."

"OK," Lipscom said. "Office space, computers. What else?"

"Housing."

"Housing for who?"

For *whom*, Rich thought. When did the mastery of basic grammar cease to be expected of people in higher education, of people who earned Ph.D.s and therefore presumably wrote grammatically correct dissertations? Were their dissertations grammatically correct?

"For my people," Rich said. "To start with, for my administrators. I've talked to those I've been able to locate. Some are nearby. A couple even have houses up here, so they're all right. Ben Turner's got his in-laws' place."

Turner had indeed booked a room at the Waldorf to ride out the storm, and, as a result, he was briefly stranded when the city flooded. Elsewhere in the city, less fortunate people found themselves trapped in the Arrowdome and the Choctaw Center while neither FEMA nor Alkansea Governor Harlan Lebear was able to mobilize a relief plan for nearly four, miserable, deadly days. But sensitive about its five-star image, the Waldorf Corporation had gotten buses to the front door of its hotel to evacuate guest residents within twenty-four hours, a feat Turner and others cited as an example of how free enterprise trumped government bureaucracy every time.

"Saw Ben last Thursday right after he got to Mayflower," Lipscom said, cocking his head and looking pointedly at Rich. "*He* stayed in the state and was on the job when you were godknowswhere."

"His wife's family is here," Rich said.

"Yeah, well, maybe you ought to have your wife's family move here," Lipscom said, grinning to show his canines.

"I'll tell them you think so," Rich said.

"Turner invited me and Margaret out to a nice lunch. I hadn't known him very well. I think he's a pretty impressive guy, credit to you as one of your deans."

"He is," Rich said. "Although I don't deserve the credit since I didn't appoint him. He didn't mention that he'd stopped over here, but I'm glad he did. He's one of my people I'm not going to have to worry about. His wife's parents have taken off to their place in Acapulco so Ben and their daughter can have their place for the duration of this mess. But Ben's situation is the exception. A lot of my folks are living in horrible circumstances. OK, horrible is too strong. They have a roof over their heads. And they're still getting paid, so they won't starve. But my vice rector for research is sleeping on the couch of some people he's met because they're the cousins of a friend of his daughter's. Frank Schwehn. Good man."

"I know Frank," Lipscom said.

"Cecilia, as you know, is living in a dorm right now. She's seventy-five years old, and she's having to go down the hall to shower."

"That's a sight I'd pay not to see," Lipscom said.

Rich felt a surge of temper he had to tamp down. This man was his boss. In so many ways, this crude, ridiculous, old-boy-connected man held the fate of Rich's university in his hands, and right now Rich wanted to grab him around the neck and pound his head into mush.

"I know you like the old biddy," Lipscom said. "But she's a pushy old broad. Gets my dander up."

"She shouldn't have to live in a dorm."

"OK, she shouldn't, but what am I going to do about it," Lipscom said. "I'd buy her a motel room out of my own pocket. Only there aren't any motel rooms available. As you found out. Where are you staying, by the way?"

Rich told him, and Lipscom pursed his lips and whistled.

"That *is* pretty grim," the viceroy said. "I'll ask around to see what I can find for you. And your provost. OK?"

"I was thinking you might give us Monster House."

"Give you Monster House? Are you crazy?"

Rich shrugged. "Evidently," he said. "But I was still hoping you might give us Monster House. I've stayed there repeatedly when I've been up here for Trustees meetings. It could provide each of my people a comfortable room. They could eat three meals a day there. And we could use the meeting space. It's new, clean, well appointed."

"It's also full."

"Yes, but whom is it full with? Business sorts who could work by phone and fax? Or Choctaw evacuees? In fact, do you have any evacuees in there at all?"

"You understand that Monster House doesn't report to me?" Lipscom said. "It's an ASU operation. And that means it reports to Stephen Hopkins."

"Yes, but Stephen Hopkins reports to you. You're the Viceroy for Higher Education."

"Coach, Coach, Coach," Lipscom said, sighing. "I can see how you won all those championships. You're one tenacious sombitch.

But you gotta understand. I can't just go order Stephen Hopkins to start throwing people out of Monster House so you can move in. The governor might chew me a new one if I did that."

"I wouldn't want you to throw anyone out. But, number one, I've got a feeling that the place isn't even full. And number two, I've got a stronger feeling that it's not going to stay full if it is full. All I'm asking is that you have Stephen give me and my people priority."

"You understand you'd have to pay," Lipscom said. "If I could pull this off for some of you, that is, whoever stays in Monster House has to pay. The operation is an ASU profit center."

Rich wanted to say, *And I wouldn't want something like a massive natural disaster to interfere with one of ASU's profit centers.* But he didn't, discretion being a central part of valor.

Instead, Rich said, "I speak for all the members of the Urban administrative team, Elia, when I say that we'd appreciate any influence on this matter you could exercise on our behalf."

"I'll see what I can do," Lipscom said. "I'll try to get to Hopkins tomorrow. Jesus. Anything *else*?"

"I think I've asked for plenty for the moment."

"Thank goodness. I thought you were going to ask for my first born next."

"Only if your first born is living at Monster House."

"Ha ha ha," Lipscom said. "OK. Now to my agenda. I presume you want to go down to Choctaw with us this afternoon."

"You can get there?"

"*I* can get there? I'm the fucking Viceroy for Higher Education. I can go where I goddamn want."

"Sure, I'll go. What's the deal? Can I bring Cally? Or can we follow you?"

"What?" Lipscom said. "Who's Cally? Your wife?"

"Yes."

"We're not going down there for a social event, Coach. The goddamn city is under water. And you can't follow us unless you've got your own fucking helicopter. National Guard has agreed to chopper me and some staff down to check on the condition of things at Urban and the community colleges. Now that you're here, I figure you ought to go along."

"I'm in," Rich said.

"Then be back here at 1 p.m. I'll have Vance drive us over to the Guard base." Vance was Lipscom's driver. *Viceroys get drivers, which even a 370-year-old Indian can grasp is a pretty swell perk.* "We lift off at 1:30. So don't be late."

WHEN RICH SHOWED UP at the Trustees Building, Lipscom, Margaret Lockhart and Ronnie Shade were all waiting for him in the parking lot. The day was warm, but in preparation for their helicopter flight, they were all wearing sunglasses and brown and green ASU Monster windbreakers. Rich thought they looked like secret service operatives from a banana republic. He kept this opinion to himself.

The flight to Choctaw took an hour and fifteen minutes. They flew over Lake De Soto and crossed over the Urban campus, which stretched along the southern shore of the lake in the northernmost part of the city. The pilot kept his altitude, but everyone could see that the southern third of the campus was under water. Remarkably, the northern two-thirds was dry. The chopper banked sharply left and flew over to the east where Choctaw Community College spread along the banks of the Desoto River. The school that people in Choctaw called "CCC-1" or "3C1" sat completely inundated, the water up to the middle of the first floor windows. Turning south again, the helicopter flew over the levee breach on the De Soto River just blocks from Carver Community College (CCC-2 or 3C2), the city's historically black public institution. The water in the river and the water in the city stood at the same level, here up to the eaves of two-story buildings. As the pilot turned west Rich could see two yawning breaches on the Saybrook Canal.

To complete the circle, the helicopter turned back north along the banks of the Alkansea. Here the levees had held. The areas right along the river were dry for perhaps a dozen blocks eastward before the city began to fall away into its historically swampy bowl. As the helicopter flew over Rich's neighborhood, he was distressed to see that the whole area was covered with water. As the Alkansea bent to the northwest, the pilot banked right and took the helicopter back to Lake De Soto. The lake levees had also held but the land behind them was low, and the breaches had filled it up to within blocks of the lake. The pilot turned the chopper back over the Urban campus and its central quad which was dry.

Here they hovered at about sixty feet, and Rich was able to look down on the most baffling sight. The quad was lined with majestic oak trees running in parallel lines from north to south down to the columns of the Urban Union where Rich had interacted with his students on the last night before the evacuation. In between the oaks was an expanse of grass, peopled when school was in session with students spinning Frisbees or tossing footballs. But now that grass was cluttered with objects that shouldn't have been there: hundreds of chairs, vaguely arranged in rows, as if someone had recently given a speech before an outdoor audience, and flanking the chairs in no formation whatsoever, were at least a hundred red plastic grocery carts.

Rich pointed to the floor of the helicopter and yelled at Elia, "Let's take her down."

Lipscom grimaced and cupped a hand behind his ear.

"Get the pilot to set it down," Rich shouted. "Let's take a look at what's going on down there. Assess the damage."

Lipscom shook his head and made a crossing motion with his arms. "No can do," he yelled. "Pilot's got orders."

After hovering over the quad for a few minutes, the pilot climbed and flew around the perimeter of the campus, and Rich realized for the first time how much elevation change there was on an expanse of campus land he had always regarded as basically flat. Flying at perhaps one hundred feet, Rich could see that the buildings on the southern end of campus were in bad shape. They would need a great deal of repair before they were usable again. Rich spotted bad roof damage on the Union and Ungulate Arena. That was worrisome. And as they came along the campus' western edge, he spotted any number of windows that had been blown out. A great deal of blowing water damage had no doubt followed.

Since normal conversation was almost impossible in the helicopter, Rich had to wait until the administrators had returned to Mayflower to ask why they hadn't been allowed to land on the Urban campus. "Danger from hostiles," the pilot said.

"Should have told you that Urban was used as a massing location," Lipscom said.

"Meaning?" Rich asked.

"Where our choppers took all the folks they plucked off rooftops?" the pilot said behind his opaque shades. He waited a second, tugging on the bill of his green cap as if Rich was supposed to say something. "The Urban campus. North part anyway. Never did flood. Easy to set down. Got them out of their attics."

"But why didn't you take them down to the Arrowdome or Choctaw Center?"

"Urban was closer. Flooding was deepest just south of there. People on their roofs. Already lots of floaters." *Floaters*, Rich thought. Jesus. Human drowning victims. Now *floaters*.

"How many did you drop off on our campus?" Rich asked.

"Round three thousand."

"Three thousand people!" Rich said.

"Give or take," the pilot said.

"Why didn't you take them out beyond the levees to the Interstate? The Interstate was dry all the way to Mayflower."

"Further," the pilot said.

"It's not that much farther," Rich said.

"Little further," the pilot said. "And the campus afforded them some shelter rather than just parking them under an overpass."

"But the campus was locked down," Rich said.

"Told 'em to just go ahead and bust in."

"You told them to break into our buildings? Three thousand people?"

"Not me personally. But that's the directive we followed."

"Jesus," Rich said, imagining the shattered glass in the hallways of all his buildings.

"Wouldn't a been right to ask these folks, most of 'em soaked to the skin, to just lie out on the grass. Least they had a roof over their heads till we could move 'em out."

"You had to leave them overnight?" Rich asked.

"Had to leave the first of 'em five days. Most of 'em four, three minimum."

"For Christ's sake," Rich said. "How hard was it to bring in buses and drive people out of our godforsaken city?"

"Not my detail, sir. I'm a chopper pilot just like the other men that worked the roofs. Have to ask somebody higher up than me about the buses."

"I'm surprised you didn't have people starve to death," Rich said.

"Well, I think they pretty much helped themselves to whatever y'all had in your cafeteria refrigerators."

"Thank goodness," Rich said. "I hadn't thought of that. That's good."

"Bunch of 'em walked the levee over a ways to the Piggly Wiggly that didn't flood and brought back whatever they could carry."

"And that explains the grocery carts."

"Yep."

"Why all the lined up chairs?"

"They weren't too happy about getting left for five days," the pilot said, "and they got kind of unruly. Had to put three squads on the ground on Saturday with M-16s to get their attention. Made 'em carry chairs out and sit their asses down if they wanted us to transport 'em out. Most of 'em finally decided to behave themselves. But some of them were so angry they cursed us and ran back in the buildings. Lucky some of our guys didn't put a plink or two in their butts."

"So those were the hostiles you were talking about."

"Yes, sir."

"And they're still in my buildings?"

"Naw. I don't rightly suspect they are. I suspect they came to their senses, hauled out chairs and lined up like they were supposed to. Can't be sure though."

"So I have all my chairs on the quad, and I may have dead bodies fouling my buildings."

"Like I said, I suspect they came out. But if you haven't thought of it, your buildings are pretty foul without any dead bodies."

"Why is that?" Rich asked.

"Three thousand people needing to tend to their bodily functions when there isn't any running water. Some of the guys went into the buildings at first on Saturday to roust people out, but they didn't stay very long. Everything smelled like a zoo. Only not that good."

ON THE WAY TO the Feasters' that night, Rich stopped at a liquor store and bought two fifths of Black and White Scotch, a bottle of vodka for Cally, a small ice chest and a shrink-wrapped package with two tumblers in it. Then he stopped at a convenience store to fill the chest with crushed ice. All of this he carried into the Feasters' guest room. After the dinner that Althea prepared for them, desperately wishing to intrude as little as possible, Rich and Cally turned down an invitation to watch television with their hosts and retreated to their room. Rich fixed Cally a light vodka soda, which she sipped as he filled her in on the details of his helicopter trip and what he'd learned from the pilot. She did not finish her drink. Rich continued to splash Scotch into his glass even after Cally had climbed under the covers and turned off her light.

Cally was asleep when Rich finally crawled into bed next to her. He didn't feel drunk. And he didn't feel sleepy. He lay on his back staring into the dark for a long time. He didn't know for how long. An hour perhaps. Maybe longer. He should have been planning his next step, he thought. But he couldn't seem to focus. He mentally walked the halls of his university, kicking glass into corners, avoiding pools of urine, side-stepping piles of human excrement. When he finally closed his eyes his chest heaved. He tried to steady himself, but then his chest heaved again. He was so afraid that his shaking would wake Cally that he got out of bed and lay on the floor with his new pillows his only comfort. His chest heaved again, and he let the shaking overtake him, mindful only not to utter a sound.

WHEN RICH ARRIVED AT the Trustees Building on Tuesday morning, he was met there by Cecilia as the two had planned the evening before. They were shown to a small third-floor office with a telephone and a computer. A second desk had been installed against the wall where visitors would normally sit. From this space Rich and Cecilia were to attend to the business of Urban University, a place that now existed only as an idea in the heads and hearts of those who had previously worked and studied there. Rich always traveled with his laptop, so he let Cecilia, who hadn't carried hers along with her bedroll, sit at the larger desk with the computer and arranged himself at the desk facing the wall. They moved the phone between them so that they could both use it. Attacking the problems that lay before them seemed like trying to dig up a mountain with a teaspoon and transport it elsewhere in a matchbox.

In the late morning, Urban Director of Public Information Sally Reasoner arrived at Rich's office. Working through a church network she had managed to find housing in the home of a complete stranger. Sally was fast talking, sometimes strong willed, short and chunky. She was also beautiful: she had the idea that got them started.

Sally said to Rich, "I'm going to get you on every radio and TV station in this town and any town we can get to that will have us. We will do interviews with every reporter who has a microphone or a notebook."

In the early afternoon, Urban's Director of University Computing, Jose Najera, arrived. Tall, thin and russet-skinned, Jose resembled the actor Jimmy Smits. Rich thought Jose was a technological genius. On Rich's watch in the Urban administration, he'd never encountered a communications problem that Jose couldn't resolve. The problem at the moment was that Urban lacked all electronic communications. Senior administrators had been requested to establish alternative email addresses, and most had. Some had evacuated without laptops, however. Some had landed in the homes of friends and family without computers. A week after the storm, and Rich still had not been able to exchange even cursory information with all his deans and vice rectors. Jose, his wife and children had evacuated to Nuevo Laredo where they had family. Now Jose had driven back alone. He was sleeping on a cot in the garage of an acquaintance of his wife's brother. His host was an electrician and father of five, his children filling all his small house's bedrooms. He made available to Jose the best that he had, a dry place to sleep, access to a bathroom in the house and a section of shelf in the fridge.

"I need you to give me some exhausting assignments," Jose told Rich. "The people I am staying with are wonderful. But there's not a lot to go home to."

"I want you to rebuild our electronic infrastructure," Rich told him. "And I want you to have at least a rudimentary website in two days and some kind of Urban University email address I can start announcing tomorrow."

"That should meet the exhausting requirements," Jose said. "What will you need?"

"We're starting completely from scratch?"

"You tell me."

"Any chance of getting our servers off campus?"

"None whatsoever," Rich said. "Your building is standing in about five feet of water. The north end of campus is dry, but it's literally an island. Only ways to get there would be by sea or air. I did a helicopter flyover with the National Guard yesterday, and they wouldn't even set down on campus for fear of what they called hostiles."

"What about our back-up tapes downtown? On the fifth floor of Choctaw Bank."

"Might be able to get them at some point," Rich said. "But how soon is anybody's guess. The city is one-way only at this point. Anybody who's there is being moved out. Nobody but the Guard is being let in. Can you do what we need from scratch?"

"Looks like I'm going to have to."

"So, from scratch, what'll you need?"

"Six servers to start. More later. And people."

"What people?" Rich asked.

"My people. I've got some friends here on the ASU campus who can probably help me in their spare time. So I can probably get you something that will pop up if someone types in www. uu.edu, something that you can use to post bulletins. But if you want anything beyond a rudimentary email system, I need to get my guys in here."

"Get me the bulletin board," Rich said. "That's a good start. You got any place for your people to stay?"

"I'm sleeping on a cot in a garage," Jose said.

"Of course. Forgive me. I'm an idiot."

"You're not an idiot, boss. None of us has any experience at this."

"I'll see what I can do to find some place for your guys to bunk."

Jose handed Rich one of his business cards. On the back he had written the office phone number of his ASU computing contact. "I'll hang out here," Jose said. "Till our cell phones finally start working again, this will be the best place to reach me."

Rich took out his billfold, slid Jose's card into it, slipped out his American Express card, and extended it to Jose. "Use this for the servers and whatever else you need."

"That's your personal credit card, boss."

"So?"

"Not right for you to spend your own money."

"Bring me the receipt. Hue will reimburse me."

Jose shook his head. "Let me see what my friends can help me with. I'll come back when I have no choice but to buy something."

"Can I run interference for you?" Rich asked. "Talk to the viceroy or Rector Hopkins about assigning some of the ASU staff to you?"

"I wouldn't," Jose responded.

"No?" Rich wondered. "Why not?"

"If the computer guys here can help me, they will. They won't need to be told. So the only thing that happens different if you ask their bosses is that they get told not to help us."

Jesus, Rich thought, Jose had sized up the situation faster than Rich had.

When Jose left, Rich asked Cecilia to draft something to serve as the stock talking points he'd use when he started doing Sally's radio and television appearances. Then he rode the elevator up to the fifth floor and asked to see Viceroy Lipscom. The secretary asked him to be seated and wondered if he'd like some water or a cup of coffee. The viceroy was on the phone with Rector Hopkins. She didn't expect him to be long, but one never knew.

Rich had finished about half a cup of coffee when the secretary said he could go in. Before he could gulp down the rest, the viceroy opened the door to his office, poked his head out and spotted Rich. His eyes swept up and down Rich's body as Rich stood up, seeming to linger on his jeans and running shoes.

"Come on in, Coach," Viceroy Lipscom said. "Hope you haven't been out here long."

"No problem," Rich said.

"Rather than your just cooling your heels and shooting the breeze with Ethyl," Lipscom said, as they got seated on either side of his desk, "you should just call for an appointment. Save you a trip upstairs for nothing if I'm not available." The viceroy smiled broadly.

"No problem," Rich said. "I needed to stretch my legs anyway. Desk I'm working at down there is kind of shallow."

Lipscom wrinkled his forehead. "I thought we had you in a regular office."

"Well, you do. But there are two of us. Me and Cecilia."

"But there's a regular desk?"

"Yeah, one regular desk. I've got Cecilia there. She doesn't have a lap—"

"This old biddy got naked pictures of you, buddy?" Lipscom asked.

"I'm sorry?" Rich said, shaking his head.

The viceroy laughed. "Just an expression, Coach. Seems like you're always unduly concerned about the well-being of your centenarian provost."

To avoid openly rolling his eyes, Rich looked down at his feet. "I didn't come up here to register anything about Cecilia," he said.

"No, evidently you came up to complain that your desk is giving you leg cramps."

"Not that either."

"What then?" Lipscom asked.

"Well, I did come up because of my desk. Not to complain about its size, but to ask if we've got any progress on getting us some working space."

"Something wrong with your office?"

"Yes, Elia, there's not nearly enough of it. I've got two desks in one office. And I've got four people here already. By the end of the week, I hope to have a dozen. If you can get me the rooms I asked for at Monster House, I may have more than that. We need a place to work. We've got a lot of things to coordinate and no location from which to do it."

"Well, then, you'll be glad to learn that's just what I was talking to Hopkins about when you came up."

"Great," Rich said.

"Not so fast," Lipscom said. "Hopkins said he didn't know of any available space on campus right off hand, but said he'd look into it and get back to me."

"Come on, Elia," Rich said. "This place has got five times the space we have at Urban and less than one and a half times the students."

Lipscom opened his eyes wide and tucked his chin back against his neck. "Last time I checked, Coach, Urban didn't have any students at all."

Rich took a long time formulating his next sentence. "I guess that's the point, isn't it," he said. "Our university is in suspension at the moment. And it's my job, the job of me and my team, to reanimate it, whatever that means and whatever that takes. To do so, I need space from which to work. I'd like it if my people had places to lay their heads. But right now, we need room to work from. We can't conceivably do it in the one office we've got right now. I'm not asking for forty percent of the space on the ASU campus. I'm not even asking for a whole building. A floor maybe. That hardly seems unreasonable."

"You've been in university administration long enough now to know that after their own salaries, faculty, deans and chairs are most protective of their space allocations. I've heard of fistfights breaking out over a lab or a seminar room. I bet it's even true of basketball coaches."

Rich let the last sentence pass without comment. "I know how territorial people are about their space. But on the other hand, we've never had a crisis like this before. ASU and Urban are supposed to be sister institutions. We just need some room in which to do our jobs. That hardly seems so much to ask."

"I've made the point to Rector Hopkins," Lipscom said. "Let's see what he has to say."

Rich had every sour confidence that Stephen Hopkins would report back to the viceroy that, unfortunately, with the influx of all these new students displaced by the flood, the ASU campus just hadn't any room to surrender. If that was the case, he presumed that Elia Lipscom wouldn't make him come up with any. And that's just what happened: Hopkins balked and Lipscom acquiesced. For anyone holding power in Alkansea, ASU was all that mattered. And Lipscom couldn't be seen as damaging the flagship's interests if he someday wanted to lead it.

The viceroy informed Rich of Hopkins' decision the next morning, but cheerily encouraged Rich that he was working on the situation and had a number of good leads, none of which he would divulge. For Rich, some good news followed as that Wednesday went along. CFO Hue Nguyen showed up. She and her husband had been offered a room in the home of a Vietnamese-American couple. An hour later, Urban's Vice Rector for Facilities, Charles Lobovich, arrived. Rich needed them both. But he had no place for them to sit. Rich gave his own desk to Hue and told her to do whatever was necessary to make sure that people got paid two days hence. He asked Charlie to make contact with his counterpart at ASU and feel him out about anything on the Mayflower campus that was going unused.

With those meager orders to his staff, Rich went off to the first of the interviews Sally Reasoner had set up for him. Frank Coughlin was lucky to have chosen radio as his medium, Rich thought, when they were introduced. His sparse hair was dyed shoe-polish black. Rich couldn't tell if Coughlin had neglected to shave for the last couple of weeks or was just unsuccessful at growing much of a beard. His stubble was completely gray. Coughlin was dressed in black corduroys and a black sweatshirt with the word "Monsters!" emblazoned across the chest in luminescent green. The sleeves of the shirt were cut off at the shoulder, revealing tufts of underarm hair every time Coughlin raised his hand to point across the desk at Rich.

Coughlin started the interview by professing sympathy for Rich, the people of Choctaw and all the employees of Urban University. But then he launched into an attack on the stranded people at the Arrowdome and Choctaw Center, saying that they'd revealed themselves to be little better than animals. Rich pointed out that the people who hadn't been able to evacuate were poor and desperate and that it seemed to him that Coughlin was blaming the victims rather than recognizing their circumstances. Rich also commented that "governmental authorities" hadn't responded to this crisis very well.

"Are you telling me that the Coast Guard and National Guard did a poor job of saving people's lives?" Coughlin asked.

"No, I'm not," Rich responded. "I can't speak with any greater expertise than what I witnessed on television, but those two units seem to me to have done an admirable job of getting stranded people into better situations." He thought of mentioning their leaving 3,000 people to befoul the Urban campus but decided against it.

"So you concede that some governmental agencies performed well in this crisis."

"Yes," Rich said, "some did. We just talked about a couple that did."

"Which ones didn't, in your estimation?"

Rich laughed dryly and said, "I guess we could start with the Army Corps of Engineers."

"Everybody's favorite whipping boy of the moment," Coughlin said. "So you blame the Corps of Engineers for what happened down in Choctaw?"

"The levees breached, didn't they?" Rich said. "The Corps built them, and the Corps was responsible for maintaining them. But they failed, not one levee or even two, but almost every levee erected to protect our city. Of course, I blame the Corps."

"Isn't it true that Congress failed to appropriate all the money the Corps asked for?"

"I'm happy to blame Congress for any shortfall in funding."

"I'm sure your Congressman will be happy to hear that."

This was getting fucked up, Rich thought. He didn't want and couldn't afford to offend those in a position to help him.

"I don't blame *my* Congressman," Rich said. "I am fully confident he's doing everything he can to assist his constituents in our damaged city. I don't blame Congressman Billy St. Clair or either of our two Senators. All are outstanding public servants."

"Do you know how they voted on funding for the Corps?"

"I don't." Rich didn't know, but he couldn't imagine that south Alkansea's Congressional representatives had voted against funding the levees.

"Then, when you blame Congress in general, you don't know whether you're blaming Alkansea Congressmen or not. How about that, folks? Man's for 'em unless he's agin' 'em and agin' 'em till he's for 'em."

Rich looked through the glass of the studio where Sally made her hand into the shape of a pistol and pointed it at her head, dropping her thumb down onto the barrel of her index finger.

"I'm for the people of Choctaw," Rich said. "The Corps of Engineers was in charge of building secure levees to protect the homes and businesses of people who live there. They didn't do their job. If they were underfunded, then they should have said so a lot louder and a lot clearer and a lot sooner than they did."

"But why should the federal government in the form of the Corps of Engineers provide protection for a place that's below sea level? Why should taxpayers from Des Moines, Iowa, pay to build levees around Choctaw, Alkansea? Why shouldn't we, the people of the greater United States, cut our losses and let Choctaw sink back into the swamps it came from?"

"That's a bogus argument," Rich said. "And I suspect you know it."

"Oh yeah, Mr. University Rector? How's it bogus? Tell the people of Mayflower, who are also going to have their tax money donated to you, just how it's bogus."

"The Corps is responsible for all the levees in this country. Those protecting Washington from the Potomac, St. Louis from the Mississippi, and Fargo, North Dakota, from the Red River. Taxpayers from Des Moines are paying to build levees in all those places. They're also paying to build Interstate highways over earthquake faults in California. And they're paying for farm subsidies that go to agri-business corporations in their own state. Taxpayers in Mayflower are paying for levees in Choctaw. And taxpayers in Choctaw are paying for tornado repairs here in Mayflower. That's the way the system works and the way it's supposed to work."

"So you're one of those tax-and-spend kind of university officials."

"That's not what I said, Frank."

"What did you say, then?"

"I think the original question was whether I held governmental officials responsible for some of the suffering experienced by the people of Choctaw."

"OK. You hold anybody else responsible beside the Corps of Engineers?"

"I sure think we ought to have done a better job of getting relief to the people in Choctaw unable to evacuate. We didn't provide them food or clean water. And most amazing to me, we didn't get them out of there for days after the storm passed. The Interstate was clear all the way from the Arrowdome to Monster Arena. Where were the buses to transport them?"

"You're sure buses could get into the heart of Choctaw right after the storm?"

"I know it," Rich said. "One of my colleagues at Urban, Dean Ben Turner, took refuge in one of the downtown hotels. Pretty miserable experience it turned out. But the very next day, his hotel, one of the city's nicest ones to be sure, got buses into the city and got all its guests out."

"So you're saying that the rich got buses and the poor got the finger."

"Your words, Frank, not mine."

"And you think that government should have been responsible for evacuating people too stupid to leave a city below sea level when being approached by a Category 5 hurricane?"

"I object to describing people as stupid because they were without resources to evacuate."

"What government should have been responsible for evacuating these people? State? Local? Federal?"

"Let's start with all of them," Rich said.

Coughlin laughed. "If they'd all shown up to evacuate the poor folks, then we could have wasted even more taxpayer money."

"If they had cooperated, if they'd had a proper emergency plan in place, then the evacuations could have been executed without waste."

"Well, we know what you think of the feds. The Corps anyway. Want to place FEMA on your blame card? How about President Bush?"

"FEMA performed pretty poorly. Why the president couldn't get a bus convoy to Choctaw is a mystery to me."

"How about Governor Lebear? Wanna give him some demerits?"

"I think there's plenty enough blame to go around."

"So you think Governor Lebear performed poorly too."

"I didn't say that. I said there's plenty enough blame to go around. We made some mistakes at Urban. Our electronic back-up failed. And now we're having to build a new communications system from scratch. That's on me. And it's something I hope you give me an opportunity to talk a bit about."

"First, let me ask just what you blame on Governor Lebear?"

"I don't blame anything specific on Governor Lebear."

"So you'd say the governor's performance was perfect. A-plus."

"Again, I didn't say that. A mess this huge, nobody gets an A."

"Then where did he mess up?"

"It's not my job to assess the performance of the governor. We all make mistakes. I made some; I'm sure he did too. That's for him to say and to learn from so as to do better next time."

"We've been talking with Urban University Rector Richard Janus, folks. Rector Janus, I'm afraid we're out of time, but I'd love to talk with you at greater length."

"I'm really looking for the opportunity to get word to Urban employees about our initial steps—"

"And we'll try to have you back to do just that," Coughlin interrupted. "You're a kick, Rec. You know how to point a finger and make sure it doesn't point at anyone who might point back. This is Frank Coughlin for WNUZ, and you've been listening to 'Up Against the Wall.'"

Walking out of the radio station, Rich kept shaking his head until Sally finally put her short arm around his waist.

"That was really screwed," Rich said.

"I'm sorry," Sally said. "I didn't have time to research the guy. I presumed we could count on a certain public spiritedness in a time like this."

"I think I really fucked up."

"Well, you didn't grab Coughlin by the throat and wring his neck."

"But I wanted to."

"Oh, how I know."

"How much damage did I do?"

"Well," Sally said, "you didn't hold the president personally responsible for all the people who died in the storm."

"Only I do hold him responsible," Rich said.

"All the better you didn't say so," Sally said, and gave Rich a swat on his rump as he slid behind the driver's seat of his Escape.

On the way back to the Trustees Building, as they were crossing the ASU campus, Rich noticed a boarded-up building. He asked Sally if she knew what it was, but she only shrugged and shook her head. "Find out," he told her.

Later that afternoon, Sally and Charles Lobovich came into the single office that was the physical entirety of Urban University. Rich had commandeered a hard plastic chair from the Trustees Building lunch room and had set himself up at the flyleaf on Cecilia's desk.

To avoid bothering Hue and Cecilia, who were working with University Computing Director Jose Najera on figuring out how to do a payroll (Hue had been brilliant enough to evacuate with a copy of Urban's budget), Rich and Sally and Charlie first stepped into the hall and then, not wanting to be overheard by passersby, took their meeting out into the stifling heat on the front steps of the Trustees Building.

Charlie had found out that the boarded-up building Rich had spotted earlier was the Alpha Sigma Pi fraternity house. The Alpha Sigs had been deactivated and ordered off campus. ASU bought the house from the national out from under the occupants.

"In response," Charlie said, "the Alpha Sigs threw what they called a 'death kegger' to commemorate the demise of their fraternity. Way I heard the story, before they got themselves drunker than a crew of cattle drivers in the Long Branch Saloon, they forked over a hundred bucks for a junker, towed it to the front yard of their house and sold the right to smash it with a sledge hammer to anyone willing to fork over a dollar for the pleasure."

"Aren't you glad most Urban kids have to work?" Sally said to Rich.

"So they started drinking and passing out cups of beer to anyone who walked by," Charlie continued. "And every time they'd drain a keg, a car load of them would take their sledge hammer dollars and stagger out to buy a fresh keg. Started this nonsense before noon. By late afternoon they were so drunk they weren't even human anymore. They'd managed to smash off the entire roof of the junker and otherwise beaten it down so much that they couldn't do it any more damage and couldn't get anybody to pay them any more for the right to bash it."

"Jesus Christ," Rich said. "Why would university officials even let this go on?"

"Well, get this. The Alpha Sigs even applied to the Inter-Fraternity Council for an alcohol permit. Approved, of course. Had the required university policeman on the grounds."

"What'd he do?"

Charlie laughed. "It's really not funny, so I shouldn't laugh," he said. "They kept feeding the cop cups of beer till he was shit-faced blind and staggered into the frat house to sleep it off."

"I've been at Urban nearly thirty years," Sally said. "We haven't ever had anything like this on our campus."

"It gets better," Charlie said.

"Or worse," Sally said.

"Or worse," Charlie agreed. "Since they couldn't get anybody to pay them any more to smash the junker, they decided they'd sell the right to smash the car parked on the street in front of their house. Didn't belong to anybody at the kegger, right, so what the hell did they care? They'd already bashed out the windows and lights on this second car when the owner arrives and begins pitching an understandably furious fit. Seems the car belonged to one of their own fraternity brothers. But they were too drunk to recognize his car. Anyway, he's sober and calls the city police who arrive with sirens wailing and roof lights swirling. The cops arrest the guy who's holding the sledge hammer at the moment, but it turns out he's not even an Alpha Sig, just a student walking by who paid a buck to club a car. Meanwhile, the Alpha Sigs scatter like roaches under a light. The cops don't manage to catch but the one guy. Later that night a bunch of these assholes sneak back into the house and try to set it on fire. If they can't live in it, then nobody will. They do manage to get a blaze going in the kitchen, but the fire department arrived before too much damage took place. Kitchen's kind of messed up, but otherwise the place is usable. So I'm told. And the kitchen, obviously, could be fixed."

"How many of these jackasses got arrested?" Rich asked.

"Only the guy with the sledge hammer."

"None of the frat guys?"

"You know how it goes, boss. Frat guys mostly got rich daddies with downtown stroke. Nobody died. Although the university cop might have, had the bastards really managed to torch the place. He was still passed out in the frat chapter room when the fire department arrived."

"What happened to the university cop?" Rich asked.

"Fired, of course."

"The way of the bleeping world, isn't it?" Rich said.

"But here's the good news," Sally said. "My ASU counterpart says the university never has decided what to do with the building. Didn't want to do something because doing most anything would bring the whole matter back up again. So they've just been sitting on it, waiting for the public memory to fade."

"How much room does it have?" Rich asked.

"Plenty," Charlie said. "Place is gigantic. It's got twenty small bedrooms, if you can believe it, each, as I understand it, with a set of bunk beds and two small desks. It's got six multi-toilet, multi-stall bathrooms, a big dining room, a huge, almost industrial kitchen, although one now in need of repair, and a chapter meeting room large enough to encompass the entire fraternity membership, those who lived in the house and those who didn't."

"It's what we need," Rich said. "Can you get me in to see it?"

Charlie grinned broadly and held up a lanyard dangling two keys.

The old Alpha Sigma Pi house smelled of smoke and mildew. But with enough elbow grease and determination, the place could be turned into a working Urban University in exile. The dining room and chapter room could each be outfitted with multiple work stations. Some of the fraternity bedrooms could be turned into small offices. And because of the showers and toilets, they could preserve some of the bedrooms as they were. That would enable more of Urban's staff who were unable to find local lodging to come into Mayflower to lend a hand in the university's resurrection. Such accommodations would not be ideal, of course. But they were better than anyone on Rich's administrative team enjoyed at the moment.

The first thing the next morning, as soon as he could get into Elia Lipscom's office, Rich asked the viceroy for the Alpha Sigma Pi house. The canny among you who have grown up in a country founded by Winslows and governed by Bushes won't be surprised that Lipscom said Urban couldn't have it. "No can do," is the way the viceroy stated the proposition.

"Why not?" Rich asked. "It's vacant, it's damaged, and my people are willing to put in the money and the sweat equity necessary to make it usable."

"Very admirable," Lipscom said. "But still no can do. The place is not mine to give."

Rich was immediately furious. "Are you telling me that son of a bitch Stephen Hopkins won't let our stricken university have a goddamn vacant fraternity house?"

"Simmer down, Coach," Lipscom said.

"I'm gonna snap that bastard's back like a dry twig."

"Hey, be still my heart. If I knew I might have been able to provoke fisticuffs, I would have sicced you on the fucker a long time ago."

"You're his goddamn boss. Make him give me the building."

"Would that I could, my friend. Would that I could."

"What in the hell does that mean?" Rich demanded.

"Means Hopkins already gave the building away. You know how he's always patting himself on the back with how public spirited he is. Has the local media thinking he rushed down to Choctaw and drove a boat around rescuing people. Well, there's some group calling itself the Hosea Rescue Alliance that is recruiting volunteers from all over the country. Soon as the Guard or FEMA or the governor or whoever makes the decision to open the city back up, this HRA group plans to rush in and put Choctaw back together before anybody can say Jack be nimble. Hopkins has committed the Alpha Sigma Pi house for their Alkansea headquarters."

"I haven't heard a peep about this."

"Yeah, but the deal is done. They've just worked out everybody's schedules. Governor, Hopkins, HRA head. They're calling a press conference for tomorrow so they can stand around and congratulate themselves on what good Christians they are."

Rich sat down and put his head in his hands. "And you didn't stop the bastard," he said.

"You know the fucker doesn't ask my permission for anything."

"But you can make him reverse himself," Rich said. "That house is empty and I need it."

"To quote old George the First, that wouldn't seem prudent. Not at this point when the HRA has already been promised the property. You can't really be against a do-gooder organization in the national publicity spotlight."

"I sure hope there's a judgment day," Rich said. "Then maybe some people will get in the afterlife what they've managed to dodge in this one."

See, Richard Janus, that's just why I need you to tell my story.

"Basketball and theology too," Lipscom said. Rich did not respond. "Well, the news isn't all bad. You can't have the Alpha Sigma house, but I have got two pieces of good news."

The viceroy's eyes lit up in almost impish delight as he opened a drawer, brought out two envelopes and slid them across the desk. Each had a four digit number written on the outside. Rich opened the first envelope. Inside was a plastic card the size of a credit card.

"Electronic keys, my man," Lipscom said. "To rooms in Monster House, just like you asked. One for you. One for someone else you want to make happy. Your pushy old provost if you want. I don't like her. But you said you wanted to get her out of the dorm. So be my guest."

Rich wanted enough rooms in Monster House to accommodate his entire administrative team. Get them off garage cots and living room couches. Now he had two. Better than nothing, he guessed. Don't look a gift horse in the mouth and all that. But Lipscom's self-satisfaction at having come up with two rooms instead of twenty made Rich want to pop him in the face.

"You're welcome," Lipscom said.

"Right. Sorry," Rich said. "Thanks for these. I know they'll be appreciated."

"Don't go play Jesus Christ the long sufferer now. One of those rooms is for you and your bride. Don't want it bandied about that we couldn't find accommodations for the rector of our sister school." Rich couldn't help but note Lipscom's undisguised identification with ASU. "I'm serious now. If I find out that you've given your room to someone else, I'll take it back."

Rich nodded. He hadn't gotten all the way to thinking about how to handle the rooms. A selfish part of him was glad that he'd evidently have to take one or see it go to waste. But a better part resented being told how to allocate what meager resources were being put at his disposal.

Rich picked up the two envelopes and waved them before slipping them into the inside pocket of his blazer. "These the two pieces of good news?" he said. "Room one and room two?"

"I like the way you think," Lipscom said jovially. "I've got *three* pieces of good news. Two rooms at Monster House for the sleeping hours. And for working hours, I've cleared out some space for you right next door at Friendship House. Come to think of it, make that *four* pieces of good news, because technically I've got you two separate spaces in Friendship House."

Friendship House was a sterile, two-story building that housed the Board's public school outreach programs, three classrooms downstairs, offices up. The staff did tutoring and counseling for high schoolers who wanted to go to ASU but lacked the grades or board scores. Mostly minority kids. Few improved their records sufficiently to be admitted to any four-year college. So Friendship House was primarily a public relations operation, a way for the state to claim extraordinary efforts to serve the poorly prepared.

"Now my staff over at Friendship is mightily unhappy about this," the viceroy said. "But I told them that comes with the territory of crisis. They're going to have to conduct all their business in just one classroom, where they're used to all three. The other two I'm giving to you. Also, I've given Stephen Hopkins no uncertain directions that he's to come up with the computers you've asked for. The building is equipped with wireless connection to MonsterNet, so you and your people should be good to go. Hopkins will have the stuff to you by tomorrow. No ifs, ands or buts. You can keep your office here on three. If you need to see your people, you're about forty-five seconds away. Not the Alpha Sigma Pi house, I'll grant. But we're making progress. If and when I see the opportunity, I'll get you more space still."

This last was another in a series of promises the viceroy failed to keep. Or perhaps, for the viceroy and men like him, the prospect of *keeping* played no role in the process of *promising*.

That afternoon, Jose told Rich that he had the university's website in a primitive state of functionality. Jose also had established a limited email system that would serve senior administrators. Unfortunately, they were still at least a week away from restoring email for all campus users. And to achieve that, Jose needed to spend nearly $250,000 on additional servers, disk recorders and other equipment. Not entirely knowing where the money was to come from, Rich told him to buy what he needed and move forward as quickly as possible.

And later that afternoon, Sally got Rich onto a radio-in-exile program, a Choctaw station broadcasting out of Mayflower but largely aimed at dislocated Choctaws who could receive the signal. On this station Rich got a far more sympathetic hearing, and he was able to start delivering his message for all students and employees: Urban University was coming back.

THAT NIGHT, RICH AND Cally informed the Feasters that they would be leaving for Monster House. Althea insisted on cooking for Rich and Cally one more time, and while Cally assisted with the dinner, Rich went out and bought a bottle of champagne which he poured as an after-dinner drink. "To Althea and Robert," Rich said, raising his glass. He wished what he said next was more original, but his words were genuinely and completely heartfelt. "To friends in need."

"Shoot," Robert said. "Althea and I thought y'all were going to stay six months."

31

What's remarkable, from my perspective, is how easy That Vicious Lying Rat Bastard's contemporaries went on him. The New Englanders of the 1670s remind me of the Republicans during the reign of George W. Bush who kept stubbornly singing their leader's praises even as his policies in the Middle East made America an international pariah, even as he thwarted scientific research in both the medical and environmental fields, even as he steered the American economy right off a cliff.

That Vicious Lying Rat Bastard led his men into a horrible battle they shouldn't have fought. Then, when he had the shelter of the Narragansett fort in his hands and could have provided warmth, more than ample rations, and time to treat his wounded, his urgency to take Indian life was so great that he burned down edifices that could have saved the lives of dozens of his own men who would expire of their wounds as Winslow marched them through a long night of suffering back to Wickford. Even the old self-aggrandizer Benjamin Church tried to convince him not to do this. But as was always true, the sneering Plymouth Governor wouldn't listen, and his soldiers were among those who paid the price of his inhumanity. But despite these colossal errors in judgment, That Vicious Lying Rat Bastard Josiah Winslow ultimately rode back into Plymouth a hero and remained so for centuries to come.

SOMEHOW, NIGH MIRACULOUSLY, CANONCHET, Quinnapin, and Weetamoo kept the surviving Narragansett warriors, and the few members of their families who escaped with them, alive and together in the Rhode Island woods over the next several weeks of brutally freezing weather. Their greatest challenges during this time were the unrelenting cold and the specter of starvation, their winter food having been lost in the inferno of their fort. The cold was, in a way, however, also an ally for my one-time Narragansett neighbors. For the men of That Vicious Lying Rat Bastard were also freezing in their paltry encampment at Wickford. Boston Harbor had iced over, as had large swaths of Narragansett Bay and the whole of the Connecticut River. As a result, resupply via boat from any of the three colonies was impossible, and the English troops with Winslow were faring as poorly as the people with Canonchet, Weetamoo and Quinnapin. The English were reduced to eating their horses, and my allies would gladly have eaten their animals had they had any. And even That Vicious Lying Rat Bastard knew better than to order men so miserable to undertake another offensive into the Narragansett woods.

While the Narragansetts were trying to hold themselves together in hastily constructed and inadequately finished *nashweetoos*, Weetamoo sent for me. She felt I could now convince Canonchet and her husband to join me in Nipmuck country. I marched down with a party of a dozen Wampanoags, half Pocassets, half Pokanokets, arriving in fierce *Pequahokesos* on the first day of 1676.

Diplomacy is a delicate art. The Narragansetts should have listened to me. If they had formed the defensive alliance I had proposed two years earlier, the English might have been persuaded to leave me alone or they might have turned tail instantly if Narragansett canoes had landed by the hundreds on the western shores of Montaup Peninsula. If they had stood with me, then all their loved ones given up to That Vicious Lying Rat Bastard's flames would still be with them. But I could say none of this. I had to surrender the divided past to the past. For now we needed to forge a common future.

Remarkably, or perhaps not, the Narragansetts wanted to hear the story of the steps I had taken to sidestep the war the English had forced upon me. Weetamoo had told them her account of my efforts, but they wanted to hear from me again how I had released Englishmen that we had captured and how, even after the first blood had been shed, I had directed our men to shoot near but not at the English for an entire day during the Pease Field Fight. Then the Narragansetts wanted to tell me their story of how they met with the English repeatedly, even going so far as to send Canonchet to Boston to try to turn aside the rush to war. How they'd required Canonchet to bank the fire of his fierce indignation after the Bostonians had threatened him and forced him to sign another of their strong-arm treaties. How they choked down the urge for retribution when That Vicious Lying Rat Bastard burned their towns in the north. How desperately they had hoped the implantation of their swamp fortress would dissuade the English from pressing forward.

"This is not easy," Quinnapin said, rocking forward on his haunches as we squatted around the fire in his *nashweetoo*. "We were foolish. We were vain. We thought we were immune, and we were not. We should have joined you when you asked." He placed his hand on Weetamoo's knee. "My wife warned me that the English would never turn away from war. But I hoped otherwise and did not heed her wisdom. I am sorry."

"What is done cannot be undone," I said.

Canonchet then related how disrespectfully he was treated during his diplomatic mission to Boston, and how humiliated he felt when under duress he inked the document reaffirming the July 15 treaty. "I knew two things even as I signed," he said. "I knew that Quinnapin would hunt down and kill anyone among our people who tried to curry favor with the English by turning over our Wampanoag guests. And I knew that the English would use our refusal as an excuse to attack. That is why we worked so hard during the summer to complete our fortress."

"I too tried to accommodate and negotiate," I said. "For as long as I could. But the English are without principle."

Canonchet snorted in derision. "They gave me a copy of their treaty before I left Boston. I nailed it over the door of my *nashweetoo* so they would find it after I escaped the great fort."

"It is not too late," I said. "We have driven them out of the west. Nipmuck country is ours alone. And from there we will push them back until they beg us to show them the mercy they have never shown us."

"We will come to you," Quinnapin said.

"We will come in the spring," Canonchet said. "We are still many enough that we must wait until the snow is gone so that the English cannot track us."

This plan made sense, and we agreed upon it.

"We have learned this hard lesson from Weetamoo and you," Quinnapin said. "Like you before us, we find ourselves in a situation where we can only hope to retain the land of our fathers by leaving it."

I departed the next morning, and after spending only two nights at Menameset, I made a journey I had been planning beyond the Connecticut River and into the colony of New York.

As it happened, the surviving Narragansetts did not have to wait until spring to move their people to Nipmuck country. Starting on January 15, New England enjoyed an unusual thaw, and within a week the snow was gone. Canonchet, Weetamoo, and Quinnapin had their people on the trail to the northwest by January 21.

That Vicious Lying Rat Bastard Josiah Winslow learned of the Narragansetts' flight within forty-eight hours. His instinct was to give chase, but in the interim, the soldiers from Connecticut, who had taken the worst losses in the Great Swamp Fight, had departed Wickford to return home. Winslow didn't feel strong enough without them. Moreover, he still didn't have an adequately supplied force under his command. The thaw was causing the ice to break up, but ships from Boston with needed food had yet to arrive. Winslow sent urgent messages to New London for Major Treat to bring his Connecticut troops back, and Treat was back in Wickford by the 26th. (Why, I cannot imagine.) But a supply ship had still not arrived by the time That Vicious Lying Rat Bastard ordered his force to move out in pursuit of the Narragansetts on January 27.

Trouble bubbled up almost immediately. A score of Plymouth soldiers simply left the column on January 29 and went back to their homes in Taunton. That Vicious Lying Rat Bastard claimed that he caught sight of the Narragansetts on several occasions, but that's just another case of his habitual prevarication. The Narragansetts were long gone by the time he got his army on the move. And the English were in such bad shape after six weeks in the open field that they hardly moved very fast.

The white soldiers called this expedition "The Hungry March," for they spent as much time trying to find game to roast as they did moving forward. The prospect of an open mutiny increased with every step That Vicious Lying Rat Bastard tried to force his men to take to the northwest. Finally, after a week, Winslow gave it up and ordered his army to turn east. On February 5, he led those still with him into Boston and finally let them go home.

Why is this murderous, profoundly incompetent man not remembered as one of the biggest and vilest fuck-ups in history? Well, all you have to consider is who wrote the history.

32

Rich and Cally's room at Monster House was bigger and much cooler than the guest bedroom at the Feasters' and much better for sleeping. The drapes were lined and thick and kept out the early morning sun. The king-sized bed was bigger and more comfortable. The furniture included a fridge and a desk. Instead of going to the local Starbucks, Cally was able to work in the room. And the room had its own bathroom, of course. That one feature, alone, suddenly now seemed like a luxury.

On their first night there, after storing their few possessions in the room's large closet and its wardrobe and bedside-table drawers, Rich and Cally got undressed earlier than usual and into bed where they curled against each other in a way they hadn't since leaving Richmond. Rich hoped that they might make love (a rector perhaps, but first and always a man). But as they talked about the next day's schedule and segued into the uncertainty of their long-range plans, he didn't make any motion of foreplay save to brush his lips against the hairline on Cally's forehead as she lay with her head on his chest. Finally, he felt the wetness of tears on his skin.

"I wish I thought we deserved them," she said.

"The Feasters?" he asked.

"Uh huh."

"We'll do something really nice for them."

"Good. Of course," Cally said. "But that won't make us even."

THE NEXT DAY THE Urban exiles took up operations at Friendship House. The viceroy made good on at least one more of his promises. Like his other promises: sort of. ASU officials delivered forty laptop computers for Rich to distribute to his staff. The computers they delivered were at least two generations old and looked as if they had arrived directly from a battlefield in the Middle East. These were computers that ASU had retired from its executive MBA program.

Cecilia remarked as she took possession of her computer, "This horse looks like it's been rode hard and put up wet."

Still, only two of them failed to operate. This was a beginning.

In her inimitable way, Cecilia called Dell Computers in Austin, Texas, and insisted on talking to Michael Dell himself. Unlikely as it seems, the combination of her pluck and the importance of her story saw her through. She actually got Dell on the phone, explained what Urban was up against, and elicited his promise of a fifty-computer donation to be shipped immediately at the computer company's expense.

By mid-afternoon, Jose and those of his staff who were in Mayflower had set up the two rooms the viceroy had given them. In one room, Rich put the midlevel staff and directed them to begin answering the barrage of questions that were flowing in by email. In the days to come, Jose would also equip this room, which the staff took to calling "the Boiler Room," with a dozen phone lines to handle questions at one of four numbers posted on the website. The phone lines were busy twelve hours a day without surcease for the next four weeks.

Rich had Jose and Charlie set up the other room for use by senior administrators. Charlie used saw horses, sheets of plywood and banquet-room tablecloths to create a large table, around which he placed fifteen, butt-numbing metal folding chairs that he'd scrounged from his Mayflower contact. Jose brought in enough electrical extension cords and power strips so that the laptops positioned on the table didn't have to rely on their ancient batteries. Here Urban's administrators, as they were able to find housing in Mayflower, gathered to plan and orchestrate their university's resurrection, each one with no more space than the square of table in front of him occupied by a scarred computer and little additional room for more than a cup of coffee.

Over time, most of Urban's deans and vice rectors took up stations in Friendship House. But the vaunted Shelby Clay, Urban's Dean of Architecture and Urban Planning, joined them only irregularly. Tall, gray, faintly rumpled, but resolutely cultured and always prepared with a wry quip, the sixty-eight-year-old Dean Clay was Urban's most visible academic employee, and he spent little time in Friendship House because he was almost constantly on television, offering his expert testimony on what challenges and opportunities lay ahead in rebuilding Choctaw.

A native of Choctaw, Clay had earned his architecture degrees at Harvard and had worked for two award-winning decades in New York before deciding to take early retirement in his hometown. Only two years later, however, at age fifty, bored and restless, Clay was appointed dean and from that position quickly became the city's leading authority on urban renewal and development. He was constantly quoted in *The Straight Arrow* and on local TV.

As the years went by, Clay became particularly well known for his advocacy and redesign of public housing in a metropolitan area where decent, low-cost rental units were essential for the sizeable portion of the population living at or below the poverty line. Shelby Clay had been born in Choctaw's old money Exchange District and like others reared there, his accent seemed more Virginia Piedmont than Gulf South. But despite the ring of plantation owner in his voice, he was an eloquent advocate for the needs of the underprivileged.

Inside the university, Clay had created the Urban Housing Institute and had populated it with grant writers constantly trolling for external funding opportunities that might translate into new public housing initiatives. Clay was always the public face of these initiatives, always the man at the center of first the ground-breaking and later the opening ceremonies, his thatch of gray hair wild on a windy day, toting a silver shovel at the beginning or wielding giant scissors to slice through red ribbon at the end, always surrounded by grinning black mothers holding the hands of their children, the new project's future residents.

Now, with Choctaw devastated and empty, Shelby Clay was the spokesman for the promise of recovery. He insisted that the city could be rebuilt and emerge from this crisis better than ever. He was telegenic, articulate and passionate. And he did Urban University proud every time a camera trained on his weathered face and ran his dean's title underneath it.

People in Choctaw thought Shelby Clay was a saint. Rich Janus and Cally Martin were among them. So Rich didn't mind that Dean Clay missed most of the Friendship House deliberations that focused on resurrecting the university rather than the city at large. Clay was doing too much good for Rich to insist that he restrict his activities to those taking place in the crowded space the men and women who worked there twelve and more hours a day over the next six weeks dubbed "the War Room."

The War Room. It would seem that we could convict Rich and his harried colleagues of hyperbole. I know something about war, of course, having had one named for me. But invoking the metaphor of war was more appropriate than they themselves first understood. Their city had been destroyed as certainly as had my village on Montaup. And real lives were at stake. The lives of working class and middle-class young people for whom Urban University represented the only rung within reach on the ladder to a better life.

ON FRIDAY OF THE second week after the storm, Rich's inherited assistant for special projects, Sheila Pyrite, showed up at the War Room dressed as if she were about to preside at a corporate board meeting. She was wearing a black suit, with a ruffled candy-apple red blouse, black stockings and open-toed high heels. Everybody else in the room had on blue jeans, T-shirts and jogging shoes. She plopped down in an empty chair and began to talk without pause as if she feared taking a breath might allow someone to interrupt her.

"It's so good to see everybody," she announced, addressing the room but staring intently at Rich alone. "I have been worried absolutely sick to death about everybody. But here you all are as well as can be expected, I'm sure. I will have to ask every one of you what happened and where you went and did you lose your house and all those horrible things that I know happened to just everybody. But look at you, everybody here cozy around the table. I'm sure you've all told your stories to each other by now." She unsnapped her purse, reached inside and pulled out a stack of photographs. "I have had just a terrible time. I'm sure you all have. Here are pictures of my wonderful house. My former house. Ha ha ha."

Without turning or making eye contact, she passed the photos to Cecilia who was sitting on her right. "I lived down in Alkansea Beach. I bet some of you didn't even know that. We are all so professional and never talk about our personal lives. Though we should. Just a little sometimes. Don't you think? My beautiful house, right on the beach. My back gate opened right on the sand. I could tiptoe into the water in the blink of a cat's eye. Gone now. Gone with the wind as they say. You can see from the photos. Nothing at all. My new friend Stanley took those. My beach lot now, he says. We got back to it, but there was nothing there. Washed out to sea. Stanley said as long as we were there we might as well go swimming. That's why I'm wearing my bathing suit. It's a two piece, a bikini I guess you'd say, so you fellas had better not look too long. Not that anything's indecent. Stanley just said we should photograph me on my property. And that's what we did. I don't know what it means. My deed and all my other papers were in the house. So I hope there's some office somewhere that shows the land belongs to me, you know the measurements about where my property starts and stops and everything. It's mine. My first husband bought it. And my second husband paid for it. Ha ha ha."

Cecilia had finished looking at the half-dozen pictures and was holding them just above the keypad on her computer. Without speaking to Cecilia, Sheila took the photos from her and handed them across the table to Rich. "You should see these too, Rector. Just don't look at my bathing suit. Ha ha ha. I don't know why I ever let Stanley take these with me in them. But I want you to see what I lost. You probably lost the same. Maybe even more. Probably everybody did. You haven't told me about your losses. But as you can see, I lost everything. I don't know what I would have done if Stanley hadn't come along. A true Good Samaritan. If it weren't for Stanley, I wouldn't have a roof over my head or even a stitch to wear."

Finally she stopped. Rich handed the photos back to her. "I'm sorry, Sheila," he said. "These are such hard times for so many people."

"Yes," she said. "I guess y'all have been wondering where I was and all."

"People are all over the place," Cecilia said.

"Stanley has a place in Tallahassee, and we've been there. But then I heard y'all were here, and I had him bring me, but we haven't been able to find a motel or anything." Sheila sat straight upright, her arms tucked into her sides and both hands gripping her purse.

"We're allowing people to work wherever they find themselves," Rich said.

"Can you manage your projects from Tallahassee?" Cecilia asked.

"I'm sure," Sheila said. "Yes."

"Well, that's probably a better plan for now," Rich said. "You stay in touch by email, and if housing comes open here we'll let you know."

"That's our plan, then," Sheila said.

"Keep us abreast of what you're up to," Rich said.

"I will," she said. "I won't let you down. You can count on me."

THE NEXT MORNING, THE Saturday of that second week after the storm, Rich was greeted at Friendship House by Alphonse Jackson, the star player of Rich's first team at Choctaw High. Alphonse was on his way to Choctaw to post a story about the condition of his old schools.

"Flood water's way down," Rich told him. "A lot of places anyway. That's what the news channels report, anyway. But the city's still closed. Nothing works. Water. Gas. Electricity. Nothing. As I understand things, you can drive down the Interstate a hundred twenty-five miles, but then they're going to turn you around."

Alphonse laughed, showing his gleaming teeth against his almost purple skin. "You are so old school, Coach," he said. "First of all, I could figure out how to get into town by hook or crook if I had to. Don't grow up the way I did and not know how to slip the Man when you need to. Sweet thing is I don't. Word is they're going to start letting demolition and construction crews in tomorrow or Monday anyway. But as a member of the Fifth Estate, I can get in right now." He reached inside his knit shirt and pulled out a plastic press badge hanging around his neck. "Keys to the kingdom. The story must be told. Might not get in if you only lived there, but if you just want to write about how nobody's home, all you need is this." He waved his badge.

"Ah, my journalist success story," Rich said, kidding him. "Didn't I teach you everything you know? About everything?"

Rich expected Alphonse to laugh and fire back a shot of his own. But instead, Alphonse responded seriously. "You did, Coach. I am forever in your debt. You taught me I could do anything. Now here I am. Who woulda thought a skinny guy out of Choctaw High would be a reporter for *Newsday*?"

Rich couldn't think of anything to say that wouldn't sound sappy. Alphonse Jackson was one of the finest kids he'd ever been blessed to be around. "So what's caused you to stop by here?" Rich said. "I already knew you were a big deal."

Alphonse laughed. "I got this idea for how to make my story work," he said. "Me and you. We go around to the gym at C-High and then out to Ungulate Arena. Old player and his coach checking it out. To anchor the connection, the piece will establish how the author was a central figure in the old coach's bestselling memoir. Then we'll check out how fucked up stuff is. Get the photos of the mess and the waste. But all the while remember the old days. Make it personal. Kick around the thirty-one point licking Urban put on ASU my last year. I need you to go with me. You're a writer. So we do a joint by-line thing."

"You're the writer now, Phonse, not me," Rich said. "You're the *Newsday* guy. I don't have any credentials."

"Wrong you are," Alphonse said. He reached into the front pocket of his jeans and pulled out another press badge. This one had the name *Richard Janus* on it. "Got the picture out of my yearbook. My editor took to the idea like a Cajun to crawfish. How soon can you roll?"

Rich looked at his watch. He didn't know about the idea of co-authoring a story with Alphonse. But he really liked the possibility of getting into the city for reasons both professional and personal. If he could get on campus, he could perhaps gauge how soon they could get the place opened up again. And he wanted to see his house. He'd seen water in his neighborhood from the helicopter. But he couldn't tell how much might have gotten into his house.

The basement had presumably flooded, and water had probably gotten into the ground level of the house with its washer, dryer, freezer, Cally's home office and their two-car garage. But the house was a split-level design, and the main living area stood five feet above the street. The damage they had suffered would depend on the depth of the water on their property. If Alphonse could get him into the city, he could assess what repairs he and Cally were facing.

"Give me a second," Rich said to Alphonse.

Rich walked over and sat down next to Cecilia and explained that a former student had credentials to get him into Choctaw. "I'm assuming you can hold down the fort," he told her.

"I'll hold it down if you want," she said. "And if you give me permission, I'll invade the fort across the street. Lot of people over there need my foot up their butts."

Rich laughed. "Hold if you can," he said. "Invade if you have to."

"Bring us back some good news," she said.

Rich told Alphonse that he would go on several not too complicated conditions. First and most important, Alphonse had to agree to let him bring Cally along. Second, Alphonse had to agree to take him by his house. Third, Alphonse had to promise not to hold him to the joint-by-line proposal. "I'll do the photo stuff," Rich said. "And I'll work with you back and forth on appropriate quotes. And I'll otherwise provide as much help with the article as I can, but given what I'm facing here, I can't really promise to make a contribution worth attribution."

"Old Tricks, my mentor the poet," Alphonse said, laughing and invoking Rich's nickname from his own playing days. "A conjurer with the ball, now a magician with words."

"What I need is a magic wand," Rich said. "Wave it and make all this go away."

THE DRIVE FROM MAYFLOWER to Choctaw was uneventful until they reached a National Guard roadblock about twenty-five miles north of town where no one seemed to be getting turned away. When Alphonse rolled his rented Jeep Laredo next to the guardsman checking credentials, he lowered his window and lifted the badge around his neck up to his chin. The soldier barely glanced at it before he waved them through.

They were stopped again at the city limits, this time by Guardsmen exhibiting a little more interest. National news organizations had reported widespread looting, and at least one motivation for the roadblocks was to deter criminals from carting the city away. The soldiers who came to either side of the truck looked twelve years old. The man on the driver's side made Alphonse take off his badge and hand it to him.

"*Newsday*, huh?" he said.

"Right," Alphonse said. He pointed at Rich with his thumb. "Coach is my partner."

The soldier didn't inquire as to the identity of "Coach," but he did lift his chin toward the back seat. "Who's she?" he asked of Cally.

"Photographer," Alphonse replied, delivering the line he and Rich had concocted. He was not required to add that she lacked a press credential because they had hired her locally.

The soldier gestured forward with his index finger. "Just get it right," he said.

The Choctaw they found nearly two weeks after the storm was a messy place. Alphonse had to steer around downed trees in almost every block. But clearly some agency had dragged enough debris aside to make passable those major thoroughfares from which the water had drained. They came into the city along the Alkansea river whose nearby neighborhoods remained dry, but they could tell instantly when they passed into areas that had flooded because there all the lawns were brown and the air smelled like mildewed hay.

They couldn't get to Alphonse's grammar school, which was in a neighborhood still under water and smelled of motor oil and sewage. But using his telephoto lens, Alphonse took pictures to document the condition of the area where he'd grown up. The neighborhood was impoverished to begin with. Abandoned and mired in water still up to front porches, it looked like something out of a nightmare, something sagging and melted that Dali might have imagined.

The Choctaw High Campus was dry, but all the doors to the school were locked, and the old gym, which sat behind the classroom building, was padlocked. The breezeway roof that once connected the two was blown about twenty-five yards away into the chain-link fence that marked the boundary of the school property. The support poles had either been pulled out of the ground or sheared off from the torque of the wind under the flat roof. The waterline on the gym was shoulder height for Rich, almost over Cally's head.

"I know you wanted to get in," Rich said, pointing to the padlock on the clasp across the double doors. "But I guess we're not going to be able to."

"The hell," Alphonse said and grinned. "This thing's been sitting in Lake De Soto water, and it's so rusty I'm surprised it hasn't fallen off all by itself. Let me see if I can give it some help?" He walked away with his eyes on the ground.

"I hope you don't plan to break that lock," Rich said. "*Newsday* won't be pleased if one of its reporters gets arrested."

"Unless you or Miss Cally is secretly a cop," Alphonse replied, "I don't think I have too much to worry about."

Alphonse returned with a rock the size of a softball and gave the padlock a smack that snapped it open.

"Oh great," Rich said. "Now I'm a criminal. Just what I always wanted."

"Like I said, Coach, you are *old* Old School."

"You used to smoke dope," Cally said to Rich. "That's criminal."

"I don't want to hear it," Alphonse said. "I've got this mentor thing, and I want to keep it that way." He pulled open one of the double doors to the gym and stepped inside.

As he did so, Cally put her mouth up to Rich's ear and whispered. "And you like to do some things in bed that are against the law in forty-seven states, Guam and Puerto Rico."

"That's just entering," Rich said. "What we're up to here is *breaking* and entering."

"Always with the I wasn't a virgin when you married me," Cally said.

"You may not have *been* a virgin, but you were *like* a virgin, either that or like Madonna or at least like a Madonna, whatever that is."

"Please shut up now."

"Fine. Why?"

"So I won't have to bonk you with Alphonse's rock." Cally grasped Rich's hand as they followed Alphonse into the space where Rich had earned his living for sixteen years.

Inside, the gym was a wreck. The wooden bleachers had been left pulled out, and all the lower risers were warped. They would never fold back against the wall again. The floor of the basketball court was buckled, some slats curled and sticking almost straight up, and all covered in green slime. The place smelled like a stagnant pond. The boys' locker smelled even worse, and the concrete floor was so slippery they backed out after one step. The water had tipped over the metal shelves holding the wire baskets where students stored their P.E. uniforms, making the locker room look as if it had been shaken by an earthquake. Matted paper, its ink run and unreadable, was all over the floor, debris, they supposed, floated away from the teachers' desks.

Back in the green-house-hot gym, uncertain of what he might need or want for his story, Alphonse posed Rich for a photo on the warped bleacher seat that used to be his when he was Alphonse's coach. He had Cally take shots of him and Rich together on the sidelines, under the basket and pointing up at the clock. Then he had Rich and Cally sit together four rows up at mid-court, ghost fans at a court that would never hear another whistle.

From C-High, they drove up to Urban where Rich could use his university master key so Alphonse wouldn't have to commit another B & E. When Rich had made his helicopter tour of the Urban campus, he'd seen why Ungulate Arena wasn't used like the Arrowdome as a sanctuary for the refugees they had plucked off rooftops. The Arena would not have provided any refuge whatsoever. Hosea had peeled its roof back like the top of a sardine can.

The seats at the Arena were fixed, of course. But they were as ruined as the bleachers at Choctaw High. With no roof to shield them, they had been drenched during Hosea and several times since. The cloth-covered seat cushions and backs were soaked. Many sprouted mushrooms. The basketball court was beyond repair. And right in the middle, stretching from key top to key top sat the Urban scoreboard, blown down from the rafters, its thousands of red, white, blue and green lights shattered on the ruined floor, glinting in the sunlight that fell through the vanished roof. What little repartee the three of them had sustained even through their visit to Choctaw High fell away now. Alphonse took the pictures he wanted or had Cally take them, and Rich let himself be moved around like a mannequin. The task ahead was even more imposing than he had heretofore understood. The shell of the Arena was probably structurally stable. But everything inside its walls was going to have to be replaced, a reconstruction process he knew would only be funded with the blood of indignation and incessant insistence.

When Alphonse had everything he thought he needed at the Arena, the three of them walked the campus where more horrors loomed at every stop. As they stood in the middle of the quad, amid the chairs and grocery carts, a pack of two dozen dogs scampered out from under the raised bottom floor of the library and went panting and yelping past them toward the southern end of campus. Most of the dogs seemed to be wearing collars. They were abandoned pets, fending for themselves, taking shelter under Urban buildings and feeding off whatever they could find in the drowned neighborhoods south of campus. Another bizarre thing for Rich to worry about and deal with, the latter a task that would be made almost impossible over the next year with the disappearance of the City Pound.

The water on the southern part of campus had drained away. But the ground levels of the buildings located there were completely ruined, their floors covered with a brown sludge as slick as thawing ice. The situation was little better in the middle and northern parts of campus, which had escaped the flood waters. Most of the windows were blown out, and the building interiors had suffered untold damage from blowing rain. None of the roofs on the academic buildings had blown off, that Rich could see, but he presumed they would discover extensive roof damage once they were properly inspected. At least one glass entrance door was smashed on every building. This, Rich and the others concluded, was the work not of Hurricane Hosea, but of human hands. The refugees that the Coast Guard had left on campus unsupervised for five days had used large planters or in some cases metal benches to smash their way inside every building on campus.

Once inside, the refugees had pulled fire extinguishers off corridor walls and used them to shatter the glass doors of all major office suites. They pillaged office refrigerators for what unspoiled food they could find and rifled through desk drawers in search of potato chips, nuts and candy. Desperate for potable water, they had drained the water coolers throughout campus. And they had tipped over all the soft drink machines in unrealized hopes of getting at the beverages inside. Rich didn't blame people for doing what they needed to do to keep themselves alive. He didn't blame them for breaking into the Piggly Wiggly even though the campus was strewn with the cans and bottles, plastic containers and foil wraps of all they'd stolen. No, Rich blamed governmental authorities who had abandoned people in such harrowing circumstances.

He did blame the refugees, at least somewhat, though, for the way they'd dealt with other bodily needs. Since the city's water system was wrecked by the storm, the toilets in all the buildings were soon full. And they evidently made no effort to fashion latrines for themselves, even though they had broken into Building 16 which housed Facilities Services where shovels and picks and hoes were in plentiful supply. Instead, they had relieved themselves in classrooms and offices all over campus. From the amount of human waste Rich and Cally and Alphonse discovered in some rooms, the refugees had turned certain spaces into makeshift toilets. That suggested at least some degree of human restraint, much more so than did those rooms with only one deposit of feces or one circle of stained carpet or wall corner splashed with urine.

The stench from this waste was so powerful that Rich and the others could smell it as soon as they entered a building. "Place smells like an outhouse," Alphonse said when they first entered Building 14 which housed the Engineering College.

"It's disgusting," Cally said and went back outside with her hand over her mouth.

"The people in here allowed themselves to behave like animals," Alphonse said as he and Rich moved deeper into the building and the smell became more overwhelming. Pretty soon, both of them were covering their faces with handkerchiefs.

"It's like *Lord of the Flies*," Rich said, when they were back outside 14 with Cally. "All order must have broken down at some point, and no one must have stepped forward to convince everybody that for their own health and well being they needed to organize a latrine detail."

Alphonse said, "And I'm like the appalled character who thinks that people would do better than this."

"I wonder if we'd have done any better," Rich said.

"What this campus shows," Cally said, "is how close we twenty-first-century human beings remain to the clammy caves of our ancestors."

RICH AND CALLY WERE confronted with a new set of sensations as they entered their own neighborhood and got out of Alphonse's truck at their house on Venice Boulevard. They were standing in the driveway looking up at their roof and inspecting an indecipherable insignia that, as on the homes of their neighbors, had been spray painted on the front wall of their house, when four National Guardsmen in dappled fatigues, M-16s in their hands, turned the corner at the end of the block and walked toward them. Rich and Cally and Alphonse waited for them, and the guardsmen asked all three to produce identification. Rich pointed out the address on his driver's license that showed he was standing in front of his own house.

"Y'all still aren't supposed to be here," the group leader said. "City's closed."

"We're here on assignment," Alphonse said and produced his credential from *Newsday*.

The guardsman looked at him. "You writing a story about this guy's house?" he asked, causing Alphonse to laugh.

"We're partners on the story," Rich said, pulling out his own *Newsday* badge. "About some schools in town. Choctaw High and Urban University."

"Who are you?" the soldier asked Cally.

"Photographer," she said.

"And while you were in town, you just stopped by to check on your house," the guardsman said.

"Can't blame us, can you?" Rich said.

The soldiers seemed to relax when Rich said this. "Naw, I can't, I guess," the head guardsman said. "Do me a favor, though. Get out of here before dark. We have no idea who's still in this city. But I suspect it's nobody you want to run into." With that the soldiers marched on down the street, gesticulating at each house they passed. Rich and Cally later learned that small National Guard squads like this were the ones who had marked the exterior wall of each house as they searched for dead bodies, kicking through one front door after another.

Rich and Cally quickly inspected their property and found that their five majestic oaks had come through the storm upright. But two crepe myrtles were down as was the sixty-foot hackberry that had straddled the back property line. Two Savannah hollies, eight ligustrums, a Japanese magnolia and a sweet olive tree were standing but dead, smothered by the flood water.

They let themselves into the house through the broken front door. Hope is an amazingly resilient quality of the human psyche. In the Choctaw heat of September of 2004, everything Rich and Cally knew about Hosea's flooding warned them that they were in for bad news inside their house. Nonetheless, both dared to hope the water had not gotten inside their house. This was, in essence, to hope that what they knew within all reason to be true was, somehow, not true. Both knew such hope was crazy. But each of them clung to it anyway. So it is with human beings. And in this way we show ourselves at our most persistently foolish, and all at once, oddly, at our stubborn best.

The watermark on the ground floor stood at forty-seven inches, and thus the basement below it was full to the brim with sludgy black brine. The heating and cooling systems there were lost. On the ground floor, which had stood in the four feet of brackish water, the washer, dryer, water heater, and freezer were ruined. Cally's office was beyond recovery. The old desk in the room had collapsed, dumping her papers and student files into the muck. Soft bricks of papers and folders lay in gluey clumps on the ruined hardwood floor. The worst news was in the garage. Flooded up to the steering wheels, their cars had become colorful and perhaps toxic terraria. Sickly orange mushrooms sprouted from the upholstery and dashboards; powdery golden mold grew on all surfaces save the glass, and the cars smelled of noxious rot.

While Rich and Cally tried to assess the clean-up tasks that would confront them in the days to come, Alphonse laid his hand on the handle of the upright freezer. Fortunately, before he could open it, Cally screamed out, "Stop!"

"What?" Alphonse said.

"It's full of meat," Cally said, "including a twelve-pound turkey my sister bought last Christmas but decided not to roast. And it's been sitting in there in the heat for two weeks."

"Putrefaction," Alphonse said.

"Serious putrefaction," Cally said.

"Thanks for stopping me," Alphonse said.

"You're welcome."

"I've always had a weak stomach."

"Then we're all glad you didn't open the freezer," Rich said.

"Jesus," Alphonse said, "I'm glad my momma didn't live to go through this."

Upstairs the news was better. The water had stopped short of reaching the living room floor, though the hardwood floors were slimy with green mildew which also crept up the wooden legs of their furniture. They needed to get back to the house again as soon as possible, this time equipped with disinfectants to wipe down practically every surface on the house's two lower levels and some kind of pump to get the water out of the basement. Remarkably, they discovered that they still had running water, presumably not potable, but useful for hosing the basement if they could get it drained. As they were preparing to depart, they decided to take what they could of their clothes, packing out their suits, shirts and blouses, jackets and slacks, underwear and shoes until the cargo space of the Laredo was filled with musty-smelling clothes, all of which would need to be laundered or dry cleaned.

On the way out of town, they stopped briefly at Cally's old apartment in Riverside, only a couple of miles, but an entirely different circumstance, away. Snug to the Alkansea River levee, Riverside was one of the few areas of the city that had not flooded. Cally's apartment was dusty and hot and stank of being closed up. But it had smelled that way before the storm. They drove back to Mayflower in a daze. When Alphonse dropped Rich and Cally off at Monster House, he stood in the late summer heat with them for a moment. He gave each of them a hug. "I got some time coming, Coach," he said. "I'll get this piece on the schools filed, then come back down to lend you a hand. Don't tell me you can't use it."

AFTER ALPHONSE LEFT FOR the airport to catch his flight back to New York, Rich called Robert Feaster, explained the situation with his basement and inquired if Robert knew where he might rent a gasoline-powered pump. A half hour later, Robert called back to say he had borrowed the pump and an F-150 pick-up truck to haul it. "We'll take it down tomorrow," Robert said.

"Oh, you don't have to go, Robert," Rich said. "That's asking too much."

Robert said, "I don't want to sound like a smart butt, but do you know how to use this pump?"

"No," Rich admitted.

"Well, I do," Robert said. "And anyway, the one I'm getting is a big honker, and it's going to take two of us to get it off the truck."

The next morning, Sunday, September 12, Robert drove Rich down to Choctaw to drain the basement. Althea came along to help Cally wipe down the floors and furniture upstairs. The pump Robert had borrowed had some mileage on it and was seriously heavy. But the men were able to wrestle it off the truck, onto a dolly the owner had provided, and through the door from the backyard patio into the utility room. Once they had the pump inside, they dropped the vacuum hose over the ledge and down into the pool of smelly water that filled the basement's twelve feet square, ten feet deep space. The pump was loud and gave off an oily smell, but it worked, and the water level dropped steadily.

While the water drained by a long hose into the street, Rich and Robert carried garbage cans into the utility room and began to fill them with debris. When the cans were full, the men carried them to the street where they would sit uncollected for two months by a city garbage collection division that no longer functioned. Rich and Robert then decided to use the dolly to move the meat-packed freezer from the utility room to the street. Rich figured he would decide later whether to try to clean the freezer of its contents or just abandon it, but he was certain he didn't want to open the appliance inside the house. They found a coil of wet rope and used it to wrap around the freezer to tie its doors shut. This, they hoped, would enable them to tilt the freezer backwards onto the dolly and roll it out of the house without exposing the horrors inside.

Their plan didn't work. As soon as they tilted the freezer back, foul fluid began to run out, producing the worst smell either Rich or Robert had ever encountered. Both had been around the incredible stench of a hog farm. But this was worse. They rolled the freezer outside as fast as they could and practically ran it down the driveway all the way to the street. Rich fought mightily to control his gag reflex, knowing that if he let himself so much as cough, he'd lose the contents of his stomach. Once they had set the reeking freezer down and lifted it away from the dolly, both men stalked briskly away, trying not to breathe. They sat on the porch, away from its poisonous odor. Neither spoke for a while.

Finally, Rich said, "I am sorry, man. That was some record-setting stink."

For whatever reason, Robert found that comment hilarious and began to laugh uproariously. Between guffaws, he managed to rasp, "You have said a mouthful, brother."

But then Rich announced, "I don't even want to think about my mouth." And that set both of them to howling.

When they finally calmed down, Rich told Robert to stay seated. He fetched a towel out of a box in the F-150 and tied it around his head like a Western outlaw's bandana mask. Then he went back to the patio, unfurled the garden hose, thanking God they had running water, dragged the hose inside the utility room and began to flush the freezer's still reeking fluid down the floor drain in front of the ruined washing machine. But the smell lingered even after Rich was certain he'd washed all the freezer water away, so he went back to the truck for a bottle of bleach and poured its contents on the utility room floor until his eyes burned and he was being sickened by the smell of chlorine rather than decaying meat.

When the pump had mostly emptied the basement, Robert insisted on putting on waders he'd thought to bring along and climbing down the slickened concrete steps to finish the job that required manual handling of the vacuum hose. Rich protested that Robert shouldn't assign himself such a dirty task, and that Rich should handle it himself.

But Robert said, "I let you wash that freezer water out. You didn't see me trying to talk you out of that job."

"It's my house," Rich said.

"These are my waders," Robert said. "And I've watched how you walk, brother. I'm afraid you try to go down those steps you're going to fall on your behind and break something. Big as you are, if that happens, we'd just have to leave you here."

Before heading back to Mayflower that day, Rich and Cally had Robert make a quick drive out to campus for a look around. On the way, they drove past the Water Oaks subdivision where Cecilia had lived for five decades. The streets in the area were still flooded. Since her house was one story and built on a concrete slab, it had no doubt suffered devastating damage. Rich ached with the horror of what Cecilia was facing.

RICH ARRIVED AT FRIENDSHIP House the next morning at 7 a.m. Since he'd brought back dress clothes from Choctaw, musty though they were, he might have dressed like a rector. Instead, he dressed in what had now become his crisis uniform: black knit shirt, jeans, running shoes and his blue blazer. Charlie Lobovich and Cecilia were already there, both dressed in overalls. With the city now open for work details, Charlie wasn't going to delay even a day. He had put together a crew of his facilities people who had found lodging in Mayflower, and he had managed to borrow three pickups from facilities management friends at ASU. He wanted to assess the damage on campus so he could begin the daunting process of putting the place back together. He had already purchased enough bleach to swab out the Augean Stables. Rich asked Cecilia if she was dressed in overalls as a gesture of sympathy.

"I'm going with him," she replied.

"Why?" Rich inquired.

"Because Charlie said he'd take me."

"And what do you think you're going to do down there?" Rich asked.

"You think I don't know how to scrub up shit?" she said. "I'm a nurse, for chrissake."

"Cecilia," Rich said. "If I'm not mistaken you have grandchildren."

"And I've had to clean up their poop plenty of times. Literally as well as metaphorically."

Rich shook his head. "You are *not* going to work as one of Charlie's laborers," he said. "You're our provost, goddamn it. I absolutely forbid it."

"You think I'm too good for such work?" Cecilia demanded.

"Yes," Rich said. "OK, no. Of course, not. None of us is too good for whatever has to be done. But I am your boss, and I am still forbidding you from doing it. It's hot as hell. Our buildings are disease factories. And frankly, Cecilia, you'll want to remember that there aren't any restroom facilities."

"Sounds to me like I can pick any classroom I want to squat in."

"You are deliberately trying to gross me out, aren't you," Rich said.

"You're gonna boss me around, I'm gonna gross you out."

In the end they decided that Cecilia could ride down to Choctaw with Charlie, but she had to agree not to do janitorial work. She could work in her office in 6, if it hadn't been used as a toilet room. And she could gather any materials she might find useful for their workspace at Friendship House. If she had time, she could inspect other buildings and report back on the their conditions.

"I want to inspect the dorms," she said. "We won't be back in business in any full measure until we get the dorms operational."

"That's a good idea," Rich said. "But the first floors of all those on the southern end of campus are going to be in bad shape."

"I'll check upstairs. Maybe kids will be able to live on the upper floors while Charlie does repairs downstairs."

EVERY WEEKEND FOR THE rest of September, Rich and Cally drove down to Choctaw, often accompanied by Robert and Althea who demanded to go along. By mid-September, they were joined by Alphonse Jackson, who had an aunt in Mayflower he could stay with. Because he had such deep roots in Choctaw, *Newsday* assigned him to report on the disaster, so he didn't have to cash vacation time. The weekend help he provided Rich and Cally with their house was a personal gesture of giving back.

Rich and Cally, Alphonse and the Feasters first emptied the ground level of all its destroyed contents. Their washer and dryer took up curbside residence next to the freezer, which managed to reek even though its doors remained tied shut. Nothing in Cally's home office was salvageable. Her collapsed desk was so softened from the flood waters that Rich was able to break it into pieces no bigger than a TV tray using nothing but a rubber mallet.

Once everything moveable had been carted to the street, the men took after the sheet-rocked walls and ceiling with claw hammer and crowbar, tearing out the soggy, chalky wall board and adding it to the growing refuse pile in front of the house. When they finally had the ground floor torn out to bare stud, they sprayed every surface with moldicide. And while the men worked downstairs, Cally and Althea undertook salvaging the kitchen refrigerator, which was only one month old when the storm hit. This was not as disgusting a job as cleaning the freezer would have been, but it was bad enough. Everything inside was thrown directly into contractor-strength plastic bags, which were carried to the street as soon as they were filled and tied off. No triage was attempted on items like canned soft drinks or bottles of beer. Anything in the fridge was out.

Once the refrigerator was emptied, Cally and Althea pulled out all the shelves and bins and scrubbed them and the entire interior with bleach and water. To combat any lingering odor, open bowls of baking soda and charcoal briquettes were set inside. These efforts were heroic. But to Cally's horror and dismay, she continued to find little dead black flies in the refrigerator for the next year. Where they were coming from, she was never able to determine.

By the end of September, people were coming to deal with their flooded homes throughout the city. One could measure the progress by the ironic yardstick of the foul heaps of refuse that grew like cancerous goiters on the curbside in front of house after house, one stinking refrigerator, freezer, washer, dryer, clump of broken wall board, fungus-sprouting furniture or wad of ruined clothing after another. By October, FEMA money finally began to flow and mercenary truckers poured into the city. Their trucks drove the refuse away to dump sites where FEMA officials compensated the drivers by the load. The front nine of a golf course in Municipal Park was turned into a waste holding center outfitted with diesel shovels and huge earth movers that stacked Hosea's detritus into a mountain that climbed five stories high and filled a hundred square blocks of land. And yet, in front of all the houses in Choctaw, those festering refrigerators and freezers were left behind for nearly a year while FEMA tried to figure out what to do with them. Among the miracles was that the city managed to dodge an outbreak of some pestilential plague spawned by the jettisoned appliances that remained in the midst of the population, each smiling the white-toothed grin of a poisonous jack-o-lantern.

LIKE THE OTHER PEOPLE of Choctaw, Rich and Cally felt angry and depressed over the circumstances fate had dealt them. At the same time, in a stew of conflicting emotions, they knew and acknowledged themselves to be fortunate. They were astonished and humbled by the generosity of Alphonse Jackson and Robert and Althea Feaster. And they knew their losses were manageable in comparison to those who lost much more and had inadequate insurance or none whatsoever. So they were lucky and constantly told themselves so, even though a large part of them felt anything but.

ON THE MONDAY THREE weeks after Hosea flooded Choctaw, Cecilia arrived at the War Room in a fury. She had been in contact with Dell Computers, and they had told her that the computers she had solicited had been delivered to the ASU campus and signed for at the receiving dock. When she went to the receiving dock, however, she was told that they were not holding computers for the staff of Urban University. They had indeed received a mysterious shipment of fifty Dell computers for a Dr. Cecilia Provost. Not knowing who that was, they sought guidance up the organizational chart. Finally, someone from Rector Hopkins' office arrived in a van, signed for the computers and took them away.

When she related this story to the others in the War Room, the outrage was almost palpable. Rich immediately called Hopkins' office but was told Hopkins was in a meeting.

"Is the meeting there in his office?" Rich asked. "I'm supposed to be in that meeting, but I don't have the location on my calendar."

"Yyyes," the receptionist said. "Here in Rector Hopkins' office. May I say—"

Rich hung up and started for the ASU administration building, about a ten-minute walk away. He was completely red in the face. Everybody in the room had heard Rich's exchange and understood that he was headed to confront Hopkins personally.

"You don't mind, boss," Charlie Lobovich said, "I'll walk over there with you."

"Me too," Jose Najera said. "I'm the computer guy after all."

"Hell, I might as well go too," Ben Turner said. "Make things into a parade."

"You know I'm going," Cecilia added.

Rich neither answered nor waited for them and was already across the street by the time they got to the front stoop of Friendship House.

"How has a man with a bad leg gotten that far ahead of us?" Ben asked the others as they broke into a trot to catch up.

"Rich limps," Cecilia said. "But he limps fast."

Charlie, Jose and Cecilia were breathing hard by the time they caught Rich about halfway to Hopkins' office. So was Rich, whose sling-leg gait took more out of him than a normal stride. Turner, a regular jogger, was in better shape.

They entered Hopkins' office single file, Rich first, Ben last. Rich walked straight past the receptionist to Hopkins' secretary and asked to see her boss. The secretary's name plate said "Karen Walsh." She was in her mid-thirties, brown-haired and a little fleshy, but quite attractive. But like most every white person in Mayflower, Karen spoke in the north Alkansea drawl that had come to grate on Rich's nerves.

"He's in a meeting," Karen said, making a five syllable sentence into eight.

"We'll wait," Rich said and plunked himself down on one of the two sofas provided for waiting visitors. The other four sat down too. On the march across campus, Rich had planned to slam directly into Hopkins' office, to kick down the door if he had to. But he had collected himself a bit. If a scene were necessary, he'd try to make it out of the eyesight of Hopkins' staff.

"Rector Hopkins has another meeting right after this one," Karen said. "Could I make an appointment for you?" Her hand brushed back and forth lightly across her telephone, and Rich suspected that she was contemplating a call to security.

"I'm Richard Janus," Rich said without smiling. He could tell that his name meant nothing to her. In hierarchical theory, he was Stephen Hopkins' equal, the CEO of a sister school, but his name lit up not one neuron in her brain. The people of Mayflower lived in the hub of their own universe. The existence of outlying planets was only a rumor of little interest to them. "I'm rector at Urban University," Rich added to her blank face. "Down in Choctaw."

Ben Turner stood, walked to her desk, and extended his hand. "I'm Benjamin Turner," he said. "Dean of the College of Humanities and Social Sciences at Urban." He smiled broadly. And did he actually wink at her? "I was chairman of the Political Science Department here at ASU before moving down to Urban ten years ago, probably about the time you graduated. You're Karen Walsh, I see. Did I ever have you in class?"

Karen blushed. "I graduated in 1988," she said.

"You did not," Ben said. "You mean 1998. I probably had you your freshman year."

She giggled lightly, high in her throat. "1988," she said.

"Well, that's sure hard to believe," Ben said. "But I was here then too. Did I have you in class?"

"I don't think so," she said. "I would remember if I had."

"Well, aren't you sweet," he said.

She blushed again, fluttered her fingers on the keyboard of her computer, and said, "I could maybe squeeze y'all in for just a minute after this meeting. Would that help?"

"That would be really nice," Ben said. "Thank you."

He sat back down next to Rich, covered his mouth with his hand and said under his breath, "Honey, not vinegar, boss."

That was no doubt good advice, but Rich wasn't in a play-nice mood. He was exhausted from working at his house all weekend and, at the moment, a little unfairly resentful that Ben's house in the Exchange District hadn't flooded, that Rich and

Cally were living in a motel room at Monster House while Ben and his wife had moved into her family's Mayflower mansion. These were uncharitable and unreasonable jealousies, though, and Rich stomped on them as well as he could whenever they rose to his consciousness. Mostly, though, Rich was just pissed about somebody at ASU stealing Cecilia's computers. So he didn't wait for the secretary to announce him when Hopkins' guests exited the rector's office. Rich was on his feet the moment the door opened, and he practically pushed past the two men leaving as he barged into Hopkins' office.

"I've come to talk to you about our computers," Rich said by way of greeting.

Hopkins stood up from his desk as Rich came in. His fine manner of dressing reminded Rich of Elia Lipscom and Ben Turner, though otherwise the three men did not resemble each other physically. Hopkins was almost as tall as Rich and considerably leaner. His thin hatchet-blade face resembled pictures Rich had seen of the writer John Updike. He had a prominent nose and emerald eyes. He spoke with a Boston accent and bragged that he was a direct descendant of one of the founders of Plymouth Plantation. He wasn't handsome exactly, but in his tailored suits and monogrammed shirts, he was routinely described as distinguished looking.

"I didn't realize you were on my schedule today," Hopkins said.

"I want my computers," Rich said, moving to the edge of Hopkins' desk.

"I had my guys deliver ASU computers to Friendship House some time ago."

"Not those dinosaurs, Hopkins, *my* Dells," Rich snapped, placing his hands on the desk top and leaning over toward Hopkins in naked belligerence. Cecilia, Charlie and Jose had come into the office behind Rich. Ben stood in the doorway until Hopkins' secretary nudged him all the way inside and closed the door behind him.

"I am sure I have no idea what you're talking about."

"Oh Christ, man. You can do better than that. Michael Dell has donated $100,000 worth of computers to Urban University. They arrived here in Mayflower. Your man signed for them, and then he contacted your office to ask what to do with them. We know that."

"OK, now I know what you're talking about," Hopkins said. "A bunch of computers came in. But how was I to know that they were for you? The shipment didn't say so. They were sent to someone we didn't recognize. We assumed they were sent as hurricane relief."

"They *were* sent as hurricane relief, you moron. To us. To the relief of people displaced and dispossessed by the hurricane. That would be people associated with Urban University."

"Those of us here in Mayflower were affected by the hurricane, too. Our town is full of refugees. Our classes are full of your students."

"Which I haven't noticed you turning away, and whom you have been charging tuition, even though Viceroy Lipscom told you not to. Now you've stolen my fucking computers."

"I have done nothing of the kind."

Rich lowered his voice and switched into a flat tone that Charlie and Jose thought so absolutely terrifying they moved closer to him so they could hold him off if he exploded. "I want my computers. And I want them now."

"I think they've already been distributed."

That's when Rich started around the desk after him, still speaking in that low voice, "I am going to break you up into tiny pieces and shove the parts up your ass."

Fortunately, for Hopkins and Rich both, Charlie rushed forward and put Rich in a bear hug from behind, pulling him backwards toward the door. Charlie was almost a head shorter than Rich, but he had been a college wrestler, and he was strong.

"Let Charlie take you out, boss," Cecilia said.

"I'm calling security," Hopkins said.

Jose turned to him, his black eyes locking hard on Hopkins' green ones. "I really don't think that's necessary, do you?" Hopkins' hand moved toward his phone. "Please don't do that," Jose said. "Things are under control here. You do that, and they're going to get out of control. I'm a hot-headed Latino, and you never know *what* people like me are going to do."

Charlie still held Rich in the bear hug, but he stopped trying to back Rich out of the room, and Rich stopped squirming. Cecilia had moved next to Rich and placed her hand on his forearm.

"Those computers are payback for the ones the viceroy made me lend you," Hopkins said, contradicting his statement that he was unaware the Dell shipment had been for Urban.

"That is such bullshit," Rich said, lunging against Charlie's strong arms.

"Rich!" Cecilia said.

"It's the absolute truth," Hopkins said. "We gave you computers when we were asked to, and we assumed you ordered these to make things square."

"Brand new computers are a lot more than square for the beat-up and outdated machines you provided us," Jose said.

"Pop," Rich said to Hopkins. "That's a finger. Like a twig. Pop. That's a wrist bone."

"What the fuck are you talking about," Hopkins said, his hands trembling.

"Snap," Rich said. "That's an elbow. My man Charlie will eventually let me go. And I know where you live. I've been to your house."

"You're insane," Hopkins said.

"Then you better give me our computers," Rich said.

"Look," Jose said to Hopkins. "I'm Urban's computer guy. You tell me where the computers are right now, and I'll have my guys go pick them up."

"Snap," Rich said.

"This is all just a total misunderstanding," Hopkins said. "Now that y'all have clarified matters, of course, we'll see that the computers are delivered to you. We'll bring them to you at Friendship House. I will see it done immediately."

"Snap," Rich said. "That's what happens if you're lying."

"It's just a misunderstanding," Hopkins said, lying, his face the color of typing paper.

"MAN," BEN TURNER SAID as the five Urbanians walked back to Friendship House. "Hopkins completely caved once Rich went all Clint Eastwood on his ass."

"I just hope that's the end of it," Charlie said.

"We get the computers back, that *is* the end of it," Jose said. "I think the man's too scared to take this anywhere else. He didn't even try to call security while we were there."

Ben Turner laughed. "Not a lot of episodes in the history of higher ed where two university rectors come to fisticuffs. Kind of like it. But not so dignified."

"Didn't happen," Charlie said. "Like Hopkins himself said, just a misunderstanding."

"You think he'll report you to the viceroy?" Ben asked Rich.

"I don't know," Rich said. "Maybe not. Probably."

"Nothing to tell," Charlie said. "Nothing happened. A misunderstanding got cleared up."

Ben laughed again. "Hopkins hasn't got any witnesses. That's the good thing."

But Hopkins had four witnesses, Rich thought. He didn't want his colleagues to feel they had to lie for him. His threats were melodramatic and stupid. But they were threats, and he had made them. Worse, he'd brought Jose into it. That was more inexcusable than threatening Hopkins himself.

Anger's adrenaline draining from his system, Rich felt so weak he was afraid he couldn't make it all the way back to Friendship House. His ankle ached, and when he stepped in a shallow spot in the grass, it rolled the way it always did, and he stumbled forward to keep from falling. He felt exhausted and stretched and limp, like an overinflated balloon from which all the air has been released. And he felt ashamed. He hated Stephen Hopkins. But he violated his own principles when he resorted to threats of violence. He recognized that he might have struck Hopkins had Charlie not grabbed him. What was the storm turning him into? What was this storm revealing about him that he had always managed to keep hidden?

ETHYL SCRANTON TELEPHONED FRIENDSHIP House the next morning and asked Rich to come over to the Trustees Building to meet with the viceroy.

"See you got all dressed up for me again," Lipscom said as Rich walked in.

Cally had taken the clothes they had brought up from Choctaw to a dry cleaner, but they weren't ready yet. So Rich was wearing the same basic outfit he'd worn since arriving in Mayflower. Today's jeans were black. Why did Lipscom care how he dressed?

"Didn't know you were such a fashionista, Elia," Rich said. He felt a surge of the kind of anger he'd unleashed on Stephen Hopkins the day before, and he tried to mask it in flippancy.

"Ha, ha," Lipscom said. "Nice term, fashionista. You make that up?"

"No. I heard it somewhere."

"We don't hear smart-ass little phrases like that in Mayflower. Too backwater, I guess."

Rich made no further comment.

"I'm serious when I'm telling you to go buy yourself a suit, Coach. We got Trustees want in on the story of what's going on at Urban, and I don't want the boss of the place looking like the Urban Cowboy."

Rich looked down at himself. What about his attire looked Western?

"*Urban Cowboy*. Get it?" Lipscom said.

Rich nodded and smiled, though the gesture made his face hurt. "The movie. John Travolta."

"And Debra Winger," Lipscom said. "She get naked in that movie?"

"I don't recall," Rich said.

"She got naked in that or the other one, you know, the one with Richard Gere."

"*An Officer and a Gentleman.*"

"Yeah, that one. She got naked with either Richard Gere or John Travolta in *Urban Cowboy*, right?"

"I don't remember," Rich said.

"You don't remember, but now you are the Urban Cowboy."

Rich didn't know what to say.

"You work at Urban. You dress in jeans. You act like a cowboy."

Rich licked his lips.

"Guess you city guys aren't the only phrase turners. You writers. Is that how you'd classify yourself? A writer who once coached basketball? Or do you think of yourself as a basketball coach who once wrote a couple of books?"

"Right now, I'm thinking of myself as a university administrator with an institution in a lot of trouble."

"And that excuses your making threats to an administrator at another university?" Lipscom said.

So Hopkins had reported him. Rich felt his anger flare again. And Lipscom was pissing him off with his stupid game playing. Rich took a very large breath and exhaled slowly.

"Stephen and I had a misunderstanding," Rich said. "I think it's settled now. But I'll apologize to him if you like."

"Why the fuck would I care if you apologized to him?" Lipscom said.

"I suppose because it would be the right thing to do if he felt threatened."

"I like that you threatened him," Lipscom said, grinning broadly. "OK, I really don't. So I'm telling you that you're not to do it again."

"Of course not," Rich said. "Absolutely."

"Although I really don't give a shit," Lipscom said. "Might do him a world of good if you had punched him in the nose. But you didn't hear that from me."

"Of course not," Rich said.

"So we're clear on this Hopkins business," Lipscom said.

"Yes," Rich said. "I promise not to make any more threats, just as you've advised me."

"Excellent," Lipscom said. "I am delighted to have you on tape admitting that you have been properly advised."

"You're taping this conversation?" Rich asked.

"No," Lipscom said. "Should I be? Are you?"

"Taping this conversation?" Rich said. "Of course not."

"Excellent," Lipscom said. "I'm glad that's settled. But that's not why I asked you to come see me. I was just talking to Al Bendorf about the situation you got yourself in Choctaw." Bendorf was one of the trustees. His district was in northwest Alkansea, an area of the state historically and culturally divorced from Choctaw. "He wonders if y'all don't need to close up shop for a year. Furlough everybody but maybe a half dozen of your top people. Get the students situated up here or wherever. Save the state a ton of money. Reevaluate things in January maybe. Idea's got some merit, you gotta admit that."

"You're saying Bendorf is proposing laying off all but a half dozen of Urban's employees?"

"OK, maybe a dozen. Your top people. Your pushy nurse provost. Whoever you need to hold down the fort. Hell, you might be able to demand two dozen for all I know."

"Elia, you said that Urban would be 'utterly protected.'"

"Up to me, maybe it would. But I work for the Trustees. They make the decision on this. I just implement their plan."

"Then you have to convince them the idea is disastrous. We're talking about full-time employment for nearly 3,000 people. People whose homes and possessions are under water. People who need paychecks to pay the motels they're staying in. People who need their salaries to pay mortgages on homes they can't even live in. People who need to eat. People who need to return to Choctaw to fix their houses so that the city can be rebuilt. People who are critical to the area's economic survival and recovery. You can't just pull the goddamn plug on people in this situation, Elia. It isn't human. It's fucking indecent."

"Listen, Coach. You don't have to convince me. I don't give a shit what you do with state money. But Ronnie told me there's some kind of law that says you can't pay people who aren't working. It's a pretty explicit law with a lot of unpleasant penalties. And I'm not going to be a party to any kind of fraud. You can count on that. So you don't want the Board to vote to furlough your whole institution, you better come up with some kind of plan."

"I've got a plan," Rich said, though he didn't.

"Yeah, in a nutshell what's that?"

"We're going to open back up."

"Great, but even if you open up in the spring, you're still going to have to furlough everybody this fall. I can probably talk the Trustees into paying everybody through the end of the month. After that, no work, no pay. Ronnie says that's the law. That puts us back to your dozen or so essential staff. That's Bendorf's notion. I suspect the others will buy it real quick."

"Yeah, well, we're going to open back up this fall," Rich said.

"Right," Lipscom said. "When?"

"October 18. Urban University will be open and teaching classes on October 18. That's a promise."

But even then, it was a promise Richard Janus had no idea how to keep.

33

While Canonchet, Weetamoo and Quinnapin were leading their surviving Wampanoags and Narragansetts to Menameset in *Pequahokesos*, or January, of 1676, I set off to New York to forge what I hoped would prove decisive alliances in the war the English libelously named for me. My goals were several. And to accomplish them, I contacted the Dutch settlers who had lost their authority in the region and had retreated to land on the upper Hudson. When my runners returned with the word that our mission would be welcome and our arrival would not be confided to the English under Governor Andros on the lower Hudson, I set out from Menameset with a party of fifty Wampanoags, including Wootonekanuske, Adonoshonk and Annawon, along with representatives of the Narragansetts and the Nipmucks. I established a base camp among the Dutch at Schaghticoke on the Hoosic River, which flowed west into the Hudson and provided me rapid access to all the parties with whom I wanted to undertake diplomatic negotiations. Even as my men began building our cedar-bark-roofed *nashweetoos*, I started my conversations with the Dutch, pleased that they offered me and my ambassadors refuge in their homes on the Hudson.

The Dutch were represented by Klaus Vanderlichten, chief officer of the Noordam Company that traded with the Indians and the French to the north. A large, barrel-chested man with red hair and a bushy red beard, Vanderlichten had once maintained his headquarters on Long Island where he traded with Narragansetts and Wampanoags both. As a younger man, he had known and maintained good relations with my father.

"We Dutch are no friends of the English," Vanderlichten assured me as we sipped warmed cider at the fireplace hearth in his drafty wooden home. The temperature outside was in the upper thirties but it felt little warmer inside save right next to the fire. "We Dutch founded this trade on the Hudson, and now we have been driven from our posts at the river's mouth."

"But I have been told," I said, "that you and your countrymen have pledged fealty to Governor Andros and his authority in this territory."

"What choice did we have?" Vanderlichten said. "The English control the lower river. And we Dutch must be seen as docile citizens if we are to be allowed to move the furs we acquire from our Indian trading partners onto vessels bound for the markets of Europe. This is the life we have made for ourselves in this new world. But whereas once we were rich, today we are barely surviving. We haven't the force to stand against Andros. So we have to cooperate with him. But he inflates the cost of trade goods he sells to us and then taxes us heavily on our furs."

"I'm sure you hate this," I said.

"I dream of revenge every night," Vanderlichten said and spit into the fire.

"I can imagine, my friend," I said. "We share a similar fate at English hands."

"But we hear that you have set the English colonies ablaze and sent many to the claws of Old Scratch."

"We are indeed at war," I said. "And that is why I am here. I think we are natural allies, you Dutch and those of my brothers in the field against Plymouth, Massachusetts and Connecticut." I listed for him and his lieutenants our series of victories, and I gauged that he and his men were impressed.

"We would like to join with you," Vanderlichten said, "as I assume is your purpose here. But I don't know how much we can help. I have no fighting men or even muskets to spare."

"We need safe passage," I explained. "We have other negotiations to pursue, and we seek confidence that you have no reason to resist arms, ammunition, and other supplies moving through this area to reach us in our strongholds on the eastern side of the Connecticut."

"You are not here," Vanderlichten said and threw his head back laughing. "None of you. Not here." He pointed at Annawon and Adonoshonk, saying to each in turn, "I don't see you, and I don't see you." He turned to me. "And I especially don't see the Great Metacom, King Philip of the Wampanoags. He wouldn't dare come into my realm." He laughed again and lit his pipe, puffing on it and passing it across to me. "Let us smoke together in agreement that we have not met since you were a boy mooning around after a Pocasset girl."

"But we should meet someday. I would like that," I said, putting the pipe to my lips.

WITH THE ACQUIESCENCE OF the Dutch to our activities attained, I turned my efforts in Schaghticoke to forging a desired alliance with the Muhhekunneuws or Mahicans, our Algonquian cousins on the upper Hudson. I hoped to enlist their support in any way possible, best of all by having them contribute warriors to our fighting force. Once our *nashweetoos* were complete and ready to provide hospitality, I sent my runners to Mahican Sachem Wannuaucon to ask that he join me at Schaghticoke for a meal. He came with a party of twenty, and we provided bear stew and roast venison for all. Once our greetings were completed, we slipped under the flap of my *nashweetoo*, each of us attended by five captains. Wannuaucon was well versed in our struggles over the last half year, but after we had spread our robes on the sleeping platforms and adjusted ourselves to the warmth, as was our way, I recited for him the genocidal atrocities the English had committed since their arrival against the Pequots, the Massachusetts, the Wampanoags and most recently the Narragansetts. A fit man about my own age, Wannuaucon said he was horrified by all that I listed and informed me that a relative of his had married a Narragansett man and had lost her life in the Great Swamp fight.

"Regrettably," I said, "our Narragansett cousins did not see the wisdom of joining our fight until after so many of their fathers and mothers, brothers and sisters were burned alive."

Wannuaucon nodded somberly, lit his pipe, smoked and handed it to me.

"I have come to ask you and your warriors to join us," I said, "and to help me recruit others of our tongue in the area who also can be led to understand that this may be the last chance we have to push the English out of our midst, first where they have spread out from Boston and Plymouth and once that is done from the mouth of the Hudson as well."

Wannuaucon responded with details about his own problems with the English in New York, particularly as they manifested themselves in their covenant with the Mohawks, whom the English had given free rein to prey on Mahicans and any other of their Algonquian neighbors. "I hate the English," Wannuaucon said. "But I hate the Mohawks more. They are the point of the English spear. They cut my people out of trade with the Dutch before I was born, and when the English replaced the Dutch, nothing changed for us. We get only what dribbles from the kettles in the Mohawk longhouses. We have not known freedom from their dominance in my lifetime."

This was an uncomfortable conversation. I understood Wannuaucon's hatred of the Mohawks. But we were in a season now when we had to transcend old grievances. But I did not argue for this attitude with my Mahican brother, for I doubted that he could let go of his bitterness. Instead, unwisely, I assured him that, if the day came that we had no alternative, we would face the Mohawks together. In the meantime, I beseeched him to see the fight to his east not as my fight, but our fight.

"Everything is at stake," I said, as we kept the fire around which we sat bright with embers by stirring it with sticks we had stacked by the woodpile for just this purpose. "We must prevail, we the Wampanoags and the Nipmucks and the Narragansetts and the Mahicans, too. For if we do not prevail, we are lost. We will never again farm the fields of our mothers or hunt the woods of our fathers. We will not teach our children the games of our own youth and race with them along the hard beach sand of the summer; we will not sing the songs of our ancestors around the fires of our *nashweetoos* in winter; we will not fetch our flutes and our drums to the meadows of spring to dance with our children under the planting moon. For if we do not prevail, we will cease to be. This you can be assured is the express intention of the English. Already they snatch our people when they can and bind them aboard the great ships, never to be seen again. If you and your warriors stand with us, victory is in our grasp. If you do not, and I say this with sorrow, not with warning, then, when the English come for you, and they will, we will not be there to stand at your side."

Wannuaucon was an intelligent man, and he agreed to join our campaign because he saw that what I presented to him was indisputably true. He not only pledged to lead his warriors east with us, but to raise others among people with whom he traded to the north and the west. In addition, he proved incredibly useful as an ally because he brought an ambassador from New France, Francois de la Manse, to meet with the two of us in Schaghticoke.

De la Manse looked every bit the part of the backwoodsman he was. His skin was weathered and brown like leather dried hard after being left in the rain. He had a sharp face and a long hank of hair that hung out of his black cap all the way to his shoulders. He kept a tin of whisky always in his coat, but he was generous in offering it to those in his company, and he fixed each of us who spoke with keen and receptive eyes. We knew that those of our neighbors who dealt with the French found them accepting and reliable. And I very much liked de la Manse's enthusiasm for my entreaties that we become allies against the English.

"We are at peace with the Mohawks," he said, "and we trade with them regularly. But our relationship with them has always been uneasy. They block our opportunities to expand our number of trading partners, wanting everything to move through them. Moreover, the Mohawks' true allegiance lies with the English, and it will always lie with whatever power controls the mouth of the Hudson, once the Dutch, now Governor Andros. My Huron and other Indian allies in New France are enemies of the Mohawks, but cannot stand against them. They can easily see the advantages of joining you against the English as a way of flanking the Mohawk."

De la Manse said that he could deliver to our cause at least three hundred warriors. As men will, he exaggerated, but he was truer to his pledge than most white men with whom I had dealt, and we were ultimately joined in Schaghticoke by nearly two-hundred native Canadian fighting men. Moreover, de la Manse promised to keep us supplied with all the powder and shot that we could use. Last, he promised that he would convince his government to blockade the ports at Boston, Plymouth, New London and Saybrook so that the English could not be resupplied. If that were to happen, victory would be ours.

De la Manse had but one request of us, that we comport ourselves as if we possessed the neutron bomb. "In every way I and my French countrymen can assist you, we will. We will praise Holy God in the name of our father the Pope as you kill all the English in New England. But when you do, we beseech you to restrain yourselves from burning the homes, barns, churches, and meeting houses of the English blasphemers. We are men who live in peace with the Indians we found here. And when the English are expunged, we will be eager to come among you for our mutual benefit. We will be able to do so more quickly and easily if we can occupy the buildings erected there now."

"What you ask is perfectly reasonable," I told him. "And I shall pass this condition along to those who lead our men into battle." For obvious reasons, I did not inform him that the torch was as important a weapon in this war as the musket.

With these significant pledges of support accomplished, I undertook the last of my initiatives while at Schaghticoke. I sent runners to the long houses of the Mohawks and invited them to dine with me and to discuss pressing matters of mutual interest. They agreed to send three of their leaders to meet with me, Satekarihwate, Deionhehkon, and Rastawentherontha. Hudson Valley neighbors of the Mahicans, but their traditional enemies, the ferocious Mohawks were the strongest Indian nation in our greater region, and, unfortunately, they were not on friendly terms with any of the Algonquians of New England, not the nearby Mahicans or any of the nations east of the Connecticut.

Despite the Mohawks' adroit change of alliance from the Dutch to the English, the relationship between the Mohawks and the authorities of New York was young enough for me to regard it as fragile. The Mohawks would undertake whatever strategy they concluded would best serve their own interests. My job, now, was to convince their leaders that they should employ their considerable military might on our side. I recognized how very uncomfortable success in this mission would make our Mahican cousins, but I felt certain that if the Mohawks joined our martial confederacy, we would prevail in New England and after that could drive the English off the Hudson as well. Widely united in this way, we natives could control the trade that had led the pinkskins to move in with us and help themselves to what was ours. Surely the Mohawks could see the wisdom of this strategy.

34

The atmosphere of inhospitality in Mayflower toward the thousands of evacuees from Choctaw came to light almost as soon as Hosea's winds blew away to reveal that broken levees had flooded the city and that the people from Choctaw weren't going home anytime soon. There were, of course, people of unfathomable generosity like Althea and Robert Feaster. But the more prevalent attitude could be captured in countless snipes of appalling hostility of the sort that Rich and Cally heard at Wal-Mart soon after their arrival. "When are these people going back where they came from?" was a common refrain uttered as if Choctaws had arrived in Mayflower by choice and remained there out of desire rather than necessity.

Though seldom baldly stated as such, the nasty, unsympathetic comments were usually uttered by white people and aimed at black people. Rich and Cally were not black and thus were often mistaken for Mayflowers, a presumption that made them furious. The superiority and heartlessness of so many people in Mayflower made Rich and Cally want to return to Choctaw with every fiber of their being. Their own house in Choctaw was so badly damaged it would require months of repairs before it could be inhabited again. But once power and clean water were restored to the unflooded areas of town, Rich and Cally could move into her old apartment. It would require a monumental feat of cleaning and the relocation of furniture, but it could be lived in as soon as the city could be reoccupied. In the meantime, their room at Monster House, they knew, provided a vastly better daily living circumstance than that consigned to the thousands of their fellow Choctaws still living in shelters. So, despite the rental charge and notwithstanding their love for the Feasters, Rich and Cally were grateful for their room at Monster House and for the comparative privacy it afforded them.

Then on the evening of Tuesday, September 21, when Rich and Cally returned to Monster House after eating still another meal at the Chinese buffet about ten minutes from the ASU campus, they found a handwritten note in an envelope that had been slipped underneath their door. The note read:

Dear Rector Janus:

I hope that I might have the privilege of speaking with you about your accommodations first thing in the morning.

Cordially,
Bertram Weekly
Manager

"What the fuck is this about?" Cally wondered aloud. "He want to raise our rate?"

"Maybe the rectoral suite has come available," Rich said. "I am, after all, a rector."

"*Interim* rector, dear. Don't inflate yourself."

"I've been inflating myself since I was in sixth grade."

"Aren't you ashamed?"

"Yes. Why did I waste all those early years?"

Cally laughed. "If you didn't have such a dirty mind, you could wear a hat two sizes smaller."

"So you're saying bigger is better. I thought as a dedicated feminist you were required to deny that."

"I deny that you ever miss an opportunity to engage in sexual innuendo."

"Me? Am I the one who walks around with such great tits, ass and pussy? That's sexual innuendo so powerful it doesn't even require words."

"I thought you said my pussy needed to be shaved."

"Darling, a warning to be fair: were you bare down there, you'd never leave my lair."

"You are incorrigible," Cally said, laughing and kissing him quickly. "But you still haven't told me what you think Bertie wants to see us about."

"Maybe he really does have a suite for us."

"My incorrigible optimist," she said.

"Does that mean I might get lucky tonight?"

"Maybe."

"Maybe means yes, right?"

"Yes means yes."

"Yes! Then I do feel lucky tonight."

NEITHER ONE OF THEM felt lucky the next morning when they stopped by the front desk and asked to see Mr. Weekly. He was eating a muffin at his desk. He licked quickly at the fingers of his right hand and then flicked with the back of his fingertips at the front of his chocolate brown Monster blazer, brushing away a dropped crumb. Weekly was short, thin, fiftyish and tired looking. His skin was gray, his black hair slicked back and in need of washing, as was his face.

"Ah yes, Mr. Janus," Weekly said. "Mrs. Janus." He had been told at least twice that Cally's last name was Martin, but he either couldn't remember or couldn't bring himself to use a last name different from Rich's. "Thank you so much for stopping by this morning. I hope you slept well last night." Weekly persisted in relating to them as if they were routine hotel guests stopping in for a night or two, soon to return home. "I hope you are finding everything satisfactory here at Monster House."

Rich glanced at his wristwatch. Rich had so much to do every day that he suffered from the daylong feeling that whatever he *was* doing was less urgent than what he *wasn't* doing. "Things are fine, Mr. Weekly. Thank you."

"Thank you for your concern for our comfort," Cally said.

"Yes, well," Weekly said. "We've been very privileged to serve you. And we hope you will return again soon. But we will need you to vacate your room by noon tomorrow so that we can prepare the room for our next guests."

"Excuse me?" Rich said.

Rich stared at the man until Weekly finally understood that he was to elaborate.

"Yes, well, I am sure you understand," Weekly said, touching at his hairline with a bowed index finger. "It's the Alabama game."

"No, I'm sure I don't understand," Rich said.

"Well, yes, it *is* the Alabama game," Weekly said.

Big a sports fan as he was, much as Rich rooted against the Monsters no matter the sport, he'd been far too distracted since the storm to have followed their football season.

"The Alabama game?" Rich said.

"Yes," Weekly said and smiled.

"So?" Rich said.

"Well, so, we will need you to vacate your room by noon tomorrow."

"Why?" Rich said.

"Why, so that Mr. Whitehorse can have his room."

"Mr. Whitehorse's room?"

"Yes," Weekly said and smiled again.

"Our room?"

"Well, your room right at the moment. But it's been Mr. Whitehorse's room for years. He has a standing reservation."

"For the Alabama game," Cally said.

"Well, yes, for the Alabama game and all the home games here at Monster Stadium. Mr. Whitehorse is a very big supporter of Monster Athletics." Weekly lowered his voice as if he were confiding a secret. "I understand that he's one of our most faithful donors. He's quite a big man in the northern part of the state. Oil, of course."

"So you're telling us that you're kicking us out of our room for a football game," Cally said. "For this weekend and every subsequent weekend when there's a football game?"

"Well, I don't think I'd say that I'm kicking you out. I wouldn't say that at all. No. I'm just honoring Mr. Whitehorse's standing reservation. As I said, he's a very big supporter. And he's had his reservation for years."

"But you *are* asking us to leave our room?" Cally said.

"Well, yes," Weekly said. "I have no choice really. But you are more than welcome to return on Monday. In fact, I will be happy to take your reservation for Monday right now."

"We can make a reservation for our own room?" Rich said.

"Yes, I'd be happy to," Weekly said. He stepped to his side, opened a leatherette-bound date book on the counter between them and took a pen from his shirt pocket. He looked up at them with his pen poised. "We'll put this on the computer, of course, but I do like to note things in my reservation book as a failsafe. What with the hurricanes and all, computers *do* fail."

"You'll take our reservation to return to our own room next Monday," Cally said, her voice registering her exasperated incredulity.

"Yes," Weeks said. "We can do that right now."

"But we can only stay until Thursday noon," Rich said, "on those weekends the Monsters play here in Mayflower."

"Yes, that's quite it," Weekly said. "I assume you have those other dates."

"Why would we have the other dates?" Cally wondered.

"Well, I can give them to you," Weekly said. "They're right here." He stretched his hand to the far side of the registration desk and plucked the top card from a stack and handed it to Cally. "Here's our schedule for this year. Our home games are bolded, as you can see."

Cally looked at the schedule card as if it were written in Sanskrit.

"We are at home seven times this fall," Weekly said, gesturing toward the card in Cally's hand. "Not unusual really. We once had eight home games in a season. But that hasn't happened but the one time, I don't think. Teams not in our conference have no choice but to come to Mayflower if they want to play us. National championships will do that."

"Let's go back a ways," Rich said. "You're saying that we have to be out of our room at noon tomorrow and every Thursday there's a home game? Seven times in all this fall?"

"Yes," Weekly said. "We're at home each of the next three weeks."

"So for the next three weeks," Rich said, "we can stay in our room only Monday through Wednesday?"

"Well, Mr. Whitehorse does have the room reserved Thursday through Sunday, and he always pays in full even though he sometimes doesn't get in until Friday and seldom stays Sunday night. But he does like to sleep late on Sunday, especially after a big game."

"We're going to be kicked out of our room for four days," Rich said, "for a man who most likely will use that room only two of the nights."

"I really wish you wouldn't say I'm kicking you out. I don't look at it that way at all. I'm just honoring a reservation by a very important person."

"And you know who I am?" Rich said. He hated feeling he had no choice but to play this card. It made him uncomfortable, made him fear he was becoming the very kind of self-important asshole he detested. On the other hand, the idea that he was being booted from the only home he had at the moment was really pissing him off.

Weekly looked at Rich with darting, blinking eyes.

"You know that I am rector of Urban University, the second largest university in Alkansea."

"Yes, sir," Weekly said. "Well, I don't know if anyone mentioned that Urban is the second largest university in the state. I don't recall that. I thought Ettons was the second largest. But, yes, I was told that you were the rector at Urban when the viceroy's office asked me to find a room for you and Ms. Lagasse."

"Speaking of which," Rich said. "Are you kicking Cecilia out as well?"

Weekly swallowed visibly, his Adam's apple moving up and down his thin neck. "Well, Mr. Charles Baron does have a standing reservation for the room where Ms. Lagasse is staying. Mr. Baron is another of our faithful benefactors."

"Also from the northern part of the state?" Cally asked in a sneer that Weeks seemed not to recognize.

"I believe he is," Weekly said. "I understand that he's in pharmaceuticals, although I may have that wrong."

"But you understand that Dr. Lagasse is the provost at our university?" Rich said, adding for spite, "The second largest university in our state."

"I was told that," Weekly said. "Though I don't know what a provost is. It sounds like an important position."

"Cecilia and I are the two top executives at Urban," Rich said. "We're here in Mayflower because our homes in Choctaw are flooded. We have nowhere to live for now but here in Mayflower. Here at Monster House."

Weekly began to straighten items on the registration desk, pushing the stack of Monster football schedule cards into tighter alignment, arranging a pen in a parallel line with the bottom of the leatherette book.

"You understand that Dr. Lagasse, who is seventy-five years old, is *home*less, just as Cally and I are. Homeless in an immediate and very real sense. We have no place to live other than here."

"I am very sorry, sir," Weekly said. "I know that we have many people such as yourself and Mrs. Janus here in Mayflower at the present. It's all very regrettable."

"And you understand," Cally said, "that Governor Lebear has issued an executive order that homeless people aren't to be kicked out of their hotel rooms anywhere in the state."

"Oh, yes," Weekly said. "I read that in *The Monitor*. Very interesting, I must say."

"It even applies to people who aren't able to pay their lodging bills," Cally pointed out.

"Oh, I didn't understand that. No," Weekly said. "I must not have read the whole article."

"But Rich and I have paid our bill, correct?"

"Yes, of course," Weekly said.

"And yet, you are kicking us out," Rich said.

"I am honoring reservations," Weekly said. "Nothing more."

"In defiance of the governor's orders."

"Oh no," Weekly said. "I would never defy the governor. No."

"The governor said you couldn't kick us out, but that's what you're doing," Cally said.

"No," Weekly said. "No, no. The governor's order was directed at hotels and motels. This is Monster House. It doesn't apply to us. It can't."

"People rent rooms here on a nightly basis, but you aren't a hotel?" Cally said.

"This is Monster House. We're here to serve the guests of Alkansea State University. That's our charge. We wouldn't ever want to disappoint ASU guests."

Rich reflected with bitter humor that he and Cecilia and Cally indeed were not guests of Alkansea State University however much he might argue that as the CEO at Urban he was a guest of the State of Alkansea.

"You realize how completely fucked this is," Cally said.

The color drained from Weekly's face. "Please, please," he said. "My hands are truly tied. We have reservations. Surely you must understand. It's the Alabama game."

LATER THAT MORNING, RICH was ushered into Elia Lipscom's office, where Rich informed the viceroy what was happening at Monster House. The viceroy said Ethyl had already fielded a phone call from Bertram Weekly worrying that Rich and Cally were upset with him but that his hands were tied. "You got us the rooms in the first place," Rich said. "I am assuming you can insist that the man follow the directives of the governor's executive order."

"I'm not sure about that," Lipscom said. "Monster House is a public entity. I think the governor's directive was aimed at privately owned and operated hotels and motels."

"You can't be serious," Rich said. "The governor is trying to keep those people with a temporary roof over their heads from being pushed onto the street."

The viceroy shrugged. "I guess we could ask the governor for a ruling."

"How do we go about that?" Rich asked.

"Beats me."

"You know I'm right about this, Elia," Rich said.

"I also know it's the Alabama game. Governor knows it, too. You can bet on that."

"I'm getting kicked out of my room, I a homeless person, I the CEO of the state's second largest university, I am getting kicked out of my room for a couple of honchos who lay big bucks on the Monster football team. Who gives a shit? Why would the governor give a shit?"

"Honchos who lay big bucks on Monster football," Lipscom said, "frequently lay big bucks on governors' races. And even if they haven't, they've got big bucks. Governors like people with big bucks. Might give the governor some of that money. Might give it to someone running against the governor if the governor gets on their wrong side."

"That seems like bullshit to me," Rich said. "I don't have a clue who these two guys Whitehorse and Baron are. But Weekly said they're from the northern part of the state. Ten to one says they're Republicans."

"Oh, they're Republicans all right. Big Bush guys."

"Then Lebear really doesn't give a shit, does he?" Rich said.

"He's a Democrat. You can count on one hand the number of votes he got in the northern counties. He's governor because of the votes he got in Choctaw and the rest of the southern part of the state."

Lipscom laughed. "You really don't know a thing about politics, do you?"

"On the contrary," Rich said. "I consider myself pretty well informed."

Lipscom laughed harder. "I'm not talking about the politics you read about in the newspaper. I'm talking about the politics that takes place when politicians get in a room with people who have money. Most of the rich guys in this state donate money to both the Republicans *and* the Democrats. They *care* who wins. But they want stroke with *whoever* wins, even if it's not their guy. And guys who run for governor need money, so they never piss off folks who have it. You don't seem to understand that at all. But I'll bet you do understand that rich guys in this state just love their Monsters. Especially their Monsters of the gridiron."

"Yeah, well, Lebear was elected by people who send their kids to Urban."

"Absolutely right," Lipscom said, chuckling again. He shook his head. "But how many of those people consider themselves Ungulates? Five? Ten?" He laughed. "Everybody in this state north, south and in between considers himself a Monster. See where I'm going."

"So you're not going to turn this around for me."

"No can do, Coach. For the time being, I like being viceroy. Really beats working for a living."

"For Christ sake. Forget about me. My provost is seventy-five years old, and she has nowhere to go. We've got Jose Najera in her dorm room now."

"You know you aren't going to win any points with me by worrying about your pushy old granny provost."

"That's shameful, Elia. Really."

"Ah, you know I'm just yanking your chain. I love the old unqualified biddy you've got running Academic Affairs for you. But I just can't help you. Would if I could, but I can't."

"I'll take this to the governor himself."

"Be my guest."

"And if the governor won't intercede, I'll take it to the press. The media would love a story about how the governor refuses to enforce his own executive order. All the more so, given that with me they've got a known commodity. I grant that nobody in this town gives a shit about Urban University, but kicking its rector out is still a juicy story."

The viceroy didn't like this. He doubted that Rich could get any kind of ruling out of the governor. The governor wouldn't want to piss off the rich guys. On the other hand, he wouldn't want to countermand his own executive order. So the viceroy was pretty confident Rich was gearing up to slam into a stone wall. If that really led Rich to go public with his complaint, the governor was going to be furious. With Rich for sure. But probably also with Elia Lipscom for letting it happen. And Lipscom needed good standing with the governor when he finally figured out how to get rid of Stephen Hopkins. The appointment to the presidency of ASU was formally the prerogative of the Board of Trustees, but the governor appointed the Board, and no one who wanted to remain on the Board would defy the wishes of the governor. What a fucking shit biscuit this was. And what a shithead Richard Janus was. He'd already gone public with his intention to reopen Urban on October 18, a decision that nobody on the Board liked but no one was willing to attack openly. It was just a matter of time before the viceroy got blamed for that. Now Janus was threatening to embarrass the governor for not enforcing his own rulings. Why couldn't underlings be subservient and docile the way they were supposed to be?

"Look, look," Lipscom said. "Let's not go off half cocked about this matter. I can see you're upset. Let me see what I can do. Let me make some calls."

An hour later, Ethyl called Rich at Friendship House and asked him to return to the viceroy's office. "I think he's got good news for you," she confided conspiratorially.

"I think I've got your issues under control," Lipscom said when Rich was again seated in his office. "I've found situations for both you and your provost, so I assume we can put to rest any idea of publicly challenging the governor."

"What do you mean *situations*?" Rich asked. "We're losing our rooms at Monster House. I'm not liking this from the get-go."

Lipscom said, "Well, I'll admit that the best I've been able to do for your provost so far is to find her another dorm room. But I remind you that's what she first asked for."

"No deal," Rich said.

"Now, now," Lipscom said. "Hear me out. I'll keep working on a better situation for granny."

"Stop calling her that, Elia."

"You Urban people certainly lack any sense of humor."

"Trade places with me and see how funny you find things."

"Oh boy, forever the guilt trip," Lipscom said. "OK, look. I'll stop razzing your provost. I can see you're loyal to her."

"Thank you."

"And I'll see if I can find her something better. It's only been an hour. Meanwhile, I've got a situation for you and your wife that I think you'll really like. So let me tell you about that."

"Go ahead," Rich said.

"Conlin O'Hara, you know who he is?"

"No."

"Very wealthy man. Used to be in shipping. Tugboats, barges. That sort of thing. Now he's in, well, everything. Very good man. Very good friend of this university."

"*This* university?" Rich asked.

"I'm sorry. Very good friend of the flagship. And as I said, he's a very good man. Very genuine. He's chairman of the deacons at First Baptist Church. Not a pious Peter or anything. Likes his Courvoisier with a good cigar. Can tell an off-color joke. But he's the kind of man who is serious about his obligations to those in need. He's past chairman of the United Way and every other charity in this town. That kind of man."

"OK," Rich said.

"What I'm saying is that Conlin is a good guy. And he's loaded. He owns what's practically a palace south of town out Highway 49."

"And?"

"And he and I talked after you left earlier, and he's extending you and your wife an invitation to come and live at his house. As I said, he and his wife Julie are terrific people."

"Elia," Rich said. "If I am reduced to living in someone's spare bedroom, I'd go back to my friends the Feasters. They have been wonderful to us. But what I want in these awful, awful times is some semblance of a place of my own. However cramped, some privacy. I understand that for the moment that's going to mean a three-hundred-square-foot hotel room. I thought you were going to find a way to let us stay in Monster House."

"Just hear me out, OK? As I recall when you first informed me about your situation at your friends' place, all they have to offer is the bedroom itself."

"That's correct," Rich said.

"Well, the O'Haras are offering you an entire wing of their house. Like I said, their place is like a mansion. When Conlin built it, he had this whole wing constructed for Julie's mother, who passed away two years ago. It's got its own bathroom and sitting room as well as bedroom."

"Kitchen?" Rich asked.

"No, I don't think it has its own kitchen," Lipscom said. "But you don't have a kitchen at Monster House, either."

"Fair enough," Rich admitted.

"This mother-in-law wing even has its own entrance as I understand it."

Rich began to chew at his lower lip. "So we wouldn't have to go through the house."

"No, you wouldn't," Lipscom said. "But I do want to be clear about this. The O'Haras are very wealthy, as I said. They have a cook, and some other help, and by reputation, they dine every night as if at a five-star restaurant. They want to share that with you."

"I'm not getting any exercise as it is," Rich said. "Last thing I need is a five-star meal every night. My butt is already arriving two minutes after I do. I'll bet I've gained ten pounds."

Lipscom looked at Rich without comment.

"All right," Rich said. "I'm being an asshole."

"See, we agree on something after all," Lipscom said, chortling. "I'm kidding; I'm kidding."

"No, I appreciate your helping with this, Elia."

"So I've sparked your interest?"

"Yes."

"So can I tell the O'Haras that you accept their invitation?"

Rich took a deep breath. "I will need to talk to Cally first," he said. "And though I *am* interested, and I appreciate the O'Haras' generosity, I won't be able to accept their invitation if Cecilia is having to return to a dorm room. That's a deal breaker."

"The two aren't even connected," Lipscom said, his irritation unconcealed.

"They're connected in my mind," Rich said. "We're both living in Monster House. And we're both getting kicked out in defiance of the governor's orders."

"The O'Haras are offering you something so far superior to a room at Monster House that the two don't reside in the same universe."

"Perhaps so," Rich said. "And the wing of a mansion and a dorm room don't reside in the same universe either."

"Jesus, man, there is just no pleasing you."

"You can please me by ordering Bertram Weekly to leave Cecilia in her room or finding other acceptable accommodations for her."

"And you can please me, I am your boss after all, by agreeing to accept the O'Haras' hospitality. Conlin and Julie were grateful when I called them, they said. And I enjoy having a man like Conlin O'Hara feeling grateful to me. When I called, he said that he and Julie had been feeling guilty about not opening their home to someone from Choctaw and that as a white professional couple you and your wife would be the perfect guests."

"He said he wanted me and Cally because we're a 'white professional couple'?"

"Yeah, something like that," Lipscom shrugged.

"Well, fuck him," Rich said.

"What?"

"Fuck him and his wife and all the deacons in his church. I'd sleep under a piss-reeking overpass before I'd stay with someone who'd say something like that."

"It's not like it sounds," Lipscom said. "I mean, Conlin O'Hara is no racist."

"Fuck him," Rich said.

"Come on, Coach," Lipscom said. "O'Hara isn't being unreasonable. Even a bleeding heart like you knows that this town is full of an awful lot of riffraff that the hurricane washed up here. The words *white* and *professional* were just a shorthand for not wanting to open his home to someone who might take advantage, might, I don't know, steal the silverware or something."

The words *fuck you* were in Rich's mouth, but he managed to restrain himself this little bit. "Fuck him," he said instead. "If he talked that way around Cally, she wouldn't steal his silverware; she'd steal his butcher knife and put it through his chest."

"I'm just trying to help you," Lipscom said.

"Well, tell Bert Weekly to back off and let us stay in Monster House, or find us an acceptable alternative. All of us. Me and Cally and Cecilia too."

But Elia Lipscom wasn't willing to piss off either Whitehorse or Baron, and he was unable to find anywhere else to offer as an alternative. Luckily, Rich was able to secure Keisha's room for Cecilia at the Feasters', Dr. Flanagan having used up his vacation and returned home to Philadelphia. And so, only days after leaving, Rich and Cally returned to the Feasters', the crowded situation there unchanged save for Cecilia's replacing the physician across the hall. That night, Rich sat in the tiny rocking chair in the Feasters' guest bedroom and ate half a medium-sized bag of M&Ms washed down by half a bottle of Black and White. The liquor and the candy were the temporary fire extinguishers for his fury. But they did not work. So after every handful of chocolate, Rich chewed a Rolaids tablet. But he was unable to douse the ball of fire he seemed to have swallowed.

Friday morning, Rich tried several times to make contact with the governor. Even he wasn't surprised that he was unable to do so. At two o'clock on Friday afternoon, he watched from Friendship House as employees streamed away from the ASU campus and the drumbeats of a pep rally began. Monster Madness was under way. The home contest festivity for the Alabama game that would not kick off for thirty hours was already under way.

The rank indifference of this football celebration to the plight of all the Choctaws in Mayflower infuriated Rich. Seething, he picked up the War Room phone and dialed the *Mayflower Monitor* to report that the governor's executive order on housing was being defied on the ASU campus. To his surprise he managed to get a reporter who at least pretended a sympathetic ear. Rich told his story about getting kicked out of Monster House in order to accommodate people from north Alkansea who were in town to watch a football game. The reporter, a young woman named Sonia Wright, clucked in the right places and several times interjected the word, "Unbelievable." Rich could hear the keys on her computer clacking as he talked, and several times she asked him to repeat things or read back a phrase. She was taking notes, and Rich hoped the story she wrote would cause a shit storm.

The next day's *Monitor* carried no story by Sonia Wright at all. Of course, that was Saturday, and the entire paper was devoted to the Alabama game that night. The sports pages analyzed the two teams and their coaches. The cover of the front section had a full color photo of the scoreboard at the end of last year's game, and a long article on the history of the fierce rivalry. Another story detailed the bet the two state governors had waged on the game, Governor Lebear putting up a tub of Gulf shrimp and the Alabama governor a bushel of sweet potatoes. Coverage continued into the Living Section where the Monster cheerleaders were compared to those from Alabama. Another story consisted of a joint interview conducted with the wives of the two head coaches. A third focused on the tailgating rituals at the two schools.

Wright's story also didn't run in Sunday's paper, which was full of the accounts of the game and the Monsters' come-from-behind victory. When it didn't run in Monday's paper either, Rich called Wright at the *Monitor* and asked for an update. Her tone of voice was a lot less sympathetic than it had been just a few days earlier.

"I checked up on your story, sir," she said, "and it didn't pan out."

"What?" Rich said. "What in the world are you talking about?"

"I called Monster House for a corroboration. I talked to a Mr. Bertram Weekly, the manager."

"That little . . . he didn't deny kicking me out, did he?"

"He explained that he had long-standing reservations that he had to honor."

"I told you that was his excuse last Friday."

"Yes, but you didn't tell me that he had informed you of this situation when you first took a room at Monster House, that you knew from the beginning that you wouldn't be able to use the rooms on football weekends."

"That's a damnable lie," Rich said. "No such conversation ever took place."

"That's not the case according to Viceroy Lipscom."

"You talked to Elia Lipscom about this?"

"Yes. Mr. Weekly said that you and a Cecilia Lagasse had been referred to him by the viceroy's office. He had been specially requested to find rooms for the two of you because of your leadership positions at Urban University."

"That part is true," Rich said. "What did the viceroy say?"

"He said that the rooms were made available for you except for football weekends."

"And he says I was told this?"

"Yes."

"That lying son of a bitch. He and Weekly are both lying."

"Are we on the record?" Wright asked.

"On the record? Why?"

"Dr. Lipscom is your boss."

Rich was pissed, but he wrenched himself under better control. "Of course we're not on the record," he said. "I should perhaps not say *lying*. But I will say that there's a colossal memory failure at work here, and it's not mine."

"Dr. Lipscom said you knew you would have to vacate your room, but that he promised to find other accommodations for you, your wife and Dr. Lagasse and that he did so."

"Did he tell you that the accommodation for Cecilia was a dorm room with the toilet and shower down the hall?"

"He said that both you and Dr. Lagasse were offered housing with prominent Mayflower citizens."

"I will grant that I was," Rich said, a cord of awareness winding itself about him. He wanted to bring up the whole business of a *white professional couple* but understood that to do so was to light a fuse that would only blow himself up. "I was. But Cecilia absolutely was not."

"According to the viceroy, Dr. Lagasse is staying with the family of a local educator."

That description sounded to Rich like someone on Lipscom's staff or an administrator at ASU. "Did he say with whom he arranged for Dr. Lagasse to reside on football weekends?"

"I asked him," the reporter said. "But he declined to provide the names. He said that the benefactors had a right to their anonymity."

Then the twist dawned on Rich. "Wait a minute," he said. "Cecilia and I are both staying at the home of a Mayflower High teacher. Is that the 'local educator' he was referring to?"

"I don't know," Wright said. "I asked him for names, and he wouldn't give them."

"*I* found the accommodations we're using now," Rich said. "The people we're staying with are friends of *mine*. The viceroy didn't have anything to do with our staying there."

"But you admit that you do have a place to stay, then?" Wright said.

"Yes," Rich said.

"So it's not really true as you told me on Friday that the manager at Monster House was putting you on the street in defiance of the governor's executive order."

"As far as he was concerned, that's what he was doing. He didn't make any other arrangements."

"But the viceroy did," Wright said. "You acknowledged that just a few minutes ago."

Rich started to try to explain, but he saw that it was hopeless.

RICH ALSO FOUND IT hopeless trying to get head basketball coach Jimmy Prince to see anything from a perspective other than his own. Rich didn't like Prince, and he didn't like the way the man handled players. Rich thought Prince was a poor bench coach whose outstanding record would have been even better had he known how to motivate through something other than fear and intimidation and had he known when and whom to substitute in key situations and when to call a timeout. But Prince could flat out recruit. He had those national championships, and kids saw him as a winner and wanted to play for him. He had been successful before he came to Urban, and he was successful at Urban too. Rich hadn't gotten any of his teams into the NCAA tournament. Prince's Ungulate teams had landed NCAA bids both of his years at Urban, albeit, Rich secretly noted, with a core of players that Rich himself had recruited. So even though Rich didn't like the man's methods, he considered Prince's job secure.

But then Prince announced that he didn't intend to return his team to Choctaw for the 2004-2005 season. Prince and his players had evacuated before the storm to the University of Memphis, where former Urban Rector Francis Saurian was now president and eager for a public gesture of charity that would help him land his coveted presidency at an SEC or even a Big Ten university. Rich knew how Saurian thought and what he was up to, but Rich was entirely grateful that Memphis had extended weeks of hospitality to Urban's basketball team members and its entire coaching staff. Memphis provided dorm rooms and meal plan tickets to all the players and found housing for all the coaches. Rich couldn't help but note that Memphis treated Urban students and staff members better than Urban's sister, ASU, treated anyone from Urban, including its rector.

Now, Saurian had offered to let Urban play its entire home season in the Memphis arena, and Jimmy Prince thought that was just grand, so grand he accepted the offer without consulting Rich. Rich was ballistically furious. Here he was trying to move heaven and earth to get Urban reopened in the fall, and Jimmy Prince was telling sports reporters around the country that he thought the city of Choctaw was unsafe, the air full of pathogens, the water toxic and the school's campus not fit for occupation.

Prince was so self-centered and myopic that he was surprised when Rich unloaded on him. Prince had always seen himself and his basketball teams as fundamentally unattached to the university whose jerseys they wore. He had never seen himself as part of a larger university operation. So it had never occurred to him that his statements about the safety of Choctaw and the ultimate readiness of the Urban campus to house and teach students were anybody's business but his own. When Rich had him on the phone and pointed out that the publicity Prince had generated with those statements was undermining the efforts of everybody else who worked at Urban, Prince responded that he lived in a free country and had a right to his own opinion.

"Let's cut to the chase," Rich said.

"Yes, let's do that," Prince said.

"You're bringing your team to Choctaw in the middle of October, and you will play all your home games at *home*."

"No, I won't."

"You will indeed," Rich said.

"The Ungulate Arena doesn't even have a roof on it," Prince said. "So how are we going to play *at* home?"

"By *at home*, I obviously mean, *in Choctaw*."

"Well, I'm the head coach, and I'd rather play up here. My kids are comfortable here, and so is my staff. Nothing's going to be really fixed in Choctaw. My house flooded, and I don't even have a place to live. It's not a good environment, and I'm not going to do it."

"My house flooded," Rich said. "And I'm going to do it. Provost Lagasse's house flooded. She's going to do it. The houses of eighty percent of our employees flooded. They're all going to do it. And so are you."

"You make this team come back to Choctaw, and you'll have to find yourself another head basketball coach. I ain't fooling. I'll tell my kids they ought not go either."

"You do that," Rich said, "and you can forget about ever landing another head coaching job anywhere. You can demean secretaries and belittle players, and people like Francis Saurian will still hire you as long as you can put up the Ws. But you maliciously destroy a program and you're finished. Moreover,

I will sue you for damages. And when I win you'll wish you had another job because I'm going to take every cent you ever earned. "

"Fuck you."

"Fuck you back, you son of a bitch."

"You just been waiting for something like this, haven't you?" Prince said. "I was nauseated when a little high school pipsqueak like you got to be my fucking boss."

"That might make a lick of sense if I had ever threatened you in any way. It might make some sense if I were intending to fire you now. But even though you are a selfish, insubordinate smear of shit, I'll give you one more chance. You commit to bringing our team home and working on whatever schedule adjustments are necessary to play in Choctaw venues that didn't flood, and I'll forget we ever had this conversation."

A different kind of man would have submitted at this point, would have recognized that he had come up against someone he couldn't bully. But Jimmy Prince's colossal sense of self-importance overrode all else. He refused to capitulate. And Rich told him he considered that Prince had abandoned his job starting immediately. Rich finally deduced that Prince simply didn't want to put up with the numbing effort it would require to see his home repaired. Prince never returned to the city, and Rich learned later that he'd collected his insurance money and sold his home to a speculator willing to undertake the gutting and restoration. Prince did not follow through on his threat to dissuade his players from returning, however. And he moved quickly to announce that Rich's decision to return the team to Choctaw had led to his "resignation" (rather than his firing). In Prince's telling, a heart attack he'd had several years ago and a history of allergies had led his physician to advise that he step aside. Rich didn't stoop to contradicting him in the media. He promoted the chief assistant, Chuck Fuller, to head coach and turned his attention to other matters. He had a university to reopen in less than a month.

35

While I was in Schaghticoke, Muttaump, Matoonas, Canonchet, Quinnapin, Weetamoo and Awashonks applied unrelenting pressure throughout the townships to the east of Nipmuck country. After the early days of the Wampanoags' retreat from Montaup Bay, save for the horror of the Great Swamp Fight, we had successfully carried the fight to the English at almost every turn. In the winter of 1676, we continued to do so.

Following That Vicious Lying Rat Bastard Josiah Winslow's ignominious retreat to Boston in the first week of February, we followed up with a concerted February 10 assault on the town of Lancaster. In preparing our attack on Lancaster, we first burned the river bridge that connected it with the garrison town of Marlborough, from which reinforcements would surely ride. Then, we hit the town hard, burning all buildings except for the garrison house. We took fifty English lives that day, and carried away with us twenty-three captives, including Mary Rowlandson who would become world famous through her book *The Sovereignty and Goodness of God* about living as our prisoner. Troopers from Marlborough did finally arrive, but it was too late; Lancaster was already laid waste. Several weeks later, the people of Lancaster who survived in the garrison houses abandoned their settlement, the latest group in a now long line to do so.

In reaction to the latest pasting we put on the English, Boston dispatched that vile racist Samuel Moseley and a brigade of soldiers to the central town of Sudbury with instructions to provide support to any additional town we might attack. From Sudbury, he was in good position to provide quick reinforcement to the towns of Concord, Marlborough and Framingham, in particular. Understanding that, we let Moseley get nice and settled in. Then on February 21, we attacked Medfield, twenty miles to the southwest of Boston. We killed twenty-three and burned fifty houses and barns. We also left the English a handwritten note that told them we were not done and that they could rely on safety from us nowhere in the region. As we made our escape, we burned down the bridge over the Charles River on the road to Sherborn.

Stirring itself to another offensive, Massachusetts dispatched a new force of 600 mounted troopers under Major Thomas Savage with instructions to establish headquarters in Marlborough and from there to conduct search and destroy missions into Nipmuck country. The Vietcong obviously studied our response to this initiative. The English called us cowards throughout this entire war because of the way we fought them. Even Roger Williams, who liked to portray himself as a friend to the Indians, did so. But we would not fight them on their terms. Why should we? When they marched out to find us, we disappeared into the woods. We fought them fiercely, but only on ground that we chose and on those occasions when we judged ourselves in possession of the advantage. Isn't this the way you are supposed to behave in a war?

Our flight before Savage provides a crucial example. The English had identified our concentration at Menameset where 2,000 Nipmucks, Narragansetts and Wampanoags were now living, the majority of them women and children. But when we determined that Savage and his cavalry were going to ride down on us, we did as we had so many times before. We abandoned our *nashweetoos*, strapped our possessions to our bodies, grasped our children in our arms, carried on our backs those of our old people who were lame, and melted into the woods.

Mary Rowlandson was among the many captives we took with us on this latest testing trek. As the wife of a minister, and therefore a woman of some standing in Lancaster, she was assigned to a sachem, in this case Weetamoo and her husband Quinnapin. But despite the fact that for the whole time she was with us, we fed her better than we ourselves ate and provided her a Bible to assist in her prayers, she still whined and complained so much that Weetamoo thought often about dashing out Rolandson's brains with a good whack from her war club. Cooler heads talked Weetamoo out of that, but Weetamoo became so irritated by Rowlandson that Weetamoo handed Rowlandson over to my supervision. Rowlandson never did manage much gratitude for our sparing her, though she subsequently got along better with Wootonekanuske and Neksonauket than she did with Weetamoo.

Because we were so many, Savage was able to trail us. But he could not catch us. Time and again we were able to stage diversions that took him away from our main body. Near the end of our journey late in *Sequocheekesos*, in the first week of March, we had to build rafts to cross the Bacquag River, a deep eastern tributary of the Connecticut. We did so, moving all our people safely to the north side of the river. When Savage arrived at the same point, he judged the crossing too dangerous to attempt and turned his troops south toward those English settlements still holding out on the Connecticut.

So while our diversionary forces led Savage on wild goose chases through Nipmuck country so successfully that he ended up in Northampton without ever even managing to engage us, others of us struck on February 25 and burned buildings in the Atlantic coast town of Weymouth only twelve miles south of Boston. This attack was a strategic twin to one we launched a couple of weeks later when we sent Totoson to attack Clark's Garrison only three miles south of Plymouth. We killed eleven and burned all the buildings at Clark's Garrison, but the message was the important thing for us. As we had pointed out in the letter we left at Medfield, we wanted the English to feel that they were safe nowhere in their colonies. We had whipped them on both sides of Nipmuck country, and now we had taken the fight to the coast.

Connected to this strategy was that of our taking hostages. We hadn't started this cruel war, but we were not closed to the idea of negotiating its end. I dreamed of such assistance from the Mohawks that we could achieve total victory and stand on the Atlantic Coast of Cape Cod to watch the English sail away forever. But short of that, if short of it we need be, we determined that if the English felt vulnerable enough, and if they understood that an end of hostilities would mean the return of their loved ones, maybe they might finally negotiate with us in good faith. To that end, after the residents of Menameset had relocated across the Bacquag River, I called Mary Rowlandson to me, asked her to dine with me and my family and fed her amply.

Though she portrayed us as savages in her book, even there she admitted that I treated her with kindness and courtesy. That first night we visited, Wootonekanuske made a tasty flatbread with slices of bear meat, and Rowlandson gobbled it down without noticing that her portion was larger than that Wootonekanuske served either herself or our son. Rowlandson did admit in her book, though, that in Wootonekanuske's cooking she "never tasted pleasanter meat in her life." I told Rowlandson that I hoped she would soon be restored to the arms of her husband and loved ones, and she cried. When I asked her if she thought the time had come to end this bloody war, she said yes, and I told her I thought so too.

While under Wootonekanuske's supervision, Rolandson knitted a shirt and a cap for Neksonauket, of whom she became noticeably fond. I was glad that after we released her we were able to restore to her maternal bosom both her ten-year-old daughter, Mary, and her eleven-year-old son, Joseph, whom we had also captured at Lancaster. But she never forgave me or any of my people for the fact that her six-year-old daughter Sarah died of wounds she suffered when we attacked their town. Our babies died; their babies died. This is what happens when men make war. I am horrified by the death of Sarah Rowlandson, and as I am not forgiven, I do not forgive Josiah Winslow and those who assisted him in bringing such suffering to pass.

THROUGHOUT THE LAST MONTH of winter, our pressure remained relentless. As we moved to the moon of *Namassackesos*, on March 13, Monoco led a Nipmuck raid on Groton where we burned the meeting house and many of the dwellings. Shortly later the English deserted the town. The next day Wampanoags and Pocassets attacked Northampton and fled with a herd of horses and a flock of sheep that we needed for food. The English were so confused they ordered Savage back to Boston to account for his inability to find an enemy who seemed to be everywhere at once.

The threat of being everywhere at once led to our multiple strikes on March 26. A force of Nipmucks attacked and largely destroyed the headquarters town of Marlborough. We often chose not to sacrifice the men necessary to take a town's garrison house, and that was our choice again here. Massachusetts continued to use the Marlborough garrison building as a military base for some time to come, but the terrified townspeople had endured enough and abandoned their settlement.

Meanwhile, a battalion of Wampanoags, Pocassets and Sakonnets, led by Adonoshonk, sacked the frontier village of Simsbury, Connecticut, our first foray that far south along the Connecticut River. At the same time, Canonchet and Quinnapin's Narragansetts attacked Rehoboth and appeared to run away in terror when Captain Michael Pierce's Plymouth regiment put up a stout defense. The English just could not stop stepping on the ambush hoe. Pierce gave the Narragansetts chase until he and his men found themselves surrounded and outnumbered. Sixty-five English musketeers, Captain Pierce included, gave up the ghost that day outside Rehoboth.

Two days later, the Narragansetts attacked Rehoboth again. This time we burned all the buildings there, seventy-two total, except for the garrison house. And on the next day, March 29, the Narragansetts attacked Providence and burned a score of houses, including that of Roger Williams, who had lobbied with the Narragansett leadership to stand aside when the English first attacked me and who sat silent as his Rhode Island colony provided naval support and refuge to That Vicious Lying Rat Bastard's army before, during and after The Great Swamp Fight.

At age 77, Williams was not without courage. Unarmed, he marched out to confront Quinnapin while his house burned behind him.

"Quinnapin," Williams demanded. "You are known to me. Do you know me not in return?"

"I know you, Parson Williams," Quinnapin said.

"I have lived in this territory for over four decades."

"Yes, I know this."

"Then why have you burned my house? You, a Narragansett sachem? Why are you doing this to a man who has always sought to be a friend to your people?"

"You sought to be our friend on your terms," Quinnapin replied. "Never on equal terms and certainly never on ours. When we lost our homes, you gave us no assistance. Now you have lost yours. In memory of the friendship you *did* show, I am sparing your life. If the time comes that we are defeated and I am captured, your people will not recall nor honor the mercy I showed, nor will they be nearly so generous as to spare my life in repayment for yours."

Roger Williams did not answer because he knew what Quinnapin said was true.

36

On the weekends that they lived again with the Feasters, while the Monsters put lopsided lickings on overmatched teams from Jackson State and Troy, Rich and Cally and Alphonse traveled back and forth to Choctaw where they labored during the daylight hours to prepare Cally's old apartment for their occupation once city utilities were restored in the unflooded areas. The weekend of the Jackson State game, they took Cecilia with them and drove her out to the Water Oaks Subdivision, not far from the south end of the Urban campus, where Cecilia had lived with her husband for forty-eight years until his death in 1999. They had raised their three children there in a brick ranch-style house that was quite fashionable when they bought it in 1951 right after she finished nursing school.

As the years passed, posher neighborhoods were built on other parcels of drained land. Cecilia and her ophthalmologist husband could have afforded one of the newer, fancier houses. But their home was close to Urban where Cecilia was on the faculty, and with a bedroom for each child, two girls and a boy, it was sufficient, and the house brimmed with family devotion. The Lagasses loved to barbecue and boil shrimp and crabs for parties in their large back yard. As the children grew up and distinguished themselves in school and in year-round sports, the house grew full of the memorabilia of five active lives.

Cecilia had invited Rich and Cally to dinner after he asked her to serve as his interim provost. Cecilia's children were grown, and even her grandchildren were adults. The house was full of pictures, curling on cork boards, crowded together in tarnished metal frames, and seemed to vibrate with a mother and grandmother's love. Rich and Cally were perhaps all the more touched by it because they did not have children themselves.

Water Oaks was one of the last areas of Choctaw to drain. Cecilia had tried to check on her house when she went to campus two weeks after the storm, but flooded streets kept her from getting there. Today the mud in the street was still wet underneath a dry, gray crust, but the house was finally accessible, and Rich was able to steer his Escape down her street. The neighborhood lawns were not visible under a layer of silt that stood a foot deep in places against the houses, risen into ridges even higher in some spots, as if a rippling lake had been frozen into sculpture. All this dirt came from a canal levee that had "heaved," that is, had been undermined by the high water levels and then exploded from underneath for a quarter-mile length. As the water gushed through the breach, it pushed all the crowned earth in front of it, rushing down streets, filling up homes.

The views on Cecilia's street were surreal. Directly across the street from Cecilia's house, a white Cadillac rested upright on its front bumper, the undercarriage of its trunk leaning against an oak. It was as if the car had tried to escape the flood waters by backing into the tree's branches. Cecilia's own car, a two-year-old Toyota Camry, had been floated over on its side, some electronic death twitch causing its trunk to pop open. In Cecilia's front yard, a child's red wagon nestled in lower oak branches as if an ornament in the Christmas tree of a giant. A plastic swimming pool hung from limbs in another yard, as elsewhere did a round, zinc icing tub.

A sidewalk once ran from the street to the six-inch-tall stoop at Cecilia's front door. But it was invisible now under the mud. The mud curled up against the house's red brick as if someone had begun a gray plaster veneer and quit after two feet. The old-fashioned screen door at the front was trapped by the thick cake of dirt at its foot. And then, most distressing, the streak of brown water line which marked houses throughout the city, including Rich and Cally's, was not visible. The flood waters had risen above the eaves. Every surface on the inside had been touched by water, even the house's cramped storage space in the attic. Nothing Cecilia owned that she hadn't taken with her to Mayflower had escaped.

"Want us to try to go in with you?" Cally asked, as the three of them sat otherwise stunned out of conversation.

Cecilia took a deep, audible breath. "No," she said. "Not today. Y'all need to get on over to Cally's apartment, and I think I'll just lend a hand there."

"Don't worry about us," Rich said. "We'll be happy to take a look at things here."

"No," Cecilia said. "I'll let you help assess things later. I've seen enough for now. I'll come back later and see what can be done."

They did come back later, but not until late October after Urban had made its coughing restart and they had all returned to Choctaw and Cecilia had taken up residence in the second bedroom at Cally's apartment. By then a Home Depot had reopened, and Rich had been able to purchase shovels and an axe that allowed him and Alphonse and Robert Feaster to enter Cecilia's house. They had to splinter the swollen front door to get in. Once they saw what they were facing in the house, they returned to Home Depot for knee-high rubber boots.

Cecilia said little as she sloshed through her home. All that once had stood on the house's bookshelves had been washed into the muck and destroyed. Robert used an axe to break into the built-in drawers in the den where Cecilia had kept her photo albums and loose pictures. Everything there was ruined as well. They all watched as Cecilia's face sagged with each new disappointment. Though she never uttered a word of complaint, they all knew how wrenching this must be for her. After a while, Cecilia's hidden distress seemed to transfer itself to Cally who had to leave the reeking house to keep herself from bursting into the tears that Cecilia repressed. After several fruitless hours of searching for anything to salvage, they left the house, stripped off their filthy boots, wiped down their hands and "washed" them with germicide gel, got in their cars and drove away. They didn't even bother to try boarding up the door. Nothing inside was worth protecting. Nothing of even sentimental value had survived the deluge.

For a time that fall, Cecilia talked of having the house raised on stilts so that it would stand above the flood level, but she learned from an architect that was impractical. Later she speculated about demolishing the house and building a new cottage on her lot, also raised. But early in the new year, she sold the property to a speculator, who had bought several other destroyed homes in Water Oaks. Within a matter of weeks, once the buyer had the required deeds and permits, he brought in bulldozers and leveled every house on Cecilia's block. On the way back to Cally's old apartment one afternoon after work, Rich and Cecilia drove down her unrecognizable street and parked in front of the space where her house once stood.

"I'm sorry," Rich said.

"Don't be," Cecilia said. "I still possess all that was in that house." She pointed with her thumb at her chest. "I have everything that matters, right in here."

THE FIVE WEEKS BETWEEN the middle of September and October 18 remained a blur to Rich as he worked twelve and fourteen hours a day trying to orchestrate Urban University's reopening. The task was a Herculean jigsaw puzzle. Many of Urban's senior faculty members, in refuge all around the country, with no homes in Choctaw to return to, opted for immediate retirement. Some junior faculty, with no deep roots in south Alkansea, landed emergency fellowships or even late appointments at other institutions and also chose not to return. Under normal circumstances the sudden loss of so many full-time faculty would have proved an unmanageable disaster.

But in these circumstances, the departure of so many professors became an unanticipated blessing because everyone who retired or relocated was someone Rich didn't have to find money to pay. In order to protect the university from an indefinite shutdown, Rich believed it was essential to have a fall semester somehow. But he didn't know how many students would or could take advantage of the reopening. Many were already enrolled elsewhere, including the despicable ASU. Meanwhile, the great majority of housing in Choctaw was damaged and not yet ready for reoccupation. And this included 5,000 beds in the stretch of Urban dorms along the flooded south end of campus. So it wasn't clear where students and faculty were going to live in order to attend and teach classes. Many faculty and students both, who might want to return, would be unable to because they had no place to live.

Rich and his administrators invented strategy as they went along. They decided that they had no choice but to offer hundreds of classes on the Internet *by* professors and *for* students marooned outside the city. For those teachers and students who could find housing in the city's undamaged areas, Urban would offer classes in select buildings on the campus' unflooded northern two-thirds. A lot of this was like a game of pin the tail on the donkey. Rich and his associates had no idea how many students fell into which category and how many would seek to participate in the reengineered semester they were designing. Rich, Cecilia and the academic deans assigned either Internet or on-campus classes to those faculty ready to teach and hoped that students would register for them.

In the end, 9,000 students enrolled that fall. More than 11,000 students disappeared in an eye blink. Still, 9,000 were more than studied that fall anywhere else in the state save at the Mayflower flagship. Nine thousand students were a viable number and provided Rich the ammunition he needed for holding on to his state allocation, which made up slightly more than fifty percent of Urban's operating budget. With so many faculty and staff retired or resigned, and with fewer buildings to heat, cool, light and clean for the time being, Rich felt that he had adequate revenues to meet his operating expenses and keep his people paid. This was a significant victory although one, he took note, never commented on, much less celebrated by, the State Board of Trustees for Higher Education.

Urban treated itself to a celebration on opening day, however. Jose Najera set up a sound system in the shaded, paved courtyard flanked by the Ungulate Arena and Buildings 5 and 81. Food service provided tubs of soft drinks, urns of coffee, and boxes of donuts. And the university jazz combo played. People who hadn't seen each other hugged and cried and shared their evacuation stories. Of the 9,000 students who enrolled that fall, only about 4,000 registered for classes on campus. The rest studied online. But over half the registrants, Rich guessed, showed up that day. Those faculty and staff returned to the city were there almost to the person. The day was overcast, but a predicted drizzle held off, and the temperature was pleasant. Those in attendance were exultant.

Cecilia went to the mike first and received a long round of applause. She expressed her appreciation to the deans and vice rectors who reported to her, to the faculty for persevering under unprecedented circumstances and to the students for coming back.

"I want to emphasize something," Cecilia said as she was concluding her remarks, "that many of you, most of you probably, already know. Many, many people, many people in attendance today, labored probably harder than ever before in their consistently hard-working lives in order for us to gather here this morning, to reopen this university that we cherish, to begin anew the study and the teaching and the research that is so vital to the well-being of our state and the resurrection of our beloved city. But if you do not know it, and most of you probably do, if you do not know it, you should. You should know that we wouldn't be standing here today if it weren't for the anger, the determination, the stubbornness, the gall, the devotion and the vision of your rector, my boss, our leader, Doctor Richard Albert Janus."

The applause that greeted Rich as he stepped to the microphone was stunning. As a player and a coach, he had heard cheers, but this was a reaction unlike any before it. The clapping and the whistling and the deep-throated roars went on and on, filling the courtyard with a reverberating sound no doubt rivaling that of Hosea as it caused the havoc that led to this day. Rich was deeply touched and ultimately grateful that the ovation lasted long enough for him to gather his emotions under control.

When the crowd finally quieted, Rich said, "Ungulates rule!" which elicited laughter and applause.

Some of the students made the snorting noises of a bull and posted index fingers on either side of their heads. Someone started a chant of "Ur ban, Ur ban, Ur ban."

When they finally settled down again, Rich said, "In case anyone is down here spying for the State Board of Trustees, I probably ought to correct an item in Cecilia's introduction and note that my official title isn't Rector but *Interim* Rector."

"No," one voice rang out, echoed by many others that responded, "No. No."

"You are our rector," someone called out.

"You got us here," someone else shouted. "You take us from here."

"Rec tor, Rec tor, Rec tor."

Rich raised his hands to quiet them down. He then thanked the people Cecilia had thanked and expressed his especial gratitude to the students for coming back to a place that was so damaged. "Those of us who are employed here," he said, "earn our livings in providing education for you. God willing, we will endure this hardship and be here to greet your younger brothers and sisters when you have graduated. Things, no doubt, will eventually get better, and the faculty and staff, I hope, will be here to see our return to the way we were before the storm. But it's going to take time. And it's going to be a time that you, our students, will not get back."

He pointed to Building 5, the student center, with its entrances boarded up. "Your union is closed. This fall you will have to bring lunch or dine out of vending machines." He pointed behind him to the Ungulate Arena with its peeled-back roof. "Our basketball teams will have to play their home games across town at Ettons Fieldhouse, this season and maybe next year too."

He pointed across campus at the academic buildings which stood behind the crowd. "None of your classrooms is any longer carpeted. The seats in many lecture halls lack cushions. You will probably be physically uncomfortable while you study. These are genuine hardships, and I have barely begun the list of indignities you ought not to have to endure, but will. So thank you for being here anyway. And hear me when I talk of the wonder of our being here at all. Cecilia has tried to give me more credit than I deserve. What Facilities Vice Rector Charles Lobovich has accomplished since the storm is nothing short of a miracle. As soon as he had a dry way to get here, Charlie and his people moved in with the unstinting determination of the soldiers who stormed Normandy Beach. As soon as they had water and electricity, they literally moved onto campus so that they could maximize their working hours. As you walk around campus today and in the days to come, you will find much that still needs to be fixed. Try always to recall what has *been* fixed and say a prayer of gratitude for Charlie and his team. Without their effort, we wouldn't be here today."

Rich raised a fist and shook it. "I cannot promise you that your remaining days at Urban will be as comfortable as they ought to be. I cannot promise you that you will enjoy the amenities that ought to be yours without question. But I will promise you that we will work on these issues every day. And most important, I will promise you that the education you will get in this semester and through to the day of your graduation will be every bit as good as ever before. And for enduring in this time of hardship, when your degree is in your hand, you will cherish your accomplishment all the more. I promise you that too."

"Rec tor, Rec tor, Rec tor," people chanted as Rich started away from the microphone.

He stepped back and said, "As *interim* rector, it is now my duty to tell you all, teachers and faculty alike—go to class."

"Rec tor, Rec tor, Rec tor."

Someone else started the chant, "Run, Rich, run. Run, Rich, run."

Facing away from the crowd, Rich raised his arm high over his head and waved his hand in acknowledgment. He embraced first Cecilia and then Cally who had stood listening to his speech behind him. Rich had given little previous thought to the idea of seeking a regular appointment as rector. As a condition of his becoming interim rector, he had agreed not to. He was a coach, not an administrator. He wanted to work with young people, not attend meetings and wrangle with bureaucrats. He wanted to write again, about Hosea, try his hand at a novel perhaps, or maybe take up that dissertation he'd never finished, the one about me. But those things seemed secondary now. This was his school. These were his students. These were his colleagues and employees. They were all his responsibility. The obstacles they were facing were many and difficult, but if they wanted him, he would serve. They were his chance.

THE EUPHORIA OVER GETTING the university reopened was sweet, but it didn't last long, on Rich's part or most anybody else's. Cally's classes on Classical Greek Drama and Mediterranean and Middle-Eastern Myth didn't attract sufficient enrollment to be offered on campus, and she had to teach them via the Internet, a process that she found unsatisfactory in a lot of different ways. The cable company announced that it would not open new accounts until service had been restored for all their customers who were returned to the city. A certain respectable logic guided this policy, but it meant Rich and Cally weren't able to have Internet service installed so she could work at home. The building that housed her office on campus was still closed. The entire campus lacked wifi, and in the Urban library she had to battle students for the use of a hard-wired computer. So she did most of her work at a coffee shop in an environment she couldn't control, one where she was constantly interrupted by the noise of nearby conversations and the frequent appearance of acquaintances eager to sit and chat with her "for just a minute."

Moreover, even when she was left undisturbed, she didn't like the process of teaching her classes online. She had never done this kind of teaching before, and she struggled to adapt her classes, which she had always run, not as lectures, but as Socratic discussions over assigned readings. Since her Internet classes were not offered in real time, the back and forth of question, answer, follow-up question and solicited elaboration was practically impossible to accomplish. Instead, she felt as if she was practically running a series of private tutorials for the twenty or so students in each of her classes. The need to respond to each student's questions on an almost individual basis meant that the process of running her class was far more labor intensive than classroom teaching, leaving her exhausted and irritable.

In addition, she just didn't feel well. She had always suffered from allergies. And her entire world now was abuzz with swirling particles of dust, mold, torn-out fiberglass, ripped down asbestos, sawdust, fumes from curbside refrigerators, you name it. Her eyes were habitually red and runny. And she felt faintly nauseated all the time, it seemed, a condition that did not usually accompany her allergic reactions. She suspected that despite a concerted effort on the part of city health inspectors, the food supply, both in groceries and in restaurants, was being contaminated in some way. The miracle was, she guessed, that some deadly epidemic didn't break out in a city struggling to deal with an explosion of garbage. Cally kept wondering when she was going to get a serious case of food poisoning, but Rich was the one who was knocked down with fever and chills after dining on seafood one night.

Despite her unhappiness over her classes and her battle with allergies, Cally took the lead on getting their house restored, an infuriating process of trying to corral harried building contractors depending on an inadequate labor force. After getting stood up by three different contractors, she decided to work directly with the electricians, plumbers, roofers, heating and air-conditioning men, sheetrock hangers, carpenters, phone company employees and cable installers. She was no doubt right that managing the work herself moved the sundry projects ahead at a faster pace, but these duties proved endlessly frustrating as workmen could not be counted on to show up in a timely manner, including even the agreed-upon day.

Cally also took the lead with their insurance companies. Their car insurance company was prompt and fair. But the handling of their home insurance was infuriating and altogether too typical of what the people of Choctaw had to face in the aftermath of the great flood of 2004. The homeowners' company insured Rich and Cally's home for wind damage; a separate flood company insured for water damage. And representatives from each one constantly claimed that acknowledged loss was the responsibility of the other company. Too often, neither paid.

During this hectic time, Cally felt emotionally separated from Rich in a way she hadn't since they had reunited. He was overwhelmed with trying to lead Urban away from the brink on which it still teetered. Elia Lipscom was constantly nagging Rich about his fiduciary responsibilities to live within his budget, a prospect Rich had many strategies for achieving, none of them certain. She sometimes felt he cared more about Urban University than he did about her.

All of this was aggravated by the fact that they had so little private time. While still in Mayflower, they were constantly shuffling back and forth between the Feasters' and Monster House. Once they arrived back in Choctaw, they had offered the second bedroom in Cally's apartment to Cecilia. This they had to do. Rich and Cally loved Cecilia. And Cecilia was a perfectly lovely housemate. Still, Cecilia's nightly presence in the house meant that common intimacies could not be enjoyed, not just sex, which they were too embarrassed to have on the other side of a paper-thin wall, but all manners of nuzzling and touching that had been their common practice. Cally had been happy before the storm. She wasn't happy anymore.

Cecilia wasn't happy either, although she would never confide that fact to a soul. She really didn't care about most of her destroyed possessions. She made enough money to replace lost furniture and clothes. But she missed the photos she'd taken of her children when they were little, their innocent eyes still welled with wonder. She missed the snapshot of her two daughters sitting together astride a Shetland pony and the one of her son before his first Little League baseball game wearing a too-large, dark blue cap that sat down over his ears. After her husband died, she would often spend evenings with an album on her lap smiling over the photos they had taken while playing with their kids. She missed her husband terribly, but, oddly, less so when she looked at the pictures of their family. He seemed with her then, looking over her shoulder, resting a hand at the curve of her neck and telling her as he had sundry times as their children grew, "We done good, my love, don't know how, but we done good, haven't we now."

Cecilia would never tell Rich and Cally, but she hated living with them. She hated it more than living alone after her husband's death. She loved them enormously. She was grateful for a place to stay. She didn't know what she would have done had they not taken her in. But she felt so intrusive. Much as she wished her presence made no difference, she knew it did.

It had to. She was happy to take responsibility for most of the cooking. She liked that, liked being of use in that way. But she really wished they would let her just go off to her bedroom as soon as dinner was over so that they could have some waking time apart from her. She absolutely wouldn't have minded and would happily have spent more reading time with a succession of books.

They wouldn't though. They insisted that she join them in the small living room to visit or to watch a DVD. She adored their company and loved movies. She enjoyed the Jack Daniel's splashed with Angostura Bitters Rich poured her every night, too, though she wished he didn't drink so much Black and White himself. She did enjoy being with them. But she felt guilty. And love them though she did, she was determined to be the first Urban faculty member to move into the trailer village once FEMA got it erected on the east side of campus. Rich had made her the university's chief trailer liaison, and she worked on some aspect of it every day, her own private desires adding to her determination to see residences, however flimsy and cramped, provided for those university employees and students who had no other place to live.

Though none of them confessed the fact to the other two, Rich and Cally and Cecilia were all distracted and unhappy. Save for fleeting moments diverting himself with Scotch and handfuls of M&Ms, Rich couldn't get the trials of his job out of his head. Nothing was moving forward at the pace it should. He and Charlie had hoped the repairs on Building 5 would restore campus dining before the end of the fall semester. The damage was more extensive than they had originally estimated, however, and it seemed unlikely now that they would have the student center back even by the end of the spring. Worse, repairs on the south dormitories had come to a complete halt. Whatever rabbit Rich managed to pull out of the hat with this year's budget, the future well-being of the university was inextricably tied to a return of the student body, which was now standing at under forty-five percent of its pre-storm enrollment. Both Building 5 and the dorms had asbestos problems that changed the whole approach to their repair. Asbestos was such a problem in the dorms that FEMA had ordered work on them stopped until a decision could be reached about condemning them entirely.

With the southside dorms out of service for the indefinite future, Cecilia's effort to get trailers established on campus became paramount, distasteful as the idea was to Rich to see the Urban campus turned into the world's largest trailer park, its expansive green spaces, usually devoted to softball diamonds and touch football and soccer fields, dug up for sewer lines and planted with raw wood poles and vines of electrical wires. He could probably authorize a second consecutive semester of extensive online instruction, but to keep the howling wolves of the Board of Trustees off his back, he had to show substantial progress in returning the university to some semblance of its former state.

Voices on the Board were already complaining that Rich had reopened the university without seeking their consultation on the matter and that he was turning the school into a travesty. He didn't believe that was true. He was confident that Urban would enjoy a significant increase in on-campus enrollment in the spring. And he also believed that dedicated teaching and a willingness to innovate could make online education successful. He didn't even have the full support of Cally on that second position, however. She maintained that she could provide *adequate* instruction via the Internet but never *equivalent* instruction. But what choice did he have? Housing was insufficient on campus and off, and until the housing crisis was solved, faculty couldn't live in the city to perform their duties in person and students couldn't be present to take their classes on campus.

The Bush administration promised that thousands of trailers would be delivered to the city within weeks of the storm. People could park them in their driveways. Large-scale employers could set up concentrated villages in parking lots or other parcels of land they controlled. And all of this would be provided by FEMA without charge to the person who took emergency refuge in the tiny aluminum boxes that crammed two sleeping areas, a bathroom and a living/dining area into 256 square feet. Life in the trailer would be claustrophobic, especially for couples, more so for couples with even one child. Rich could barely stand the idea of crowding three college students into each of these grim spaces, but he recognized that FEMA trailers, lousy as they were, constituted the university's best option for providing housing to his students until FEMA issued a ruling on Urban's asbestos-infected dorms.

If a building was fifty-one percent damaged, it had to be torn down and rebuilt. FEMA would pay. If, on the other hand, a building was only forty-nine percent damaged, then FEMA would provide what it estimated to be the cost of repairing it. A series of FEMA-designated experts delivered a wide range of damage estimates on both sides of the tear-down/repair divide. And FEMA would not give Charlie Lobovich permission to undertake any action whatsoever until the agency made its funding decision, whenever that might be. Of course, Rich could tell Charlie to tear the dorms down and rebuild them. But if he did so, and FEMA later ruled they were not at least fifty-one percent damaged, then it would compensate Urban only that damage percentage *on the old dorm* that its experts finally agreed on. Rich didn't know how he was going to balance the budget as it was. If he guessed wrong and started building new dorms, he would be short millions of dollars for which he had no revenue sources. New dorms wouldn't be ready for at least a year anyway, and Urban needed student housing by the middle of January.

So trailers it would have to be. And right after Thanksgiving, Cecilia appeared to have them on track for the start of spring term. After having it reviewed by University Attorney Regan Hooks, Cecilia brought Rich a FEMA contract calling for the implantation of five hundred trailers for faculty and staff, to be located on the northeast side of campus, and one thousand trailers to house three students each, to be located starting just south of the employee enclave and stretching along the southern boundary of campus in every conceivable open area where one could be put and connected to power, water, and sewerage. Heat and cooking gas was to be provided by a propane tank at the nose of each unit. What an unholy mess, Rich thought, as he paged through the contract before signing it.

Federal government employees didn't do the actual work. This was contracted to a huge, politically well-connected Mayflower company. As Halliburton was to Iraq, Damm Engineering was to Hurricane Hosea. So the contract wasn't with FEMA but rather with Damm, which agreed to use its trucks to pick up the trailers at a huge federal trailer depot in Mississippi and haul them to the Urban campus. Damm also agreed to erect the required utility poles, run and install all necessary wiring, dig needed trenches, implant and connect sewer lines, pave between the trailers with crushed concrete, supply each trailer with a filled propane tank and subsequently operate a propane resupply service. For this work, Damm would be paid $30,000 per trailer, or for the lot of them, $45,000,000. A frightful amount of money, Rich thought, but since that was FEMA's recovery plan for residents of the whole city, he embraced it.

Problems arose when Damm didn't start work by December 1, as they said they would need to do, if the trailers were to be ready for occupancy by the beginning of classes in mid-January. After consulting with the Damm vice president in charge of the project and being guaranteed that work would commence on the trailer village by December 15, Rich moved the first classes of spring semester back two weeks to January 31.

Additional complications began when Rich received a phone call on December 7 from Margaret Lockhart. How she had learned that Rich had moved the spring term back to a

January 31 start date, she never said, but she wanted to know on whose authority he had done so.

Rich was perplexed by the question. "My own authority," he told her. "I am the university's chief executive officer."

"But . . . but you report to the viceroy," she said.

"Yes," Rich replied.

"And Viceroy Lipscom was not . . . was not consulted."

"I am expected to consult him about the timing of our academic calendar?"

"Do you not send copies of . . . copies of your calendar to the viceroy via . . . via my office every year?"

"Yes," Rich said. "I did that when I was provost. I assume Cecilia still does."

"She does. But neither she, nor you, nor anyone . . . anyone else at Ewe Ewe sent any document to us . . . to us about this start date switch from January 17 to January 31." Nobody in Choctaw liked the habit people in Mayflower had of calling Urban University "U.U." But when Margaret Lockhart did so, she dragged out the initials with a sniff as if she'd just smelled something disgusting. "You are supposed to ask . . . supposed to ask for the viceroy's authorization . . . authorization to make any such changes as this. He's the one . . . the one . . . the one who has to answer to the Board. He's the one who will have to explain if anyone complains to a board member about this change. And we get . . . get complaints to the Board about such matters all the . . . the time."

"Someone has complained?" Rich asked.

"As of this time, no . . . no. But the viceroy has asked that you . . . asked that you send him a formal request for this change, stating . . . stating your reasons."

"He's not going to reverse me, I hope."

"No, he won't need to reverse you, but, but he will want a paper trail on your reasons."

"We've decided to move the start of the semester back to give our trailer installation company time to have housing ready for students who need it."

"You don't have adequate housing in place...in place now?" Lockhart asked, her question sounding like an accusation.

Rich hesitated before answering. "We've got most of our north dorms ready for occupancy. We were able to accommodate some of our students there this fall. We'll have more room there by the time school starts. I am also hoping to have a thousand trailers."

"Hoping?"

"Well, I have a contract with Damm Engineering."

"But Damm isn't guaranteeing that you'll have how many. . . how many beds ready?"

"Three thousand."

"Lot of beds," Lockhart said. "But you have no. . . have no guarantee they'll be ready."

"I have a contract, Margaret, but things are like a third world country down here."

"I've heard people say that...say that about Choctaw before the storm."

Rich counted to five. "So now maybe we're a fourth world country."

"Well, whatever . . . whatever world you live in," she said, "it seems to me that you're running...running radio, print, television and Internet ads promoting Ewe Ewe's readiness to . . . to resume fulltime operations on campus, and you don't...you don't know if you can even house . . . house the students who may be . . . may be relying on your word. I am very concerned about this, and I am sure . . . sure the viceroy will be . . . will be too. I guess it's beginning to seem to us...seem to us up here at the Board that you are making decisions based on your desire . . . desire to keep your institution operating rather than making de . . . making de . . . cisions based on the best interests of the students you are charged to serve."

"I presume that you are not trying to insult me, Margaret," Rich said, knowing full well that she had just insulted him and had done it with malicious delight. Nobody in Alkansea higher education played *gotcha* like Margaret Lockhart.

"I'm just . . . just making an observation. And I'm not the first . . . not the first to have made it. Some of the Board members . . . Board members have worried about this very thing."

Rich felt in his marrow that this last sentence was complete bullshit. Whenever Lipscom or Lockhart or Ronnie Shade wanted to bully one of the state system's rectors, they alleged that the concern of the moment had been raised by a board member. Every time Shade called Rich with an accusation twisted into a question, he maintained that he was following up on a board member's inquiry, a board member, Shade always assured Rich, who was only interested in making sure that every university was "cupping the mustard."

But this "board member" question was always malarkey. The frigging board members were a bunch of rich businessmen and lawyers who liked to pad their resumes. Mostly they liked the free suite tickets they got to Monster football games.

"You know, Margaret," Rich said, "you may not be trying to insult me, but let me confess that you're beginning to hurt my feelings. I moved the start of the semester back not because I'm *indifferent* to my students but because I'm *concerned* about my students. Damm was supposed to have the trailers ready by mid-January. When it became clear to me that they weren't going to make that deadline, I pushed school back a couple of weeks. In the grand scheme of things that can hardly be a big deal, but for Urban students it may be critical."

"But you admit . . . you admit that you have no guarantee the trailers will be ready . . . will be ready by the end of January either."

"In the post-Hosea world, nothing is guaranteed," Rich said.

"And yet you are accepting enrollments . . . enrollments from students who may have no place . . . place to live. Many of those students are currently enrolled . . . are currently enrolled here at the flagship. Is it really wise . . . really wise to encourage them to leave?"

And there you had it, the snake of motivation out of the grass and slithering about in plain sight. The nearly 4,000 Urban students who had enrolled at ASU in the fall had provided the "flagship" a financial windfall. Why let them go now?

"Damm Engineering is the largest company in the state," Rich said. "I think we have good reason to rely on them. I think they'll have the trailers ready by January 31."

But they didn't.

37

In the two weeks after we sacked Providence, we staged raids on Andover, Billerica, Braintree, Bridgewater, Chelmsford, Woburn and Wrentham. And thus on April 15, the United Colonies ordered all the people on the Connecticut River to take refuge in Hadley and to abandon the standing towns of Hatfield and Northampton. Further, they advised the people still living on the eastern side of Nipmuck country to take refuge in larger, better fortified settlements. The English were rocked back on their heels. If we'd had a navy, we would have finished them, for we could have stopped them from being resupplied by mother England. Francois de la Manse assured us that the French would blockade all New England ports, but we never spotted the French white naval flag fluttering from a single mast in a single New England harbor.

I RETURNED TO THE Nipmuck Country from New York at the end of February to plan and direct the attacks of March and April. Our string of victories continued, but my experience on the upper Hudson altered my strategy. I now believed that we needed to find a way to bring this war to an end as quickly as possible, because, unfortunately, my mission to Schaghticoke failed to result in the diplomatic and then military triumph that I had hoped.

Initially I was encouraged. I was successful with the Dutch and the Mahicans. The French promised impressive assistance and provided some. Though still notably European, the French maintained more honorable relations with the Indians with whom they interacted than did the English. And after Francois de la Manse took his leave of my *nashweetoo* on the Hoosic, his people made good on at least parts of what they offered. Within the month, I was joined in Schaghticoke by two hundred Canadian Iroquois. Added to the men I had brought with me and the 400 Mahicans who also joined my forces, I now possessed a fighting force approaching 700, enough to make a difference when we marched back to Massachusetts.

Had I to do it over again, I would have returned to the shifting fronts of the war in early February when we might have forced the United Colonies to sue for peace. But here, to my eternal regret, I overplayed my hand. I was intoxicated by the notion of bringing the Mohawks into the war on our side, for I knew that their assistance would deliver victory. But by delaying my departure from the Hudson Valley, I exposed myself in a way I did not foresee.

I held my enhanced battalion on the Hoosic around me until I could receive the Mohawk ambassadors Satekarihwate, Deionhehkon, and Rastawentherontha. While we waited for their arrival on a brutally cold day, gathered around the fire in my *nashweetoo*, my allies, captains and I undertook much discussion about the wisdom of negotiating with the Mohawks.

My Mahican friend Wannuacon was strenuously opposed. "You have not lived in this region, Metacom," he said. "I know from first-hand experience how ruthless the Mohawk are. They do not feel bound to any agreement they make outside their own longhouses. They have knifed my people in the back more than once. They will do the same to you. They are without conscience when their current advantage lies in reneging on earlier commitments. I strongly recommend that you return east with the warriors we have already assembled and forget about any kind of relationship with people who are so untrustworthy."

Wannuacon's sentiments echoed those of Weetamoo who had counseled me the last time I saw her before I left for Schaghticoke to be wary of the Mohawks. "They speak a different tongue," she said. "They live a different way. They are strong and fearless, but they are not civilized the way we are. They delight in butchering their enemies, and they have contempt for all of us who are unlike them. It is said they do not even regard us as human."

Wootonekanuske reminded me of her sister's advice now, speaking as she prepared us *sobaheg*, a corn stew with ruffed grouse and woodcock. "I don't know that Wannuacon is correct we shouldn't even meet with the Mohawks," she said. "But I think we should be cautious, and I think we should seek guarantees for any pledges they make to us."

"What kind of guarantees?" Wannuacon asked.

"Guns, powder," Wootonekanuske said.

"They'll never do it," Wannuacon said. "They're more likely to demand arms from us."

"How about we ask them to surrender hostages to us as a pledge of their faith?" Adonoshonk said. He and Wootonekanuske frequently saw things similarly, and they had grown closer during our time on the Hoosic. While Annawon and I conducted our negotiations with the Dutch, Adonoshonk led the building of our *nashweetoos*, and when he contracted frostbite on his toes, Wootonekanuske treated him with a salve of fir sap and crushed moss. When he caught a bad cold, Wootonekanuske treated his chest congestion with a salve made from wild cherry bark and his sore throat with blackberry root gargle.

"The idea of hostages you can certainly set aside," Wannuacon said. "The Mohawks hold the family sacred."

"What then?" Adonoshonk asked.

"That's just it," Wannuacon replied. "There's isn't anything."

"Then we must make them see their interests in joining us," Annawon said.

"Exactly," I said.

"I urge you, Metacom," Wannuacon said. "Your time here has accomplished a great deal. If you fear my enmity for the Mohawks too greatly influences how I see things, take the advice of the great Sachem Weetamoo and the caution expressed by some of your captains and your own bride. You achieved more already than you had any reason to anticipate when you crossed the Connecticut River. Please don't push your luck with people I guarantee you cannot trust."

But thinking I had solved the military riddle of victory, I did not heed this counsel. We were not able to reach consensus. Out of personal loyalty, I now believe, Annawon and Pawtonomi stood with me, Tuspaquin with Wannuacon, Wootonekanuske and Adonoshonk. To my sorrow, I was not swayed by those who saw things in this matter more clearly than did I.

I hoped to capitalize on the uncertainties surrounding the European occupation of the area. New York was founded as the Dutch colony of New Netherlands in 1613, and, though the Dutch were as capable of racial violence as any of the other white invaders, their primary interest was the fur trade rather than colonial settlement. The Mohawks were powerful before the Dutch arrived and became more so through their symbiotic domination of the fur trade. The English had acquired title to the Dutch holdings in New Netherlands in 1664, but the English had only secured control of Manhattan and the Hudson in 1674. So the Mohawks had a new group of white men to deal with, men, I hoped to demonstrate, who had a thirst for land ownership and domination that the Mohawks had never encountered with the Dutch. That I had hit upon sensitivity in Mohawk thinking is demonstrated by the fact that they undertook serious discussions with me. And for one giddy period when I thought I had them convinced, the prospect of victory danced vividly in my brain.

Having seen the likes of That Vicious Lying Rat Bastard Josiah Winslow up close for so many years, I possessed unqualified conviction that some version of a Pan-Indian alliance constituted the only long-run hope for the survival of our culture as it existed when the invaders first moved in with us. The Mohawks *should* join us, I fervently believed, so my job was to make them *understand* that they should.

And I remain loyal to my Pan-Indian convictions to this day. But, to be fair, I *must* concede that Mohawk defenders can wage a powerful counterargument, for long after the Wampanoags and I were just an ill-remembered footnote, the Mohawks were still around having things largely their own way. They were still around to fight on the side of the English against the French in the French and Indian War and against the Americans in both the Revolutionary War and the War of 1812. I still think they were wrong not to have joined me, but for a century and a half after they didn't, I couldn't have found one of their number to have agreed with me.

Nonetheless, I was indisputably correct to have seen that the Mohawks were at a pivotal point in their history when we discussed their joining me in the winter of 1676. They were not certain if their relationship with the English in Albany and at the mouth of the Hudson would mirror the successful relationship they had maintained with the Dutch for over sixty years. And by reciting the bitter experiences my brother Wamsutta and I had encountered with the English, I tried to convince the Mohawk emissaries that if they joined the war on our side, we could drive the English from the region, and they could resume the satisfactory relationship they had long enjoyed with the Dutch.

But in hindsight I can see that all my talk of universal Indian brotherhood was no more persuasive to them than it had been to the Narragansetts before the Great Swamp Fight. The English had convinced me that no long-term accommodation was possible with them as partners. The Mohawks, hardly indefensibly, were looking out for their own interests. They had not experienced what my people had, and when they looked at Europeans and Algonquians, they saw peoples both vastly different from themselves.

Meanwhile, all the time the Mohawk diplomats were talking to me in the upper Hudson Valley, three other Mohawk ambassadors were at the mouth of the river negotiating with New York's Governor Andros. Which entity could offer the greatest prospect of economic advantage: the Algonquians of New England or the English? In my pan-Indian idealism, I did not understand this, but they were going to ally themselves with the highest bidder. And that, to the ultimate demise of New England Indiandom, was Governor Andros.

Andros offered the Mohawks unqualified control of all fur and skin trade, which remained considerable (though contested in Canada by the French), in the reaches above Albany and into the north country where Europeans had yet to establish settlements. This dominance would keep the Mohawks in arms and powder and prized European goods to fill their longhouses for more than a century to come. My us-versus-them argument proved no match for Andros' specific, immediate, and as it happened, long lasting, material deal. For among the Mohawks there was no us that included the Algonquians. In addition, the Mohawks had no trust for those who had already joined me at Schaghticoke. The Mahicans were not just Algonquian but also the Mohawks' traditional enemies. And the northern Iroquois were in league with the French, whom the Mohawks despised and correctly regarded as their economic rivals.

An infamous story about my negotiations with the Mohawks persists and is sometimes believed to this day, though honest historians, if they pass it along, concede that it is uncorroborated. That Notorious Praying Prevaricator Increase Mather made the story up from whole cloth. Mather is the Puritan bigot who wrote that the land of New England Algonquians was "The land the Lord God of our Fathers hath given to us for our rightful possession." Probably not the same Lord God Jesus who said in the Sermon on the Mount that the meek, not the bellicose, would inherit the earth. Mather's story is that in order to trick the Mohawks into allying with me I ambushed a squad of Mohawks and then tried to blame the murders on the English. When the Mohawks found out that I was the killer, they turned on me. Is such a cold-blooded action consistent with any other that I took in this whole heartbreaking affair? Moreover, consider That Notorious Praying Prevaricator's insidious, deeply racist motives. He wouldn't have it that Indian people could, in this case the Mohawks, calculate their interests and take action accordingly. No, he had to reduce all Indian actions as those proceeding from hot blood. In one fell swoop I was a despicable felon, and the Mohawks were mindless reactionaries.

The truth is I possessed too little with which to entice the Mohawks. What Andros had to offer was concrete, whereas my entreaties were speculative and rhetorical.

I undertook my negotiations with the Mohawks because I was not satisfied with what I had earlier accomplished at Schaghticoke. Just as Wannuacon and Wootonekanuske warned me against, I tried for too much. And as is so often the case in human affairs when one overreaches, I got less than I could have had. Had I returned to Massachusetts in early February, I would have arrived with open supply lines and a fresh fighting force. Instead, I kept working on the Mohawks until they had, unbeknownst to me, sealed their deal with Andros.

Under the terms of their agreement with Andros, the Mohawks were obligated to attack my camp at Schaghticoke. And that's just what they did. They circled to the south and came in with the sun from the west. We had stationed guards, but some had their throats cut before they could sound the alarm, and those that made it back to camp succeeded in raising us too late. The Mohawks had surprise and numbers on their side. Our defeat was devastating.

We lost the essential leadership of Wannuacon who was felled by a Mohawk musket then scalped. The Mahican sachem was clearly targeted, almost certainly pointed out by a traitor. His death accomplished exactly what the Mohawks sought. The Mahicans, defeated by the Mohawks so often in the past, were terrified. They broke ranks and returned to the porous refuge of their own territory. Similarly, the French Indians also deserted us. Their interest in joining us was heightened by what they had heard of our long string of victories. But then their first experience with us was that of chilling defeat. Many of their force were killed, and those who survived fled. My own warriors, hardened from fighting the English, fought well, and our losses were few. But as we marched out of New York in February, we were no more than those who had arrived. Our short-term gains were squandered. Our grander plans were shattered. And Mohawk raiding parties harassed our retreat until we crossed the Connecticut River.

This bitter defeat hardly brought That Vicious Lying Rat Bastard's War to an end, but it did change the nature of our expectations and the development of our strategy. Many victories still lay ahead. But I now surrendered any hopes for the kind of total triumph I dared dream of in alliance with the Mohawks. We were still basically untouched and even untouchable in the trackless refuge of Nipmuck Country. But in the area at large, we remained outnumbered by the English more than two to one and, with the Mohawks now menacing our west, surrounded on all sides save the north. Moreover, despite our daring raids against Weymouth and Clark's Garrison, we were cut off from the sea.

And this last fact had a direct, economic impact because the Narragansetts, Pocassets, Sakonnets and Pokanokets were all people who derived much of our food from fishing, crabbing and clamming. In terrifying ways, now, hunger was as much our enemy as the English. All of us who lived on Narragansett and

Montaup Bays had been forced to flee and to abandon our crops in the ground and our carefully maintained stores of food. As the spring of 1676 arrived we were still separated from the fields of our foremothers.

Now, it was planting season, and save for our Nipmuck brothers we were far from home.

38

On December 10, Rich received another of many annoying phone calls from the viceroy's office, this one from Elia Lipscom himself.

Lipscom began the conversation with a gleeful trip down ASU football memory lane, recounting for Rich's delectation the Monsters' season-ending triumph over Georgia and ASU's invitation to the Orange Bowl. Rich despised the way Mayflower people just presumed that everyone they knew was a Monster fan. Rich wasn't a Monster fan. Rich was a Monster anti-fan. He rooted against the Monsters no matter the sport and no matter the opponent. He would root against them in tiddlywinks if they had a tiddlywinks team, he liked to joke to those, unlike Elia Lipscom, who would find such a line funny. If the Monsters were to play a team from Hell, Rich would watch the game outfitted with a pitchfork and a sack of brimstone.

Rich let Lipscom blabber on without a single verbal cue to continue until eventually the viceroy came to the end of his football exultation and told Rich he had some bad news for him. "The Board has decided to cut your state allocation this year by eight million dollars," he said, then continued on as if he just stated the temperature. "Hell of a thing, Governor Lebear gave us a cut figure, so we had no choice. Governor says that Hosea is going to break state government, and he's not going to let that happen on his watch."

"Hosea is going to prove a cash cow for this state," Rich said. "FEMA and the Bushcovites may have screwed up everything they've touched, but the money is starting to flow already, and it's going to turn into a torrent."

"He's been told that, but he says he prefers to err on the safe side."

"This is hard and fast?" Rich asked.

"Hard as calculus and fast as a drunk teenager."

"Eight million?"

"'Fraid so."

"I can't conceivably do it."

"You've got no choice. That much money simply will not be made available for you. That's the way it works."

"I won't be able to meet payroll."

"You're going to have to lay people off. The sooner you start, the easier it will be at the end of the fiscal year."

"You told me this wouldn't happen, Elia. You said we would be 'utterly protected.' Now we're going to be destroyed. First by the hurricane, now by you."

"Hey, don't blame me for this, Coach. I'm just the messenger. The governor cut higher education, and the Board had no recourse but to notify the individual institutions of their share."

"What was the total cut?" Rich asked.

"Fifty-seven million."

"Jesus Christ. Fifty-seven million with half the fiscal year gone," Rich said. Something was wrong with that number. Rich picked up the calculator that sat as always on the top of his desk. He punched in the numbers. "Wait a minute, our budget is seven percent of state higher ed. Seven percent of fifty-seven million is four million, not eight."

"Yeah, well," Lipscom said. "Right. We had to redo your number because you're only half as big as you were when you were at seven percent."

"You mean half as big because we're only teaching half as many students this fall?"

"Not even that many, are you?"

"But that's just this fall. We'll have more students in the spring."

"How many more?"

"We don't know, of course."

"But you won't be back at twenty thousand, will you?"

"That's not likely," Rich said. "The city is too damaged. Housing is a major issue."

"Yeah," Lipscom said. "Margaret tells me you've concocted a plan to pack your kids into trailers. Don't know how wise I think that is."

"It's our only hope of getting our students back."

"Well, there you have it," Lipscom said. "How wise is getting your students back? Maybe your students would be better off staying wherever they are now. Did you ever think of that? We've got quite a few of them here at the flagship, and I don't know why it's in their interest to return to Choctaw and live in a trailer."

"First of all, Elia, I can't *coerce* students to do anything. They can stay where they are if they choose, and many no doubt will. But it seems to me it's my job to *provide* for my students. Those in the middle of their degree work always lose credits when they transfer schools. Charlie is getting our physical facilities back online. And that's a miracle, I have to tell you. But we have adequate teaching space. The students want to finish their degrees. We have teachers to teach them. We're ready to do our jobs down here."

"You don't have all your teachers. You've told me previously that a whole bunch of them retired in the weeks right after the storm. Or found other jobs. Or, I guess, just up and quit."

"That's true. But we have plenty enough remaining faculty to teach 16,000 students."

"Is that how many students you think you will have in the spring? Eighty percent?"

"I doubt it," Rich admitted. "We're kind of hoping for seventy-five percent. 15,000."

"So what you're telling me is that you have more faculty than you need. That's where you can find the money for your cut. If you have faculty to teach sixteen thousand, and you're only teaching nine thousand this fall, then you have a *lot* more faculty than you need. I'm not saying this will be easy, Coach, but it appears you do have some slack to work with."

"I can't lay off people in the middle of the year, Elia. It isn't right. A faculty member can't find a new job in a month."

"Well, you've got to do something. Why don't you eliminate athletics?"

"I'm not going to cut athletics. I've only got about two million general fund dollars in athletics anyway, so that wouldn't get me anywhere near where you say I have to cut."

"I don't know, man. You start laying off faculty and longtime staff, you're going to get a lot of pushback if they see the old coach unwilling to cut the sports program."

"The pitiful way you fund us, this has come up before. A lot of short-sighted academics think athletics is a luxury. But we've done our homework, Elia. Kids associate Division I athletic programs with a big-time university. Long-term recruiting would fall off a cliff if we eliminated athletics, which is a free advertising engine for schools like us. Puts our name in the papers all across the South every time we show up for a game."

"Man, that water y'all are drinking down there is doing something to you. You don't even have a football team. The only thing that really matters to folks in these parts is football and even an old round baller like yourself ought to know that."

"We don't have a football team because the Board has blocked it for decades."

"The Board has blocked it," Lipscom said, "because it's too goddamned expensive."

"Bullshit," Rich replied. "We know how mid-major schools like ours manage a football program. We take a bunch of guaranteed-revenue away games with the likes of Alabama and LSU, and we can cover our entire athletic nut. Guys like your ASU Monsters get the thrill of kicking our ass sixty-two to nothing in football, and we can run basketball, baseball, volleyball and softball programs just as good as those at the flagship schools."

"Yeah, maybe," Lipscom said. "But the facts of the moment are you don't have a football team, and you're not going to get one in time to save the rest of your athletics. I recommend you cut your sports. But that's just me. It's your call. Just hear me that you gotta do something."

"The question is, Elia, why do I have to do something? Or at least, why do I have to do an eight-million-dollar something? That's just not a fair number. I'd have a hell of a time finding four million dollars. But maybe I could do *that*. What is the Board thinking in doubling Urban's share of the cut?"

"The Board is thinking you are allocated a certain amount of money every year to teach so many students and you're not even teaching half of them. You've got more money than you have a right to. That's what the Board is thinking."

"But that takes no account of the fact that we're the victims in all this. The storm happened to us, to our faculty, our staff, our students. Our faculty have moved heaven and earth to teach this fall when they have no houses to live in. Now you want me to take away the livelihood of people who have already lost everything they owned. Where's the conscience in all this? Where's the morality?"

"The Board's not in the conscience and morality business, Coach. They're in the higher education business. And your business is bankrupt. You talk as if we ought to ask the other institutions in the state to take an unfair cut, when you aren't holding up your end."

"How much of a cut is the Mayflower campus taking?" Rich asked.

"It is the wisdom of the Board that the flagship be spared a cut. After all, we are picking up your slack already. We're teaching students that you're not teaching. We are facing increased responsibilities with increased costs."

"And FEMA is forking over 2,000 dollars for every Urban student ASU is teaching."

"But that hardly meets the cost of providing full-time college education. How would you like it if all you got from the state was two thousand bucks per student?"

"Come on, Elia, I assume you know better than all that. Most of our students are federal grant recipients. So the feds are already paying ASU what we get for teaching them. And they're getting FEMA's two grand on top of that. This storm is a fricking cash cow for Stephen Hopkins. I doubt he even had to add more than a handful of adjunct instructors. The kind of student increase he's *benefitting* from can be dealt with simply by adding Urban students to classes that were already being offered at ASU. You say we have more teachers than we need. The Mayflower campus obviously has more *money* than it needs."

"I don't run the Board, Coach. It does what it wants. And you can complain about this cut all you want, but you're going to have to deal with it. Maybe now you can see why I wanted you to think about shutting down this entire year."

"Elia, if I had shut down, I would have laid everybody off at the end of September. Everybody. At least I got them paid through this fall term."

"Well, you're not going to get them all paid through the spring term. Not unless you've got somebody down there who can spin brown grass into gold."

RICH DID MANAGE TO spin brown grass into gold. But he got his hands dirty in a way he never thought he'd have to. And if had it to do over, he'd do the same thing again.

Rich was determined not to lay off any of his employees in the fiscal year of the hurricane. And that meant he now had to find eight million dollars on top of the lost tuition revenue that wasn't offset by utility and other operating savings from being closed down for nearly two months and functioning without a number of buildings during the year. All told, he needed to raise twelve million dollars to keep his budget balanced. He had a pledge of one million dollars from the Fortran Foundation which had a long history of support for higher education. In his younger days he and Cally had been Fortran Graduate Fellows, and that fact got him an audience with its board, which listened with sympathy and quickly wrote him a check.

He also lucked into a two-million-dollar grant from the Sultan of Bahresh, who decided to employ his billions to cultivate popular standing in the United States by being a post-Hosea benefactor. He gave the same amount of money to Ettons University, the preppy private school across town that hardly needed it as much as Urban did. The Sultan actually handed out less money than he made in a single day's interest, but he succeeded in having his largesse contrasted on CNN and in other media with the ineptitude of the Bush administration. But the Sultan still didn't get his money's worth in the state of Alkansea. Most of Ettons' students came from the Northeast, so locals weren't emotionally connected to a gift to the private school, and nobody outside Choctaw really cared what happened to Urban.

Rich also got a million dollars from Beatrice Florin, the proprietress of her late husband's off-shore drilling empire. Florin had gotten mad at Urban during the late days of the Francis Saurian administration, and Rich's overtures toward her after he became interim rector had all been politely rebuffed. Ben Turner, however, who knew Florin socially, alerted Rich to the fact that she was concerned the storm might result in damage to Urban's Geology Department, which had historically trained a significant number of Florin Oil's employees. Ben set

456   Fredrick Barton

up a lunch with Florin to discuss the situation, and Rich spoke
with such passion about Urban's importance to their city that
she volunteered to write a check. He didn't even state a number,
and she offered it up with no strings attached. Beatrice Florin's
donation balanced Urban's projected revenue versus expenditure
shortfall and brought Rich back to the eight million dollars
the state was chopping in mid-year. She helped with that too
by providing Rich an introduction and some critical financial
grease. This was the dirty part.

Bushian ineptitude had embarrassed even his heretofore
slavishly subservient Republican Party members in Congress.
Few of them really had any sympathy for the victims of Hosea,
but they didn't like that fact being made apparent. In addition,
most of them campaigned on pro-education platforms, even
though few of them ever voted in favor of increased funding
for education. They were for it, but they were for tax cuts a
whole lot more. They were for education as a philosophical way
of condemning *ignorance*, which they used as a code word for
impoverished minorities and recent immigrants. Now, though,
after all the bungling, and the white hot indignation of the
national reaction to the incompetence, the Republicans who
controlled Congress yearned to make some display of concern.
This was particularly true of Republicans in swing districts who
had been able to milk Bush's War on Terror for the crossover
votes needed to hold onto their seats. After Hurricane Hosea,
compassion was expedient.

Rich was ushered into this fertile greenhouse of possibility
by Beatrice Florin and her longstanding connections. Money
buys friends, a lot of money a lot of friends, big money friends
with big sticks. Rich didn't have to do anything other than
figuratively hold his nose and close his eyes. First Beatrice put
Rich in contact with the Washington lobbying firm of Piaster,
Pye and Associates. A conservative Democrat, Stan Piaster
formerly represented Alkansea in the United States Senate.
He was sixty, trim, handsome and smooth as silk. He had left

the Senate after three terms for reasons that were never clear. Unpublished rumors whispered that a political opponent had pictures of him in a slinky black dress, mesh stockings and stiletto heels. Rich didn't know if a smidgen of truth adhered to these whispers. But Stan Piaster made no pretense that he intended to do anything other than use his influence to get as rich as possible and as quickly as possible, and that's just what he did once leaving office.

Piaster's partner was Bridgette Pye, a former Republican Congresswoman from Mayflower's fourth district. Pye was forty-nine and as coarse and difficult as Piaster was charming. She was barely five feet tall in her stacked pumps and was built like a fireplug, a fact she sought to disguise by dressing only in black. She was pro-flag, pro-gun and pro-life. She had become a significant Congressional player during Newt Gingrich's "Contract with America" campaign and captured her seat on a right-wing platform that included the promise she would serve only three terms. This was a promise she kept, leaving Congress as George the Second was coming in. She was a perfect mate for Stan Piaster. He had the style, but in the Republican Congress of the era, she had the contacts.

Beatrice Florin never told Rich how much she paid Piaster and Pye to work their magic for him. Rich always assumed Beatrice paid them and thus never believed their protestations that they assisted him because of their concern for the people of Choctaw. Bridgette Pye had never done a thing for Choctaw as far as Rich knew. Piaster had a better record as far as Choctaw went—as a Democrat, he had needed Choctaw's African-American vote to win his Senate seat. But no Choctaws considered Piaster their knight in shining armor. Perhaps Piaster and Pye assisted Rich as a favor to Beatrice, but Rich assumed that Florin Oil paid them straight out.

Pye accompanied Rich to a private meeting she arranged with Illinois Congressman Shale Whittenburg, chairman of the House Education Committee. They waited for a short time in the Congressman's outer office, and when the door to the inner office opened, Rich was shocked to see Sheila Pyrite, his own mysterious assistant for special projects, emerge with the Congressman who was holding Sheila's hand. She was dressed in a smart beige suit and a ruffled black scoop-necked blouse over which lay a strand of pearls.

"Sheila?" Rich said, just as she accepted a kiss on the cheek from the Congressman.

"Hello, Rector," she replied and winked at him.

"What are you doing here?" Rich asked.

"I just popped in to see Shale," she said. "We're old friends. He mentioned that you were coming to see him. Which you really should have told me about. But no matter. I told him all about you and how hard you're working to save our school."

"Come right in," the Congressman said and turned immediately back into his office where he walked toward his desk.

"But what are you doing in Washington?" Rich asked Sheila.

"Well, I was working on a project, of course," she said and laughed.

"We shouldn't keep the Congressman waiting," Bridgette Pye said, grasping Rich by his upper arm and using the heel of her hand to urge him forward.

"What project?" Rich asked, as Bridgette propelled him into the next room.

"I'll give you a full report when we get back to Choctaw," Sheila said.

The Congressman stood behind his desk and opened his palms toward the two chairs across from him, indicating that Rich and Bridgette should sit. There were three aides in the room, two twentysomething men in suits and a fortyish woman in a white blouse and black skirt. The Congressman didn't bother to introduce them. Nor did he ever make reference to the fact that he'd just had some kind of private meeting with Sheila Pyrite.

Short and shaped like an olive, Whittenburg had represented a district on the southwest side of Chicago for twenty years. Once a safe, middle-class white Republican enclave, full of homes built in the 1950s, the district was now twenty-five percent African-American and twenty-two percent Hispanic. In the most recent election, the Congressman had held onto his seat by only two points, and he was eager for an opportunity to court minority voters. Showing concern for the people of Choctaw was a good vehicle for that strategy. Directing some recovery funding to the largest institution of higher education in Choctaw was a tactic for doing so.

Rich began his best pitch, and was startled when the Congressman said, bluntly, "How much are you asking for?" Rich had come asking for "help." He didn't have a figure in mind and had no idea he'd be asked to provide one quite so baldly. Rich almost said, eight million, since that's how much he needed. But he forced himself to pause, take a deep breath, and try to look needy without looking pitiful. Was eight million so much he'd get nothing? Or if he asked for eight million, might he leave money on the table?

"Our problem requires at least ten million dollars in the next few months," Rich said. "Of course . . ."

Rich was going to try to do a little dance that would push the idea of ten million while assuring the Congressman that less was more than acceptable, but Whittenburg interrupted him to ask, "Have you seen anyone else about this funding?"

"Anyone else?" Rich said, not sure what the Congressman was asking him.

"Have you approached anyone else on the hill?" Whittenburg said. "Your own representative, for instance?"

"Congressman St. Clair?"

"He's your rep, right?"

"Yes, Billy St. Clair represents the first district of Alkansea, which is most of Choctaw. Urban University is in that district."

"And you have approached him for this support?" Whittenburg asked again.

Rich knew nothing about proper protocol. Was he supposed to have approached his own rep first? "You're the first person here in Washington that I've talked to," Rich said.

"Excellent," Whittenburg said. "Perfect. We will start the ball rolling from our side. Our colleagues across the aisle can join in as they choose." Translation: if Whittenburg was going to lace some education recovery money for Urban into an emergency relief package, he was damn sure not going to let the credit go to Billy St. Clair just because Urban was in St. Clair's district. Once Whittenburg soaked up the lion's share of credit for being a compassionate conservative, he would collect an IOU from St. Clair by letting him hang around in any photo ops the matter might generate.

"Please forgive my lack of experience at this process, Congressman," Rich said, "but are you saying that you think you can help us with some portion of the ten million we need?"

"I think we probably ought to do better than that," Whittenburg replied. He turned toward the row of aides, each taking notes but otherwise not participating in the conversation. "Let's put Dr. Janus' Urban University down for thirty million in the forthcoming emergency relief bill." He turned back to Rich. "I am just supposing that it will take you several years to get back on your feet. Three years. Ten million. I assume thirty million all told will help."

Rich felt beads of sweat on his face as he stammered his astonished gratitude.

"Now remember," Whittenburg said, as he stood to usher Rich out, "mum's the word for now. You let me be the one to confide the good news to Congressman St. Clair. We find too few opportunities to reach out to the other side, and we like to savor them when the chance arises."

In the days ahead, Rich got a glimpse at how the system worked. Congressman Whittenburg arranged a "fact-finding

tour" of Choctaw and south Alkansea. Piaster and Pye arranged
a trip to the levee breaches and through the blight of the most
severely flooded neighborhoods. Whittenburg stood on the floor
of Ungulate Arena in a shaft of sunlight pouring through the
roof. And later that night Beatrice Florin hosted Whittenburg at
a two-thousand-dollar-a-plate reelection campaign fundraising
dinner for five hundred of her closest friends. How many of
those dinners she paid for herself by one method or another
never came to light. But whoever paid, the Illinois congressman
walked away with a million dollars for his war chest.

Of course, that didn't mean Urban got thirty million dollars,
which would indeed have funded its recovery pretty thoroughly,
especially with FEMA paying for repairs to Urban's buildings.
Remarkably, though, thirty million *is* what Whittenburg
introduced. Not surprisingly, that's not what Congress passed.
Who knows if Whittenburg was in on this sleight of hand? He
introduced what he promised to introduce. He walked away
with his million bucks. And then the legislation got amended,
and despite his chairmanship of the Education Committee,
Whittenburg was only one congressman pouring money into
the public trough where there were a lot of different mouths
jockeying to feed. Rich couldn't even rightly complain. He may
have been promised thirty million. But he'd only asked for ten.
And that's what he got.

But before he got it, Rich got a call from Margaret Lockhart
directing him to drive up to Mayflower for a special meeting
with the viceroy. When Rich inquired about the reason for the
meeting, Lockhart pleaded ignorance other than to say, "I know
y'all talk on the phone all the time, but just because y'all are a
ways away . . . a ways away, it doesn't mean y'all ought not to talk
face to face once in a . . . once in a while. He's very concerned
about *Ewe Ewe*, you know, and I'm sure he just wants . . . just
wants to discuss some things."

Rich hated such a summons, which always felt demeaning
even though routine. He already had to drive up to Mayflower

462   Fredrick Barton

once a month to attend the Board meetings. And the viceroy

462   Fredrick Barton

once a month to attend the Board meetings. And the viceroy usually found an additional reason a month to summon his rectors, either individually or as a group. Driving seventy-five up the Interstate, Rich could make the trip in a little over two hours. But the drive was followed by the inevitable waiting. Nothing ever started on time. A meeting that began only a half hour late was early.

Then Lipscom could never finish *any* meeting in less than two hours. And those were the short ones. The languid way Lipscom ran his meetings made Rich think the viceroy's job required too little of him and that he had time to squander, not understanding that his rectors didn't. In sum, a trip to Mayflower killed an entire day. So Rich was never in a good mood arriving in Mayflower. His mood got lots worse this trip when the viceroy greeted him by saying, "Just who in the fuck authorized you to go ask Congress for money?"

It seemed to Rich that much of his job as Urban's CEO consisted of getting hit with blows he didn't see coming. He despised being attacked this way and wanted to fight back. But he managed a calm response. "I thought fund raising was central among my responsibilities."

"That's just bullshit, Coach," Lipscom responded, leaning over his desk as if he were a junior high principal and Rich a troublesome eighth-grader. "Bull. Shit."

"I am truly mystified," Rich said, "that you are angry I was out raising money to offset the state budget cut. I am just trying to protect my institution, to keep my people drawing their salaries and to balance my budget as you've made amply clear I will be required to do."

"By fishing in my pond, Coach, by fishing in my pond. The federal budget belongs to the state as a whole. If someone is going to ask the feds for money to support public higher education in this state, that person has to be me or someone who reports to me."

Rich did not point out that *he* reported to the viceroy.

"This state is hurting, Coach. Higher ed is getting hammered. We're facing a fifty-seven million dollar budget cut to be absorbed by *all* the institutions in the state, and I come to find out that you've gotten to some jack wad from Iowa or somewhere and convinced him to put you in for thirty million all by yourself. You know how that plays in this town, Coach? That plays like we've got a man on our team who isn't in the huddle, a man running his own end around when the rest of us are trying to run off tackle."

"Well, the funding Congressman Whittenburg put us in for was in an emergency relief bill. I don't think the other schools would qualify."

"That's for me to determine, Coach. I would say all our institutions need some emergency relief because the storm has resulted in a huge cut to higher ed. And, anyway, I've got two community colleges in and around Choctaw to manage. Did you talk the Congressman into support for Carver or Choctaw C.C.?"

Rich didn't know whether Lipscom had a point there or not. Rich bore no responsibility to raise money for the community colleges. And Carver only had about one thousand students. But should he have asked the Choctaw C.C. rector to accompany him to see Whittenburg?

"And you Choctaw folks," Lipscom said, knocking on his desk with his knuckles for emphasis, "persist in maintaining that Hosea happened only to you and nobody else in this state. We've been over this before. Right here in Mayflower, the flagship has stepped up and undertaken an education burden it's never been asked to carry before."

Rather than arguing, as he had before, that ASU had financially benefitted from the storm, Rich inquired, "Just for curiosity's sake, how did you learn of my meeting with Congressman Whittenburg?"

"I learned it from Stephen Hopkins," Lipscom said. "Stephen has this brilliant idea about starting a coastal wetlands preservation and restoration institute here at the flagship, and he was hoping a federal grant would provide needed start-up funds. But he was basically told that your buddy Whittenburg had provided all the money for the state of Alkansea a Congressman could afford to jam into one bill. Especially a Congressman who answers to voters from somewhere else. Way Hopkins sees it, way a lot of important supporters of our campus here see it and are gonna see it, you ran off with money that the flagship could have used. And that gets on me, Coach. My job is to make sure that things are equitably distributed. My job is to make sure none of my people is the Lonesome Fucking End."

No, Rich thought, apparently your job is to make sure that ASU gets the loaf and all other state institutions pretend to be deliriously happy with the crumbs. Rich didn't inquire if Hopkins had received Lipscom's permission to pursue Congressional funding for a new institute, one, as it happened, that duplicated a research center at Urban where it was more properly placed.

"We gotta be clear on this from here on out, Coach," Lipscom said. "You want to go ask Congress for money, you clear it with me first. We all have to be on the same page of the playbook. We all have to put the educational ball in the end zone as a *team*."

So Elia Lipscom and his supporters on the Board were able to get Rich's thirty million dollars reduced by two thirds. Lipscom pulled that off by successfully soliciting the support of Billy St. Clair, who was pissed that Rich had "gone around him" to Whittenburg, and Frank McSeveney, the Republican who had succeeded Bridgette Pye as Mayflower's representative in the fourth district, who was pissed that no money was directed to the flagship. McSeveney was so angry about the deal and at his former supporter Bridgette Pye that he introduced legislation to prohibit former Congressmen from working as lobbyists after they'd left office.

As a publicity gimmick to demonstrate the solidarity of Alkansea, St. Clair and McSeveney were photographed in the House standing on chairs on opposite sides of the center aisle and leaning toward each other to shake hands. They had managed to convince Congress to pass a thirty million dollar educational recovery component that included ten million for Urban, ten million for Ettons University, three and a half million for Choctaw Community College, and one and a half million for Carver. Though Rich was royally annoyed that Lipscom and his collaborators took even the first dollar out of Urban's thirty million dollar pot, he didn't feel too bad about the money going to the community colleges. They had suffered damages just as significant as those at Urban. And they were public institutions. Rich was more angered about the money, an identical sum to Urban's, that went to Ettons, a private school that suffered far less damage than Urban had and taught very few students from Choctaw or elsewhere in Alkansea. That deal got swung to please the U.S. senator from New Jersey whose daughter was an Ettons sophomore and who promised to kill the whole package if Ettons didn't get the same amount of money as this "Urban University that nobody has ever heard of."

But if Rich was pissed about the money for Ettons, he was enraged that the last five million of the thirty million dollars originally targeted for Urban went to the Monsters at ASU.

STILL, FRUSTRATED AND ANGRY though he was that political machinations and rank human selfishness and greed had diminished the security that the whole thirty million dollars would have meant to Urban University's recovery, Rich was pleased that ten million would enable him to protect his employees for fiscal 2004-2005. As an athlete and coach, Rich had always concentrated on victory, but in the world of sport, victories were clearly delineated in a way that they weren't in life. Losing twenty million dollars could be considered a defeat, but gaining ten could be viewed as a significant victory. Some part of the former attitude gnawed at him in the middle of the night and awoke him with a pounding in his chest, but in his waking hours he consciously decided to emphasize the positive.

All things considered, the restarted fall semester of 2004 ended in an orderly fashion with the last of final exams on Saturday, December 18. Commencement ceremonies were held on December 23 when an amazing, stubbornly determined 1,075 students walked across the stage to receive their degrees. The event would remain in Rich's heart for the rest of his life.

Urban usually held its graduations in Ungulate Arena. But that facility was unusable and would so remain for the next three years, another victim of FEMA red tape. It took longer, in fact, to repair the damaged building than it took to build it in the first place. With the arena not usable, Rich had to move graduation to one of the huge exhibition halls in the Civic Center. This wasn't ideal because, unlike Urban's basketball facility, the exhibition hall lacked any tier seating. A high stage was erected, but the faculty, graduates and their families had to sit on folding chairs that stretched away from the stage in two long three-thousand-seat blocks on either side of a center aisle. From the back, figures on stage looked like ants. To ameliorate this problem, Rich had Drama and Film Chair Joe Alter broadcast the event on closed circuit television with a giant screen above and behind the stage and six large screens spaced down the outside aisles. Despite the fact that many people had to watch the proceedings electronically in order to see them clearly, the Civic Center space was packed and electric with emotion.

Rich dispensed with a traditional graduation speaker. Instead, he gave the program over to a series of speakers chosen from the campus community: one faculty member, one non-faculty staff member, one undergraduate and one graduate student. Each was asked to speak for a few minutes about his or her experiences during the storm and in returning to the university afterwards either to work or study. People in the audience cried all the way through, cried at the speakers' stories, cried in memory of their own stories, which differed in detail but not in kind.

Rich presided at the ceremony, and right after the processional, when he stepped to the microphone to say a few words of welcome and briefly introduce the first speaker, he was greeted with a standing ovation. When the speeches ended and after all the degrees had been awarded, once the last of the graduates was reseated, he stepped to the microphone for some closing remarks and was welcomed with a second round of applause that gradually turned into another, sustained standing ovation.

When the crowd finally quieted, Rich said, "The program reads that we're now supposed to sing the alma mater and go home, but before we do that I want to keep you together on this remarkable occasion for just a few moments longer."

"You talk now, Coach," one of the student athletes called out.

"Yeah, you talk, Rector Janus," someone rejoined, a female voice, an older student or maybe someone's mother.

Another round of applause burst out.

"I want to speak directly to tonight's graduates," Rich said, "although what I want to say, directly from my heart, applies in many ways to everybody in this room, whether graduate, faculty member, loyal, long-suffering Urban staff member or proud parent, spouse, child or other loved one. People who know the unusual way that I came to hold the office that places me before you now, know that I did not seek my current position. But it has been my privilege to hold it."

Applause broke out again.

"Run, Rich, run," someone called out, and the remark was greeted with laughter. Rich smiled and continued, "Barring unforeseen circumstances, tonight is not the last Urban University graduation over which it will be my privilege to preside. Life granting, I'll be back in the spring. But I don't know that any commencement can ever top this one. I am so proud of all of you that at times I think my heart may burst."

Applause again.

"As you perhaps know, I did not attend Urban as an undergraduate, but I did earn my Ph.D. here at Urban in 1994, so as a fellow alumnus of this vital institution, I am proud to welcome you. Those of you who have graduated tonight have done so in unprecedented times, and I want to emphasize the depth of my admiration for you for accomplishing what you have under circumstances when many would not have persevered. You returned to Urban this fall when this fiercely determined institution rose up from the flood waters of Hurricane Hosea and opened its doors when every other institution in this great city remained dark."

Another round of sustained applause.

"I thank you for coming back when others did not and would not. I thank you for your loyalty to this treasured place when in our city's darkest hours Urban University was one of the few places where lights dared shine."

Applause.

"I thank you. But I want to apologize to you too. I apologize that you spent your last semester without a student union. I apologize that you spent your last semester without a dining facility on campus. I apologize that we are holding this ceremony tonight, not in Ungulate Arena, but in this Civic Center space quite clearly designed for events unlike this one. So I thank you for your understanding and for your devotion despite the lack of amenities that you would have found most anywhere else. It has been four months since the storm. Through the leadership and ceaseless hard work of Vice Rector Charles Lobovich, we were able to get many of our buildings reopened. But we did what we did in defiance of the absence of crucial support, yes from the widely derided FEMA, but also from our state government. With proper resources put at our disposal, the union could have been and should have been open when you returned to school in October. But it isn't open now, and it probably won't open for your former classmates this spring. With proper resources put at our disposal, we could be meeting tonight under a repaired roof in our arena, an arena whose repair work couldn't have been entirely completed by tonight, but an arena that could have been usable tonight. So yes, I thank you, and again I apologize that you have had to endure under conditions that are a mark of shame upon our state.

"So let me ask you all a question. An overarching question. It is a question that I suggest influence you as you think about governmental leadership for our city and our state in the days and years ahead. As a graduate of this stubborn, resourceful, defiant institution, it is a question I suggest you keep foremost in your mind as you enter voting booths for the rest of your life to choose those who will make decisions that will affect the future of Urban University. The question is this: Is there *one* among you? Is there even one among you, who thinks the State of Alkansea would not have repaired these facilities had Hurricane Hosea blown not through Choctaw but through Mayflower and those facilities been damaged not at Urban but rather on the flagship campus of ASU? Is there even *one* among you?"

A thunder of applause broke out, and Rich had to shout into the microphone, "A *single* one among you?"

The crowd was on its feet again, as he roared, "A. Single. One?"

When they had finally quieted and reseated themselves, Rich began again, "So I thank you for your courageous persistence and your understanding. And as I am thanking you, I want you to thank the determined, self-sacrificing faculty and staff of this university who would not say die when quitting would have been easy and flight would have been understood and forgivable. Would the faculty and staff of Urban please stand to be recognized."

They did, and the applause for them lasted a full minute.

"In their brief comments from the podium today, the deans of your colleges have told you how good you are and how proud they are of you. You deserve such praise. And I repeat it once again. You are the very best. Now I want to tell you how good I want you always to be. Good to your family. Good to your community. Good to Urban University. Your days here are not ending. We don't call this ceremony a commencement, a beginning, for nothing. Your days of being connected to Urban are just getting under way. To be enduringly good, you must be with Urban, not just today, but as long as you live. You need to remember this place that has provided you with the skills you will now employ for successful lives. You need to remember Urban by joining the Alumni Association and by rooting ferociously for our Ungulates, the way those green and brownies up the Interstate root for their Monsters. You need to remember your alma mater with your financial support. And no amount is too little. And I am serious about that. Five dollars. Twenty-five dollars. Someday soon maybe five hundred dollars. For those of you who will get rich, and some of you will, five million dollars. Start thinking about that now. I am."

Laughter and applause.

"Here are the facts about your alma mater, graduates. Urban University is not the biggest university, but by God it's the toughest university. Our faculty and staff are far, indecently far, from the best paid university employees, but they are without a shadow of a doubt the most dedicated. And if they weren't, then you wouldn't, you couldn't, be sitting here today with diplomas in your hands."

Applause again.

"Sometime after the storm, in my deep yearning for the survival and recovery and ultimate prospering of this place that I hold so fervently in my heart, I began to have a dream. And in that dream all the graduates from the nearly fifty years of this institution's history were gathered together in the quad in front of the library. All eighty-five thousand of them. A bonfire was burning as if for a pep rally. And everyone there was dressed in Urban black and orange. And the graduates joined hands. And in unison they began to chant 'Urban is Choctaw. Choctaw is Urban. We are Urban. We are Choctaw.' This bonfire in my recurring dream captures my understanding of what this institution is and who its graduates are. You are, we are, this city. We are Choctaw. We are the Choctaw as it is now. And we are the Choctaw of the future. Those of you in this room, those who graduated from Urban before you and those who will graduate after you, we are Choctaw. Ettons University gets a lot of national press and likes to compare itself to places like Duke and Vanderbilt. But Ettons isn't Choctaw. Ettons is New Jersey."

This last comment was greeted with laughter and then applause.

"Urban is Choctaw. So as you leave here today, graduates, keep this city and this great institution close to your heart, whether you remain here or support us from some other place that life may take you. Yes, help us with your dollars. But equally important, help us with your votes and your advocacy. From this day forward, insist of every candidate running for every office in this city and state, and of every official running for federal office *from* this city and state, insist that every one of them support this institution fairly the way it has never, not once in its five-decade history, been supported on any governmental level."

Applause.

"Hosea was a disaster which should have called upon our elected leaders to rise above the usual infighting of their political affiliations. But that hasn't happened, and the residents of our city are suffering from it, still waiting for FEMA and the State of Alkansea to cut its bureaucratic red tape so that the people who live here can begin rebuilding their lives. We Choctaws know something about the great flood of 2004 that America as a whole has yet to grasp. It was a disaster made not by nature but by man. The waters of Hurricane Hosea did not sweep over our city; they broke through to our city. Our levees were high enough,

Fredrick Barton

but they were not strong enough. Our homes were lost, our lives were altered, our university crippled, not by an act of God, but by an act of negligence, not as the product of inevitability but as the byproduct of irresponsibility. Moreover, it was a disaster that didn't end when the flood waters were pumped away. It is a disaster that continues, one all of us know has barely yet been addressed. If our public officials don't begin to act for the public good, it is a disaster that may not be over for years to come. Yet, in whatever atmosphere of sadness and indignation, we fight on, don't we?"

Sustained applause.

"At Urban University half of us are still missing, but tonight I celebrate and embrace the half who are home. And about my Urban University colleagues, my fellow Urban University graduates and all my fellow citizens in our unique city, I think of language from Shakespeare's *Henry V*, for Hosea was our St. Crispin's Day, and we will forever fiercely 'stand a tip-toe when the day is named . . . and strip our sleeves to show our wounds . . . we band of brothers and sisters who shed together our blood and our tears.'"

Rich paused a long second, his head bowed over the scratch of outline he had before him. Then he looked up and said, "We have not been treated fairly. We are not *being* treated fairly." He raised a clenched fist over his head, and emphasized each of his last five words: "But. We. Will. Not. Surrender."

39

As spring bloomed on New England in 1676, the great Indian confederacy of Wampanoags, Nipmucks and Narragansetts found itself in a frustrating and perilous circumstance. We had carried the day militarily. And yet we were in big-time trouble. We were still getting adequate supplies of powder and shot through our French connection, but we were close to the breaking point in terms of food.

Denied safe access to the sea, we were trying to fish the inland waters wherever we could, but that required a dangerous dilution of our military forces. The women were gamely trying to plant corn in isolated meadows, but everyone was afraid to engage in the settled farming we had done all our lives because it made us so vulnerable to destruction by an English cavalry charge. Thus we huddled under *apawonks*, our lean-to shade arbors, far less warm and comfortable than we would have preferred, and we kept our possessions bundled and ready for movement on a moment's notice. This was not a felicitous way to live, but we had no choice.

More problematic than our physical discomfort, there wasn't enough available land in Nipmuck country to feed all of us, nor was there enough seed. Thus, beginning in late March, we began to consider adjusting our strategy. Voices among the Nipmucks began to be raised in favor of abandoning the war effort. Chief among these was a Prayer known as Sagamore Sam.

"Not on your life," Annawon said when Sagamore Sam made his view known in council. "We have these bastards on the run. If the idea of peace arises, let it come from the English."

Muttaump knew that many of his people now worried that he and other Nipmuck sachems had been rash in leading them to join with my Wampanoags. They were not assuaged by our long list of victories because they had been forced to move throughout the fall and winter, and now that planting season had come, they were having to share their farmland with Wampanoag and Narragansett women. Still, Muttaump was of no mind to call the war off. He and his Nipmucks had enjoyed greater isolation and independence from the English than had my Wampanoags. He had heard our tales, though, and now he had seen the villainy of the English up close. "We fight until we can no longer sing our call to war," Muttaump said. "I agree with Annawon. Let the English come to us."

I accepted the pipe from Muttaump and drew upon it. "I have talked openly and often," I said, "about pushing the English back onto the great ships that brought them here. We did not start this war, but the hearts of our fighting men encouraged me to believe that we could prevail. We have accomplished much. English habitation on the Connecticut River is reduced now to a single town. We have burned villages between here and the Great Sea, including towns just outside Boston and Plymouth. We have carried the fight into the colony of Connecticut. We have driven the dual-tongued Roger Williams and his Rhode Islanders out of their capital at Providence and into sanctuary on Aquidneck Island. We have even learned how to make our own bullets and repair our own rifles, skills we had not learned before this war began. But our people are hungry and our storage baskets are nearly depleted."

I looked hard at Sagamore Sam and his ally Prayer Sagamore John. "Not one among us would bend a knee to these vicious men in our midst," I continued. "But as their Bible says, for everything there is a season. And now is the season for planting. We cannot fight on empty stomachs. So from the position of military strength and momentum we enjoy at the moment, we should communicate to the English that we are open to negotiating a cessation of hostilities."

Muttaump shrugged in recognition of the power of my argument.

But bold Canonchet objected: "No," he said. "These vile English must beg us for peace. My aunts and uncles perished in the great fire at our fort. We should fight them until they kneel." He turned to me. "We do need food, so I will go get it." With a sweep of his hand he indicated Weetamoo, Awashonks and Quinnapin. "We all have food pits on our own land."

"As do we at Montaup," Adonoshonk interjected.

"Yes," Canonchet said. "And accompanied by a troop of the strong and the brave, I will bring back our storage baskets and kill any English we encounter on the way there and back."

"I will certainly go with you," Totoson said.

"As will I," Pawtonomi said.

Adonoshonk also volunteered to go, but I directed that he remain with me.

Amid vigorous dissent, we decided to try to feed ourselves and fight on. But without permission, Sagamore Sam sent a letter to the English offering a settled peace. I had argued for this position, but he should not have taken this action on his own. Decisions of such significance required consensus. Moreover, the letter succeeded in encouraging our enemy to think that we were weakening. Had I drafted it myself, I would have used less supplicant language.

But all the while, the war continued, still largely at our direction. When we dealt critical blows to Rehoboth and Providence in the last days of March, we seized a moment of control over a swath of territory that had been lost to us since the beginning of the war. Canonchet led these battles, and he was magnificent, a fierce fighter and a brilliant tactician. These constituted significant victories, for my Wampanoags had a stash of critically needed seed corn buried in our former land just south of Swansea. From Rehoboth, Canonchet led two dozen men, half Narragansetts, half Wampanoags, into the neck of Montaup to collect the seed. The mission was a success, and the Wampanoags made ready to return with the seed to the north Connecticut Valley where our women would plant it as soon as they could hoe the land into corn hillocks.

Before Totoson and Pawtonomi led their contingent of Wampanoags back to our camps on the Connecticut, though, Canonchet announced that he was going to lead another raid into his own old territory to locate Narragansett storage pits.

"The more food and the more seed we can gather," he told my men, "the longer we can carry the fight to the English. And if Metacom's strategy is ultimately what we need to do, the more of their towns we burn, the sooner they will beg to end this war and let us return permanently to the land and coastlines of our grandmothers and grandfathers."

"But you know we can't go with you," Totoson said. "It's essential to get the seed we've already gathered into the ground as soon as possible."

"No, no," Canonchet explained. "I am not asking you to delay your return. You must go immediately, and you must travel fast."

"But you will have only half as many warriors with you," Pawtonomi said.

Canonchet laughed. "Yes," he said. "I'll have only a dozen men. That means the English will have to bring over one hundred against us to have any chance."

"I think you Narragansetts should come with us," Totoson said. "We deliver what we have, and then we ask Metacom to let us return. You and us together."

"Not necessary and too long," Canonchet said. "Quinnapin and I have sent runners into our homeland repeatedly. No one's there. The English want our land, but they can't occupy it in the middle of this war. They marched away immediately after they burned our fort, and they can't put a force together to return without exposing more of their towns to our torches. I don't fear the English when I face them. Why would I fear them when I won't have to face them? You two need to get on the trail, or I'm going to grab my corn and beat you back."

Totoson and Pawtonomi were reluctant to assent, but they were without the authority to stop him. So they wished him the Creator's guidance and a swift return to their company.

What Canonchet did not know was that after marching its men away after the Great Swamp Fight, Connecticut had ordered regular patrols through Narragansett country. The Connecticut regiment wasn't sent because they had any inkling that a Narragansett squad might return. In typical me-first fashion, Connecticut was guarding against any initiatives by Massachusetts or Plymouth to establish a presence and therefore claims to the valuable area.

In our months together, I had become very fond of Canonchet. He was strong, brave, steadfast, true and bright. I listened to him in council, and I watched him on the battlefield, and I thought, that's what I was like when I was his age. That's what I hope I was like.

Canonchet made his excursion into his homeland, located additional food reserves, and set out to return to us. He had reached the confluence of the Blackstone and the Seekonk rivers on April 9 when he and his tiny band of men were intercepted by a Connecticut regiment under Captain George Dennison. Just a few more miles and he would have been beyond the range of Dennison's patrol. Caught in the open, Canonchet and his men scattered as was our strategy. But shit-headed Niantics who were with Dennison were able to identify Canonchet by the silver-trimmed jacket the Bostonians gave him and the large belt of wampum shells he wore across his breechclout. Ignoring the rest of the Narragansetts, the Connecticut soldiers concentrated on Canonchet. He was fleeter than any of the English, and he would have escaped had not the Creator turned his face away at the crucial moment. As he attempted to cross the Blackstone, Canonchet lost his footing and slipped under the water. His wet musket was unusable. And his soaked moccasins and leggings weighed on him like stones. He shed the jacket. And he flung off the wampum belt which had long been a trademark of his attire. But he was slow now, and defenseless, and he was shortly run down and captured, and marched off to Stonington, the closest Connecticut town.

Canonchet was offered to have his life spared if he would lead the English to me. His response was one of contemptuous defiance. He would not cooperate with them in any way. So they stood him before a firing squad, executed him, and then quartered his body. His young handsome head was cut off and sent to Hartford where it was displayed on a stake in the town square.

Rest in peace, Canonchet, my ally, my friend. Would that all we knew have had your heart.

40

As Rich led the recessional from the Civic Center stage on the night of his Fall, 2004, graduation speech, people stuck out their hands to him, first members of his faculty as he walked through their ranks, then his students. Two students stepped into the aisle and hugged him. So did two of his students' mothers. The whole way through the crowd, people called out, "Great speech, Rector." Several chanted, "Urban is Choctaw." Someone even yelled out, "Richard Janus for Governor," a remark that shook Rich out of his emotional reserve and made him chuckle.

In the dressing room where the platform party changed out of their graduation regalia, Rich was congratulated by most of his vice rectors and deans. Drama and Film Chair Joe Alter stepped forward beaming and shook Rich's hand vigorously, his bush of red hair bouncing with enthusiasm. "I'm proud to serve with you, Rector," he said. "Very proud. Very proud indeed."

Cecilia Lagasse wrapped Rich in a long hug and whispered, "I love you, boss."

As he was removing his academic robe and putting his tam back into its box, he was approached by Ben Turner, who shook his hand and said, "You got balls, my friend. I'll give you that. Your speech was dynamite."

"Thanks, Ben," Rich said.

"Of course, the problem with dynamite is its annoying tendency to blow things up."

"Meaning?" Rich said, as he slipped his arms into the sleeves of his suit coat.

"Big bullies you're poking in the eye. Ettons may have more alums residing in the Northeast than in Choctaw, but those who are here pack a lot of wallet."

"Aw, come on," Rich said. "All I did was tease them a little bit. They're big boys. They should be able to take it."

"Maybe," Ben said. "But I wouldn't have picked a fight with the viceroy."

"I didn't pick a fight with the viceroy. I didn't pick a fight with any specific person."

"The viceroy might disagree."

"I didn't even mention the viceroy."

"Well, you said that we haven't been fairly funded in our entire history."

"We haven't," Rich said.

"I hardly disagree, but the viceroy would dispute that. It's a big part of his job to say that everything is equitable."

"Which is bullshit."

"Yes, but saying so publicly just pisses people off. Especially people who hear you say it firsthand and can't discount it as a rumor."

"People like who?" Rich asked.

"Like the viceroy, Coach. Like the viceroy."

"Lipscom wasn't here."

"Yeah, he was."

"You're just jerking my chain," Rich said. "You know how he is. If he had been here, he'd have had a robe on and been up on the platform shaking hands like he had something to do with our students earning their degrees."

Turner shrugged. "Maybe he got a late start and got here too late. I know he didn't get a chair. Saw him standing at the back with his arms folded. Didn't look like a happy camper."

"You're a liar," Rich said and laughed.

"Saw what I saw."

"Seriously, Ben? Lipscom was here and didn't even let me know?"

"I guess it could have been his twin brother. I was on the stage, and the viceroy was standing behind the last row of chairs. Long way back there, and it's been a while since my vision was twenty-twenty."

"So you *are* just yanking me," Rich said.

Turner didn't smile. "No, I'm not. I guess it could have just been someone who looked like him, but I sure thought it was him."

Rich lifted his eyebrows, then pursed his lips and wiggled them. "Well, I said what I said. I told the truth. I've said as much to Elia's face, so he won't be surprised. Speak truth to power and let the chips fall where they may."

"Well," Turner said, "that sounds all straight up, I guess. But when you start chipping away at a tree, you better watch out that it doesn't fall on you."

THE NEXT NIGHT WAS Christmas Eve. Cecilia had left on an early plane to spend the holidays with her oldest daughter in Seattle. Rich and Cally had hoped to be back in their house so they could celebrate the holidays in their own home. But the date for reoccupation kept drifting further into the future. Though the work was completed, the house remained without electricity or gas because its safety inspections had not yet been conducted, and the city couldn't say if the inspections would take place within a week or two weeks or two months. Matters were little different in other neighborhoods that had taken water.

So Rich and Cally's pledge to themselves that they would be home for Christmas was broken, although definitely through no fault of Cally's management of the Sisyphean repair process. The twin duties of online teaching and the constant need to meet workmen and prepare countless insurance forms had worn her out. She had lost fifteen pounds and looked almost gaunt. The stress of all she was handling also afflicted her with a nagging indigestion that matched Rich's lifelong heartburn. Between them, a jar of Rolaids didn't survive two weeks.

Since they had expected to be back in their house by Christmas, they had found one of the few Christmas tree lots that was open in the city, had bought a Fraser fir and placed it, as usual, in the wide archway between their living room and den. They had planned to celebrate with a traditional turkey dinner, enlivened by a bottle of Sauvignon Blanc and then maybe a second. But they had no gas to cook the turkey, no electricity to run the refrigerator, no lights to see by. And they had no heat on what turned out to be a night in the upper thirties.

But Rich and Cally were not people to be thwarted. They had planned a Christmas Eve celebration at their house, and so they would have it no matter how impractical. They placed two four-inch-thick candles in a tool box along with two lantern-style flashlights. On the way from Cally's apartment, they stopped at a Rite-Aid for a sack of ice. Two cold bottles of wine clanked in a grocery bag on the back seat of Rich's truck. A second bag contained a roll of goat cheese, a jar of Greek olives, a box of crackers and a sleeve of clear plastic cups. Pulling up to the drive-thru lane at Popeye's, they purchased four pieces of chicken with mashed potatoes and coleslaw.

When they got to their home, Cally spread a linen cloth on the dining table and lit the candles. Rich opened a bottle of wine, and they spread goat cheese on the crackers with a plastic knife and speared olives with a plastic fork. When they had finished this appetizer course, they used plastic forks for the potatoes and coleslaw and their fingers for the chicken. The night was so cold they ate with their winter coats still on. Cally kept her black and orange Ungulate stretch cap pulled down around her ears. Rich ate with his sweatshirt hood up.

"It's great to be home," Cally said, smiling at Rich, licking her fingers.

"No place like it, I've heard," Rich replied. "Or is it there's no place like Rome?"

"This would be very elegant if we weren't freezing to death," she said. "We're using only the finest in plastic and paper."

Rich swept a lock of hair off his forehead with the back of his wrist. "I love you," he said.

"I know," she said. "That's because you're smart. And because I'm your construction slave. Don't forget that."

"That's why I'm smart. Because you're my construction slave. Also because you're beautiful."

"I'm too thin."

"You can never be too thin or too rich. Someone said that. A thin Republican, no doubt."

"I'm too thin," Cally said. She took a long swallow of wine. "And you're Rich. But not too Rich."

"You're too rich," Rich said.

"I am rich in love," she said.

"No," he said. "I am Rich in love."

"Oh, that's right," Cally said. "But I am in love with Rich."

ON JANUARY 4, 2005, Elia Lipscom called Rich to say that he was finally empanelling a search committee for the Urban rectorship.

"Y'all got so many problems down there," he said. "I think we need to get a permanent leader in place. An interim can only do so much."

Rich wasn't sure whether he should hear that comment as an insult or not.

"I mean, for an old ball coach," Lipscom said, "you've done a commendable job of sticking up for your place. I'll hand you that. People say you did a great job at your graduation right before Christmas. That's the word that filtered back up here anyway, and I'm sure it's true. Said you gave a corker of a speech. Don't happen to have a copy, do you?"

"No," Rich said. "It wasn't written out. Just notes scratched on the back of the program."

"Too bad," Lipscom said. "I would like to have read it. Have to give a graduation speech now and again myself. Always looking for good ideas. People say it was a stem winder."

"Should I hear that as a compliment?" Rich asked.

"Why shouldn't you?" Lipscom replied. "But anyway, as I said, I will want you to assist me with the composition of the search committee. I'm going to ask a couple of members of the Board. Then we'll want a couple of people from the business community. I have some ideas, but you should pass along your suggestions. Same about somebody active with the alumni association. I'm going to need the most help with faculty and staff. I know very few of your people, I'm sorry to say. We'll want some senior administrator who is well thought of. And no, don't recommend your pushy provost. And one staff member from a mid-level position. Last, current faculty. Somebody from one of the professional colleges and somebody from Arts, Humanities or Sciences. Why don't you give us a couple of names in each category."

"I'll get working on names for you immediately."

"Oh, and I almost forgot," Lipscom said. "We'd like you to serve on the committee. Not a bad deal, huh? You get to be in on picking your own boss."

"Well, I've been meaning to talk to you about this, Elia. I'm kind of thinking of standing for the position on a permanent basis."

A long silence followed.

Finally, Lipscom responded, "As I recall, when I appointed you interim, you said you had no interest in becoming rector on a permanent basis."

"I did say that," Rich admitted. "And that was true at the time, but things have changed."

"What's changed?"

"Well, Hosea, for instance."

"Jesus Christ, all anybody from Choctaw can ever talk about is that fucking hurricane."

"If you lived down here, Elia, that's all you'd talk about, too."

"Oh Christ. All right. Why should I give a shit? You want to apply, have at it. But I should warn you. You probably think you have some support about now. On the heels of that crackerjack graduation speech and all. But in a couple of months things will probably be a lot different."

"What's going to be different two months or so from now?"

"The other reason I'm calling. The governor's office is making the fifty-seven-million dollar cut permanent. That's eight million for you. And even if you get the fifteen thousand students you're hoping for, that's another twenty million bucks, Ronnie tells me, in lost tuition next year. The Board will ask you to prepare a budget for 2005-2006 to reflect that. Ronnie says you can't possibly accomplish that kind of cut without the official authority of Financial Exigency, which we will request the Board grant you. I hate to say this, but however much people seem to love you right now, Coach, after you whack a few programs and lay off a few tenured faculty, you're not going to stay so popular."

RICH ENJOYED BEING LIKED as much as anybody, but popularity, insofar as that meant being well-regarded by those around him, was something Rich had always enjoyed, and he therefore took it for granted. However, popularity in normal times was one thing. Serving as the captain of a sinking ship with an inadequate number of lifeboats and having to decide who gets to live and who has to die was something else entirely. Not much popularity is available in the latter circumstance.

Nor will one discover much popularity in the obligation to topple an icon. Outing corruption in his or her organization is a key duty of any leader. So is knowing when, how, and how much to compromise. The conflict between those two responsibilities provides any leader a key test. Rich would come to believe that he failed this test at a pivotal moment.

The test began when Urban's Internal Auditor, Chandler Piehl, alerted Rich to her concern about a conflict of interest on the part of Architecture and Urban Planning Dean Shelby Clay, who was widely viewed as a secular saint. Piehl worried that he was a crook.

In what started out as a routine procedure, Piehl audited the recent activities of the Housing Institute Clay ran, which involved cooperative venture projects with private construction companies to build low-rent apartments for poor and working-class families. Piehl became curious when she noticed that the construction contracts for the housing units were signed by Dennis Stitch, President of Deep South Construction and Engineering. Piehl remembered that when she'd audited an earlier Housing Institute contract that Stitch had signed that as well. When she checked, she found that Stitch had signed the earlier contract as President of Choctaw First Builders. Perhaps he had simply changed employers in the intervening three years. But when she pulled the contracts for the other Housing Institute projects, she found that Dennis Stitch had signed all of them, although never as the president of the same company twice in a row. Perturbed, Piehl then discovered that the state's blind bid requirements were often satisfied by bids from more than one company for which Dennis Stitch was CEO. This was bad, but it was much worse that Dennis Stitch was Shelby Clay's late wife's sister's husband.

Deeply upset by this information, Rich shared it immediately with University Attorney Regan Hooks, who advised him to take the issue to the viceroy immediately. With some reluctance, Rich did so. He liked Shelby personally, and Rich was among the great majority of Choctaws who thought that Shelby Clay was one of the good guys.

"Oh Jesus, Coach, what do you want to go around stirring up shit like this for?" Elia Lipscom asked when Rich sketched out the situation as he understood it.

Rich protested that he hadn't gone looking for this information, that it had been brought to him, and that he and Regan presumed that Rich couldn't just ignore what the auditor had found. "It looks bad, Elia," Rich said.

"But that doesn't mean it *is* bad," Lipscom said.

"No, I guess not," Rich admitted. "I would be among the first to hope that there's some kind of acceptable explanation. But we won't know that until we get to the bottom of things."

"Get to the bottom of things?" Lipscom asked. "Meaning what?"

"I don't know," Rich said. "I've never had a situation like this before. We've got to do an investigation, don't we?"

"An investigation. Yes, I suppose you do."

"How do you suggest we begin?"

"You aren't by any chance taping this conversation are you, Coach?" Elia asked.

"No, why would I be taping this?"

"Well, I remind you that state law prohibits your taping this conversation without my permission, and I have not given you such permission."

"I'm not taping," Rich said.

"Good. Because I need to give you some important advice."

"That's what I called you for."

"You are right. Given what your auditor has uncovered, you are obligated to undertake an investigation," Lipscom said and cleared his throat. "But you want to be smart about this, Coach. Shelby Clay is a 900-pound gorilla. He brings in more grant money than anybody else you've got down there in Choc Town, and he brings it in *for* Choc Town. You see what I'm saying? Every Democrat who runs for statewide office in Alkansea aims for a photo shoot with Shelby Clay. You don't want to go tugging on Superman's cape, Coach."

"I thought you said I needed to launch an investigation. Now what are you saying?"

"Let me repeat, you are absolutely obligated to investigate this situation," Lipscom said. He snuffled and cleared his throat again. "But you've got lots of other things to think about too."

"Meaning?"

"Well, you've got the whole exigency crisis to manage. And that sure ain't no cake walk. And last we talked you said you wanted to have the interim yanked off your title."

"Yes?"

"The best investigations are the quietest investigations. If Clay has untoward shenanigans going on with some public housing construction contracts, you want to do your digging with a teaspoon and not with a jackhammer. You get my drift? Clay's got a lot of friends and admirers with a lot of money. What seems clear as a bright spring day when you're looking at documents in the privacy of your office becomes as murky as a catfish pond once complicated explanations and heated denials are published in the papers. If I were you, I'd keep the jackhammer in my truck at least until after the Rector Search Committee had set the crown on my head."

"You're telling me to investigate, but to go slow."

"I'm telling you to be smart, Coach. Look out for number one."

"I'll have Chandler go forward and prepare me a thorough and detailed report. Then, once the search committee has made its decision, I will be fully prepared for the next step."

"Jesus, Coach. I've gotten to where I really hate it when you call up here."

JANUARY OF 2005 WAS a hopeful time for Urban University. All through the holidays, Damm Engineering had continued to work on Urban's massive mobile housing project, Ford F150 pickups arriving in convoys every day with a stream of dim white travel trailers. By the tenth of the month, the northeast side of campus, where faculty and staff were to live, had its sewerage trenches and utility poles installed. And by the fifteenth, the first section of the employee trailers was ready for occupancy. Cecilia Lagasse was the first to move in, an event covered by *The Straight Arrow* and the network television stations in town.

Rich and Cally had tried to talk Cecilia out of this move. The weather had been colder than usual, and no one believed that the trailers would prove very warm, all the more so because they stood on the south rim of the lake and were therefore exposed to the unbroken blast of the north winter wind. Moreover, Rich and Cally pointed out, their own house could be ready for reoccupation soon, any day, in fact. And the moment their house was available, they were moving into it. So Cecilia was more than welcome to stay in Cally's apartment for as long as she wanted. They understood that Cecilia urgently wanted to give them back their privacy, but they had all lived together for three months, and they could handle a while longer.

But Cecilia was insistent that she move. That some of the senior members of the administration live in the trailer village, she argued, was important for campus morale. What better emblem of shared hardship than that the chief academic officer reside there? As it happened, Peter Alexander, the seventy-year-old Dean of the Engineering School, opted to live in one of the trailers too. Peter and his wife had been living with their son north of Lake De Soto since the storm, and he was tired of the eighty-mile round-trip commute to work every day. If Peter could manage it, Cecilia maintained, so could she.

Cecilia was right about one thing that remained unspoken. Rich and Cally did feel a certain measure of relief when she was gone. Their feelings were akin to those when they left Althea and Robert Feaster's guest bedroom for Monster House. They loved the Feasters, but they weren't ever comfortable in a shared space. Cally was able to return to padding around after work in slippers, panties and her favorite orange Ungulate T-shirt. Rich could lounge about in running shorts without underwear. He could slip his hands underneath Cally's scanty outfit whenever he wanted to again, a luxury of a loving relationship that had been impossible now for half a year. All the same, Cecilia hadn't been gone two days when competing emotions arose. They missed her. And they recognized that they would never be so close to her again.

The move into the faculty-staff trailer village went smoothly. What followed did not. The work on the utility poles and the sewer trenches for the student trailers continued on a two-shift-a-day operation even as the faculty and staff were settling into their mobile units. But then, two days after the faculty were moved in, Damm Vice President and Urban trailer project manager Buzz Pasmore showed up in Rich's office with a puzzling, then outrageous, demand. Since the work was one third done, he said he wanted Rich to cut him a check for one third of the total obligation. $16,500,000 he said.

There were several problems associated with this surprise request. First, the contract Rich had signed contained *no* provision for payments in stages as the work went along. This, Pasmore explained, was standard operating procedure. "It's always one third, one third, one third, unless otherwise stipulated in the contract."

"If it's standard operating procedure, then why isn't it *stipulated* in the contract?" Rich wanted to know.

Pasmore shrugged, and brushed his callused hands through his flattop of sandy hair. "I don't know. We did this deal on the hurry up. I guess it should have been."

"Well, since the contract doesn't call for this payment," Rich said, "I'd say any discussion about money changing hands is premature."

"I'll have to check in with Arlin about that," Pasmore said. Arlin was Arlin Damm, the company's founder and CEO, and after Beatrice Florin, the second richest individual in the state.

"Yeah, while you're checking in with Mr. Damm," Rich said, "have him explain the request for $16,500,000. The contract calls for one payment, once the project is completed, of forty-five million, one third of which is fifteen million, not sixteen point five."

"Oh, I know the answer to that." Pasmore brushed his hand through his brush cut again. "The one point five mil is our profit. Ten percent of the overall price of the project."

Rich laughed out loud. "You're kidding, of course."

But Pasmore didn't smile. "No, sir, I'm not. We might have asked for twelve percent. Some companies build in fifteen percent in case there's a run of bad weather or other surprises. But we held at ten percent. Which I think is more than fair."

"You realize how bizarrely unorthodox this is?"

"No, sir."

"Well, I know we did, as you put it, a hurry-up deal on these trailers, but a contract sets out the terms of a business arrangement. I may be just an old basketball coach and English teacher, but I know that. And our contract, signed by me, Arlin Damm, and FEMA, said that you would get paid forty-five million dollars for fifteen hundred installed and operational travel trailers. The document contained no mention of payments to be made in thirds and certainly no language about a ten percent profit on top of the forty-five million."

"I understand FEMA authorized fifty million dollars for this project," Pasmore said.

"Whatever FEMA authorized, your company bid forty-five million."

"Plus ten percent profit."

Rich laughed again. "I admire your persistence, Mr. Pasmore, but the contract nowhere mentions that extra four and half million dollars."

"Well, I'll admit these were our mistakes," Pasmore said. "But we can still fix them."

"Look," Rich said. "Your being here talking to me isn't where you want to be in the first place. I know you're the guy on the ground, getting the trailers hauled, the earth moved and the wires strung, but I assume you understand the role of contracts. This is a larger operation than others, but it's no different in kind. I signed the contract because I am granting FEMA, and through FEMA Damm Engineering, the right to park trailers on university property. FEMA signs the contract because it has agreed to a price with you to do the work. And ultimately FEMA pays you. So rather than talking to me about most any of this, you need to be talking to FEMA. They have a contract to pay you forty-five million dollars when the work is complete. But if they want to pay you one third now, that's up to them. And if they want to pay you forty-nine and a half million dollars instead of forty-five, that's also up to them. I think there's something strange about a profit that's not included in the contract, but, frankly, right now, all I care about is getting those trailers in place before school starts. So if FEMA doesn't want to hold you to the contract, that's their business, not mine."

"OK," Passmore said. "But the point is that we're a third finished and you got your people moved in, so we're going to need sixteen point five to go forward from here."

"And my point is that you're talking to the wrong guy."

"Well, you're the guy who cares about these trailers and how fast they get set up. You pay me. FEMA reimburses you. You get what you want. Our company gets what it needs."

"*No* provision required Urban University to front a dime on this project, much less eleven cents on every dime *in* the contract. You want to get paid, you're gonna have to ask FEMA."

"Well, we can do that, I guess. But dealing with FEMA is not what anybody would call a speedy process. And if we have to stop what we're doing to deal with FEMA, then I don't think we're going to have those trailers installed for the start of your school."

So that was the game, Rich realized. In fact, that was probably the game all along. Damm Engineering could point to the trailers that were already operational, the others on site, and the trench digging and utility pole installation underway as an indication of its good faith. Rich had no idea how long it took FEMA to pay. But clearly FEMA had a whole lot less incentive to move quickly than Rich did. And Damm Engineering had figured that out. But they hadn't figured out that Rich didn't have $16.5 million to hand over to Damm. He needed every nickel he had to meet payroll and operating expenses.

Rich never knew what Arlin Damm's motivations were in this business. Had he made some sort of gross miscalculation? Was it possible that he could lose money on this project? Was it that he could make *more* money on some alternative project? Damm's company was based in Mayflower where all things ASU were first-rate and gold-plated. Was he so soaked in the ASU culture that he didn't understand the stepchild status of Urban? Federal money was pouring into Mayflower in such a torrent, did he not grasp the desperate financial situation that attended most everything in Choctaw, public higher education in particular?

Or, Rich wondered, was there something nefarious behind this. Like most every rich person in the state, save for Beatrice Florin who didn't give a shit about Monster football, Arlin Damm was a big-time ASU booster. Had he been manipulated to stop the trailer park at Urban so that Urban students who had enrolled at ASU in the fall would stay there in the spring? Was

Damm trying to hurt Urban on purpose? Was such speculation purely paranoid?

Probably, Rich hoped, but he never could get it out of his head.

Rich and Arlin Damm talked on the phone the next day to no avail. Just as Buzz Pasmore had done a day earlier, Damm kept repeating that what his company was asking for was standard operating procedure and pretended astonishment that Rich was not aware of such. This was complete bullshit, of course. Regan assured Rich of what he was already confident about, that assertions of "common practice" didn't alter the terms of a written contract. But Damm wouldn't budge. He would not go forward until he was paid the $16,500,000.

Rich immediately tried to meet with Gloria Ruff, the FEMA representative who had signed the contract along with Rich and Arlin Damm. But Ruff no longer worked for FEMA. So Rich met with Edna Uehling, who had replaced Ruff. Uehling said that she couldn't just cut a check for $16,500,000 of the taxpayers' money without reviewing all of the pertinent contract information. Rich urged her to understand that time was of the essence.

"Why is that?" Uehling wanted to know.

"Because we're trying to get our students into their trailers by the beginning of the semester."

"Students?" Uehling said. "You've ordered FEMA trailers for your students?"

"Yes," Rich said.

"Well," Uehling said. "The first thing I'm going to have to determine is whether students are even *eligible* for FEMA trailers."

Edna Uehling's examination of the pertinent documents was not completed by January 31, during which time Damm stopped all work on Urban's trailer project. School started for the spring semester without enough housing for students. Many enrollments were cancelled at the last minute. And many other students were frustrated by having to commute into campus from places distant from the city. Rich tried to explain what had happened in an email to the students, but so many were angered about the now broken promise of a place to live on campus that Rich agreed to meet with students to discuss the matter. Rich scheduled the meeting in a large lecture hall in Building 8. But over eight hundred students showed up, twice the room's capacity, so he had to move the meeting outside into a cold and overcast afternoon. Rich's people scrambled and got a P.A. system set up on the steps of the library so that Rich could be seen and heard. But waiting in the chill chafed the students' already raw feelings.

"The trailers are on campus," an unhappy student stated early on. He was dressed in knee length black satin shorts, tennis shoes with black socks pulled up over his calves, a hooded orange sweatshirt and a baseball cap turned backwards on his head. "They're right there." He pointed through the quad to a pack of trailers. "Why won't you just let us move into them?"

Rich explained that the trailers were not hooked up to sewerage or water or electrical power, that they weren't yet usable.

"Then hook them up," another student said, this one dressed in jeans and a T-shirt. He was cold and had his arms folded across his chest.

"I'm trying to get them hooked up, believe me. I am terribly embarrassed that many of you were counting on housing that we're not able to provide at the moment. We hope to have that problem rectified in the near future."

"You promised us housing before the semester *started*," Black Shorts said.

"And I wanted to *have* housing for you before the semester started," Rich said. "A lot of students aren't enrolled this semester because we don't have those trailers operational."

"But a lot of us did enroll because housing would be available," another student said, a girl in a wool skirt and cardigan sweater.

"We relied on what you told us."

"Some of us wouldn't have enrolled if we knew we wouldn't have a place to live," said a second girl, dressed in a black sweatsuit.

"Look," Rich said. "I am sorrier about this than you can know. I thought we had a deal with the company who is installing the trailers. But complications have arisen."

"Well, you're the rector," Cardigan Girl said. "Why can't you just tell them they have to hook up the trailers."

Rich laughed, though he shouldn't have. "It doesn't work that way. The people putting in the trailers don't work for me. They work for an engineering company."

"Well, get guys who do work for you to hook them up," Black Shorts said. "The trailers are already here."

Rich laughed again and this time heard someone mumble, "I'm glad he thinks this is funny."

"Guys," Rich said. "I know this is more complicated than any of you have any desire to be concerned with. But I can't just order University employees to install those trailers. Those are FEMA trailers, and they have to be installed under the terms of a FEMA contract which is with a private company and not with the University."

"But you're the rector," Cardigan Sweater said.

"And it's not within my power."

"Then maybe you shouldn't be the rector," Black Shorts said.

The cold kid in the T-shirt said, "I'm not saying you shouldn't be the rector, but a lot of us think that if the situation is as complicated as you say, then you should have taken that into consideration before you ran those ads saying housing would be available."

The matter was far more complicated than Rich was able to communicate successfully. But in part, he felt, the students were right. He had promised them housing, and he had failed to deliver it. He might be caught in the crossfire between greed and bureaucratic incompetence and indifference, but the fault was still his. His job was to deliver, and he hadn't. And to make matters all the more galling, that meant Margaret Lockhart was right.

Edna Uehling released her decision at the end of the second week in February when she ruled that only homeowners or renters were eligible for FEMA trailers and that college students were neither. Rich appealed her judgment, arguing first, that FEMA couldn't change its mind after a contract had already been signed, and, second, that students were indeed renters; they were renters of dorm rooms in dorms that were flooded and couldn't be lived in. Uehling said she would take the matter to her supervisors. But then she was promoted to a position at FEMA in Washington, and the whole issue landed on the desk of *her* replacement who needed time, he said, to acquaint himself with the matter before authorizing anyone to go forward.

Eventually the replacement ruled that FEMA would cover the cost of installing the trailers, but by then there were only two weeks left in the spring semester and no one was any longer interested in moving into them. By fall, Charlie Lobovich would have the dorms habitable again.

But all winter and spring, students arrived at Urban and walked past and around those empty trailers that sat crowded together on the eastern and southern perimeters of campus and saw them as an infuriating taunt, a herd of inert white elephants trumpeting Richard Janus' failure to deliver on his promise to students he claimed to care about. They were never hooked up, their usefulness on Urban's campus past. In the first week of June, a fleet of Ford F150s arrived and began gradually hauling them away. Damm Engineering began sending Rich demand letters for the $16,500,000 they claimed they were owed for the installation of the employees' village. Regan responded in polite legalese that they could go fuck themselves. They threatened to sue. But they never did. Eventually, Rich always presumed, FEMA paid them because the letters stopped. Whether FEMA paid them fifteen million or sixteen and a half, Rich never knew.

41

S ome historians have called Canonchet's death the turning
point in the war they pinned on me. These are historians
who like to say both that I started the war and was irrelevant to
it, that the real Indian hero of the conflict was Canonchet, and
that once he was gone, we were lost. I shake my head. After he
joined us in the aftermath of the Great Swamp Fight, I came to
have great regard for the young Narragansett sachem. As Tom
Wolfe would term things, he had the right stuff. Canonchet was
indeed a great hero in this war, courageous in battle, defiant in
defeat, loyal to the very end. But losing Canonchet wasn't the
turning point in the war. The course of a war never rests on the
shoulders of one man, no matter how broad. And I include
myself in that analysis. The Greeks didn't lose the Trojan War
when Paris killed Achilles, and the Trojans didn't lose it because
Achilles slew Hector. We had three nations fighting against the
English, and many sachems involved in devising our strategy.
Canonchet's loss was tragic because he was so young and
charismatic, but his death wasn't pivotal.

Less than two weeks after Canonchet's death, we hammered
the English still again, this time only seventeen miles from
Boston, when we attacked the garrison town of Sudbury. Our
men surrounded Sudbury on the night of April 20, hid in the
thickets of white alder and red pine, and unleashed hostilities at
dawn the next morning. Five different troops of Massachusetts
soldiers rode to Sudbury's defense. Those from Watertown and
Charlestown and a passing company from Boston on its way

toward the Connecticut Valley all made their way into the town and helped protect Sudbury from the extent of devastation we were sometimes able to wreak.

Troops from Concord and Marlborough met with a more bitter fate. Concord was able to muster only a dozen men for its rescue mission. We cut them off, killed ten and took two captive. Captain Samuel Wadsworth led a much larger force of fifty men from Marlborough. Wadsworth was another hoe stomper. Given that human life was at stake, I should probably not reach for the humorous analogy. But the English were like an undisciplined high school basketball team that always went for the same fake and always surrendered the same backdoor layup. We let Wadsworth spot a small number of us who pretended to be frightened and ran away. As so many of his predecessors had, Wadsworth ordered his men to chase us—which they did, right into our trusty old ambush. By the time the fighting was concluded, the Marlborough company had lost more than thirty of its men, including Captain Wadsworth. All told, we took seventy-five English lives at Sudbury. More important, though we took some scrapes here and there, we escaped this long day of fighting without a single mortal casualty.

So the death of Canonchet wasn't the turning point of the war for which they framed me. A month into the spring of 1676, we still had the English completely on the defensive, without a military answer for our withering hit-and-run tactics. But we nonetheless knew we had to get this war over with very soon. Our women needed to get crops into the ground fast, lest, come fall, our empty bellies would bring us the defeat that English muskets could not.

On March 26, our destruction of the Connecticut town of Simsbury yielded some hope that our far-flung victories might get the English to negotiate. For on March 28 Connecticut dispatched an offer of a peace conference with discussions to include a prisoner exchange. Our council over this proposal proved unusually heated. Sagamore Sam argued strenuously that we needed to seize this opportunity for peace. Muttaump said little but seemed open to the idea of a treaty negotiation. I, too, said little since I had made clear that I was open to a negotiated peace as long as the terms included a return to our homelands.

But in the days after Connecticut executed Canonchet, Quinnapin and the Narragansetts became adamantly opposed to negotiations. "This is just another of the white men's tricks," Quinnapin said. "We are kicking their ass, and so they want a peace conference. What they want is a breather from our burning down their towns. And we've just gotten started with the Connecticut invaders. But they've seen what we've done to Plymouth and Massachusetts, and they're anxious to avoid the same fate. So, of course, they want to parley. But take note of what hypocrites they are. They want to discuss an exchange of prisoners. Did they discuss exchanging Canonchet for one of theirs? We all know the answer to that. So I say fie on their peace conference."

Weetamoo stood with her husband. "Quinnapin is right," she argued. "The Connecticut settlers' murder of Canonchet means that they aren't sincere about prisoner exchanges. And that is probably reason enough to reject their overture. But our war is with Josiah Winslow and his enablers in Boston, and I don't see *them* proposing a negotiated settlement. If Connecticut is offering us a separate peace, that means little to us. Let them bring their brothers aboard, and I might look at matters differently. I am not opposed to the idea of exchanging prisoners, but such a practice must be a step toward ending the war on terms that we can accept."

Then in mid-April, Massachusetts contacted our contingent in Nipmuck country with an offer for a prisoner exchange as well, and we responded positively to this overture. But Massachusetts did not really have any prisoners to trade us. Throughout the war, any Indians they didn't kill, they sold to the next slave ship out of Boston, justifying such inhumanity as necessary to finance the war. Now, when they received an indication that

we'd trade prisoners with them, their next move was to direct
Major Daniel Gookin to undertake raids into Indian country for
the express purpose of taking captives they could trade back to us.

These guys were really something else, no?

Nevertheless, early in planting season of *Sequannikesos*, on
May 2, we released Mary Rowlandson, just as I promised her
we would, and when Gookin was unable to procure captives
enough to trade, we began to accept ransom payments for other
captives, money we needed to pay the French for our arms.
Being the stingy jerks that they were, the English complained
mightily about having to pay to get their loved ones returned.
But by *Nimockkesos*, the time for weeding of plants, too few of
which we had in the ground, by June, we had returned twenty
people to their families.

This policy was not universally endorsed in our Council
of Sachems. With hunger every day a graver concern, most of
our council members acceded to the idea of trading prisoners
for money. Prisoners we had to feed. Money bought us powder
and shot. But Awashonks' Sakonnet captain, Nompash, spoke
fiercely against the policy. "If we want the English to sue for
peace," he insisted, "then rather than trading our captives,
we should kill them. Execute them just as Connecticut did
Canonchet and the others have so many of our people. If we
hatchet off the heads of their loved ones, and place them on the
pikes of their garrison houses next to those of our people rotting
there, we'll get the white devils to the negotiating table far faster
than any policy of mercy. We can expect no leniency from them,
so what logic suggests that we should show them any?"

"We do not kill captives," Wootonekanuske said. "That has
never been our way. If we start acting like they do, we will be no
better than the savages they are."

Most in the council agreed with Wootonekanuske, and the
idea of killing captives was rejected as unAlgonquian.

Like my wife and most of the others, I did not agree with
Nompash, but I was not entirely happy with our captive exchange

policy, either. I wanted to commence a process that might result in peace, and that is why I released Mary Rowlandson. I wanted to demonstrate that we were reasonable men and women and that calm conversation could perhaps lead to terms by which the fighting could be ended. Despite our need of money for arms, however, I was less enthusiastic about the larger scale return of our captives. The French would not supply us without adequate payment forever, but they were much heartened by our military domination to this point, and their interests were completely served by maintaining us as a viable fighting force.

In the meantime, I didn't want to surrender an advantage we had carefully amassed over many hard months. Our possession of the captives created a critical incentive for the English to continue negotiating with us. Our releasing of captives en masse would deprive us of a significant bargaining chip. But my opinion did not prevail in our Council of Sachems. The logic of trading captives that we had to feed and house and drag along with us when we moved, for money we needed for arms, prevailed, and once started we traded captives on a regular basis for the rest of the war. However, and forever after, those who have told my story have usually failed to grasp the intricacies of my thinking and have depicted me as sullenly opposed to the peace dialogue.

To which I have to say, immoderately, why don't you guys just go fly a library of Puritan documents up your own butts.

UNFORTUNATELY, FOR US, THE English understood the bind they had us in. Aside from engaging in the prisoner exchanges, the English met our overtures for peace by their demand for an unconditional surrender. To this point we had carried the day militarily, but the English were eating, and we were not. Even our release of Mary Rowlandson backfired on us because she refused to communicate our civil nature but did report to them how little food we had.

We offered a cease fire and a return to the status quo ante bellum. We would both just quit fighting, and everybody could go home. The Nipmucks could stay where they were, and the English would leave them alone. The Narragansetts would go back to their country in western Rhode Island, and Massachusetts and Connecticut would leave them alone. Weetamoo would return to Pocasset. I would lead my Pokanokets back to Montaup. And That Vicious Lying Rat Bastard Josiah Winslow would kiss my ass and then he and Plymouth would leave us alone. The English could rebuild their towns, and we would leave them alone. We would plant our fields, hunt the woods of our lands, and fish the waters that the Creator had made to sustain us. We would ask no reparations from them; they would require none from us. A decent proposal, one I'd argue vigorously to be entirely consistent with the New Testament the English professed so mightily to venerate.

But, surprise, surprise, the English would have none of it. We could surrender, and then they would deal with us as they chose. That meant, of course, that as they had done with Canonchet, our leaders would be executed. It also meant that untold numbers of us would be rounded up and sold into slavery. Bills to pay, you know. So ever hungrier, we fought on.

But the tide had turned against us. The English changed tactics in critical ways. First, they started using as soldiers and guides certain Atlantic coast Indians and some Prayers they had heretofore scorned. Connecticut had supplemented its troops with Mohegans from the beginning. In the immediate vicinities of Boston and Plymouth, a number of Indian villages, close and vulnerable, had remained neutral throughout the war. Now the English called on those of our own native blood to serve with them. Sadly, more than a few did, most usefully as scouts. They knew our ways and could find us where the English had been unable. The English also began to send indentured servants into the field with the promise that they could buy out their indentures with the proceeds from any captured Indians sold as slaves. This policy emphasizes the desperation the war had produced, for freed indentured servants would mean greater demand and competition for that most scarce and treasured commodity: land. But desperate though it was, this strategy outfitted their battle units with men marching with a considerable private incentive to do us harm.

Last, and most important, the pinks figured out that their single best strategy was to disrupt our ability to farm and fish. They looked for us along stream and pond banks where we could only be successful in limited and therefore vulnerable numbers. And if they could stage expeditions to attack our settlements with sufficient men and finally avoid ambush, they didn't necessarily even have to kill us. They needed simply to take advantage of our established strategy of refusing to meet them in open ground. If they could force us to flee, they could seize whatever we couldn't carry with us, and they could trample under whatever we had put in the ground to feed ourselves in the future.

After the Sudbury attack, most of our warriors remained for a time in Nipmuck country while messages were sent back and forth with Boston about the fleeting prospects for a negotiated peace. Meanwhile, many of our people went west to fish along the Connecticut River and to plant corn and other crops in areas that we controlled. We made a large settlement near the shallow Fall River at Peskeompscut about five miles north of Deerfield. The elderly people, women and children there could have remained content at Peskeompscut with bellies full of fish and tubers for the rest of the summer, all the way to harvest time.

Unfortunately, the English farther south learned of our whereabouts and put together a ragtag military company of 150 mounted troopers. Captain William Turner was reluctant to lead this band of irregulars, some stationed militia, some townspeople, some rambunctious teenage boys, out against us until he was informed that the Peskeompscut encampment had few warriors in residence. At that point his reluctance turned to eagerness. On the night of May 18, he and his regiment rode out of Hatfield on the well-established river trail to the north.

He tied his horses in the woods and crept to the edge of our village by dawn. At first light, his men flung back the flaps of our *weetoos* and opened up on our loved ones as they slept. Few in residence were able to defend themselves; most were unarmed. Initially, anyway, Turner was luckier than he knew, and we more bitterly unfortunate, for some fifty of our warriors were out on a fishing trip higher on the river. So Turner and his men were able to kill the defenseless without resistance.

But the luck of Turner and the Hatfield men did not hold. Our warriors learned of the attack and rushed back to Peskeompscut, circled south of the village and loosed most of Turner's horses. Forced to engage fighting men rather than those who lacked the capacity to fight back, Turner and his men showed themselves the cowards they were. Our warriors routed and humiliated Turner's army. We killed half the Hatfield men we met that day, including Captain Turner himself. His men fled in terror, knocking each other off horses in hopes of escape, abandoning each other in a disgraceful panic.

But our embarrassing the heartless murderers provided no solace. We had driven the cowards away. But before we did so, they had taken the lives of several hundred members of our families.

42

Not long after Urban reopened in October, 2004, Ronnie Shade came down with paranoia that someone was going to sue Urban and therefore the Board of Trustees for opening unsafe buildings. Ronnie had read an article about "black mold" and was now terrified that those buildings Charlie Lobovich had already reopened and those he was still repairing must be giant toxic pustules of black mold that would drop from light fixtures or escape from air vents or burst from the crevasses of inadequately scrubbed classroom furniture to jam down the throats and up the noses of unsuspecting students, faculty or staff who would then spin around and demand millions of dollars from the Board. Ronnie Shade wouldn't have that, by God. He was CFO for all of public higher education in the State of Alkansea, and he sure wasn't going to let lawsuits at Urban soak up money that could be better used at ASU.

"This situation is unparalyzed in the history of our state," Shade urged upon Charlie when Shade called the vice rector to warn him about the situation.

"Jesus Christ," Charlie replied. "What next? A plague of frogs? We've got to get those buildings reopened, Ronnie. That has been my entire focus since the flood waters ebbed."

"Well, my concern at this point," Shade said, "is that you guys at Ewe Ewe have developed channel vision. All you can see is what's good for your school, but not what's good for public safety. We could be talking life and debt here."

"Send me what you got that has your boxers in a twist," Charlie said before ringing off, "and I'll have a look at it."

Charlie Lobovich and Ronnie Shade couldn't have been more different. Charlie was stocky and thick from years of pumping iron in the Urban fitness center. He wore his hair short and his shirts a little tight, and his personality was as blunt as his build. Ronnie was skinny but not fit looking. His persistent deviousness carried an undertone of hysteria.

"This black mold business is a bunch of hooey," Charlie told Shade when they met a week later at the Board of Trustees building in Mayflower to discuss Shade's concerns.

"That's not what the paper says," Shade replied. "I faxed you that article. I want you to take it seriously."

"I did take it seriously. I took it to the chair of our Department of Biology who just happens to be an expert on algae and mold. He says the whole thing is completely overblown."

"What's Algean mold?" Shade asked. "I sent you an article about black mold, not Algean mold."

"Algae, Ronnie, algae. Green scum."

"What's green scum got to do with black mold? It's the black mold I'm worried about."

Charlie took a deep breath and attempted a different tack. "Look," he said. "First of all, our Biology Chair says that if we wipe everything down with disinfectant that we will kill anything that might be dangerous. He reminded me that black mold is ubiquitous in moist climates like that of Choctaw. It's in every breath of air we breathe. It can make you sick if you collect it in a test tube and snort it, I guess, but other than that we spray everything down really well, wipe everything up, and there's nothing to worry about."

"Why would anybody snort a test tube of black mold? You got some sick sombitches down at Ewe Ewe just to think of something so stupid."

Charlie rubbed his eyes and caught himself before he scratched the backs of his hands which were raw from long months of supervising projects in the fall and winter. He didn't want Shade to accuse him of suffering from black mold himself.

Shade said, "I'm not gonna let haste and channel vision from you Ewe Ewe guys expose us to lawsuits we can't afford."

"We're doing the same things in the buildings we haven't reopened," Charlie pointed out, "that we did in those we opened in October. We've been using those buildings for four months, and nobody's sued yet."

"That don't mean they won't."

"If they were to sue, they couldn't prove they inhaled the black mold on our campus. They could just as well have gotten sick in their own homes."

"Quite a place y'all got down there. Remind me not to visit."

"The point is no one is going to get sick from mold in our buildings. I've got the testimony of a scientific expert on that point."

But Charlie's scientific support meant nothing to Ronnie Shade whose malaprop brain was already made up. He hired Trost Environmental Specialists, a company from Mayflower that claimed to specialize in mold remediation and told Charlie that Urban had to follow their directions. Trost was started up in the immediate aftermath of Hurricane Hosea and was owned by Martin Trost, a big supporter of the Monster Athletic Association. Over the next several months, Trost put a halt to Charlie's efforts to return the Urban campus to its pre-storm status. Using the authority granted by the Board, Trost closed buildings that Charlie had cleared to reopen, stretched what seemed miles of plastic air conduits down hallways and into offices and classrooms, and connected the conduits to huge compressors that circulated air for what purpose no one could determine. When Charlie asked whether air was being blown in or sucked out, he was told "whichever is appropriate."

Meanwhile, the men and women who were employed by Trost, and were the only personnel authorized to enter the "hazardous" buildings, removed everything that wasn't nailed down. Steel and plastic chairs and wooden office furniture, all of which had been wiped down and could have been saved, were simply pitched into dump trucks and hauled away. Computers, audio/visual equipment, radios and television sets, Trost guys simply stole outright. Like all of Choctaw, the Urban University campus was knocked flat by Hurricane Hosea, and while it was down, Ronnie Shade sent Trost Environmental in to pick the victim's pocket.

Among the Urban property that disappeared during the Trost pillage was the entire contents of the Theater Department's costume and set-building shops. By the time Trost finally surrendered its control of Urban buildings back to Charlie Lobovitch in mid-January, the "mold remediators" had thrown away or pilfered thousands of clothing items and thousands of dollars worth of tools. Rich sent a formal demand for restitution by Trost, but no Trost official ever responded. When Rich tried to pursue the matter through the Board, he was told by Ronnie Shade that Trost had performed the function for which it was hired. Rich insisted that millions of dollars' worth of valuable equipment and furnishings had been needlessly lost. Shade advised Rich against making such "slanterous" statements and went on to declare that he was sure that any instances of thievery were no doubt perpetrated by "the Spicanics Trost had been forced to employ." Shade directed Rich and Charlie to itemize everything that Trost had removed and claimed that the Board would put those materials on the list for FEMA reimbursement. Rich was never told how much Trost got paid, but by any rough calculation Rich figured that Trost's fee, plus the value of jettisoned property, exceeded what the state might have paid in "mold infection" lawsuits, not one of which was ever filed.

Drama and Film Department Chair Joe Alter was heart sickened by what the mold remediators had done to his costume and set shops. He was the first person back into Building 12 the day after Trost pulled out, and he called Charlie in a panic when he discovered his shops, which were in raised and unflooded areas, completely bare. Where were his costumes and building tools? Joe had a play to produce. He had not been able to stage a production during the jumpstarted and abbreviated fall semester, but he planned to mount *The Glass Menagerie*, which had been originally scheduled for the fall. That would be impossible without costumes and sets.

Joe was walking around in circles and crying when Rich and Charlie arrived at Building 12. Charlie's inspections, alarming at every turn, had not yet included Building 12. Quietly, Charlie explained to Joe that he had found things equally distressing everywhere on campus where Trost had worked.

"I see," Joe said, swallowing hard, trying to staunch the tears which rolled down his ruddy cheeks. "So we in the theater have not been singled out."

"No," Charlie said. "I'm afraid something similar has happened everywhere."

"I really don't know what we're going to do," Joe said. "We have to produce plays. You can't learn theater from a book."

"I know," Rich said.

Joe mopped under his eyes with the back of his right hand. "I apologize to both of you," he said. "I must be more of a man."

"Don't talk like that," Rich said.

"This is a blow," Joe said, and his lips trembled. He stuck out his hand to Charlie who shook it. "Thanks for all you have done." He then extended his hand to Rich. "And, you, too, Rector. You have done so much to bring us back. But this is such a blow."

Rich shook Joe's hand, and reached out to touch Joe's shoulder. When he did so, Joe embraced Rich completely and laid his bushy red hair against Rich's chest and neck, unable any longer to stop himself from sobbing. After a half-minute Joe pushed himself away and snuffled, "I am so very sorry. Please forgive me." Then he turned and walked briskly out of the room.

That night Joe called Rich at home, an unprecedented act. Joe had never called Rich before at home or in his office. "I wanted to apologize once again," he explained.

Rich told him he had nothing to apologize for. These were hard times, and what Joe had discovered was, indeed, as he had put it, "a blow." Rich knew, moreover, that Joe had lost his home and all his possessions in the flood and that he was now living in the faculty/staff trailer park. A lifelong bachelor who had devoted himself to university drama and the training of Urban students in the theatrical arts, he had now lost still more.

"But I am still ashamed of my behavior," Joe said. "I hope you will forgive me."

"No forgiveness is required," Rich said. "You've no reason to be ashamed."

"In times like these, real men don't cry over their losses," Joe said. "They calculate their responses. Since leaving you and Vice Rector Lobovich today, I have done just that."

"I would have expected nothing less," Rich said.

"Yes, well, thank you, of course," Joe said. "My plan is this. We will go forward as planned with a production for the last two weekends in February. We can't do the Williams. And without seats in the theater, we can't utilize our usual performance space. So I have decided on *Godot*. We can acquire the costumes from the Salvation Army who may even agree to donate them. Save for the tree which we can get potted at Home Depot, the stage is bare. And we will perform it in the student amphitheater. Vice Rector Lobovich will help me arrange the necessary lighting, I'm sure. I am concerned that the concrete seats will be cold and damp. We will address that by collecting squares of corrugated cardboard to hand out to the audience as they arrive and will notify people that they might want to bring blankets."

Rich and Cally, along with Cecilia Lagasse, were there for the first performance. They were the first to arrive on a chilly February Thursday, bundled up in hats, scarves, gloves and overcoats. The players had gathered in a classroom in Building 6 to stay warm, and some of the crew were still working on lighting adjustments. Joe Alter was wandering the grassy perimeters of the amphitheater through which members of the audience might stroll to reach their seats. He had a garden trowel in his right hand and a handled paper grocery bag in his left. Squinting in the poor light, he was scooping up dog shit.

The dog pack that Rich and Cally and Alphonse had spotted on their first day on campus two weeks after the storm still housed themselves under the library and still roamed the campus at will, defecating in every green space. Charlie had been at his wits' end dealing with this disgusting nuisance. He had been unable to receive assistance from either the SPCA or the City Pound, neither of which had yet returned to operation after the storm. Charlie had given serious consideration to having campus police shoot the dogs on sight, but he and Rich both worried about the public relations backlash. Not long ago, each of these animals had been someone's pet.

"Whatya doin?" Rich asked Joe, though he could plainly see.

"One of the kids stepped in some of this mess, and I almost did too. Can't have that happen to any of our audience."

"Did you try to get hold of Charlie to have him send over one of his grounds maintenance guys?" Rich asked.

"Wasn't really time." He rolled his left wrist and looked at his watch. "Curtain is in seventeen minutes."

"So you're just taking care of the problem yourself," Rich said, stating the obvious.

Joe Alter shrugged and stooped back to his work. "Not exactly the kind of job you can in good conscience assign to someone else, I guess."

The night grew chillier as the play ran on. But the production was altogether magnificent, no surprise from a director of Joe Alter's sensitivity, keen sense of theatricality and thorough preparation. And, at least as far as Rich heard, no one stepped in dog shit. The only untoward thing that happened was that Cecilia caught such a chill, she was shivering by the time Rich and Cally dropped her off at the trailer park. They insisted that she drive back to Cally's apartment with them and spend the night in her old bedroom. But she adamantly refused.

AFTER ELIA LIPSCOM INFORMED Rich in early January that the Board would declare Urban in financial exigency at its March meeting, Rich spent frenzied weeks trying to head off that necessity. Without success, he begged Lipscom to ask the Board to provide Urban a grace year. He wanted to attack the projected twenty-eight-million-dollar shortfall on a number of fronts at once. He would lobby the governor to restore the eight-million-dollar cut. He would go back to Washington to beg for additional federal assistance. He would refuse to hire new faculty or replace staff vacancies. He would call again on Beatrice Florin and ask her to lead a fund-raising campaign to raise five million dollars in three months. He even dared hope that Florin would write a check for that amount herself.

To Rich such a plan seemed reasonable, but Lipscom would not agree to intercede with the Board on Urban's behalf. Rich then asked Lipscom to allow him to make a grace-year request of the Board himself. The viceroy refused, warning Rich that such an appeal would not meet a friendly reception.

So all the while Rich was watching his plans for a student trailer complex collapse, he was also trying with elusive success to line up other supplemental support for his 2005-2006 budget. Governor Lebear would not meet with Rich about the eight-million-dollar state appropriation reduction. Rich did secure a meeting on the issue with the governor's chief administrative officer but she said that decisions on the fifty-seven-million cut were "history" and "at this point set in stone."

The cut to higher education had been justified, Rich argued, as being needed to offset a projected state budget deficit. But that deficit had not materialized. In fact, the state was running a huge surplus. The CAO said this made her hope the state would soon be able to make restorations, perhaps as early as for the 2006-2007 fiscal year. Rich pointed out that by proceeding as she had outlined, Urban University would be forced to disrupt the lives of employees by making numerous layoffs in positions that might be restored in a year's time. Careers would be injured needlessly, and his university would suffer damage to its programs that couldn't be easily restored when the funding returned.

"I hear your concern," she said, "but I'm sure matters aren't quite as dire as you suggest."

ASIDE FROM THE UNIVERSITY'S fiscal nightmare, Rich suddenly had an even more important matter to worry about. After the chill she caught at *Waiting for Godot*, Cecilia came down with a chest cold that progressed to pneumonia. She was stuffed full of antibiotics and told not to leave her bed. Rich and Cally tried to get her to return to the second bedroom in Cally's apartment. But she wouldn't consider it. So either Rich or Cally, Cally usually, dropped in at her trailer late each afternoon to make sure that she was getting proper nutrition and to handle such purchases as Cecilia might need from a drugstore or grocery. Rich was concerned foremost with Cecilia's health, but he also missed her leadership, her daily presence at his side and the value of her professional advice.

AND NOW MOST EVERYTHING Rich tried either stalled or failed. He didn't get a five-million-dollar check from Beatrice Florin. She agreed to head Urban's crisis fund-raising drive and to approach friends to support the campaign. But she warned Rich that raising so much money in only three months would prove a difficult, if not impossible, task. It proved the latter.

Enrollment constituted still another serious problem. Lacking that needed housing from the trailer complex, instead of enrolling the 15,000 students he hoped for in the Spring, 2005, semester, Urban enrolled only 14,000. That reduced the university's tuition revenues, and the shortfall ate up most of the two million dollars left from Urban's ten-million-dollar share of the federal relief package. Rich had hoped to roll over that two million against the twenty-eight million needed for 2005-2006, but now he would need it to balance the fiscal 2004-2005 budget.

Rich couldn't complain, though, that Beatrice let him down. She did promise him another million dollar check and agreed to pay for and facilitate another fund-raising trip to Washington. Most important, Beatrice hosted Rich at a small dinner party at her home. The entire guest list included Rich, Cally and Alkansea's senior United States Senator Marilynn Williams, a cagey moderate Democrat in an increasingly conservative Republican state. The senator's husband was also invited but could not attend. Only someone with the checkbook stature of Beatrice Florin could have commanded a U.S. Senator's undivided attention for an entire evening.

Beatrice was a big supporter of Senator Williams, and as it happened, Rich and Cally were also admirers. They didn't always agree with some of the senator's positions, but they knew and understood the politics behind them. She was not popular with environmentalists of one stripe because of her ardent support for the oil and gas industries, which were major employers in Alkansea. She was a strong proponent of coastal restoration initiatives, however, also something good for Alkansea, and therefore she was liked by those who worried about wetlands and Gulf marine life issues.

Senator Williams was also a Choctaw and made no secret of her love for the city where she had grown up and attended public schools. She had been wily enough, eventually, after turning forty, to marry a wealthy businessman from Mayflower who gave her needed credibility north of Lake De Soto. But she was always, often to her political detriment, identified with her hometown. At age sixty-five, she was now in the middle of her fourth senate term even though she had never gotten more than fifty-two percent of the vote. She campaigned with great ease in the African-American community that supported her with ninety-eight percent of its ballots. But she ran hard to the middle, targeting her ads and speeches to the economic concerns of specific areas. This strategy enabled her to blunt the Republicans' efforts to savage her as a "liberal" who was "pro-abortion" and "weak on national defense."

Marilynn Williams was decent and likable, and now that Beatrice was providing him the chance to make his pitch to her personally, Rich thought Williams would help him if she could. His major concern was that she had received both her undergraduate and her law degrees at Ettons and was widely known to help Ettons whenever possible. So Rich would have to mask any irritation he felt about Ettons' drinking at the public trough.

Senator Williams was a bright, committed and unusually well-informed politician. Still, even she failed to understand the systematic way in which Urban was discriminated against in the state higher education funding process. She knew that ASU was funded at a "flagship" rate whereas Urban was funded at the lesser, so-called, "Research II" rate. But at Beatrice Florin's dinner, Rich was able to lay out the disparity in wrenching detail. He was also able to emphasize once again the economic impact of Urban University on the City of Choctaw. The senator knew this but stated she found it useful to hear the details again. Most important, Rich was able to stress how the Board was utilizing Urban's student enrollment decline to double its cut.

"When Urban was founded in the mid-fifties," Rich said, "the state legislature spoke of creating a higher education system modeled on the University of California. ASU would be Cal Berkeley; Urban would be UCLA."

"I hadn't ever heard that," the senator said, shaking her shoulder-length black pageboy. "But that's exactly what we should aspire to for the benefit of our state and its young people."

"What I am afraid of," Rich said, "is that in the aftermath of Hosea, that idea will be permanently shelved. The legislatures of the sixties and the seventies moved us in that direction, however minimally. But Monster proponents have fought us every step of the way. You may remember our struggle in the sixties to be allowed to field athletic teams and our fight in the seventies to move from Division II athletics to Division I."

The senator laughed. "This confession will have to remain in this room," she said. "But I'm not much of a sports fan. I root for Ettons against ASU, which is the privilege of an alum. Otherwise, I root for the Monsters because I like serving in the Senate, if you follow my thinking. But I don't really know anything about athletics except that the Monsters are usually very good in football. And I know almost nothing about athletics at Urban." With both hands, she smoothed the fabric of her navy blue suit coat down over her waist.

Rich explained the role athletics played in student recruiting and a university's general public profile. "But I was using athletics only as an example. We don't do a good job funding higher education in this state," Rich said. "Few states in the Deep South do. But we're at the bottom. Lower even than Louisiana and Mississippi. And inside Alkansea, only ASU is funded at the same level as its peers. When funding for Urban is compared to Memphis, Georgia State, Alabama Birmingham, the University of Houston, we want to commit suicide."

"I'm sorry, Dr. Janus," Senator Williams said.

"Well, we've lived with this for a long, long time."

"You shouldn't have to. But as I am sure you understand, all these funding issues are those of the state legislature and the Board of Trustees, not the United States Senate."

"Yes, of course," Rich said. "In the long run, we must get our student enrollment back to the level we enjoyed before the storm. Until that happens we remain at peril. And at present, I'm afraid that the negative attitude the rest of the state holds toward Choctaw, combined with the ASU-centric attitude of the Board, may result in Urban suffering damage in the near term that could last a generation. I brought up the example of athletics. If *I* may keep something in the room, I am under

pressure from the viceroy himself to address the severe budget
cuts I am facing, by, among other things, eliminating our
athletic program. I am resistant to this pressure, not because
I'm a former basketball coach, but because of the damage such a
move would inflict on our public image and thereby on student
recruiting and hence our ability to recover."

"How can I help?" the senator inquired.

Rich took a deep breath and then laughed. "Is there any
possibility that Congress might make a special allocation to the
higher education institutions of Choctaw?"

"On top of the FEMA rebuilding money you're in line for?"

"Yes," Rich said.

"How much are we talking?"

"I can only answer that question for Urban. But added
together, the two community colleges would require perhaps
one-third again what we need."

"And Urban would need?"

"To avoid making any further cuts, we would need twenty
million dollars. We're going to need to cut twenty-eight million
from the current fiscal year's budget. One way or another I
can find the first eight. After that, we're going to be radically
changing the nature of the university. We're going to have to lay
off staff and faculty, including tenured faculty."

"Can you lay off tenured faculty?" the senator asked, shaking
her head.

"We won't have any choice."

"And how long are we talking about? I assume more than
one year."

"Well, right now, I'm talking about one year," Rich said.
"But I suspect it will take at least three years to recapture our
pre-storm enrollments. And that, of course, may be optimistic."

"So let's assume you have some tuition grow back over
three years," the senator said, "then I guess we're talking about
one hundred fifty million over three years to be fair to all
constituents."

"No, no," Rich said. "Only half that, right?"

"Not if we include Ettons and Saint Augustine." Saint Augustine was the small historically black Catholic college in Choctaw.

Rich chafed that neither Ettons nor Saint Augustine had suffered the kind of physical damage or student enrollment loss that Urban had, but he knew to keep his eye on the prize. If the senator could deliver the money he needed, he couldn't concern himself with others getting money perhaps beyond their needs. Wasn't that the lesson of the parable about the workers in the vineyard? Senator Williams had her alma mater to protect, and she had her African-American constituency to satisfy.

"Well, then yes," Rich said. "Forgive me for addressing you only about public higher education."

"One hundred fifty million spread over three years," the senator said, obviously calculating.

"I guess," Rich said. "A lot of money, I know."

"An educational relief package."

"Yes," Rich said.

"An emergency and recovery package."

"Yes," Rich said. "To protect, as we were once promised, Choctaw universities from a tragedy beyond its control."

"Hmm," the senator said. "What if we did it as a loan? My Republican colleagues would respond better if we structured it as a low-interest loan."

"OK," Rich said.

"We give you the money in fifty-million-dollar payouts for three years. No interest applies for the first five years. Then each institution begins to pay the loan back at one percent interest over forty years."

Rich did the math in his head. Urban would get a total of sixty million dollars that it would have to repay over forty-five years.

"So our share would run us less than one point four million per year," Rich said, "once we started the repayment."

Senator Williams shrugged. "Unless Congress decided to forgive the loan at some point."

"How likely is that?" Rich asked.

"Loan forgiveness draws a lot less attention than the original dedication of relief money."

"Well, if you could get us from here to 2010, I feel totally confident we can handle the one point four after that."

"If necessary," the senator said, smiling.

"If necessary," Rich said, "but even then, with gratitude."

Senator Williams turned to Beatrice and said, "I wonder if you might pour us all a brandy." Underneath the table, Cally squeezed Rich's knee.

Rich had complete faith that Marilynn Williams would do her best to get him the sixty million they'd discussed. But Congress does not act swiftly, not even in response to historic disasters. And many Republicans, who controlled both houses, expressed a need to make sure the funding was not wasted. Some Republicans wondered aloud if "the country was wise to invest taxpayer dollars in a place like Choctaw." They defended such statements as expressing a concern about the intrinsic vulnerability of low lying coastal cities. Of course, Choctaw had a black majority population. No Republican seemed to include in such statements a concern about whiter places like, for instance, Houston. So Rich understood the delicate negotiations Senator Williams was going to have to undertake. And while Rich waited for her to work a miracle, he was forced by the dictates of the Board of Trustees to move forward with a plan of financial exigency to reduce expenditures in Urban's 2005-2006 budget by twenty-eight million dollars.

Then the new year of 2005 turned crueler yet. Each time Cally visited her, Cecilia seemed more shrunken, only her caustic wit indicating the fight she was putting up. On March 4, Rich and Cally took a cake to Cecilia's trailer to celebrate her seventy-sixth birthday. She did not try to get out of bed, but she did sit up to visit with her friends.

"I'd like this with a single malt chaser," she told Rich when he'd brought her a saucer of cake. "I've got some Oban in the kitchen. Make mine neat and plentiful." She smiled like a Cheshire. "No booze, no birthday."

"Honey, drinking alcohol isn't so good when you're on antibiotics," Cally said.

"Why should I care?" Cecilia said. "I'm old. I can't expect to live all that much longer. And why would I want to if I can't have a single malt on my birthday?"

"You can have a Scotch as soon as you're better," Rich said. "I'll buy you a bottle of Johnnie Walker Blue. You and I will drink the whole bottle just the two of us. We'll make Cally bring us ice and feed us slices of blue cheese on thin crackers."

"Hey, how did I get to be the waitress in this thing?" Cally asked, laughing.

"You don't drink Scotch," Rich said.

"You don't ever drink Scotch?" Cecilia said. "That's the first untoward thing I've ever heard about you. Have you ever tried single malt and chocolate chip cookies?"

"No," Cally said, "although Rich probably has. He drinks Scotch and eats M&Ms."

Cecilia turned to Rich, her eyes glassy but penetrating. "I know he does that," she said. "And as a health professional, I hereby advise him to stop it."

"Second," Cally said.

"Hey, how did this get to be about me?" Rich asked.

"Because you're the rector," Cecilia said. "Unless you're drinking Scotch and eating M&Ms. Then you're the rectum. And we need you to be the rector, not just another asshole."

"I love the way you talk," Cally said. "And he needs to hear it."

"Then bring me a glass of Oban," Cecilia said. "It's my birthday.

"No," Cally said. "Not till you're well."

"Oh Jesus fucking Christ," Cecilia said. "Rich, go in the kitchen of this tin can and pour me two fingers of Oban. Bring it in here and hand it to me. I promise I'll just sniff it."

"Promise?" Rich said.

"Jesus Christ," Cecilia said. "I'm *seventy*-six, not *six*."

Cally signaled Rich with her eyes to comply. He poured the Scotch and brought it back. Cecilia held the glass to her face and took a deep breath. Then she started coughing so violently Rich and Cally had to take the cake dish and the drink away from her lest she spill them.

When she finally recovered, she grinned triumphantly and said, "Goddamn but that was one great snort. Now you drink that up, boss, before I make you give it back to me."

A week later, on March 11, when Cally stopped by, she found Cecilia lying unconscious on the floor in front of the bathroom. Cally called an ambulance, and Cecilia was taken to the hospital where she drifted in and out of wakefulness for the next seven days. Rich and Cally spent time at her bedside. Five days into Cecilia's hospitalization, at her doctors' direction, Cally notified Cecilia's family that she was in crisis, and they began to arrive to be with her.

Cecilia's children and some of her grandchildren were with her at the end. Cally and Rich were there too, thank God. Historians would someday record the number of fatalities that Hurricane Hosea had caused. Cecilia Lagasse's death would not be in that number, but she was every bit as much a casualty of that storm and the official neglect that allowed it to do so much damage as those who were its immediate victims. Cecilia Lagasse, their fellow soldier in the post-hurricane fight, Rich's incredible hero for her courage and self-sacrifice, Cecilia Lagasse, their housemate, Cecilia Lagasse, their cherished friend, was gone.

43

From our village on the upper Connecticut River, where our families were slaughtered, many of us returned to Nipmuck country and erected our *weetoos* in the area of Mount Wachusett. In early June, five hundred men rode out of Boston under our old buddy Daniel Henchman with orders to proceed west to Hadley where he was to rendezvous with Connecticut forces and drive our remaining people away from the Connecticut River.

Major John Talcott led a Connecticut regiment out of Norwich on June 2 and surprised a small settlement of Narragansetts trying to farm an area in Wabaquasset on the Massachusetts border. Talcott's men killed fifty-two, mostly women and children. Henchman, meanwhile, en route west, surprised a group of Wampanoags fishing at Washaccum Pond. He killed seven and took twenty-nine prisoners to be traded back to us or sold at the slave block. But we gave him enough of a battle that he depleted his ammunition and had to march to the garrison at Marlborough for resupply.

Then, as if things weren't going badly enough for us as we tried to feed ourselves, on June 12, in service of their partners in Manhattan, the Mohawks attacked our people on the Connecticut River before Talcott and Henchman could get there. If the Mohawks drove us out of the Connecticut River Valley, then Massachusetts could not lay claim to land west of the Connecticut by right of conquest. Since Massachusetts and New York had not yet settled their borders in this area, neither wanted to concede an advantage to the other. We were their scoreboard.

The Mohawk intrusion into the Connecticut River area made matters much worse for us. We had planted corn and other crops there, but now we felt unsafe to stay in the region or even return for harvest time. Almost equally as bad, the Mohawk activity in the west disrupted our supply lines to the French.

After a general council meeting of our leaders, we decided that the Narragansetts and Wampanoags would return south into the land of our mothers and fathers. Muttaump and Matoonas were solicitous in their offer for us to stay. But we knew that other Nipmuck leaders like Sagamore Sam and Sagamore John were anxious for us to depart. And though we were in no hurry to do the bidding of the Prayers, we knew that we must seek the farmlands and seacoasts of our heritage or stay and cause the Nipmucks to starve along with us.

So near the beginning of *Towwakesos*, in mid-June, we set out together, a thousand of us, Quinnapin, leading the Narragansetts, and I, leading the Wampanoags. I had good, loyal people with me, Weetamoo and her Pocassets, Awashonks and the Sakonnets. And we had excellent captains in Adonoshonk, Annawon, my sister Amie's husband Tuspaquin, my uncle Akkompoin, and the Sakonnets Totoson and Nompash. We did not know what we would find, and we assumed we would not be left unmolested. But all of us still had storage pits of food in our home territories. If we could reach them, they might sustain us until we could get crops in the ground. And maybe we could secure access to the bays of our homelands so that we could provide ourselves with needed protein from seafood. And whatever we faced from the English, at least we would once again be fighting from the advantage of our own land.

Together on June 16, Narragansetts and Wampanoags attacked Swansea in hopes of driving the Plymouthites as far away from us as possible. Several garrison houses withstood our onslaught, but we took all the food we could find and burned the rest of the town to the ground. Thereafter, we necessarily began to disperse. Some of the Narragansetts headed west to their country, though Quinnapin and others remained with me, as did Weetamoo and her Pocassets; Awashonks led her people back to the southeastern coast of the Sakonnet River. Those with me intended to settle first in Pocasset country and someday, with the Creator's blessing, farm again the soil on Montaup.

Hunger had returned us to the shores of Narragansett Bay, from whence we had fled. And in our isolation from each other, things fell apart with astonishing, deflating rapidity. Our problem was that in our historic homeland area, the English were too close and could strike at us too easily, particularly given that we were weakened by starvation that daily took the lives of our young and old. Those of our wives who were nursing found their milk drying up. As we buried our babes, we buried our future every day. The racists who were starving us now started a rumor that we were killing our children in order not to have to feed them. The murderer pinning the blame for his crimes on the victims. We lived rich but careful lives before these horrible times. And we exercised our care on behalf of our children. Like people anywhere on this tormented globe, we lived for our children. That's a basic human trait that we would not question even of those hated English who tortured us so.

We were able to retrieve food from some of our storage pits, but we were not ever able to settle. Upon our arrival back in Plymouth, That Vicious Lying Rat Bastard Josiah Winslow and his colony councilmen sent Major William Bradford and still another army after us, five hundred men, more fighters than we had left, this time with Indian scouts who could track where the English themselves would have stopped in utter confusion and built a fort. By June 27, Bradford was at Pocasset, keeping us from our original plan of reestablishing a settlement there. From Pocasset, Bradford marched his men out after us whenever we were spotted. Our sole advantage now rested on our knowledge of the land. But we were forced to remain constantly on the move, and Bradford's scouts enabled him to follow where the English never had been before.

Then that little bantam blowhard Benjamin Church got involved in a way that dealt us another cruel blow. As you may recall, before the war, he had maintained a farm in Sakonnet territory, and during that time, had cultivated a relationship with Awashonks. Church was no different from the other belted hats who moved in with us in the seventeenth century. He considered himself one of the elect and saw God's approving hand in every bit of good fortune that came his way. What set him apart, and what blinded Awashonks to his evil, was that unlike monsters such as Josiah Winslow, Miles Standish, and his contemporary clones, Sam Moseley and John Talcott, Church so liked to hear himself talk that he'd talk to anyone, even an Indian. He considered himself a charmer, and as we know, some people can be charmed by a man just because he's endeavoring to charm.

The rocky, seacoast land of the Sakonnets was so isolated that they had never felt the pressure of human habitation that the Pokanokets, Pocassets and even the Narragansetts had known for some time before the war. Church was the only white man who had yet moved in close by. So, for a short while anyway, Awashonks was able to reoccupy her territory without attracting the kind of attention from Bradford that we were drawing farther north. But then, Church, who had relocated to Aquidneck Island across the Sakonnet River, noticed her men out fishing and made cautious contact. His very cockiness carried the day for him. He was willing to approach the Sakonnets unarmed, and he was willing to talk. All through New England, Indians were exhausted by the totality of this war, so, of course, they were intrigued by the approach of a white man who wasn't cursing and shooting at them.

Eventually, Church got the audience with Awashonks that he wanted. He knew that she had a drinking problem, so he didn't forget to arrive with a bottle of rum. He proposed that Awashonks agree to a separate peace, and for that I could have forgiven her. Her people yearned to rest and return to the lives they had known before the war. But Church would not grant her wish simply to stop fighting and remain neutral. She could switch sides or be regarded an enemy combatant and subject to Plymouth's judgmental fury. Choosing the former meant supplying men to fight against me and providing scouts and trackers to follow my people as we sought to escape. Urging Awashonks to agree to Church's terms was Nompash, that fierce captain who not long earlier had argued that we kill our captives and post their heads atop the fortified walls of the English garrison houses. He had never forgiven all of us who had spoken out against that savagery when the issue was brought before our council. Persistently drunk, Awashonks formally sued for peace on June 28 and assigned men who were our own blood, men who had fought beside us for over a year, to stalk and kill us.

So then we were hounded by two Plymouth groups, one under Bradford, a second with the assistance of the Sakonnets, under Church. Awashonks' decision did not produce the darkest day in my life. That was yet to come. But her betrayal made my heart heavy with dismay. Such is the way total war manifests itself, an alien universe where honor shrivels into dust to be blown away by the hurricane of defeat, desperation and despair.

Comparable tragic developments followed in Narragansett Country. Since the Mohawks now controlled the Connecticut River, Talcott turned southeast into Rhode Island. There on July 2 he surprised a settlement of Narragansetts desperately trying to plant crops in their old homeland. Meeting little resistance, Talcott's men slew 171 of our allies, mostly women and children, and among them the beloved "Old Queen" Quaiapen, whom Talcott sneeringly described as "an ugly old piece of meat."

Talcott's unopposed butchery prompted the Narragansett Sachem Potuck to lead eighty of his people to what was left of Providence to surrender. The Rhode Islanders, who had never joined the English military confederacy, told Potuck that they were not at war with the Narragansetts, so he could not surrender to them. They said he would have to meet with Massachusetts leaders in Boston. Worn out, urgent for surcease, Potuck asked if the Providence men would assist him, and they provided a sloop to transport him to Boston under a flag of truce. But the Rhode Islanders also insisted that Potuck's people wait for him in Warwick. Having been attacked by Canonchet and Quinnapin as recently as late March, they were nervous about so many Indians in their midst, starving and destitute though they appeared.

Potuck agreed to this arrangement. But while Potuck was en route to Boston, Talcott's fiends attacked those at Warwick, killed sixty-seven of them, carried some off to the forest to be tortured by their historic Mohegan enemies and sold the rest into slavery. By the time Potuck reached Boston, he was suing for peace on behalf of a contingent of people no longer living.

In Boston the Bay Colony leadership took no notice of Potuck's arrival under a truce flag. The Rhode Islanders weren't at war with the Narragansetts, they told him, and therefore no one from Rhode Island had the authority to offer him safe passage. With that, they arrested him and had him executed on Boston Commons.

This is what happens when people at odds regard their enemy as *other*, a lesson that Israelis and Palestinians, Muslims and Christians, Hutus and Tutsis, Somalis and Kenyans, Americans and Arabs haven't learned all these centuries later. If your enemy is *other*, you don't have to treat him as you yourself would insist on being treated were you his captive rather than he yours. It is despicable for our enemies to torture us but fair for us to torture our enemies if they are *other*, as our enemies always are.

When, Rich Janus, will you tell this story?

44

Rich Janus' financial exigency plan was an exercise in institutional mutilation. After achieving the first five million dollars in reductions by redlining vacant positions, many of which sorely needed filling, Rich asked each of his vice rectors and deans to study their budgets and come back to him with cut recommendations. Their total recommendations, all painful, came to only six million dollars. When he added in the million from Beatrice Florin and the two million he got from the Urban University Foundation, he was still short fourteen million dollars.

So now came the bloodletting.

Rich told his non-academic vice rectors that they each had to cut ten percent from their remaining budgets. They told him it could not be done, that they could not accomplish their organizational obligations if they had to make additional cuts of that magnitude, cuts that were stacked on top of the vacant positions Rich had already eliminated and the round of additional "voluntary" cuts they'd already made. He told them they had no choice. He called in the Athletic Director and told him that Urban would cut back from fifteen sports to just four teams: men's and women's basketball, men's baseball and women's softball. The A.D. was to prepare appeals to the NCAA and the Deep South Athletic Conference for waiver of its membership regulations. The NCAA required at least fourteen sports for Division I status, and the Deep South required fifteen. The A.D. was to request exemptions from those requirements. But even though there were now voices inside Urban, as well as those of the viceroy and members of the Board, demanding that he do so, Rich would not eliminate athletics in their entirety. He was determined to save the most popular programs and gamble that NCAA and conference waivers would allow Urban to remain a Division I school.

Rich gave his academic deans a different task. He directed that they rank their departments from bottom to top. They were to consider issues such as student demand, cost of instruction, and comparative standing versus regional and national competitors. Rich's initial plan was to put all his deans in a single room and force them to prepare a programmatic elimination list that would achieve the last fourteen million dollars in savings the Board required. In the pitiless aftermath of Hurricane Hosea, Urban University now found itself in the late winter of 2005 in an open lifeboat that was sinking. Surviving at all demanded throwing overboard a large number of programs and the people who derived their livelihoods from teaching and staffing them.

The final structure of Rich's plan was influenced considerably by a suggestion from Peter Alexander, the seventy-year-old Dean of Engineering, who volunteered to retire and recommended that he not be replaced. He proposed instead that a new college title be created that folded Engineering into another unit. The reduction in administrative costs would save the university another half million dollars, requiring the layoff of fewer faculty. Peter had come to Urban from the faculty at Alabama and had only eighteen years in Urban's retirement program. He had planned to work another two years, and retiring at this stage would reduce his pension because he fell short of the twenty-year threshold. But stepping down was for the good of the order, he said, a small sacrifice in a time that demanded people rise above themselves.

He was one of the heroes.

Another of the heroes was the woman for whom Rich would have given his life. Cally recommended that she, too, take early retirement, and that Rich move the rest of the faculty in her Classics Department into other units. The Latin and Greek professors could be transferred to the Department of Foreign Languages. The expert in Classical Art and Architecture could move to the Art Department. Her colleague who taught classes on Plato, Aristotle and Marcus Aurelius could relocate to Philosophy. The new classical dramatist, Karl Gelderman, who might otherwise lose his job, could join Drama and Film. By scratching Cally's salary and benefits and all support funds for her department, Rich could put another $125,000 into his cut pile.

"That's my plan and I'm sticking to it," Cally said while moving arugula leaves from a plastic box into salad bowls as they were preparing dinner. Rich was drizzling a salmon filet with olive oil and coating it with black pepper and garlic salt. He had not anticipated Cally's offering to sacrifice herself, and he wasn't remotely ready to embrace her suggestion.

"Not in a million years," Rich said. "You love teaching."

"I do. I still do. I acknowledge that," she said. "But I've had a thirty-year career."

"I'm not going to do it," Rich said.

"You have to, Rich."

"I don't have to do anything. I'm the boss, remember?"

"You know that our majors aren't where they ought to be. The Board has us on probation as a low completer. With the enrollment fall off from Hosea, the Board's going to cut us anyway. You do it this way, my colleagues will get to keep their jobs. And people will see how even-handed you are. You even took down your own wife's department and forced her to retire."

"No," Rich said.

"Yes, Boo. Yes. You have to. I've had a wonderful career. I can still do my research. And I'll get my book finished a lot sooner if I don't have to do committee work anymore."

"You'll miss the students."

"I will," she said. "But I'll get Joe Alter to let me teach a class in Aeschylus once in a while. Karl doesn't like him. I could also do a graduate seminar on Sophocles. Karl might feel pinched about that, I guess, but hey, I'm sleeping with the rector in order to save his job."

"I can't do it. I'm going to have blood on my hands. But I won't have yours." He stood next to her at the kitchen counter, a shaker of tarragon poised over a plastic carton of sour cream.

"Sweetie, you have to." She took the tarragon from him, set it on the scratched Formica, and turned him to face her. "You have to, Rich. It's the right thing." She laid her head against his chest and circled his waist with her arms. He wrapped his arms around her back. "I'll make it worth your while." She giggled into his shirt. "I'll have a lot of time on my hands."

Rich laughed. "You're offering to bribe me with sex to put you on the cut list?"

"It's the right thing," she said.

IN THE DAYS AHEAD, Peter Alexander and Cally Martin set examples that were embraced by others who were near the ends of their careers, professors who had planned before the storm to continue working another three to five years but now stepped aside sooner so that the jobs of younger colleagues might be spared. The storm produced much selfishness at Urban and elsewhere in the damaged region, but it also produced bracing acts of self-sacrifice like those of Peter and Cally and others who followed their lead.

Rich was greatly enlightened by Dean Alexander's proposal, which he accepted with gratitude. At the time of the storm, Urban had ten colleges: Architecture and Urban Planning, Arts and Music, Business, Education, Engineering, Humanities and Social Sciences, Law, Natural Sciences, Nursing, and Pharmacy. Expanding upon Alexander's idea, Rich presented his deans with a reorganization plan on Wednesday, March 30, that would reduce additional administrative costs by another million dollars by creating a new line-up of colleges. Arts and Music, Humanities and Social Sciences, and Architecture and Urban

Planning colleges would be combined to form the College of Liberal Arts. The Engineering and Natural Sciences colleges would be gathered into the College of Natural and Applied Sciences. The College of Pharmacy would be renamed the School of Pharmacy and would be headed by a director rather than a dean. The Dean of Nursing would take on the additional title of Director of Pharmacy. And the College of Education would be renamed the School of Graduate Education, would eliminate its undergraduate curriculum, be led by a director and report to the graduate dean. The Department of Counseling would be combined with the Psychology Department to achieve further cost savings. And all statistics would now be taught by the Math Department.

When Rich presented his plan to the Council of Academic Deans, Pharmacy Dean John Leake objected strenuously to Rich's outline, but the other deans said next to nothing. That didn't mean they embraced the plan, however. Amanda Josef, the popular Dean of Education, had been on the job market since the previous September. She had lost her home, had stated that she never wanted to go through another hurricane, and had accepted a job at Middle Tennessee a week earlier. Her decision to relocate had nothing to do with Rich's reorganization plan, but few people on campus were willing to accept that. That was because she didn't like how Rich decided to handle Education and said so publicly when asked. Even Ben Turner was snippy with Rich when Rich first revealed his plan. As they were leaving the rector's conference room after Deans Council concluded, Ben curtly asked to see Rich privately.

"I want to know if this is going to cost me my deanship," Ben said as he followed Rich into his office and closed the door.

"These are wretched times, Ben," Rich replied. "There aren't any easy choices here."

"So the answer is yes."

"I think it's only fair that Shirley lead Liberal Arts," Rich said, referring to Shirley Johnson, Dean of the College of Arts and Music. Rich sat at his desk. "She's the longest serving dean of the three areas we're putting together to form the new college."

A look of indignation bristled on Turner's face as he sat in a chair across from Rich. "This is one fine deal, Rich. I thought we were friends. Who did you come to when Francis Saurian first cooked up the kooky idea of making you provost?"

"Just wait a second, Ben. You're the most capable academic administrator . . ."

"You admit that but . . ."

"And that's why I'm offering you Cecilia's position."

"Cecilia's position? Provost?"

"Well, interim provost," Rich said.

"Effective when?"

"Immediately."

Turner was quiet for a time. "So I lose my deanship."

"But you become the provost."

"Interim provost, you said."

"I'd appoint you provost without the interim designation, but the viceroy won't let me. Says an interim rector shouldn't be making permanent appointments. Probably even right, I guess. Although I hate admitting that Elia is ever right about anything."

"At Cecilia's salary," Ben said.

Rich laughed. "You wouldn't like that. Cecilia made less than you do."

"Jesus," Ben said.

"So you can keep your current salary."

"You didn't give Cecilia some kind of stipend for moving to Academic Affairs?"

"I did. Fifteen K."

"So I get my current salary plus the fifteen K?"

Rich sighed and shook his head. "No, Ben, in this situation I can't do that. We're laying off people in the hundreds. I can't be handing out raises in the same season. It wouldn't fly, and it wouldn't be right if it did fly."

"This kind of sucks, Rich. I'm sure you can see that."

"Everything about Hosea sucks, everything that has happened to our city and our university this entire year."

"I'm losing a deanship that I've held for ten years."

"And I'm offering you the chance to become Chief Academic Officer."

"With no pay increase and on an interim basis."

"With no pay increase for the moment and on an interim basis for the moment."

"Meaning?" Ben asked.

"Well," Rich said, "I've applied for the rectorship and . . ."

"I thought you'd ruled that out." Ben Turner's eyebrows gathered in a knot over his nose.

"I did, but Hosea changed my mind."

"Hmm," Ben said. "I hadn't realized."

"If I get the position," Rich said, "I'll appoint you provost permanently. And as soon as we get this financial crisis behind us, I will raise your salary to what I was making when I was provost. That'll be a lot more than a fifteen thousand dollar increase for you."

"And if you don't get the position?"

"Well, if I don't get the position, the next rector will decide who serves as provost."

"I remember from a Scotchy conversation one night that seems a lifetime ago you saying Elia agreed that you'd return to Academic Affairs when the new rector was appointed."

"That was the deal," Rich said.

"So where does that leave me?"

"If that's what happens, then there are no guarantees," Rich said. "The new rector will do what he or she wants. But I will agree to the following. If I am not appointed rector on a permanent basis, I will go to the new rector and recommend that you stay on in Academic Affairs. I'll go teach English and do some volunteer coaching for the city recreation department."

"Maybe we could get you to take back the reins of Ungulate basketball," Ben said. "The kid you put in when Prince walked didn't do dick. No way with the players we had we should have gone fourteen and eighteen this year. Jimmy would have had them in the NIT at the least. Chuck had the one and done in the conference tournament. Big-time boo."

Rich said, "I'm not sure John Wooden could have managed a winning record with the problems we had. Players who lost their belongings in the flooded dorms. No campus food service after the storm. Compressed fall semester which demanded more study in less time, just as the season was getting underway. Et cetera, et cetera. Sure the kid's green. He probably needed a few more years as an assistant. But he's earned his shot."

"This is sure some fucked-up shit," Ben said.

"That mean we have a deal?"

"Sure. Fuck it, right? Anyway, what choice do I have?"

"None," Rich said. "None better than this, anyway."

RICH AND CALLY WERE finally able to move back into their house on April 7. They invited the Feasters down from Mayflower to celebrate with them two days later and stay over that Saturday night. Rich bought four thick filets and prepared them for the barbecue. Cally made a Bordelaise sauce of butter, olive oil, chopped shallots, parsley and garlic. While Rich and Robert fired up the grill on the patio, they talked about the recent NCAA basketball tournament and sipped their drinks, a beer for Robert, a tall stiff Scotch for Rich. Upstairs, Althea tore up lettuce and grated cheese for a salad while Cally chopped cucumbers, red peppers and tomatoes into a blender for fresh gazpacho. Rich had bought ice cream to be topped with Chambord for dessert.

The dinner and dessert conversation, filled with reminiscences about bluffing their way into Choctaw not long after the storm and the many long, hot weekends of dirty labor in September and October, lasted late into the night. They talked about their mutual fondness for Cecilia, and how sad that she wasn't with them right now. They also talked about missing Alphonse who had worked with them on so many occasions before returning to New York after Christmas. All through dinner and the conversation afterwards, Rich filled Scotch glass after Scotch glass, and before they went to bed, he was slurring his words. Rich had more than doubled his alcohol intake since the storm, a semiconscious act of self-anesthetization, but he hadn't gotten sloppy before, and he was ashamed of himself even before falling asleep. Once they were in bed and the light was out, he apologized repeatedly to Cally, who responded by rubbing his shoulder and slipping under his left arm to lay her head on his chest.

"It's OK, baby," she assured him.

"No, it's not," he said. "I've embarrassed myself. And I'm sure I embarrassed you, too."

"Everybody understands the pressure you're under, Boo," she said, her hand moving in slow circles on his stomach. "Give yourself a break."

"No," Rich said. "I'm ashamed." His stomach burned, and he shook out two Rolaids tablets from the jar by the bed. "These fine people. These wonderful friends. In front of them."

"It's OK, sweetie," she said. He didn't say anything. She laughed a little. "It's OK, that is, if you don't barf in my hair."

Rich snorted. "You haven't ever known me to throw up, have you?"

"I haven't ever known you to drink so much, either."

"So you *are* embarrassed."

"No, I'm not. I promise. It's OK. Really, it's OK." Her hand continued to caress his stomach, and he didn't say anything. She giggled again. "It's OK, if you don't barf in my hair."

Rich took a deep breath and blew the air out so hard she could feel it on her arm. "I'm not going to barf," he said.

"In your hair," he added.

ON MONDAY, APRIL 11, Rich met with Ben Turner and the other Urban deans to discuss the list of academic programs that would be cut. As requested, he had received the deans' priority lists on Friday, and he had studied them with a pounding hangover the afternoon after the Feasters had departed for Mayflower. Each dean's program list had been distributed to all the others, and Rich had instructed them to prepare a cut list of ten programs from the departments outside their own colleges. His intent was to tally all the recommended cuts, and then allow each dean to defend programs in his or her college that other deans had proposed to cut. After the discussion, he would ask the deans to vote again and to hand their ballots to him without revealing their final recommendations. After listening to the discussion and studying both rounds of balloting, he would make the final cut decisions and communicate them to an open faculty meeting set for three o'clock on Wednesday afternoon.

This process had been communicated to the deans the week before. They understood what Rich wanted them to do. But they didn't do it, and the meeting around the football-shaped table in the rector's conference room ultimately turned into the kind of mutiny that would have been led by Bartleby the Scrivener. When Rich asked the ten deans, Ben still representing Humanities and Social Sciences, to pass over their recommended cuts, they simply didn't do so. The silence that followed his request was broken only by the occasional cough, the squeak of a chair rocking back or the scrape of a shoe on the bare floor that had yet to be re-carpeted.

"OK, guys," Rich said. "What gives?"

Nobody responded until, finally, Engineering Dean Peter Alexander said, "Several deans would like to discuss the proposed procedure itself before we move forward."

Rich didn't usually think this way, but he thought now that he hadn't *proposed* a procedure; he had *set out* a procedure.

"There is disagreement among us on this issue," Alexander continued, "but the majority felt we should discuss the procedure before executing it."

"I see," Rich said.

Rich had spent most of his professional life as a basketball coach whose players and assistants did what he told them. Universities required a more collaborative style, and Rich understood that. But he had no eagerness for the kind of debate now confronting him. Life-changing decisions had to be made, and they had to be presented to the Board of Trustees in little over a week. Rich's restructuring plan had already been presented to the deans, who were supposed to have kept it secret until the departments to be eliminated were incorporated into the proposal. But the reorganization was already being discussed among the faculty. The part of Rich that had been stirred by idealism for most of his life wanted to believe better of the people sitting around the table with him. But some of them would be directly affected by the changes and were obviously angry about it. One of them, perhaps more than one of them, had revealed details about Rich's plan and fanned the fires of the faculty rumor mill. Now this.

"When did you reach the decision to defy my instructions?" Rich asked.

Ben said, "I don't think it's fair to characterize the request for a discussion as defiance."

"I hope not," Alexander said. "I know that some of us have the requested lists with us and have arrived prepared to do what you ask, Rector. I know that I have." He took a folded piece of paper from the inside pocket of his suit jacket and laid it on the table.

"More than one of us have prepared our lists," Ben said.

"I certainly haven't," Pharmacy Dean John Leake said. "I'm losing my deanship. My colleagues are losing their college. This is appalling. Name one other university in America that houses Pharmacy in the same college as Nursing."

Rich said in a tone of controlled flatness, "Pharmacy is *not* being housed with Nursing, John. Both units will simply be led by the same person. There's a difference. Meanwhile, name one other university with a College of Pharmacy that has been hit by a hurricane and forced to cut twenty percent of its budget in one year."

"I don't even know why I'm here," Leake said. "This isn't even my job anymore if this sorry plan goes through."

"You're here, John," Rich said, "because until this sorry plan does go through, you're the Dean of the College of Pharmacy."

"No, I'm not," Leake said. "I'm not the Dean of Pharmacy. She is." He stabbed his finger venomously toward Nursing Dean Rene Walsh.

"You act as if this was my decision, John," Walsh said. "The rector made this decision, not me."

"You have a job to do, John," Rich said. "We all do."

"I *had* a job to do," Leake said.

"Enough," Rich said.

"You know what," Leake said. "Enough is precisely the right word. The very idea of a basketball coach being our rector. I'm not putting up with this one more second." He snatched up the pad that lay on the table in front of him, rose from his chair and strode from the room, slamming the door behind him.

A long stunned silence followed.

"This wasn't supposed to happen," Education Dean Amanda Josef said.

"No, it wasn't," Law School Dean Sharon Meyer concurred.

"Did you have some sort of meeting to discuss what's happening here now?" Rich asked.

"John has been very upset about losing his deanship," Architecture and Urban Planning Dean Shelby Clay said. "Heck, all of us who are losing our leadership posts have. I don't know how I'll be able to get up in the morning if my wife doesn't call me Dean Clay anymore." Clay looked around the table, probably expecting laughter that he hadn't elicited. "Anyway," he continued, "John's been calling all of us repeatedly since last Wednesday. We agreed to meet for breakfast yesterday. We all have our concerns. Apart from ourselves, our faculties are upset about the changes you're proposing."

Rich leaned back in his chair and rubbed two fingers across his lips. "I have several comments about that," he said. "First of all, why are faculty already discussing a plan that hasn't even been finalized? The structural changes I plan to submit to the Board were supposed to have been held in the strictest confidence. But that confidence has obviously been broken by one of you, maybe more. I am not happy about that."

Rich tucked his chin down toward his chest and raised his eyes to each of the nine deans remaining in the room. In turn they darted their eyes away from him.

"In case this hasn't been plain, I am also not happy about what we are being forced to do. I have argued against it with the viceroy and with each member of the Board. But we are being shown no mercy. It has occurred to me that I ought to resign rather than execute this exigency procedure, which is unnecessary given the state's current financial situation. The cuts we are being forced to make are in all ways detrimental to the interest of the people of our city, our current students and our future students. If I thought my resignation would cause the governor, the viceroy and the Board to reverse themselves, I would not hesitate a second before drafting my letter. But I don't think a reversal would result from such a gesture. And I'm pretty sure we'd prefer to manage this ourselves rather than have a restructuring forced on us."

Rich leaned forward to rest his elbows on the table. "I prepared the reorganization plan for the express purpose of sacrificing administrative efficiency in order to save as many faculty and staff jobs as possible. I presented the plan to you and asked for your response. John raised his objection, but the rest of you sat silent. I took your silence as consent."

"I think we were all just stunned," Ben said. "I know I was, and that's why you and I spoke immediately after the meeting."

Sharon Meyer said, "I think all of us but Peter were thrown off balance by the sweeping nature of the restructuring. I was shocked, and to this point the Law School isn't even affected."

"Am I now to gather that John is not the only one who objects?" Rich asked, again looking at each of his deans.

Once more, no one would meet his eyes.

"Your plan has my strongest endorsement," Peter said. "The engineering faculty will not like it, but in a situation this tough, this is a better plan than eliminating more departments and the faculty and staff employed in them."

"Well," Rich said, "I would have liked to have had this discussion last week, but the plan has not been released, so we can have it now. Let me start with this question: can we agree that a restructuring plan that saves twenty-five faculty and fifteen staff positions is superior to remaining structured as we are now?"

Peter and Ben both mumbled, "Yes." The others remained silent.

"Maybe we should have a show of hands," Rich said, and he asked them again if they endorsed the strategy of reorganizing to save jobs.

All raised their hands, including Amanda Josef, whose unit would lose its status as a college under Rich's plan.

"Good," Rich said. "That's a start. Now let's discuss how we might make the plan I presented to you last week more palatable. I am very serious when I say I am open to any suggestions you want to make as long as we save the same number or perhaps even more jobs."

"We could eliminate Athletics," Amanda said.

"It wouldn't save us any money," Rich said.

"Why not?" Rene Walsh inquired.

"The Athletics budget comes largely from a dedicated student fee," Rich said. "We are legally bound to use that fee only for Athletics. It cannot supplement the general fund."

"That's correct," Ben said. He had been a longtime member of the Athletics Council, and he knew how sports funding worked.

"But surely Athletics is funded beyond the proceeds of the dedicated fee," Shirley Johnson said.

"It has been," Rich said. "But my proposal calls for dropping eleven sports. The fee will cover the costs of the remaining four. In fact, it will generate a surplus, which will assist with restart-up costs when this crisis is over and we begin to restore the sports we're cutting now."

"Maybe we just ought to drop all of Athletics anyway," Rene said.

"For what purpose?" Rich asked.

"A demonstration to the faculty," Amanda Josef said. "You know, a demonstration that we have focused on sparing our academic programs."

"But that would be a false and pointless sacrifice," Rich said. "And I am not into empty gestures."

Another round of silence followed Rich's rejection of the idea of reducing intercollegiate athletics beyond what he had already proposed.

"Any other suggestions?" Rich asked.

"We could cut the Law School," Business Dean Adam Cain said.

"Say what?" Sharon Meyer interjected. "You can't be serious."

"I don't feel comfortable saying this in front of you, Sharon," Adam said, "but your professors make the most money far and away. Ettons has a law school. The state law school is at the flagship. So ours isn't really required, and if we cut it, then we wouldn't have to do the other things the rector has proposed. You guys have a salary budget that's way greater than the savings we have on the table now. What's more, your guys are all lawyers, and if we eliminate their teaching jobs, they can go practice."

"That is such a crock of unadulterated shit," Sharon said.

"Frankly, Adam," Shelby said, "what's good for the goose is good for the gander. The only salaries at this university that approximate those in the law school are paid in your college. So let's eliminate the Business School. It's considerably bigger than the Law School, so the savings would be even greater. And your people are all trained business professionals who perpetually claim they could make more money outside the university, so, in actuality, we'd be doing them a financial favor by laying them off."

"That is patently ridiculous," Adam said. "Business has the largest number of undergraduate majors on campus, and our MBA is Urban's largest graduate program."

Sharon said, "And the Law School earns the university an annual *profit* of two point five million dollars. Cut us, and the university is worse off, not better."

"Is this getting us anywhere, Rich?" Ben asked.

"I don't know," Rich said. "I hope we can conclude that whatever we are finally forced to cut, it won't be the Business School or the Law School."

Another round of silence followed. Rich let it linger until everybody in the room was restless with discomfort.

Finally, Rich said, "Are there any more suggestions?"

They looked at him sullenly, each like a child defeated in argument, devoid of further response but bitter to be absent further answers.

"I won't ask you to vote on the proposal," Rich said. "I had hoped you would embrace the reorganization, but despite what I see as the lack of a reasonable alternative, I can see that you don't. I will present it to the faculty on Wednesday as my plan, and you can characterize it that way if you choose."

"I will let my faculty know that I endorse the plan," Peter said.

"I don't really have a faculty anymore, of course," Ben said, "but I'm with you, boss."

The others said nothing.

"All right," Rich said. "However unhappily, we will treat the matter of restructuring as settled. Let's now turn to the original agenda of this meeting which is to work our way toward a programmatic cut list. However difficult the reorganization, we were talking of ways to save jobs. Now we're going to need to address the far more painful decision about who we're going to put out of work. So let's turn to the lists I asked you to make."

The silence that had dominated the day's meeting reigned, and the deans twisted about in their chairs as if each was trying to stretch out a knotted muscle.

"I didn't prepare a list," Sharon said. "Your instructions said to list programs in the other colleges, but I just didn't feel qualified to make such a judgment. I mean, what we do in the Law School is so different."

"I felt the same way," Adam said.

"Me too," Rene said.

"I could have made a list about some of the colleges," Amanda said, "but I feel incompetent to comment on anything in Pharmacy, Nursing and Law."

"You have all ranked your own programs from top to bottom," Rich said. "If I were to take one program from each of you, I would know your recommendation. But if we are to be strategic, then perhaps we should take more than one program from some colleges and none from others. I had hoped, as academic leaders, in the painful service of the whole university, you would assist me in making the worst, most objectionable decision of my life."

"Well, that's just it, Rector," Shirley said. "You asked me to make a list of programs I'd cut outside of Arts and Music. And I did. But I have no confidence in it. In the end, and I think I speak for most of us, I just think it needs to be your call."

If only slightly, heads nodded around the table.

"Is that the consensus, then?" Rich asked.

"You can certainly have my list, Rector," Peter said, sliding the folded sheet of paper across the table.

"Thank you," Rich said, moving the paper in front of him.

"I'll get you mine," Ben said. He pointed at his temple. "I brought it up here."

"Anybody else?" Rich asked. "Shirley, you made a list. Whatever your reservations, would you mind sharing it with me?"

She looked first at her colleagues and then down at the table. "I'd prefer not to," she said.

45

By July of 1676, Bradford's relentless pursuit kept us from establishing any settlement and therefore from acquiring any chance of long-term survival. Those still with me were reduced to staging raids on poorly defended villages and isolated farms to capture whatever food we could find. We endured desertions on a daily basis as individual warriors and their families peeled away in hopes of finding some place of refuge where they might find hunting or a path to the sea. Many, many of these people were swept up in Church's dragnet as the Sakonnet scouts identified recently traveled trails to small camps made by people no longer possessing the strength to fight.

Church became a great hero during this time and bragged about his exploits for the rest of his life, finally gathering all his self-aggrandizement into his book *Entertaining Passages Related to King Philip's War*, a collection of embellished tales designed to capture the same market which made a bestseller

of Mary Rowlandson's myopic, self-pitying jeremiad. Church
was celebrated by his fellow Plymouthites because he brought
in far more captives than did Bradford, and he was hailed, by
himself for certain, as the man who brought King Philip's War
to a close. What Church really accomplished was becoming the
largest individual slaver in the history of New England.

My spirits fell lower when, on one of our raids, my warriors
killed Hezekiah Willet, a young Englishman who lived not far
from Montaup Peninsula. I had known Hezekiah since he was
a child. My father was a particular friend of his family, and not
long before his death Massassoit had made me and Wamsutta
promise that we would always be respectful, kind and loyal to
the Willets. Now a white man who had done me no harm, a
man I would never have ordered attacked, had been killed by
men under my command. War is a self-sustaining maelstrom,
easy to unleash but stoppable only by catastrophic dying. I was
no longer able to imagine any acceptable ending for this war
that had turned tauntingly against us. So Hezekiah Willet, a
decent, innocent person, died for nothing whatsoever.

And yet my sadness about Hezekiah's death tormented
me over the hypocrisy of my own feelings. We were starving.
Our only access to food lay in the larders of white men who
had come into our country unbidden. My men raided farms
like Hezekiah's for days, with my permission and under my
direction. We had been sacking whole towns throughout New
England for over a year. Many had died at the hands of men I
had sent to shoot, to bludgeon, to cut and to burn. Some of
them were our true enemies. But some were not. How many,
like Hezekiah Willet, were not? I did not choose this war they
named for me. But how many innocent lives had I taken in
resisting that which was thrust upon me? How does one define
innocence, and how does one define victim? Can those who
stand on the other side ever be innocent, even if they point no
musket in your direction? Can those who do not stand beside
you ever be victim?

Who knows the answers to such questions when the sanctity of life is no longer acknowledged? Willet was not my enemy, but neither was he my ally. And so what do we conclude? How about this: no matter the righteousness of defense, killing is still killing. And I had sent my men to kill those whose skin was lighter than our own. And in doing so, how much had I let Josiah Winslow trap me into thinking about the world in terms like his own?

WE MADE PLANS FOR another attack on Taunton. But Church intercepted us, killing my uncle Akkompoin and scores of others. My warriors were so weak with hunger and fatigue from constant flight, they could not hold their muskets steady enough to draw bead on Church's troops. With only forty men, twenty-two of them now well-fed Sakonnets under his command, Church was able to take 173 Wampanoags and Narragansetts prisoner. We were defeated, but what were we to do? If we surrendered, the lucky ones among us would be those they executed. The unlucky ones would be sold into slavery to live out short, miserable lives in the brutal sugar fields of the West Indies.

Our only course, then, was to try to choose the location of our dying. Each of us still alive chose home. Totoson returned to the Sakonnet country he had abandoned when Awashonks turned on me. Quinnapin led what few of his people remained with him back to Narragansett country. Though she knew that she would likely fall to either Bradford or Church, Weetamoo set out to reach Pocasset. With Annawon at my side, I went to my ancestral Montaup. All of us sought to breathe our last on the soil from which we sprang.

The end came swiftly. Early in *Lawawkesos* of the year the English numbered 1676, on August 6, Weetamoo was spotted trying to cross the Taunton River and in trying to dodge the bullets of our enemies, fell into the water and drowned. When the English found her body, they cut off her head and displayed it on a stake in the town square at Taunton. Or, at least, that's the way the English have preserved the story. They note that when her body was discovered Weetamoo was naked, but that fact is never commented upon.

What really happened was that a squad of Bradford's men caught Weetamoo with just five warriors in her immediate party. The English killed Weetamoo's security team. Then they stripped her naked and bade her to dance for their amusement. She refused. So they beat her and a dozen of them raped her. This was not common in the war they named for me. We did not condone raping the women of our enemies. And neither did the white men of New England at the time. So throughout the war, the instances of rape were few. But Weetamoo, my beautiful sister-in-law, was a despised antagonist, a defiant warrior queen. And when she would not bow to their determination to humiliate her, they taught her the lesson they judged she needed. She was just a woman. And she was put to the use for which women were brought into the world.

Weetamoo passed out while being brutalized, and they left her, still naked, unconscious, on the ground overnight. She never awoke. The next morning, fearful that their violation of taboo might be discovered, they threw her body into the river. Weetamoo was my brother's wife and my wife's sister. She was twice my own blood. She was an emblem of our unyielding resistance. She was as good and as true and as brave a person as has ever been. You knew too little of it in your lifetime, dear sister, but may your journey in this next life be one of peace.

Weetamoo's last husband, Quinnapin, was captured shortly after he arrived in Narragansett country. He was executed in Newport on August 25. People who had known and traded with him for years said that he was so gaunt they weren't certain of his identity.

Matoonas was betrayed and taken prisoner by Sagamore John, then brought into Boston. To crown his treachery and earn a pardon for himself, Sagamore John tied Matoonas to a tree on the Commons and shot him to death with an English musket.

Not long later, Sagamore Sam also sought a pardon by luring Muttaump and the rest of the Nipmuck leadership to Boston with the promise of peace negotiations. Sagamore Sam's treason bought him nothing. He was in the line of Nipmucks who were marched before a firing squad and executed on August 27.

The great Totoson, who led our attack on Dartmouth that allowed the bulk of us to escape from Pocasset Swamp, grieving over the death of his malnourished and enfeebled eight-year-old son, lay down in the forest one night, starving himself, and never awoke.

Some of these outlived me, though not by long, and not meaningfully. The end of the war was proclaimed when English lead, fired from the musket held by John Alderman, a Praying Pocasset, serving with the forces of Big Mouth Benjamin Church, sent me finally, gratefully, into the dirt. As the word of my demise spread, church bells rang throughout New England. And the English congratulated themselves that they were the Almighty's Elect, and I was the banished Satan Incarnate.

But there were sour notes in the hosannas they sang to themselves. This war they had named for and blamed on me had cost them the lives of nearly ten percent of their male population, a greater percentage of their young men under age thirty. To put that loss in perspective, the male death rate during the bloody American Civil War, counting the casualties on both sides, was less than half what the English suffered in 1675 and 1676. Had the United States suffered comparable battle deaths in World War II, the body count would have come to nearly five and a half million, rather than the actual figure of under 300,000. And the libelously designated King Philip's War had cost the Puritans treasure in proportions so great that they would not approach the same level of per capita income they enjoyed before attacking me for an entire century.

But compared with us, of course, the English losses were negligible. They sacrificed much in their greed to get our land. But we lost everything trying to defend it. Eighty percent of our population either died or was sold into slavery. Most of those who survived unchained moved either north or west as fast as they could go, not always warmly received by the native peoples who resided in those locations first. Narragansett Country and Montaup Peninsula, the entire coast of Narragansett Bay, once so vibrant with the fullness of human life, were left barren of their indigenous populations.

46

With input from only two of his ten deans, trying to preserve areas of academic strength while maximizing his dollar savings, hardly always overlapping objectives, Rich decided to cut Anthropology, Chemical Engineering, Classics, Economics, Finance, Geology, Mass Communications, Nursing Administration, Physical Education, Social Work and Special Education. Seventy-nine faculty were to be terminated, including fifty-four tenured professors. Nineteen staff members who worked in those departments were also to be laid off.

He would rather have amputated a leg.

At three o'clock on March 23, Rich met with the Urban faculty in the largest functioning room on campus, the still uncarpeted King Auditorium in Building 9. The room had seats for 505, but people were seated down all the aisle steps and were standing crowded together in the back of the room. Rich estimated there were at least 650 people in attendance. Earlier in the day, he had emailed a copy of his exigency plan to all faculty and staff, and the room was full of people who were facing layoffs at the end of the semester. Those who had survived the cuts were there as well, some sympathetic to and supportive of what Rich had to do, most not.

A general hubbub arose as Rich made his way to the front of the room. As he took his position at the lectern, a round of applause broke out, followed immediately by hisses and boos. Rich waited until they quieted. Then, he outlined the major points in his exigency plan, both the restructuring and the program terminations. He stated that he despised having to do this, but that he had been ordered to do so by the governor and the Board of Trustees. Rich hoped that those who survived this holocaust would be relieved and grateful for the structural changes that saved a significant number of jobs.

To the contrary, once the exigency plan was revealed in its entirety, those who remained employed were as outraged as those who were terminated. Several professors in programs that required statistics insisted that they had to have their own professors do the teaching. Numerous voices in those colleges that were to be merged into others demanded that the decision be reversed. An Education professor waved a letter she claimed had the signature of everyone in her college decrying Rich's having humiliated Amanda Josef by "downgrading their college" to a school and having forced her resignation. The faculty in the surviving Engineering departments had signed a petition insisting that they not be "subordinated" to the Science programs, that their college be reinstated, and that the chair of Civil Engineering be designated their dean, since, the petition stated, the Civil Engineering chair "had been in line for the deanship for years."

After listening to a series of these complaints and demands, some of which he answered directly, Rich reiterated his regret and emphasized how frustrated and bitter he was to have had to prepare the document he had sent them earlier in the day.

"Yeah, but you sent it, didn't you," someone called out. Rich didn't see who said it and didn't recognize the voice.

"Well, I have sent it to you," Rich said. "I have shown it to the deans and vice rectors. Nobody who has seen it likes it very much. But I have not yet presented it to the Board of Trustees. That is scheduled for a week from today."

"If this is all just *fait accompli*," someone called out, "why are we having this meeting?"

"The proposal isn't final until it's approved by the Board," Rich replied.

"Why haven't faculty been involved in this process?" someone else called out.

"Faculty have been involved," Rich said. "As soon as we were informed by Viceroy Lipscom that we had to make cuts, former Provost Lagasse and I met with the academic deans and asked them to meet with their department chairs and with the faculties of their colleges. They did so. Faculty input was solicited at every stage."

"I don't recall being asked to vote on doing away with the College of Engineering," someone said.

Rich responded, "We haven't voted on anything. It is inconceivable to me that we *could* have voted on anything. No one would have voted to eliminate his own department or the department of his friend. Who would? And yet we have to submit a plan that cuts twenty-eight million dollars from next year's budget. I don't want to make these cuts, but I am forced to."

"We understand this whole plan is yours and yours alone," someone said.

"I take full responsibility for the plan," Rich said. "I took advice from many people, but the final decision is mine."

Peter Alexander stood up. "For those of you who don't know me, I am Peter Alexander, Dean of Engineering. I am one of the people whose advice the rector both sought and took. I recommended Engineering be combined with Science in a college led by only one dean."

"Traitor," someone called out.

"Shame. Shame on you," another voice said.

A slightly built, tawny-skinned man stood up and said with a heavy accent, "I address this to both Dean Alexander and Rector Janus. My name is Abeer Mahbudin. I am assistant professor of Chemical Engineering. Your document eliminate my job and my salary. I have wife and two children. How will I live now? You must show me. Our apartment. All lost in storm. I ask please Dean, please Rector, do not do this. How will I live?"

"I am profoundly sorry, Professor Mahbudin," Rich said. "It is very little consolation, I know, but Dean Alexander and I will do everything we can to help you find another position."

John Leake jumped to his feet and said in a loud voice, "Are you going to help me find another position, Mr. Rector? How are you going to manage that since this university runs the only Pharmacy program in the state?"

"Your position as a faculty member hasn't been terminated, John," Rich said. "In fact, the plan as currently drafted does not include the elimination of any faculty positions in Pharmacy."

"But I am not a *faculty* member in the College of Pharmacy," Leake said. "I am *Dean* of Pharmacy. And I presume I will be relegated to a faculty member's nine-month salary, a vicious cut in pay for someone who has served this university with distinction for over three decades."

"Frankly, John," Rich said, "you and I both know that with thirty-four years of service, which you will have at the end of this semester, you would make more money from the State Employees Retirement System than by continuing to work. If you think it is beneath you to teach, you can retire and improve your financial situation with one signature."

"You have just spoken publicly about a private matter, *Rector* Janus," Leake said, eyes gleaming, "and you will rue the day you have done so in front of this many witnesses. I am going to sue this university for violation of my privacy rights, and I am going to sue you personally."

With that threat, Leake made a departure from the room that was a lot less dramatic than he would have liked because he was sitting in the middle of a row and had to climb over a half dozen people just to reach the aisle where his way was blocked by the people seated there. So instead of an indignant stalk, his exit was a series of stumbles. Remarkably, as far as Rich was concerned, given that the cruel axe of exigency hadn't fallen on any of them, a lot of Pharmacy faculty walked out with him.

As Leake was leaving, Economics Professor Sean Macreedy stood up. He didn't identify himself, but Rich knew who he was because he had repeatedly filed grievances against his chair after receiving the lowest raises in his department. "I want you to look at this face, Richard Janus," he said. "Mr. *Basketball* Rector. Look at this face closely. I have taught here for seventeen years, and you are putting me on the street. You are taking food from my mouth and a roof from over my head. I have a son and a daughter in college. Who is going to pay their tuition now? We all feel sorry for Professor Mahbudin who spoke earlier. But he doesn't have tenure. I have tenure. What gives you the right to take that away from me?"

"Unfortunately for you and me both, Professor Macreedy," Rich said, quietly, "the State of Alkansea Board of Trustees for Higher Education has given me the power and the responsibility to cut twenty-eight million dollars out of our budget. You and your family are among the many who are affected. I so wish this wasn't happening."

"Yeah," Macreedy said, "Your decisions have cost me my job. They'll cost you your soul."

"The problem for me, sir," Rich said, "is that I fear you may be right."

CALLY WAS PRESENT FOR the pain and acrimony in King Hall, and she and Rich rode home from campus largely in silence. Later, as they ate dinner and sat afterwards in their reading chairs in the den, they discussed what had happened. She didn't try to sugarcoat the horror of what Rich had endured. But she did insist that he had handled himself well. He had faced up to the attacks, had fielded hot questions with calm answers, had met accusations with explanations and always with an expression of regret, which no one in the room could conceivably disbelieve. Rich drank constantly as they talked, first at dinner, then in the den. He mixed his Scotch with water, but by the time Cally went to bed at 10:30, he had killed half a fifth of Black and White. By the time he went to bed two hours later, the bottle was empty.

He awoke at 3:45 with tingling in his left arm. He thought he had trapped it under his body as he slept. The pains in his chest started shortly later. He felt as if a huge weight was pressing down on him, something as heavy as a car, he felt, compressing his diaphragm and blocking his ability to breathe. He woke Cally, and she rushed him to the hospital, where they immediately put him on a heparin drip and no doubt prevented a far more serious heart attack. Later that morning they performed an angiogram, discovered a blockage and then cleared it with angioplasty. The only good news was that he had evidently sustained no lasting damage to the heart muscle. But before releasing him to go home on the following Monday, the doctors told him that his blood pressure was dangerously high and that he had to take actions to reduce stress. They wrote him prescriptions for the blood pressure medicines Diovan and Verapamil and for the blood thinner Coumadin. And they recommended that he take an immediate vacation.

But he did not. How could he?

On Wednesday, two days out of the hospital, Rich drove to Mayflower to present his exigency document to the Board. Cally went along to provide moral support. She knew the Board meeting was going to generate the very kind of stress Rich ought to be avoiding, but even she couldn't figure out a way for him to hand off this duty.

Before distributing copies of his proposal, Rich asked to address the Board on what was about to happen. The viceroy replied with unveiled impatience that Rich could have three minutes. Rich quickly listed ten Urban programs that were ranked higher than those in the same areas at ASU, though he did not point this out. He simply stated national rankings

for his top ten departments and compared Urban's rankings in
those programs to their competitors at such bellwether places
as Vanderbilt and Duke and such flagship public institutions as
the Universities of North Carolina, Virginia and Florida. All
these programs would survive the cuts forthcoming he said, but
the overall university was being damaged in a way that it could
not recover from for many years. When he finished, not one
Board member made a single comment. They didn't even ask
him where the departments at ASU ranked, compared to those
he had listed for Urban. Their interest in Urban didn't include
enough curiosity to stimulate them to do so.

Rich then distributed copies and outlined the proposal's
principal provisions. When he finished, the Board members
pawed through pages for a few seconds before one of the
Trustees moved that Rich's proposal be accepted. No other
comments were made. In one fell swoop, they laid off well over a
hundred individuals including fifty-four professors with tenure
and embraced a plan that reduced Urban's colleges from ten to
five and eliminated eleven departments.

At the end of the meeting, as he always did, the viceroy
sang out "Go Monsters" as he banged down the dismissing
gavel. Urban, an institution that had been compared at birth to
UCLA, had just been exposed to crude amputation and was left
crippled for the foreseeable future. But no one with the power
to have stopped the operation seemed even to notice.

Rich was so disgusted with the entire proceedings that
he wanted to get out of the Board of Trustees Building, and
Mayflower entirely, just as quickly as he could. But Elia Lipscom
stopped Rich and asked him up to his office, telling Cally where
she could find a soft drink machine. Elia then took Rich by
himself into his office.

"I got some bad news for you, Coach," Lipscom said when
they were seated.

"Different bad news than what we just went through?" Rich
asked.

"'Fraid so."

"I don't have a firstborn for you to take, Elia."

Lipscom laughed. "Like that sense of humor. Black, but still a sense of humor. Born of experience, huh? Even with a record like yours, you got beat a lot over the years. Am I right?"

"I've never had a loss like this. No. Never in my career. Nothing like it at all."

"Well, sorry to stack this on top. Especially since we'd heard you had a little scare over the weekend."

"Who told you I had a scare over the weekend?" Rich asked.

"Oh, we've got our sources. I wouldn't be much of a viceroy if I didn't have some reliable people on all my campuses."

"Nice, Elia."

"It is nice, isn't it? Very helpful to know if I'm getting the straight poop from the people who report to me."

"I've always been straightforward with you, Elia."

"Yeah, you probably have." Lipscom laughed. "Not always to your advantage, I must say. We've managed to be pretty civil. But I will confess your doggedness could really piss me off sometimes."

"So what's the additional bad news?" Rich asked.

"Sorry to tell you this, Coach, but come July 1, we're gonna go in a different direction."

Rich was embarrassedly slow to understand what he was being told.

"I'm afraid you didn't find much support on the search committee," Lipscom added.

Finally Rich got it, and it sucked the air out of him for a second.

"The Urban Rector Search Committee," Lipscom said.

"I see," Rich finally managed.

"People on your campus gave you a lot of credit for getting the school opened up again last fall, but that wasn't an opinion shared by many of the folks up these ways."

"Kept the vultures from shutting us down," Rich said. "I'll wear that badge for a long time."

"I'll give you that," Lipscom said. "Though you might have played it the go-along way and come out ahead. Never know. Certain people on the Board felt you opened that school back up without their permission."

"I'll wear that as a badge of honor too."

"You're a bullheaded S.O.B.; I'll sure give you that."

"So I'm done as rector June 30," Rich said.

"Well, technically. You'll keep the title till then. You can do the ribbon cutting stuff and the public face appearances. Whatever you want in that regard. Or not is OK too. It's really up to you. I understand your doctors have recommended a vacation, and I think you definitely deserve one. So we'll go ahead and transfer day-to-day power to your successor right away."

"Right away, meaning?"

"Well," Lipscom said, looking at a wall clock which read 5:05, "five minutes ago actually."

Rich laughed with shock. He felt so ashamed. He knew he had poked people in the eye a few times. And he knew the exigency process had turned campus admirers into enemies. But he had not seen this coming, and he felt like a complete fool. People sneered at him as "Coach," and he now realized that they were right to. He came out of the world of athletics, which absolutely had its share of assholes, bullies, blowhards, fakers and cheats. But sport was still a world where openness and hard work could produce success. You couldn't politic an L into a W. But being a university CEO, particularly a campus head at a public university, was almost entirely about political maneuvering. Rich realized that at times. But just as often he'd ignored it. Paying it too little heed, he'd not calculated when he should have, not kissed all the ass he should have, so the poisonous snake of politics coiled in the grass waiting for him, struck when it had the chance, and he was incautiously and deservedly dead.

"I didn't even make the short list," Rich said.

"No," Lipscom agreed.

"I didn't even realize y'all had done interviews."

"Well, we didn't. Under the circumstances, exigency and all, people pretty riled up down there, the committee felt we would just go ahead and get the candidate we wanted in place."

"And he takes over immediately."

"As executive vice rector, yes. Until July 1. We can talk now or later about how we want to release all this to the public. I can announce publicly that a provision of your serving as interim rector was that you would not be a candidate for the position. That *was* the original deal. So it wouldn't even be a lie. It'll probably leak that you *did* apply for the position, but you could deny that, and I'll back you up. We could say that you *offered* to serve until a successor was appointed. That would counter the application leak."

"Why would I want to do any of that?" Rich asked.

"I'm just trying to help you save face, Coach."

"Only place I need to save face is when I look in the mirror."

Lipscom laughed. "Nice line. Why you didn't get the job, but goddamned nice line."

"My successor must be someone currently at Urban," Rich said.

"Yes."

"Ben Turner," Rich said.

Lipscom laughed again. "Good guess, Coach. How'd you know?"

"Aside from Cally, Ben is the only person at Urban who knows I've been in the hospital."

RICH WAS NUMB ON the drive home. He had surprised himself by taking to his job as Urban's rector, surprised himself in wanting it permanently and ultimately wanting it badly. He thought back to his days in college, always expecting to be a university professor, and his days in graduate school planning to devote his professorial career, or at least its beginning, to writing about me, then, the long years of doing something else entirely, something he loved.

Rich enjoyed coaching basketball so much he hadn't ever imagined he would want to give it up. And even when he accepted Francis Saurian's cockeyed plan to become Urban's provost, he nurtured in the back of his mind that he'd return to coaching some day. Dreamed about it quite often. Dreamed of the smell of the hardwood and the ingrained sweat of the locker room. Dreamed of himself once again with a whistle around his neck and his arm draped over the soaking shoulders of a player to whom he was offering instructions.

But then, especially after Saurian resigned and Rich became rector, he fell in love with that too. Or better, he fell in love with Urban University, with its students, with its role in educating the broad spectrum of middle- and working-class students in Choctaw who wouldn't otherwise get college degrees. The challenge was different than that of running a basketball program. The job was bigger and more complicated, and its rules were less clear. Ultimately, he judged, he just wasn't up to it.

In his playing days, Rich always had a good jump shot. And so long ago in a Division II league, he was big enough at only 6'3" to take his man down low and work a little bit of the power game. He was a good passer too. With the right partner, he could make a killing on the pick and roll. But he was never more than average as a ball handler. So he turned it over more than he wanted. And he wasn't elusive enough to take it to the hole through a crowd. His strengths were focus, will, and the discipline to stay within himself. These traits made him a successful small-college basketball player. And they made him a good coach. But they didn't serve him well as a university CEO. He wasn't a good glad-hander. And that crucial lack of elusiveness was a killer.

Rich had wanted to succeed as Urban's rector. And he clearly hadn't. Not because he hadn't been appointed rector on a permanent basis, but, far more important, because he hadn't won the war with the Board of Trustees. Whatever it took, he didn't have it. Such was the analysis Rich shared with Cally as they drove back to Choctaw.

Cally would have none of it. "You're blaming yourself for the failures of others."

"No," he argued. "That's not what I'm doing. I am who I am. I don't think I could have played my cards any other way."

"Exactly," she said. "The cards were stacked against you."

"They were. I agree. The cards have been stacked against Urban since the day of its creation. Everybody in Alkansea would benefit if Urban became the state's UCLA, but the only people who believe that are at Urban, or at least in Choctaw, and they don't have the power to make it come true in the face of the withering opposition in Mayflower."

"So how can you see your not being named rector on a permanent basis as *your* fault?" she asked. "As the product of something lacking in yourself?"

"I think it's like this," Rich said. "Urban needs somebody who can take the stacked cards and win anyway. I couldn't do it."

"Jesus, you're an idiot," Cally said. "If the storm hadn't come along, if the Governor hadn't panicked, if the Board hadn't forced us into exigency, you might well have been named rector, and you would have done an excellent job. Led us toward that UCLA goal."

"No I wouldn't," Rich said. "I would have done the best job I could. I wouldn't have had all the people on campus hating me because I developed a restructuring plan they despise. But I wouldn't have succeeded in turning us into UCLA. That's what I would have tried to do, and I wouldn't have succeeded."

"Because they wouldn't let you, Rich. Because they wouldn't let you."

"No, they wouldn't. But that's no excuse. To have a chance to move forward, I had to make the governor or the Board or somebody in this state see the right thing and do it, and that was to provide us enough emergency funding so we could avoid gutting the place. My job was to convince them of that, and I didn't get it done."

"What if Marilynn Williams comes through with that one hundred fifty million you two talked about at Beatrice Florin's? Then you will have succeeded."

Rich laughed, "From your lips to God's ears."

THE NEXT DAY, RICH and Ben talked about the transition. They sat across from each other on the two facing sofas in the rector's office that Rich had not changed since he'd taken over from Francis Saurian. Each had a cup of coffee that Rich poured from the pot he kept simmering all day long. He wasn't supposed to be drinking coffee, but that didn't stop him.

"I didn't think you were a candidate," Ben said. "When I applied, I understood that Elia appointed you interim with the express condition that you *not* become a candidate."

"That was the original understanding."

"Thank goodness," Ben said. "If I'd known you'd applied, I wouldn't have."

"I told Lipscom in January that I'd decided I'd like to keep the job. Told you too, if you recall." Rich shrugged. "Anyway, Elia agreed to let me apply."

Ben laughed. "Your star was shining brightly in January, but I'd applied myself by then."

"I only thought it was a star," Rich said. "Asteroid is more like it. Meteor, actually."

"Well, you can't expect to remain popular when you're firing people and changing things in ways folks don't like. If you'd managed to hold everybody with you, I'd have dropped out."

Rich felt certain this wasn't true, but he didn't say so.

"When do you want to swap offices?" Rich asked. "I can have my stuff cleared out of here in an hour. Less. Most of my books are still in Cecilia's office anyway. Yours, that is."

"Swap offices?" Ben said. "What do you mean?"

"Lipscom explained that he's already appointed you executive vice rector with day-to-day authority over the campus. Said I'm to do the public stuff until July 1. That doesn't make a lick of sense to me. The public side of this job isn't even my long suit. You're better at it; you ought to do it. Starting right now. Lipscom says he wants to help me save face. But that seems a pointless charade to me. You have the authority now; you should have the title too. I'll just go back to my job as provost. I liked that well enough."

Ben sighed deeply, sipped his coffee and held the cup in front of his face for a moment before setting it back down on the coffee table. "Well, that's something we need to talk about then," he said. "Just like Elia. He was supposed to fill you in, but apparently he didn't."

Rich felt like a fighter already reeling from one thunderous blow who fails to see the punch that knocks him out. "I'm not going to be provost, either," he said.

Turner made an exaggerated face and clicked his front teeth together. "If I'm going to have half a chance to pull this place back together," he said, "then I've got to shed as much of the exigency baggage as I can."

"Meaning me," Rich said. "The embodiment of exigency baggage."

"Not the best choice of words," Turner acknowledged but then added, "but you'll admit you're not the most popular guy on campus."

Rich laughed dryly. "No, I guess I'm not."

"Rotten shame, of course," Ben said. "Completely unfair and all."

"But there it is."

"Yes," Ben said. "There it is. And I wouldn't be fair to myself and what I hope to accomplish by saddling myself with all the hostility that's directed at you by keeping you on as my number two." He picked up his cup and drank from it again. "I'm sure you understand."

Rich understood that he was a naïve idiot, that loyalty was a virtue little known in the contemporary world.

"So who are you going to bring in?" Rich asked.

"I've asked Amanda," Ben said.

"She'll have to back out on the job at Middle Tennessee."

"She has."

"Already?"

"Well, we need to hit the ground running."

"Then you've known about this for a while."

"Well, yes. I thought Elia was going to explain to you yesterday how things would go."

"I see. So, given the way Amanda kept our restructuring plan confidential, I will probably start getting condolences and raspberries about the time this meeting concludes."

Turner laughed. "I agree she's going to have to learn to zip her lip. But she brings a lot to the table. The way I look at it, it's always a good idea to get some split tail in the upper administration. Keeps the beaver contingent out in the paddies confident their interests are being looked after and therefore happy to just slather more mud on their little academic dams. And with Amanda as provost, I can at least halfway settle down the Education people. They'll never forgive you for demoting them from a college to a school."

"If you're going to make Amanda the provost," Rich said, "you could have Education report directly to her instead of through the Graduate School."

"I thought of that," Ben said. "But I don't want to give anybody the idea that we can revisit the plan you just got approved by the Board."

"But you could do that at the next Board meeting. Those guys don't give a shit who reports where down here. You ask them to do that, the only danger you'd encounter is the storm of halitosis as they yawn in your face."

Ben laughed. "But you're missing my point. If I tinker with one thing, then by implication I can tinker with lots of things. The Education people don't like what you did to them. But the Pharmacy people don't like what you did to *them*. And the Engineers. And everybody with a friend in one of the departments that you cut, which is to say, *every*body. I change something for one group, pretty soon I've got a line from here to the lake wanting to dismantle the whole exigency plan. And you had to make the cuts because you had to balance the budget. So better to leave the whole thing intact."

Rich took notice of Ben's casting of the cuts as belonging to Rich alone, and he realized that Ben fully well intended to preserve the cuts because without relief from the Board and the Governor, the cuts were necessary. At the same time, Rich realized that Ben would never embrace the cuts publicly but always blame them on the "faulty decision-making" of the "previous administration," that is, on Rich. Ben would use what Rich had done, all the while decrying it as heartless and miscalculated. Rich started to point this out, but sighed and let it go.

"So what do you have in mind for me?" Rich asked instead.

"Well," Ben said and laughed a single ha. "I thought about asking you to take over the basketball team again."

"I wouldn't push the kid out," Rich said. "Chuck stepped up when Jimmy bailed on us, and he deserves his shot."

"Chuck will announce his resignation before the end of business today. Jimmy has been offered the top spot at Oklahoma State, and he's bringing Chuck up as associate head coach."

"Chuck is giving up a head coaching position to become an assistant again?" Rich asked.

"Head coaching position at a school in financial exigency," Ben said. "Recruiting has been a bitch. Everybody we compete against is telling kids that we may close down. You know all that as well as I do. Better. But, anyway, Jimmy says this is his last stop, three, four years only, five at the most. Once he steps down, the job is Chuck's. That's the deal. Chuck figures it's the fast lane to the Big Twelve. Seems to him a surer bet than staying here and having to win enough games to get hired at a place like Oklahoma State."

"So you're serious about asking me to go back to the Arena?" Rich said, Charlie Brown allowing Lucy to tee up the football one more time.

"Unfortunately, no," Ben said. "I've given this a lot of thought. I've kicked it around with Elia for a couple of hours. If we were going to stay with an athletics program, I'd be begging you to step in and plug the gap. But I think we have to let the whole of athletics go."

"You're not serious," Rich said, shocked and alarmed.

"I'm not happy," Ben said. "But I'm serious."

"Why in the fuck are you doing this? It's purposeless. You know as well as I do that it won't save us any money."

"It's not about the money at this point," Ben said. "Your cuts have got the budget in balance. So it's not about that."

"So what's it fucking about?"

"It's about how we get the people at this institution turned and marching in the same direction. They hate what you've done. And they look and see that you wiped out eleven academic departments but you didn't wipe out the Athletics Department and it pisses them off. They think you did it because you used to be the basketball coach."

"I shut down all but four sports," Rich said.

"Yeah, but the four you left are the only ones they knew about anyway, so to them you didn't do anything to athletics at all."

"I left those four sports in place because they're the ones the students care most about. And I left them in place because with our five-year waiver from the NCAA we can remain a Division I institution. Go ask Hart how important Division I is for recruiting, not athletes, but everyday kids looking to major in accounting or biology or English or civil engineering. Kids don't even know what it means exactly, but they know they want to go to a Division I school."

"People know that Hart says that, Rich, but they think he says it because *you* want to hear it. Because you used to be the basketball coach and because you still sit center court and cheer louder than anybody else at all the games."

"That is unadulterated bullshit," Rich said. "And you of all people fucking well know it."

"Bullshit is beside the point. People are completely pissed off. They hate the exigency plan. And I need to give them something. They want athletics; I'm giving them athletics."

"They only think they want that, Ben. They're scared, and they're angry. But they don't really want to teach and work at an institution so damaged that it had to give up one of its most public emblems. You'd go broke trying to buy the ink an athletic program brings the university for free. Every time one of our teams plays out of town, that's a host of free ads directed at every high school kid who reads a newspaper, listens to the radio or watches TV. I promise you, it's going to hurt general student recruiting, and that's going to cripple the grow-back that's our only long term hope for recovery."

Ben shrugged. "I hope you're wrong."

"I know I'm right," Rich said. "Please listen to me. Don't do this."

"It's already done. Elia and I agreed this was the best way to pull the university together."

"I hope you're not operating under the deluded presumption that Elia Lipscom has the first, tiniest, remotest concern for the wellbeing of Urban University."

"Elia is my boss, OK. He thinks we should do this. He thinks it will provide me a boost of support as I take the reins. I think he's right."

"He's mostly right for himself. Every time we beat ASU in any sport, the people in Mayflower turn purple. Every time a kid they recruit signs up with us, they get apoplectic. They tried to stop us from having athletics in the first place, and they'd love to shut our programs down. They don't call 'em Monsters for nothing. Elia is getting you to do what he hasn't got the balls to do himself. You do this, and you'll go down in the history of this school as the rector who dumped athletics. Whatever recovery you manage to orchestrate, and doing this will make it tougher – mark my words – whatever you accomplish, you'll be known forever as the rector who dumped athletics. Don't do this, man. You should refuse the job rather than do this."

"I suppose you'd refuse the job rather than do this," Ben said.

"You goddamn well know I would."

"And you didn't get the job, did you?"

47

In my last days, heartbroken and eager for the release from sorrow the Creator devised for us when he invented death, I made my way across the uprise at the tip of Montaup Peninsula. Several of my very good men had survived to be with me, my first captain Annawon among them. We were fewer than twenty now, and we were cornered. We knew this. We knew that we measured our time among the silver maple, black birch and white oak of our home in days and shortly hours. The despicable Benjamin Church and his men came at dawn on August 12. We fought to the end, but we had no strength and no chance. The ball of metal that tore through my chest granted me final discharge from the onerous duty of resistance. It is said that the bullet tore my heart apart. But I had no heart left to destroy.

The English dragged my body through the mud like that of a slaughtered hog pulled from the sty. That righteous Christian hero Benjamin Church declared that I was such a vile man I was not to be buried but left to rot, my flesh to be picked at by birds and nested in by vermin. He ordered me drawn and quartered. And so I was disemboweled and beheaded, and the rest of my body hatcheted into four parts. Church then ordered that my right hand be chopped off and given to the Praying Pocasset traitor John Alderman as a trophy for shooting me. My head they fetched away with them to Plymouth where it was displayed on a stake not far from where Miles Standish placed the head of Wituwamat a half century earlier. Soon, the heads of Annawon and Tuspaquin would flank mine. Those of my colleagues were taken down after a time, but mine was left to fester and then to blanch in the Plymouth sun, snow and rain for an entire generation.

THOUGH I RESISTED TILL the end, death came to me not as defeat but as escape. By the time the English bullet put me out of my misery, I had lost everything that mattered. I stopped breathing on August 12, 1676, but I died on August 2.

We had just taken another in a series of defeats. We were starving and sick. And those few of us who remained had concluded that what slim hopes we had required that we part with one another, those who had clung together and fought side by side for so long. The parting was wrenching, for the hardship had made us close, had spawned friendships, between me and Quinnapin, for instance, where none had existed before the war, had tightened bonds, between me and Weetamoo, between Weetamoo and Wootonekanuske where strong connections already existed.

On the night before the Narragansetts and Pocassets were to depart from us to return to their own homelands, we were all camped in the woods near the Matfield River. We butchered a sheep that we had taken off an English farm, and one of our warriors had brought down a young doe. This was not food enough to fill all our bellies, but it was food enough to provide at least a taste of meat. And we treated the occasion as if it were a feast and not a last supper. We spoke not of what most of us knew would prove true: that we would likely not see one another again in this life. Instead, we told stories of our youth, the funny mistakes each of us had made as children. We spoke of the love we felt for those who had raised us and for those who now depended on us. We recounted the triumphs we had enjoyed in this war which pressed in upon us, of our astonishment that we were able to trick the English into ambush over and over again. We did not speak of our hatred for the English, not even of our hatred for the likes of Josiah Winslow. But we did speak of our affection for each other.

As the night grew late, and the campfires tumbled to ember, we danced together one last time. We did not use our drums for fear of alerting the English to our whereabouts, but kept the rhythm on our knees and with hands smacked against the ground. We danced the dance of resistance, for we knew that wherever we ran, the English would follow, though in low voices we sang not of the defeat that awaited us but of the victories we proclaimed to lie ahead.

I let Neksonauket, who was nine now, dance with us that night. I had made him a bow with which he hunted squirrels and rabbits and was occasionally able to supplement our meals. I had let him smear himself with warriors' paint, but he had never seen battle, and I hoped he never would. He danced well, and afterwards he sat at my right side, flushed and sweaty but erect and sinewy, thinner in the face and torso than he had been when he was a year younger, but taller, his young legs rippling from the endless days he had spent with us on the trail.

Neksonauket joined with us in keeping the rhythm for those still dancing. He was my son, and I was proud of him.

That night, after the dancing ended, as the three of us huddled together in the *apawonk* we had erected for shelter, Wootonekanuske and I simply held each other until we could tell from Neksonauket's breathing that he was asleep. Then I whispered to her the plan I had devised with Adonoshonk and Annawon. We would wait a day after Quinnapin and Weetamoo led their people out. Then we would depart ourselves. Our main body would indeed go into the Montaup woods and try to hide from the English raiders. But when all of us reached Swansea, Wootonekanuske, Neksonauket and I would turn to the northwest, just the three of us, lying low in the day, traveling at night. If I found the chance, I would steal a horse, or better, two. But I would never hobble it near our place of hiding.

We would make our way back to Nipmuck country where we would find our allies, I knew, doing only a little better than ourselves. But with only the three of us, we could count on shelter and sustenance. And after meeting with the Nipmuck sachems, we would continue on to the north. If we could reach the Merrimack River, we could join with the Abenakis and the Penacooks who had not suffered nearly the hardships of those of us in southern New England. From this north country we could attempt to reestablish our contacts with the French, to council with them about ways they could assist in diverting the English with a naval attack on Boston or Plymouth, ways in which they could supply food that the French Indians could help us import into Nipmuck country and make it possible for an alliance of Nipmucks, Abenakis and Penacooks to make the English sue for a peace that would include the Pokanokets and our southern Indian allies as well. Such an undertaking, I whispered as Wootonekanuske steadily stroked my arm and sometimes my face, such an undertaking, I admitted, would be difficult, but not impossible. And as the tide turned and food supply lines were opened, we would be joined in the north country first by Adonoshonk and Annawon and our own people and soon thereafter by Quinnapin and Weetamoo and theirs too.

"We will, my love," Wootonekanuske said. "You will lead us, and we will."

THE NARRAGANSETTS AND POCASSETS were ready to move out not long after first light, their only repast a boiled mush of dried ground nuts seasoned with wild onions and what flesh could be stripped off the bones remaining from the prior evening. There were no more than a few spoonfuls for each person.

As they had done when they were about to part after the fight at Nipsachuck, Weetamoo and Wootonekanuske once more walked away together out of earshot. Through the trees we could see them talking and then for a long hard time embracing, their arms around each other, lips moving against ears. Quinnapin couldn't watch and turned away to make his final preparations. Neksonauket stood close by me, his eyes brimming.

When the two women returned, Weetamoo touched Neksonauket on his head, and he grabbed her fiercely around her waist. "We go now, brother," she said to me. "We will watch the bright star, and think of you on your travels."

"I am taking fifteen men to accompany you upstream," I said. "Pawtonomi and Annawon will come with me. Adonoshonk will be in command here. When you and Quinnapin cross the Matfield, we will erase your tracks so that Awashonks' men cannot trail you."

As my men and I started down the trail behind our friends, Wootonekanuske called after me, "Come right back, my love. Protect my sister, but then hurry back."

Neksonauket stood beside her, a war club he'd acquired without my knowledge tucked in his waistband. He swiped at his cheek with the back of his wrist, then lifted his bow above his head and waved at me with it as he stepped closer to his mother and put an arm around her waist. I waved back. I loved my family with every fiber of my being. And Wootonekanuske remained the most beautiful person upon whom I had ever cast eyes.

When we reached the crossing point of wide shallows, Quinnapin, Weetamoo and I stood together as their people waded across. Annawon and the others with me began the task of wiping the trail. As the last of the Narragansetts and Pocassets began to cross, Quinnapin turned to me and said, "History will record that our council was wrong."

I shook my head and shrugged.

"Wrong twice," he said. "Had we openly allied with you a year ago spring, this would not have happened. Had we listened to Weetamoo when she first came to us, we wouldn't have sacrificed so many of our families in our great fort. I know you have accepted us. But that was strategic. I don't know how you can forgive us."

"I can forgive you twice," I said. "I can forgive you because you took Weetamoo in and protected her and our kin when I could not begin to do so. And I forgive you because you sacrificed so much in refusing to give her up when the English demanded that you do so."

Weetamoo laid her arm on mine. "Your father was a great man," she said. "You are worthy of being his son."

"I will say the same to you," I said. "Our fathers came together to make the Wampanoag nation. You have served your people bravely. It has been my privilege to fight at your side."

She embraced me, holding me as she had her sister earlier. Then together Quinnapin and Weetamoo waded into the water. I stood on the bank and watched them until they disappeared.

"We should head back," Annawon said. And so we turned in the direction of our camp, erasing our own tracks and those of the Narragansetts and Pocassets as we made our return.

But our care was misplaced. And we were already too late. Awashonks' scouts led Church and his English monsters into our camp less than a half hour after I departed. The fighting was brief, as Church's men gunned down Pokanoket warriors too weakened to resist. Adonoshonk was hit in the back in the first volley and crawled into the brush where we found him mortally wounded. With his dying breaths he told us what had happened.

The Sakonnets recognized Wootonekanuske and pointed her out to Church who ordered that she not be harmed. She made a run toward the river, Neksonauket at her side, but she was overtaken by two men. Since the English who took hold of Wootonekanuske were interested only in her, our son might have escaped had he kept running. But he stopped to defend his mother. With his war club he hammered on the arms of one of the men who held fast to a struggling Wootonekanuske. He was only nine, but the blows hurt, and the Englishman elbowed him hard in the face, breaking a tooth and knocking him flat.

Wootonekanuske screamed with a ferocity that startled even her captors, twisted free and threw herself over Neksonauket. "You touch my son again, and I will claw you to pieces," she hissed. "I will scrape out your eyes before you can raise a hand to your face."

But her threat was empty, and they laughed at her. She was rail thin, and neither was afraid of her. "Your son?" one said.

"My son," Wootonekanuske said. "Yes, you devils, my son."

"Our lucky day," one Englishman said to the other. "King Philip's bitch and his pup too."

"And a pretty penny each will fetch when the next slaver docks at Plymouth Bay."

The soldiers tied the hands of Wootonekanuske and Neksonauket, yanked them to their feet and started to push them down the trail. The soldier Neksonauket had struck stopped and picked up the war club Neksonauket had dropped when he was knocked down. The soldier flipped the weapon end over end as he walked behind my son, catching it by the handle, once, twice, a third time. Then, with tremendous force, he swung the club into Neksonauket's arm just below the shoulder. The blow snapped his humerus like a dry twig. Screaming again, Wootonekanuske turned on the soldier and tried to bite him, but the other one hit her across the back of her head with the butt of his musket, knocking her out.

Benjamin Church understood the value of my wife and son, took them to Plymouth and delivered them to Josiah Winslow.

Years later Church claimed he had recommended that Winslow use Wootonekanuske and Neksonauket to lure me to surrender. But Winslow was frightened at the very idea of holding them, terrified that he was personally in danger every minute they remained in Plymouth. He had them transported to the slaver immediately.

Once the slave ship had docked in Bridgetown, Barbados, Wootonekanuske was washed, dressed in frills and lace, and paraded on the block under a pitiless sun. A plantation owner, who sneered that he did not want to lie with any of the African women he owned, bought her to serve as his mistress. But he raped her only the one time. Afterwards, he shot her in a fury, because when he bent to nuzzle her, she bit off his right earlobe.

Neksonauket was taken to Jamaica. His first week as a field hand, he was beaten to death because his broken arm prevented him from carrying his assigned bundles of cane.

After Wootonekanuske and Neksonauket were taken from me, the rage I felt seemed to eat me up from the inside. When we reached Swansea, Annawon asked if I wanted to take a man or two with me toward Nipmuck country. I told him that I would not go, that I would continue on with the few left to Montaup. Annawon started to try to convince me otherwise, but then he shrugged, and we marched on toward our destiny in the emptiness of home.

A remarkable thing happened to me as we trudged our way from the banks of the Matfield down onto the peninsula the English took, ironically, to calling Mount Hope. I would have predicted that my rage would lead me to seek out the English so that I could butcher as many white men as possible and die covered in their blood with a raised hatchet of defiance clenched in my fist. But that's not what happened. The loss of my wife and son drained the hate out of me as if I were a water sack shot through with a musket ball. All our efforts proved so futile, our fate so cruel. Without Wootonekanuske and Neksonauket, I had no reason to continue. I was finished. In Montaup, I made camp and waited for the English to come so that I might stand and defy them one last time.

48

As Rich prepared to leave the rector's office, he called in Urban attorney Regan Hooks to ask her advice about a file he'd received earlier in the morning from auditor Chandler Piehl. Chandler's thorough investigation left little doubt that Shelby Clay had personally profited from the federal-grant-funded building programs of his Urban Housing Institute.

"Got to bust him," Regan said. "Take away his deanship immediately. Suspend all his grants until we get this whole thing formally answered."

"The question is whether we have to turn this material over to the U.S. Attorney."

Regan pursed her lips and blew out a long, whistling breath. She shook her head of black hair back and forth. "Above my pay grade," she said.

"But you agree that we are looking at criminal activity," Rich said.

"It certainly *appears* to be criminal activity," Regan replied. "But we're also talking about the biggest swinging dick on this campus and one of the BSDs in this city. I'm not going to advise you to drop a dime on him. And I'm certainly not going to do it."

"We can't just sweep this under the rug, Regan. That would make us accessories after the fact, wouldn't it?"

"Not what I am saying at all," she countered. "My advice is that a thing this explosive is above your pay grade too. You need to write Shelby a letter saying he's being returned to faculty status and relieved of his duties at the Housing Institute pending appropriate inquiries into what Chandler has dug up. You go any further than that without Elia Lipscom's permission, and you can forget about remaining rector."

Rich laughed and told Regan that Ben Turner was already her new boss. Regan was shocked into silence. Finally, she said, "Why bother with this pile of Shelby Clay shit then? If Ben is now the COO, let him deal with it."

"Ben and Shelby are old friends," Rich replied. "He's not going to want to do it."

"He better do it," Regan said. "Gets his own ass in a crack if he doesn't."

"Maybe not the best way to go," Rich said. "Ben is trying to come out of the exigency mess as a hero. Kind of pisses me off, of course. But from the institution's perspective, maybe he's right to put as much distance between me and him as possible. Might as well add this noxious business to the poop suit I get to wear out of here."

Rich did not tell Regan why he planned to take the responsibility for Clay on himself. The looming Clay scandal involved a compromise he was ashamed of himself for making. He hadn't buried it. But he hadn't faced up to it immediately either. In pursuit of the permanent rector's job, he'd let Elia Lipscom convince him to wait. Now, he feared that Ben Turner and the viceroy would conspire to let Clay skate.

"I'll demote Shelby," Rich said to Regan. "After that, I'm out, and you'll need to lead Ben through due process in case exculpatory explanations exist that we aren't seeing."

"If you relieve Shelby of his administrative responsibilities, and he fights back, then we follow the Faculty Handbook procedures. If he doesn't protest or just retires, then that's the end of it as far as Urban University is concerned."

"Unless we turn the file over to the feds."

"I think that's a decision that Elia Lipscom has to make," Regan said. "I'm just a pipsqueak, one person, regional campus, girl attorney. Lipscom has a whole legal staff. If we're talking something as big as a federal indictment, then he and his guys should make the call."

"So I demote Shelby, hand that over to Ben and send the file up to Elia?"

"Exactly," Regan said. "You go to the feds yourself and Shelby's got a way to turn this shit into sunshine, then he can sue you for everything you've got. Your due diligence is to turn everything you've gathered over to your boss."

When Regan returned to her own office, Rich wrote Lipscom a cover letter and attached it to the auditor's Shelby Clay file. Rich also drafted a demotion letter to Clay and included a copy with the material he sent to Lipscom. Following Regan's advice, the letter to Clay raised Rich's concerns about evidence of Clay's rigging state bidding procedures as well as what could be construed as repeated instances of financial kickbacks. And Rich's letter to Lipscom asked that the viceroy and his staff determine what further legal steps should be taken. Rich closed his letter to Lipscom by resigning his position as interim rector effective immediately. Finally, Rich made a copy of everything he was sending to Elia Lipscom and had it hand delivered to Ben Turner.

IN THE DAYS THAT followed, while waiting for a response on the Shelby Clay mess, Rich arranged teaching assignments for himself on the fall English schedule and began to prepare classes that he'd never taught before. On the blustery day that he moved his office from Building 6 to Building 1, while pushing a metal flatbed hand truck full of books across campus, Rich was stopped by Joe Alter, whose path Rich crossed in front of the library. After greetings and unmemorable small talk, Joe said, "If I may speak openly, Rector, I was very sorry when I learned that you weren't going to continue in your leadership position."

"Thank you, Joe," Rich replied. "Coming from you, especially, that means a lot to me."

"I'm sure you're relieved, of course," Joe said, bouncing nervously on his toes. The wind stirred and lifted the curls of Joe's red hair like flapping wings on either side of his face, making it appear as if he might rise off his feet and take flight. "I can only imagine what an awful burden you had to bear, and I know you ended up in the hospital with heart problems. So I'm sure you're glad to step away."

Rich bit at the lumpy flesh inside his lower lip. He thought of telling the truth to this man whom he barely knew on a personal level but so liked and appreciated. He thought of confiding that he wasn't relieved but rather that he was pissed, that he felt violated. But what good could come of such a confession? So he shrugged and said nothing.

"I am not alone in thinking that you did a magnificent job," Joe said. "I felt like you got this place reopened by sheer force of will. It's no telling how many jobs you saved."

"Thank you, Joe. But Charlie Lobovich and lots of others deserve most of the credit."

"Well, I appreciate what everybody did. But you were our leader."

"An awful lot of your colleagues, our colleagues, won't ever forgive me for a lot of the exigency decisions I made. And it's hard to blame those who lost their jobs. I don't forgive myself for not figuring out how to protect them."

Joe grimaced. "These are hard times, Rector. But a lot of people understand that you had the brutal job of throwing some people overboard, in order to save as many as you could."

Rich took a deep breath.

"This sounds corny, I guess," Joe said, "but you're my hero."

Rich felt his eyes glass in the wind. "I'm just an old ball coach who lost the biggest contest of his life," Rich said. "But thanks. Your kind words have made my day."

As they moved apart Rich reflected that Joe Alter was Rich's hero, Joe Alter, who never heard the thunderous applause that Rich had heard all his life, as a player, as a coach, as Urban's rector at its triumphant post-Hosea graduation, Joe Alter who had devoted his life to teaching others to stand in the limelight while he himself always stood in the shadows, Joe Alter who beamed at the applause others received, Joe Alter who took pride in the talents of others, talents he often didn't possess himself, Joe Alter who lost his stage and his costumes and sets but put on a production anyway, Joe Alter who picked up dog shit so that his audience members wouldn't step in it, who picked it up himself because it had to be done and it wasn't the kind of job you could in good conscience assign to someone else.

IN THE LAST WEEK of June, shortly before the beginning of the new fiscal year, Ben Turner called a press conference. When the lights were shining and the cameras were rolling, Turner introduced Senator Marilynn Williams who announced that she had secured a one hundred fifty million dollar commitment from Congress for an emergency relief and recovery package for higher education in Choctaw. Urban was scheduled to get twenty million a year for three consecutive years, with payback to start in five years and to be spread over forty years. Interest was set at one percent. In almost every detail, Senator Williams' recovery package reflected the plan she had worked out with Rich. Rich could not fairly say that the plan was his, rather than the Senator's, but he took pride in having initiated it. Turner did not invite Rich to the press conference. At no point did Turner mention Rich's name or acknowledge the role he played in securing the Senator's support.

Senator Williams did thank "former Rector Richard Janus for helping me formulate the ideas and strategies of this recovery legislation." But no one in the local media picked up on the remark. The video footage aired by the four Choctaw television news channel did not include it, nor was it mentioned in the front-page article in the next morning's *Straight Arrow*. As far as history would ever understand, the money had been captured by Benjamin Turner.

Rich had hoped the federal cash would come through in time to head off the exigency plan he had presented to the Board. It didn't. But had he still been Urban's CEO, he would have insisted on cancelling the faculty and staff layoffs. He didn't know how the Board would have reacted. But had they tried to block him, he would have fought. And he would have won, he believed. He would have had a united campus at his back once he announced the restorations, and the Board would have been facing a frightening revolt and a public relations nightmare had they tried to enforce the exigency plan in the face of funding that made it unnecessary.

After consulting with Elia Lipscom, Ben Turner did nothing of the kind. Lipscom was infuriated that Congress had chosen to give this kind of money to Ettons and Urban while designating none at all for ASU. In fact, as it had happened on his watch as viceroy, Lipscom was afraid this federal bequest could torpedo his plans to oust Stephen Hopkins and finally take his rightful place as ASU rector. In a rage, he told Turner that the Urban rector could forget about spending one dime of that sixty million because he was going to have the Board cut Urban's budget by another twenty million annually.

Here Turner rose up on his knees. And he and Lipscom came to the following agreement: The twenty million would be placed in Urban's budget, so that Turner could show the Senator where her funds had gone. Half of the money would go into dummy lines from which Turner would spend nothing. This ten million dollars would be available to cover overages Elia Lipscom could now allow himself to run in his own budget, funds he could devote to curry favor with the rich and influential and therefore to his campaign to unseat Stephen Hopkins. Once Hopkins was finally vanquished and Lipscom was ensconced in the rector's office at ASU,

Lipscom would nominate Turner to succeed him as viceroy, one little bloody hand washing the other.

Turner counted on his faculty not to understand the implications of what Marilynn Williams' money meant. If and when necessary, he would explain that the federal support funds could not be used for continuing expenses and thus could not be employed to restore the previous administration's cuts. For, after all, this was just loan money that had to be paid back. And it would run out in only three years. Had Rich been in charge, he would have restored the cuts on the presumption that Urban's enrollment would recover in three years and that tuition revenues would then supplant the federal dollars. But he was wrong in that presumption. Urban's enrollment never again reached the 20,000 students it had on the eve of Hurricane Hosea. And yet, Rich's determination to cancel the exigency layoffs would have worked. As Senator Williams had predicted from the beginning, Congress forgave the loan before the first repayment installment was due. And through careful management of the inevitable employee attrition resulting from retirements and other resignations, Rich's plan would have succeeded. A lot fewer people would have been cast into the darkness of immediate unemployment and all the financial, emotional and physical dislocation that accompanies it.

But Rich wasn't in charge, and Ben Turner spread perfumed bullshit about what he couldn't do. To underscore the limitations on what the federal money meant, he pointed out that it would not enable him to restore Urban's athletic program, proof positive to the cynical that Turner was telling the truth. Of course, the absence of an athletic program impeded recruiting and resulted in the firing of Hart Thompkins who never stopped saying so. In his best move, Turner made himself a hero to continuing faculty by securing permission from Elia Lipscom to use a portion of the federal relief money that Lipscom let him keep to fund across-the-board faculty pay increases of nearly 10%. In the minds of those who kept their jobs at Urban University after Hurricane Hosea, Ben Turner was their angel. Rich was still the devil.

Rich would have festered over these developments considerably more had other, more important matters not commandeered his attention. He never got those new classes prepared that summer of 2005, and he never taught a single section of English at Urban University. While he was still battling depression over the way his administrative career at Urban ended, he got news that made him forget all his professional setbacks. For in the first week of May, with the repairs on their house completed, and with her spring semester completed, Cally finally went in for the mammogram she was scheduled to have had two days after the storm.

The X-ray showed a tumor the size of a walnut cut in half, flat side out, so deep in her left breast that it nestled directly against the underlying muscles of her chest. Because of its structure, she hadn't been able to feel it in her regular self-examinations. But it was there, and a needle biopsy established that it was malignant. The mastectomy that followed revealed that she had Stage IIIB cancer. The underside of the tumor had invaded the muscle tissue of the chest wall and the three axillary lymph nodes near her sternum. The surgeons believed that they were able to excise all the cancerous tissue, but they followed up with a course of radiation and after that a regimen of chemotherapy.

Rich joined Cally in retirement as soon as she was diagnosed. He accompanied her to all her procedures and every meeting with her doctors. He helped her through the indignities of her chemotherapy side effects. Cally had always had a highly sensitive system. Pollen made her miserable every spring. Exposure to wool made her skin break out in a rash. Two shots of vodka would cause her face to redden from cheekbone to cheekbone. So, not unpredictably, she didn't handle the chemotherapy well. She suffered from diarrhea, persistent nausea and bouts of vomiting. She contracted ulcerated sores in her nose and

mouth. Her beautiful, thick hair fell out in clumps. And Rich
held her as she cried herself to sleep every night.

But Cally refused to show her dismay to anyone save her
husband. The wig they bought irritated her scalp, so she seldom
wore it around the house, covering her head when she was home
with an Urban baseball cap. But she did wear the wig when she
went out, and they both thought it looked reasonably good.
People wouldn't have commented, of course, but they thought
that most people genuinely didn't notice. Her additional weight
loss was less than her doctors predicted, only about ten pounds,
but she bragged that she could now wear clothes from high
school. And when asked how she was feeling, she would say that
she felt fine.

Though she cried at night, she remained defiantly upbeat
even with Rich during the day, fortifying herself with a steady
stream of black humor. When she found that she could wear a
white suit she hadn't had on in a decade, she put on high heels
and modeled it for Rich.

"How do I look?" she asked in a breathy Marilyn Monroe
meow. She twisted away and looked back at him over her
shoulder.

"Like a movie star," he said.

"Yeah," she replied. "Like Yul Brenner."

"Well, maybe like Sinead O'Connor."

She turned to face him, shifted her weight onto one leg
and put a fist on her hip. "That's so sweet," she said. "I've got
cancer. And my husband says I look like a fucking nutbag Irish
singer. How flattering. And she's a lesbian too. Not that there's
anything wrong with that."

"She's a lesbian, and we have something in common. We
both want to eat your pussy."

"You'd be disgusting if I ever listened to a thing you say."

"The virtues of cunnilingus notwithstanding, I don't really
think you look like Sinead O'Connor," Rich said. "Just a lot
more like Sinead O'Connor than Telly Savalas."

"Yul Brenner," Cally said.

"Well, you look more like Yul Brenner than Telly Savalas, I guess."

"That's because Telly Savalas has tits, whereas Yul and I have just one between us."

"I think you look like Michelle Pfeiffer," Rich said.

"That's a good one. I wouldn't look like Michelle Pfeiffer if she was bald and had only one tit."

"She only had one tit in *A Thousand Acres*. And she looked pretty good to me."

"She may have had only one tit, but she wasn't bald."

"If she were bald, she would look pretty good to me. But never as good as you."

"Is that because I'm bald and have only one tit or because all my pubic hair fell out?"

"A silver lining to every cloud. But since you keep harping on this bald business, I am going to shave my head and pubes so we can be all bald together. That sounds deliciously kinky to me."

"I may have cancer, but you're the one who is sick."

"I'm going to get balded tomorrow. Hi and low."

"No, you're not."

"Yes, I am. I'm serious."

"No, you're not. I'm serious."

"I don't want you to feel alone, so I'm going to do it."

"If you do it, I will feel completely alone. I look in the mirror, and I see a stranger. If you shave your head, there will be two strangers living in our house, and I will completely freak out."

"I love you," Rich said.

"I know you do, Boo. And that's why I'm going to beat this fucking cancer because you'd be too lonely if I don't. On the other hand, if you shave your head, I will have to kill you, and then I'd be too lonely, and I would have beaten this fucking cancer for nothing."

"OK, I won't shave my head. But, you know, what about down there?"

"Well, that's another matter."

WHEN CALLY FINISHED HER chemotherapy treatments, she was cancer free, and she was told that her five-year survival prospect was better than fifty-fifty. In fact, she lived to age eighty-five. She died in 2033, three months after Rich. Her cancer never reappeared.

Cally Martin did not become a casualty of Hurricane Hosea, but her illness, or at least the seriousness of it, was another product of the storm that history would never document. Cally's willful survival saved her husband. Had she succumbed, he probably would have climbed into a bottle of Black and White and drowned within a matter of months.

The impulse to covet the end is something I experienced, and it's something I particularly understand in the context of losing your wife. I lost my home and my entire people, but had Wootonekanuske still been with me, I would have tried to make it north of the Merrimack River as Annawon encouraged me. Perhaps there, with Wootonekanuske at my side, I might have lived another forty years or so if the English had left me alone. I had good genes for that, recall. My father Ousamequin lived to age 80. But with Wootonekanuske taken away from me, I greeted John Alderman's bullet with a raised middle finger of relief.

My friend Rich Janus fared better, and for that I thank the Creator. Cally lived, and thus he did too. And together they took themselves away from Choctaw and the entire State of Alkansea and at the age of fifty-seven added additional chapters to their blessing of life together.

EPILOGUE

Since my own story ended in the seventeenth century, and since everybody about whom I cared and with whom I fought for freedom died either before me or with me, or, as in the case of Annawon, shortly after me, I haven't much to add to most of their stories. That Vicious Lying Rat Bastard Josiah Winslow was still alive when I expired in 1676. He remained as Governor of Plymouth after he achieved his life's objective of ridding his part of the universe of most everyone who looked like me. Ethnic cleansing a later monster would term it. A year after my death Winslow was charged with irregularities in his management of Plymouth Colony, but he managed to stave off these allegations by demonstrating how much money he had made selling my kinsmen into slavery. Winslow was born eleven years before me and died four years after I did. I begrudge him every one of the nearly 5,500 days he drew breath longer than I did. He finally expired in 1680. The Creator's response to his arrival was not as Winslow had arrogantly anticipated, given that he was a true believer in his own status as *elected*. Not surprising for a man who oversaw the genocidal eradication of entire nations, he resides in Hell, where, given the nature of our Merciful Maker, his torments are less than he deserves.

Many of those who played central roles in Richard Janus' life were still in place when I ended my narration about his efforts to save Urban University in the aftermath of Hurricane Hosea. Here is a short account of what happened to some of them:

In 2016, Senator Marilynn Williams became America's first female president.

In 2007, Beatrice Florin appeared in the *Forbes 400* list of the nation's richest people.

In 2006, retired and relocated to Santa Fe, former Urban Pharmacy Dean John Leake was shot dead by a policeman in a passing cruiser when he became enraged and attacked a meter maid for posting a ticket on his car. While slapping her on her face and ears, he kept screaming, "I'm only three minutes late," and the sound of his own screeching voice drowned out the passing officer's order to cease and desist.

Alphonse Jackson won a Pulitzer for his moving essay on his flooded hometown that included a long passage of tribute to his high school basketball coach. A few years later Alphonse won a second Pulitzer for his book on Barack Obama's 2008 presidential campaign.

Althea Feaster won a first and then a second state basketball championship in 2008 and 2009. Her husband Robert sat directly behind her at every game. For the semi-finals and finals both seasons, Rich and Cally sat next to Robert and cheered their lungs out.

Not long after Rich resigned from Urban to devote himself to Cally's fulltime care, Stephen Hopkins resigned as rector of Alkansea State when auditors discovered that he had been using the university plane, Sky Monster, to ferry his daughter back and forth between Mayflower and Los Angeles where the twenty-year-old ASU drama major was auditioning for soap opera roles. The flights were paid for by the ASU Foundation and defended by Hopkins as a "student support initiative." Even the people of Mayflower were outraged.

Elia Lipscom finally became ASU rector and watched his salary vault from $290,000 to $440,000, plus the house, the expense allowance and all the other perks of flagship rectoring that made his total annual compensation package worth close to $700,000. That sum was supplemented by his quick appointment to a dozen corporate boards that paid him an average of $50,000 each to sit in a few meetings every year. Lipscom loved his job until the very minute he had a fatal heart attack while having sexual intercourse with a pair of Monster cheerleaders.

Sheila Pyrite continued in her position at Urban University as Assistant to the Rector for Special Projects until her death in 2017. Ben Turner and his successors never figured out what she did any better than Rich or Francis Saurian ever did, but she was often seen in the offices of leaders in the United States Congress.

Margaret Lockhart succeeded Elia Lipscom as viceroy and immediately demanded that all the state's rectors attend monthly meetings of the Board of Trustees in their ceremonial academic regalia. She presided over these meetings in her own robe and a tam the size of a cocktail tray. She also directed that all paperwork forwarded to her office be sent with five copies, each in a different pastel hue: eggshell, pearl, ash, primrose and peach. Aside from the rectors at ASU whom she left entirely alone, she liked to call the other rectors ten minutes before the beginning of the workday. Lockhart was sixty-nine years old when she became viceroy and held the position until she died at age ninety. She died at her desk, left instructions that she be buried in her academic robe and requested that those attending her funeral dress the same way.

Ben Turner was supposed to become viceroy after Lipscom went to ASU as rector, but Lipscom reneged on his promise to nominate him. As an administrator from Urban and a resident of Choctaw, Turner did not make the short list. He remained as rector at Urban for four years, during which time he tried in vain to get Lockhart to let him restart the Ungulate athletic program. His initial support among the faculty waned quickly, and he became so unpopular among faculty and students that he rarely made public appearances on campus. He did, however, become active in the most prestigious and exclusive Choctaw carnival organization and attended its ball every year wearing a powder blue gaucho costume with silver spurs and a hat that dangled twined white balls from its brim. In the last half of his

590   Fredrick Barton

rectorship, his alcohol consumption increased to the point that he smelled of booze from several feet away.

Ben lost his position when the FBI arrested him, along with Dennis Stitch and Shelby Clay, whose demotion by Rich, Ben had instantly reversed. Ben claimed he did not know about Clay's kickback scheme. But federal investigators found copies of Chandler Piehl's investigative report and Rich's cover letter transmitting it to Turner in both Turner's and Clay's personnel files. Turner had destroyed the original and had seized and shredded a copy he had found in the front of Clay's file. It never occurred to Turner to look in his own file or that Rich would have placed multiple copies in Clay's. Turner was sentenced to two years for his cover-up. His rich, well-connected wife left him while he was in prison, and he spent the rest of his life mostly on the porch of his Exchange District house, always with a glass of Early Times in his hand, usually dressed in sandals and a painter's smock, odd, since he didn't paint. On Mardi Gras Day he took to erecting a small perch for himself halfway up an Old Town light pole where he clung for several hours clad only in a green eyeshade, a puka bead necklace, a red, white and blue jockstrap, black leather cowboy boots, and chaps. In the history of Urban University that was written for its seventy-fifth birthday, he was identified only as the rector who dropped intercollegiate athletics.

Shelby Clay entered a plea bargain agreement with federal prosecutors and testified both against Dennis Stitch, whom he blamed for the kickback schemes, and Ben Turner, whom Clay claimed tried to extract campus political support for rescinding Clay's demotion. Clay was sentenced to eighteen months of probation and sixty hours of community service. When he died, his obituary in *The Straight Arrow* made no mention of his brief period of disgrace.

Richard Janus' entry in the school's history volume included, "Interim Rector Janus provided strong leadership after Hurricane Hosea and got the campus reopened less than two months after the storm, the only Choctaw university to hold classes that fall of 2004. Janus was not successful in working with FEMA to provide needed student housing, however, and Urban suffered a devastating loss of student enrollment which diminished its stature for many years."

After Cally Martin fully recovered from her breast cancer, she and Rich moved to Rockwood, Tennessee, where Rich's old family friend Jerry Schwartz recommended him for the head basketball coaching position at the local high school. Alphonse Jackson wrote him a letter of recommendation that the Rockwood Principal called the most passionate and well-written letter he'd ever received. Alphonse also included a copy of his Pulitzer-Prize-winning *Newsday* essay with its tribute to Rich's coaching. That didn't hurt.

Cally taught in the Classics Department at the University of Tennessee for many years as an adjunct. She was offered but turned down a full-time position. She finished her book on Sophocles and then another on Euripides. She was at work on a volume about the plays of Aristophanes when she died. She never missed one of Rich's basketball games.

Rich coached at Rockwood for seven years, winning a state championship in his third. Every year, Rich looked forward to the coming of school and the comforting echo of balls bouncing on hardwood, the smell of sweat in the locker room and of sore muscle balm in the training room. He eagerly anticipated the annual challenge of teaching a new team how to play together and how to win. But in the summers, he turned his attention to something else. He had heard the call to write for some time, and now he responded to the urge, perhaps like a loving mother in her late thirties, desiring to bear another child. He thought about his topic for a long time and took notes for nearly a year. Finally at the desk in his den on a mild summer day, he opened his computer and set his fingers on the keys.

This is how he began:

"Call me Metacom."